Sexy . . . swank . . . and sophisticated . . .
their intimate games bred reckless desires.
Their money made it easy.
Their ambitions made it dangerous.

At 305 East, the "in" crowd were in all the way. When their passions reached the flash-point, 305 East would be blown wide open.

305 EAST

by
Paul Gillette

To Shelly

305 EAST
A Bantam Book / published by arrangement with
Arbor House Publishing Company, Inc.

PRINTING HISTORY
Arbor House edition published March 1977
Bantam edition / February 1978

ISBN 0-553-11281-3

Published simultaneously in the United States and Canada

Bantam Books are published by Bantam Books, Inc. Its trademark, consisting of the words "Bantam Books" and the portrayal of a bantam, is registered in the United States Patent Office and in other countries. Marca Registrada. Bantam Books, Inc., 666 Fifth Avenue, New York, New York 10019.

PRINTED IN THE UNITED STATES OF AMERICA

Profuse thanks to my old buddy,
Carl Ain, for suggesting the title.

When he was twelve years old, Ted Vassilikos went with his father and mother to his Uncle George's in Pottsville for his cousin Tina's wedding. As they were leaving the church and everybody was lined up to kiss Tina, Ted saw his uncle's face take on a strange expression. The loose skin of his cheeks started to shake, and his eyes bulged as if someone were blowing up a balloon inside his head.

Ted looked to where his uncle was looking and saw a tall man with huge shoulders. His shiny brown suit fit very tightly, and he had greasy black curly hair. His eyes were so deep inside his head that he seemed to be peering through two tunnels.

Ted looked back to his uncle and saw now that his forehead was sweating. Ted's father must have realized that something was wrong, because he came around from the other side of Tina and took his brother's arm. Ted went over next to them and watched as the tall man came down the line. As he approached Tina, he smiled at George Vassilikos but did not shake his hand as the others on the line had been doing. He only kissed Tina, said "Congratulations" to her husband and walked away. Watching him from behind, Ted mostly noticed the size of his neck and shoulders. The man looked as if he were carrying a hundred pound bag of cement under his coat.

As they rode from the church to the reception, Ted asked his father who the man was and why Uncle George was so scared of him.

"Don't ask questions," said Demetrios Vassilikos. "It doesn't concern you."

There was a band at the reception, and lots of food—*moussaka* and *dolmadakia* and *spanakopitis* and *taramasalata* and *psari mayoneza* and *arni psito* and *pastichio* and all sorts of other things that people ate only on holidays—and Ted forgot about the man at the church. Everyone else seemed to forget him, too. Ted's father got drunk and went up on the stage and started dancing alone in front of the band. Uncle George and Aunt Maroula went around the hall kissing everybody.

Then, just after Tina's husband carried her away while everyone threw rice, the man in the brown suit came into the hall. Ted watched as he looked around, found Uncle George, and walked over to him. Ted's father saw them from the stage, jumped down, and hurried to George's side.

The man stood in front of Uncle George, smiled, and for a long time didn't say anything. Two other men who were dressed the same way came over and stood slightly behind him. Uncle George's cheeks were shaking again and Aunt Maroula stood behind him in a funny position with one hand over her mouth and the other hand over the first hand.

The band kept playing but everyone in the room stopped talking and gathered around. Ted looked back and forth from his Uncle George to the smiling man in the brown suit, waiting for one of them to say something. Neither did.

Ted's father broke the silence. "What kind of animals are you?" he asked the man in brown. "You come on the day of his daughter's wedding? Don't you have any decency?"

One of the men started toward him, but the one in brown held out an arm to stop him. Then the one in brown slowly unbuttoned his jacket, pushed back the sides, and standing with his fists on his hips slowly turned a complete circle so everyone could see he had a gun in a shoulder holster.

Now he looked again at Uncle George and, after a moment, leaned forward and tucked two fingers into the older man's lapel pocket. He glanced around, as if to make sure everyone was watching. Then he tugged sharply and, with a loud *r-i-p-p,* pulled the pocket off the suit.

A hushed groan went through the crowd as people realized what they were seeing. Demetrios Vassilikos and another man tried to intervene but were quickly pushed back by the friends of the man in the brown suit. One of the friends opened his jacket and held his hand over the stock of his pistol. Everyone shied away as if the man had actually taken the weapon out and pointed it.

Now the band stopped and the musicians stood at the edge of the stage watching the drama on the dance floor. George Vassilikos's eyes rolled upward, as if they were trying to find a hiding place somewhere behind his forehead.

The man in the brown suit, still smiling, surveyed the crowd like a stage magician who wanted to make sure everyone was paying attention before he did his next trick. Then he balled up one of George Vassilikos's side pockets in his fist, gave it a tug, and ripped it off. George stood there, the midnight-blue of his tuxedo peeling away to reveal wide swaths of whitish-tan, gauzelike undercoating.

"You don't think I'm decent?" the man in the brown suit asked Ted's father. "I waited till the bride and groom left, didn't I?" He laughed uproariously, displaying a huge set of yellow-brown teeth. Then he quickly reached for George's remaining pocket, balled it up in his fist and pulled it off the coat.

Ted shrank up against his mother's side. The man in the brown suit again surveyed the audience, then seized Uncle George's tie by the knot. He gave it a few experimental tugs that made Uncle George's head bobble about like a puppet's. Then he tugged sharply and hard, snapping the tie and seeming almost to snap George's neck as well.

The man, like a stage magician, gave everyone another smile, then put two fingers behind George's collar and ripped the shirt down the front. Next he reached for George's belt. George backed away, crossing his arms over his crotch. The man laughed, stepped toward him and pushed him hard on the shoulder. As George struggled to regain his balance, the man's foot came up. The instep caught the older man in the crotch. George gasped and coughed, then held his cupped hands in front of his mouth and spit his set of false teeth into them.

Ted's father and two other men made another attempt to intervene and again were shoved back. The man, laughing, slapped George's cupped hands with the back of one of his, sending the dental plate skidding across the floor. He then reached inside to George's undershirt, balled it up in his fist and pulled George's face close to his own.

"Now listen, you fucken Greek, from now on, when somebody tells you you have a partner, you have a partner. Get the message?"

Ted watched his Uncle George, who previously had seemed so capable and strong, bob his head up and down while he tried to articulate "yes" with his toothless mouth.

The man glared silently at him for a moment, then pushed him back into the arms of Ted's father.

George Vassilikos fell to one knee, sobbing. The man looked at him contemptuously, turned on a smile for the crowd and strode out of the hall followed by his acolytes, who backed toward the door, hands hovering near their pistols, till they were almost outside.

When they were gone the crowd swarmed around George, the men muttering incredulously, the women uttering the soft shrieklike sounds of mourners. One woman found his cracked dental plate and offered it on her palm. He only stared at it.

"Okay, it's all over," said Demetrios Vassilikos, gesturing for them to disperse. "Leave him alone."

"Call the police," someone said. "They can't get away with that."

"We'll call the police," said Demetrios, clearing a path for his brother. "Now don't worry about it. Everyone go home."

Ted followed as his father led Uncle George outside. But his father raised a hand as Ted tried to get into the car with them. "Go with Momma," he said.

Ted went back into the hall and found his mother and they drove to Uncle George's apartment with Aunt Maroula. Someone produced some desserts that no one at the reception had got around to eating, *galatabourikos* and *baklava*. *"Na fataì,"* said Aunt Maroula, putting a plate in front of Ted and his younger cousin Matthaios. "Eat."

It was almost midnight when Ted's father and Uncle George got home. Ted waited until his father and mother were alone, then asked what had happened.

"Don't ask questions," said Demetrios Vassilikos. "It doesn't concern you."

Ted tried again the next morning and the next afternoon. His father remained unresponsive. But on the ride home to Nanticoke, while Ted pretended to sleep, his father and mother discussed the strange intruders.

"They're Mafia," Demetrios Vassilikos said. "They want half his business."

"But they can't do that. This is America. He should call the police."

Demetrios groaned. "Sure he should call the police. And if they arrest the *choìros* who threatened him, two weeks after they're in jail some of their friends will carve their initials in Maroula's forehead. Or kidnap young Matthaios on his way home from school."

"So he must give them his business, no questions asked?"

"If he listened to me he'd've sold his business six months ago. Right after they first started bothering him. But no. I'm only his older brother. I live in a hick town like Nanticoke with all the coal miners. What do we know about the way things are done in the great metropolis of Pottsville?"

"So he didn't listen to you. What must he do now? Become their partner?"

Demetrios waited a long time, then said, "I wish I knew, I wish I knew."

Ted Vassilikos struggled to understand the conversation. It made no sense to him that something or somebody called "Mafia" could demand half his uncle's business and come to his daughter's wedding with guns when he refused to give it to them. But he understood that his father, who normally was not afraid of anything, now was afraid for Uncle George. And he could not forget the picture of the man in the brown suit, grinning as he displayed his pistol, like a villain in one of the gangster movies Ted saw on Saturday afternoons at the Majestic Theatre.

Two months later Ted's Uncle George died of a heart attack.

When the man in the porkpie hat sat next to him at the bar in the My-O-My, Ted Vassily took him for another alumnus looking to rub elbows with The Star.

"Gonna be an easy one this Saturday, 'ey, Mister T?"

Ted made himself smile. "They're never easy."

The man gestured to the bartender, who brought two beers. Ted wanted to refuse his and spare himself the inevitable bullshit but felt it would be easier to chug it and cut out than go through a whole number about why he wouldn't accept it.

"The sportswriters are giving you thirty-six points," the man in the porkpie said. "That sounds like a real piece of cake to me."

"Tell you what," said Ted. He chugged the beer. "Tomorrow morning you go up to Rec Hall and tell Pater Noster you want to play quarterback this Saturday. If it's okay with him, it's okay with me."

"Oh, shit, man, now don't go getting pissed." He waved to the bartender, who promptly replaced Ted's empty mug. "I'm just tryin' a be friendly. You oughtta try bein' nicer to people, man. It might work to your advantage."

Ted ignored the fresh beer and started scooping up his change from the bar.

"Really, man, you never know who can help you out. Like me, for instance. Here you are treating me like shit but who knows, maybe I'm the guy who can set you up with that house you're interested in buying on College Avenue."

Ted tried to conceal his surprise. No one was supposed to know about his interest in the house but the old man who owned it.

The man laughed. "You wonder how I found out? I should make you work for the information. That's what you'd do to me. But I'm a nice guy so I'll tell you." He gestured to the bartender, ordered a package of beer nuts and took a long time opening them, enjoying keeping Ted in suspense.

Ted silently sipped the newly headed beer.

"Simple deduction," the man said finally. "Last year, according to the records at the courthouse, you bought a whole block of buildings on South Atherton. This year you bought all of a block on College except for one house in the middle. So obviously you're interested in it. Okay, maybe I can help you get it. One hand washes the other, they say."

"How do I wash yours?"

The man laughed. "Information."

"Like?"

"Like the score this Saturday."

"Come to the game. See for yourself."

"Well, see, that's the whole point, Mister T. I wanna know *before* the game, like those other folks you're feedin'. That way, my people and I can take care of ourselves and of you too."

"I don't follow you."

"Come on, Vassily, you came here on scholarship from a broken down coal-mine town like Nanticoke. Your old man is a Greek immigrant who runs a hot dog stand. So last year you buy a hundred thousand dollars' worth of real estate, and this year you buy a hundred thou more. Where'd the money come from?"

"Hey, you accusing me of throwing games?"

"Not throwing them. Just being smart about them." He popped a fistful of peanuts into his mouth and chewed thoughtfully. "You're not going to tell me you never bet on a game, Mister T."

Ted drained his beer. "I'm not going to tell you anything, mister. Except goodbye."

He started out. The man caught his sleeve. Ted tried to shake his hand away; he held on.

"Now, look, Vassily," he said quietly, "I can do this the easy way or I can do it the hard way. I'm tryin' to do it the easy way."

"Get your hand off my jacket, or I'll break your nose."

The man smiled in a way that Ted found eerily familiar. He kept his hold on the sleeve and, with his free hand, unbuttoned his jacket, revealing a shoulder holster. "You won't break my nose, Teddy, 'cause if you did you'd have to explain to the cops how we happened to be talking about what we're talking about. And then they might want to ask who else you've talked about it with. And they might also want to know how a twenty-year-old quarterback whose old man runs a hot dog stand gets his hands on a quarter of a million dollars if he ain't shavin' points."

He let go of Ted's sleeve and rebuttoned his own jacket. "Now you don't want to talk to the cops, and I don't particularly want to talk to the cops. So why don't we forget about the cops and just talk to each other."

"Not here," Ted said. "Outside. Let's take a walk."

He grinned. "Yeah, Ted. Sure. It's a lovely night. I think a stroll could prove very pleasant." He flipped a half dollar toward the bartender and pocketed the rest of his change.

They walked outside. He started toward the parking lot. "Not in a car," Ted said. "It's too suspicious-looking. Let's just walk around campus as if we didn't care who saw us."

His grin broadened. "Yeah. Sure, Teddy. Very bright. I like the way you think, kid."

They crossed College Avenue and went through the main gate, then headed up the mall.

"Now start at the beginning," Ted said. "Never mind what I might have going with anyone else. Tell me exactly how you and I would work it."

"Very simple. We pick games like next Saturday's where you're heavily favored. My people place a few bets at a lower point spread. For every one we place for ourselves, we place one for you."

"How low a spread?"

"That depends. Next Saturday we could probably get away with fourteen. With a stronger team, it'd have to be seven or even three."

"And it's my job to see Penn State doesn't win by more? I fumble, or throw away passes, or do whatever I have to do?"

"Now you've got it." He hesitated. "Hey, are you putting me on? Don't tell me this is all new to you."

"I just want it all spelled out from the beginning, so there aren't any misunderstandings. Now, the games that we fix: How much money do you place for me?"

"A thousand of our own each game, plus whatever you give us to bet."

"How do I know I can trust you to bring back what I win?"

"We'd be foolish to screw you, Ted. That'd be killing the goose that lays the golden eggs."

"But if I gave you a pile of money to bet, and it was near the end of the season? . . . Maybe you'd figure you got all you could out of me."

"We don't work that way, Teddy. Once a man becomes our friend, he stays our friend. We never let a friend down."

They passed the Sparks Building and were in the clearing next to Pattee Library. The area was deserted, and the huge hedges cast eerie shadows across the spare, leaf-strewn lawn.

"These guys you're tied in with, how tough are they?"

"Pretty tough, kid."

"Suppose I told you I didn't want to go along with it? Suppose I said I didn't want to mess with guys like that? Any chance they'd bother my family or my girl friend?"

"Let's hope it'd never come to that . . ."

"But if it did? Could I tell you tonight that I'm not interested and have that be the end of it?"

He smiled uncomfortably. "I can't speak for anyone else, Ted. I can't promise what other people would do or not do. But obviously they'd be very disappointed."

"So someone could get hurt—my father, my mother, my girl friend . . ."

"Well, let's hope it won't come to that . . ."

"You're fucken-A it won't, dick-face." Ted had the move timed, letting the man get a full step in front of him before throwing the punch. It caught him in the back of the head, just below the porkpie hat and behind the ear, and Ted knew from feeling his fist land that a second hit wouldn't be necessary.

He wasn't, however, going to leave anything to chance. As the man stumbled forward, Ted kicked him hard in the stomach. He seemed for a moment to be trying to spin around, but somehow his legs wouldn't go along with the rest of him—they kept moving in the initial direction and finally buckled.

He fell to his hands and knees. Ted shoved him to the ground with a knee in his back, picked up his head by the hair and slammed his face into the dirt—once, twice, three times.

Ted turned him over. The entire side of his face was red with brush burns. Two rivulets of blood flowed from the corners of his mouth. They made his jaw resemble a ventriloquist's dummy's.

Ted ripped open the man's jacket and took the gun from his shoulder holster. It was a thirty-eight automatic, loaded, but with no bullet in the chamber that presently was in firing position. Evidently he didn't expect he'd have to use it in a hurry.

Ted stared at the gun, strangely fascinated. It wasn't the first he had seen at close range. He'd fired a forty-five and a rifle at the National Guard, and a high school buddy who now was a cop in Nanticoke had taken him target shooting with a police thirty-eight. But he'd never touched a gun whose sole purpose was evil, whose owner's only intent was to intimidate and if necessary kill innocent people like his Uncle George. Or himself.

He emptied the bullets and stuffed them into his jeans pocket, then sat with the barrel in the man's face, waiting for him to come to. The man woke a few seconds later, coughing blood, spitting, then blinking incredulously as he realized what had happened.

"I've got something for you to tell your people," Ted said. "You can tell them the nephew of a guy they killed in Pottsville made you eat your gun."

The man smiled weakly, then his face froze in an expression of shocked disbelief as Ted jammed the barrel into his mouth.

He hadn't realized until too late that it was coming. He couldn't open his mouth quite far enough to get his teeth out of the way. The barrel cracked the two front ones, breaking them off, then ripped into the roof of his mouth.

A glistening puddle of bright red formed around the cold steel in Ted's hand. The man gagged and tried to turn his head to keep from choking, which worsened the damage the barrel was doing to the roof of his mouth. He gagged twice more, then passed out.

Ted withdrew the gun and slapped the man back to consciousness. It took nearly a minute to get him to open his eyes. "Get up," Ted said. "We're going to police headquarters."

He half pushed and half kicked the man back across campus to the small State College police station. "This clown pulled a gun on me," he told the cop at the desk. "I had to take it from him."

The cop surveyed the man in the porkpie hat. "Who helped you, Ted? The whole offensive line?"

"I didn't mean to hurt him as much as I did, officer. I guess I panicked. He's Mafia. They killed my uncle years ago, now they're trying to get me to shave points . . ."

The man now seemed to be trying to say something, then apparently changed his mind and only spit blood onto the floor.

"I better call the D.A.," the cop said. "And an ambulance."

"Just call the D.A.," Ted said. "Maybe he'll bleed to death."

The man looked up at Ted as the cop went to the phone and dialed. "You're gonna pay for this, fucker," he said softly. "It may take fifty years, but you're gonna pay."

ONE

Hartford Loomis did not notice anything at first. It was a lovely, cold Sunday morning without a trace of the usual midweek haze marring the cloudless blue sky. Looking out from his terrace he could see across the East River to Queens and beyond, somewhere near the airport. With binoculars, he reflected, he probably could see Fire Island. He gazed at the horizon and smiled contentedly. Manhattan early on Sunday morning was as tranquil and pleasant a place as there was. That had been true when Edward Hopper painted the picture a half century ago, and it remained true today. It was one of the few things about New York that wasn't constantly changing, and one of the things Hartford Loomis liked best.

He leaned back in his lounge chair, tucked his blanket up under his armpits, then flipped through the *Times* for the business section. One of the reporters had been by the bank to interview him for a profile. He'd hoped it might run today, with his daughter Nan home from Kansas City. If so, he'd pretend he didn't see it and leave the paper lying around for her to find. No luck. This week's profile was Ed Blocker, the oilman. Hartford Loomis put the section aside, sipped his coffee, and searched for the arts and leisure section.

Suddenly through the wrought iron spindles of the terrace he noted two men in work clothes on the roof of one of the brownstones across Second Avenue. Thinking they might be burglars he sat up for a better look. There were three men, and they were not burglars: they were surveyors.

Hartford Loomis watched for a moment, then went to the phone on the windowsill and pushed the buttons of a familiar number. "George," he said, "have you heard anything about a construction project on Second Avenue across from my apartment?"

"Hart," replied George DelVecchio, "it's eight o'clock Sunday morning."

"I know the time and day, George. What I want to know is if you've heard anything about a construction project across from my apartment."

George DelVecchio hadn't become the youngest senior vice president in the history of BankUS without knowing when to back down. Smoothly shifting gears, he said, "Hart, actually we have been involved in some preliminary talks with the outfit . . ."

"Well, if some son of a bitch is putting up a building between me and my river view, I want to know immediately and I sure as hell don't want to pay for it." He slammed the telephone receiver into its cradle and glared across the avenue at the surveyors.

"Well," said a delicate voice in the doorway, "who's in a grumpy mood this morning?"

"Nanny." His frown immediately vanished. "What got you up so early?"

His daughter kissed him on the cheek, then brought her cup of coffee to the table. "When I was a little girl, this grumpy old man I know was always telling me something about early birds catching worms. Now what's this about some son of a bitch putting up a building between you and your view?"

He gestured toward the surveyors and shrugged. "Seriously, hon, why so early? You didn't get much sleep."

"I've decided to fly back today, Daddy. So I wanted some time to visit with you." She noticed his half-empty cup. "Fill it for you?"

"Not yet, thanks." He started to reach for her hand but felt awkward about it, so he finished the movement by going for his cup. "Nanny," he said after a moment, "what would you say if I told you I wished you'd reconsider your choice of careers?"

She smiled in a way uniquely hers, almost motherly. "Same thing I said last time you told me, Daddy. It's not my *lifelong* career. I'll quit in a year or two. But I'm not ready to settle down yet. I like the idea of seeing the world first."

"But as a flying waitress—?"

"Being a flight attendant," she answered in suddenly clipped tones, "is the nicest way I know of doing it."

"Well, far be it from me to argue with a bright young lady whose mind is made up. But Uncle Ben tells me Joseph Williams will be giving a special series of music appreciation lectures at the university this summer. He's holding an enrollment open for you, just in case."

She smiled again as she got up and came over to his chair. Her coat was open, and he could see the movement of her breasts beneath her sweater. They were huge breasts, much bigger than he'd ever noticed on a girl with her bone structure. And she was wearing no bra, of course. She never did. He wondered how she could avoid being embarrassed when men gawked. As they surely did.

"Daddy," she said, snuggling against him, "you know my mind is made up. But I'm not going to put in for Los Angeles as my permanent base when I finish training. I'm putting in for New York, and that means we'll see a lot more of each other than you thought."

"Why, great! I'll tell your brother to forget his plans to move into your room—"

"Uh, Daddy, don't do that. Some girls and I've been talking about taking an apartment together." Almost as an afterthought, she said, "You know, out near the airport. It'll be more convenient."

He said nothing. He wondered if she thought he was too out-of-touch to realize that most New York-based stewardesses had apartments right in Manhattan.

"You don't object to that, Daddy. Do you?"

He made himself smile. "No. I've always said, Nanny, you've got to make your own decisions."

She threw her arms around his neck and uninhibitedly pressed her body against his. He felt the soft fullness of her breasts, and was embarrassed.

"Then you'll back me if Mom raises a stink?"

"I'll stay neutral." He recalled that the fellow she was

with last night was a first date. And it was almost four a.m. when she got in. He hoped she hadn't . . . done it with him. Not that he expected her to be a virgin. Not in this day and age. Certainly not at twenty-two. But he didn't want her to be a first-nighter, either. He didn't want it to be possible for every hardhat, bookkeeper, and errand boy who came along to say he had screwed Nanny Loomis on the first date.

For a moment, he had a nightmarelike vision of her lying on a beach, legs spread wide, her enormous breasts rolling about as her glorious body (he knew it was glorious; he had, after all, seen her often enough in a bikini) thrashed and strained against one after another in a long line of bricklayers, truck drivers, messenger boys, firemen, postal workers, mechanics, welders, steamfitters, pool room knockabouts—blue-collars one and all, each queueing up for a shot at the goddess, each smirking as he swaggered away, pleased as punch that he'd put the blocks to Hartford Loomis's daughter. Hartford Loomis struggled to suppress a wince.

"About that building across the street," Nan was saying, "could it be this one?" She rummaged through the *Times* and came up with the real estate section.

Hartford Loomis read the headline: "Ex-Football Great Ted Vassily Will Build 'American Dream' on 2nd Ave."

Joseph Williams woke to a rendition of one of Chopin's nocturnes—opus thirty-seven, number two, though you could hardly tell from the way it was being butchered. He rubbed the sleep from his eyes, pulled on a bathrobe, and went into the living room. The girl behind his Steinway beamed proudly and hit a fistful of wrong notes as he entered.

"Good mor-ning!" she sang, the unmistakable throaty timbre of the Seven Sisters colleges in her voice. She continued to assault the piano.

Joseph Williams searched the bar and finally found a bottle of soda water. "My dear Buffy," he said, coming up behind her and bringing his mouth to her ear, "I apologize profusely for not having the piano tuned before you came. If you promise to stop immediately, I promise to have it taken care of first thing tomorrow morning."

It took a moment for the message to sink in. When it did, she smiled and lifted her hands from the keyboard. "I haven't played in quite a long time, I'm afraid."

"Not long enough," Joseph Williams murmured, stuffing ice cubes into a glass and pouring the fizzing soda over them.

"Pardon?"

"I said, 'Without practice, one's playing tends to get rough.' " He went to the terrace door and looked outside. "Lovely day, isn't it?"

For a moment she said nothing, then slowly got up from the piano and came to his side. "Joseph, if you'd like me to leave, don't think you have to spare my feelings."

"The thought never entered my mind."

"I mean it, Joseph. I didn't fuck you last night out of any misguided sense of lasting affection. It was strictly recreational—at least from my point of view."

He tried to put his arm around her. She backed away. He took a swallow of soda water and went back to the bar. He wished he could learn to be nicer to them the morning after. Granted, they should know better than to play his piano—as every last one of them apparently felt compelled to do. Still, if he could just bring himself to be civil it would make life considerably easier. They'd be back for encores, which would free him from having to chase after so many of them.

"I don't need your patronage, Joseph," she continued. "I can handle a quickie as well as you. I don't have to feel I'm in love with a man to fuck him."

He draped his body over a bar stool and stared at her around the side of his glass. She was really excellent looking. And, in bed at least, she performed in bravura fashion. All that and brains, too. What was it the magazines called her? "Ms. Perfection." He didn't want to push her out of his life after only one night. He owed it to himself to investigate. After all, how many women had even the potential to sustain his interest?

He watched her wait for his reply. He wondered whether to be conciliatory or take the offensive. The decision practically made itself. With her sort, one always took the offensive.

"My dear Buffy," he said, lowering his voice, "you needn't advertise your liberation. I understood your availability when I asked you here. It was my primary reason for asking you. Using naughty words, however, doesn't make you sound tougher, freer, less dependent . . . or whatever it is you're trying to affect. It makes you sound like a child."

He watched her face recompose into an expression approximating respect. And this was the fiery lady lawyer whom everyone was hailing as the messiah of women's lib? She was caving in as fast as any flustered Cliffie thirty years ago when he was at Harvard.

"You're really sick, Joseph," she tried weakly. "If you feel this sort of compulsion to degrade a woman you've just gone to bed with, you ought to see a psychiatrist—"

"You ought to get some new lines, dear Buffy. That amateur analyst's routine was stale when I was your age. Fact is, I rather like you. But I don't like your piano playing. So now that you've stopped, why don't we act like two civilized adults who've just had a most satisfying night in bed and make ourselves some breakfast?"

The corners of her mouth rose in a tentative smile. When he smiled back, she made it a full smile. He extended his arms, and she stepped into his embrace. He felt as he imagined Pavlov must have when he rang the bell and watched his dogs salivate.

She pressed her body against his, kissed him on the cheek, then rested her head against his chest. "I guess it was sort of presumptuous of me to play the piano of the great music director of the New York Symphony Orchestra. Himself, yet."

He managed a chuckle, enjoyed the feel of her small firm breasts against his chest, then released his hold. "Now then, some cappuccino? And a croissant?"

She started toward the kitchen. "I'll take care of it, if you like."

"Wouldn't think of it. If your sisters ever heard they'd drum you out of the movement."

"Oh, now, we're not—" She stopped when she decided he was joking.

He popped two croissants into the warming oven and ground the coffee beans. While the coffee drained he watched her pore over his record albums. She was indeed attractive! She must be thirty-five by now, had been a celebrity for almost ten years, but she maintained the body of a twenty-two-year-old—none of the flab or looseness most women start developing at twenty-five. He smiled . . . if only she'd emancipate herself from those ridiculous tinted glasses. Last night she actually wore them to bed and didn't take them off until he made a joke about it.

She took an album now from the cabinet and started toward the turntable. "I'll do it," he said, intercepting her. He hated anyone using his delicate equipment.

He put the album on the spindle. Ingrid Haebler playing Chopin. Very good choice. Buffy Weiss's taste was obviously better than her performing skill. He went back to the kitchen, held a cup of milk under the air hose on the cappuccino maker, then blended it with the coffee.

"By the way," he said, setting the cups on the table, "how did you happen to wake up so early this morning?"

She smiled. "I'm always up early. I've already read halfway through the *Times*. Are you a late sleeper?"

"I try to be, but the damned construction in this neighborhood during the week makes it impossible." He gestured to the skeleton of a new building outside the window. "Another six weeks and I'll lose my view. I'm thinking seriously of looking for another apartment, except with service the way it is in New York these days I wouldn't know where to begin. Service in this place is bad enough but at least I know what to expect. The Irish have a saying: 'Don't trade the devil you know for a devil you don't know.' "

She nodded, then went to the couch and found the real estate section of the *Times*. "Maybe you'd be interested in this. A new building on Second Avenue. Ted Vassily, the football player, is building it. Get this: 'Mr. Vassily has budgeted $100.00 per square foot of rentable space, which will make this structure the most expensive apartment building ever erected in New York. He said, 'Three-oh-five East will be a truly luxurious building in a city where genuine luxury has become all but impossible to find.' "

She handed Williams the paper. He scanned the article. The building would occupy the entire block between First and Second Avenues. The architect was Axel Wessman, who had come out of retirement at age eighty-six to design it. Going against the modern trend of rippleless planes of glass and concrete, he had contrived a structure reminiscent of the Florentine palace of Lorenzo de Medici. It would be granite and feature a four-story base built right to the edge of the property line. The interior would be for parking. The roof of the garage would be a block-sized garden and mall with shopping facilities and professional offices. A residential tower, reminiscent of Giotto's in Florence, would rise from each corner; tower heights would range from thirty to forty-eight stories.

"The thing that impresses me most," said Buffy Weiss, "is the allocation for lower income occupancy."

Joseph Williams' eyes went to the relevant paragraph. Vassily planned to set aside twenty percent of the apartments for rental at a token sum to the disadvantaged. The cost would be absorbed by the other apartments. Combined with the building's luxury services, this would result in an initial rental of about three hundred dollars per month per room, highest in New York.

"Mr. Vassily," he read aloud, "said he believed there were more than enough well-to-do New Yorkers who would be willing to undergo the extra cost in order to make it possible for disadvantaged people to enjoy a truly equal life style."

"I do, too," said Buffy Weiss. "In fact, I'm thinking of moving in myself. Don't you see, Joseph, this is a direct challenge to all of us who like to think of ourselves as liberals or even"—she smiled—"progressives. It's one thing to talk about equality of opportunity, but this man is really putting his money where his mouth is. And he's asking us to do the same."

Joseph Williams stared thoughtfully at the page. Partly he was wondering how a single girl like Buffy Weiss, celebrity or no, could afford the six hundred or nine hundred dollars a month that even a small apartment would cost. Partly he was toying with the idea of making the move himself. He agreed that the Vassily project was a real challenge to liberals. How could you say you believed all people were equal if you refused to live with some of them? He wouldn't undergo the discomforts of a slum, of course, but if 305 East proved out to be as luxurious as its builder promised, why not live in it? He'd be happy to pay a slightly higher rental to help poor people share that luxury. What the hell, *noblesse oblige.*

He'd need much the same setup he had here on Park Avenue: six or seven rooms for his family quarters and a second apartment for his office and studio. The family apartment should be a penthouse, or at least a duplex on a high floor. The studio would have to be soundproofed and contain a bedroom and kitchen, and it would have to be several floors distant from the family quarters lest his wife Maria observe the female traffic. But all this should be easy enough to arrange if he took action promptly.

"You're not listening to me," Buffy Weiss was saying.

He smiled. "My dear Buffy, I not only have been listening to you, I've been convinced by you. Good works should not go unrewarded. I'm going to move into Three-oh-five East."

"Are you serious?"

In reply, he took a telephone receiver from the shelf adjoining the table and punched out a number. "My business manager," he explained. Into the receiver he said, "Dave, sorry to bother you on a Sunday but there's something I want to take immediate action on. A new building going up, it's called Three-oh-five East. Details are in this morning's *Times.* Check it out, and if everything is bona fide, set me up there."

As he hung up he noted Buffy Weiss's expression. It was the same look he often saw in students' eyes when he lectured. And in the eyes of young lady reporters who came to interview him. It lay somewhere between worship and adoration. It was pleasant to look upon. Most pleasant.

"Joseph," she said, covering his hand with hers, "I'm impressed, I really am."

He leaned across the table to kiss her. She opened her

mouth to take his tongue. His hand eased across the table, and her breast fitted conveniently into it. He liked the feel of it: firm, full. Lovely.

There was no need to say anything. He stood. She stood. They embraced. He took her hand and started toward the bedroom.

"Oh, just a moment," he said midway across the room. He went back to the telephone and again pushed the buttons for his business manager's number. "Dave, on Three-oh-five East, it occurs to me that the best approach might be to have my press agent tie in with the building's press agent. It should help them to publicize that I'm going to be a tenant."

"How do you know the building has a press agent?" Buffy Weiss asked as they continued into the bedroom.

Williams smiled. "How do you think the story got in the *Times,* my dear? That football hero certainly didn't write it himself."

John Malloy read the story on the plane to Florida. It was one of several dozen clippings in an envelope prepared by his chief of staff Tom Donohue.

Tom Donohue had been one of the bright young guys on the fringes of the Kennedy administration before that fateful November day when Lee Harvey Oswald brought down the curtain on Camelot. Though Donohue's personal role in Camelot was a walk-on, that was enough for John Malloy, who regarded John Fitzgerald Kennedy as the greatest politician of modern times.

One of Kennedy's greatest strengths, John Malloy believed, was his refusal to let yes-men insulate him from the outside world. He read several newspapers daily and the three news magazines weekly. So did John Malloy. He had staff men scan the papers he himself did not have time to read and clip items they thought warranted his attention. So did John Malloy.

"305 East ideal base if we go ahead with Project RFK," read Tom Donohue's note, stapled to the clipping. Project RFK was John Malloy's plan to take a page from the book of Robert Kennedy and move to New York to run for the Senate. New York was the only state in the union where a charismatic outsider with enough media money could put the blocks to the local pols. And, of course, New Yorkers were much more receptive to the Malloy charisma than the folks in his home state of Connecticut.

As he read the story on 305 East, John Malloy felt it couldn't be more right for him if he'd designed it himself.

"Johnny," he said to his twelve-year-old son, who sat next to him on the plane, "how'd you like to live in an apartment building that's being built by Ted Vassily?"

"Who's Ted Vassily?"

John Malloy smiled. It didn't *seem* that long ago. "Probably the greatest quarterback that ever lived," he said.

"Did he play at Yale?"

"No, Penn State. Then pro ball in New York . . . he eventually even bought the team, then sold it."

"Jeez, the name sounds familiar. But he was way before my time, Pop."

John Malloy's smile broadened as he remembered that day in September—was it really fifteen years ago? There were eighteen seconds on the clock. New York was down by three points. The ball was on the Cleveland forty-five, second down and short yardage.

Against a prevent defense, Vassily had used short passes to move forty yards in six plays. New York still had one time-out left. Another short completion would mean excellent field goal range. Cleveland tightened up.

And Vassily opened up. He took the snap from center and did his characteristic back-pedaling dance into the pocket. Mikey DeAngelico, his favorite receiver, was in heavy traffic in the flat. Vassily's arm came back, then forward, and John Malloy's eyes automatically had gone to DeAngelico—who didn't get the ball. Now, as two Cleveland defensemen broke into the pocket, Vassily uncorked one. Long. Incredibly long. He was standing on his own forty when he threw it. And it just kept going and going, high and far, to Emerson Wade, the lanky rookie wide receiver, who was alone in the end zone. And dropped it.

John Malloy had almost expected the New York fans to storm the field and assault Wade. The pass had been perfect. And had traveled an astonishing sixty-four yards in the air.

New York huddled. The clock was stopped at nine seconds. There was still time for the short completion, a time-out, and a field goal attempt. But it would be close.

Vassily took the snap. Back into the pocket. Defense charging. DeAngelico in the flat. Another fake. And another bomb. And, to John Malloy's disbelief, right after Vassily let go of the ball, he turned and started off the field.

Emerson Wade wasn't alone this time. The Cleveland safety was on his heels. The ball followed the exact same arcing path of the first pass and stuck to Wade's outstretched fingers inside the end zone. The official measurement: sixty-four yards in the air. Touchdown. Game. Conference championship.

After the game, reporters asked Vassily why he had started off the field. He told them, "Wade knew better than to drop two in a row."

"Ted Vassily could, as they say, thread a needle at seventy yards," John Malloy told his son, then told him the story of the championship pass. "They used to call him Instant Replay. He liked to cross up the defense by calling the same play twice in a row. You'd think after ten years they'd have been able to anticipate it, but about the only times they did was when he didn't do it."

That afternoon, once John Malloy and his family had settled into their waterfront home in Palm Beach, he had his advance man Ed O'Hora set up a conference call with Donohue in Philadelphia and Ted Vassily.

"Ted," said John Malloy, "I want to tell you I admire what you're doing and I want to give you all the support I can. In fact, I'd like to rent an apartment in your new building—eight to ten rooms and preferably on the same floor with one or more of the subsidized apartments. Tom Donohue will work out the details. Perhaps I can also arrange some financial support during construction if you need it."

Tom Donohue stayed on the line after Ted Vassily had hung up. "Tom," said John Malloy, "I assume that Vassily is perfectly legitimate, but run the usual investigation and shitcan the whole thing if anything unsavory turns up."

"I've already developed some information, John. You'll want to think about it. He sold his interest in the ball club five years ago and went into the construction business specializing in low-income housing. Federally financed."

"Some pretty nasty people in that."

"Yeah, and Vassily rubbed elbows with a few of them—though I think he himself was on the up-and-up. There was quite a scandal in Michigan involving one of his projects. A building collapsed, killed twenty-six people."

"Oh, yeah, I remember reading something about that. I didn't know it was his building."

"His corporation, T. V. Construction, was the general contractor. An investigation showed one of the subcontractors had used substandard materials and bribed the federal inspector to let them pass. The investigation cleared Vassily and his people, but he apparently blamed himself for not having stayed sufficiently on top of the situation. He got out of the construction business then and joined the faculty of some small college in California, teaching business administration. That was year before last. He's apparently been in hibernation between then and now."

John Malloy stared thoughtfully at the Atlantic horizon outside his window. "So old Instant Replay is either a con artist with a new scheme or an honest man who got taken and wants to show the world he's absolutely legit."

"Yeah . . . show the world, I'd say. Or maybe just show himself. One more thing, John. The subcontractor and the bribed federal inspector are both dead. They were beaten to death, apparently by a man who used his bare fists. One bought it in Michigan, the other in Arizona. Nobody was ever arrested, let alone convicted. Vassily was never a suspect in either case. But if you remember him on the football field, well, it doesn't exactly stagger the imagination . . ."

John Malloy next changed into his swim trunks, hunted up a football in one of the closets and went down to the beach with his son.

"Goin' long, dad," Johnny called over his shoulder as he raced along the surf.

His father gave him a lead of twenty-five yards, then put the ball in the air. It was a beautiful pass—high, long, good spiral. He would have been damn pleased with it when he was quarterbacking Yale. Of course, Yale was not Penn State. And he was not Ted Vassily . . .

Johnny now saw the ball over his head and accelerated. It was slightly to his left, over the water, and he pumped his legs high as he splashed in after it, not taking his eyes from the ball or slowing down as he kept his arms out in front of him. The ball landed flat in his palms, bobbled there for a moment, then stuck. He pulled it against his chest, took another half dozen steps into the surf, turned around, jumped into the air, and exultantly tried to spike the ball the way the pros always did on TV.

"All right!" he called back, dancing with one fist high over his head. "All right!"

John smiled as Johnny retrieved the ball and jogged back up the beach. "Jeez, Dad, you're a regular Ted Vaseline. That must've gone sixty yards easy."

John laughed. "Vassily, Johnny. And it was more like forty."

"No, it was farther than that."

"Well, let's try it again." John took the ball, gripped it with his baby and ring fingers against the laces, and danced back into an imaginary pocket. He really did hope that Ted Vassily was legit.

Eddie Spats Johnson, Jr., had read the story on the plane from California. Normally he did not read the *New York Times.* He preferred the *Daily News.* But on airplanes he was a compulsive reader to keep down jet nerves, and he'd already finished the *Reporter* and *Variety* he'd brought from L.A. He was desperate enough to ask the guy in the aisle seat who wasn't reading his paper if he could borrow it, and then proceeded to devour it, including the real estate section, where a headline especially caught his eye: "Ex-Football Great Ted Vassily Will Build 'American Dream' on 2nd Ave."

Eddie Spats Johnson, Jr., loved football. When he saw that the ex-great was Ted Vassily, he read with special attention.

Next to Sammy Davis, Jr., now retired, who in Eddie's own field had demonstrated such versatility, talent and drive, Eddie probably admired Ted Vassily more than any other man. And Eddie had, over the years, won more money on Ted Vassily than on any other human or animal in sports. Indeed, if he'd limited his wagering to games in which Ted Vassily played he'd have been tens of thousands of dollars ahead now rather than hundreds of thousands behind.

He remembered his two biggest scores: the last two games Ted Vassily had played. It was after Vassily had retired from active play but still owned the team and traditionally opened each season by putting himself in at quarterback for the first offensive play.

The first year, from his own thirty-five, he'd passed to Mikey DeAngelico for a touchdown. Eddie *didn't* have a bet on that game. But the next year, when Vassily announced that he'd take the first play from scrimmage again, Eddie phoned his man in Vegas: "Give me a hundred to one he can't do it again."

"Thirty to one," said the book.

Eddie insisted on fifty to one—which was still ridiculously low, the odds against a touchdown pass on the first play from scrimmage being something like eight hundred thou to one.

"Tell you what," said the book. "Forty to one against a first-play touchdown, no matter how it's scored."

Which was pretty ridiculous also, since Ted Vassily obviously was not going to put himself in the game for one play and then hand off to the fullback. He was filling the stadium with people who wanted one more look at the old man throwing a bomb.

But Eddie Spats took the bet. It was the kind of situation where his hunch was too strong to resist . . . and if he ignored it and Vassily actually scored a first-play touchdown, well, Eddie would have had nightmares over it for the rest of his life.

He bet modestly. One thousand dollars. And he was sure he'd lost it when the Chicago kicker booted into the end zone, which meant the ball would be put into play on the New York twenty. Chicago, of course, would play prevent on the well-advertised first play, determined not to let Vassily do what he had done last year.

The snapback from center. Vassily into the pocket. No defensemen coming at him, with all the linebackers and safeties back in the prevent zone. DeAngelico double-teamed. Wade covered. "Peanuts" Huddleston covered. In fact, every eligible receiver was covered. Except Walt Kulikowski.

The burly fullback, who probably hadn't caught ten passes in as many years, suddenly released the tackle he'd been blocking and stepped out into the flat. As the tackle now charged in, Vassily popped the ball over his head and into Kulikowski's hands. By the time the defense realized what was happening, Kulikowski was running with the momentum of a locomotive. Meanwhile, the downfield receivers were throwing blocks at their surprised defenders.

Two defenders did manage to get close to Kulikowski at the thirty. He drove straight into them, head down, and they fell away like bowling pins. Someone got a fistful of his jersey at the ten yard line, and Kulikowski carried him across the goal line. Eddie Spats Johnson, Jr., had won forty thousand dollars.

Two months before the next year's opening game with Pittsburgh Eddie started getting the old vibes again. He wanted to bet the whole forty thou. He couldn't get coverage for it but he did manage to cover eighteen, half in Vegas, the rest spread out in New York, L.A., Chicago, Miami, and New Orleans. His odds ranged from thirty to one to a hundred to one—still ridiculously low.

He couldn't sleep for three days before the game. There was some talk Vassily had decided not to put himself in. Kickoff time. Eddie sat in Joe Mandino's private booth at the stadium. When Vassily came onto the field, wearing his familiar green jersey with the number 13, the crowd roared its pleasure and anticipation. Eddie had been on stage before a hundred thousand lonely and entertainment-starved GI's, but they hadn't approached anything like this.

Pittsburgh had won the toss, elected to receive, and fumbled on its own twenty-eight. Eddie's heart was beating so loudly he thought it would just up and blow out. What a setup for a one-play touchdown!

Vassily bent over his center, and for a moment it looked as though something had gone wrong. The New York line didn't move, except for "Nasty" Nate Elefante, the right tackle. And the backfield.

Eddie thought it was a busted play, maybe an offside or illegal procedure. So, apparently, did everyone else. Including Pittsburgh. It wasn't until Vassily was halfway to the end zone that the defenders realized what had happened. And he was across the goal line before the crowd caught on.

Eddie had to watch the play a dozen times on film before he finally figured out what happened. And even then he didn't believe it.

What happened was, the center had snapped the ball back to Vassily as Nate Elefante hit through the line. That automatically ruled out the possibility of a pass because Nasty Nate, an ineligible receiver, was downfield. But everything happened too fast for Pittsburgh. As Elefante shot through, two of the backs came up to Vassily's quarterback slot, as in a running play, then mysteriously dropped back. Now the guards and left tackle dropped back, too, forming the familiar pocket that Vassily liked to throw from. But in Vassily's place in the pocket was Hank Manheimer, the slotback. And while he was posturing as if about to pass, he didn't have the ball.

By the time Pittsburgh read the fake, Vassily was ten yards past the line of scrimmage. The linebackers had blitzed and were out of the action. The cornerback had a shot at him, but Elefante had a line on the cornerback. He threw a block, and Ted Vassily, the quarterback who hated to run—in fact, as statistics later would show, the quarterback who had not run ten yards in ten years as a pro—ran a quarterback sneak for a twenty-eight yard touchdown.

Eddie won more than half a million dollars. Joe Mandino, who had to intercede to get some of the bigger losers to pay off, at first suspected that Eddie had some advance knowledge of the play. It was only after he'd worked out in his mind the possible ways to a fix and had decided you'd have to cut too many defense players into the action that he believed Eddie really was operating on a pure hunch. . . .

Now, on the airplane from Los Angeles to New York, Eddie read about Ted Vassily's new construction project and couldn't help comparing the course of his own life with the quarterback's. Vassily had walked out a winner.

He had hung up his cleats after that game and had sold his interest in the team midway through the season. New York never won another championship. Five years later, Vassily was a wealthy man devoting his time to humanitarian projects.

And Eddie Spats Johnson, Jr.? He was on his ass. Again. He had invested three mil in two movies, with himself as the star and director. Both bombed. He was in hock in Vegas for the entire hundred thou he would earn for his annual four weeks at The Purple Sage. He hadn't had a hit record in fifteen years. And the only movie and TV work he could get was cameo or guest-star stuff thrown his way by friends who felt sorry for him.

Eddie Spats Johnson, Jr., who as a five-year-old was earning fifty dollars a week playing the clarinet; Eddie Spats Johnson, Jr., who had more hit singles than any other black entertainer, *including* the great Sammy Davis; Eddie Spats Johnson, Jr., who went bust and came back to win two Oscars and host the highest-rated variety show on TV; Eddie Spats Johnson, Jr., who had sung in the White House and got a commendation from the president; Eddie Spats Johnson, Jr., who at one point was even being considered a possible candidate for governor of California (what the hell, if Reagan could do it . . .)—Eddie Spats Johnson, Jr., was on his ass again.

How? How could he have pissed away every last penny of the more than fifteen million dollars he had earned since that first gig on clarinet in his daddy's Dixieland band?

Granted, he had always been a high roller. Granted, he'd given more than three mil to charity and made bad investments with about five mil more. Still, to be broke at age forty-five after nearly three decades of international superstardom . . .

And now here he was on his way to New York again, just like when he got out of the army, starting from scratch. Well, not quite from scratch. He wasn't an unknown. But in some ways he'd be better off if he were—better an unknown than a guy with a reputation as a loser.

Worst of all, he was broke. Not only would he have to hassle the has-been shit, he'd also have to sweat coming up with the ten thousand dollars a month he needed to maintain his place in L.A., his alimony payments, his contributions to the Black Scholarship Fund, and his professional staff. His personal manager Manny Greenberg advised cutting back on everything: sell the L.A. place, fire the staff, declare personal bankruptcy, live in a modest apartment for a year or two while he worked on a comeback. But Spats couldn't handle that. He had the feeling—as strong as the one that impelled him to bet eighteen thousand dollars that Ted Vassily would score a first-play touchdown—that it would be the end of the line for him if he ever cut back on expenses. He just couldn't hack the shame—never mind the discomfort.

But the fact was, the dollars had stopped coming, and he was out of his mind trying to figure out how to get them rolling again. Movies were out. After his last two bombs, no one would touch him. Records ditto. He could produce his own session with just a few thou, but he didn't have material he liked and he was too hassled to go looking for new stuff. TV was a blank: variety shows were dead, and the pilot he'd done for a black adventure series got no takers. Manny Greenberg suggested capitalizing on the big-band re-revival by putting a group together and going on the road, but after expenses he'd be lucky to clear two or three thou a week. Meanwhile the road shit would tie up so much of his time that he'd never be able to work on getting something else going.

What he'd really like to try was hosting his own talk-and-variety show, in the old Johnny Carson slot of 11:15 to 1:00 a.m. But Manny Greenberg got him two weeks subbing on "The Show" and the ratings dropped like a dead bird. After that, no one would touch him.

He could only think of one person to turn to, one person with the power to help him, who'd never let him down in the past. He didn't want to do it this way, he preferred to do it on his own or with the help of show-biz friends, but it was too late for that now. Another month or two without something happening would mean Tap City. He needed help fast. When his plane landed in New York, he took a taxi to Fifth Avenue and Sixty-eighth Street.

"Mr. Johnson for Mr. Mandino," he told the doorman, who eyed him warily.

"Who?"

Eddie felt his anger rising. Did the doorman find it so fucken odd for a black man to come to his building? Did you have to be in white tie and tails for the bastards to treat you with a little respect? "Johnson," he repeated with exaggerated enunciation. "For Mandino."

"Jansen?"

"Johnson, goddamn it. Eddie Spats Johnson. Don't you ever go to the movies, man? You been dead or something, man?"

"Does Mr. Mandino expect you?"

"No, dumb-dumb, I just go around ringing people's doorbells in the middle of the night to shake them up. What the fuck business is it of yours if he's expecting me? Ring the fucken bell and tell him I'm here."

The doorman planted his hands on his hips. "Look, fella, don't talk that way to me." A buzzer summoned him to his switchboard but he ignored it. "I don't care *who* you are, you don't talk that way to me."

Eddie actually felt heat in the back of his neck. He wanted to punch out the doorman, except he didn't dare step out of line . . . the fucker'd have him arrested and he'd blow the next two months fighting an assault charge.

The doorman glared at him for another moment, then went to the switchboard and got into a conversation with one of the building's tenants.

Eddie was seething. What the fuck did the guy expect him to do—stand here in the doorway all night? He hesitated a second, then strode across the lobby.

"Wait a minute—" the doorman called, chasing after him.

Eddie kept walking until the elevator operator blocked his path. The doorman moved in behind him, and both hovered as if about to throw him out. They were each over six feet.

"Now look, you fuckers," he said, reaching over his head to shake a finger in their faces, "I'm Eddie Spats Johnson and Mr. Mandino expects me. So watch your goddamn asses or you're gonna both be in more trouble than you can handle, I guarantee you."

"If Mister Mandino expects you," said the doorman, "he'll tell me on the phone. Until then you're not getting on that elevator." With deliberate slowness, he waddled back to the door and lifted the switchboard phone. There was an exchange of words, then he replaced the receiver. He didn't come back to Eddie Spats. He didn't say anything.

"Well?" Eddie prodded.

The doorman, after a long pause, said, "Mr. Mandino is sending someone down."

A moment later a man of about seventy with an often-broken nose and one cauliflower ear shuffled into the lobby. He wore a tuxedo, and his voice was raspy to the point of near-inaudibility. "Little Spats!" he beamed, throwing his arms wide. "It's good to have you back!"

"Hi, Angie." Eddie smiled. "How's my man?"

They embraced, then Angie led the way into the elevator and inserted a key into the keyhole between the buttons labeled 18 and 20.

"Uncle Joe has the whole floor, Spats," Angie said. "So we had them put a special lock on the elevator buttons. That way nobody gets in that we don't want. Smart, eh?"

Spats smiled. It was good hearing one of the old guys boast of his shrewdness. It reminded you of the old days. "Smart, Angie," he agreed, touching an index finger to his temple.

"You okay, Spats? Everything all right?"

Spats kept his smile in place. You don't reveal your problems to the flunkies. "Terrif, Angie. Never been better."

"You look it, Spats. Good to see you."

The elevator opened into a huge foyer with a pale pink marble floor and pillars. The entrance was flanked by mirrors in ornate gold frames.

"Some spread," said Spats under his breath.

"Wait till you see the inside." Angie led him to the living room, which wasn't much smaller than a basketball court. The pink marble floor of the foyer gave way to one of deep forest-green laced with pink. A lighter green marble continued three feet up the wall, giving way after a trim of more forest-green to a rich olive-green silk wallcloth. The wall facing the entrance was consumed by a picture window that looked out over Central Park. A fireplace of forest-green marble dominated one of the flanking walls; a large marine scene by Clyde Prettyman hung over it. The opposite wall featured three twelve-by-sixteen portraits in a neo-Byzantine style by the Sicilian artist, Saro.

"Eddie, my boy," beamed Joe Mandino from the center of the room. "Come in! Come in!" He stood before a fountain featuring four fish heads spitting streams of water onto the body of a large, reclining, white marble nude. Joe was tall and slender in an impeccably tailored three-piece blue serge suit. His thinning brownish-gray hair was slicked down in a style reminiscent of the nineteen fifties.

Eddie felt underdressed and ill-at-ease in his tight stovepipe slacks and open-throat, black lace sport shirt—even though he'd worn the same outfit with comfort on real formal deals in California. "Uncle Joe!" he said, making loud sounds with his cleats as he ran across the marble floor. "Uncle Joe, I really missed you!"

Joe Mandino kissed him twice on each cheek, then threw an arm over his shoulder and led him to the couch. "Ah, my little boy," he sighed. *"Mio piccolo cioccolato."* He hugged Eddie, cuffed him on both shoulders, then hugged him again, held him at arm's length and gazed sorrowfully into his face. "So long your Uncle Joe doesn't see you, *piccolo*. So long."

Eddie grinned sheepishly. "You know how it is, Uncle. We get busy, we get tied up, one thing leads to another, next thing you know five years gone down the tube."

"I know, *bello*, I know." He took one of Spats's cheeks between the thumb and forefinger of each hand and pinched vigorously. "Ah, *mio bello, mio carissimo bello!*" He sighed mightily. "Too long, *bello*. Too long." He hugged him again. "But you never have to worry about your uncle, *bello*. I know how it is. And I know how my boy feels about me."

Eddie patted him affectionately on the back, then slowly eased his way out of the clinch. Much as he loved his many friends of Italian ancestry, he could never get completely comfortable about their penchant for physical intimacy. "It's a beautiful place you have here, Uncle Joe." He made a sweeping gesture to encompass it all. "It reflects your taste."

"Grazie, piccino. I'm glad you like it. Now we have a

drink together, you and your uncle, eh? We drink to old times. And new times." He gestured to Angie, who already had poured the glasses of *amaretto* and now hurried over with them. "To Eddie Spats, one of the finest men I've ever known. And one of the most talented. Drink, *bello*. Drink. You're with your uncle now. You can relax."

They drank and hugged and drank some more. Angie then fetched a fresh round, and Joe Mandino led the way out to his terrace overlooking Central Park. "Eddie," he said softly, "I should tell you something while Angie isn't here to listen. With the doormen, Eddie—with the elevator operators, with waiters and taxi guys and people like that—with these *scugnizzi,* Eddie, we never let go of the control, eh, goombah? *Giammai perdere la faccia,* eh? They're not worth it, *bello*. You understand?"

"I'm sorry, Uncle. I guess I got a little upset. You know, the black thing and all."

Joe Mandino raised his hand in a manner that bordered on the papal. "I understand, *bello*. I understand. But we don't do it anyway, you know? Because we don't want, for the sake of some *scugnizzi* like these, to get a fight going and have the cops come around and embarrass some people that don't deserve to be embarrassed, you see what I mean, *bello*? Now, enough of this subject, eh? It's very unpleasant. No more. Okay?" He put his arms around Eddie and patted him on the back.

Eddie returned the hug.

"You understand. Good," Joe continued without waiting for acknowledgment, "it's hard enough in these days of persecution and prejudice, *bello,* the goddamn D.A.s don't have enough to do without going around harassing law-abiding citizens, the newspapers can't leave an innocent man alone—you see the paper this morning, by any chance? You see the story about me?" Without waiting for an answer, Joe stepped back into the living room and went to an antique secretary, from one of whose shelves he withdrew a copy of the newspaper folded to an inside page. Eddie dutifully followed.

"You see this? And the writer's name? Gershman? Gershwin? Some kike, in any case. You see what he writes: 'Police believe the city's five Mafia families are engaged in another full-scale program of investing in legitimate businesses in order to infiltrate and ultimately take control of them. Masterminds of the operation are said to be Manhattan superboss Joseph "Coffee Joe" Mandino and Brooklyn chieftain Anthony "Tony Bags" Bagatello.'

"You ever hear anything like that in your life, Little Spats? What's this superboss nonsense? Not once do they show a drop of evidence I ever committed a crime. But they call me a Mafia superboss right in the paper, plain as day. Is that right? You tell me, is it *right*?"

He slapped the paper vigorously with the back of his hand. "And what's this 'Coffee Joe' business? And 'Tony Bags'? A wasp Wall Street lawyer commits a crime, do you see them calling him names? A cop makes an arrest, do they say 'Edward "Shit-the-Pants" McDonough was the arresting officer'? Like hell they do, even though his friends have been calling him 'Shit-the-Pants' since he was four years old. And 'Baby-face' Rockefeller. And 'Actor' Lindsay. Or whatever they used to call those fine statesmen. Do you see that in the papers? But let some poor Italian blow a fart off-key and out come the cute names. Coffee Joe. Coffee Joe!

"Twenty-two years ago I happen to be in some guy's kitchen in Chicago making coffee, when the Cook County sheriff's detectives bust the place without a warrant. The F.B.I. decides it's an international crime convention and ask me what I heard people say. I tell them I didn't hear anything because I was in the kitchen making coffee. From that minute on, I'm 'Coffee Joe' Mandino, including in the great so-called liberal press."

He threw the paper disgustedly into the secretary, then looked up and, almost magically, replaced his scowl with a smile. "But Eddie Spats, we don't wanna talk about this boring stuff, do we? We want to talk about my dear friend Spats." He gave him another pinch on both cheeks. "*Andiamo, bello*. We go outside on the terrace. You tell your Uncle Joe what you've been doing lately . . . how you feel . . . what's bothering you . . ."

Eddie stared out at the darkness over Central Park and briefly remembered the nights, almost four decades ago, when his father would walk him into the park when they came home from a gig at four or five in the morning and sat on a bench and waited for sunrise. And Eddie Spats Johnson, Sr., would tell him about places in the United States that he had played on "Orpheum Time" and other vaudeville circuits—places where the whole town was like this park, with streets that wound along rivers and houses that never were more than two stories high, and people would sit on their porches at night and never worry about being assaulted or robbed.

"I'm in bad shape, Uncle," Eddie said softly, almost confessionally. "I'm on my ass."

Mandino nodded. "You get in trouble, Eddie, 'cause you piss people off. You mouth off to doormen and you play house with white women. You have to learn, *piccino*—never piss people off unless there's a profit in it."

Eddie did not choose to argue this point. He knew Joe Mandino was his last hope. "I'm learning, Uncle. It's hard, but I'm learning."

"Good, *bello*. That's what I want to hear. Now your troubles. Tell me."

Eddie related his failures and hard times over the past three years. "I don't know where to turn, Uncle—except to you."

"You did the right thing, Eddie. I can help you. Now that talk show—that doesn't sound like such a bad idea. Maybe if one or two big sponsors went to a network and said they'd like to get involved, the network would reconsider, don't you think?"

"Hell, yes. Do you know somebody who would?"

"I'll look around. I'll see." He draped his arm over Eddie's shoulders. "Don't you worry about a thing, *bello*. You go back to California and fuck some of those big-titted blondes. I'll do what I can and call you when it's done."

"Uh, Uncle, there's just one problem. A big problem." Eddie explained his money situation and the ten thou a month he'd need to keep afloat.

Joe whistled under his breath. "You really know how to spend it, eh, *bello?* But don't worry. It's taken care of. I'll have the lawyers set something up."

"Uh, Uncle, just one more thing, I've been thinking, maybe it wouldn't be a bad idea to live here in New York for a while. You know. Change my luck. Be on the scene. Where the action is. There's this apartment building I've been thinking about. Maybe you saw the story in today's papers . . ."

Joe hadn't, and now got the real estate section from the secretary. "Why would you want to live in a building with poor people?" he asked as he finished reading.

"They're my people, Uncle. They're the ones I grew up with and the ones that buy my records. They keep me in business." He smiled awkwardly. "Besides, it won't be bad for the old image. That old flashy Sammy Davis stuff with a Rolls Royce and four hundred dollar suits is out nowadays. People want an entertainer to be more down-to-earth, man of the people . . ."

Joe screwed up his face thoughtfully. "I think you may have a very good idea there."

"I think lots of important people will be doing it, Uncle. I mean, it's a natural. You know. For politicians, actors, anybody that needs an image. And it's not like you'd have to make any big sacrifice if the guy does what he says he'll do. All the luxury services should be there . . ."

Joe Mandino seemed not to be listening. His eyes stared somewhere beyond Eddie.

"You dig, Uncle? Okay for me to do it?"

Joe made a sort of shooing gesture with one hand, as if to brush away a fly, then went to the secretary and found an unopened bottle of *amaretto*. "You know," he said, refilling both glasses, "you people have the right idea about this image shit. We Italians could learn from you."

"Then you'll help me set up at this Three-oh-five East?"

"I want to ask you a question, *piccolo,* and I want a straight answer. Don't be afraid." He peered somberly over the rim of his glass. "If I thought about moving into that building myself—I mean, if I checked it out and decided it was worth moving into, tell me the truth now, no bullshit—would it hurt you in any way, *piccolo,* if I happened to live in the same building?"

Eddie hesitated. "Well, if there were just the two of us, Uncle—maybe—but if a lot of other big shots lived there . . . you know what I mean . . .?"

Joe nodded, then looked down at the newspaper.

"Three-oh-five East, eh? Maybe it'll be a better address than Fifth Avenue." He smiled. "Maybe they'll have doormen there who treat a man's guests with respect."

Grace Colello almost didn't read the *Times* story. A political science major at City College, she allowed herself only one day of recreational reading, which was Sunday, and though most of it was given over to the *Times*, the real estate section was not on her list of priorities.

However, on this particular Sunday she was flirting with the idea of moving out of her parents' Brooklyn apartment and taking a place in Manhattan with some girls from school. After scanning the classified columns and circling a few ads, she let herself browse some of the pages with display ads for luxury apartment buildings—the sort of life style she and her friends professed to hold in contempt but about which she occasionally still had fantasies.

The headline caught her eye: "Ex-Football Great Ted Vassily Will Build 'American Dream' on 2nd Ave."

Now what was the "American dream"? Heart-shaped bathtubs and electric douche bags? She read the article, ready to sneer, and was astounded to find that Ted Vassily's American Dream was not so far removed from her own. Even more astounding, she might qualify to live in the building—not as a single girl but with her family.

"Dad," she said, showing him the newspaper, "why don't we put in an application for this?"

Marty Colello scanned the story, then winced. "You never learn, do you?"

"Oh, don't be such a cynic. It says twenty percent of the apartments will be rented to low-income people at scaled prices. What's so suspicious about that?"

"Why do you think they're doing it? Because they feel sorry for us? Come on, grow up."

"Why do you care why they're doing it? If it gratifies your sense of paranoia, say they're doing it for a tax write-off. The fact remains, they're doing it, and we may be eligible."

He sighed. "Look, Gracie, I may not be one of your smart-guy college professors but I've been around a little longer than you have and I know which end is up. Mark my words, if these Jew bastards are giving up twenty apartments to poor people, you can bet they're in the cellar and full of rats and Christ-knows-what-else—"

"How do you know they're Jews? Where does it say they're Jews? And anyway—"

"Who else would be doing something like this? Who else does anything in this goddamn city? Anyway, they gotta be garbage apartments and if they aren't, there's some other gimmick. Cause there's one thing you're not gonna change in this world, young lady—not you, not your college professors, not anybody else—the one thing you're not gonna change is that there's no such thing as a free lunch."

"You're so . . . so *damned* cynical!" She clenched her fists and looked for something to bang them on. She wanted to say "fucking cynical," but she didn't dare. Not to *her* father. "You always suspect everyone's motives. And demean everyone's intelligence." She took a deep breath, as if to fuel herself for an extended tirade, then slowly let it all out. There was no point in railing at him. He was hopeless.

"Well," he said, "I may not be one of your goddamn Einsteins from City College, but I've got eyes, I can see. And one thing I've seen these long fifty-five years is that nobody ever gave Marty Colello a goddamn thing he didn't work for. So put that in your pipe and smoke it, Miss College Girl."

She made herself smile. There was no other way with him. "Suppose I put in an application for us. Would you mind that?"

"Save your time. If the apartments aren't in the goddamn cellar, some Jews that work in the *Times* composing room rented all goddamn twenty percent of them two days before the paper hit the newsstands."

"It's my time. So let me waste it."

"If the apartments aren't already rented they gotta be crap."

"If they're crap we don't have to move into one. We can stay in this lovely palace."

"I'm telling you, you're wasting your time."

"So let me waste it."

"All right, fill out the goddamn application. See for yourself. Like I've had to all these years."

Hartford Loomis scanned the report on his desk. "With a background like this," he told George DelVecchio, "I don't think Mr. Vassily is going to have a very easy time coming up with either money or tenants."

"I hate to be contrary, Hart, but I think you're wrong."

"Would you want to live in a building put up by a guy whose last one collapsed?"

"I wouldn't mind living in this one, if I were in that financial league. And judging from the feedback I've been getting, lots of people feel the same way. Vassily's rental agent tells me some very big names have already put down deposits for apartments. Big names in show business, politics—"

"Yes, that's the kind of character this thing would appeal to. But they're not going to get their apartments if he can't find the money to put up the building."

He lowered his gaze to the folder on his desk, signaling DelVecchio to leave, then leaned back in his chair, put his feet on the beige Brazilian leather hassock alongside the desk and stared pensively out his window over the roofs of the neighboring buildings. It was another clear day, just like the day before, and looking to the northeast he could see beyond the Manhattan Bridge to the tenements of Bedford-Stuyvesant, then the smokestacks of industrial Brooklyn. God, how he loved the views of New York. There wasn't another city in the world with anything that rivaled them—not even San Francisco. It would be intolerable if he lost the view from his apartment. He couldn't bear waking each morning and looking out the window at someone else's wall.

He picked up the Vassily folder and flipped through it, letting his eyes rest on the various documents without actually reading them. Finally he buzzed his secretary and asked her to send in George DelVecchio.

"This feedback you've been getting," he said, "are you sure it's an accurate picture?"

DelVecchio shrugged. "I haven't tried to verify anything, but I have no reason to doubt anything I've been told."

"Well, make a few more inquiries. Verify. And if it seems likely that Vassily's going to succeed getting the building up, rent me the northeast penthouse. Be damn careful about putting our own money in it, though . . ."

George DelVecchio chuckled. "Hart, would you want to live in a building put up by a guy whose last one collapsed?"

Hartford Loomis smiled mirthlessly. "I like the neighborhood, George."

When George DelVecchio got back to his own office, his intercom was buzzing.

"George," said Hartford Loomis, "make that two apartments. The northeast penthouse for me and something smaller for Nan. Maybe a large studio or a small one-bedroom. On a different floor, of course. So she'll have some privacy. She's a big girl now." She certainly was.

TWO

TWO MONTHS later.

Ted slept through the landing. Usually he didn't. Usually his eyes were fixed to the window, scanning the terrain—a holdover from the days when he was so afraid to fly that he didn't dare shift in his seat for fear the slight rearrangement of his weight would upset the plane's balance. Not tonight. Tonight he conked out at thirty-seven thousand feet and didn't wake until the plane was on the ground and two hundred screaming assholes were jamming the aisles wrestling with each other for access to the overhead storage bins while a frazzled stewardess on the public address system urged them to remain in their seats until the aircraft had come to a complete halt (can aircraft come to a partial halt?) at the terminal. These same screaming people, Ted reflected, had been the paradigm of courtesy in Los Angeles four hours and forty-eight minutes ago. New York, it seemed, could bring out the worst in everybody.

While he waited for the aisles to clear, he tried rubbing some of the pain and stiffness out of his knees, which were inflicting their usual punishment with unusual gusto—probably the rain. As he followed the crowd out of the airplane the stewardess at the door flashed a waxey professional smile as he neared. " 'Bye, now."

"Eat dick," he murmured. Up in the air he had asked for her phone number and she'd brushed him off.

She kept smiling, but now there seemed to be a slight

quiver at one corner of her mouth, as if she had heard him and were fighting to hold on to the smile. He looked to her eyes. Their immaculate blankness persuaded him that nothing had registered. That, he told himself, was what was wrong with the world: horny pricks like himself were always reading things into a girl's expression just because she had big tits and a cute ass.

He followed the crowd to the baggage area, spotted his battered old pullman, retrieved it from between two characters with purple double-knit blazers who were taking over the area around the carousel as if they were blocking the old Minnesota front four on third and long, and went out to the place on the sidewalk where the Carey bus should stop unless they were on strike or the Port Authority had changed the procedures for the umpteenth time in a week and a half or something else had gotten fouled up. To his surprise, a bus was there.

So was one of the original all-pro front four, Natale Nasty Nate Elefante, all two hundred and eighty pounds of him. "Teddy, baby!" he called, charging across the sidewalk, his enormous gut leading the rest of him on a power sweep. "Good ta see ya, my man! Good ta see ya!"

"Hi, fucker." Ted grinned and made a fist, which he planted in Nate's midsection. It nearly disappeared before meeting the resistance of a solid wall of muscle.

Nate put his head back and laughed, then uncorked his own punch. Ted barely saw it coming, flexed, and smiled as it met the rock-wall resistance of his own abdominals. Actually, the shot hurt some, and the smile suppressed a wince.

Nate enjoyed putting on a show. "My man, my man, what a gas this is!" He wrapped his arms around Ted and hoisted him into the air. "Instant Replay, you old fucker. The Man with the Golden Arm. Mr. Clean, the Mean Thirteen." He spun Ted around, then set him down and held him at arm's length, as if to make sure he hadn't picked up someone else by mistake. "You get yo'se'f lots a tail in California? You bury yo' face in lots a that triple-C clean California cunt? Man, what broads they got out there. I'd eat a mile a their shit just ta kiss their ass."

"That was always your problem, Nate. You were kissing it when you should've been kicking it."

"Shee-it," Nate sputtered, clutching his gut. Finally he straightened up and punched Ted on the arm. "Replay, you still the same old prick." He led the way to a double-parked white Cadillac and put Ted's pullman in the trunk. "Hey, you weren't really plannin' on takin' that bus, were you?"

"Yeah."

"Man, you kiddin'? With your bread?"

"You know how cabdrivers get to me. One of 'em would mouth me about a small tip and I'd want to bust his head. Too much hassle."

"Whyn't you call me to pick you up? I hadda call your secretary to find out the flight."

"Thanks, man."

"Shee-it." Nate got in the driver's side and leaned across to open the door. "It's good ta see ya, fucker." He pulled into traffic. "Welcome home."

"New York's not home anymore, Nate. It's just another city now."

"Oh yeah? Then how come you just bet your ass you can whip the town again? How much you got ridin' on this caper, Mr. Clean? Five mil? Ten?"

Ted smiled. "How's your mother, Nate?"

"Just great, Ted." There was a pause, then he laughed. "Don' wanna tell me, huh? Replay, you ol' fuck, you haven't changed a bit." He drove out of the airport, turned on the radio and fiddled with the dial as the car headed west on the Van Wyck Expressway. Eventually he found some piano music. "WNCN," he reported. "See—I even remembered your old radio station. Do I take good care of my man?"

"The greatest, Nate." Ted leaned back and stared at the early evening sky blackened by the tinted glass of the windshield. For an instant, fifteen years flashed away and he was on the field in his first pro-college all star game. . . .

First play from scrimmage. Pater Noster wanted to send the fullback off tackle. Ted scanned the defense and audibled a pass.

As he dropped back into the pocket he saw the pro end to his right fighting past the blocker. He found Mikey DeAngelico in the flat and fired a quick one. Three full seconds later, from his blind side, came what he imagined a building would feel like if it fell on you. Everything went black, and when he came to this mountain in a gold and white uniform was helping him up. He looked from the 77 on the jersey to the goateed face of Nasty Nate Elefante gloating evilly behind the bars of his mask. "Hi, college boy," he said. "Welcome to the pros."

"That was an illegal hit," Ted muttered.

Nate laughed. "So go call a cop." . . .

Now, in the car, Ted noticed the sky again, and the moon glowing dully through the tinted windshield.

"Everybody's really pissin' about the meeting being at midnight," Nate said. "You figure on that?"

"Yep."

"How come you wanna piss them off?"

"How come you always used to rough up a quarterback the first time you sacked him?"

"That's different. These guys are on your side."

"Everybody's on his own side."

Ted stared out the window at the dingy buildings of Queens. He remembered reading in the newspapers as a twelve-year-old about places called Queens and Brooklyn and the Bronx and thinking of them as glamorous and romantic, full of adventure and excitement. When he actually got to see New York the sense of adventure and excitement was confirmed. He and his high school buddies would take the bus from Wilkes-Barre and check in at the George Sloane Y.M.C.A. They'd spend the whole weekend just strutting around town and riding subways to Queens and Brooklyn and the Bronx, then go back home thinking they were the hottest studs that ever drew breath.

The pages of a few calendars flipped by, and now Ted was playing ball in New York. Queens, Brooklyn and the Bronx promptly lost their glamor, became enclaves of folks who, along with their brothers in more glamorous Manhattan, fucked you for practice when they ran out of ways to do it for profit. Just like, come to think of it, most of the rest of the world.

Nate maneuvered the Caddy through the heavy traffic on the Grand Central Parkway, then turned onto the Long Island Expressway, where traffic was lighter. "Oh, I almost forgot," he said, turning down the radio, "Eddie Fassnacht called. He can't meet with you past ten tonight so he wants to set the meeting back from nine to eight. If that's not okay, he can meet you tomorrow for breakfast."

"What happens after ten?"

"Something about his kid being interviewed on some radio show. He wants to listen. So maybe eight-thirty?"

"Nine. If he wants to leave at ten, let him leave. I don't have that much to say to him anyway."

Nate raised the volume a shade more and drove silently into Manhattan. He let Ted out in front of the Tuscany Hotel on Thirty-ninth Street, then went looking for a parking place while Ted checked in. When he got back he phoned Fassnacht while Ted unpacked. Afterward they strolled down Lexington to Thirty-fourth and across to the Golden Coach on Second Avenue.

On, the captain with a name that belonged in an old Abbott and Costello routine, was on duty. He welcomed Ted with profuse handshaking, a bottle of Wan Fu, heaping platters of Tsing Tsau Niu Yiu Shi and Lobster Ding, and the Coach's crowning glory, steamed bass in black-bean sauce. Everything was so good that Ted and Nate had him repeat the whole meal, top to bottom, after which they strolled back to the Tuscany.

Eddie Fassnacht was waiting in the lobby. And fuming. It was nine-fifteen. "You know, Vassily," he said as they rode up in the elevator, "some people might get the impression you're not all that interested in happy relations with your unions."

Ted smiled. "I guess it all depends on your point of view. The way I look at it, my unions should be worrying about having happy relations with me."

"Oh, now wait a minute, fella. I don't know what the unions were like out in Kalamazoo or wherever the hell you put up your other buildings, but you're in New York now. If you think you're going to pull that shit on us, you've got another think coming."

Ted's smile broadened. "You weren't listening, Fassnacht. I said, the way I look at it, you should be worrying about having happy relations with me. Now, if you don't share that point of view you're always free to tell me to go fuck myself and let me try putting up my building with nonunion workers."

"Are you serious? In New York? You'd never get your first brick laid."

"Thanks for the warning."

"Seriously. There are no skilled workers in New York that aren't in the union. A small-time contractor up in the Bronx a few years ago got on our unfair list and tried to put up a little six-story brownstone with nonunion men. Within three weeks he was back at our headquarters begging us to let him settle up."

"What was he offering the scabs? A buck-fifty an hour?"

They were at Ted's door. He opened it and gestured for Fassnacht and Nate to precede him inside. Nate hovered near the pantry, waiting for Ted to offer a round of drinks. Ted didn't.

"Fassnacht," he said, flopping down in the room's one reclining chair, "I'll bet I could put an ad in tomorrow's papers offering fifty bucks an hour for laborers and have half your membership standing in line to take jobs under fake names."

"How could you pay fifty an hour? Your cost would be more than double union scale."

"I'd get the building up, wouldn't I?"

"You're not making sense. Why pay more than you have to?"

"I don't intend to, but if they'd work for fifty an hour, plenty of them would work for forty, wouldn't they? And if they'd work for forty, some of them would work for thirty. And on some jobs, where your laborers are getting seven to ten an hour today, they'd jump at the chance to work for fifteen."

Fassnacht busied himself deciding where to sit and finally settled for the sofa.

Ted took a small notebook from his pocket. "I've had my engineers spec out some recent New York construction jobs of approximately the same scope as Three-oh-five East. The way we figure it, if we divided among our actual bona fide workers the amount of money that normally gets paid to the shop stewards and business agents and dummy workers and other featherbedding assholes that you characters stick the average contractor with, we could raise every worker's paycheck by fifteen to twenty percent. And we'd get a better job too—not one of these typical New York horror stories with loose bricks and chipped marble and walls so crooked they drive the bubble in the level right off the bar."

Fassnacht said nothing. Ted gave him another smile. "Tell me I couldn't get myself a full crew of competent men for fifteen to twenty percent over scale. In fact, don't just tell me—bet me a few hundred thousand that I can't do it. I'll give fifty-to-one odds."

"Oh, I don't say you couldn't assemble a crew. But getting the building up would be another story. No union trucker would carry materials to your site. And if you decided to try with nonunion truckers, some people might get a little irritated that you were trying to bust up their union and decide to bust back."

"Fassnacht, I don't know whether you're tougher or dumber than you look. I figure you for at least sixty so it must be the latter. I also figure you never heard what happened to the last business agent that tried to muscle—"

"I'm not trying to muscle—"

Ted raised a hand to silence him. "It was about this same time of night, and I'd just had a magnificent dinner, just as I did tonight, and I had this natural healthy desire to take a natural healthy crap, which I did, except I didn't flush the toilet. Instead I came out and persuaded this business agent to come in and then I told him I was going to hold his head underwater until he either ate my shit or drowned."

Fassnacht looked green.

"You know something," Ted continued, "I never realized how much fun it could be to watch a union boss eat shit."

Fassnacht looked at his watch, he brushed off his clothes, he played with his hair, he adjusted his belt. "I think," he said finally, "we've reached an impasse." He started to get up. "Why don't I just run along now, my son's on the radio tonight and I want to hear the program, tomorrow I'll have someone else from the union get in touch with you. Perhaps you'll be more compatible with him—"

"Don't get off that couch." Ted stood. Fassnacht eased

back against the upholstery. Ted smiled at Nate. "Hey, buddy, maybe things would get friendlier if we all had a friendly drink."

Nate grinned. "Yeah. Maybe so."

Ted watched Nate pour Scotch-on-the-rocks. Fassnacht sipped his as if afraid it might contain strychnine.

"Fassnacht," Ted said finally, "I'd like nothing better than to have amiable relations with New York's building trades, but I'm putting you on notice . . . I know how you guys come sniffing around as soon as a new project is announced, looking for a little something on the side in exchange for your promise that you'll smooth the way for the contractor. All he has to do is put your uncle or brother or wife on the payroll in some job that never gets done. If he does, everything goes just fine. If he doesn't, he gets slowdowns and fuckups and disasters up the ass.

"Well, I don't play. I pay for eight hours' work, and I demand it from every swinging dick on my payroll. I don't ask for favors on the classification of different jobs. I decide the classification, and you go along with it. I decide the number of men that work, and when they work, and where they work, and for whom they work, and how they work. And if your men want to work my job, those are the rules."

Fassnacht started to talk, but Ted cut him off. "I don't ask your people to work without pay. I pay full union scale for each job classification. But I decide the classification. You think it's unfair, that's your problem. As I said, you don't like the way I do business, you tell me to go fuck myself and you keep your men off my job. But if a man works my job, he works my way on my terms." He smiled. "But I didn't bring you here just to give you bad news. I operate on an incentive system. I give bonus money for speed and more bonus money for efficiency. Before work starts my superintendent will go over the plan with all the men. My goal is to get an expertly crafted building as quickly as possible. If your guys can produce quality at ninety percent my usual costs, I don't mind splitting the remaining ten percent with them. This approach won't mean as many jobs for as long a time, but for the individual skilled worker it means a higher hourly wage than he ever made.

"And to encourage pride and craftsmanship I've decided to make it possible for some of the men who work on Three-oh-five East eventually to live in the building. I don't know how many apartments I'll be able to make available or at what price, but you can be sure it'll be a tremendous value. The workers will enjoy luxury no different from that of tenants paying three hundred dollars a room monthly rent. They'll live with these tenants, socialize with them if they like, and have every other benefit that comes from living in Three-oh-five East. I offer this to my workers—not as charity or a bribe, but as incentive. I want every person who has anything to do with Three-oh-five East to feel about it as if he were building his own house."

"Well, Mr. Vassily," Fassnacht said, sipping his Scotch—Ted noted his finally using "mister"—"maybe we aren't as far apart as it seemed. I admit I'm not accustomed to meeting contractors like you, but I can understand that maybe you had some unpleasant union dealings in the past and are overreacting . . . in any case we're—"

Ted grinned. "Save your bullshit diagnosis of my union attitudes for your next group therapy session. If we're less far apart than you thought, let's explore our areas of agreement without any patronizing jabs at the other guy's motives."

Fassnacht got angry again. "All I'm trying to say, Mr. Vassily, is that maybe we can work something out. Now, this incentive system is by no means foreign to us. We're not opposed to quality workmanship done at reasonable speed. If it can be done consistent with the safety and welfare of our men, we're all for it. And we agree that excellence should be rewarded. That's what unionism is all about." He smiled. "Now, once we've come to agreement on the scope of the project and the basic job classifications, we'll be happy to sit down with you and work out a system of incentives. We'll provide expert inspectors of each job—"

"You're missing the point, Fassnacht. I decide everything—the job classifications, the incentive system, the inspectors, the works. I'm ready to spend a pile of money on this building, but I want every goddamn penny to count."

Fassnacht sighed. "Vassily, be sensible. I can't go back to my bosses and say I've given you a blank check to do whatever the hell you like."

"I don't see where you have any choice. I'm putting up what probably is going to be the most publicized apartment building in the history of New York City. Its publicity will come from luxury apartments being made inexpensively available to people who otherwise couldn't afford them. You're not going to win friends for your union by opposing or delaying this kind of project. Matter of fact, you'll contribute greatly to the anti-union sentiments that have been building in this country since the late Mr. Hoffa and his goons started running wild in the late fifties. I've got superintendents and work crews in other cities where I've built. If I have to, I'm prepared to fly these crews in to work nonunion here until my building is finished. I'm prepared to bivouac them on the construction site and have them under armed guard, just in case *your* goon squads try to disrupt proceedings. Hopefully none of this will be necessary, because as I said I'm also prepared to use New York union crews if we can agree that I offer monetary concessions and fringe benefits in exchange for control."

Ted looked at his watch. "Mr. Fassnacht, it's a quarter to ten. I understand you want to hear your son on the radio tonight. I've said all I have to say, so there's no point keeping you any longer."

Fassnacht followed Ted to the door, hesitated a moment, then tentatively offered his hand. Ted gave him the vise-grip he reserved for people who were impressed by that sort of thing.

"Jeez," Nate said as he closed the door, "why the rough stuff?"

Ted sipped his drink. "Nate, it's an unfortunate law of life that the only people sons of bitches respect are bigger sons of bitches."

"Did you really hold that guy's head in the toilet until he ate shit?"

"How's your mother, Nate?"

"Oh, man—" he sighed "—man, you're one frustrating fucker."

He was also one tired fucker. He found verbal combat even more fatiguing than the physical type. And his biggest battle of the night remained to be fought. He wanted to get ready for it. That meant relaxing. And that meant getting rid of Nate. "I'm not going to be very good company for the next couple hours," Ted said, undoing his tie. "You're welcome to hang around, though, if you want to."

Nate's eyebrows arched. "You're not pissed off at me?"

"No." Ted flashed a smile, gave Nate a couple of jabs on the shoulder, then a hard right to the stomach. Nate struggled to conceal that it hurt. "When I'm pissed off," Ted reminded him, "I never hit you."

Ted knew a return punch was coming, and he was set for it.

Nate laughed. "I'm not pissed off at you either, Replay. When I'm pissed, I never hit back." He drained his drink, brought the glass to the pantry and washed it, then took his jacket from the closet. "I'm gonna see if I can scare us up a few broads for an all-skate after the meeting."

"Skinny with big tits."

"Don't worry. Only grade-A merchandise. See ya."

When he was gone, Ted took a long hot shower, shaved, gave his aching knees an hour under the heat lamp, set the alarm for eleven-thirty, turned on the bed vibrator and lay down.

It really felt strange being back in New York. He'd been away for only five years, but somehow it seemed much longer. Of course, a good deal had happened during that time. He'd put up twenty-nine buildings. And seen one fall down. He'd made a lot of money. And lost a wife. He'd tried to play Thoreau and found he wasn't very good at it. And he'd tried to play Joe Superstud and found he really wasn't very good at that either—which came as quite a surprise because it used to be the thing he did best.

Yes, they had been an enlightening five years. When he left New York he was ready to set the world on its ass. He was going to build so many apartments that not one poor person in the country would have to live in a slum. In his spare time he'd give interviews telling how he'd done it so others could follow his example. Let a few years pass and there'd be "draft Ted Vassily" movements at all the major political conventions. And then? My fellow Americans, it's indeed a privilege and pleasure to address you on this occasion . . .

Well, no, not really. He never really quite had fantasies of the White House. But he did have visions, not at all precise, of being involved in some important way in what was going on in the country. He certainly never saw himself teaching business administration in California and spending most of his time chasing twenty-two-year-old twat.

And now here he was, back in New York. Just like old times. Except that he was five years older. And losing his hair. And hurting more than ever in the knees. And not doing very much with a football anymore. And Chris wasn't with him.

Chris. He felt a pang just thinking the name. The rule—the ironclad rule that he'd lived by in the three years since the breakup—was never to think the name. Because the second you thought the name, you started thinking about the things you did together. And the way she looked. And the sound of her voice. And the smell of her perfume. And the way her body felt when you were fucking. And when you were just lying together without fucking. And the more you let yourself think about things like that the more you'd think about giving her a call, asking if she would consider trying to make a go of it again. And that was foolish, because you knew her answer would be a very polite and pleasant no.

It would be easier to cope with if it were an angry no. Or an uncertain no. Or a bitter no. Because that would give you something to work with. But the polite and pleasant no meant no hope. You were like a movie she had seen too many times. No way she'd sit through it again.

Chris. Damn, what breasts she had! When she was on the beach you could practically hear guys' necks squeak as they craned toward her. And when she went bra-less around town . . . Ted once saw a guy actually wreck his car staring at them instead of watching the road. It wasn't so much that she flaunted them. She enjoyed having people notice, but she didn't wear see-through material, plunging necklines or other stuff to flag attention. Usually she wore very conservative outfits designed, if anything, to divert attention from them.

Chris. Her breasts weren't her main attraction, of course—although some of her one-note women's lib asshole girl friends worked on persuading her that Ted felt that way. Actually what Ted missed most about her was her inventiveness. She was always springing a notion that, when you considered it, you immediately recognized as the unique solution to your problem—but you'd never think of it till she sprang it.

When she'd come back from shopping to their place on Twenty-eighth Street she'd not only be loaded with the stuff she went out for but also, for example, a certain kind of belt he'd been trying unsuccessfully to find for the last four years, and a set of coasters that matched perfectly with a cocktail shaker somebody had given them, and three magazines he hadn't seen that had stories about him, and a goddamn special kind of ballpoint pen Nasty Nate had told her he was looking for, and two reissued Caruso albums that previously had been impossible to find, and a leatherbound original edition of her favorite writer, Henry James, that just happened to be marked down to seventy-five cents . . .

What an incredible woman! She hated football. She refused to come to the stadium, and she never watched the games on TV because every time he got tackled she would go crazy with fear he would never get up. She had it worked out with Bernie DeAngelico, Mikey's wife, that Bernie would phone her immediately after the game to let her know he was okay. Actually, he never took a really serious hit the whole time she knew him. It was a good thing for her peace of mind, though, that she didn't meet him back in the days before he turned coward.

Still, though she hated the game—or said she hated it —the strategy intrigued her. In fact it was she who gave Ted the idea for that quarterback sneak that faked the whole world out if its jock in his last game.

"Are you going to do your ego trip again this year?" she'd said a few weeks before the game. She never was one for euphemisms.

"I think I'll put myself in for the first play from scrimmage, sure."

"Well, maybe you'd reduce your chances of getting killed if you did something unexpected. Like running with the ball."

He laughed. "Honey, I haven't run with the goddamn ball since I was a sophomore in college. And I tried not to do it too much then."

"Exactly. Which is why nobody would expect a bootleg."

Ted didn't know what struck him funnier, her use of a term like "bootleg" or his thinking of an old horse like himself trying to get around Pittsburgh's front four. Even if he faked everybody out, he'd be lucky to get ten yards before the fake was read and the whole goddamn defense caved in on him. The only thing that could save him would be an epidemic of Pittsburgh heart attacks.

But the idea of a running play of some sort turned him on. He'd made his reputation doing the unexpected, and what could be less expected from a chickenshit no-run quarterback like Instant Replay? He toyed with the possibility of letting Walt Kulikowski lead him on a power sweep, or maybe even handing off to someone. Then the idea of a sneak hit him. He certainly wouldn't try it from too far out. But if by some chance that first play ran from in close, and if the defense was set in a way that favored it, he might just give it a shot.

He diagrammed an elaborate fake involving the slotback and Nasty Nate at right tackle. It would work only if Pittsburgh tried a safety blitz, but within their own thirty they very well might.

Ted didn't really expect to use the play. He had five pass patterns that almost certainly would be better calls in any situation he faced. But he had the guys work up the sneak anyway—just in case.

When New York recovered the Pittsburgh fumble on the twenty-eight, the sneak became a possibility. Not a strong one. But in the ball park. In the huddle Ted called a tricky post pattern with DeAngelico as primary receiver. He was all set to go with it when Rube Tomlinson, the Pittsburgh defensive captain, called the shift that Ted diagnosed as an upcoming blitz. Then he noticed the rookie right linebacker, Oskie Andrews, playing the tight end wider than he should. Okay! With Tomlinson head-on to Ted's left guard, Andrews was the only guy he had to get by. He was never mistaken for the Metroliner, but with Andrews that wide he could be across the twenty before anyone realized what was up. He audibled the sneak, millions of people across the nation were astonished, and one in the stands named Eddie Spats Johnson was considerably richer.

"Well, hero," Chris said as they watched it replayed half a dozen times on the eleven o'clock news, "how does it feel to take the glory for a play that your wife called."

"That wasn't a bootleg," Ted laughed, grabbing for her breast.

They balled about five times that night—not bad after two years of marriage. . . .

Chris. The only solution was not to think about her. Which was difficult. In California it hadn't been so bad because that was new terrain and he was living a whole new life style. If he worked at it, he could almost believe that no person named Chris Jenkins ever existed, except maybe in his dream life. But New York was their town. Every Saturday night they used to walk from the apartment on Twenty-eighth Street to the corner of Thirty-fourth and Third for the Sunday *Times*. They had a subscription to the New York City Opera and another at the Philharmonic. Mondays they'd often go down to the Vanguard to hear the Thad Jones–Mel Lewis band. They'd stayed together at the Tuscany for the six weeks between giving up the apartment and making the move to Michigan. . . . It was impossible to be anywhere in this goddamn town without somehow flashing back and believing the years hadn't passed, the bubble hadn't burst, Chris had just stepped around the corner and would be back any second. . . .

He forced himself to look at his watch. Quarter to eleven. Too early to get up. Too late to do much of anything else. Well, action is always preferable to inaction, as Pater Noster used to say. He got up, gave his knees another shot under the lamp, dressed and went for a walk up to Grand Central to pick up the next morning's *Times*.

Eleven-thirty. He poured a Scotch and sat with the newspaper until Nate checked in fifteen minutes later. "No broads," he reported. "Jesus, I've been getting howitzered so much lately I don't know how to react when a broad treats me nice."

"It's age," Ted said. "You know you've had it when they start looking surprised that you came on to them."

"That happen to you, too?"

"Yeah. In California. Two out of three at the college would do this surprise routine, as though they figured I only intended to play big brother. It shocked them that an old fuck like me would want into their pants."

"Shee-it. And I thought it was just 'cause I'm fat and ugly. It's a good thing I have you to straighten me out, Replay. I was starting to get an inferiority complex."

"Glad to oblige."

"Yeah. Now I'm not just fat and ugly. I'm old, fat and ugly." He laughed. "What next? You can go downhill only so far, then you hit bottom of the hill."

"It's a bitch," Ted acknowledged.

"Seriously, man. You were always the guy with the ideas. Whattaya do when you know it's over? Or almost over? Cut your cock off? Blow your brains out? Hire hookers?"

"You play it one down at a time, Nate. And when you hurt, you do yourself a favor and try not to think about it. Otherwise you hurt more and don't play as well and the coach takes you out—"

"Hey, did Witt ever take you out when you owned the team?" Fortunately for Ted's mood of the moment, Nate had the attention span of a six-year-old.

"A couple times."

"How could he do that? If you owned the team, you coulda told him to fuck off if you still wanted to play, right?"

"Sometimes it's good to have someone else calling shots for you, Nate. Sometimes the guy on the sidelines can see things you don't."

"Yeah, I guess so." He was silent a moment, then laughed. "Hey, you know something? We gotta be crazy. I mean, here we are, both of us retired, both of us doing a thousand things not connected to football, and still we talk about the game all goddamn day. I mean, shee-it, even when we're not talking about it, we're talking about it."

The door buzzer rescued Ted from the conversation, and Nate ushered in the designer of 305 East, Axel Wessman. He was eighty-six and didn't walk very well anymore, Ted noted, but his eyes were clear as crystal and so was his brain. "Sorry I'm early, Ted," he said, "but I wanted to talk to you before anyone else got here."

Ted shook his hand and led him to a chair. "You didn't have to come at all, Axel. I told you that."

"I wanted to, Ted. Something's up and I have to tell you about it." Ted winced as he watched the old man lower himself gingerly into his seat. Knowing how his own knees hurt at less than half that age, he could imagine the pain Axel was suffering.

The elderly architect accepted a glass of Scotch, touched it to his lips, then lowered it with shaking hand to the arm of the chair. "Ted," he said softly, "I've brought you my resignation."

"I don't understand, Axel."

"I'm not a kid anymore, Ted. I'm not even an old man. I'm a very old man. This project is going to need someone who can stay with it for a while. I'll be happy to stay on as consultant, if you want me. But I think the ultimate responsibility should belong to another designer."

Ted was sure he wasn't leveling. "Is it your health? Some doctor find something you haven't told me about?"

He shook his head. "But you never can tell at my age. My resignation is right here." He reached into his jacket.

Ted held up his hand to reject the envelope. "You're not giving me a straight count, Axel. Who's been muscling you?"

"No one."

Ted went to the window and stared out. "Five years ago, buddy, no other architect would talk to me. Dummy football player, they all thought. No experience in high-rise construction. He'll go out of business before the foundation is even laid. You listened to me, Axel. You took my ideas and developed them into buildings—buildings that poor people could afford and could live comfortably in. I needed you then, Axel. I need you now. Axel Wessman doesn't walk out on a friend who needs him."

Axel allowed a small smile. "You don't need me, Ted. You saw *Banker's Daily*. They virtually accused us of playing a practical joke on the financial community."

"So that's it? You can't take the flak?"

"I'm just being practical."

"If I never did anything impractical, Axel, I'd still be back in Nanticoke, Pennsylvania, making chili-burgers in my old man's diner."

"But this—" Axel gestured toward the architect's drawing of 305 East that Nate had tacked over the mantel, "—they hate it, Ted. Not the critics, maybe. Not the *Times*. But the people whose money you need—they hate it."

"I love it," Ted replied. "I told you to pull out all the stops and, damn it, you gave me exactly what I wanted. I wouldn't put up anything else. I'd rather build nothing at all."

"But I've saddled you with a hundred dollars a square foot. It's going to be impossible to rent these apartments at the prices you have to charge to accommodate all my frills and subsidize your low-income people too."

"Who's been talking to you? DelVecchio from BankUS or Kraft from Chase?"

Axel pretended for a moment not to understand, then looked sheepishly at Ted. "DelVecchio. But he made sense, Ted."

"Did he tell you he'd cut off my money if you didn't back out?"

"No. He simply asked if I'd consider cutting back in certain areas. And he pointed out that neither his bank nor any other would consider Three-oh-five East mortgage-worthy as plans now stand."

Ted was furious. He expected bankers to do their talking with him, not his designer.

"He made sense, Ted. It's fine to think of ourselves as building another Duomo or Giotto's Tower. But we're not using government dollars. We've got to pay our way. And we need bank money to do it." Softly he added, "They didn't say so in as many words, but I got the feeling the bankers would be considerably less uncomfortable if you had, well, a firm like S.O.M. on the job . . . or one of the hot young firms, like Roche and Dinkeloo or

Mitchell and Guirgola . . . Face it, Ted, I've never designed anything of even half this scope. And I'm a very old man. Nobody wants anything to do with very old men."

Ted looked at him silently for a moment, then held out his hand. "Give me your letter, Axel."

The old man slowly took it from his pocket. Ted ripped it in four and dropped the pieces into the wastebasket. "We're putting up your building," he said. "Now you can stay for the meeting, if you like, or you can go back to your drawing board and start work on the one we'll put up when this one is finished."

Nate broke the tension with, "You better listen to Ted," and clapped Axel on the shoulder. "You know, buddy, just 'cause your name is Axel, that doesn't mean you're a big wheel."

Ted couldn't help laughing, and when Axel joined in Nate declared it time for another drink and made the rounds with the Scotch bottle.

Almost as if on cue, the door buzzer sounded again. Ted went to his reclining chair as Nate answered.

"Hey, Superspook!" he boomed from the foyer.

"Hey, Elephant!" The voice belonged to Emerson Wade. They half-wrestled, half-danced into the living room. Together, their bodies reminded Ted of the figure 10. Emerson stood six-eight and had magically stayed at his playing weight of two-ten. On a frame as big as his, two-ten makes a fellow look downright emaciated.

"Hey, Replay!"

"Hey, Emer!" Ted met him halfway across the room.

"I've been trying to get in touch with you all night," Emerson said, "but the desk told me you left instructions not to ring. I've got something really hot."

"Money?"

He looked warily at Axel.

"You can speak freely," Ted said.

"Piles of money," Emerson replied. "All we need."

"Who's Santa Claus?"

"The Ron-Cor Corp."

Ted's eyebrows arched. "They're too big to be interested in an apartment house. And this isn't their kind of deal.

They like asset plays—low multiple companies with big book value."

Emerson shrugged. "All I know, my man, is they have an acquisitions vee pee named Frank Keegan who bought me a thirty-dollar lunch with a sixty-dollar bottle of wine and told me he thinks you've come up with the greatest idea since the wheel. Plus he thinks you and I were the greatest passing combination the sport has ever known, and he would love one of these days to take us and our foxes out with him and his wife and their son and daughter-in-law."

"I don't want their C.E.O. calling my shots. They could suck us in and spit us out bald-headed."

"I told Keegan how you operate. That doesn't bother him. He'll settle for a small piece, if that's all you want to give up. And get this for a kicker—Ron-Cor will be our guarantor for notes equal to the amount of stock we make available to them."

Ted whistled under his breath. "If we only gave them twenty percent, it'd solve our mortgage problem."

"Right-toe, my man. I'd like to take credit for being the financial genius who devised that little scheme and twisted Mr. Keegan's arm to accept it, but the fact is he waltzed in and laid it on the table for me."

"So how come I'm not jumping in the air clicking my heels?"

"You perceive a honkey in the woodpile?"

Ted nodded. "I don't know a hell of a lot about Ron-Cor, but I know they're not running a charity."

"Maybe," Nate contributed, "they just like hanging around football players."

"Enough to pay a few million dollars for the privilege?"

Emerson smiled. "Well, lots of busted-down old jocks make a good living selling life insurance or stocks to people who don't need them but can't resist the opportunity to say they bought their policy from good old Joe Blow, the fastest running back in the N.F.L. in nineteen sixty-who. The dollars for our deal are bigger, but some corporate honchos are pretty generous with stockholders' money. And don't forget the prestige angle . . . a company like Ron-Cor wouldn't hurt its image a bit by backing a project that'll put poor people in rich men's apartments. Corporate social conscience and all that jazz."

"I still get bad vibes. I don't know why, but I smell mob money."

"You saying the Mafia owns a four-billion-dollar company?" Nate asked.

"Not outright, but the boys may have substantial holdings, enough to influence if not control. Anyway, you know how I feel about the mob."

"Sure, Replay," Emerson said, "and I feel the same way, but you'd be mighty pissed off if I told Keegan 'no' without even bringing you the offer, wouldn't you?"

"I can't believe you guys," Nate said. "Here we are scratchin' our asses for bread, somebody comes along with the keys to Fort Knox and you're turning him down 'cause you heard maybe they got some guys didn't make Eagle Scout."

"I don't like hoods, Nate."

"Who does? But so far all you have is vibes. Shouldn't you at least investigate?"

"I think he's right, Ted," Emerson said. "And remember, we're not doing a one-on-one with some punk button man asking you to shave points in a game. Ron-Cor is a public corporation with an SEC guardian angel. I don't think there's reason to be afraid of hassles with the mob even if your vibes are true, which is by no means certain."

"I suppose you're right," Ted said. "Anyway, if things go right tonight we shouldn't need them." He held his glass out to Nate, who promptly refilled it.

The buzzer sounded once again, and this time it was Eddie Witkowski.

"Coach," Ted said, "thanks for coming."

"Thanks for the invite, Ted. Glad you've decided to give me the opportunity to make some more money for myself."

It was good to hear Witt's down-home, coal-cracker accent again. Ted introduced Witkowski to Axel Wessman as the door buzzed again. Nate welcomed Mikey DeAngelico. By the time he'd said hello to everyone, p.r. man Burr Whiteside and Jay Kasselman, the rental agent, had arrived.

"Ted," Witt said, taking him aside, "you're looking well. I was sorry to hear about you and Chris. I would've written, but frankly I couldn't think of anything to say."

"Thanks, coach. You just said it."

"I'm glad you got yourself right into this project. It's not such a hot idea to sit and brood about things—"

The buzzer again, heralding George DelVecchio and Tom Martinson of BankUS, followed by Frank Sanchez of the *Post* and Eddie Wayne of the *Daily News.* They did a double take as they recognized the old ballplayers. "Hey, Ted," Sanchez said, "is this supposed to be a business meeting or a Superbowl replay?"

Mikey DeAngelico guffawed. "Where you goin', 'replay,' man? This is the real thing."

The buzzer again sounded, and as Burr Whiteside went to answer it DelVecchio promptly moved over to Ted. "What's this with the press?" he demanded.

"When you throw the party, Mr. DelVecchio, you make out the guest list. This is my party."

"You misled us, Mr. Vassily. We understood we'd be meeting privately with you and your investors."

"I have no secrets, Mr. DelVecchio. Do you?"

"You're a wise guy, aren't you, Mr. Vassily? You want to embarrass the bank by having us turn you down with the press on hand."

"Far from it," Ted said. "I want to help you show the world what a humane institution your bank is—by having you offer financing when the press is on hand to witness it."

"Sorry, Mr. Vassily. It's BankUS policy to keep all transactions strictly private."

"That'll look beautiful in tomorrow's papers, Mr. DelVecchio: all these poor people having to live in their slums another few years because BankUS wouldn't even *discuss* Three-oh-five East with me."

His face momentarily took on the look a quarterback's sometimes does when a monster like Nasty Nate breaks into the pocket and there's nothing to do with the ball but eat it. He stared at Ted for a moment, turned and started to walk away, then promptly wheeled back when he saw the latest arrival—Stan Kraft, from Chase. "Oh, now come on, Vassily, what the hell is this? Am I supposed to bid against Chase for your business? With the press looking over my shoulder?"

"If you'd like to make a private preemptive offer I'd be glad to hear it."

"Thanks." He saw that Stan Kraft had seen him. "Thanks a lot."

Ted went over to Kraft, shook hands, turned him over to Burr Whiteside, then gestured to Nate, who ushered everyone to seats and saw that all the Scotch glasses were full. Ted then went to the fireplace.

"Gentlemen," he said, "you've had plenty of time to review the prospectus and the cost and income projections that my secretary sent out so I won't waste time going over them again. Tonight's meeting is to update you on subsequent developments and wrap up loose ends.

"First, I know some of you felt my projections on labor costs were unreasonably low. Earlier tonight I had a good meeting with Mr. Fassnacht of the union, and I think I can confidently say there's no need to change the projections.

"Second, on funding, I personally have purchased enough stock in the Three-oh-five Corp. to cover fifteen percent of the total projected costs of construction and operation until rental income starts coming in; Athletes Investments, Inc., representing Eddie Witkowski, Mikey DeAngelico, Nate Elefante, Emerson Wade, and myself, has purchased an additional thirteen percent. That totals three percent more cash equity than you bankers ordinarily demand for New York residential construction.

"Projected net income from rentals, assuming one hundred percent occupancy and allowing a stockholders' dividend of ten percent earnings, will amortize the mortgage in twenty years. In the unlikely event that occupancy falls below one hundred percent, the deficit will naturally be charged against dividends, not amortization.

"On the subject of rentals, Jay Kasselman, your closing figures as of today show how many vacancies?"

Jay smiled. "Eight, of a total of four hundred apartments. Leases have been signed on two hundred and ten, and we've taken deposits on the remaining one hundred and eighty-two. All that's without putting a single ad in the paper—strictly business generated by our publicity. Obviously this is one hell of a popular apartment building." Jay couldn't resist the impulse to hype.

"Well," Ted said, "that covers it from my end. If you gentlemen have any questions, let's hear them."

George DelVecchio took off his glasses and massaged the bridge of his nose. "Not so much a question as an objection. Those leases you have are only for two years."

"That's standard in New York."

"I know. But what happens when the leases expire? What's to stop your tenants from evacuating en masse? And if they do, how does the bank recover its investment?"

Ted had anticipated the question. "They'll have no reason to evacuate. Three-oh-five isn't being built in a decaying neighborhood where encroaching slums would make people change their minds about wanting to live there. Our location is in the heart of one of the most desirable residential neighborhoods in the city. Tenants will have airtight security. They'll enjoy a level of luxury that can't be matched anywhere in New York. They'll have substantial investments in the furnishing of their apartments. So why not renew the lease? I don't doubt we'll have an occasional vacancy. But wholesale evacuation? No way."

"You're leaving out cost. The extra twenty percent these tenants are paying to subsidize the low income apartments doesn't bring them appreciable benefits. You say, probably truthfully, that you'll provide a level of luxury unavailable elsewhere, and this, presumably combined with social conscience, will motivate them to pay that extra twenty percent. But what happens if some other developer decides to go after a piece of your market? Suppose he puts up an equally luxurious building without subsidized apartments—and therefore can charge twenty percent *less* than you?"

"Given the realities of New York real estate, that's highly unlikely."

"Unlikely, but not impossible. And if it happens, you're relying on social conscience to keep your tenants from going to him. Sorry—BankUS admires your faith in human nature, but we're not willing to underwrite seventy-two percent of your investment without something more tangible."

Ted looked to Stan Kraft of Chase.

"I'm afraid every bank you talk to would say the same thing, Mr. Vassily. We're impressed that you signed so many tenants so soon. We concede you've got one hell of an idea, and it really does seem to have caught on with New York. But that's part of the problem. New York is very quick to ride a trend and just as quick to desert it."

"I agree," said Tom Martinson of BankUS. "Today it may be groovy to live with poor people. But let a murder or rape take place in Three-oh-five East, or even a mugging, then let one or two big-name tenants move out and it could very well start an exodus."

He had a point, Ted thought. But these guys had hustled their tails to a midnight meeting simply to tell him he was full of it. "Okay, gentlemen," he said, shrugging, "I'm sorry I wasted your time. Thanks for considering my proposition." He started toward the bedroom. There were gasps—mostly from his own people, who, he realized, were trying to lay it on for the bankers' benefit.

"Mind you, Mr. Vassily," George DelVecchio said, "BankUS supports your efforts to provide superior housing for low-income people." He paused to let it sink in with the newsmen. "All we ask is that you meet us half way."

"By firing my designer?"

DelVecchio flushed. Apparently he didn't expect Ted would bring the thing into the open with Axel present. But he recovered quickly. "By reviewing some architectural decisions. For example, custom designed apartments with different floor plans for each floor. Oversized rooms, balconies, cathedral ceilings, paned windows—for a start. No offense to Mr. Wessman, who over the years has made many great contributions to architecture, but this approach"—he gestured to the diagram over the mantel—"is frankly impractical. If you cut back on some of the more extravagant frills, you should be able to reduce costs by twenty percent without losing an inch of rentable space."

Ted smiled. "Mr. DelVecchio, I didn't come back to this

shithouse you call a city to put up just one more of those steel and glass matchboxes everyone else is building. You don't convert a slum into a luxury apartment by putting a canopy over the door and hiring a guy in a fancy uniform to stand there."

"I agree. Most so-called luxury buildings in New York are anything but, and there's a definite market for the real thing. That's why I'm here in the first place. But this—" DelVecchio gestured toward the diagram—"special elevators with individual keyholes instead of buttons, marble floors and wallpaper in every corridor, working fireplaces, French doors . . . That kind of luxury might've worked in the thirites and forties when land was cheap and labor and materials were cheaper. But—no offense, Mr. Wessman—it just isn't economically feasible today."

Ted looked at Axel. DelVecchio's "no offense" notwithstanding, the old man was obviously hurt. "One of the reasons this country is on its ass," Ted said, "is because we've let you guys with the pocket calculators seduce us away from what we had in the thirties and forties. Look around this room—" he made a sweeping gesture that took in the Tuscany's high, beamed ceiling and thick plaster walls—"look at this hotel and compare it to the dumps they're putting up today. For Three-oh-five to work it's got to get back to the standard of excellence we used to take for granted in this country. Anything else would be worse than nothing at all."

DelVecchio shrugged and went back to his chair. "As I said, Mr. Vassily, we'd like to support you, we admire your goals, but BankUS has to have a substantial reduction in the cost per foot of rentable space or we're just not going to be able to provide financing."

Stan Kraft of Chase nodded his agreement.

Ted surveyed the faces of his colleagues in Athletes Investments, Inc. "Suppose," he said, watching carefully for reaction, "we came up with an additional two percent cash equity. That would bring us to five percent above the usual twenty-five percent level."

"Okay by me," Mikey DeAngelico said quickly.

"Ditto," said Emerson Wade.

"Me too," echoed Nasty Nate.

Ted had hoped for their reaction. It was one of the

reasons he'd invited them all to the meeting instead of trying to work things out with DelVecchio and Kraft privately.

DelVecchio shook his head. "Sorry, it isn't the cash that bothers us. We've got to have a substantial reduction in the cost-income ratio."

Axel cleared his throat. "If you like, Ted, I'll review my plans and see—"

Ted raised a palm to silence him. "Bankers don't make my decisions for me." He turned to DelVecchio. "Tell you what I'll do. I've got holdings in Michigan and Maryland that I hadn't planned on mortgaging, but if you'll meet me half way I'll put them on the line. They'll boost cash equity to thirty-two percent—a full *seven* points more than you'd usually demand."

He expected at worst a request for a point or two more, and was prepared to go to thirty-five, even though it would break him. To his surprise, DelVecchio began putting his papers back into his attaché case. "You've got a great idea, Mr. Vassily, but I'm certain my directors wouldn't go for it."

Kraft followed suit.

"What the fuck do they want?" Nate said aloud to Emerson. "A mortgage on his cock and balls?"

"How many points do I need, gentlemen?" Ted pressed. "Forty? Fifty?"

Mikey DeAngelico got up from his chair. "I got a chain of car-washes. And I'm A-rated in Dun and Bradstreet. If it'll help the deal I'll throw them into the pot."

Kraft forced a smile. "Mister DeAngelico, I'm afraid you don't understand how banks work—"

"Yeah, and you don't know shit from Shinola about catching a pass, which makes us even. What I'm saying is I got a goddamn A-rated fucken car-wash chain worth two million beanies. Now fuck how banks work, that's gotta mean something."

"I'm sorry," Kraft said, edging toward the door.

Eddie Witkowski stood. "Mr. Kraft," he said softly, "I'm just an old Pennsylvania coal cracker and I'll be the first to admit I feel a little out of place among all this high-finance talk, but where I come from it's considered bad manners to walk out on people before they've finished talking."

Kraft halted in his tracks.

"These young men have invested a lot of energy and hard work in this idea," he continued. "I think the least you could do is hear them out. You've rejected thirty-two points plus an A-rated car-wash chain worth two million dollars. Is it possible this idea is so terrible no offer they make would be acceptable?"

"The idea's far from terrible, Mr. Witkowski. It's just . . ." He let the sentence trail off.

Witkowski smiled and looked around the room, eye-to-eye, person-to-person, then capped his Knute Rockne halftime routine by massaging his jaw. Finally he looked around again. The room was silent.

"Mr. Kraft," he said so softly you had to strain to hear him, "I'm principal stockholder in a football team that's pretty highly thought of. A month ago a fella offered me ten million for my piece of the franchise. Now suppose I personally took a second mortgage on Three-oh-five East and pledged my stock as further collateral for your first mortgage. Would you be ready to talk business?"

George DelVecchio answered before Kraft. "BankUS would, Mr. Witkowski."

"Of course, Chase would also," Kraft added quickly.

Witkowski's smile broadened. "Okay, then with Ted's permission, why don't we adjourn this meeting with an announcement that both BankUS and Chase are prepared to finance the project and that details will be revealed in a few days."

"Right, coach," Ted put in quickly. Good old Eddie Witt not only had wrapped the package but had tied it with a pink ribbon. "Our financial v.p., Mr. Wade, will be in touch with both banks. Meanwhile, Frank and Eddie" —Ted turned to Sanchez of the *Post* and Wayne of the *News*—"our p.r. honcho Burr Whiteside has more material on our building plans—how applications for the subsidized units should be filed, energy-conservation measures in the building design, et cetera. And Axel Wessman is here to explain anything in his area that you think might interest your readers."

The meeting broke up. Nate joined Ted as he walked the bankers to the door.

"You know, Mr. Vassily," DelVecchio said, "this whole scene was unnecessary. All you needed to do was tell us Mr. Witkowski was prepared to commit his stock. We'd have had the papers ready for signature and our cashier's check made out."

"And the press," Kraft echoed. "Totally unnecessary, Mr. Vassily."

Ted smiled. "Being a prick means never having to say you're sorry."

"Don't bump your ass on the door on the way out, fellas," Nate added.

Back in the room Ted found Eddie Witkowski putting on his topcoat. "You saved my ass, coach. I was confident they'd jump at thirty points, especially with the newspaper guys here."

"Didn't mean to call the play for you, Ted, but I felt the momentum slipping. Of course, even without the team stock they'd probably back down and accept twenty-seven or twenty-eight after the newspapers worked them over about it. If you want to keep the points down I can always withdraw my offer after they accept it. Meantime, they'll be on the hook with the press for okaying the loan."

Ted laughed. "I thought I was the only devious bastard on this team."

Witkowski buttoned his coat, started toward the door, then turned back. "I'm serious about pledging my stock. As much collateral as you need, Teddy—it's yours."

"You know I'd never let you underwrite the note, coach."

"Be damned sore if you didn't, Ted."

"I couldn't let you risk it. The project's too speculative."

"Anything worth gambling on is speculative, Teddy. But I believe in Three-oh-five East. And, buddy, I believe in you." He took Ted by both shoulders and stared him straight in the eyes when he said it. Only Eddie Witkowski could pull off a line like that with a straight face. "I'll be in touch," Eddie said, and walked out.

Ted returned to the living room and poured himself a

stiff Scotch. "Jeez, Replay," Nate said, materializing alongside him, "what kinda voodoo did you put on Witt?"

"We're old friends," Ted said. "He was my high school coach."

"Shee-it, stuff like that never stopped you before. Seriously, you don't expect me to believe he just offered up his whole goddamn share of the team, do you?"

"His offer was spontaneous, Nate. And I'm deeply moved by it."

Nate laughed. "Replay, you prick, you had it set up."

Ted gave him a believe-whatever-you-like grin and went over to the newspaper guys. They'd already put away the p.r. stuff Whiteside had given them and now were jazzing with Mikey DeAngelico and Emerson Wade about the one thing none of them ever got tired of jazzing about.

"Hey, remember the Cinderella Bowl?" Frank Sanchez was asking Eddie Wayne. "Remember the look on Lombardi's face the time Max McGee faked the punt, then ran it for a first down?"

"You think that was something," Mikey said, "you shoulda been on the Penn State bench during the Orange Bowl when Replay refused a fifteen yard penalty that would of meant a first down on the Notre Dame five with eight seconds to go. Pater Noster practically shit his pants."

"How'd you know about that, Pint-size?" Emerson Wade asked. "From what I hear, they wouldn't let you in Penn State."

"That's right. 'Cause I was too fucken dumb. So I went down to Alabama and graduated valedictorian. And that was before they started lettin' you spooks in to lower the curve, Emer—so it's one fucken big-dick accomplishment, if I must say so myself."

Emer reacted with the mock-disdain suitable to a Penn State honors grad who'd spent two years as a Rhodes scholar before turning pro. Everyone else gave Mikey the big laugh.

Sanchez noticed that Ted had joined the group. "Hey, Replay, all shit aside—and everything off the record—what's the story on that penalty call? Were you groggy?"

"The story, Pancho, is what I said right after the game. I didn't like that Notre Dame goal-line defense. I decided

I'd rather take my chances throwing passes from forty yards out."

"Oh, come on, Ted," Eddie Wayne said, "you couldn't've figured the thing in the few seconds it took to refuse the penalty. You had to have been groggy."

"This one's always groggy," Nate contributed. "Groggy like a fox."

Ted winked—he felt it was expected of him—and through his other eye noticed Axel Wessman had put on his coat and was standing at the edge of the group. "I remember that Notre Dame game," Axel said. "I heard it on the radio. It seems, as they say, like only yesterday." He paused, then said as much to himself as anyone, "Everything does, these days. Well, I think I'll be leaving, Ted. Thanks. For everything."

Ted walked him to the elevators. "Axel, suppose Three-oh-five East goes up exactly according to plan. And I go broke. Or something else happens, forcing the project to be abandoned. What value could the buildings have to an outside corporation that took them over?"

"You mean Ron-Cor?"

"Yeah. Would it be worth their while?"

"No question about it, Ted."

"How?"

"First, evict the occupants of subsidized apartments and rent them at full price. Then start cutting back on services and maintenance. It would take a year, perhaps two, given the current real estate situation, to price the building out of the luxury market. Meanwhile, one refinances. And leaves the stockholders and financiers pretty much holding the bag."

"Do you think that's what Ron-Cor has in mind?"

"Possibly. Or they may be looking for a high-prestige enterprise to offset the unfavorable publicity that attaches to their alleged connections."

"What do you believe? Could they turn a profit?"

"It would depend, of course, on how much money they put up and how long you kept afloat. If they took twenty percent and guaranteed another twenty, as you suggested, their profit point would be somewhere around the three-year mark. The less they put up, naturally, the less time you'd have to last to make it worth their while."

"And the more they put up, the more control they'd have. Which is why I wouldn't let them have more than twenty points, no matter how strapped I was. Which they know. Which is why they told Emer they're willing to place more-or-less unlimited funds at my disposal. Which offer they can always withdraw if I ask for too much."

Axel nodded.

Ted pressed the button for the elevator. "Thanks for everything, Axel."

"Thank you, Ted." The elevator arrived. He got in, then blocked the door. "Ted"—he hesitated—"I'm serious about what I said earlier. If you decide you want to cut back, if you want me to redesign, just say the word."

Ted smiled. "Would Lorenzo ask Brunelleschi to redesign Il Duomo?" The reference, he knew, was off by a few centuries, but who kept that stuff straight at—he looked at his watch—four in the morning?

He went back to the living room. Everyone was still jawing about football. "Hey, T-Bone," Mikey DeAngelico said, "you feel like throwing a few? Emer has a ball in his car. We can all go up to Central Park, it'll be daylight in half an hour . . ."

Ted laughed. "You characters have to be out of your minds."

"Why not, Ted?" Frank Sanchez asked. "We can play some two-hand touch."

Ted hadn't thrown a football in more than six months. And that was to college kids, not all-pro receivers like Mikey DeAngelico and Emerson Wade. "You got air in that ball, Emer?"

"If it's flat, I've got a pump." Good old Boy Scout Emer, always prepared.

They piled out of the Tuscany and jogged to Park Avenue to hail a cab. When none came within five minutes Nate said they might as well jog to the park. Everyone felt goofy enough—and had drunk enough Scotch—to think the idea was just great.

They formed a double file, Nate alongside like a platoon sergeant, and jogged up Park to Grand Central, west to Fifth, then up past the Plaza and into the park. Along the way they passed a half dozen drunks who had a hard time believing they weren't hallucinating.

In the park they chucked the ball around a few times, then picked sides. Those who'd played pro ball split up, with Mikey, Burr Whiteside and Ted on one team, Nate and Emer on the other. Ted's team also took Frank Sanchez, and the other got Eddie Wayne, who'd been a high school quarterback, and rental agent Jay Kasselman.

They ran about twenty plays, but it was no contest. Emer couldn't defend against Mikey, and Eddie Wayne couldn't pass against Ted. They tried switching things around, but that didn't work either. Mikey couldn't defend against Emer—both were receivers, not cornerbacks—and Eddie Wayne still couldn't pass against Ted. They started getting bored, and when Nasty put an unnecessarily hard hit on Frank Sanchez, who had a rough time getting up after it, the game broke up.

"Shit, T-Bone," Mikey said as the civilians said their goodbyes and headed toward Fifth Avenue, "we can't call it quits now. I haven't chased passes like that for five years. Throw a few more."

Ted was game, as were Emer and Nate. They ran a few patterns, with Emer and Mikey at ends and Nate filling in at center. At first their timing was a little ragged, but before long things started to click. Ted sent Emer on a fly and waited till he was some forty yards away before letting the ball go. It hit his outstretched fingertips about eighty yards out, and he pulled it in like a lady plucking laundry from her clothesline. "Hey, Replay," he shouted as he trotted back, "where'd you get the cannon?"

Ted smiled. It felt nice to know he could still get that kind of distance on a ball.

They ran a few sideline patterns, then Ted called another fly—this one to Mikey. He knew when he released it that the ball had wings. Mikey kept looking over his shoulder, waiting for it to start coming down. Finally, at what must have been nearly a hundred yards out, he had to turn around and start back for it. He took it right on the sternum, clutched it to him and continued running toward Ted.

"My God," said a voice behind Ted, "is there helium in that damn thing?"

The vocal timbre was strangely familiar. Ted turned and saw a shortish guy, skinny as a yard-marker. He wore a tuxedo and ruffled lace shirt open at the neck, his bow tie untied and its ends dangling.

"All right, you guys," he said, doing an old Sammy Davis takeoff of Jimmy Cagney with his forearms against his abdomen, "I know you gotta be some pro team's new secret weapon. Now all you gotta do is tell me who so I can put a couple bucks on the next game. I promise not to let a soul know what you're up to."

Nate, who'd been pantomiming a block against a non-existent defensive tackle, sidled up to the newcomer. "Hey," he said, "you're Spats Johnson."

"All right," said Spats, "so much for my career as an N.F.L. spy. The question is, who are you, big fella? And who's this man with the golden arm? I haven't seen a pass like that since old Ted Vassily hung up his jock. . . ."

Ted introduced himself.

"Oh, wow!" Eddie Spats took Ted's hand in both of his. "I just rented an apartment in your building, man. It's great. The whole idea, I mean. Just what I'd expect from a guy like you."

Ted thanked him as Mikey and Emer came back from their patterns, and Ted introduced them as well as Nasty Nate.

"Hey," Spats enthused, handshaking all around, "talk about an all-time, all-pro group! Like, Super-Duper Bowl, here we come. You know something, fellas? I'm on my way home from a gig at the Place, y'know? I just had a goodnight drink with a few guys with lots of bucks. They also like to wager here and there when an interesting proposition presents itself, y'dig? Well, if I said to those dudes, 'Whattaya wanna bet on my way home through Central Park tonight I run into Ted Vassily, Emerson Wade, Mikey DeAngelico and Nasty Nate Elefante running pass patterns?' "—he sighed and threw his arms out in wonderment—"man, do you have any idea what odds those dudes'd've laid me?" He laughed so hard he doubled over. "Oh, man, what a gas this is! Hey, guys, you know what's always been my life's ambition? To catch one of this dude's passes. Like some jocks wanna be actors, this actor wants to be a flanker. What say, big man, you gonna let me run a few?"

"Why not?" Ted said. "It's a crazy night."

Nate hunched over the ball, and Ted called for the snap. Mikey and Emer jogged out casually, and Ted watched Eddie run a flag route. For a guy who wasn't an athlete, he moved well. Ted waited until he was twenty yards out, then lobbed one that would be easy to catch. Eddie looked around just in time to see it at his shoulder, then turned into it and clamped his hands around it as it hit his chest.

"All right!" he grinned, holding it triumphantly in the air as he returned to the impromptu line of scrimmage. "Did I do it or did I do it?" His voice rose a few tones in pitch and took on the cadence of Howard Cosell. "Eddie Spats Johnson, ladies and gentlemen. Pulls it in at the forty. The pass was slightly underthrown, but we can't blame Vassily for that, can we? He's been winging them well all evening. . . . Seriously, Vassily," Eddie continued, now taking on a British accent as he chucked the ball back, "do try to put a bit more oomph into the next one. Frightfully difficult holding on to them, you know, when they don't have that swift."

Ted sent him on a buttonhook and put a little power into the throw to teach him some manners. Eddie fielded the ball without obvious trouble, but Ted could tell from his expression as he jogged back that it had hurt. They ran one more buttonhook, which Ted let up on, then started throwing to the whole group again. After half a dozen plays, Eddie pleaded exhaustion and sat on the sidelines, cheering as Mikey and Emer hauled in long ones.

They kept at it for half an hour, then headed back to the hotel. Eddie considered joining them for coffee but decided not to. "Gotta be up by two p.m.," he explained. "I'm taping for my new TV show. Hey, Ted, I gotta have you on some night. In fact, all you dudes. We'll rap about old times. Plus Three-oh-five East. In fact, anything. It's a very loose atmosphere. You got a phone number where my producer can reach you? I'll talk to him this afternoon."

Ted gave him the number at the Tuscany, then shook hands goodbye. Eddie jogged fifty yards toward the west end of the park, turned to wave, then resumed his jog. Nate, Emer, Mikey and Ted started back downtown.

"That Ron-Cor deal, Emer," Ted said after they'd walked a few blocks in silence, "any chance they'd accept non-voting stock?"

"I'll ask Keegan, Replay." He hesitated. "You don't want to go with Witt's guarantee?"

"Not if I can help it. Or Mike's car-washes."

"You think it's a little shaky, T-Bone?" Mikey asked. "You lookin' to get sacked?"

"No reason to play with your friends' money when you can play with a stranger's, Mike."

"No reason we shouldn't be able to keep the figure under thirty-five points," Emerson said. "If we sold six to Ron-Cor and took advantage of their offer to guarantee an equal amount, we'd limit our outlay to the twenty-eight originally budgeted."

"Even with voting stock," Ted thought aloud, "they couldn't be too much of a pain in the ass with six points."

Emerson hesitated, then smiled. "I'm waiting for your on-the-other-hand."

"On the other hand, they can't help but know that we know it. So would they come in on those terms just for the p.r. value? Or on the outside chance we'd default and they'd take over the whole deal?"

Emerson shrugged. "We could always go back to Plan One. I suspect those bankers will soften a little after a couple weeks of having to walk through poor peoples' picket lines to get to their offices."

Ted shook his head. "That was my first miscalculation, Emer. A few years ago it would've worked. But these guys were too tough tonight, and it wasn't a bluff. They know the public climate has shifted. They could tell us to shit in our hats, and after a few days no one would care."

"We could try anyway. If it didn't work, we could always go back to Ron-Cor. Or develop additional resources of our own, either through Eddie Witt or someone else."

"No. If our first play bombed, Ron-Cor could raise the price of its money."

"T-Bone," Mikey said, "maybe I'm just a dumb-ass wide receiver that couldn't get into Penn State, but this whole thing doesn't make sense to me. I mean, if you really believe in Three-oh-five East, why not go all-out with Witt's money, mine and everybody else's? And if you don't believe in it, why not get the fuck out now?"

Ted shook his head. "You're right, Mikey. It doesn't make sense. And I'm getting tired even thinking about it. Let's talk football."

Which was always a safe out. Ted knew the group could relive the glory days for hours on end without getting bored. They did remember-whens all the way downtown to the Tuscany and through breakfast.

"Well," said Emerson, stretching as he polished off a second cup of coffee, "eight a.m. and time for the office. If you want anything tonight, Replay, don't bother to phone, because mine will be off the hook."

"I oughtta run, too," Mikey said. "Bernie's probably watching the TV news to see if I got mugged."

Nate and Ted walked them outside. "Gonna hit the sack, Replay?" Nate asked after the others left.

Ted took a deep breath. The morning air was cool and clear, the sky overcast in a way that gave the city a feeling of intimacy, muffling its noise and some of the nastiness of the people who lived in it. "I think I'll take a little walk first."

"Wanna be alone?"

"Come along if you like."

They walked up Lex to Forty-second, then east to Third, then uptown again. Nate noticed Ted was limping. "You hurt it when we were juking around?"

"No. Just the usual stiffness, I think."

"Now if only you could transfer it to your dick, huh. You know what your problem was as a quarterback, Replay? You took too many hits before you got smart and hired me to protect you."

"One of those hits, as I recall, was put on me by Nasty Nate Elefante."

"Yeah, but you gotta admit I made up for it after I started playing offense."

"No argument, Nate."

"You'd be back in that pocket, ol' Nate out in front givin' them defense fuckers all sorts a shit—you could hold the ball till hell froze over an' nobody'd get within twenty feet of you."

"Well, not too often, anyway."

"Okay, couple a times, maybe. I mean, there's such a thing as the safety blitz. But you gotta admit, Replay, thanks to me you had the lowest sack average in the league."

"Hey, Nate, I'm with you, and by the way, what makes your performance all the more remarkable, as old Howard Cosell might have said, was that you made the transition from defense to offense. I don't think I've ever heard of another lineman doing it. How come?"

"Thought you'd never ask, Replay. Seriously, no put-on, I always had this tremendous feeling for being part of a team. That might not be the kind of thing people expect to hear from me. I know my image—I guess I used to encourage it, at least when I played—but I'll tell you something, guys like you that were superstars in your diapers might've never found it out, but I did very early, playin' high school ball under a really good coach—when you're part of a really first-rate team, it's a feeling nothing in the world can match . . . Like, when I was with Pittsburgh we had dissension up the ass. The offense hated the defense, the tackles hated the ends, we'd even try to make each other look bad on the field sometimes. I'd see guys like you an' Mikey and Emer and ol' Walt Kulikowski, and I'd say to myself, 'That's what you call a *team.*' No wonder I started losing my stuff there, or that they eventually put me on waivers."

"They made a mistake."

"Not really. See, that's what I'm tryin' to say, when they put me on waivers I really was shit. I *deserved* bein' on waivers. But it was you guys that put me back together again. I think Witt read it that way from the beginning. When he first sounded me out about getting my head straight, I told him, 'Witt, you wanna really see what I can do, give me a shot on offense.' I wanted to be part of you guys. Not just on the squad but in there with you and Mikey and Emer, runnin' the plays, givin' you what I had, bein' part of—"

"Part, hell, you were essential, Nate."

"We *all* were essential, man, that's what I'm tryin' a say. And that's probably why we all quit when you did —me, Mikey, Emer—the only guy that hung in was

Kulikowski and he was on the toboggan for the rest of his career. I could've stayed around. I mean, as a lineman I was good for another ten years . . ."

Ted made himself laugh. "Ten more years of taking hits. It hurts me just to think about it."

"That's 'cause you were never a hitter. You know somethin', man, there's two kinds a guys play this game —those that love contact and those that hate it. No in-betweens. Most guys in the pits, plus a few running backs like Kulikowski or Jimmy Brown or Larry Czonka, they loved the hits. It didn't matter whether they were getting or giving. Of course, they'd rather give than get. But they didn't *mind* getting, if you know what I mean. Guys like you are different. You'd sell your mother to avoid it. No offense, Replay, but I always wondered, when you hate gettin' hit so much, why the hell even bother to play football?"

"Nobody plays ball that doesn't like contact, Nate—at least in the beginning. It's that first serious injury that changes you. You can't forget the pain. And you remember how easily it happened. You weren't doing anything differently than you usually do. So it could happen again anytime. And next time it might be worse, hurt more, cost you your career. So now you're playing survival ball, a sort of prevent offense. Every play is another opportunity for it to happen, and you do whatever you can to tip the odds against it."

"Why not just quit, if that's the way you feel."

"Most guys would, I think. But they don't want to let go, don't want to think of themselves as over the hill."

"Goofy world. Guys gettin' hit that don't want to, gettin' their brains beat out just for some stupid game they're playin' in their heads."

"Tell me it's so different in real life."

They walked a few blocks in silence, then turned east. Nate smiled as they approached the Second Avenue intersection. "I had a hunch you'd want to come here. Looks good, doesn't it?"

Actually it didn't look anything. There was just a blue construction fence, and inside a few of the old buildings the demolition people hadn't gotten to yet. There was a big sign at the corner: a black background, painted with a marble effect, and superimposed on it, in gold letters, a big "305" and, underneath, "EAST."

Ted let them through the fence with his key. The grounds foreman recognized him and came over to pay his respects, but Ted waved him away. Nate and Ted found a plank to sit on and watched a demolition crew at the opposite end of the lot gutting a three-story brick job.

"Replay," Nate said after a while, "I've been thinking, a guy like me could really be a lot of help to you once the building is open."

"Of course. That's why you're on the board of directors, man."

"Not only that. I mean in more practical ways. Like building superintendent."

Ted's eyebrows arched.

"Think about it, Replay, it ain't such a bad idea. I mean, having a celebrity super. Granted, I'm not a big name like you, but people know who I am. It'd be one more plus for the building, don'tcha think?"

Ted didn't answer immediately.

"I could do it, Reep. Okay, I don't have experience. But I could learn, right? All the workers'd listen to me. Nobody ever back-talks a fucker my size."

"Why would you want it? It pays only a couple bills a week. And there's headaches up the ass."

"There's headaches in everything. And what the fuck'm I doin' now? Drifting from one thing to another, sellin' cars, sellin' insurance, anything where there's a chance to get a little mileage out of my name."

Ted felt a slight uncertainty he didn't want to voice.

"And I'd have my own apartment, right? Without payin' rent? I checked it out, that's always part of a super's deal. So I'd get to meet all the broads in the building. I could red-flag the knockouts for you—you know, the ones I'd probably never be able to do business with myself. And when you weren't too busy, maybe we could knock around sometimes, like the old days. I wouldn't be in your hair when you had other stuff to do." His eyes found Ted's. "Whattaya think, Replay? Sound good?"

"Nate, you're one of the best friends a guy could have—"

Nate's expression darkened. He suspected an end run. "You don't think I'd make a good super?"

"The best, Nate . . . If you want the job, it's yours."

"Really, Reep?" The sun came out again. "You mean it? Hey, terrific, man!" He whacked Ted on the back. It felt like getting hit with a side of beef. "You won't be sorry, T. I swear, first week on the job, I'll scout more dynamite cunt than you see all year. No doggos. All eights or better. Dig?"

"I dig, Nate."

They fell silent again. Ted watched the demolition crew work on the three-story brick job. In the time he and Nate had been sitting there, they'd leveled an entire outer wall and now were tearing apart the inner walls. Another few hours and the building would be razed.

There was something sad about seeing it come down. Ted wondered about the guy who had put it up—probably sometime around the turn of the century—wondered what had been on his mind. Was he just another builder, making a buck? Or did the building mean something personal to him? Maybe he was a guy like Ted's old man, working 'round the clock in a diner for ten years to salt away enough dough to buy land, then busting ass for ten more to get a building up—and hoping to collect enough in rents to make his mortgage payments. All that sweat and strain, then finally he's okay. And then half a century later, some smart-ass ex-football player comes along and tells a few guys this and that, and the building comes down in less than a day.

Ted kept watching the workers and tried not to think about the builder. Soon he felt his body relaxing. The demolition noises and street noises began blending in his mind. His body was nicely tired, the muscles feeling good after the workout, despite the stiffness in his knee and a little soreness in his throwing arm.

He let his eyes range over the lot and pictured Axel Wessman's towers rising in the four corners. They actually seemed to be materializing in front of him, slowly, one floor at a time, as if the whole building had been in storage underground and now was being raised into place by some unseen magical elevator. The towers continued up, then the connecting wings came into place. Then the inner core filled in, and trees and grass grew, and people materialized walking back and forth. And Ted was sitting on a bench near a fountain, watching it happen all around him.

For a moment, for just the fleetingest instant, he sensed Chris on the bench beside him. Her perfume, that one fragrance she always loved, seemed very real. He almost expected to feel her leaning toward him, her body brushing his, one exquisite breast flattening against his arm as she drew close and said something to him. And then they'd hug, and she'd fit her body into the crook of his arm the way she always did. And they'd sit there for hours, looking at the whole scene together.

The fantasy lasted just long enough to jar him when he came awake and realized it wasn't real.

"My man," Nate said, "you're nodding out."

"Yeah." Ted looked at his watch. "Almost ten. I think I'll pack it in."

Nate got up with him. "Wanna walk back or take a cab?"

"Walk."

They headed for the gate. Ted stopped in front for one last look at the lot.

Nate stared at him curiously. "Replay?"

Ted waited.

"You're a little scared, aren't you?"

"Scared?"

"I mean, of the whole thing."

Ted thought about it. "Not scared, really. Just getting up for it, I guess. Like for a game."

"That's a good thing. You know how it is if you're not up for a game. You can get careless. And you can wind up getting cold-cocked. . . ."

"Yeah."

They started west toward Third.

THREE

Eddie Spats Johnson knew when he hit the bed that it was going to be a bitch of a night. He'd hoped all that running in the park with Vassily and those other jocks would have tired him out. But as soon as his body was between the sheets, his eyes sprang open like those jacks-in-the-box they used to show on TV cartoons. He tossed and turned and flopped and squirmed and . . . nothing. After half an hour he was wider awake than ever.

He considered a Valium but looked at the luminous clock on the dresser and decided against it. It was already seven. The Valium wouldn't work till eight, even with some beer as a booster, and then he'd be semi-zapped for the afternoon taping. On the other hand if he didn't zonk out on Valium, he could wind up lying here all morning with his eyes wide open and be completely zonko-bedonko for the taping.

The problem was, they taped the show at five in the goddamn afternoon. Now, if they ran it live, everything would be fine. In fact, it'd be just like a gig with the band. He'd fall out of bed somewhere around five, take two hours to shower, dress and read the papers, have a nice dinner, jazz around for another hour or so . . . beautiful. But this reveille shit! It wouldn't be bad once a week. But every day!

He laughed mirthlessly. Little man, he told himself in a voice that sounded more like his father's than his own, you oughtta have your ass kicked. Twenty-five years ago you were standing reveille in the army at five a.m., not two p.m., and were glad to have the three squares a day it brought you. Two months ago you'd've given the left side of your ass for a steady gig, *any* steady gig—even some horseshit game show at nine in the morning that meant getting up at six. Now you're sitting on one of the hottest TV properties around, you're doubling with the big band at the Place, you're pulling down five thou a week and it could be fifty by the end of the year—and you're bitching about having to get up at two in the afternoon!

Well, okay, it was unreasonable to bitch. Still, the alarm was set for two, it was now seven—no, seven-twenty—and he still was nowhere near conking out.

What he needed, he reflected, was a broad. Some nice, lush, hot-boxed number with tits the size of cantaloupes and wearing a tight skimpy halter that made them look as though they were trying to bust out. He'd bury his face between them and breathe in till their flesh clogged his nostrils and made him feel he was going to suffocate, and even then he wouldn't back away, he'd just keep pressing the big gloppy fuckers against his face, feeling their fantastic texture, loving their softness, grooving on the pulse of her heart that vibrated through them. Ah, fuck—tits! My kingdom for a pair of tits!

But, no, that wasn't what he really needed. There were tits galore at the Place—all over New York. He could've picked up half a dozen broads tonight if he wanted them—sleaze shots, with their too-much eye shadow and cigarette breath and horsey hips and smelly cunts—those were always around for the taking, particularly now that he was hot again with the TV thing. But he didn't want that. He didn't want just a hole to empty it in. He wanted . . .

Well, he wanted a Clean. One of those super-scrubbed college types, with her trench coat and Weejuns and nice bare legs moving under a short skirt while her bra-less tits bounced like cheerleader's pompoms when she walked. A broad that looked like ice to the rest of the world; one you figured you wouldn't be able to fuck if your life depended on it. But you came on to her anyway, because it's better to go down swinging than get called out on strikes. And to your surprise, she was interested. Not too interested. But interested enough to make it worth working at. And then, after you finally got her back to your place, you went into the kitchen to make her a drink and came back to find her sitting on the couch with a button open on her blouse that you knew wasn't open before. And that's when you knew you'd won. And the knowledge was enough to give you a stiff dick for the next six weeks.

Yep, that's what he needed. And that, he suddenly realized—although he should have known it all along—was Francesca. Goddamn it, everything always came back to Francesca. Even after five years, he couldn't get her out of his head. Of course, they'd been married for close to eight. But the last four were hasslesville, with both of them knowing it couldn't last. Was it possible even now—four plus five—nine years later, he was *still* thinking about her?

Not only possible. It was fact. He'd been thinking about her ever since the breakup, but particularly since he left the Coast. Somehow the East, with its intellectual types and gloomy weather and whatever the fuck else it had that he identified with their early days together—somehow all this made him want her more than out on the Coast where, if you really got horny, it was just a matter of picking up the phone and for a C-note you'd get a Clean with fantastic jugs and a great body and an I.Q. of 186 who was just filling in as a hook while waiting for U.C.L.A. to approve her doctoral thesis. Or you could drive over to Malibu, or up to the nudie beaches of Santa Barbara and watch cream-skinned, golden-haired fuck-goddesses strut their stuff all day; and if you came on to five of them, you'd be sure of hitting at least one that recognized you and was hot to make it with a celebrity and didn't have a hang-up about the race bit. So you could block Francesca out of your mind, if you kept your dick active enough. And even though the block wasn't complete, even though she snuck in every now and then to take a few shots at you, at least you could get a decent night's sleep.

But now? A quarter to eight and he was still wide awake. He should've taken the Valium.

What he really needed here in New York, he told himself as he flopped into a new position and tried to get comfortable on the pillow, was some male friends. Guys like Ernie Rose and Gene Carter and all the old gang on the Coast back in the good old days when any one of their names on a picture would mean the studio would get its money back—and all of the names would be a surefire box-office bonanza. "The Mickey Mouse Club," newspaper guys used to call them. Probably on the theory that it was childish to spend all your time boozing and chasing broads and hanging out in nightclubs and pulling down close to a mil a year working just a few hours a day. Yeah, childish. Go find a newspaper guy that wouldn't give the left side of his ass to trade places with you. Go find anybody! The Mickey Mouse Club!

But. But . . . BUT—no denying it, that was when he lost Francesca. He couldn't blame her, really. How can you blame a girl for walking out when you spend eighty percent of your time with your wonderful good buddies? Sometimes weeks'd pass that he wasn't in touch with her. And she worried a lot. She was that kind of chick. Other wives'd imagine their husbands screwing some big-titted fuckbird. She'd imagine him lying somewhere bleeding on the highway and be relieved to learn from the newspaper columns the next day that he'd only been screwing some bit-titted fuckbird.

Yeah, no question, he'd been unfair to her. But the thing was, when she finally laid it out for him, when she finally issued the ultimatum, he reformed. He really did. He cut out broads, stopped running with the gang, even stopped smoking grass. And then—who could figure it out?—*then,* when she finally had him where she'd always said she wanted him . . . that's when she ankled. Who could figure it out? Who could figure *anything* out these days?

He got up and took a Valium, chasing it with a beer. Better semi-snorked than zonko-bedonko, right?

He went back to bed. Hell with Francesca. It was over. Period. Meanwhile . . . meanwhile, it wouldn't hurt to tie in with some buddies like Ted Vassily and his boys running pass patterns this morning. Now, they really had it made. You put in four, five years playing ball, bet shrewdly on a few games to build up a nest egg, then retire and tell the whole world to shit in its hat. If you want to run pass patterns in Central Park at five in the morning, fuck it, you run pass patterns in Central Park at five in the morning.

Eddie smiled. Vassily and the others would be fun to hang out with. In fact, it could beat the old days with Ernie Rose. Vassily looked like a goddamn Adonis. He should be the best door-opener since Errol Flynn.

Yeah, Spats would have to make it a point to shine up to Vassily once 305 East got opened. Invite him to dinner some night. Suggest a double date. Maybe fix him up with one of the Place's tit-dummies, just to break the ice. Also have him on the TV show, of course.

The show. That reminded him. He'd invited Vassily. It was a good idea, too. Everybody was football crazy. People'd tune in who normally couldn't stand old Eddie Spats Johnson. He'd tell the producer Vince Sanders this afternoon. Should make a note of it. He'd probably forget without a note. He couldn't remember anything lately. The old mind going. Deterioration. Encroaching senility. Ah, he felt nice and relaxed now. The Valium was taking hold. Without it, he hadn't had a decent night's sleep in close to ten years. What time was it now, anyway? Quarter to nine? That late?

He woke to the ringing doorbell. He looked at the clock on the dresser and couldn't believe it. Eleven o'clock? Who would be waking him at eleven o'clock? He turned over and hoped they'd go away. No way! The bell rang and rang and rang. Where was the doorman? Didn't he have instructions to keep everybody away unless he was told someone was expected? What kind of building was this?

Bing-bong, bing-bong, bing-bing-bong . . .

It was never going to stop. And now he was awake anyway. Might as well answer it.

His caller was a kid with a huge basket of flowers—big round yellow ones, smaller orange ones, a couple dozen scattered ones that looked like roses (Eddie wasn't too up on flowers' names), and, in the center, a wreath of green flowers around a red background that had a figure in the middle made of white and dark blue flowers—the figure of his long-time trademark, a clarinet next to a pair of spats.

He took the basket from the kid and started to unpin

the envelope attached to the ribbon, then decided not to. He was still zonked enough from the Valium that he might be able to get right back to sleep. He started for the bed and suddenly realized the door was still open. The kid was standing there, waiting for a tip. He found some bills, barely glanced at the one he pulled from the wad, and shoved it at the kid. "Here," he murmured, starting to close the door.

"Mr. Johnson?"

Oh, God, kid, what more do you want?

"I'd like to shake hands. . . ."

Eddie Johnson suddenly felt about four inches tall. The effects of the Valium seemed to vanish, like a curtain being lifted, and here was this kid standing there, maybe eleven or twelve years old, cute as a button, big brown eyes, close-cropped afro, great big teeth. . . . How many people shit on a kid like this in the course of a day? Bad enough to have the white folks doing it to you, but when a brother did—

"Sure, big fella," Spats said, taking the boy's hand. "Sorry I'm a little grumpy this morning, but I'm not feeling too well, didn't get very much sleep. . . ."

The kid smiled. "That's okay. I just wanted to shake your hand so I could tell the guys in the neighborhood. You know?"

Eddie knew. There was a time when he was that kid. Hundreds, thousands of times back stage in the old days with dad and the band, he'd collected celebrities' handshakes for his mental scrapbook—Jack Benny, the Marx Brothers, Sammy Davis, Louis "Satchmo" Armstrong, Bojangles . . .

He made himself smile. "Come on in, pal, I gotta do better than just a handshake for a buddy, don't I?" He went to the refrigerator. "You drink beer? I don't have any soft drinks. Maybe some Scotch? O.J.?"

"Beer'd be terrific," the astonished kid replied.

Eddie opened two bottles. "Now tell me about yourself." He ushered the kid to an armchair. "Where do you live? Do you have a family? Do you play a musical instrument?"

He lived on 135th Street. Deep poverty. One of five kids. All with momma. Assorted fathers, whereabouts unknown. He wanted to play electric guitar, couldn't afford one.

"Do you sing? Good enough to try out for TV?"

The kid ducked his head. "Shee-it, I can't do much of anything, Mr. Johnson."

Eddie was stumped. What can you do for a kid that can't do much of anything and knows it? "Well, I'm glad to see you working," he said. "Lots of kids, they take what they think is the easy way, they hang around the street and hustle a buck here and there. They wind up in jail. And then they get out and next thing you know some honkey cop shoots 'em. It's corny but it's better to play it straight, ol' buddy. Take it from me."

He went to his jacket and picked through the wad of bills. He came back with three fifties. "I want you to do something for me, big fella. I want you to take this"—he gave the kid a fifty—"and buy something nice for yourself. Whatever you want. Not to share with your family or anybody else. Just you. It's your personal birthday present from Eddie Spats Johnson." He gave him the second fifty. "Now, with this, buy something for your family. Something you think they'd really like. Okay? And with this"—third fifty—"buy some books for yourself. Not comic books or porno stuff. Books that tell you how to do things, how to get along in the world. Ask your teacher or the librarian to recommend some, okay? Hell, I wouldn't have a clue."

The kid examined the bills, then neatly folded them and put them into his pocket.

"You wanna come see my show?" Eddie continued, "Give me your address. I'll have my producer mail tickets. You, your momma, the whole family. A couple for your friends too. Then after the show you can come backstage and see the cameras and stuff. You think you'd like that?"

The kid nodded, speechless.

"Okay, that's how Eddie Spats takes care of his buddies. Now"—he smiled as he hoisted his beer bottle in toast—"let's polish these off so old Spats can get back to bed, okay, big fella?"

The kid finished his beer, murmured "thanks," and left. Spats opened another bottle for himself and opened the envelope that came with the flowers. The card was signed,

"*Auguri,* Joe Mandino." It was accompanied by a clip from *Variety* that revealed why Spats was being congratulated—after a month on the air his show had topped the Nielsen ratings for his time slot. Of course it happened on only one night—and during a week when the opposition was using a substitute host. Still, it was no small accomplishment.

Eddie took a long pull on his bottle of beer and sighed contentedly. The Nielsen thing by no means meant he was back on top again. It would be a long hard climb under the best of circumstances. But at least he was going in the right direction.

Now if only he could sleep. Because, goddamn it, if he didn't start sleeping regularly he'd blow the Nielsens and everything else. You don't top the ratings if you show up for work every day so zonked you can't deliver your best.

He looked at his watch. Eleven-forty-five. And he was beat. If he didn't get at least two more hours he'd be a walking zombie for the taping and he'd be lucky to get through the gig at The Place. Should he take another Valium, just for insurance? No. That would waste him completely and he'd feel depressed as hell later. Better just do a little more beer to boost the one he took earlier.

He opened another bottle and placed it on the table next to the unfinished one, took another long pull from the unfinished one, stared at the floral arrangement and tried not to think about anything that would keep him awake.

How, he wondered, could he have come to this? Even in the worst of the old days, even when he was flat-ass busted, he never had trouble sleeping. Of course during the hassles with Francesca he leaned heavily on grass and booze. But he was drinking now. And while he didn't get plastered every night, like in the old days, he was certainly consuming enough to bring him down after the gig. Worse yet, when he did get plastered nowadays, when he drank enough that he barely made it to bed before passing out, he'd wake a few hours later and not be able to get back to sleep.

What he needed was exercise. Not just a walk across the park after the gig. A full-scale exercise program. Weights, running, calisthenics, the whole shmear. But he couldn't do that stuff alone. It bored him. Maybe after he got set up in 305 East. Maybe he'd hang around with Vassily and those guys. They probably exercised all the time. You don't get a physique like Vassily's sitting around in saloons every night.

And a broad. That was still what he needed most of all. A Clean. Where the fuck did you find a Clean that was going to ball a black entertainer? Or any black man? The only white chicks that balled blacks were nymphomaniacs, freakos, social workers, show business assholes, and other professional liberals.

Maybe a black chick? Sure. Go find one. The black Cleans wouldn't look twice at a guy in show business. They all wanted N.A.A.C.P. chaps with law degrees. Say "man" or "dig" or "chick" or some word like that in front of them and they looked at you as if you just laid a fart. They considered you a street-corner ditty-bop.

Meanwhile, it was five minutes before noon, and how did you get to sleep?

Spats polished off the first bottle, started on the second, stared at the flowers and tried not to think about chicks. Chicks were the worst thing to think about when you wanted to sleep.

The flowers. What a super gesture on Coffee Joe's part. Who else? Name one other person in the entire fucken universe who ever cared for him that way. Sure, everybody said Coffee Joe was using him. But what was the big deal? You sang a couple weeks at a mob club. You showed up at a few parties where they needed celebrities. Small price to pay for the kind of treatment he got from Coffee Joe. Using him? Name one person he knew who *wasn't* using him. The only difference was, Coffee Joe paid back.

If you could even call it using. Joe paid back far out of proportion to anything Spats had ever done for him.

So okay, you signed with Blackjack for your record label, and Joe owned a piece of it. But you got the same deal with them as any record company. C.B.S. and R.C.A. weren't angels, either! And when you worked a mob joint, you got top dollar.

No, what it really was with Joe and him, he believed, was—corny as it might sound—affection. Nothing more complicated. Joe was a warm-hearted guy. There weren't too many people he could trust. He liked doing things for people he liked. And he liked Eddie Spats.

Eddie remembered their first meeting. It was in Atlantic City at Fatty Barbera's joint. Eddie's father's Dixieland band was playing breaks for the room's big band, and Eddie was doing a feature spot with vocals and a dance routine. He was, as he remembered it, around twelve years old.

Coffee Joe had a ringside table. He was with a gorgeous blonde with big tits. Little Eddie saw the couple smiling and digging him while he did his routine, so he played up to them. They led the applause after each tune and kept applauding for a few more beats after everyone else had stopped. When the set was over and he'd gone backstage, one of Fatty's bouncers told him Mr. Mandino would like him to join them for a drink.

Eddie's father was against it. "You know that ain't permitted."

The bouncer smiled. "Don't worry, if Coffee Joe wants Little Spats at his table, nobody's gonna say no."

The bouncer escorted him to the table, and Eddie looked around the room in disbelief. How strange it felt, surrounded by all these white people, watching the main show right up on stage. The house rule was that no black person could be in the room, except on stage, and to get to and from the stage you had to use a back entrance.

Joe Mandino asked him if he wanted something to drink.

Eddie hesitated. Surely Fatty Barbera would never stand for that.

"Don't worry," Joe said, anticipating the objection, "it's okay."

Eddie ordered a Coke. The waiter brought it in a tall, frosted glass filled to the brim with ice, and with a cherry on top. Eddie sipped it. Nothing ever tasted so good.

The blonde with the big tits touched his face—curiously, as if she wondered if the brown would rub off. "He's so *cute,*" she said. "Just like a little chocolate Easter bunny."

Joe smiled. "That's what he is. *Mio piccolo cioccolato.*" He took Eddie's face in both hands, then pinched both cheeks. "A very talented boy, this fellow. He's going to be a big star somedav. Aren't you, *bello?*"

"*Bello* means handsome," the girl told him. "You're a handsome young fellow, Eddie."

He felt very strange, having these people touch him and talk Italian and say nice things about him. "I hope to be," he said in answer to Joe's question.

"Would you like something to eat?"

Little Spats hesitated.

"Don't worrv, it's okay." Joe snapped his fingers and the waiter brought a menu. "Anything you want, *piccolo.* Don't worrv about getting back on stage. They can do the next set without you."

Eddie ate two hamburgers and a turkey sandwich and drank three more Cokes. He watched as the show concluded, the Dixieland band did its set and the big band returned for the next show.

"*Allora, piccolo,*" Joe Mandino said, shaking his hand, "I'll let you get back to work now."

"Thanks . . . thanks for everything," Eddie said. He started away from the table, then turned back. "Oh, do you have a favorite song, sir?"

" 'Please Don't Talk About Me When I'm Gone,' " Joe said. "Do you know it, *piccolo?*"

"I'll learn it during the break," Eddie said.

Joe shoved something in his pocket, and he went backstage feeling warmer and happier than he could ever remember. No one had ever been that nice to him before. Certainly no white person. He wondered if they'd throw away the dishes now that he ate from them. Backstage, he fished into the lapel pocket of his tuxedo and found what Joe had put there. He could hardly believe his eyes. He'd never seen a hundred-dollar bill before. . . .

Eddie now stared at the floral array. You had to hand it to Coffee Joe, he traveled first class. And wasn't that what really counted? So what if he cut a few corners? What was the law anyway but a set of rules established by the rich cats to keep the loot from changing hands? That was Joe's line, but it was also true. The law, the svstem, the establishment—they weren't too crazy about the average man. Democracy, communism, socialism, all the fucken isms—whoever ran the show, the fat cats got fatter and the little man got screwed. That's what Joe said, and who could show him wrong? Not Eddie Johnson. So the only thing to do was get yours where you could, hopefully without hurting anyone. If you were a rich kid, you went to Harvard and pulled down a hundred thou a year as a lawyer. If you were poor, well . . . you had to be a little more imaginative.

Eddie yawned. The beers had done their work. He glanced at the clock. Twelve-fifteen. Late, but at least he'd get a good hour and forty-five minutes' sleep. He considered phoning his answering service to push his wake-up order back to two-thirty, but he was afraid talking to the operator would upset his drowsiness. He polished off the last beer and went to bed. He was asleep within a minute.

He was jarred awake half an hour later by the phone. He looked at his clock and trembled with rage. "What the fuck's the matter with ya, calling an hour early?" he screamed into the receiver. "Didn't I fucken tell you two o'clock?"

There was a moment's silence, then Joe Mandino replied, *"Piano, piccolo, piano.* It's only me. I'm sorry I woke you."

Eddie apologized profusely and thanked him for the flowers. "I'm a nervous wreck, Uncle," he added. "I can't get any sleep. Then I get up and I can't function."

"Maybe you should see a doctor. I know a good one. I'll set something up. Now why I called . . . this friend of mine, Vinnie DeAngelis, in from out of town. He's gonna catch your second show at the Place tonight. I just thought, if you wouldn't mind, you could stop over at his table, say hello, let him buy you a drink, make him feel good rubbing elbows with a celebrity, eh?"

"Sure, Uncle, glad to." Eddie felt he had to say something more about the way he answered the phone, but he couldn't figure what. To buy time he asked, "You pick out your apartment yet at Three-oh-five East?"

"No. There's a few hassles. Nothing important. So I'm sorry I disturbed you, eh, *bello?* Now back to sleep, eh? . . . And Eddie—you know, when the phone rings sometimes, *bello,* even if you don't expect it, even if it wakes you up at a bad time—be nice, eh? No dirty words, okay? Who knows, it might be some nun calling a wrong number. You wouldn't want to ruin her whole day, would you?"

Eddie chuckled sheepishly. "No, Uncle. You're right. Sorry. *Ciao*, now, okay? I'll see you."

He hung up, considered another beer, then realized he had only forty-five minutes of sleep-time. Might as well stay up.

He stumbled into the bathroom, looked at his face in the mirror, and winced. His skin was almost gray. He looked as though he needed a blood transfusion. And skinny! His weight probably was down to one-twenty. Flyweight! He would have to shape up. Really shape up.

He stared at himself and tried to summon the energy to turn on the shower. He really had to do something about the doorbell and telephone. He could turn off the bell on the telephone, but then he wouldn't be able to get a wake-up call from his answering service. And that was the only thing that could wake him permanently: if he used the alarm clock, he'd always turn it off and go back to sleep. And the doorbell? Well, that was the building's fault. It should stop being a problem when he moved into 305 East. In fact, he'd read in the brochure that 305 East would also have a special wake-up service for tenants, so the phone problem would be solved too. Maybe everything would be solved. Maybe.

The phone jarred Ted Vassily awake, and for a moment he didn't know where he was. Opening his eyes, he half-expected to see the familiar view of the Pacific from his Malibu beach house. Instead, he saw the art deco print curtains of the Tuscany, alive with afternoon sunlight.

He'd forgotten to tell the desk he wasn't taking calls. He picked up the receiver. "Hi," said a youngish female voice, "I'm Buffy Weiss. Do you have a few minutes?"

In the fuzziness of coming awake he couldn't place the name.

"I hope I didn't get you at a bad time, but I happened to be in the neighborhood, so I thought I'd give it a try. I'm in the lobby now. Can I come up?"

She obviously thought he should know her name, and

while it was definitely familiar he didn't quite have the handle yet . . . "I'm still in bed," he said.

"That doesn't bother me if it doesn't bother you."

She had one of those flat, sexy, Seven Sisters voices that had always turned him on. Well, this wouldn't be the first time he'd fallen into something decent via an unexpected telephone call. In the old days it used to happen all the time . . .

"Well, can I come up?"

"Sure." The worst that could happen was he wouldn't like her and he'd get rid of her. "Stop by the desk on the way and have room service send up some coffee. Unless you'd prefer something else."

"Coffee's fine. See you in a jiff."

He went to the bathroom and was in the process of giving his teeth a brisk brushing when she came into perspective for him . . . Buffy Weiss, sure, the famous lady bleeding-heart lawyer, had her picture on some magazine lately, he'd seen her name on the early rental list for 305 East . . . Buffy Weiss . . . well, well . . . this could be interesting. . . . The door buzzer was ringing just as he finished.

"Hello," she said, extending her hand. He noticed her eyes do a frank head-to-toe check-out.

He returned it and liked what he saw. Trim body. Breasts could be bigger, but acceptable. Good legs and ass, accented by tight-fitting, well tailored jeans. A straight little nose, a sexy smile, and rose-tinted glasses that did interesting things to her eyes.

He ushered her into the living room, considered trying to sit on the couch with her, then decided to stay with separate seats until he diagnosed the direction of the play. He motioned her to the couch, took the armchair alongside it and waited for her to say something.

She was waiting for *him* to say something. "Well," she said finally, "you're probably wondering why I'm here."

"The question crossed my mind."

"I've heard you're one hell of a fuck, and I want to see if it's true."

He'd been around aggressive women before, but none that ever quite popped him one like that. He offered a smile that he hoped seemed as nonchalant as he intended. "Right now? Or would you rather wait till we have our coffee?"

She smiled back. Either he was super-cool or super-dumb. "I can wait," she said. "Actually, that isn't all I came for. You see, Mr. Vassily—Ted?—I've heard a good deal about Three-oh-five East; in fact, I'm going to be one of your tenants. I admire what you're doing, so I wanted to meet you. I may even write something about you."

"Oh, are you a writer or something?" He was careful to say it with a straight face, as though he really didn't know who her famous person was.

Her eyebrows arched. Had she mumbled her name on the phone? Or was it possible he really didn't know? "I'm Buffy Weiss," she said.

"Name sounds familiar, but I'm afraid I haven't read any of your stuff. Of course I've been away from New York a few years."

Was he putting her on? Or was he trying to piss her off? "I'm published nationally. Of course, I don't write sports, so maybe that explains it."

He grinned. Should he give her a shot back? Or should he punt? What would save the fuck? "Yeah," he murmured, opting for plan one, "football dummies like me usually confine ourselves to the sports pages. And the comics. We can handle pictures okay. It's the words that strain."

"I didn't mean it that way." She smiled pleasantly. "I guess I have become sort of presumptuous with all the publicity I've had lately. I'm sure plenty of people wouldn't recognize my name."

Talk about one-upmanship. No question, he was back in New York. Should he try to disarm her by playing it straight? "I get most of the national magazines. Where should I have read about you?"

"Well, I was the subject of a *Newsweek* cover story last month."

"Hey, that's terrific. I haven't had a *Newsweek* cover since I left pro ball. *Time,* either, for that matter."

She smiled. "Why don't we cut out this bullshit and go to bed?"

He stood, bowed slightly, and gestured toward the door. She preceded him into the bedroom, hesitated a moment alongside the bed, then started to unbutton her blouse. As if on cue, room service arrived with the coffee. Ted tipped the waiter, locked the door, turned on the "Do Not Disturb" light and came back into the bedroom.

She was standing where he had left her, the blouse unbuttoned but still on her shoulders. His eyes traced the narrow expanse of bare flesh it exposed—the lovely softness of her throat, the full curves of the inner slopes of her breasts, which were fuller than they'd seemed when the blouse was buttoned. There was no interruption in her suntan line, and the idea of her sunbathing topless added to his turn-on.

He waited for her to take off the blouse.

"I don't really want to do it this way," she said. "I don't want it to be just one more quick ball with a guy I'll forget an hour after it's over."

He didn't answer.

"I came here expecting to meet a guy who's supposed to be a big man in *every* department. I'll feel cheated if all I get from you is a warm body and a hard cock." She touched her index finger to her temple. "I want some of what's up here."

"Coffee break," he said.

They went back into the living room. He poured two cups, put them on the coffee table, and sat on the couch next to her.

"Let's start at the beginning," she said, seeming to put on a new face. "My name is Buffy Weiss. I'm thirty-one years old. I'm a lawyer and, among other things, I make my living bringing class actions against companies who rip off the little man. *Newsweek* calls me 'the female Ralph Nader,' which I resent as oversimplification as well as being sexist. But let it pass, it's handily descriptive. Anyway, I also do a lot of writing. And I think your plan for Three-oh-five East is one of the most exciting innovations in the history of urban development. Not that vest-pocket housing is all that novel. But that someone would have the imagination to attempt it in a purely commercial venture. And apparently succeed . . . I saw in this afternoon's *Post* that BankUS and Chase are bidding to be your banker."

"Thirty-one . . ." he said, giving her another careful look. "You know, I'd never have guessed you for over twenty-five. When you just said you were going to be my tenant, I figured you'd be moving in with your parents or something . . ."

"Oh, come off it, Vassily. You're not going to turn me on with that old cutesy-pie sexist horseshit. I'm not a Miss America contestant."

He sighed. "What's the big crime about telling you I find you attractive?"

"Well, I *know* you find me attractive, asshole. You've been undressing me ever since I came into the room. And if that's all you've got in you—if all you're good for is a fuck—well, fine, let's do it, get it over with and go our separate ways. I mean, really, Ted, unlike some of the other ladies you may have known, I'm more than capable of accepting you on that basis. I'm also one dynamite lay, as you'll find out. So it'll be worth your while, no matter how it works out. But, goddamn it, I want more. The kind of guy who dreams up Three-oh-five East isn't just another piece of nice-looking meat with a cock sticking out of it. You've got more than that. You've *got* to have more than that. And I want it."

He shrugged. "You ain't about to get it by taking shots at me every time I say something." He noticed that her body seemed to relax, as if in acceptance of this. "I'm sorry if I'm not following the script you intended for this little *tête-à-tête*"—he felt a bit self-conscious using the expression, almost retracted it to paraphrase, then decided to go ahead—"but I'm me and you're you and that's about all there's to it. Now, you want to talk, that's okay. And you wanna go to bed, that's okay too. But, please, don't break my balls every time I say something that's not in your script."

"You're right." She sipped her coffee and looked up at him. "Back to the beginning. I think Three-oh-five East is one bitch of an idea, and I'm greatly admiring of you—God, what an awful construction that is . . . I greatly admire you for conceiving it. What made you think of it?"

"I've specialized in low-income housing for as long as I've been in construction. But you can't put up a decent building on the kind of budget you have to stay with to keep rents affordable. I got interested in vestpocket when

I heard about New York's Mitchell-Lama subsidies. But they didn't work because the buildings got the reputation of low-income projects and nobody in middle- or upper-income wanted to live there. I thought about it and decided maybe the problem was the subsidy. . . . All the non-low-income people felt they were being screwed by having their tax dollars support poor people in the very same apartments where the taxpayers were paying double or triple the rent."

"How does that differ from Three-oh-five East?"

"The government is out of it. In my experience the less government has to do with anything, the better. You give them a handle on something, the next thing you know they have you filling out five hundred forms and paying shyster lawyers two hundred bucks an hour to keep the bureaucrats off your back. At Three-oh-five East, tenants are dealing with me. If they like what I have to sell, they buy. If they don't, they tell me to go fuck myself."

"But fundamentally they're still subsidizing the low-income units."

"Wrong. They're paying me X dollars for accommodations they find worth the price. If I can do it with such efficiency that I have a few bucks left over to make some of the same apartments available to low-income people at a reduced price, that's nobody's business but mine."

"You're really into objectivism, aren't you?"

"You mean that Ann Rand philosophy?"

"Ayn, as in 'mine,'" she corrected. "I could almost believe I'm talking to Jonathan Galt."

He didn't pick up on the name.

"You know, *Atlas Shrugged.*"

"I've heard of it but never read it."

She smiled. She was starting to like him. Of course he'd never read it, but it was rare to find someone who admitted it. "Anyway, you apparently believe in its credo of *laissez faire* capitalism. . . ."

"I'm afraid I never got that heavy about it. I've concentrated on what I wanted to accomplish. And I've let other people decide what labels to put on it. Maybe I'm not seeing the forest for the trees. On the other hand, if everybody spent all his time looking at the forest, nobody would take care of the trees—and pretty soon there'd be no more forest. That's always been my big bitch against academics."

Her smile widened. His pragmatism was invigorating. She really felt like fucking him now. She hoped he'd be as *au point* in bed. She thought of reaching inside that robe and taking hold of his cock (she hoped he'd be naked underneath), but she wanted him to make the moves now. "Wouldn't it make life easier if you got some government help on Three-oh-five East?" As she spoke, she maneuvered her elbow against the side of her body in a way that would pull her unbuttoned blouse open, exposing her breast.

"I can handle it without government help. The day I have to ask those paper-clip suckers to help me is the day I forget about being in the construction business."

She wondered if her maneuver had succeeded in exposing her nipple . . . if it had, he certainly didn't seem to notice. She wanted to see for herself, but she also didn't want to glance down. . . . "Why are you so down on government officials?"

"Going in, because I'm from Pennsylvania. They've raised bureaucracy to an art there. You can't fill out a form in a county office without a lawyer, and you can't blow a fart without a license. The lawyers are almost as corrupt as they are incompetent, and they set national standards in each department. The politicians are worse, but dumber. If people get the kind of government they deserve, as Jefferson once said, Pennsylvanians have to be the undeservingest of all time."

She put more pressure on her blouse with her elbow and bicep, and felt the edge of the fabric pressing against the outer curve of her breast. No question the nipple was exposed. He still wasn't reacting.

"It goes beyond that," he went on. "I think the United States has just about made real democracy obsolete. Politicians get power by identifying problems the public wants action on, then promising laws to provide the action. The guy who persuades a plurality of the voters that he's got the solution to their problem gets into office, then passes a law against whatever it was they didn't like. The ones that opposed him have to go along with those that supported him, no matter how offensive they find it. Multiply the example by a hundred senators and however the hell many representatives and governors and state and city legislators we have, and you wind up with a hell of a lot more government than Jefferson and the other good old boys ever dreamed we'd have. Give them another few years and they'll have all of us going around in Boy Scout uniforms saying 'Yowzuh.' "

She maneuvered her other hand to the corresponding side of her blouse, down near her hips where he wouldn't see her pull it, and gradually slid it back. She kept her eyes on his but knew for certain that both breasts were now exposed.

"The only answer is for the individual to reassert control of the government. Screw their drivers' licenses; drive without one. Let the bureaucracy suffocate in its own paper work." Without taking his eyes from hers, or missing a beat, he said, "You've got a pair of tits, I see."

He came over to the couch and knelt at her knees and took a breast in each hand and studied them admiringly for a moment, then brought his face against them and rubbed them gently against his cheek, then found the nipple of one with his tongue.

She reached inside his robe and explored him, delighting in the firmness of his pectoral muscles, the washboard hardness of his gut. Then reaching downward through a forest of abdominal and pubic hair she found his penis, rigid and throbbing.

He ran one hand gently across the breast not occupied by his mouth, then continued down her stomach to the waistband of her jeans. He was pleased—and she was astonished—at how wet she was. She couldn't remember being this wet with so little foreplay.

His mouth covered hers; his tongue explored the roof of her mouth as his finger eased inside her. The pressure of his wrist popped open the waist of her jeans. She tugged and fondled his penis until she felt she couldn't let another moment pass without having it inside her. "Let's go into the bedroom, okay?" she said.

He shucked his robe and stood alongside the bed, waiting as she slipped out of her jeans and panties. She couldn't believe his body. There were muscles on top of muscles. And not just bulk. Or raw definition, like the bodies of kids in their twenties. He had the ideal combination of solid and soft, the ideal blend of line and bulk. Only his gut, which was about three inches too big, marred perfection. She wasn't about to complain.

When she was naked he moved slowly toward her. She threw her arms around his neck, shoved her mouth against his and pressed their bodies together as if trying to fuse them. He pulled her against him, his coil-like arms powerful, hard yet supple to her touch.

He eased her onto the bed. Her legs parted in response to his hand. One finger was inside her again, then two, three—she was so wet they felt like one. Now he was on top of her, and she had all she could do to hold back a scream as his penis entered her. It hadn't seemed so big in her hand, but something about the way he came into her made it feel immense. She spread wide to accommodate it and found that she was gasping in spite of herself.

He drove hard against her, his pubis beating a rhythm against hers, stimulating her clitoris without giving it the kind of pressure she needed to go over. She felt she could almost go—but not quite. And she sensed he knew it, was holding back only to tease her.

He drove, pounded, slapped—building a fire inside her. All the while his hand explored her breasts, sides, hips and thighs as his tongue moved in and out of her mouth in rhythm with his thrusting.

Suddenly he slapped her hard on the thigh. "Put your legs down."

She didn't understand, but she obeyed.

He maneuvered his over and outside hers. "Now lift yours over mine."

She obeyed and found that in the new position her vagina felt much tighter, his penis much thicker. She dug her heels into the bed and moved against him as he lengthened his thrusts, and then she felt him seem to slip away as he lined up his pubic bone against hers.

She didn't know what he was after until she felt the tingling sensation in her clitoris. Somehow, magically, he had found the pressure point, knew how to focus on it, and now, as he rubbed his pubis against hers, it was as specific, as precise a stimulus as if she were masturbating, incredibly precise, the hard edge of his pubis pulsing against this most sensitive spot as the blunt longness of his cock thrashed around inside her. She had come for a fuck, and she was getting one!

He pushed and rubbed and pumped, and faster than she'd ever thought possible she found herself climaxing. "Oh, don't stop!" He didn't until she was fully spent. "Ohh, how good . . ."

"Take another one," he said.

"No. You. I'm wrung out."

He resumed stroking, but at a slower pace than before, and now the angle and direction of entry changed. She took up a side-to-side pattern with her hips as his strokes lengthened. "Hey, great!" he said. She widened the arcs as he intensified the strokes, and moments later she felt the explosive thrusting that told her he was coming. She played on it, stoking it, firing it, milking it, draining it, till he lay limply on top of her. Then she too relaxed and enjoyed the warm tenderness of his cheek against hers, his body over hers, his pulsing inside her.

They lay silently for long minutes. Finally he lifted himself and went into the bathroom. "Coffee?" he asked when he came back.

"Mmm."

He found a robe for her in the closet and they went into the living room. She cuddled up against him on the couch. "You know," she said, "you're just about the best lay I've had since can't-remember-when."

He didn't answer.

"Was it good for you too?"

"Very."

They sipped their coffee, which had cooled but still was warm enough.

"You're one hell of a stud," she said. She was thinking it had been too long since she was involved with someone. Ted Vassily might not score one hundred percent in every department, but so far he seemed to offer more across-the-board than anyone who came to mind.

"You're a tolerable piece yourself." And she was. He was thinking he might be able to hit something off with her. She wasn't quite what he needed to obliterate the memory of Chris, but if she kept her New York cuntiness under control things might work for a while. She'd certainly be preferable to prowling singles' bars with Nasty Nate.

A moment passed, then she laughed.

She seemed to want him to ask what was funny, so he did.

"Our vocabulary of compliments," she said. "In a pretty short time we've come a long way from the Brownings." She paused. "I mean Robert and—"

"Elizabeth Barrett? No shit. I thought you meant the automatic rifles."

"No need to get touchy about it, no offense intended—"

"I wonder."

"Hey, baby, don't be so hypersensitive. I . . ." She let the sentence trail off. She really didn't want to hassle now. She wanted more of that cock. And more of the nice feeling of mutual digging they'd shared until a few seconds ago. "Okay," she said, "I guess I was condescending. I apologize."

"Accepted." He kissed her on the nose. If she moved off that easily they'd get along just fine.

They sipped some more coffee and she curled up in the crook of his arm. "You know, I've never eaten crow like that with another man."

He reached inside her robe and let her breast rest in his palm. Hearing her say that, he realized, made him feel cocky, like some high school kid. Well, what the hell . . . he was a man who'd once made a living playing a boy's game. Whoever said he'd grown up anyway? . . . or even wanted to. . . .

They snuggled silently for a while, then he said, "I don't have a hell of a lot on for today. How about you?"

"Is that invitation or investigation?"

"Invitation. How about dinner tonight?"

"Sure."

"Good. Now let's go back to bed and see if we can figure out what to do till then."

It didn't take long for him to get another erection. This time, though, the fuck went much slower and the climax was exhausting. They fell asleep in each other's arms.

He woke to the ringing telephone. "Jay, Ted," said his

rental agent Jay Kasselman. "Sorry to bother you with this but I didn't want to make the final decision on my own."

"Shoot."

"I turned down an applicant for an apartment. A Mafia biggie . . . Joe Mandino. I figured you wouldn't want that type in Three-oh-five. Well, his lawyer called today. They're going to sue if we don't rent to him. Says they'll claim discrimination. They may also picket."

Ted was incredulous. "The Mafia's going to picket us?"

"Not exactly. Mandino has formed an organization called the Italo-American Rights Organization. They'd do the picketing. Some big people are in the outfit—politicians, entertainers. The lawyer says he wants to talk to you personally. He thinks you'll okay the application once you hear him out."

"That sounds like a lift from *The Godfather*—the Hollywood meeting, the horse's head in the guy's bed . . ."

"This lawyer didn't come across that way. Maybe he was saving it for you. Anyway I figured you wouldn't want me to tell him to go fuck himself unless I checked with you first."

"I'll think about it and get back to you."

Buffy watched him hang up the phone. "To say I'm curious would be understatement."

He filled her in on the parts of the conversation she hadn't heard.

"Have your lawyer see him," she said. "It shields you from receiving the threat. If they try to transmit one through the lawyer, they could be liable for prosecution for extortion." She paused. "Unless you're afraid that won't stop them."

"I don't have a lawyer."

"You've got to be kidding."

"I hate the whole lousy parasite profession."

"Which comment I, being a lawyer, should take gracefully."

"Nothing personal. I'm sure you and a few others are paragon exceptions. But the ones I've done business with are bloodsuckers. I don't like them or trust them, and I don't have time to go hunting for one I do like and trust so

I keep the hell away from them except for the few things it's illegal to handle myself, like making court appearances on behalf of a corporation."

"But a lawyer's advice—"

He held up a hand. "Look, Buffy, when I want a lawyer's advice I'll ask you. And if you don't like this loutish attitude toward your profession, and I can see why you might not, maybe we ought to call it a day right now. Frankly, I've got enough trouble without getting sour vibes from my dinner dates."

"You know something, Ted Vassily? You're a prick."

He thought of his line the night before about being a prick meaning never having to say you're sorry. Instead he decided on Nate's "Don't bump your ass with the door on the way out."

She stalked out of the bedroom with her clothes in her arms. He heard her make rustling noises in the living room, as if she were dressing. He waited for more footsteps and the slamming door as she exited.

None yet. Either she was a very slow dresser or she was waiting for an apology and retraction.

He really wanted to spend the night with her. But he'd also been through this routine too many times. Give a lady her way when she acts cunty and from then on every time she wants her way you get the same treatment. Tell her to go fuck herself the first time, and seven out of ten will cut out—but the three who stay are hassle-free.

He lay back on the bed with his arms folded under his head and waited for the exit footsteps. If she was going to give in, there were two moves: (a) Come back into the room and ask, "Do you really want me to leave?" (b) Slam the door, then come back, ring the bell, and ask, "Do you really want me to leave?" ("No, dear, frankly I don't, but . . ." And that was when to make one thing perfectly clear . . .)

A minute passed. The rustling stopped. But still no footsteps.

He waited. Another minute. Now the footsteps. Slam! Now the doorbell?

He waited. Half a minute later she stood naked in the bedroom doorway. "I didn't much fool you, did I?"

He let himself laugh.

"You smug bastard."

He laughed harder.

She laughed now, too. "Will you reinstate the invitation?"

He got up and took her in his arms. "Buffy, I do believe I'm in danger of getting to like you—"

"Fuck me, you silly bastard."

He carried her to the bed and did. He was surprised he was able to get it up for a third in such a short time, but of course it had been a long while since her predecessor.

"You know," she said, "you ought to leave your cock to Harvard Medical School."

"Penn State," he said. "More deserving people would benefit."

"You're really into that reverse snobbism thing, aren't you?"

"I'm into equality of opportunity—which I'd expect a poor people's advocate like yourself to share my enthusiasm for."

She looked at him sharply. "You *do* know who I am. You did from the beginning. I've said nothing so far about poor people! Just consumers. You were putting me on . . . oh, you bastard," and while he laughed she threw her arms around his neck, pressed her body against his, reached down and caressed his cock. "You're a sadist. You really enjoy pissing me off."

"Naturally. Let's get dressed, we'll walk some before dinner."

They walked to Twenty-third Street, then east to the river and along the esplanade.

"Where are we going for dinner?" she asked.

"The Golden Coach."

"May I take you somewhere afterwards for a drink?"

"Certainly."

"Would you like to know where?"

"If you want to tell me."

"My very favorite place in New York—the Algonquin lobby. Have you been there?"

"I don't think so."

"It's just terrific. Beautiful wood, Great Gatsby ambience, armchairs and sofas all around—that's where they serve the drinks—and absolutely no hustle, you can relax as long as you like."

"Sounds great."

They walked to the baseball diamonds near Houston Street, then headed back uptown. She noted that he seemed preoccupied.

"The Mafia thing," he explained. "Mind if I ask that lawyer to stop by the hotel later tonight?"

Normally she'd resent the intrusion but she wanted to see him in action. "Why not ask him to join us at the Algonquin?" she said, knowing she couldn't be excluded from the conversation there.

They found a phone booth. Ted reached Kasselman, got the lawyer's number and arranged the meeting. Then they resumed walking, which she seemed to relish. He liked that.

"You know, Buffy Weiss," he said, "you're a pleasure to be with."

"You know, Ted Vassily, if you get a little more unprickish, I might start liking you even more. The operative word being 'even.' Dig?"

"You, I do. Very much." Maybe it sounded sort of corny-sincere but he didn't feel self-conscious saying it, and she didn't put him down about it . . . just snuggled against him and let him feel the pressure of her breast.

They walked a few blocks more, found themselves on Second Avenue, window-shopped the antique places, then continued uptown to the Golden Coach. Afterward they had half an hour alone in the Algonquin lobby before Mandino's lawyer was due.

"Well," she said, "do you like it?"

"Very much. It's what a lobby should be. In fact"—he leaned over and kissed her on the cheek—"if you'll give me permission I'm going to ask my architect about doing the same thing at Three-oh-five East."

"Really? I think that'd be fabulous. . . . But why do you need my permission?"

"It's your very favorite spot in New York. I wouldn't want to dilute it for you."

She snuggled against him as well as she could from another armchair. "You know one of the things I like best about you? You've got an open mind."

"I take it that's not another put-down."

"No. Seriously. I mean, how many people would be

flexible enough to see something they like and immediately change plans the way you just did?"

"Well, shucks, ma'm—but seriously, I do try not to get locked into fixed positions. Maybe it comes from being a quarterback. You know, fifty percent of the plays are audibles . . . new calls made from the line of scrimmage—"

"I know what an audible is." She kissed him. "And I know that right now I'd like to reach over and stroke your cock. Audible that."

He laughed. "If I didn't have a meeting with a lawyer, I'd ask you to step outside and repeat that."

The lawyer arrived exactly on time and was not the stereotype Ted had expected. He was tall, slim and sandy-haired with pale blue eyes and a bland, serene expression. Except for his impeccably tailored three-piece suit, Ted would have taken him for a tourist. Even with it, his style suggested more farm boy than mob lawyer. "Jack Perkins, Mr. Vassily," he introduced himself. His twang suggested the Midwest; the cadence and dropped "r" on "mister" suggested the South. "Mrs. Vassily?" he inquired of Buffy.

"Miss Weiss," Ted said.

Perkins shook her hand, then turned back to Ted. "I'm mighty obliged you took the trouble to see me so soon, Mr. Vassily. I think if we hear each other out, we can resolve this to everyone's satisfaction."

"I'll hear you out, Mr. Perkins." Ted motioned to the waiter for drinks.

Perkins ordered bourbon and branch, and recalled some of Ted's football glories while he waited for it to arrive. When it did, he sipped it, nodded his satisfaction, put the cellophane stirrer in his mouth like a piece of straw and leaned back in his chair.

"Mr. Vassily, my client is a citizen of the United States and the State of New York. When he applied for an apartment in your building he was rejected. No reason was stated for the rejection, but our investigation shows you do in fact have vacancies. Mr. Vassily, my client's credit record is impeccable and his bank references are superior. Indeed, if you chose to investigate you would find that his net worth is considerably greater than that of many people whom you have accepted as tenants. You would also find that he is a decent, sober man who in forty-four years as a tenant in New York City has not once had a dispute with a landlord. We're prepared to obtain, if you want them, letters from his current and several previous landlords to the effect that he has been a model tenant. All this being so, your rejection of his application may be interpreted as an act of discrimination within the meaning of the Civil Rights Act of 1964 and the 1968 Open Housing Act."

Ted smiled. "You left only one thing out of his résumé—he's the Manhattan overboss of the Mafia."

Perkins remained expressionless. "You certainly don't know that, Mr. Vassily. Fact is, no one has established that such an organization even exists in the United States. Many Italo-Americans feel police officials indiscriminately apply the name of the Sicilian terrorist society, Mafia, to all unsolved crimes that appear to have an element of organization about them. In any case, and more pertinent, Mr. Mandino has never been convicted of a crime. That being the case—"

"He's been arrested," Buffy interrupted.

Ted looked to silence her.

"An arrest, Miss Weiss," Perkins said, "is not a conviction. As I recall, you have made your reputation representing certain minority defendants against unjust and unfounded accusations."

Ted admired Perkins' style. He wondered when the lawyer realized that Buffy was *the* Miss . . . Ms. . . . Weiss.

"I've never defended mobsters," she said.

This time Ted put pressure on her arm to silence her.

"I've never defended niggers, Miss Weiss," Perkins replied. "Now you might take offense that I refer to your clients as niggers. And you would be justified in so doing; the term is a vile epithet which insults the black man. But I submit to you that it is no less offensive to an Italo-American to be referred to as a mobster, particularly when there is not one scintilla of evidence that he is guilty of any crime."

Buffy seemed about to say something else, but Ted increased pressure on her arm. Biting her lower lip, she leaned back silently in her chair.

"Mr. Vassily," Perkins continued, "the Italo-American

Civil Rights League protests your rejection of Mr. Mandino's application. I've spoken with officers of the organization, and they assure me they will picket the building if you don't rescind your decision. They also will initiate a mail and telephone campaign to persuade Italo-Americans in the construction trade not to work on the building, and to persuade newspapers to publicize your discriminatory rental procedures. Finally, they are considering action to enjoin you from continuing your discriminatory practices and to seek compensatory and punitive damages."

Ted forced a laugh. "Perkins, you got to be out of your bird to think a lawsuit is going to scare me into changing my mind. You know you're not going to subject Joe Mandino to cross-examination about his moral character."

"That may not be necessary, Mr. Vassily. His moral character isn't at issue here. What's at issue is the right of a man who has never been convicted of a crime and who qualifies in every other legal respect to rent an apartment in the building of his choice. I might add that it's far from my intention to, as you put it, scare you. I hope to reason with you, to appeal to your sense of fairness and justice. Failing that, it's my obligation to my client to warn you of the action he and the Italo-American Civil Rights League will take."

"And failing that, two of Coffee Joe's goons break both my arms and legs, right?"

Perkins stayed cool. "You insult my client, Mr. Vassily. And you insult me when you imply I might permit myself to be used to convey such a threat. The fact is, I'm here on my own initiative. Mr. Mandino doesn't even know I've come. He assumes that if I fail to get satisfaction from your rental agent, he and the Italo-American Civil Rights League will take the actions they have planned. But I came to you personally because I know something about you and your reputation for fair play."

He slouched in his chair and sipped his bourbon. "Mr. Vassily, I'm a Floridian. And I'm just a few years younger than you. Your senior year in college was my freshman year. I remember when Penn State came to Jacksonville for the Gator Bowl. And I remember a Penn State receiver named Emerson Wade, whom they didn't want to let stay in Dulong's Motel because he was black. I remember what you told the folks who run the Gator Bowl —and the couple dozen newsmen who just happened to be present. I also remember a personal apology from the mayor of Jacksonville to Emerson Wade, who slept that night in Dulong's Motel. Mr. Vassily, any man who's taken the risks you have over racial equality, both in your college career and in the pros, must have a deep respect not only for the feelings and sensitivities of minority peoples but also for the principles of equality on which this nation was founded. . . . My goodness, I'm afraid that sounded like a speech. I didn't mean to—"

"You don't seriously expect me to equate Coffee Joe with Emerson Wade."

" 'Coffee Joe.' " Perkins clucked his tongue. "Funny how we come up with all sorts of derisive slang and nicknames for people we don't respect, isn't it? You've never met the man. I'd venture you don't know many if any of his friends. Yet you don't hesitate to call him 'Coffee Joe.' Would you even *know* the nickname if it weren't that newspapers, in their biased reporting of crime stories, for years have used it as a way of holding him up to ridicule and fitting him into the public stereotype of a gangster? Well, no matter. No, Mr. Vassily, I don't expect you to equate Mr. Mandino with Mr. Wade. But I do expect you to recognize that the same mentality that led to Mr. Wade's maltreatment as a black man is behind the stereotyping of Italo-Americans as gangsters. And I expect you to treat Mr. Mandino with the same fairness and lack of prejudice you would demand of a landlord if you applied to rent an apartment. You would be irate if you were rejected because the landlord subscribed to the stereotype of Greeks as devotees of anal sex, and therefore perverts, and therefore undesirables. Why reject Mr. Mandino for his Italian ancestry?"

The bastard had a tongue on him. "I'm not rejecting him for his ancestry."

"Then why are you rejecting him?"

"Because he's—" Ted hesitated.

Perkins smiled. "You were going to say, 'Because he's a mobster,' weren't you? But as I said, you don't know he is, do you? You may suspect it, you may have read newspaper stories that intimated it. But you don't have any real knowledge of it." He sipped his bourbon. "Mr. Vassily, I think you're too fair a man—too just a man—to deny Mr. Mandino the right to live in the place of his choice without clear and convincing evidence that he's guilty of a crime. And Mr. Vassily, if you have that evidence I challenge you not only to deny him permission to rent an apartment in your building but also to present the evidence to a federal judge; because, Mr. Vassily, if you do have evidence that any person committed a felony, it's your obligation under federal law to provide that evidence to a federal judge."

Ted glanced at Buffy, who was nodding apparent agreement, then quickly turned away from her.

"I'll ask you to go one step further with me, Mr. Vassily. Let's assume, for the sake of argument, that Mr. Mandino were a convicted criminal. There are statutes prescribing maximum and minimum penalties for every crime. Do you think it's fair for private citizens to provide additional punishment, whether by discrimination in housing or other means, for whatever crimes a person may have committed?"

"There's no law," Ted replied, "that I have to rent an apartment to someone I find unacceptable."

"There is a law, Mr. Vassily, that you cannot find a person unacceptable on the basis of race, religion or national origin. If you aren't rejecting Mr. Mandino on one of those bases, I'd like to know—and the court will want to know—just what is your basis." Perkins drained his bourbon and put the empty glass on the end table alongside his chair. "May I pay the check?"

"My treat," Ted said.

Perkins stood. "Thanks for the drink, Mr. Vassily. And thanks for your time. I hope you'll decide to give Mr. Mandino the same presumption of innocence you yourself would demand—and be entitled to—if you were the accused." He shook hands and left.

"You really made me feel like a zero," Buffy told him. "I could've helped you, you know. Except you thought you were too goddamn smart to need help."

Without answering, he called for the check.

"My treat," she said, snapping it from the waiter's hand.

"Remember?" She fished a ten-dollar bill from her purse and handed it to the waiter. "Well," she said, "do I get an apology? Or are they a one-way street with you?"

He shook his head. "Buffy, if you're ever anywhere else when I'm doing my business, don't volunteer. I'll ask for your comments when I want them. If that offends you . . ." He shrugged.

The waiter brought her change. She left a dollar on the table, stood and waited for Ted to usher her outside.

"I almost believe you let that smooth-talking redneck con you into it," she said, walking a good yard distant from him as they headed east on Forty-sixth Street.

"He made some points."

"You're not seriously considering letting Mandino in. Not on the basis of that yahoo's double-talk."

"He's never been convicted of a crime, has he?"

"I can't believe I'm hearing this. Of course he hasn't been convicted. He's bought judges, juries, prosecutors—he's made a mockery of the whole system of justice—"

"So I should make a reverse mockery of it by taking the law into my own hands."

"Oh, wow. He really did con you. Man, what a disappointment you are. For a while today I really respected you, but you're—"

"Time for shaping up, eh, Buf? If I want to win back your respect, I'd better snap-to and think the way you do."

"That's not it, for Christ's sake. But at least *think*. Don't let some glib fucker turn you around with a little flattery and a few arguments any freshman law student could recognize as bullshit."

"I quote Miss Weiss's comments from earlier in the evening: one of the things she likes best about me is my flexibility, my open mind. She likes it, that is, as long as it's open to her ideas. Anybody else's are bullshit."

"That's not how I feel, and you know it."

He didn't answer. He wasn't in the mood to prolong the hassle. He was tired of hassles. He was tired of them before she'd come into his life, and he'd grown increasingly tired of them through the day. She was one hell of a chick, and if she were hassle-free he could probably work up some real interest in her. The hassles, though, red-flagged him.

She waited for him to say something. She didn't want their thing to go sour—God, when you find a stud like that you ought to walk on hot coals to keep things from going sour. But how many hot coals did he expect her to walk on? Maybe the dumb-dumbs he usually dated enjoyed being treated like decorations. Well . . . she had to draw a line.

He was startled to find that they already were at Lexington Avenue. He turned downtown, then stopped when he realized she hadn't turned with him.

"Ted," she said, "I think I ought to go back to my place."

"Whatever you say." When she didn't turn away immediately he added, "The invitation's still there if you want to come back with me."

She hesitated. "I don't think I should."

"Whatever you say." He turned down Lex.

"Ted—"

He turned back.

She smiled sheepishly. "I left my makeup kit at your hotel."

He laughed. "Come and get it."

Well, at least the night was saved, and he was glad for that. In some ways he did really like her. Matter of fact, if only she'd get her act together and stop going cunt-o on him . . .

She knew by the way he hugged her that he was glad she was coming with him. Good. She certainly didn't want to check out without at least one more lovely fuck. Matter of fact, she could conceivably enjoy a long run with him. But it was probably out of the question. He was just too into his horseshit macho white superstud bag. Oh, well, as someone said, silk purses, sow's ears . . . Not to mention gather ye rosebuds whilst ye may . . .

FOUR

IT PISSED her off that he didn't phone. The first three or four days she assumed to be the old machismo show-'em-you-don't-need-'em nonsense. But then a week passed. And another. And that *really* pissed her off.

She might not have minded so much if they hadn't had such a spectacular night when they'd gotten back to the hotel. But it had been dynamite. First another super-fuck with more of that incredible clit action that he seemed to own the patent on. Then he'd produced a bottle of the smoothest cognac she'd ever tasted, and built a fire, and they'd sat in their robes in front of the fireplace watching the flames. And she got him talking about his life, his family back in Nanny Goat or whatever the hell that Pennsylvania coal mining town was called, his football days in high school and then at Penn State, the way he'd bought up all those properties near the campus when land was cheap and built a hundred-thousand-dollar nest-egg even before he went into pro ball. . . . He seemed at first not to want to talk about it, not to want to share it with her, she had to really work to draw it out, and when she finally succeeded that made her feel even closer to him. He had done the Horatio Alger thing to the hilt. In his own maybe crude fashion he had really made one hell of a success of himself—especially considering what he had to start with. And what tied it all together was his incredibly fierce drive to—there was no other phrase for it—do good. He really was going all out on the poor people's housing thing. He wouldn't make a hell of a lot of money from it. It wasn't a limousine-liberal sort of caper. Most people would think he was an asshole for doing it. But he was doing it because he believed in it. He was really—incredible as it might seem in this day and age—well, there was only one word for it: pure. Uncorrupted. Straight.

And now the son of a bitch was playing games with her. After that magnificent night together, after a magnificent afternoon together, he was dicking her around. Why?

She replayed the night in her mind and tried to think of something she might have said or done that turned him around. Nothing. They'd sat at the fireplace and sipped their Delamain Pale Dry and talked and talked. Then they'd gotten sexy and had another fuck, right on the floor in front of the fireplace—super-groovy with the hardness of the floor beneath her and the heat of the open fire against her flesh. Then they'd gotten back on the couch, and she'd snuggled against him and they'd semi-dozed and talked some more and sipped some more Delamain. And pretty soon it was dawn. Whereupon they'd adjourned to the bedroom and felt each other up, exploring the possibilities, but didn't quite make it, and finally had fallen asleep in each other's arms. And then, around noon, they'd awakened and showered together and, though he was late for a business thing, splendidly knocked off another one, then bolted a danish and a cup of coffee before heading their separate ways. And as he'd kissed her goodbye before putting her into a cab in front of the Tuscany, he'd said he'd be in touch.

And that was the last she'd heard from him. For a while she even worried that something might have happened to him. Just like a loyal little Sheepshead Bay housewife. But then she saw his picture in the paper with the goddamn mayor and that was the end of Sheepshead Bay.

But *still* he didn't phone, and she even considered different excuses for phoning him, like maybe having an idea for something she might write about 305 East or maybe even a straight-on "I really don't want to see you, asshole, but it's been a super-busy week and I've developed this incredible set of horns, and nobody else is in town so I thought maybe I'd take advantage of your trusty old tool if it's still in working order. . . ."

But she wouldn't give him the satisfaction. If he was so goddamn independent she'd find someone else to do her . . . matter of fact, she already had . . . two new ones since she saw him last. But that, maybe, was part of the problem. Both had given her about as much satisfaction as a . . . well, compared to *him,* the prick—so why didn't he call?

She replayed their last night, searching for something that might have pissed—or turned—him off. There was only one moment she recalled when he'd acted what one might call strange. . . . She had mentioned to him, teasingly, that he wasn't the first pro football player she'd balled and he'd asked who the others were and she mentioned a few names. And then he hesitated a long moment and said, "Do you have a special thing for spades?"

She had been both unsettled and angered. Actually, when ticking off the names, it hadn't occurred to her that they were all black. Suddenly it jarred her that she'd brought up the whole subject, and it really pissed her off that Ted Vassily, the big liberal, considered her lovers' skin color significant. "Do you have something against chicks balling spades?" she had shot back.

"No, not at all." And then he'd changed the subject.

She wondered. And waited. Another week passed. And another. And she went to Los Angeles for two weeks. And when she got back and checked her answering service, he still hadn't called. She tried to purge the image of him, but that only made her want him even more (the other dudes still couldn't touch him as a lover). So finally she said fuck it, who needs Pyrrhic victories, who needs one-upmanship? And she called.

"Hey, Buf, good to hear from you!" The bastard sounded as though he really meant it.

"You were on pins and needles wondering when I'd call," she said dryly.

He ignored it. "What've you been up to?"

"Wondering why, if I'm such a great lay, you never called." Well, if you're going to eat crow, no use going half way.

"You want to get together tonight?"

The pluperfect son of a bitch—didn't even have the decency to make excuses. . . . And then she reminded herself that she wasn't looking for Pyrrhic victories. "Sure." Would anyone who knew her ever believe she'd take shit like this? *She!* And from a fucking fish-brain jockstrap from a Pennsylvania cow-college!

"Great," he said, "stop by the hotel around seven. We'll have dinner."

Oh, Jesus. Stop by the *hotel!*

"Or better yet," he said, "how would you like to see Three-oh-five East?"

"Sure." By now she was so numb from self-disbelief she couldn't manage more than a syllable at a time.

"Can you get away this afternoon? I'm on my way there now. Come by around three. Ask for me at the construction superintendent's shack. I'll leave word I'm expecting you."

"Great," she said, feeling and sounding to herself like an automaton. Keep telling yourself, she told herself, that you're just doing it for cock. Exploit the fuckers the way they've always exploited women. . . .

Except she knew she *wasn't* just doing it for cock. If she were, why would her heart be pounding this way? The fish-brain fucker. And besides, she had work to do. She really should spend at least two hours on her brief on that South Dakota Indian matter. . . .

She selected jeans that molded her pubes and ass, then hunted down a sheer embroidered pullover that would reveal her nipples. As she showered, carefully sudsing herself all over, she wondered whether he'd go down on her, and realized that he hadn't the last time—which was further testimony to what a terrific lay he was because ordinarily she would have missed it. Well, tonight she would initiate it (she felt a tingle as she thought of taking that nice fat cock in her mouth) and see if in turn he was as good with his mouth as his other equipment (and suddenly she was so turned on it took real effort to resist the urge to masturbate).

She touched herself with perfume, tugged on her jeans, admired herself topless in the mirror, put on the blouse and left for the construction site.

"Yes, ma'am, Miss Weiss," replied the guy in the super's

shack who wore a hard hat and could pass for the Marlboro man. "Mister Vassily's up in the tower. If heights don't scare you, I'll take you up. If they do, he'll come down."

"They don't scare me," she said.

He gave her a hard hat and led her through piles of bricks and stacks of metal rods to a cagelike affair inside some red metal pipes that went all the way up one side of the building. She'd seen these things on construction sites and understood vaguely that they were elevators. Suddenly she realized she was going to ride it, open air, up the outside of the building, and got a wild tingle in her crotch.

He opened the door and gestured her inside, and though she realized she could change her story about not fearing heights she didn't want to . . . there was something terrifically exciting about testing herself.

The Marlboro man clanged the gate shut, told her to hold on to a bar at one side of the car, then moved a lever. The car whooshed up and the wild tingle in her crotch suddenly shot through the rest of her and for an instant she felt woozy, almost as though she were going to pass out. Now she felt her body swaying—and tightened her grip on the bar. God, there were no *walls* on this thing! If she fainted, part of her body could protrude through the metal framework and get caught in the other pipes and—*crunch!* The lawyer in her at the same time reflected that Vassily's insurance policy almost certainly didn't cover tourists on the site. Didn't he realize he could be wiped out if something happened to her . . . ?

Her balance seemed to steady as the car continued up, but the tingle didn't abate. Now it was in her hands and feet too. What a sensation! What a *trip!* And the view was not to be believed! The whole city seemed to be expanding spherically away from her, as if her eyes were a high-powered telephoto lens doing a fast reverse zoom. And meanwhile the tingle intensified.

Suddenly the elevator slowed, and her insides seemed to drop two feet. Then it jerked to a halt, and she felt that initial woozy dizziness again. The Marlboro man, smiling amiably at her, opened the gate and gestured for her to step out, which she did onto a concrete floor beneath a plywood ceiling punctuated with thick concrete pillars but no walls. The hugeness of the place was overpowering. It seemed almost an acre square. The absence of walls—and the absence of anything but sky where the walls normally would have been—created the eerie feeling of being on some kind of windblown platform in outer space.

The Marlboro man led her past welders and carpenters and other guys carrying bunches of the metal rods she'd seen on the ground. The floor seemed even vaster from the center of it, and the hammering, welding, rod-dropping, combining with the howling of the wind, heightened her space-platform sense of isolation.

Now she finally spotted Ted standing near one of the wall-spaces talking to two other guys. He wore a white bulky-knit sweater and brown slacks. The wind blew his trousers so tightly against his legs that she could make out the shape of his muscles. He looked up as she approached, flashed a huge smile, then ran to her and took her in his arms. "Hi," he shouted over the din, then lifted her in the air and kissed her hard as he set her down.

"Hi, yourself," she replied, shouting back to be heard.

"Come over here." He led her to the guys he'd been talking to. "My construction superintendent, Pete DeAngelis," he shouted. She shook hands with a handsome, silver-sideburned man of fifty-plus with coal black eyebrows. "My general superintendent, Nate Elefante." She shook hands with what seemed like a whale with a goatee. She couldn't believe the size of his fist. It was literally three times hers.

"See you later," Ted shouted to them. "Come on, hon, I'll show you around."

The "hon," the big hug—as though she were his wife just returning from a week in the country.

He took her hand, led her to a ladder and motioned for her to climb. She emerged on a floor criss-crossed with wooden beams and metal rods. Above it was only the sky. Pillar-shaped plywood molds stood about it like tree trunks. Carpenters were hammering on them, and in one corner men were smoothing cement that another man was emptying from a huge container suspended from a crane.

She stepped onto a plank to make room for Ted. He took her hand again and led her along a network of planks toward a section of the roof where men were working with the metal rods. "We've been laying one floor a day," he shouted. "That's considered unusual for a project this size, but I've got a great crew." He pointed to a section of the floor where the cement had already been smoothed. "The surveyors get here at two-thirty every morning. By that time the previous day's cement is dry. They work with flashlights to mark positions for the carpenters, who start at five and build pillar molds and a plywood ceiling. By eight we're laying rods and by ten we're pouring cement. Everybody keeps just one step ahead of everybody else. By five or six in the afternoon the finishers have put the final touches on the cement and we're ready for the surveyors the next morning. Unions generally don't like their guys to work that fast because it shortens the job, but every worker on this project owns stock in the company. It's amazing how conscientiously a guy will work when he's paying his own salary."

Part of her mind was absorbing with fascination the incredible bustle around her, the virile ambience—all that banging and moving and *do*ing, the clean rugged smell of the wood, the sharp always-shouting voices of the men. Part was absorbing Ted's explanation. And part was being excited at being with him, being *here,* having the opportunity to get so close to something in its own way so magnificent. . . .

Another part was remembering an interview years ago with a legendary French song-and-dance man, then in his late seventies, reputed the world over for his sexual conquests, a man said to have actually bedded five thousand women in his lifetime. Buffy had asked (this was in the old days before her female-consciousness had been raised) how he explained his extraordinary seduction talents. He'd replied without hesitation, as if repeating an explanation often given before, "Let them see you at your best, doing the things you do best. Make it easy for them to admire you, and they will do the rest." Was that Vassily's game? (Had he, maybe, even read the interview!) Whatever, he was making himself look good. Goddamn good, the son of a bitch.

"We're building all four towers at once," he was saying.

"In effect, it's like building four separate buildings, which makes it a real bitch to coordinate but it's cost-effective. I've got interior finishing work being done right now on the fifth floor, electricity and plumbing up to the fifteenth, and here we are on the twenty-fourth. When we top out the skeleton on the fortieth I'll have full occupancy up to the tenth."

He took her hand and started toward the edge. Involuntarily she stiffened.

He smiled. "Feel queasy?"

She nodded, a little embarrassed for showing her weakness, then angry at herself for feeling she shouldn't show it—and even for considering it a weakness.

"I was going to give you a view of the central quadrangle," he said. "But if you'd rather not . . ."

She hesitated, then decided to let herself be as feminine-helpless as she damned well pleased. "Is it safe?" (Of course it's safe, asshole. He wouldn't invite you if he didn't think it was safe.)

He put an arm around her. "It's safe."

They went to the edge.

"Lock your foot around a rod," he said, showing her how.

She did.

"Now lean over."

She did. The tingle that had filled her body in the elevator came back with even more intensity. The wind heightened the feeling. She put pressure with her shin against the rod, as if to reassert her claim to this lifeline. And she looked down.

The view was, literally, breathtaking. The wall-less skeleton of the building seemed to angle outward from some miniature base, as in an exaggerated art-deco drawing. She was along the interior flank of the tower, which in turn was one side of the central quadrangle. An unbelievably long-necked crane stood in the center, its cab seeming toy-size so far below. The container which it previously had hoisted to this tower had been refilled and now was being hoisted to the adjacent one. Workers on all four towers were erecting molds, laying rods, spreading cement.

She looked down again at the cab of the crane and suddenly felt her body starting to sway. Almost immediately Ted's arms closed around her waist. "Let's go back," he said, leading her away from the edge.

"You've got one hell of a set of reflexes," she said, feeling steady now that thirty feet of floor were between her and the void.

"I was watching for a reaction. Most people get a little dizzy the first time."

"You know, you really shouldn't have invited me up here. I'm sure your insurance wouldn't cover it if something happened."

"Buffy, if I only did things my insurance covered, I'd be back in Nanticoke, Pennsylvania, hawking hot dogs in my father's snack bar." He took her hand and they climbed back down the ladder and went to the elevator. The tingling sensation resumed as she stepped into the cage. Then her stomach felt as if it were floating up through her head as the elevator plummeted. She instinctively gripped Ted's arm—and after the moment of panic passed, relished the feel of it.

The car clanged to a halt several floors above the ground. Ted opened the gate and led her through unpainted plaster corridors to a doorway opening onto the quadrangle. The once toylike cab of the crane seemed huge as they walked around it. She followed him to the elevator in the opposite tower. He moved a lever and they shot upward.

"Preview of coming attractions," he said, leading her out and across a floor with some interior construction but no walls. He looked around, calculated a direction, then brought her to an area midway along one of the nonwalls. "Your apartment," he said. "Like the view?"

She looked out at the East River and, beyond it, the stacked crates on the piers in Queens. "Magnificent. I wonder if it will turn me on this much when the walls and windows are up."

"For me, nothing is more exciting than seeing it in the raw—even from one of the lower floors."

He gave her a tour of the bare-bones apartment, showing where the different rooms would be, then they returned to the elevator. The Marlboro man was waiting in the quadrangle, and a tall, lean, slightly-stooped old man was with him. "Axel!" Ted clasped the elderly man's hand. "Say hello to one of our tenants, Buffy Weiss."

She shook hands and exchanged amenities with the architect, then walked across the quadrangle with him and Ted. They entered one of the other towers and climbed a stair to a finished apartment. Its quiet, after the tumult in the quadrangle and on the construction sites, was church-like. Ted took an ice bucket from a refrigerator, used tongs to put cubes in three glasses, splashed Scotch over them and passed them around.

"Axel," he said, his voice booming through the apartment, "have you ever read—" he smiled, suddenly hearing himself, then in more conversational tones began again—"have you read *Working,* a book written some years ago by Studs Terkel?"

"Heard of it," said the old man. "Never read it."

"It's a collection of interviews with working people. One of them is a construction laborer who says there should be a big concrete slab on every building with the name of every guy who worked on it. That way the guy could take his kids there one day, if he wanted to, and say, 'I helped put this up.'"

Axel's eyes seemed to take on a twinkle as he sipped his Scotch and looked at Ted over the glass.

"Actually it wouldn't have to stop with the kids. A man's grandchildren, his great-grandchildren, every descendant for as far down the line as the building stood—they could come by and look at it and remember their ancestor who did it, just like the descendants of the Astors and Morgans and all those people who founded the public library and have their names carved on marble in the foyer."

Axel chuckled. "Where do you want the slab, Ted?"

Ted feigned surprise. "I'm not saying I do, Axel. You're the designer. After all the energy and effort you put into making this building work aesthetically . . . well, I'm just tossing the idea out for you to think about."

"I'll work it in somewhere, Ted."

Buffy only half-listened as they went on to other subjects, and found herself thinking that this was the first time since her early teens that she was really flipping over a guy who didn't seem to give a shit one way or the other about her.

Ted finished his business with Axel and began walking the older man to the door. Almost as an afterthought, he turned to Buffy. "Hey, hon, come on with us. I want to show you something."

They went down the stairs, across the quadrangle, then down a small narrow stair into an enormous enclosed space. Its walls were polished beige marble, two of them featuring great arched windows looking onto the quadrangle. "Our version of the Algonquin lobby," he said, pointing to a framed architect's drawing on one wall. "Here's what it should look like when we're through."

The entrance at the opposite end of the room featured three steps, thirty feet wide and bracketed by a dark brown marble rail leading to the level where she now stood. It was flanked by two sets of stairs half its width leading to a lower level. "We'll have armchairs, couches, tables and lamps all through here," Ted explained. "They'll accommodate four hundred people. We'll have cocktail service from a bar on the west wall. The north and east walls face the quadrangle, which will be landscaped. During good weather we'll have service there too with portable tables and chairs, like in a European café."

He led her to the entrance. "The three stairs are for psychological effect. I was afraid some tenants might feel the busy lobby an infringement on their privacy—you know, people gawking at them as they walked in, that kind of thing. I put the problem to Axel and he came up with the split-level approach. Anybody who doesn't want to be seen can go down the side stairs and enter his elevator on the lower level. Someone who wants to walk through the lobby, or stop and sit awhile, enters here. To sort of reinforce the feeling that he's entering the area voluntarily, we make him climb three steps."

He led her back now through the cavernous lobby. "There are separate elevator banks for each tower, expensive but it diffuses the traffic flow. It also, I think, gives the lobby a sort of European-plaza effect, different people going in different directions for different purposes, not a whole mob running from point A to point B. We'll have a restaurant and shops with entrances on the west wall, and others across the quadrangle."

They had walked back to the architect's drawing. "The colors are meant to tie it all together," Ted continued, indicating an array of swatches tacked to a cork display board. "The dark brown and burnt orange are the area rugs, the beige is the drapes. The chairs, couches and lampshades will cover the full spectrum. They'll all be old pieces, bought at random." His eyes met hers, and for the first time since he and she had come from her soon-to-be-apartment, he seemed really to be looking at her. He smiled. "Well, what do you think?"

"Dynamite," she said. "I'm impressed."

"And this is the genius responsible for it all." He clapped Axel on the shoulder. "You've really lived up to your reputation, old buddy."

"You've done a marvelous job, Mr. Wessman," she echoed, feeling strangely uncomfortable, both for the old man and for herself.

"Thank you, Miss Weiss. I've waited all my life to design this building. Mr. Vassily gave me the opportunity."

She was doubly uncomfortable now, but Ted seemed oblivious to her feelings—or Wessman's. "Well, Axel, thanks for coming over," he said, walking the old man to the exit stair. She waited, not certain whether to follow, and since he ignored her she stayed where she was.

He walked out with the old man, then came back a moment later. "And now, Miss Weiss," he said, extending his arm theatrically, "it's time for your own personal welcome to Three-oh-five East." He went to a wall telephone. "Eddie, bring in the furniture and champagne." He hung up the phone, turned to her and extended his arms again.

She realized after a moment that he expected her to step into them. She did, slowly.

"Something wrong?" he asked.

She didn't know where to begin. "Don't you think you embarrassed Mr. Wessman?" she asked finally.

"Embarrassed." He held her at arm's length and scrutinized her face. "How?"

"You treated him like a child. In front of me. Giving

him lollypops of praise, demanding his fawning gratitude—"

" 'Lollypops of praise.' " He smiled. "You know, Buf, you've got quite a way with words."

"I was making a point. Which seems to have escaped you."

"You don't know Axel. I've known him a long time. Maybe that escaped you."

"Does that mean he has to put up with your condescension for financial reasons?"

He turned away and started toward the lobby entrance.

She tried to contain her anger. "Well?"

"Come on over here, Eddie's bringing the champagne. . . ."

"I asked you a question."

He looked over his shoulder at her. "Believe me, I know Axel. He wasn't embarrassed. Now come over here."

The way he shrugged off her comments was infuriating. . . . The fuck, she reminded herself scoldingly. Don't forget why you came here. Not for a rewarding intellectual exchange. Not for emotional union. You came for a fuck. From a guy who happens to be a superb practitioner—never mind his shortcomings of perception and sensibility.

She followed him to the entrance, where the Marlboro man had materialized with a rug and a lamp. Another hardhat carried a mahogany Victorian love seat with peach velvet fabric. Ted showed where to place them, after which the men vanished down the stairs to return with a handsome walnut end table, champagne in an ice bucket and two delicate fluted glasses.

"Taittinger Comtes de Champagne Blanc de Blanc 1969," Ted announced, displaying the bottle. "We'll christen the place with the very best." He held a palm to its side. "Not quite there yet."

She watched silently as he put it back into the bucket and considered doing him the favor of suggesting that he maybe compromised the impact of his largesse by advertising it. Doubtless the worshipful dummies he usually bedded wouldn't recognize the name and needed the *sommelier* routine . . . matter of fact, she was a little surprised at his good French pronunciation of the label. . . . Oh, cool it, she told herself. . . . The fuck, think only of the fuck. . . . First things foremost, Buffy. . . .

He sat now on the love seat and gestured for her to sit next to him. She complied, stiffly at first, then let her body fit nicely against the hardness of his. Damn, he had a good body. The moron.

"It's good being with you again, Buf," he said, pressing her shoulder in a way that made it natural for her breasts to be firmly against his rib cage. "I've thought about you a lot—"

"Which is why you phoned so many times." Even before she finished, she devoutly wished she hadn't said it. Stupid, not her style . . . or even self-serving. Get him to finish up here quickly as possible, go back to his place, take every last bit of stiffness she could get from his dick and push him out of her life till she needed another shot—which hopefully wouldn't be too soon.

"I've been putting up a building," he said. "It can keep a person busy." There was a moment's pause, then he added, "I'm sorry I didn't call. I'm glad you did."

She marveled at the change in his mood. Did he actually schedule himself? Four-fifteen, introduce her to the architect. Four-twenty-one, show her the lobby. Four-twenty-nine, champagne. Four-thirty-one, tender peace-offering. . . .

She felt his hand at her chin, tilting it toward him. She resisted for just an instant, then let him kiss her. It felt good. Damn good. Damn it. Especially that sexy thing he did with his tongue across the roof of her mouth.

His hand rested briefly on her hip, then eased up her side and cupped her breast from outside her blouse. His thumb found the nipple and massaged it sensitively.

Almost instinctively she let her hand stray to his lap. He was stiff. Four-thirty-two, kiss her. Four-thirty-two-point-five, hard-on. Four-thirty-three . . .

He held the kiss for a long moment, then moved his head and arm in a way that invited her to put her face against his chest. Funny, she thought, how two people could communicate in such body language without a word. . . . Was it a talent limited to very experienced lovers? Would evidence of it be a good way to assess a lover's track record? . . . And why was her mind wandering like this? . . . Was his personality *that* offensive—his sexual abilities notwithstanding? Was she resisting him to avoid admitting her need of him? . . . One thing was for sure . . . if he knew what she was thinking, he'd no doubt tell her she thought too damn much. . . .

"We'll make this our special table and love seat." His voice, somewhere over her ear, seemed remarkably intimate. If she closed her eyes she could persuade herself they were back in his hotel room.

What a routine . . . Jesus, would anyone believe it! Did he think she was sixteen years old? Oh, come on, play the game. She took hold of his cock—stiff, with a thickness that startled her. She had almost forgotten.

No doubt feeling like some damn concertmaster, the maestro now decided to change the mood and tempo by reaching for the champagne. "It's just right now," he pronounced, palming the bottle.

She had to fight the impulse to tell him how she was reading his every move. . . . The fuck, she told herself, wiping the mental blackboard. Take it and run.

He (correctly, she noted with interest) turned the bottle, not the cork. There was a soft little pop (as there should have been), then a wisp of smoke rising from the neck. He studied it for a moment, then splashed an ounce into one glass, nosed it without tasting and nodded his satisfaction. (Where did he learn *that* routine? Some adult-education wine-tasting course? One of those quick-study wine primers?)

He filled each glass one-third of the way, handed one to her, holding it by the base so she could take the stem. "To us," he said, lifting his in toast.

Oh God, she thought, and said, "To us," then sipped the champagne, put the glass on the table, cuddled against him again and took hold. "You've got a marvelous cock."

"Thanks."

Well, it was as good a reply as any. She enjoyed running a finger over its crescentlike span.

"You know what I'd do if you were wearing a skirt?" he said.

"No, Ted. What would you do if I were wearing a skirt?"

He brought his hand to her crotch and with uncanny accuracy managed to position his middle finger directly over her vaginal introitus. (She wondered, did the crotch of her jeans guide him?) "I'd take your panties off. Then I'd unzip my fly and have you sit on my lap." He seemed suddenly to be short of breath. Apparently the fantasy was turning him on. "And I'd make it with you."

She took the penis in her palm again and put pressure on the base with the heel of her hand. She noticed that he was getting stiffer, though she would have thought that impossible. "Why a skirt? What's wrong with jeans?"

"A skirt would cover us, in case someone happened to walk through he wouldn't know we were making it."

"Okay, next time a skirt it is. . . ."

She actually felt his heartbeat. It seemed to go *whump* just as she agreed, and it continued to go *whump*. She didn't fully understand what had got him so wound up but she delighted in being able to take part in his excitement.

"Meanwhile," she said, licking his jaw just below his ear, "what's wrong with taking off my jeans and doing it bare-ass? You can lock the doors here, can't you?"

"On this level, yeah . . ." She couldn't believe the way his heart was beating. "It's open on the lower level, though. Not that anybody'd be likely to walk through."

"And if someone did? It's your building, right?"

She almost expected his heart to explode through his chest. "Yeah, right." He got up. "I'll be right back."

She watched him walk to the rear door, enjoying his athletic stride. He really carried himself beautifully. The bastard.

He bolted the door, then went to the main entrance and latched both doors there. Her eyes fixed on his cock as he walked back. It seemed to fill the entire front of his pants. She found herself wondering when she actually made the decision to fuck him here. She'd only been teasing at first. But then . . . actually, of course, she never really made a decision. It just happened. And, she noted, his wasn't the only heart that was pounding.

She stood as he came back to the love seat. "Well, superstud," she said, popping open the waist-snap on her jeans, "do I take it off or do you?"

He took one flap in each hand, seeming to caress them.

His fingers felt good against her bare stomach. She shivered excitedly as she felt them reach into her pubic hair.

He coaxed the jeans and panties further down. "You're one hell of a turn-on, Buf." He continued to stare for a moment, then sat on the love seat as she stood in front of him and pressed his face against her belly, his mouth against the hair.

"You're not bad yourself, superstar." She reflected that she didn't feel at all self-conscious about the inane exchange. . . . Now if only, she further reflected, he could pull her entirely out of this fucking analytic head and make the experience consume every last *bit* of her awareness . . .

He was probing her pubis with his tongue, making an exciting crackling sound. And then his hands somehow materialized at both sides of her jeans, his thumbs inside the waistband of the panties. He applied pressure, and almost without her realizing it was happening both jeans and panties slid halfway down her thighs.

"You *are* deft," she said, taking his head in her hands, pressing his cool face against the heat of her belly. "You are incredibly fucking deft, you fucker."

His hands now applied different pressures, and she felt herself being turned around. It happened so fast that before she even realized she was moving she found herself in the new position—sitting on his lap, her back against his chest, her legs straddling his knees, his huge crescent cock hooking up between her legs and over her pubic hair.

He nuzzled her neck as one hand reached under her blouse to cup her bare tit and the other slipped between his cock and her pubes. Two fingers parted her vaginal lips while a third, between them—Jesus, did he ever have it down to a science!—entered the hot wetness of her vulva. He shifted his hips slightly and at the same time guided hers slightly upward. And then—hocus pocus dominocus—the fuckingmonstermarvelprick disappeared inside her.

For the minutest fraction of a second she found herself thinking how many times he must have done this before to accomplish the maneuver so smoothly, and then she was thinking nothing at all because the big fucking monster was filling her with sensation, wedging up inside her in a way that made her feel she would split in half, driving so deep and with such force that she, literally, could feel the pressure up into her chest.

She threw her head back and felt a double sort of excitement as his tongue found her adam's apple at the same time that his hand did something to her breast. And —was he a fucking octopus?—something else started happening down in her pubes. A hand? A finger? Was it outside or inside? Outside? In the pubes. Then finding the clitoris, rubbing the side of the shaft as the outer curve of his penis applied pressure from the other side. Outside, inside, tongue, tit—and getting in there with it all, magnifying it all—she had to pick and sort through the incredible barrage of sensation to identify the individual components—the roughness of the fabric of his jeans, the hardness of the zipper pressing up into the crack of her ass, driving her higher and higher, further and further into that unbelievable wild spinning-world of multiple sensation that—that—oh, God—

The orgasmic fireball seemed to start in the very pit of her abdomen. The warm glow expanded ever so slowly but always intensified. Then its speed increased. And it overtook her. Consumed her. Filled her with an incredible tingling warmth . . . pulsating . . . surging through her in waves.

Through it all she was somehow dimly aware of those bucking hips, lifting her, jouncing her into the air—that flesh-sword ripping its way up to (or so it seemed) her throat—the mesmerizing tongue, the sexy crackling sound of his saliva somehow managing to come through with the other sensations—the hard zipper, the hand on her tit, kneading, turning.

He drove on, seeming to gain momentum with each thrust, until her body went partially limp. Then he slowed but still did not stop—hips undulating now instead of bucking—tit-hand stroking, soothing—until finally she went completely limp. "You are magnificent," she whispered, letting her head fall back onto his shoulder. "You are infuckingcredible."

He said nothing for a moment, then resumed stroking her clitoris. "Another?"

"Oh, wow, it'd kill me." She reached between her legs and fondled his testicles. "Your turn."

"Okay." He ran one hand down her thigh and, as if part of a caressing maneuver, slid her jeans and panties over one ankle, then lifted her off of him, turned her and somehow managed to get her sitting on his lap again, her knees up against his armpits as he entered her. She noted that he could accomplish all this without saying anything, and she reveled in the authoritative way he went about it, taking for granted that he'd be obeyed, controlling the act the way a conductor controls his orchestra (with no put-down in that image now). Not that the domination aspect, the macho horseshit, when she thought about it, was particularly *appealing*. No, it was more the athletic grace of it that was—what? Well . . . like a ballet. . . .

Orchestra. Ballet. And suddenly she found herself thinking of Joseph Williams, whom she hadn't seen since that Sunday months ago when they read about 305 in the *Times*. She had no specific thought about him, he simply flashed through her mind like a film slide that happened to get mixed up in the wrong batch. For an instant his image filled her mental screen—she saw him vividly, in close-up, white tie and tails and holding his baton, thin straw-colored hair seeming to glisten in the beam of some distant spotlight, his eyes fixed to hers (that is, to the camera) and face with an expectant expression, as if he were about to give his orchestra the upbeat—and then he was gone, the slide was off the screen, and she was back with Ted Vassily, who (she suddenly realized) was coming.

She accelerated her hip movements, as if somehow to make up for having failed him by drifting into the Joseph Williams daydream. Why, she wondered, had she drifted? Was it some sort of mental reflex, a kind of escape from the overwhelming (threatening?) intensity of her own orgasm? Or was she blocking, trying to put some sort of barrier between her and this oh-so-self-confident stud? . . .

As she thought about it she realized she was into another drift, and she was angry with herself. He, she was certain, never drifted. He fucked with every dram of his physical and mental energy. Was it all a matter of I.Q.—genius versus animal smarts? If so, her brain was a sexual handicap. And damn it, she didn't like that. A superior brain should contribute, not detract from sexual performance. She should be able to think herself to greater heights of excellence than anyone of lesser intellect could achieve instinctively. Or was there perhaps a mutual antagonism between intellectual and physical excellence? Was that maybe why all the great athletes seemed such morons? And such good fucks? Damn it, she was *still* drifting. . . .

"Ahh, that was good," she heard Ted say, realizing at the same time that his hips had now stopped moving.

"Was it?" she purred, and realized she really didn't know.

"Yeah. Great. You are one hell of a fuck, Ms. Weiss."

She laughed, uneasily. "That sounds like an epitaph. 'Here lies Ms. Weiss, one hell of a fuck.' " She wondered what made her think of that . . . the Freudian sex-death thing? . . . *le petit mort,* as the French called orgasm . . . ?

He nuzzled her neck. "I didn't mean it was your only asset, it's just the one that happened to be on my mind at the moment."

"As well it should be." She bussed him on the cheek, then dis-impaled herself. She wanted to change the subject, she wasn't in the mood to do a big number on the sex-object thing. "May I have some more champagne?"

He poured as she got back into her panties and jeans.

"Well," he said, "when we christen a building, we really christen a building."

"You ain't kidding, superstud."

"It turned me on to do it in the open like this."

"Really? Why?"

"Who knows? It just did."

"Is it something you've done before? Or thought about doing?"

"Not exactly under these circumstances."

"But under similar circumstances?"

"I guess you could say so."

"Like what?"

"Oh, I don't know." He suddenly seemed embarrassed, which surprised her. She had begun to think he didn't have the capacity for embarrassment.

"How could you not know the circumstances? You can't think of a single instance?"

"Well, on a ship once. On a lounge chair on deck, a blanket over us . . ."

"Really? What turned you on about that?"

"Who knows?"

"But didn't you ever wonder about it?"

"Either it does something special for you or it doesn't. Who cares why?"

And that, she reflected, was probably the essential difference between them. "The forbidden fruit thing, maybe?"

"I never thought about it." He laughed. Somehow, she noted edgily, he seemed to have gotten over his embarrassment.

But damn it, she wanted to know! "Is it better if other people are nearby? If there's some chance of being discovered?"

"Who knows? Who thinks about stuff like that?" He sipped his champagne, then seemed almost to choke on it. "Hey, I forgot!" He looked at his watch. "I was supposed to meet someone at five. Come on back to the office with me. It won't take long, then we'll get the hell out of here and have the night to ourselves."

She noted that he didn't wait for her assent as he swooped up the champagne bottle in one hand, his glass in the other and started for the door. She hesitated, wanting him to wait for her, then realized he wasn't going to. She followed him.

The giant he had introduced her to up in the tower—the whale with the goatee and a name that sounded like "Elephant"—was waiting in the finished apartment where Ted had conferred with the architect. With him was another beefy number, not quite as heavy but in the same league: a steer rather than a whale. Funny, she reflected, how football types invariably reminded her of mammals.

The two men stood as she and Ted entered. The steer's physique intrigued her. He was the sturdiest looking man she'd ever seen: no taller than five-nine or -ten but well over two hundred pounds, all of it distributed as if to achieve the lowest possible center of gravity. His neck and head seemed exactly the same width. Both extended virtually to his shoulder blades. And his torso looked exactly like—well, she knew it was a cliché, she'd heard TV sportscasters use it dozens of times . . . it wasn't merely tired it was exhausted, but it really did fit—a fireplug. He seemed almost legless.

"Replay!" he beamed, his craggy face crinkling to life like a mountainside suddenly bathed in sunlight.

"Hey, Cooler!"

For a moment the two men regarded each other like wrestlers about to grapple. Then they took a step toward each other, and Ted punched Cooler in the stomach.

Buffy was stunned. She'd never seen a man strike another, except on film. The in-person reality of it was overwhelming. She could scarcely believe the force of the blow. Its sound echoed through the apartment, a riflelike crack.

The steer was unfazed. Smiling broadly, he returned the punch, for which Ted seemed to stick out his stomach. Another riflelike crack, Ted's laugh and another punch. The steer also laughed as he absorbed it, punched again.

They weren't, she realized, actually fighting, but what *were* they doing?

They traded two more sets of punches, each blow seeming harder than the last. Then, laughing raucously, they fell into each other's arms, then separated, held each other at arm's length and hugged again.

The scene embarrassed her. It was, in its own sort of super-macho way, almost homosexual. Detach, she told herself. This is an anthropologist's dream: greeting rituals of mid-twentieth century American football players. Don't judge. Study it.

They finally broke the clinch. "Buffy," Ted said, "meet the greatest fullback ever to play the game, Walt Kulikowski. Cooler, Buffy Weiss. *The* Buffy Weiss."

She offered her hand. Kulikowski seemed uncertain whether to take it. Finally he did. The size of his fist amazed her. His palm was as wide as her waist. "Pleased to meetcha," he murmured.

"Champagne, Cooler?" Ted displayed the bottle. "Or you staying with your Scotch?"

"Scotch," he said, stumbling back to retrieve his glass.

"Sit, relax." Ted gestured. Kulikowski and the whale sat. Ted remained standing. "Whatya been doing, Cooler? Seems like twenty years since I've seen you."

Buffy went to the couch across the room and only half-listened as they said jock-things to each other. She wondered if Ted realized how unpleasant this was for her. She suspected he didn't. And that he would not especially care if he did. Immaculate ignorance . . . the ultimate uncaring, mindless boor. And she, with consummate assholery, put up with it. For the sake of her twat? Maybe the sexual revolution wasn't such a good thing after all. . . .

Ted and Kulikowski did a five minute long-time-no-see routine and another five on the good old days. Each minute made her progressively angrier. Even he . . . how in hell could even *he* ignore her this way . . . and then, as if on cue, he was crossing the room in quick strides, refilling her just-emptied champagne glass and returning to Kulikowski —all of it without once looking at her.

She should leave the room, tell him she'd wait outside. Better yet, that she'd meet him back at the Tuscany. Better yet, to go fuck himself. She was waiting for a break in the conversation when it took a turn that both embarrassed and revolted her—and yet, strangely, fascinated her.

"You're probably wondering why I wanted to see you," Kulikowski said.

Ted laughed. "Not especially, Cooler. What the hell? We're old pals. It's always good to—"

"Ted . . ." His voice was pained. "Ted, let's not kid around anymore. While I've still got the balls—" He looked guiltily at Buffy. "Excuse me, while I've still got the nerve. 'Cause if I don't hurry and get it out, man, I won't be able to."

Ted regarded him with seeming astonishment. The reaction, Buffy in her wisdom decided, was exaggerated. Ted seemed to be putting the poor bastard on, making him sweat every word. . . .

"I'm broke," Kulikowski blurted out. "I'm on my ass, Ted. They repo'd my car, the goddamn rent ain't paid, I don't even own this jacket I'm wearing—I borrowed it from my goddamn brother. Can you throw something at me, man? I'll take anything. Anything at all."

The tension for Buffy was almost unbearable. The whale, she thought, obviously felt it too as he silently refilled Kulikowski's Scotch glass. Ted only continued to stare at him, as if in reproof for some great social sin.

Kulikowski took a quick slug of Scotch. "I know my track record ain't the best, man. But you gotta believe, I'm ready to give it everything this time. No more fu—uh, screwin' around with broads, no more thinkin' there's no tomorrow. Anything you give me, man—it'll be just like when I played ball. You know nobody on the team worked harder for you than I did . . ."

His voice, Buffy reflected, was low and even. He looked to Ted for encouragement, for an answer. His eyes, moist and seeming slightly swollen, testified to his pain. Ted said nothing. He looked away. And now—was it calculated? —he slowly sipped his champagne. How, she wondered, could he be so damn callous?

Kulikowski's eyes followed him for a long silent moment, then switched to the whale, who almost imperceptibly shrugged. Kulikowski took another slug of Scotch, looked back to Ted. For God's sake, Buffy silently urged, answer him!

Ted remained silent. Kulikowski moved his lips as if about to say something, then apparently changed his mind and took another drink of Scotch. Ted again sipped his champagne. Finally Kulikowski said, "What more can I tell you, Replay? I've said it all. I need help, man."

Ted nodded and after another long wait said softly, "It's kind of tight now, Cooler. I'll see if I can turn something up. But I can't promise."

Kulikowski smiled nervously. "You won't be sorry, Replay. I won't let you down this time. You've got my word." He got up and clapped Ted's shoulder. "I can do you lots of good, Reep. I know I can. Maybe you can put me in the p.r. office with old Burr. I still know all the newspaper guys, I can do a lot for you there—"

Ted held up a hand to silence him. "I'll talk to Nate, Cooler. We'll work out what we can. Right, Nasty?"

"Right, Replay."

Kulikowski shook each man's hand. "Thanks, fellas, you won't be sorry . . . I won't let you down." He looked from one to the other for encouragement, got none. "Well," he said, shifting his weight, "I guess I'll be running along. I'll give you a call, okay? Maybe tomorrow?"

"Nate'll call you soon as something turns up, Cooler."

"Yeah. Okay, Ted. Right. Thanks." He shook hands again, took a step toward the door, hesitated, found his Scotch glass, drained it, started out again. At the door he turned back. "You know, Replay, when I think of all I gave the game . . . two-thousand yards a year, two years in a row . . . never less than a thousand after my rookie year . . . I mean, what'd the damn game ever give me back? These days goddamn high school coaches make more than I did . . ."

Ted was expressionless. Kulikowski looked from Nate to Buffy. "What I should've done," he went on, inexplicably addressing her, "was make a little smart money on the side. Lay some information on guys that could pay for it. At least bet a few bucks now and then . . ." His eyes fixed to hers. She thought of Coleridge's ancient mariner, collaring a random wedding guest. "Do you have any idea how much one fumble could've been worth to me? The right drop at the right time was good for fifty thou, maybe a hundred . . . more than I got from the game in—"

"The game never made anybody play it, Cooler," Ted said.

Kulikowski's eyes held Buffy's a moment longer, then looked back to Ted. "Yeah, I suppose you're right, Replay. I guess I'm just feeling sorry for myself. Hey, thanks again. You, too, Nate. Good meeting you, Miss Weiss. Sorry to have ruined your day." He looked around the room, smiled shyly as he nodded to each of them individually, then walked out.

"Cooler's really scraping bottom," Nate said.

Ted emptied his champagne glass. "Cooler was scraping bottom when he was on top."

"You notice how he got mad at the end? After you said I'd call him? Like, what'd he expect? To go on the payroll right away?"

"That was always his problem, he got pissed when things didn't come easy. He seemed to figure the defense owed him three free yards every time he ran." Ted replenished his champagne. "You know, he was the one that missed the block when Elmo Washington destroyed this knee on me. Cooler's idea of throwing a block was to lay down and hope nobody stepped on him."

"The greatest fullback ever to play the game," Buffy said dryly.

Ted ignored her. "Give him a call in two days, Nate. No, make it three. Let him get hungry for it, then offer him doorman or security guard. Say I didn't want to give him anything, but you talked me into it."

"You think he'd take doorman or security? He was looking for something soft, like the p.r. office."

"If he doesn't want it, all the better. I don't owe him a living. I don't owe him the fucken time of day." He inspected the champagne bottle, divided half its remains between his glass and Buffy's, drained his, then emptied the bottle into it. "And now, Mr. Elefante, I've got a dinner date with a lady"—he smiled at Buffy, seeming really to notice her for the first time since they left the lobby—"so if you'll excuse me I'll get my ass the hell out of here." He raised his glass to her, then drank it down. "Awful waste of Taittinger, drinking it fast like that. We should've let Cooler wait another fifteen minutes and finished it properly in the lobby."

Nate ushered them to the door. "One thing before you go, Ted. The guy from the building inspector's office has been sniffing around again. He says we've got about fifty new violations. I know what you said about payoffs, but you know what a hassle it was correcting his last citations. If we gave him a couple thou to leave us alone, we'd save ten or twenty in the long run. . . ."

"Did he ask for the money? In so many words?"

"No, he just sort of pissed around about it. One of those raps like, 'My boss is really on me, he's used to being taken care of on these things, you builders from out of town don't know how it works in New York'—that routine. Obviously he wants me to ask how to keep everybody happy. Pete DeAngelis tells me the usual bite is four or five thou a month, but they'll go light on us because we're a high-publicity project, in good with the mayor, all that shit."

"Tape your next meeting," Buffy said. "Get him to spell out exactly what he wants. Then turn the tape over to the—"

"When will you see him again?" Ted interrupted.

"After you leave, probably. He's usually floating around

the site at quitting time, giving DeAngelis creepy looks and writing stuff down in his notebook."

"See if he's on the site now. If he is, bring him back. I'll wait here."

"Okay."

Nate left, and Ted went to the window to stare out. Buffy waited for him to say something. She wanted an apology. Actually, she felt she deserved a litany of apologies. For this new delay. For the inconvenience. For brushing off her last helpful comment. For the scene with Kulikowski . . . He shouldn't have invited her here at all if he didn't have time to pay full attention . . .

He stared out the window and said nothing.

"How much longer are we going to be here?" she asked.

"Quiet," he replied softly. "I'm trying to get myself up for something—"

"Now, look, Ted Vassily, I don't know what the hell your other playmates put up with but I didn't come here to be—"

He turned toward her. *"Then get the fuck out."*

She was stunned. She waited for him to apologize. He only turned back to the window. She waited a moment longer, considered leaving, went to the couch and sat down. For now.

Nate returned a few minutes later. With him was a paunchy disheveled man of about forty with curly steel-gray hair. Ted turned slowly from the window.

"This is Mr. Gorman," Nate said. "Mr. Gorman, Mr. Vassily."

Gorman tentatively extended his hand. Ted looked at it as if it were contaminated. "I understand you're trying to shake down my super, Gorman."

Gorman glanced at his waiting hand, as though not quite sure what to do with it. His eyes went around the room. He seemed to stiffen when he saw Buffy. "No, Mr. Vassily. Nothing of the sort. I just said there are certain violations here that need to be corrected. It's the law, Mr. Vassily. I'm only doing my job enforcing it."

"You hear that, Nate? He's calling you a liar."

"What'd you tell me," Nate said, "about your boss

needing to get taken care of? About us guys from out of town not knowing how things are done in New York?"

Gorman forced a smile. "Uh, I'm sorry, Nate, but I think you misunderstood me." He turned slightly, as if to avoid having either man directly behind him, and raised his hands. "What I said was, my boss was on me about getting the *violations* taken care of. That is . . . I said we're very strict about these things in New York. As of course we have to be, with a population concentration like ours, a traffic flow of millions of vehicles a day . . ."

Something in Ted's look seemed to silence him. Gorman glanced at Nate, then turned to Buffy. "You're aware of these things, Miss Weiss. You realize the importance of maintaining standards of safety—"

"Talk to me, Gorman, not her!"

He turned back to Ted.

"Come here," Ted said softly. "I want to show you something."

Gorman took two uneasy steps toward the window. Ted nodded and stepped back, as if to clear a path. Then with a suddenness that stopped Buffy's breath he reached out, grabbed Gorman by the hair with one hand and the neck with the other and pushed his face into the windowpane.

Buffy gasped. And her mind raced, churning up bizarre thoughts, inappropriate thoughts—thoughts no doubt intended to distract her from the horror she was witnessing . . . the sound, she thought, of the face hitting the window was perfectly characterized by that journalistic cliché "dull, sickening thud" . . . clichés did not enter the language by accident, originally they were accurate descriptives . . . and, she thought, the rear view of Gorman as he hit was comical, almost Chaplinesque, his coattails riding up over his shirt, his chunky buttocks straining the seat of his double-knit pants . . . and his socks, ankle-high instead of over-the-calf, one of them having lost its elasticity and now lying in a rumpled roll below his ankle . . . and his legs, chalk-white, as if not exposed to the sun for years, and perfectly hairless . . . and his shoes, black formal cut but old and scuffed and worn with a *brown* suit . . . surely a man who shook down builders for thousands each week should do better than brown suit with black shoes—

The flood of thoughts was cut off as (could they all have passed through her mind so fast? was she still really hearing the echo of his face hitting the pane?) he fell away from the window, tilting toward Ted like a nightclub comic's drunk, and she saw the detritus he had left on the pane . . . a big splotch of red now streaking down like the "legs" of a good full-bodied wine on the sides of the glass, and on both sides of this mess, his sweaty handprints as he tried too late to ward off the impact. . . . She sucked in her breath and was afraid she would vomit as Ted landed a punch on Gorman's back, just above the hips, then, from beneath, another one somewhere in the area of Gorman's chest, and then seemed to shove-spin Gorman around. . . .

Buffy felt herself getting dizzy as she saw Gorman's face—splotches of blood covered both cheeks, a rivulet of it came from his nose, mixed with snot, which he tried unsuccessfully to sniff back in, coughing and sputtering as he did. He held his hands in front of the mess, as if to catch it. Ted grabbed him by the hair, jerked his head back and pressed him up against the window. "Now you listen to me, creep, *nobody* shakes me down, you understand? This building is going up and nobody gets paid off. Nobody! You understand?"

Gorman nodded frantically, a nightclub comic's parody of fear, as Ted shoved him toward the door. "And tell the asshole you work for to expect a lot of people looking over his shoulder till this building is finished. If we get more citations than any other construction operation, you better be damned well prepared to show that we've done something the others haven't. You grafter bastards have had a free ride for too long. Well, the gravy train is about to stop." He looked to Nate. "Get him out of here." He turned to Buffy. "Excuse me, I'm going to wash my hands, be right back."

She watched, numb, as he walked into the next room. Suddenly she was exhausted. Too spent even to think about her reactions to what she'd just witnessed.

"This way, Mr. Gorman," Nate said, gently moving him out the door, which he then closed, went into the kitchen, returned with a bucket and washcloth and started cleaning up the mess.

Ted came out a few minutes later, looking thoroughly refreshed. "Nate," he said, "have Burr Whiteside get to his man in the mayor's office and say I had to rough up Gorman. Have him say I'm really pissin' about the shakedown try, and if there's any more trouble with those building department fuckers I'll sell the unfinished building to the highest bidder and let New York shove its poor people up its ass. They know I'm nuts enough to do it, and if I did the papers'd never let them live it down." He took Buffy's hand. "Come on, time to go." She followed him to the door. "Also, Nate, have Burr get something to the papers on this. No details. Just a sort of blind thing, maybe for one of the gossip columns, about rumors having it there were fisticuffs here when a lower-echelon building department guy tried to put the arm on Three-oh-five East. The item should strengthen our hand in the mayor's office."

"Right, Reep."

"Okay, see you tomorrow."

Buffy was silent until they were in a cab headed for the Tuscany. "Thank you for a lovely afternoon," she said.

He laughed. "Sorry about the rough stuff. I guess I should've had you wait outside."

"You also might have excluded me from that charming episode with Mr. Kulikowski."

"What bothered you about that?"

"What bothered me! Why, you humiliated the poor man. Couldn't you have let him down gently if you didn't want to help him? Or simply offer him the doorman's job before he left instead of making him wait three days for it?"

"Sure. I could've done that."

"Then why did you have to abuse him?"

"I didn't have to."

"Then for goodness' sake, why *did* you?"

"Buffy, you'll enjoy life more if you don't ask so many questions about things that aren't any of your business."

"Then let me ask a few about something that is. Do you realize—"

He raised a hand. "In the hotel. Not here."

"Why not here?"

"I don't air my personal laundry in front of cab drivers."

She fumed till they got there. "Now," she said, "do you realize the position you put me in by making me witness that beating? Do you realize I could be called to testify about it? Gorman recognized me, you know. If I'm questioned, do you expect me to perjure myself to support the lie you're putting out through your p.r. man?"

"You won't be questioned. The whole thing is going to end in the mayor's office."

"Don't be too sure. And don't be so goddamn smug every time I offer a little advice. If you'd listened to me, you'd've had the cops tape Nate and nail Gorman in the act of asking for a bribe."

"And then? Have the case get bounced by some assistant D.A. on the pad? And meanwhile have Gorman's replacement nail me with all kinds of violations from a building code that's so goddamn complex even you lawyers can't figure it out?"

"It doesn't have to happen that way. . . . Anyway, there's no justification for assaulting the man—"

"I didn't hurt him, just bloodied his nose. He'll be okay."

"It's still assault. Legally speaking, it's aggravated assault. And it was totally unnecessary. Why couldn't you—"

He raised a hand again to silence her. "Buf, one of the reasons I went into business for myself was so that I wouldn't have to spend half my life explaining my decisions to other people."

"That's a cop-out. And you always do it with me. Every time your argument is weak, you change the premise. Or you just shut me off."

He took both her hands in his and looked evenly into her eyes. "Buffy, I like you very much. I'm sorry if you were upset today. Next time I'll try to make things more enjoyable for you, but let's get something straight . . . I'm not a debater. I don't enjoy these back-and-forth hassles about who did what and why and how come it wasn't done differently. If we're going to get along, you've got to break the habit of giving me the third degree every time I do something that doesn't make sense to you."

"And if—" She cut herself off. It was, as she knew long ago—and shouldn't have let herself forget—pointless to even try with him. You know what you came for

. . . take it, and run. "Okay," she said. "End of hassles. Let's make up." She offered a big smile. "Shall we fuck first and shower later, or vice-versa?"

He managed a smile that matched hers. "Why not both together?"

They did, and while it lasted it seemed worth all the unpleasantness he'd put her through during the afternoon. . . . He held her in front of him, facing the spray, moving her body so that the hot needles of water first attacked one breast, then the other, then her pubes. She struggled playfully against him, and he tightened his grip on her. She relished the feel of his hard muscles, especially in his arms, which wrapped around her like coils of (bizarre image) rubber-coated steel. As they jostled, he dipped behind her and she felt his cock between her thighs, snaking up in front of her, burrowing through her pubes, looking from her angle as if it actually were hers. Now he raised himself again to his full height and lifted her off her feet—seeming for a moment to be doing it with his cock, though she quickly realized the main leverage came from his arms, still wrapped around her.

She wanted it in her now, she could feel her juices flowing to welcome it. But he made her wait, building her even higher. He grabbed a bar of soap, rubbed its hardness against her breasts and belly, then into her pubes—still keeping his (their) dick incongruously in place against them. He lathered her, knelt to do her legs, gently nuzzling her buttocks as he scrubbed from behind, then burrowed his face into her belly and pubes as he did her front. She gripped his hair and tried to keep from crying out, fighting a no-lose battle between greater pleasures, whether to prolong the exquisite heightening of desire or surrender to it. The sound of the water, the heat of it, the moisture in the room, the subtle fragrance of the soap—all competed with the hard muscularity of his body in an assault that seemed both to strengthen and weaken her. "Oh, God, do it now!" she finally cried out. "Do it now, you incredible fucker, do it *now!*"

He pulled her down into the tub and manipulated her thighs into a straddling position. She was so lubricated that she could scarcely feel his entry. He half rose, burying his face between her breasts, licking them, nibbling on them, taking one in each hand and slapping them against his face. He pulled her down on top of him, putting wonderful new pressures on her vagina.

She was out-of-her-mind excited . . . but something was wrong . . . the sensations she needed to propel her orgasm somehow weren't happening. He sensed her difficulty. "Try this," he said, easing a washcloth between his pubis and hers. Magic! The rough terrycloth provided the clitoral friction that soap and water apparently had been offsetting. She climaxed in less than a minute.

"Another?" he asked.

She laughed. "Oh, you madman, you unbelievable fucking madman!" She kissed him. "You go ahead, darling, have yours."

"In bed," he said.

She stood, rinsed off, and started out of the tub.

"Wait," he said. "Soap me first."

She felt slightly guilty, realizing that she'd accepted all his ministrations but offered nothing in return. She imitated the way he had soaped her. As she rinsed him off, kneeling at his feet, his prick loomed immense in front of her eyes. She took it in her mouth, enjoying the cleanness of it, still fresh with the water from the shower. She took one testicle in each hand and kneaded them as she ringed his glans with her tongue. She stood, kissed him softly on the lips. "Ready?"

They stepped out of the tub and toweled each other dry. He hugged her, arms around her waist, and dipped at the knees. His penis hooked underneath her, coming up behind her ass. "Put your legs around my waist," he told her.

She hesitated, not knowing quite how to accomplish it.

"Don't worry. I can support your weight. Just lift up."

She held around his neck and lifted her legs. His strong hands guided her into position, then he reached beneath her, positioned his penis and made a jerklike move with his hips. To her amazement she found herself impaled again. His organ seemed immense inside her.

"Look, no hands," he said, holding them wide as he walked into the bedroom, carrying her on his cock. She realized, of course, that she was supporting most of her own weight with her arms around his neck. But still—!

At the bed he gently lowered her onto her back, still not disengaging, then maneuvered both their bodies into his old reliable legs-under position. He climaxed quickly.

Lying against him afterward, she decided that on balance it hadn't been all that bad an afternoon.

"Well . . . ready for dinner?"

She snuggled against him, relishing the feel of his firm, hairy chest. "Whenever you are." How nice it was to be in bed with him, she thought as they got up. Now if only he would just manage to avoid doing something to fuck things up . . .

He did not. Even before they left the hotel he started getting on her nerves again. She couldn't even pinpoint precisely what bothered her . . . more of the same old pattern of his not understanding *her* point of view and unwillingness to articulate his own. Face it, she told herself ruefully, except for sex he's not in your league.

The irritating trivia continued on the way to the restaurant. She wanted to take a cab, he wanted to walk even though it was drizzling. He didn't consider her feelings . . . he simply decreed that they'd walk.

Then, at the restaurant, he proceeded to chew out the waiter, loudly, without the slightest self-consciousness, drawing all sorts of attention to their table. Granted the waiter had been remiss and somewhat rude, but you just didn't *do* those things in public, particularly if you were with someone likely to be recognized . . . and as a result seriously embarrassed.

Coming back to the hotel, he pointedly didn't tip the cabby. And when the guy gave him some lip, Ted told him he was a lousy asshole driver who didn't deserve to be tipped. For a moment it looked as though there'd be a replay of the afternoon's scene with Gorman.

It won't work, she told herself unhappily as the doorman ushered them into the elevator at the Tuscany. Ted Vassily may be the greatest cocksman in history, but in every other department it's just no go.

They went to bed and he gave her another bell-ringer. No special techniques this time. No new positions, just good old push-pull. But done with the master's touch. . . . He'd bring her to the edge of orgasm, then magically sense where she was and slow up so that she'd lose it, then bring her back, then make her lose it again, and on and on until, when she finally let go, she thought the top of her head was going to blow off.

"Another?" he asked afterward, as usual. And this time, as much out of curiosity as anything else (could he really sustain another?) she said yes.

Whereupon he swung right back into it, building her excitement with slow teasing rhythm, pushing harder as she got wound up, driving hard to get her to the edge, followed by more teasing action, more drive, teasing, drive, and *bwanngg!* She was so exhausted afterward that she could scarcely move her hips to help him reach his own orgasm. . . .

She woke half an hour later to find Ted wide awake. She waited for him to say something. For a long while he didn't. Finally he asked if she'd like a drink. "Snifter of Armagnac? Larressingle, ten years old?"

"You sold me."

He went to the pantry and returned with two snifters. "Let's talk bluntly about something," he said, sitting cross-legged opposite her on the bed.

She eyed him warily. "As bluntly as you like."

"Well, we have quite a sex life together but we don't do so much for each other in other departments, do we?"

She smiled. "I guess we've had our ups and downs."

"Mainly downs. Even I can see that I'm not exactly your idea of an intellectual giant or the world's most reasonable man. You like to *talk* about a lot of things I prefer to leave unsaid. What it seems to boil down to is different styles, different ways of doing things, looking at things."

She nodded. She was a little surprised, startled, that he had noticed. She took a large swallow of Armagnac. "Are you, in your ineluctably diplomatic fashion, Mr. Vassily, suggesting I get lost?"

"No. I'm trying to say that much as I like making it with you, I really meant it when I said earlier there's just no room in my life for hassles, even with an admittedly sensational lady like yourself."

She couldn't believe he was still spelling it out this way, couldn't believe his nonchalance about it after the fantastic time they'd given each other. This was *her* department

. . . her prerogative, the thanks-but-no-thanks routine . . . who in *hell* did this character think he was . . . well, at least she knew who *she* was . . . including someone who wouldn't tolerate one more second—fucking or otherwise—with this balloon-headed stud who obviously mistook himself for some kind of cock-propelled masterbuilder ready to run the world. Okay for the world, maybe . . . no way, no way in the world for Buffy Weiss . . .

Fighting for control, she carefully put the snifter on the night table, got out of bed and went to the closet.

He didn't say a word. Merely watched her closely, making her feel like something under glass.

Clothes in hand, she strode into the living room, dressed quickly, made an instant inspection of the bathroom to be certain she hadn't left something from her handbag, then went to the door. She thought for a moment of going back into the bedroom for a final word, then decided against it. She let the door slam behind her and nervously waited for the elevator, hoping he wouldn't come into the hall after her and make it necessary for her to say even one more word to him.

He didn't.

Ted sipped his Armagnac, feeling let down but relieved. She was, he decided, trouble. A flake, really. Maybe a little more superficially elegant than most others he'd dicked over the years—but when you stripped away all the degrees and the words and the rest of the bullshit, a flake nonetheless. There was, he'd learned the hard way, no point in trying to reason with flakes. It was pointless to explain anything because they already had it worked out in their heads and nothing you could say would change it for them. So the only thing to do was opt out, invite them to go their way. Which was too bad, because sometimes they really had nice things going for them . . . like Buffy Weiss. Except not enough, really, not in any department, including, as he'd learned today, sex.

Their first session had been okay, but he knew today in the lobby that something wasn't working. Namely her. She was fine during the build-up, fine till she came, and then she just tuned out. It was like being with Sleeping Beauty. No movement, no response—nothing! He'd had to fantasy Chris to come. And he hated doing that (was even embarrassed?), that was one dependency he needed to stay as far away from as possible. Or go crazy.

In the shower she'd done the same kind of tune-out. And in bed. Apparently she was, when you got down to it, a rich New York cunt accustomed to having guys kiss her ass for the pleasure of her cunt. No real give and take . . . just gimme, gimme, gimme, even in bed. Which you could put up with if you were horny enough, but eventually you had to check out.

At first it had seemed she might be interesting for other reasons. She obviously was very bright and very articulate. Seeing her could be a stimulating experience—even a learning experience. But mostly what she did was haggle over horseshit—exactly the opposite of Chris, who maybe didn't have a Seven Sisters *summa cum laude* or whatever Buffy's credentials were, but who definitely had one of the sharpest minds he'd ever known . . . and was a *nice* chick besides.

The only thing Buffy seemed willing to share with him was her body, which to tell the truth was less than sensational . . . flat tummy, good ass, decent legs, but her tits weren't as big as he liked them . . . and he'd always been a tit-man. . . . If *all* a chick was giving was her body, well, it ought to be better than Buffy Weiss's. . . .

So? So end of game. He'd known that early in the evening, even before they'd left the restaurant. The ratio of cunty demands and pouts to shareable good traits was simply too high. . . .

He sipped his Armagnac. Nothing to do for now but hang in there, take whatever action came his way over the next few weeks—if anything did—and then, after the building opened, it'd be a whole new ball game. Check that: a whole new season.

He drained his Armagnac, finished what she had left in her glass, turned off the light and got under the covers. No question, he'd have enjoyed having her body here next to him now, but . . . forget it.

He flopped over onto his stomach and enjoyed the cool feel of the pillow against his cheek. And in his head he could see the building taking final shape, the slabs of granite fitting into place up the walls until all four towers were covered, then a gala party in the lobby, a fine jazz-flavored orchestra, gorgeous women. And in his hand was a lovely breast . . . like Chris's.

FIVE

John Malloy followed the TV camera's pan across the lobby of 305 East and marveled at the public relations job Vassily and his people had done. When Malloy received the invitation to the party celebrating the building's opening, his immediate reaction had been to plead a prior commitment. Who needed another cocktail bash with publicity-seeking bores who already were on his side? But as the evening neared, it became clear that this would be the party of the year in New York and an incomparable opportunity for politicking.

Vassily's publicity barrage started with items in the gossip columns and mentions on TV talk shows. A week later there were full-length newspaper stories and filmed reports on the network evening newscasts. Then one network announced it would do a documentary on the building, and Eddie Spats Johnson began advertising that his show on the night of the party would be telecast live from the 305 lobby. The icing on the cake was the phone call Malloy received from a friend at *Time:* the week of the party, Ted Vassily and 305 East would be the magazine's cover story.

Malloy's chief of staff, Tom Donohue, promptly phoned Burr Whiteside, whose office had issued the invitation, with the good news that John Malloy had been able to get out of his previous commitment.

"We'll be arranging special entrances for V.I.P.'s who

want them," said Whiteside. "TV lights, the band playing your favorite song, Eddie Johnson identifying you for the home audience—is Mr. Malloy interested?"

Is the pope Catholic? "I'll speak to him about it, Mr. Whiteside," said Tom Donohue. "I'm reasonably confident he'll go along if you believe it'll be in the best interests of Three-oh-five East. As you know, Mr. Malloy was one of Mr. Vassily's very first supporters on this project. Anything he can do to help make the evening a success, I'm sure he'll want to do it."

Whiteside provided a schedule of available entrance times between eleven-thirty p.m. and one a.m. They ran at five-minute intervals, insuring that a new arrival would not preempt a predecessor's on-camera time.

John Malloy wanted to get on during the first half hour for maximum exposure among the early-to-bedders. Unfortunately, the time period was fully booked.

Tom Donohue noticed Joseph Williams' name in the eleven-fifty slot. "He's a very strong supporter of yours, John, maybe he'll agree to being bumped. That'd give you the best position in the lineup, far enough down so you don't seem to have been waiting in line to get in the door, early enough to catch the fast snoozers. And there's another advantage—you'll be coming on right after Jeannie Danton."

"Who the hell is Jeannie Danton?"

"A remarkably sexy actress that everyone says is going to be the next Marilyn Monroe. She made the papers a couple months ago when her tits popped out of her dress in front of the paparazzi when she left a nightclub."

"Ah, *that* Jeannie Danton. I didn't know she lived in Three-oh-five East."

"She doesn't, but she likes to come to parties where people take her picture. Anyway, bet on it, she'll be showing everything the F.C.C. will let her get away with, which should leave the audience bright-eyed and bushy-tailed when you come on after her. Shall I try to set up the switch with Williams?"

Malloy thought for a moment. "Phone him, but don't say what we have in mind. Ask him and his wife to have dinner with Peg and me—new neighbors, mutual interests, that sort of thing. He'll accept, I'm sure. Meanwhile, book my entrance for a slot further down the line. At dinner I'll jokingly mention that my late slot may cost me votes. If Williams doesn't volunteer the swap, we'll get Vassily to shoehorn me in somewhere in the first half hour."

The shoehorn hadn't been necessary, and now, sitting at the TV set in his apartment, John Malloy watched the festivities he would soon join. The scene reminded him of the old Guy Lombardo New Year's Eve broadcasts from the Waldorf, but with a much younger and with-it audience. Eddie Johnson had brought over his TV studio band, which kicked things off with a swing arrangement of old Dixieland favorites, featuring solos by Spats on clarinet and Slide Hillard on trombone. Then the band played dance music while Spats roamed the audience introducing celebrities. The dancers were mostly young, the girls mostly knockouts. Malloy suspected most of them were, like Jeannie Danton, here for tonight only.

Now he watched as the camera panned from a group of dancers to a huge reproduction of the *Time* cover—an impressionistic Clyde Prettyman painting featuring Vassily's portrait in the foreground, a sketch of 305 East immediately behind him and off to one side a drawing of old Number 13 throwing a pass. He should, Malloy reflected, explore the possibilities of a p.r. liaison for himself with Burr Whiteside; a man who could set up all this hoopla for an apartment house should be able to elect a senator single-handed.

The TV camera held on the cover for a long beat, then pulled back to reveal Spats Johnson with a fiftyish redhead who still retained much of what undoubtedly had once been a spectacular figure. "I'm with Sally Knight," Spats was saying, "the internationally syndicated columnist and star of her own afternoon interview show on this network. Sally, you've been to more than a few parties in your career. Has there ever been one like this?"

"If there was, Eddie, they didn't invite me. Why look, there's Marilyn Chase. Isn't her new show marvelous? Hi, Marilyn, come on over. . . ."

"You know, John," said Tom Donohue, "the word is the

president's men volunteered to have him make an appearance. And were turned down. It seems Vassily doesn't exactly admire him. . . ."

The orchestra sounded a fanfare and the TV cameras switched to the main entrance, where a platoon of policemen was clearing a path. "It's the mayor of New York," said Spats in voice-over as the orchestra struck up "The Sidewalks of New York." A camera panned with the mayor through the throng toward the enlargement of the *Time* cover, where Spats came forward to greet him.

Behind him John Malloy heard the clink of glass and turned to find his wife pouring from a whiskey decanter. Deciding a little diplomacy was the best policy, he waited a full minute after she left the room before following her into the kitchen.

"I dumped it down the drain," she said, giggling as she displayed her empty glass.

He kept his voice soft, trying to convey hurt more than scolding. "You did promise."

She giggled again. "I promised not to drink on public occasions in return for your promise not to check out girls on public occasions. You checked out three Tuesday night, Johnny—at least I *saw* you checking out three, who knows how many I missed." She giggled again and brandished the empty glass. "Well, this was my second drink. I've got one more coming."

Her slight thickness of speech, he told himself, probably would go unnoticed by people who didn't know her, but there was no question she'd had more than two drinks. "Would you rather not come down tonight? Johnny and I could go alone. I'll introduce him to all the football players, he'll get a kick out of that. You could stay up here and watch on TV if you prefer—"

"No thank you, Mr. Malloy. I'll accompany you. Right after I have that third drink you owe me."

He sighed deeply.

She started to giggle again, then abruptly stopped. Her eyes met his, and suddenly she seemed cold sober. "John . . . I won't embarrass you tonight. I promise. I was a lush long before you knew—or cared. I know how to handle myself."

"I'm only trying to make things easier for all of us."

"You needn't worry, John. After all . . . I've got a stake in your career too."

He made himself smile. "Promise you won't drink any more?"

She laughed. "I won't drink any more. I may not drink any less, but I won't drink any more . . . at least not after that third one you owe me."

He went to her and forced himself to take her in his arms and kiss her gently on the cheek. Fortunately the booze smell wasn't on her. She must've started just a while ago. "Do a favor for an old buddy? Forego that third one till we get back?"

"In consideration for what, counselor? Your not checking out all those long-legged ladies dying to get you into their pants?"

He raised his right hand in the oath position, extended his left onto an imaginary Bible, cast his eyes skyward and intoned, "I solemnly swear by all I hold sacred that I will not look tonight at anyone's lovely legs but my wife's."

"You're still a charmer, you bastard. No wonder they go crazy over you." She put the glass in the sink. "Okay, I'll forego, but you better too, or I'll . . . I'll walk right over and grab Spats Johnson's penis."

John visualized her doing that. Prim Peg? No way. "Fair enough," he said. "Now let's go in and watch for my cue."

He started toward the living room. She held his arm. "John?"

"Yes?"

"I'm not being so unreasonable, am I?" She stood in front of him and straightened his bow tie. "I've told you I don't care what you do when I'm not with you"—she didn't add the obvious, that it would have done precious little good if she did—"is it too much to ask that when we're together you at least make a pretense of being interested in me?"

"Please let's not go through this again." He kissed her cheek.

She seemed to think this over, then smiled. "All right, John, let's go watch for your cue."

Back in the living room the TV set showed Spats Johnson with Preston Wade, Nate Elefante and Mikey DeAngelico, all looking very dapper in tuxedos. "If you just tuned in, folks," Spats was saying, "this is not, I repeat, *not* a rerun of some old post-game footage. These gentlemen are executives of the Three-oh-five East Corporation. Well, hey, guys, I'd say that's quite a switch from the days when—" He cut himself off as the band sounded another fanfare and the TV picture again switched to the main entrance. "It's Jeannie Danton," said Spats in a voice-over as a stunning blonde girl swept up the stairway, her marvelous breasts prominent through the sheer fabric of an X-cut bodice.

"Eleven-forty-five, John," said Tom Donohue. "They want us in the foyer at eleven forty-eight."

"There's still time," said Grace Colello. "Why don't you put something on and come down?"

Her father looked up wearily from the TV set. "For the same reason I told you two hours ago. We don't belong there."

"You go," added her mother. "I'm sure you'll have a good time without us."

"You *do* belong," Grace protested. "That's what this building is all about. We are tenants here. We didn't get these invitations by mistake, for God's sake."

"Sure we belong." Marty Colello gestured at the TV screen. "What do I talk about with Sally Knight? And the president of the Bank of the United States? 'Hi, Mr. Loomis, I'm Marty Colello. I drive a laundry truck. How's things down at the Common Market these days?' "

"You don't have to talk with anyone if you don't want to. Talk to me. And drink some champagne. And dance. It's your party as much as Hartford Loomis's." She turned to her mother. "Really, mom. You'll have a great time. Imagine next Sunday at grandma's, maybe they'll even see you on TV."

"Gracie." Rose Colello smiled patiently. "We'd feel uncomfortable. We don't have anything to wear. Look at all those people in their tuxedos and gowns."

"They're not all wearing tuxedos and gowns. Look. Right now on the TV. That's Buffy Weiss. You've heard of her, right? What's she wearing? Jeans and a blouse."

Marty Colello laughed. "Buffy Weiss is famous. She can

wear her pajamas if she wants. You know what'd happen if I went in there in my dungarees? They'd think I was one of the maintenance men and tell me to take out the garbage."

"Wear one of your suits. Wear what you wore to church last Sunday. There are people there in regular street clothes—"

"Not in fifty-dollar Robert Hall exclusives, there ain't."

Grace sighed. "You know, sometimes this family really exasperates me. When I told you about this building, you couldn't believe it was for real. You were positive it was some plot by the Jews to screw us out of something. You couldn't figure what they wanted to screw us out of, but you were sure it had to be something. So I filled out the rental application myself. And we got accepted. And now we live in the swankiest apartment building in New York. We're paying two hundred dollars a month for an apartment that other people are renting at two or three thousand. And you still think somebody's trying to do a number on us."

"Gracie." Her mother smiled. "We'll be the first to admit you were right about the apartment. It's beautiful. We're thrilled to have it. But honey, really . . . we wouldn't be comfortable at the party. We'll enjoy it more on the TV. You go. We'll watch for you on the TV."

Grace left the room. "Don't be too late," her father called after her. "Get back here as soon as it's over."

In the hallway mirror she examined her cocktail dress. It was last year's. No one was wearing green this year. Or satin. Maybe she should do a Buffy Weiss. Wear jeans. She laughed as she thought of herself skipping into the party dressed super-freako, jeans and a T-shirt, no bra. Nothing unfashionable about that. Not with her breasts. She might even steal the show from Jeannie Danton. If her parents weren't watching on TV she might try to work up the courage to do it. Just to see what reaction she'd get from all those celebrities who didn't have as much up front as she did. Even Jeannie Danton, she was sure, didn't measure 40-D.

From the television set in the living room she heard a fanfare, then the voice of Spats Johnson identifying John

Malloy. A tingle of excitement went through her. The Malloy family had been her heroes since high school, her ideal of what an American family should be. She was only fourteen when Secretary of State Mark Malloy was killed in that ski accident that some people still insisted was no accident. But she remembered his elegance and style, his wit, the masterful way he conducted his news conferences (to which she had listened on her transistor radio when her girl friends were listening to the latest dee-jay). Henry Kissinger might have been a more adroit manipulator of people and nations, but no one could compare with Mark Malloy, not even that paradigm of elegance and style, the late John F. Kennedy himself.

Nor was there anyone to compare with Mark's brother, Luke. The fiery young senator had done more for the people in four years than the other ninety-nine of that august body's grafters and old windbags combined. And now John Malloy, at thirty, was about to launch his own senate campaign—in New York rather than having to battle his brother's senior colleague in their home state of Connecticut. She had written a letter volunteering to work on his campaign the very day she read the *Times* story about his likely candidacy, and within a week she'd received a reply from his chief of staff thanking her for her interest and promising to be in touch if and when a committee was organized. Now—think of it!—she was living in the very same building. Why? Because a patriotic and conscientious ex-football player named Ted Vassily had decided to help create a microcosm of the melting pot, to construct at least a piece of the American Dream here and now. Corny as it might sound to some people, including her cynical friends, to her it helped restore a young person's faith in America. Malloy and Vassily . . . what a ticket *that* would be . . . and here she was about to meet them and their people. . . .

She looked again in the mirror at her year-old green satin dress with its unstylish empire waist and the little-girl puffy sleeves with lace cuffs. She wished she had something more elegant, more sophisticated, but damn it, if 305 East was what it claimed to be—if the whole egalitarian thing wasn't a fraud dreamed up by p.r. types—it shouldn't matter.

Trying to psyche herself into feeling more confident than she did, she strode to the elevator and pressed the lobby button. Half a dozen men in tuxedos were waiting in the foyer. One of them who had a goatee and seemed big as a house smiled and executed a small bow as she approached. "May I see your invitation please?"

She handed it to him.

He glanced at it, then looked up at her and smiled again. "Hey, aren't you Grace Colello?"

She did a double take. "Do we know each other?"

"Your name's on the invitation." Laughing, he offered his hand. "I'm Nate Elefante, the building superintendent. Some people call me 'Nasty Nate.' But I couldn't be nasty to a sweetheart like you. If you ever need anything, just let me know."

He ushered her into the lobby and motioned to a white-jacketed waiter, who hurried over with a tray of champagne. Another waiter materialized with a tray of crackers and caviar.

"Will your husband be joining you later, Mrs. Colello?" Nate asked.

She smiled. "I'm not married."

"Really?" He pantomimed twirling a handlebar moustache. "Well, let me give you a tour of the building. Starting with my apartment. Seriously, come in and enjoy the party. I'll introduce you around. . . . Here's the architect of Three-oh-five East. Just because his name is Axel, he thinks he's a big wheel. . . ."

Nate left her with Axel Wessman, who asked the usual polite questions about where she was from and what line of work she was in. She told him she loved his building, and they agreed it was a lovely party. Then someone else greeted him, he excused himself, and she was alone.

She looked self-consciously around the lobby and wished the superintendent hadn't left. Everyone seemed to be with someone else, either in couples or groups. Why hadn't she had the foresight to invite a girl friend? At least she'd have someone to talk to.

She spotted a man looking at her from a dozen yards away. She smiled tentatively, he smiled back, then turned to a woman in his group and that was the end of it.

She looked around again and saw—no one. The sense

of isolation was scary. She felt like a clown in her year-old green dress. Maybe if she had another champagne she'd relax. Luckily one of the waiters was nearby. She gestured, and he hurried over to exchange her glass.

"You wanna see a pair?" Nate asked Ted, who was admiring Jeannie Danton.

"I see them!"

"I've got another pair for you, just brought her in. Real nice chick, the down-home type. And she's unattached. I left her with Axel for safekeeping."

Ted peered through the crowd. "Green dress?"

"That's the one. Name is Grace Colello." Nate jabbed him in the ribs. "Go to it, my man."

Ted started across the room. A short, slim, dapper man of forty in a flaming red dinner jacket blocked his path. "Real ass-farm you've got here, my friend."

Ted tried to get around him.

The man extended his hand. "Wattley's the name. Stoney to friends. I'm one of your tenants. Just wanna tell you, good show, fellow. Good show."

"Thanks," Ted said, "good to meet you." He tried to take his hand back.

Wattley didn't release it. "Wanna tell you something else, my friend. If you don't get more ass than a toilet seat, you should forgive the expression, you're not the Ted Vassily I used to read about. *This* is a full scale ass-farm, my friend. Full scale."

Wattley, Ted realized, was drunk. He also was—the name finally rang a bell—one Stonington Wattley, M.D., the very social plastic surgeon. "Thanks, doctor," Ted said, trying again to retrieve his hand.

"Ah, recognition!" Wattley beamed. "Damned heads-up of you, Vassily." He weaved slightly, then smiled. "I may be a little stinko tonight—but don't worry, I'm sober as a judge in the operating room. Come to think of it, that's not the best reassurance in the world, is it? I know some bench warmers who knock it back pretty good, and then have the nerve to sentence some poor wino to thirty days on a drunk-and-disorderly . . ."

"Pleasure meeting you, doctor." Ted managed to free his hand. "See you around."

"Stoney to friends," Wattley called after him. "Remember that."

Ted looked for Nate's discovery in the green dress. She was alone now, and Ted noted with pleasure that Nate had made a good call, especially on the breasts, though the rest was a little heavier than Ted preferred.

Ted started toward her, then hesitated, searching for an opening line. It annoyed him that after all this time he still felt awkward approaching a girl cold. But he always had, and it was even worse in recent years, particularly with the younger ones.

Oh, now, for God's sake, Vassily, he told himself, don't let this stupid thing out-psyche you again. Just march on over and say hello and ask if she's having a nice time. After all, you've got a legitimate interest. It's your building!

He started again toward her and found his way blocked by the Malloy family. "Ted," John said, "I've looked forward to this meeting for a long time."

Ted shook hands with the father, mother and son and exchanged the chitchat of a first meeting with people he'd known and who had known him through the newspapers for years. He paid more attention to the feel of the conversation than to the words. The feel was good.

Ted liked John Malloy. The would-be senator was articulate and bright—more of either than one would expect from a politician. Malloy also had the good taste not to lay on the bullshit, either about Ted's career or about what a wonderful humanitarian thing 305 East was. And, of course, there would always remain the fact that on the day when the first press release about 305 East made the papers, John Malloy called from Florida to pledge financial as well as moral support and to reserve an apartment. With the Ron-Cor money, Ted hadn't had to take advantage of the financial support, but it had been good to know it was there.

He also liked Peg Malloy, though he couldn't pinpoint why. She had a kind of fragile quality that he found engaging. She wasn't as pretty as in her pictures and she came across considerably older, but there was a brain behind the pretty blue eyes—not a cunt-o brain à la Buffy Weiss, forever cooking up a new assault on your balls, but a quiet supportive sort, the kind a guy should have on his side, the kind Ted had had on his side with Chris . . . or was he reading things into Peg Malloy? Looking too hard for what he'd lost . . . ?

One thing he wasn't reading into her was interest in him. There was no mistaking it. You didn't play the game as long as he had without at least learning to recognize that much from a woman's eyes. He wondered why she let herself come across that way to someone who had strong reason to be loyal to her husband. Whatever the case, he wasn't about to follow up. You don't fuck with a friend's wife—even a potential friend's wife. Not to mention early supporter.

The building chitchat inevitably gave way to football chitchat and the promise to throw a few long ones to Johnny Malloy some afternoon. "An ex-quarterback I know tells me you can thread a needle at seventy yards," said Johnny.

"These days," said Ted, "I'd be lucky to mail a ball seventy yards."

They all laughed and the Malloys said their goodbyes, John adding, "We'd love to have you over for dinner soon."

As they moved away Ted made another start toward where the green-dress lady had been. Only now she wasn't there. . . . He finally spotted her near the bandstand talking to some guy her own age. He sighed, scanned the room for another suitable target and drew a blank. Maybe he'd get to Spats Johnson after the telecast and find out if any of that show business action was available.

Hartford Loomis, finally managing to break away from the bore who'd been holding him captive, surveyed the lobby for his wife, son and daughter. He saw young Hart over by the bandstand talking to one of the starlet types. Like father, like son . . . matter of fact, young Hart seemed considerably better at it than he himself had ever been. God . . . the boy's last girl friend, that little number from New Canaan, was an absolute knockout. . . . Did his wife Ellie, he wondered, have any notion how many of his hard-ons had been inspired by conjuring up images of that little lady's hips shaped snugly in her jeans, the crotch seam pulled so tight he could actually make out the flesh of her labia? And how often he'd thought of getting something like that for himself? . . .

But thinking was all he'd done so far. The fact was, he was now at an age and station where the pursuit of sex was less an adventure than an inconvenience. The chairman and chief executive officer of the Bank of the United States simply did not roam the corridors, tweaking secretaries' asses. Nor did a man who loved his wife and family risk embarrassing them by playing around too close to home. Eliminate the office and the apartment building as locales for recruiting, and what was left? Years ago there was always the possibility of spontaneously striking up something with a girl at a party, taking her phone number, pursuing a clandestine affair on evenings when one was supposedly out of town or working late at the office. But with each passing year fewer girls responded to his passing smiles.

In fact, over the past ten years he'd managed the grand total of exactly one affair, a rather insipid one at that, with a thirty-fivish executive secretary from the bank's advertising agency. All the rest of his extramarital action had been with call girls who, their Sutton Place addresses notwithstanding, were still prostitutes. They actually dulled his appetite for variety. Even the youngest of them—eighteen, one barely seventeen—conveyed a weariness that bled the experience. Even those hired for the whole night somehow always seemed to be clock-watching. And none of them was attractive in the set-your-heart-pounding fashion of his son's little dish from New Canaan or the magnificently endowed girl in the green dress Hart Jr. was speaking to now. Or, say, Jeannie Danton.

Jeannie Danton. The whorishness of her, combined with her fantastic looks and body, was capable of triggering any man's fantasies. As no doubt they did for the people who went to her movies. He'd seen most of them, and he was not a steady moviegoer. The most exciting scene he'd ever witnessed on film was her first nude scene.

It was in a quickie potboiler about an adolescent boy's introduction to sex. Jeannie Danton played the high school bitch all the adolescents considered untouchable. Eventually she consented to a date with Our Hero and took him off to her favorite secluded beach, wearing a bulky terrycloth T-shirt so viewers couldn't be certain what she had on underneath . . . The boy strips to his swim trunks, pan to Jeannie nonchalantly lifting T-shirt, tits popping out at the audience. Camera stays close-up as she tosses the shirt aside. "Well," she says as much to the audience as to the boy, "didn't you ever see a girl's breasts before?" . . .

Seeing those marvelous boobs, in effect pushed right at him through the lens, had been powerfully arousing. The sluttishness of the girl, taunting, flaunting, challenging the viewer to take her sexuality, daring him to find an enterprise too wanton for her, too depraved . . .

Was he projecting? He smiled to himself. Maybe so. Maybe she was merely spaced out on dope and didn't even know where the camera was. Whatever, there was a fantastic sexual spark inside that girl, a mechanism that never stopped working its effect, never mind the setting or the audience.

Seeing her tonight he felt it even more. He wondered what it would take to get her into bed. How much would he pay for a complete no-clock-watching full night, for a literally once-in-a-lifetime experience? Certainly many men had spent tens of thousands over a period of time in anticipation of such an experience and wound up with only cock in hand? The rub, of course, was that it couldn't be guaranteed. If anything could, it was that the experience would fall short of expectations. It had to be noncommercial. Still, maybe a night with Jeannie Danton would be its own reward even if she did clock-watch . . . if, that is, he could ever happen on some way to arrange it. . . .

He surveyed the lobby again and felt a twinge of discomfort as he noticed his daughter Nan talking to the building superintendent, that huge fellow with the goatee. His Nan was radiant tonight, her brown eyes sparkling, the TV lights finding subtle amber and chestnut accents in her billowy soft shoulder-length hair. Her dress was casual-elegant, shorter than most girls now were wearing, sheer enough on top to show the clear outline of her breasts, yet not vulgar. No question, his Nan could hold her own with the bandstand chippie and Hart Jr.'s New Canaan piece. Maybe Jeannie Danton, too . . . and though logic told Hart he should not wish it to be otherwise—he should, in fact, be happy that she was so attractive and thus able to arouse the interest of men she found desirable —it still upset him to think of other men looking at her the way . . . well, the way, for example, he looked at other girls her age . . .

"Real ass-farm, right?"

Hartford Loomis almost literally jumped at the sound of the voice beside him and turned to find a short, slim, dapper man of forty in a flaming red dinner jacket.

"More ass here than in the proctology ward at Bellevue," the man said. "Hey, you're Hartford Loomis."

Loomis found himself assuming his frostiest banker's air. "I beg your pardon?"

"Recognize you from your picture. Nice piece about you a few Sundays ago in the *Times*. Wattley's the name. Stoney to friends. I guess we're neighbors."

"Ah—I guess so," Loomis managed.

"I'll tell you something, Loomis, you want ass, get out of banking. Be a plastic surgeon. All sorts try to bed you for a free operation—a nose job, silicone for the tits, whatever . . . of course there are disadvantages . . . mainly, you're always dealing with flawed merchandise. Except you transform it into perfect merchandise. So if you can handle the preliminary stage it can be damn gratifying at the finale—makes you feel like God and superstud combined. . . ."

"Ah, yes, excuse me, someone I have to talk to." He slipped away from Wattley and with great relief spotted his wife, her brother Ben and Ben's wife talking to the Lloyd Jordans of Connecticut Casualty.

"Hart," said Ben as he approached, "I was telling Lloyd that you and he are probably the only two families in this place that aren't card-carrying flaming liberals. You're going to feel mighty lonely after a while."

Loomis smiled. "On the other hand, there could be advantages. Maybe those college kids who've been picketing us about our holdings in South Africa will think I've had a change of heart and start bothering George Moore and David Rockefeller."

Lloyd laughed. "Let the Dow drop another two hundred points and the little bastards won't be bothering anybody."

Loomis winced at the prospect of the further drop in the market and gestured to a waiter, who produced a tray bearing champagne.

"Damned good," said Ben, sipping his. "Any idea what it is?"

"Taittinger Comte de Champagne Sixty-nine," Lloyd said. "I asked a waiter."

"Are you serious? That stuff goes for damn near thirty a bottle."

"Can you imagine serving it at an affair this size?"

Loomis smiled. "Enjoy, Lloyd. We're paying for it."

The band sounded a fanfare, then broke into the up-tempo jazz-waltz from *Broadway Fandango*. "Joseph Williams," they all said, nearly as one.

Buffy Weiss watched on the nearest TV monitor as Joseph Williams moved into the picture with Spats Johnson. It irritated her that she had not heard from him after that Sunday morning in his apartment when she introduced him to 305 East. Not that she wanted to fuck him again. Not that she even wanted to see him, pompous ass that he was. But simple courtesy should have dictated a phone call, if for no other reason than to report he'd gone ahead with his plans to move into 305 East and to ask about her plans. But expecting courtesy from a New York male these days was like expecting the Second Coming. It occurred to her that of late she was getting to be the girl least likely to be called back . . . first Williams, now Vassily . . . the bastards . . .

She emptied her champagne glass and took a fresh one from the waiter who materialized genielike alongside her. Speaking of Ted Vassily, he really should have phoned to apologize for that awful ending to their last night together. . . . She suddenly realized she was standing only a few feet from the couch where she had laid him that afternoon. . . . "We'll make this our special table and love seat. . . ." The damn cornball . . . she should find somebody else to fuck there, then make sure Vassily found out about it.

A blue-haired lady wearing too much jewelry was now sitting on the special couch and apparently thought Buffy had been looking at her. The lady smiled as if about to speak, and Buffy quickly turned away. The last thing she needed now was a verbal hand-job from a middle-aged sympathizer who admired all Buffy had done for womankind—or, worse, a sermon from one of those douche bags who felt a woman's place was in the home. Fact was, what Buffy really needed now was a guy to get her juices flowing. She'd expected there'd be at least a few prospects at the party, but pickings were unbelievably slim. Vassily—or someone—had seen to it that the place was loaded with cunt, but the only guys around were married *and* with their wives, or adolescents, or creeps like that character in the red jacket, Stoney Wattley, who slobbered over her till she thought she'd upchuck.

Now that she'd done her spot on TV, she told herself, she ought to cut out. Head up to Elaine's or someplace. Find a decent cock for the night. Or go back to the apartment and get some work done. No, she wasn't in a work mood tonight. It was a damn shame there was no one here suitable for instant fucking. She just couldn't get herself interested in guys like the banker Hartford Loomis, who'd been eyeing her earlier. If she could bring herself to it, it might be amusing to do a guy like that, get him hooked and then con him into donating a few million to her South Dakota Fourteen Defense Fund. She wondered what Loomis was doing living in 305 East. Was he a closet liberal?

Too bad, too, that she couldn't bring herself to fuck one of the football meatheads just to show Vassily that he wasn't all that damn special. Not Elefante, of course; that would backfire because it was so obvious. But maybe Emerson Wade. Or Walt Kulikowski. Yes, Kulikowski would be perfect. She could imagine the expression on Ted Vassily's face if he saw her with his *doorman*. . . . Unfortunately this whole line of thought was academic because none of them in any way appealed to her.

Oh, well, if you're not getting any dicking you might as well do some business. She noticed John Malloy and his wife and son handshaking with two middle-aged couples. Might as well go over and introduce herself. Malloy would certainly want her support in his senate race. Now was a good time to let him know he wouldn't get it automatically, he'd have to come up with something in return—maybe something for the poor Indians, or at least for a poor-people's advocate named Buffy Weiss.

Nan Loomis watched on the nearest TV monitor as Joseph Williams moved into the picture with Spats Johnson.

"He's the musical director of the New York Symphony Orchestra," Nate Elefante told her.

"I know," she said.

Nate seemed disappointed that his words weren't a revelation to her. "He was one of our first tenants."

"Really?" Nan immediately felt bad, even guilty, about disappointing him and searched for something to make him feel better. "You must have been with the building from the very beginning to know that."

"I was. The *very* beginning, even before Ted Vassily decided where to build it. I helped him select the site. You know, the old T-Bone and I go a ways back together."

"Did you play football with him?"

"Did I play football with him! Honey, I was his best blocker. Originally I used to play defense, I was all-pro on defense, but old Ted and me were such good buddies I converted to offense so I could block for him. We've been best friends ever since."

"It must be very gratifying to have a friendship like that."

"Oh, it is. Particularly with a guy like Ted Vassily. I wanna tell you, there's never been a man like him. You'll see for yourself when you meet him. In fact, I'll introduce you." He hesitated. "You're not engaged or anything, are you?"

She smiled. "Not at the moment."

"Hey, well great. I'll see if I can find him and introduce you." He started away.

She touched his arm to restrain him. "You don't have to do it right now."

"Hey, I don't mind."

"But he might be busy—"

"He won't be too busy to meet you."

"Please, Nate." She increased her pressure on his arm. "I mean, I'd like very much to meet your friend eventually but I really don't like to be . . . well, fixed-up. I prefer to let things happen naturally—"

"Of course, of course." He kept nodding agreement as

he backed out of her reach. "I'll just see if he's around anyway. No sweat, no obligations, just an introduction. Believe me."

She watched him vanish into the crowd and wished she could somehow learn to avoid situations like this. Trouble was, she was always so damn terrified of hurting the other person's feelings, especially if it was a man . . . almost any man . . . and to avoid it she'd say yes to almost anything. She had dated so many men for just that reason . . . men she didn't even particularly like. And because she still couldn't bring herself to say no there'd be a second date and a third and then the guy would be making demands on her time, wanting her to date him exclusively, wanting to control her life, and she *still* couldn't bring herself to say no. So she'd run. Which, of course, would hurt him even more than if she'd said no in the first place. She knew the pattern, but she didn't seem able to change it.

What had happened with Bob was a good example. She should have backed off . . . backed him off . . . the first time he kissed her. She should have told him right away that she didn't want to get involved with someone she worked with, especially when he was also a *married* man. But somehow she just couldn't . . . it seemed so, well, unfriendly, so . . . rude. Particularly when she couldn't be absolutely certain that he was really coming on to her. It could, after all, have been just a friendly thing on his part, just a, well, fatherly sort of kiss. So she'd kissed him back and the kisses got more intense and she couldn't reasonably resist now because she'd accepted the earlier ones—that would make her, well, a *tease* . . . so they kissed some more and then they were petting and then they were in bed.

Which in itself didn't really make her feel bad. She never could accept the line most girls drew between coitus and the other sex acts. What did it matter, really, if a guy put his finger or his penis in your vagina? So she wasn't at all hung up about "making love" to a guy, even if she didn't like him all that much. The problem was, when she did, it somehow changed the relationship for the worse.

That too had happened with Bob, an airline captain. For a while he seemed content to see her only when they both happened to be at their Kansas City base. But then he began pressuring her to bid for his flights. And pretty soon after that he started talking about leaving his wife. And she didn't *want* that. God . . . she didn't want *any* of that.

Her father would say that Bob had planned things from the very beginning, that all the men who pressured her into doing things had planned it that way. He told her how he used the technique himself in business. "The old salami game," he called it. "You start by taking a very thin slice, one so small that the opposition doesn't consider it worth fighting for. Then you take another, no bigger, and they won't fight over that either. The more slices you take, the more you condition them not to fight. And pretty soon you wind up with all the salami and they're left holding the string."

Yes, her father would say Bob deliberately, callously exploited her. But even if that were true, which was by no means certain, she would not let the experience sour her. In future situations she would still try her best to give people the benefit of the doubt. After all, to do otherwise would make her a cynic—just like her father.

Still, she wished she were at least more skillful at saying no, as when her father suggested that she live in 305 East. It wasn't that she didn't love and want to be near him, and of course her mother and brother. When she'd decided she had to get away from Bob, she'd chosen New York as her base specifically because she wanted to be near her family. But not *this* near, not just a few floors away. And yet she couldn't bring herself to refuse the apartment her father wanted to rent for her. How could she refuse when he looked at her that way and she saw how much he wanted her to have it?

It was the same even with that building superintendent. She'd been so afraid of hurting his feelings that she'd tried overly hard to make him feel good. Somewhere along the line he'd mistaken her courteous expressions of interest and too polite reluctance as meaning she really *did* want to meet Ted Vassily. Now, nothing she could say would discourage him.

Not that meeting Ted Vassily was such a terrible prospect. She'd never gone out with a professional football player. It might be interesting. He certainly was good looking. If she happened to be walking through the lobby some afternoon and he happened to be walking the other way, and if he smiled and said hello, well . . . she would probably enjoy talking with him, and if things just naturally led to an actual date, well, fine. But she didn't want to feel she was under pressure when she met him—or anyone else. All of which meant she had better not be here when the superintendent returned.

She located her brother near the huge reproduction of the cover of *Time* talking to a girl in a green dress. She hoped Hart wouldn't mind her joining them. Maybe if the superintendent saw she was not alone . . .

Eddie Spats Johnson watched the red light on the TV camera go out, then hurried into the washroom behind the blowup of the *Time* cover. He tore off his jacket, tie, shirt and T-shirt while his man Marco tied an apron around his waist. He raised his arms as Marco and Marco's assistant, Link, scrubbed him with wet sponges.

"You los' fifteen pounds tonight fo' sure," Marco observed.

Spats laughed. "No way, man. That'd put me five in the hole."

His acolytes laughed on cue, tossed their sponges into the sink and started rubbing him with Turkish towels. The large clock over the door said that seventeen seconds had expired.

"Yo' workin' very hard tonight, Little Spats," said Link.

Spats smiled as they discarded the Turkish towels and splashed his body with cologne. No question he was working his ass off tonight. Thirteen minutes on, two for commercials, thirteen on again, right down the line. In the studio it was six-and-a-half to one, which despite involving the same total of on-camera minutes was much easier. Also, of course, in the studio, except for the few times he got up to do a number with the band or with one of the guests, he spent his time sitting at a desk. Tonight he'd been hopping around like a damn monkey right from the beginning, hopping as he hadn't since the old saloon days with dad and the band. It was exhilarating, but it was also exhausting.

"Okay, Little Spats." Marco slapped him on the shoulder, signaling the end of the cologne rub as Link handed him a fresh T-shirt. Spats pulled it over his head, then stepped into the fresh dress shirt Marco was holding for him. People who noticed that he changed outfits several times during a show often considered it an affectation, part of his old ditty-bop thing. They ought to try standing under fifty thousand watts of klieg lights for two hours and see how it feels.

Besides, Spats couldn't bear to be unclean—and he didn't know how anyone could bear it. Just the thought of perspiration odor made him uncomfortable. Maybe, as a college chick he used to date once told him, he was overreacting to those long-ago years on the road when he was lucky if he got a chance to bathe once a week and people always seemed to be turning their noses away when he walked past. Maybe. But overreact or underreact, he liked to be *clean*. And now that he had a few beanies, goddamn it, he intended to stay clean. If he were down to his last twenty cents he'd probably spend it on a bar of soap.

Marco slipped a tie into place under Spats' starched pink collar as Link buttoned the front of his shirt, then knotted his tie while Marco fastened his cuff links. Spats shucked his trousers and shorts, stepped into a fresh set, tucked in his shirt and backed into the sports jacket Marco was holding.

"Hey, we jus' done it in record time," said Link.

Spats looked at the clock. Thirty-two seconds had passed. He dabbed his face with a wet towel, again with a dry one, then ran a brush through his hair and stepped onto the set. The floor director clipped a wireless lavalier microphone to his tie. "All set on the bandstand, Spats. We'll pick you up here and pan with you. You've got thirty-six seconds."

Spats glanced past the cameras, saw the girl in red and did a double take. Now *that* was a *Clean*. That was a *super*-Clean. He guessed her age at twenty-one or twenty-two, probably a college kid. Lush brown shoulder-length hair, lovely smile. *And* she was beautiful. Not in the plastic fashion of those damn actress-models but in the super-clean way of a college cheerleader. Nothing fragile or phony about those kids. None of that be-careful-you'll-spoil-my-hairdo horseshit. You probably could grab one, eat her cunt till you drove her crazy, then fuck her ass off and when you finally got off her she'd look as fresh and ready to go as when you started. *That* was a clean fuck.

And Miss Red Dress had it. Along with a body . . . slight build but no sharp angles . . . all soft and curved. And magnificent boobs, without a bra. Her dress was conservative enough so that she didn't come across slutty, even though you had no trouble making out the contours.

She had, in a word, class. The kind that said old money, good breeding, the right schools, the whole shmear. The kind that could keep him in round-the-clock hard-ons.

Of course that kind of class did not very often have—or in any event give in to—an interest in crossing the, ahem, racial barrier. But as they said about Babe Ruth, he didn't get to be a home run king by standing there with his bat on his shoulder. You gotta swing.

"Merrill," he told the floor director, "I'm gonna do a minute or two in the crowd before we go to the bandstand."

"Jeez, Spats, we're running pretty tight."

"We'll squeeze the rest of the celebs if we have to. Give me a hand mike."

They got one to him just as the floor director signaled on-the-air. "Hey, there," said Spats, beaming at the camera with the red light, "we're at the party of the year, celebrating the grand opening of New York's most talked-about apartment building, Three-oh-five East. And right now we're going to talk to some of the people who've come to celebrate with us." He walked into the audience, looked around as if searching for a suitable subject, then pushed his hand mike toward the girl in red. "Hi, there, what's your name?"

She blushed. "Nan Loomis."

"How are you enjoying the party?"

"It's nice."

"Do you live in Three-oh-five East?"

"Yes."

"You really dig long answers, don't you?" The crowd around them dutifully chuckled.

"Yes," she replied, blushing again.

"Are you married?"

"No."

"What's your apartment number?"

She hesitated.

He peered into the camera lens and did a Groucho Marx thing with his eyebrows. "Better yet, what's your phone number?"

She smiled. "I haven't had it installed yet."

"Very good answer, young lady. And I'm sure several million viewers are sorry to hear it."

That was as good an exit line as any. Besides, he had enough information to track her down later. Now to give the audience bit legitimacy by saying hello to a few more people. He looked around. A guy in a red dinner jacket was at his left staring at Nan Loomis as if he'd been hypnotized. Spats could tell from the way the dude was weaving that he'd had a taste too many. "Hello, there," he said, pushing the mike at him. "How are you enjoying the party?"

"Regular ass-farm," the guy muttered.

"Class, you say?" replied Spats, and pulled the mike away. "Yes, a classy party indeed . . . and here's a classy young lady in a classy green dress . . . hello, there, what's your name?"

"Grace Colello."

"How are you enjoying the party?"

"I'm having a wonderful time."

"Do you live in Three-oh-five East?"

"Yes, I do."

"Another young lady who likes short answers. On the other hand I'd rather short answers from you than long answers from our previous guest. Are you married, Grace Colello?"

"No, I'm not. I live with my parents."

"Are they here at the party?"

"No, they're watching on television."

Spats peered into the lens. "Mr. and Mrs. Colello, how can you possibly stay upstairs watching while such a great party is going on in your lobby?"

"They enjoy your show so much, Mr. Johnson, they wouldn't dream of missing it."

"Now that's what I call loyal fans. Thanks heaps, Mr.

and Mrs. Colello. What line of work are you in, Grace?"

"I'm a student at C.C.N.Y."

"And your folks?"

"My father drives a laundry truck. My mother is a clerk at an insurance company."

Spats' eyes met hers, and he wondered if she felt the hurt he would feel if he were in her place. He hadn't intended to embarrass her with the question. He figured she'd say the old man was president of G.E. or something like that.

But if she was embarrassed she did a fine job of hiding it. "Well, that's Three-oh-five East for you," he said lamely, realizing only after he'd said it that it made the whole bit sound even worse. Time to bail out. "Okay, folks, now for some music. Grace Colello, this song is for you, and for my good friends Mr. and Mrs. Colello, and for Miss Nan Loomis and Mr. Ted Vassily, a class gent, and all the rest of you. I'll just amble over to the bandstand right now and play some clarinet with the greatest Dixieland band ever to come up the Mississippi . . . Mr. Eddie Spats Johnson Senior and his Bourbon Street All-Stars . . ."

Burr Whiteside allowed himself a smile as the image on the TV monitor cut to the Dixieland group on the bandstand. "I'd like to take credit for setting that up, T-bone, but I had nothing to do with it."

Ted looked at him uncomprehendingly. "His father's band?"

"No, buddy, the laundry-truck driver's daughter."

"I thought it was pretty crass myself. Probably embarrassed the hell out of her. To say nothing of her folks."

"Well, anyway, I didn't set it up. It probably was spontaneous on Spats' part. There's nothing in the script about it . . . still, you've got to admit it's pretty good p.r."

Ted shook his head and walked away. He wanted a closer look at that girl in the red dress—what was her name—Nan Loomis? Probably Hartford Loomis's daughter, with her own separate apartment in 305. As he approached, she seemed to be alone, but when he got nearer he saw she was talking with the asshole in the red dinner jacket, Stonington Wattley. About to change course, he noticed that the just-identified Grace Colello was apparently looking at him. He smiled and nodded. Once he understood a girl was actually checking him out he wasn't so damn uneasy about approaching her. "Hi, Grace Colello," he said, "I'm Ted Vassily."

"Yes, I recognize you." She extended her hand. "Hey—you recognized me too. From the TV thing." She laughed. "So that's what it feels like! Public recognition, I mean."

"Good or bad?"

"Well, good. Sort of. Strange, too."

And now? He hated this part of the routine. He hated the first words. Either you asked stupid questions she didn't want to answer, or vice-versa. Or both. In any case the words were horseshit. And unless you went through with the exchange you didn't get to know the lady. Which meant, barring extraordinary circumstances, you didn't get to bed her.

"How are you enjoying the party, Grace?" Couldn't he manage something better than that? It was the exact question Spats had asked her on TV.

"It's lovely."

He waited for her to say something else. She didn't. He found himself straightening his tie. He knew he was making her uncomfortable too, but he couldn't help it. He just didn't have a talent . . . or a tolerance . . . for glib horseshit. "What's your major at City?" Good thing she was in college. What the hell would he ask if she were a secretary? How fast do you type?

"Political science."

He waited for something else. Again, nothing. He found himself clenching his fists. Was she answering in near-monosyllables because she wasn't interested? Or was she just nervous? He would try once more. Then, great tits or no, if she didn't make it easier for him, well, fuck her. Or rather don't fuck her. . . . "What do you think of Three-oh-five?"

"It's lovely, I like it very much."

He waited. Nothing. He almost burst out laughing as he said silently, Then go fuck yourself. Instead he managed a small smile and said, "If you ever need anything, let me know. I'm in penthouse east." He turned and started away.

"Mr. Vassily?"

He turned back.

She smiled hesitantly. "Please don't think I'm being deliberately standoffish. I'm not trying to be. It's just that at first I sometimes have a hard time being spontaneous with people." She came up closer to him. "I really do admire what you've done here."

Which was more like it. Feeling considerably bolder, he thanked her and asked if she'd like to see the view from his penthouse.

She hesitated only an instant. Then— "Love to." And thought, oh God, here I go again.

He couldn't quite believe she had agreed so quickly, but he wasn't about to give her time to reconsider. He led her to the east bank of elevators and inserted his key in the penthouse slot.

"You know, naïve as it may sound, I've actually never been in a penthouse before," she said as the car shot upward. "When I was a kid I heard that golden oldie 'Penthouse Serenade' and had no idea what the word meant. Finally I looked it up in the dictionary, which defined it as a house built on the roof of an apartment building."

"I think that's originally what penthouses were. Then builders started applying the term to an apartment that took up the entire top floor. Now, of course, they talk about 'penthouse apartments' plural, meaning an ordinary apartment on the top floor. Which is kind of silly."

She smiled. "Devaluation of the language. Like Hollywood calling nearly every movie 'sensational' and 'spectacular' and 'colossal' and finally 'super-colossal.' Or calling the regular size of soapsuds 'giant' and the large size 'super.' Eventually the words lose their meaning."

He nodded, and waited. . . . "Right, I agree," he prodded. She still said nothing more. "Anyway, in Three-oh-five East, a penthouse is still a penthouse. At least in the sense of occupying the entire top floor of the tower it's located in."

Grace smiled and hoped he would keep talking. It really irritated her that she was not better at small talk. And he was trying so hard to make it easy for her! She felt both foolish and a little panicky. She hoped he wouldn't get too impatient with her—as he almost did when he started walking away before she called him back and apologized. She had meant the apology too. But now here she was doing the same old silent number again! "Uh, 'major motion picture'," she said when it became obvious that he had said all he was going to about penthouse apartments.

"What?"

She felt her smile slipping away. ". . . I just thought of another ludicrous example of language escalation. You know how they put on the advertisements for books—'Soon to be a major motion picture'? I've often thought, what would they write if the book were going to be a minor motion picture? Or aren't there any minor motion pictures?"

He laughed. "They ought to try it, just for the hell of it. I'd buy it."

She echoed his laugh. But *now* what to say? She devoutly wished she'd long ago worked up some sort of all-occasions dialogue that could get her through these situations. She waited for him to say something. He clearly wasn't stupid. So why did he seem so awkward with her? Surely he wasn't bashful about being with a new girl—not with all the experience he must have had. Unless she just turned him off and he was only being polite. . . .

Still he said nothing! Was this damn elevator going to take forever to reach the top floor? At least once they got there she could carry on about how terrific his apartment was. . . .

And *still* nothing. "Who lives in the other three penthouses?" she asked, feeling desperate.

He actually seemed relieved at being asked a question. "Penthouse West is Eddie Spats Johnson. North is Hartford Loomis, president of BankUS. South is a man named Mandino."

Silence.

"Are they all the same? The apartments, I mean." Stupid question, but at least a question.

"No. Every apartment in the building was custom-designed."

Silence. Was the elevator going to just keep going up till it was in orbit? Their eyes met—in an elevator how could you avoid it?—and she smiled. It was that or scream.

He smiled back. "You know," he said after another awkward moment, "I'd very much like to kiss you," and inwardly he groaned. Jesus, Vassily, can't you do better than that!?

"That might be nice," she said, and wished she could have managed something better.

She turned her face up to meet him. Her mouth opened. He eased his tongue inside, grateful she accepted it, pleased and surprised as he felt her sucking gently on it.

Suddenly he felt very relaxed and very relieved. Interesting how physical contact could put him at ease. Well, the physical was what he had down cold. It was the verbal horseshit that he'd never mastered.

He enjoyed the cushiony soft feel of her lips and the comfortable, knowing way she moved her face against his. Did he dare risk going for her breast? Why not? Keep running the play till they stop it (and try to block those football metaphors, he silently instructed himself, realizing that it was probably a losing battle).

He eased his hand up her side as she leaned against him with her arms over his shoulders. He let his thumb linger for a moment at the base of her breast, and when she didn't ease off he slid it upward. She still didn't ease off, and now his entire thumb and the heel of his palm were over her breast—there was certainly no possible way she could interpret it as an accidental brush. And still she didn't back away. He brought his entire hand over and made a gentle caressing movement, and when this was accepted he brought his free hand to her other breast, giving both of them a firm squeeze.

They were, he found himself thinking as his heartbeat suddenly became audible to him, incredibly, wonderfully huge. And though she was wearing a bra there was no mistaking the full natural firmness underneath.

The elevator slowed and he considered releasing her, then decided to wait for her to make the move. She stayed right with him. He felt something beyond gratitude, an instant genuine affection toward her for allowing him all this absolutely hassle-free. A truly *nice* chick. What a chick should really be like. . . .

He felt the elevator come to a halt. The doors opened.

He still did not release her. She continued to kiss him, then after a long moment backed away.

"I . . . I didn't want the doors to close on us." She felt the need to explain.

"They wouldn't have. As long as the key stays in, they stay open. Anyway, *voilà.*"

She preceded him into the apartment, surprised that the elevator opened directly into his foyer. She had expected some sort of hallway and another door. "It's beautiful," she said, almost sighing as she looked across a multilevel expanse of rooms without walls. The foyer itself was bigger than her bedroom. Two stairs led down into the largest of the rooms. On one side was a sort of walkway, a yard wide. On the other were a second sitting area, about half the size of the first, then two steps up from that a dining area. Opposite her was a third sitting area, higher than even the dining area, up against a wall that was entirely window, the drapes open, the brightly moonlit sky so unexpectedly vivid that it seemed unreal, like something at the Hayden Planetarium. "Is it *ever* beautiful," she said.

"I'm glad you like it." Ted led her into the sunken section. "Ever since I designed it I've wanted to share it with someone special. I'm glad you're the first lady to see it."

"Why me?" Even as she asked the question she felt silly about it. Still, she couldn't prevent the rest of it from coming out. "What makes me special?"

He laughed easily now. "Grace Colello, if you really don't know what makes you special, I suspect I shouldn't tell you."

He stopped in the center of the room, held her against him and leaned over to kiss her. She responded as readily as in the elevator. He savored the warm wetness inside her mouth, the just-right amount of suction she was applying to his tongue. He wanted to touch her breasts again but held back. No hurry now. He knew they were available whenever he wanted them. A great feeling.

He backed away. "Champagne?"

"I've had so much already tonight. Maybe I shouldn't. You don't have to open a fresh bottle or anything, do you?"

"I plan to anyway, I'm in the mood." He liked her unsophisticated concern about opening a new bottle. He was so sick of spoiled-rich cunt-os who had no qualms about wasting things.

"Okay, then, I guess I'll have some too, thanks."

As she watched him take the stairs two at a time to the dining area, then vanish into the darkness, she realized how overwhelmed she was by him. But in a strange, special way she didn't really understand. Before she'd gotten on the elevator with him he was a fantasy figure; a romantic fantasy figure, even more, say, than John Malloy, who—however much she admired him and his family—was somehow more in her ken, the world of politics. Now, though, Ted was both more and less a fantasy. Somebody real whom she'd touched and kissed and talked to, and yet somebody who had made her feel things she'd rather not feel, unsettling feelings that took her back to other times, other places she'd rather not remember. . . .

To the time in high school, her junior year, when she finally was able to acknowledge her growing suspicion and then conviction that the Church and its priests and nuns were the imposed morality that had kept her from doing it with guys when what she felt inside told her differently. "Natural law" seemed damned unnatural, and like a revelation in reverse she proceeded to make up for lost time and opportunity, sometimes at the rate of three different guys a week. If she wanted someone, and he wanted her, that was that.

Except it really wasn't. In her wonderful revolt and new freedom she soon found herself feeling lousy, which wasn't supposed to be the idea at all. At first she thought it was a sort of backlash from her old conditioning, and maybe some of it was, but gradually she came to understand that it was something else quite different—it had to do with an unease not on so-called moral grounds but on personal grounds. . . . It had to do with a simple matter of feeling that it was a kind of unseemly and indiscriminate invasion of privacy. You didn't, after all, give or show all of yourself to everyone who came down the pike. You didn't burp in front of strangers, or tell them your family history at the first hi-there-hello, or let them watch you in the john. It wasn't *wrong* (well, not really) but it was somehow a wipeout of yourself, and it reduced you to someone without feelings, like an animal . . . not civilized, really.

So, after a rush of activity and a string of who-knew-how-many sexmates, she began to back off some. She didn't set corny schoolgirl limits like some of her friends—breasts on first date, in the pants on the second, and so forth, which was plain jerky when you thought about it. But she did insist on at least knowing a guy some, on *feeling* intimate with him before getting intimate, however many dates that took.

And then, just after starting at City College, she found herself slipping. It began, as she remembered, one night at a dance when she met someone and, without thinking or observing any of the good resolutions she'd made for herself, found herself in bed with him. And a few evenings later it was with another guy she'd met only that afternoon in the library, and then a matinee between classes with someone she'd met in the cafeteria. She was, she eventually realized, letting herself be intimidated by these college guys who seemed to know so much more than she, these guys who were so much more hip and confident than anyone she'd known before . . . especially any males, and especially—though she didn't specifically connect this—her father and his relentless suspicion of anybody who had *anything* different (for which read better) than he did—whether youth or education or job or clothes or you name it. She'd been raised in a home dominated by a father who made a career of hating the world for being better than he was—and it was catching, even if you happened to be a lovely looking girl with a brain to match your looks. Because the girl was also the daughter. . . .

When she realized what was happening, she was able to get hold of herself again, though never feeling really secure about it, never feeling really at ease. Still, things seemed pretty well under control, up to now, that is, up to Ted Vassily. . . .

He had come back with a champagne bucket and two glasses—tulip-shaped glasses, she noticed, thin and elegant. Being born in a blue collar didn't mean you had to wear one for life—fortunately for both of them.

"To the first lady to share my apartment at Three-oh-five East," he said, lifting his glass and waiting for her to touch hers to it.

She sipped. "Mmmmmm, good."

"Yup, this is the sixty-four. We're serving sixty-six downstairs—which is also great, but not quite up to this."

She sipped again. She felt a little better now, not nearly as anxious as when he'd been out of the room. "Tell me something," she said. "What makes me so special? Seriously, I won't be offended if you say I just happened to come along at the right time and you felt like inviting me here. . . ."

"That's not it."

"Then what is it?" She looked at him over the rim of her glass.

"Well, it's . . ." He really *did* feel unusually affectionate toward her, and was damned if he knew why. He'd had the feeling though, even before the business in the elevator. "Maybe it's the way you made it easy—well, easier—for me to talk to you," he managed finally, not satisfied but not inclined to search further. "I mean, that little speech about not wanting me to think you were deliberately standoffish—"

"Hey, you remember it practically verbatim."

"Yeah. Anyway, I needed it. I tend to tense up until a lady lets me know my attentions are welcome."

"You? The great Ted Vassily? 'Tense up'?" She was surprised she was being this bold with him. Well, she didn't feel at all intimidated now.

"Sorry if that disillusions you, but I guess I'm not nearly the powerhouse some people apparently expect. . . ."

She laughed and sipped some more champagne. She was starting to feel giddy. "Well, I think you're very cute."

"I'll buy that."

She laughed. "Come on, you mean my little try at making you feel at ease was the only thing that inspired you to want me to be the first lady to see your penthouse?" She found herself thinking that she really must be drunk, or getting there . . . ordinarily she wouldn't act *this* sappy. . . .

"Must've been," he said. "Because I asked you up immediately afterward, didn't I?"

"I guess you did." She sipped her champagne, told

herself not to press, went right ahead and did it anyway. "But what got you interested in me in the first place? I mean, why bother to meet me at all?" *Stop it, Grace. . . .*

He touched his glass to his lips. Was she looking for an argument or reassurance? "Why bother to meet anyone? Why bother to get up in the morning? Why bother to breathe—"

"Oh, come on, now—don't dismiss me that way."

"I mean it. Who wants to analyze things like that?"

"Well, let me put it another way . . . when did you first decide you wanted to be with me?"

He was getting irritated now. The first time I saw those incredible tits. "I didn't make a decision, it just happened."

His temperature was rising. Well, you see, honey, what it really was, there was this one in a red dress and I really wanted to make it with her but someone else tied her up while I was on my way over to her so then I caught you looking at me and I figured what the hell. "Probably, Grace, when our eyes met. Now let's try not to analyze it beyond that, okay? You seemed open and interesting, you didn't come packaged with airs and other put-ons . . . okay?"

"Okay, I'm sorry. . . ." She sipped her champagne. Actually she felt guilty for putting him through this inane line of questioning. . . . She must be drunk; she'd never badger a man this way otherwise. . . . "Anyway," she said, hoping to recoup, "I'm glad you invited me up."

He breathed easier. "So am I," he said moving closer and putting his arm around her.

She felt herself beginning to stiffen, felt the old resistance trying to assert itself, but somehow when he took her chin in his hand and tilted her face toward his she didn't resist. And when he leaned forward to kiss her, she opened her mouth to take his tongue. And loved the assertive way he thrust the whole of it deeply inside.

And then he was touching her breasts from outside her dress. And then he was easing her body back on the couch. And then his fingers somehow found their way inside her bodice, and she realized he had unbuttoned a button without her being aware of it. And she wanted to resist, she really did. Except why should she? . . . she was *enjoying* it. She liked the feel of his huge hands, they seemed gigantic, she'd never felt something that size around her breast before—and yet they were incredibly gentle. . . .

But damn it, not yet . . . it was happening too fast . . . even for Ted Vassily. "You know," she murmured, gently freeing herself, "I think I probably shouldn't stay too long. . . ."

He sat up with a swiftness that stunned her. "I don't much like being teased, Grace."

"I'm not teasing you—"

"Then I apologize for misinterpreting your—"

"No, it's not that, I like you very much, but—"

"I don't like playing dirty old man." He stood. "I don't like pushing people to do things they don't feel like doing—"

"You haven't been pushing. You . . ."

He turned toward her, seemed about to say something, then shrugged. "Sorry, I guess I have a low rejection tolerance."

"Wow. I'll say."

"Do you really have to go right away?"

"I guess not, not really."

"Good. . . . Come over here, I want to show you the view to the east." He led her to the uppermost sitting area, from which they looked out over Queens and beyond. She couldn't remember ever having been so far off the ground, except in an airplane or once on the observation tower of the Empire State Building. This was so high it seemed as though she could actually see the curvature of the earth.

"It's a little hazy tonight," Ted said, "but when it's clear you can make out Fire Island."

"It's still magnificent."

"It certainly is," he said, looking down at her. He took her in his arms and found her mouth with his.

No pulling away now, no feeling of wanting to. . . . The kiss this time was long, relaxed, the kind she'd expect from someone she'd been to bed with a dozen times. She waited for his hands to retrace their way to her breasts.

They didn't. "Let's sit here," he said. Without waiting for her to agree, he sat on a large reclining leather armchair and guided her onto his lap. She fitted herself against his body, impressed by its bigness, by how huge his chest and shoulders were—my God, at least twice the size of any other guy she'd known, or at least so it seemed. She pressed her face into the nape of his neck. The muscles there were enormous, too; they seemed like flesh pillars, no other guy in her experience had been anything but soft there. She ran her finger tips over his chest and arm, silently repeating her amazement at the size of him. Actually, she decided, it wasn't that he was so much bigger, he was just more muscular. She loved it. It was a powerful turn-on.

He kissed her again, slowly, not urgently, and enjoyed the way she seemed to come up to him, lifting her face toward him, as if there were some sort of hidden succulence somewhere inside him and the closer she pressed against him the closer she'd get to it. He had a tremendous urge to bury his face between her huge breasts, but he wouldn't rush things. He'd try not to. . . . What he was going to do was give it one more try, and if she resisted again he's simply take her back to the lobby and maybe call her some other night. Or maybe not. Because he really couldn't hack resistance. He was getting on, damn it. Something had happened to him these past few years. He'd completely lost his appetite for combat. Maybe that's what marriage does to you. . . . Or rather, marriage to Chris Jenkins. . . .

He broke the kiss, muttered something neither of them paid any attention to, then eased his hand against the underslope of her breast. No resistance. Thumb over the breast. Still no resistance. Entire hand over the breast. Still none. Now inside. None. Maybe that abrupt withdrawal after her last resistance had put some manners on her. . . . Now if only she'd get wound up enough to want it as much as he did . . . and he wanted it very much. Not that it had been so long since the last—though, come to think of it, it had been over a month—but there were things about her that would excite him no matter when the last time was. Not just her breasts, though they were masterpieces. It was her entire body . . . a little heavier, mayby, than he usually liked, but somehow that made it even more appealing, promised a different, a new kind of experience. He began to imagine all sorts of wild hotness inside her cunt, the juices brought to near-boiling by the sexy layers of fat around them. But hers wasn't flabby fat. It was all smooth and distributed evenly over her whole body. And that made a nice change of pace from his usual run of near-skinny girls. Come to think of it, she was his first with her build since before he'd started dating Chris.

"Mmmm, that feels good," she was saying.

He had her breast exposed and was running the entire length of his index finger gently over the nipple, which was rigidly erect. "This feels good too," he said, giving her full breast a loving squeeze. Gorgeous. Enormous. Gorgeously enormous. He worked his free hand around to the other one and pressed both together.

She smiled. "Do you like them?"

Do mice like cheese? "I do, I do. Cross my heart and—"

"You don't think they're too big?"

"No."

"Sometimes I'm afraid they are."

Like hell, you are. "They're perfect, absolutely perfect . . ." He lowered his face against them, pressing his cheek against the cleavage, then tickling one nipple with his tongue. He enjoyed her vanity about them, enjoyed her inviting his praise. Too often women with big breasts were worried that you wouldn't notice they had something upstairs too—all boobs and no brains—as though you couldn't possibly be interested in both, for Christ's sake.

Now he took the tip of Grace's breast into his mouth, felt the nipple going far back on his tongue, and decided to see how much of her breast he could get inside. He sucked. His mouth filled, and still most of it was outside . . . !

He went back to licking the nipple, attending to the other one with his fingers. Her hips began squirming now, ever so slightly. Good. She was beginning to get there. Now should he go on, risk another pullback . . . or try to bring her beyond the point of return?

When in doubt, procrastinate. He stroked her legs through her pantyhose. God, he hated pantyhose. "I wish you weren't wearing these. I'd really like to feel your legs."

"I'll take them off."

She got up and looked around hesitantly, as if deciding whether to take them off right there or go into the bathroom. After a moment she did it right there. He enjoyed watching her, enjoyed the sexily awkward way she bent over as she slid them down her legs. Then she held them in front of her with both empty legs hanging down, made a little movement as if to shake them out, folded them and laid them across the vacant chair next to him. He smiled. Chicks were really fun to watch when they fucked around with their things.

She returned to his lap and into position. He thrust his tongue all the way into her mouth and ran his palm up her bare thigh. They were solid legs. Firm. Not too muscular like a dancer's, but not at all flabby. And she must have just shaved them, their smoothness felt great.

He licked his way down her throat to her breasts. God, going back to those breasts was like discovering them all over again.

He kissed and licked and stroked, bringing his hand up over her panties and onto her belly, lingering there before going back to her legs. Her movements told him it probably would be okay if he went for her box right now, but he wanted to eliminate completely any possibility of rejection.

He ran his fingertips once more over the outside of the panties, then dipped inside the waistband far enough to brush her pubic hair. Now outside again, then down onto her legs. Finally into her crotch—but still staying outside her panties. She was incredibly moist. No question that she was ready. But, again—patience. No abrupt move. A sustained crotch massage, still staying outside the panties. Now into the leghole of the panties. Wet. What lovely wetness. An experimental finger into the lip area. Hold for a second, give her a chance to get comfortable about it. Now inside. Yes!

Wet! Hot and wet! He couldn't remember hotter wetness in any chick. And the way she was moving on his finger, bucking up and down on it as if trying to wrestle every last bit of sensation from it.

He partially withdrew, then eased in a second finger. No trouble. She probably was wet enough to accommodate three. He inserted two all the way, feeling the mucoid slickness of her cervix with his fingertips and wedging the two lower knuckles into the vaginal introitus, feeling its perimeter snug against them. She started squirming more forcefully now, moving her hips in wider arcs.

He shifted beneath her, still not taking his fingers from inside as he hoisted her hips up onto his abdomen, then crossed his free hand over and played with her clitoris while he withdrew the other one and took out his cock. Now, head of the cock into the hollow of her groin. Rub it there for a moment. Now against the wetness. Another rub, make her comfortable about its presence. And now in. Slowly. Ease it. Good, she's cooperating. A little more. Jesus, that feels good. Really great. What fucking hotness. And tight! Deeper now. More. Good. Still deeper. She really has a grip on it. Terrific! All the way . . . Yes! Time for bed, but he didn't want to go just yet, didn't want to interrupt the wonderful feel of that tight hotness. And now she started moving, just as she had when his fingers were inside her, but even more vigorously. He brought his fingers to her clitoris, might as well give her as much as he could, make it as good for her as possible . . . And he found himself thinking he really *wanted* to be good for her . . . not just for the buildup that would benefit him at the end . . . but, well, damn it, because he really *liked* Grace Colello. (Of course, he reminded himself, before he started awarding himself angel's wings, he should keep in mind that he felt something of this with nearly every girl at the threshold of a first fuck—a kind of tenderness bordering on gratitude for what they were allowing him—but with Grace it seemed more intense, more personalized. . . .)

"Mmm," she said, "that's lovely . . . you move so well . . ." She seemed to be scooping down for him, as if by forcing herself as low as possible into his lap she would get more of his cock. He pushed up with his hips to enhance the effect. The action of her cunt—the tightness of it, the perfect tension-level as it moved up and down his cock, almost as if milking it—sensational! He wanted it to last forever. And wanted even more to change it, wanted to get her into bed where their nude bodies could act without any restraint, drive his cock right through her, drive so hard their bodies would seem to fuse . . .

"Let's go to the bedroom," he said, stopping his movements. "It'll be better."

She followed silently, watching him begin to shed his clothes even before they were inside the room. He had a terrific cock, thick as well as long. And he seemed to know every possible good thing to do with it. The way he played with her body, he seemed to know it as intimately as she did—more so. Still, somewhere way in the back of her mind was a nagging feeling of unease. After all, if you thought about it, she didn't know him at all, and here she was fucking him as quickly as she had anybody—*anybody*—even during her Prone Joan periods. . . . But somehow—magically, thankfully—she didn't feel at all guilty or wrong about it. And it wasn't that she was just burying her old feelings in the flush of good sex and would feel lousy when it was over. She'd had good sex before. Maybe not *this* good . . . but . . .

He tossed his clothes onto the dresser and turned to her. She was just stepping out of her panties. His eyes went to her breasts and seemed incapable of turning away. Not only big but perfectly shaped. And no sag at all . . . high and firm. They were . . . they were . . . ahh, Jesus!

She stepped into his outstretched arms. His grip, his chest, his thighs—everything seemed so hard. Including his cock. It stood there between their bodies like a big, warm, flesh stick.

"Baby, you are just fantastic," she heard him say.

"You feel so good," she answered, but scarcely heard her own voice. The whole scene had an other-worldly feel to it. She was swimming in excitement.

He ripped the covers off the bed and shoved her, almost but not quite roughly, into place. She saw him smiling as he climbed gingerly into position on top of her. It was a tender smile, reassuring—and a hungry one, too.

She felt the heat of his chest and torso as he lowered himself, then felt his hand between her legs. And then the nub, that blunt hard nose at her vaginal opening, seeming even bigger now than before, wedged there.

He rubbed the head against her, lubricated it, then

pushed with it and she felt the rampart yielding, slowly, ever-so-slowly, almost painfully—had she suddenly got so tight, or had he grown even bigger? . . . And then he was in. And it was delicious. His throbbing pillar seemed to exude special sensation-causing rays, coming from every pore, suffusing her flesh, shooting through her body like bursts of electric current.

She heard him grunt. And liked the way it sounded. And she started moving—back to reality now—feeling superb, feeling a great cock that was being wielded by someone who really knew how. . . .

Now one hand gripped her thigh. "Put your legs down."

She did and felt him maneuver his over and outside hers.

"Now lift yours over mine."

She did. It was a new position for her, but it felt good, really good. And she liked being commanded this way during lovemaking. It made her feel more . . . well, more free, less responsible for pleasing him.

Now he was doing something with his hips, and she found that his pubis was putting intense pressure against her clit. . . . It was a wild sensation, something she'd never experienced. It was all the usual sensations of screwing plus this precise, pinpointed sensation that she previously had achieved only while masturbating. It was fantastic.

She arched her hips to get more of it, and in response he pressed even harder against that magic spot. Somewhere inside her she felt the warm stirrings that meant orgasm would soon be within reach.

"Oh, baby," she moaned, "it's so good." She was startled to hear herself calling him "baby" . . . realized she'd never called any other guy "baby" . . . she must've picked it up from him. . . .

He intensified his action and tried not to look down at her body. He'd allowed himself a glance moments ago, and it had almost made him come. Those unbelievable breasts . . . the way they lay there, gorgeous big gloppers wildly rolling around as her body bucked and strained against his. He wanted to grab them but knew if he did it would be the end for him . . . he'd come within seconds. And he wanted her to come first. You didn't check out on a lady without giving her a come, not if you could help it. . . .

He forced himself to focus on the sheet alongside her head, which distracted him somewhat, but he could still feel those gorgeous monsters against his chest. It was unbearable . . . He'd have to break his concentration on them or there was no way he'd be able to hold back.

He forced himself away from her, propping himself with both hands in a modified push-up position. Okay, now he wasn't touching or looking at them—but he still remembered them! He couldn't remember ever having such a rough time holding off an orgasm . . . well, not recently, anyway. Now what were those gimmicks he'd used back in college, when it was a *lot* harder to keep it back? Imagine yourself tied to a railroad track with the train bearing down on you . . . count backward from one thousand . . . go through the team roster, number by number, matching each guy's face with his jersey. . . . He tried the roster routine, using the Penn State squad of his senior year, intoning the players' names in his mind as if he were announcing them over a public address system. . . . "Ladies and gentlemen, number eleven, from McKees' Rocks, Pennsylvania, cornerback Mike Evans . . ." He got halfway through the twenties when Grace Colello let out a little moan and he couldn't resist looking at her. And the hungry expression on her face got to him enough that he couldn't resist a glimpse at her breasts. And seeing them, there was no possible way he could make himself look away. And that's the ball game, folks, Penn State wins it, forty-three zip, now y'all be sure to come back next Saturday . . .

No, he wasn't going to cheat her that way. He would let himself come—there was no way not to—but he was going to make sure she got hers even if he had to manage it with a soft dick. So he didn't thrash around on top of her, as he wanted to, while torrents of orgasm raged through him. And he didn't let himself collapse afterward. He forced himself to keep pumping, putting even more pressure now on her pubes.

His legs and back ached, and he knew he was going soft —no doubt she could feel it happening—but goddamn it, he wasn't going to stop.

So he pushed. And pumped. And now her body seemed to take on more tension, almost as if she realized she'd have to help him. She pushed down on the bed with both fists, pushed up harder with her pubes. And the tenseness in her face increased, her brow strained with the effort, her eyes were squeezed shut. She pushed harder. Harder.

And then he heard her moan. She was there, no mistaking it. She bucked so hard she lifted him right off the bed, it seemed that only her heels and the back of her head were touching. The force of her action practically knocked him out of the saddle. At the same time she let out a scream, and then her hands clamped around his back, the fingernails digging into his flesh. And he felt and heard himself laughing with pleasure . . . "Yes, baby, take it, take it . . . !"

They collapsed into each other's arms, their heavy breathing seemingly amplified a thousandfold in the room's humid stillness. She was aware again of his weight on top of her, and wondered how he managed to come exactly when she did, nobody had ever done that before. Unless he hadn't come . . . but he must have, he wouldn't have stopped if he hadn't . . . God, she hoped she had satisfied him . . .

He lay on top of her until he felt his cock begin to shrivel, and she, sensing what was happening, eased her hips back and laughed sexily as it popped out. He lay on his back then and she fitted herself into the crook of his arm, resting her head on his shoulder. And both of them felt deliciously spent. . . .

Grace Colello, he found himself thinking, was one lovely, giving girl—and with the thought came an abrupt (like a dash of cold water in the face) sense of loss, of sadness. It wasn't premonition, he told himself . . . he didn't believe in that crap. It had nothing to do with the old nonsense about post-coital sadness—who the hell was sad over pleasure, except a masochist?—and it certainly wasn't because he'd suddenly uncovered some heavy flaw in Grace Colello. The opposite, in fact—she was a fantastic lay, a special and loving person, and somebody that he felt an immediate kinship with in a way that he never could with somebody like Buffy Weiss or even, come to think of it, with Chris. Both of them shared upper-class backgrounds that gave them a head start over people like Grace Colello, and Ted Vassily, né Vassilikos. . . . And, damn it, that very feeling of being so close to her was what would probably keep them apart. *He didn't want the responsibility of caring for her!!!* Yes, Grace Colello with her blue-collar background, her smarts and her unpretentious enthusiasms, and her *niceness,* was what he *ought* to get next to on a permanent basis. But he had never been able to in the past. And thinking this, he knew it was the old guilt—silly, maybe; irrational, maybe; but there, and go argue with it and the limp dick that was eventually its casualty—the old guilt about her blue-collar origins. He could dump on a broad with bread-and-boarding school in her past without any problem . . . but with somebody like Grace, the old class loyalty—and maybe resistance to it?—reared its head.

Well, damn it, he wasn't responsible for everybody's feelings. What was this big conscience number all of a sudden? Why so much guilt? Who said he had to justify everything . . . ?

He looked over at Grace, lying there beside him, stroking him, and decided they had better get the hell out of the apartment. He wanted to take his mind off all this . . . and besides, he should be getting back to the party. Grace and he could stroll around the lobby, talk to other people, get out of themselves and they'd both feel better. . . .

Grace stared through the forest of hair on his chest, focused on a point on the far wall, and wondered why she was feeling so down, so *glum* . . . and after a terrific fuck that should have left her tremendously invigorated—and not just physically. It wasn't the old hang-up about being too casual. No, she'd gotten past that once she had committed herself to staying with him—and feeling good about it, matter of fact.

Then what was it? That he was simply too much for her?—too fantastic, out of this world, as she'd felt when she'd first stepped into the magnificence of his apartment? Fantastic lover, fantastic everything else . . . unreal, too unreal for her ever to relate to as an ordinary—that very word seemed to contradict Ted Vassily—man *and* lover. For a moment earlier she'd thought she'd glimpsed him as a very mortal sort of man, thought he was even sort of cute in his diffidence . . . but that feeling was gone now. The old sense of awe was back . . . and with it the sense of how impossible it would be for her, Grace Colello, to manage a lasting relationship with somebody like him. . . .

And feeling that, the glumness deepened to a kind of depression, because she *liked* him so much, this unattainable man. And to save herself the hurt she knew would be there if she went on seeing him, she'd have to put him off. She couldn't risk seeing him again, even if he wanted it. She just couldn't handle it. At least not yet . . .

"You know," she heard him say, "I hate to break this up but I'm afraid I should be getting downstairs . . ."

She all but sighed with relief.

"I mean, the TV thing will be wrapping up soon"—he sounded so apologetic, she felt sorry for him—"and Eddie Spats will probably want me on-camera for the close—"

"Of course." She sat up quickly.

"Hey, Grace, please don't misunderstand . . . I'd love to keep this going all night, believe me, but, well, you know, it is sort of my coming-out party. . . . I'll tell you what, we'll go down to the lobby, chat it up with a few people and then after the TV wrap-up maybe come back here for a nightcap and—"

"Thanks, but I really should be getting back to my apartment." She had already started dressing. "My dad gets uptight when I'm out too late. I'm sure you understand—"

"Sure, whatever you say. But if you change your mind . . ." He let the sentence trail, wondered if she saw through him, and tried to stop himself with a reminder that he wasn't responsible for the whole goddamn world, that she was an adult and took her chances, her risks, just as he did. . . .

He finished dressing quickly and waited for her. She couldn't find her panties, and after a long frazzled minute of embarrassed searching decided to leave without them.

"Hey, seriously," he said, ushering her out the door, "I hope I haven't said anything to offend you, believe me, I only—"

"Of course not. What a silly thing to even think." She stood on tiptoe and kissed him on the nose. "Maybe I'm giving you the wrong idea because I'm tired. It's been an exciting and long day." She smiled.

"Right." He felt better. He hugged her. He touched the elevator button and tried unsuccessfully to think of something else to say. The car arrived. He followed her inside and pressed the lobby button and hugged her—fraternally—again. "Hey, I really enjoyed tonight, Grace. Very much."

"Likewise, sir." She bussed him on the lips. "Thanks for inviting me." Standing there next to him, she was careful not to let her body touch his, embarrassed at what he would think, what he must be thinking. . . .

Looking down at her, he saw her breasts as though for the first time and silently laughed to himself that along with all his other contradictory feelings one was clear and sharp at this moment—damned if he didn't feel like doing the whole thing over again. Crazy mixed-up oversexed football player, he told himself as the door opened onto the lobby and he took Grace by the arm and led her out.

John Malloy made sure his wife was looking the other way, then glanced toward the area where Spats Johnson had just interviewed the two girls. The one in red—the Loomis girl, probably Hart's daughter—was still there, talking to that drunken fool Stoney Wattley. But the one he really was interested in, the Sophia Loren-type in the green dress who'd been talking to Vassily, had disappeared. Well, at least he remembered her name. Grace Colello. He'd put Tom Donohue to work right away.

". . . don't you think so, John?"

"Absolutely, Peg," he replied automatically, "I agree completely."

Her look told him she not only knew that he hadn't been paying attention but also why. She wasn't, though, about to make a scene now, which she no doubt felt was more consideration than he deserved. . . .

Thankfully she returned to whatever she'd been saying to whomever she'd been talking to—Joseph Williams's cousin, as John recalled. He wanted to look around again for Grace Colello but restrained himself and tried to listen to Peg. He managed to stay with her for a few sentences, then drifted again, remembering that when he looked at the area where Grace had been, Vassily wasn't there either. Was it possible that the old stud had managed to get her off someplace for a little jump? . . . He tuned back in on Peg's conversation just in time to hear a reference to the previous week's *Lucia di Lammermoor* at the City Opera. "I thought Pat Wise was a surprisingly strong Lucia for a girl her age," he said, "and I think she's going to be one of the most important singers this country has ever produced. And Sam Ramey—he gets better and better. The only bassos I'd mention in the same breath are Ezio Pinza and Emilio Mosso." There, Peggy, say I wasn't paying attention that time. . . .

He continued on good behavior, nodding in appropriate places as Peg and Williams's cousin chatted on about the opera, then allowed himself another look around the room. . . . Nothing, nothing—and then he saw Vassily, and the girl, getting into the elevator. Goddamn . . .

". . . did you, John?"

"Sorry, dear, I just noticed a few of the football stars I hadn't introduced Johnny to yet. Would you excuse us for a moment?" He quickly took Johnny off with him to the tuxedoed group near the east elevators and shook hands with Emerson Wade, Burr Whiteside and Mikey DeAngelico, swapped pleasantries with them, then turned back to where Peg had been. She was not there. He scanned the room, couldn't find her and for a moment had the panicky feeling that something awful might have happened, then relaxed, telling himself nothing could have happened in a ground floor lobby that was filled with people and security guards. At worst, she'd decided to go upstairs for a snort. He'd take advantage of the opportunity to survey the lobby.

"Hey, Johnny," he said, "there's another guy you've probably heard of. I'd no idea he was part of this operation too." He led his son to the front door and introduced him to Walt Kulikowski.

The ex-fullback, resplendent in his doorman's gold-braided uniform, pumped John's hand vigorously. "Good evening, senator. I'm honored you recognize me."

"Recognize you?" John laughed. "Why, Johnny, this fellow ran two thousand yards two years in a row—and that was when you really had to earn your yardage." He turned back to Kulikowski. "As for that 'senator' business, Walt—I appreciate the vote of confidence but I've a long way to go."

"You'll get there, senator, no doubt about it. Hell, I'd bet my life on it. . . ."

Malloy politely remembered some of Kulikowski's biggest runs, then began to move off, saying he had a few people to say hello to, so if Walt would excuse them—

"Senator," said Kulikowski, grabbing his arm, "before you go, I just wanna say—I'm only filling in here with Ted, you know—helping him out at the door till the building gets on its feet and he can get along without me. So when your campaign gets rolling, if you think you can use an extra man—maybe somebody in the bodyguard-chauffeur department—I'd sure like to team up with you. I have my chauffeur's license and my record's clean so there'd be no trouble getting licensed for a gun . . ."

"Well, thanks for letting me know you're available, Walt. I'll pass it on to my chief of staff Tom Donohue. . . . I'm not sure what the budget will permit these days, but if it's at all possible . . ." He retrieved his arm, which Kulikowski seemed reluctant to release.

"Hey, *thanks*, senator, I really appreciate it. I mean it, I won't let you down."

Malloy, his smile now frozen in place, turned back into the lobby.

"If you're looking for Mom, Dad, there she is."

The smile nearly cracked. Peg hadn't gone up for her snort, she was still talking to Williams's cousin but they'd moved from their original place and now were in the company of the maestro himself, self-impressed ass that he was. . . .

Maestro Joseph Williams half-listened to the chatter of his wife, his cousin and Peg Malloy as he surveyed the lobby and tried to pinpoint the reason for his negative feelings about this affair. It was, of course, awash with bores, but most big parties were. It was a bit pretentious with touches like the Taittinger sixty-six, which he suspected ninety-five percent of the guests were incapable of appreciating, but that wasn't the problem either, most parties tended to be vulgar. And it wasn't even the Broadway guys-and-dolls ambience that Spats Johnson provided with his retinue of off-duty prostitutes.

No, what it was, Joseph Williams suddenly realized, was the waste of a perfect opportunity to do something *really* worthwhile, beyond Vassily's self-promotion . . . a notion that took shape as his eyes fell on Buffy Weiss, who was standing off to one side of the bandstand, looking rather uncomfortable and alone. He remembered the Sunday morning at his studio when she'd introduced him to the idea of 305 East, his excitement about the potential social and even political implications of the building, which had grown as the construction work progressed—an excitement that logically should have climaxed tonight at this party. But the purpose of 305 East seemed buried beneath the evening's too-bright glitter. Except for that brief, patronizing episode on TV between Spats Johnson and that girl in the green dress, there wasn't even a hint that this party had anything to do with the city's first egalitarian luxury apartment building. It could be *any* party, something sponsored by the Symphony Guild, something Babe Paley or Truman Capote or Leonard Bernstein threw for her/his/his-her five hundred closest friends, in and out of their various closets.

What Vassily should have done—Williams wished he'd thought of it in time to have given Vassily some advice—was tie up the affair with a really important cause. Instead of picking up the tab himself Vassily should have had admission by ticket only. Make it five hundred dollars a couple—except for the building's subsidized tenants who could be admitted free. The others would've gladly paid for the advantageous public exposure. A hundred paying couples would mean fifty thousand dollars for some deserving charity, and if five hundred attended—the approximate size of tonight's crowd—the income would be a quarter of a million. The party was a major lost opportunity. Courtesy of a has-been quarterback.

Williams looked over the room and again stopped at Buffy Weiss. He remembered reading that her Indian trial in South Dakota would be getting under way in a few months. Now that was a cause worth the glitter. . . . According to the papers the Indians' defense fund was virtually bankrupt. Buffy and the other lawyers were donating what time they could spare. A little financial help might mean the difference between freedom or imprisonment for thirty-four native Americans whose only crime was that they'd tried to take back some land the country had swindled from their ancestors. . . . Joseph Williams was outraged anew just thinking about it. Tradition was something he understood and respected. . . . He wished he'd kept in touch with Buffy Weiss after that night months ago. Not that he wanted to continue a sexual or emotional relationship, but she could be useful in many ways with her media and other connections. And he, of course, could reciprocate.

Why not, as a matter of fact, initiate such an arrangement now, tonight? Except on second thought, with his wife present, it wouldn't be such a good idea. Wait till tomorrow when he could simply have his secretary get her on the phone.

His plan formulated, Williams returned his attention to his wife, his cousin and the Malloy woman, all talking the usual chitchat nonsense, which he again promptly tuned out, wondering idly where his cousin's husband was. Probably kissing the ass of his banker brother-in-law. What could Ben possibly want from a man like Hartford Loomis? Certainly not money, not with Ben's wealth. But if not money, what? Why would one even consider associating with a banker if one didn't need money?

"Oh, here are my two Johns now," he heard Peg Malloy say as her husband and son approached. Despite his self-acknowledged elegant sensibilities, Williams couldn't resist the voice inside that snickered something about one of the Johns needing flushing. Indeed . . . !

Actually, John Malloy wasn't all that bad, as politicians go . . . aside from an excessive tendency toward self-conscious nobility, which wasn't, Williams supposed, such a difficult thing to forgive in a would-be senator whose loyalties at least were to the right causes and who was pragmatic enough to forge liaisons and arrange trade-offs with opponents whom most doctrinaire liberal legislators were content to hurl insults at.

Yes, as politicans went, Malloy was reasonably sharp and worth knowing. Which was why Williams had accepted his dinner invitation two weeks ago and why, when Malloy subtly revealed his distress about not having a grand entrance during the first half hour of Spats Johnson's TV show, he'd volunteered to swap orders of appearance.

Still, valuable acquaintance as Malloy might be, he fell considerably short of the knowledgeable, cultured man-for-all-seasons that so many of his supporters in and out of the media seemed to consider him. His limitations had become apparent that evening at dinner. Talk about politics—about the current comings and goings of political figures or the status of various legislative proposals—and he was on solid ground. But talk about the broader realms outside politics, he became a treasure trove of the second hand and the secondary source. . . . At least he had the good sense not to try to discuss music with Joseph Williams, apart from expressing prosaic appreciation of the current *Tosca* at the Stuyvesant . . .

"Hello, maestro," said John Malloy, extending his hand. "How are you enjoying the party?"

Williams smiled his most luminous smile. "Not nearly as much as Maria and I enjoyed dining with you and Peg." He raised his glass. "But it is fine champagne." As the routine replies and exchanges flowed by, he kept his smile in place and let his thoughts wander. . . . What he really would like to do now, he reflected, was see Maria to her bed—her nightly headache should be due any minute—and line up one of the available ladies. Certainly there were enough of them about, even discounting Spats Johnson's garish imports. Of course, as a man of refinement, he naturally required a degree of emotional and intellectual stimulation along with his sex. Which seemed increasingly difficult to come by. . . . For a moment earlier in the evening, he thought he'd detected the promise of it in the banker's daughter—what was her name? —Nan Loomis. Certainly she was bright, and unlike most her age she was able to manage consecutive sentences without a "like," "wow," "man" or any other of the obligatory adolescent clichés mangling the language. But once he began probing for something beyond the standard cocktail party badinage that she handled with such ease, she seemed to come up empty—whether because she was afraid to express an original thought or because she didn't possess one, he couldn't tell. The world, it seemed, had turned into a parrot colony. But, Maestro Joseph Williams wryly admitted to himself, this was presently of relatively small moment to him, compared to his overriding need to—the hell with intellectual rapport—get properly laid.

"Hey, Nasty Nathan," said Spats Johnson, coming down from the bandstand, "come in here with me a second."

Nate followed him into the dressing room and watched as the two flunkies helped him out of his clothes and started scrubbing him down.

"No point in letting things fall apart while the night's so young, now is there?" Spats said. "Besides which, we've got so much female talent hereabouts, I thought I might prevail on yourself, Mister Vassily, and perhaps a few of your colleagues to help entertain them. You figure you could manage that?"

Nate laughed. "You came to the right guy, Spats. I been workin' on tonight's hard-on for the past month an' a half."

"Well, all right! Tonight you get some help with it. Right after the program. Bring yourself and Burr Whiteside and, oh, two or three other buddies. And Ted, of course. Where is the old T-Bone, by the way? I've been looking for him."

"He took off with that chick in the green dress right after you interviewed her." Nate winked as he made a pumping gesture with his fist. "Looks like the ol' T-Bone decided to start his own party early."

Spats grinned. "Well, more power to him. Meanwhile, somebody's gotta take care of the linemen, right, ol' chum?"

"Terrific, Spats. Where do we show up? Your apartment?"

Spats hesitated. The original plan was to party at Coffee Joe's. But that was when the guest list was smaller. Would Joe mind a few extras? Well, he guessed not—especially if Ted was among them. Joe had said he wanted to meet Ted. He'd probably be so glad to have him show tonight that he wouldn't even question Spats' motive for the change in plans. "My friend's apartment," Spats told

Nate. "Penthouse South. And be sure to get the T-Bone back from the taxi squad, eh, ol' buddy?"

"Penthouse South. . . ." Nate echoed. "That's Coffee Joe Mandino's apartment . . . he's your friend?"

"Yeah, and a good guy, Nate. You'll really like him. But don't say 'Coffee Joe' in front of him, okay?"

"He's Mafia, ain't he?"

Spats felt himself getting hot. "He's a gentleman, in my experience, Nate. And so far as I know he's never been arrested for so much as a traffic ticket. Now if you don't want to come to the party—"

"Hey, easy, man. Don't get nervous. I didn't say I don't wanna come. I just said—"

Spats looked at the clock over the door. Thirty-nine seconds had elapsed. "Okay then, man, no problem. Now I gotta get back to the bandstand. I'll see you in Penthouse South after the show." He buttoned the sports jacket Marco had just slipped onto his shoulders, then casually got to the real purpose behind his invitation to Nate. "Oh, one thing more, Nasty. That chick with the red dress that I interviewed at the start of the last stanza. Nan Loomis is her name . . . you know who I mean?"

"Yeah, she lives in fourteen E."

"Well, I'd like her to come to the party too. But, you know, my schedule is so goddamn hectic I probably won't be able to ask her till after the show, and she might be long gone by then. So, ol' buddy, I'd really appreciate it if you'd ask her for me." And if you say no, ol' buddy, he said to himself, you're gonna still have your hard-on tomorrow.

"Sure. No sweat, Spats."

Spats started out the door. "And don't say I want her to be my date, dig? Just that I'm having a little get-together for a few of the people who were on the show, and I asked you to invite her along with everyone else."

"Gotcha, Spats. You want me to invite the girl in green too? I mean, if Ted's finished with her?"

Merrill Wilson, the floor director, was waving frantically for Spats to hurry. "Yeah, sure, whatever you think, Nate."

"Eighteen seconds, Spats," Merrill said, fastening the

wireless mike. "No time to get you to the bandstand, so we'll pick up here and pan with you—"

"Did I hear something about a party?" said a female voice at Spats' shoulder.

He turned. She had straight shoulder-length brown hair with a blonde streak on the side and wore rose-tinted aviator glasses. "Hey, Buffy Weiss," he said.

She smiled. "Am I invited?"

"Jeez, Buff, I can't talk to you now, I'm on the air in seconds—"

"I'll make it fast, chum. I'd like to fuck you."

"Hey, not near the mike!" He covered it with his hand. He danced a couple steps away from her as Merrill Wilson quickly stepped between them. Spats glanced at the assistant director, who stood next to the camera, signaling with his outstretched fingers that the five-second cue was imminent. "Wait near the bandstand," Spats shot back over his shoulder to Buffy. "I'll come down during the solos on the next tune." He turned back to the camera just as the assistant director began the countdown. "Well, it's still party time here at Three-oh-five East," Spats said as the red light flicked on, "and we're going to have us some party music." He started toward the bandstand. "I give you Mister Eddie Spats Johnson Senior and his Bourbon Street All-Stars, with one of my all-time favorite tunes, I hope it's one of yours . . . I know it's the favorite of an old friend of mine who couldn't make it to the party tonight, but he's watching on TV. So for my good buddy Joe, here's a flashback to the old days in Atlantic City, 'Please Don't Talk about Me When I'm Gone.' Uh-one, uh-two, uh-hup, two, three, four . . ."

The drummer kicked off the intro as Spats trotted up the bandstand stairs. After the ensemble chorus, Spats took the first solo, then scooted back down the stairs as Butterball Gardner took a trumpet chorus. Buffy Weiss was waiting.

"Hey, a lady with your experience should know better than to talk that kind of jive near a live mike," Spats said, checking that his switch was off.

She smiled. "I take it you're not interested, then."

"I didn't say that."

"I know what you said. I was listening."

Spats felt like Alice on the business side of the looking glass. What the hell was this chick doing coming on to *him?* She wasn't a show-biz hanger-on. Did she have a thing for spades? Or was she trying to wig him out?

"I'm still listening," she said. "Are you talking?"

"Yeah, sure," he said. "Come to the party." What the hell, he told himself, no harm in having a little insurance in case the Loomis chick didn't field his pitch. And if she did, he could always dump Miss Wise-ass. "I'll meet you here right after I wrap up . . ."

A most subtle hint, Hartford Loomis told himself. That was the only way to approach the situation. First, of course, he'd have to get friendly with someone who had natural access to her—someone like Spats Johnson or, more realistically, someone like Vassily, who would have it through Spats. They would have to be together under fairly casual circumstances, perhaps lunch, perhaps a cocktail after work, maybe even here in the lobby. In any case, it would have to be one of those man-to-man type encounters that inspired frank talk.

But what exactly would he say? Perhaps just that he found her attractive, then let Vassily or whoever take it from there, and if that didn't work he could spell out his interest more directly. . . . Hartford Loomis actually felt himself blush at the prospect of making his pitch to Vassily, who, in any case, was definitely the first person he should approach about setting it up. After all, BankUS held the first mortgage on 305 East. Vassily should—and almost certainly would—welcome the opportunity to get to know him better. And—who could say?—even if it didn't lead to a liaison with Jeannie Danton, it might lead to other things . . . there certainly were enough girls in Vassily's circle.

He looked around the lobby. If Vassily were handy, he might even invite him to get together for a drink tomorrow. He spotted him near the elevator, talking with Joseph Williams and the young girl in the green dress Hart Jr. had been with earlier. You had to hand it to the boy. . . . Hart considered joining them, then decided against it. No point letting Williams see him approach Vassily, whatever the circumstances. Tomorrow would be time enough. He'd phone . . .

Until he happened to notice her coming out of the elevator with Ted Vassily, Joseph Williams had not even considered Grace Colello. Oh, he had noticed her, and certainly she was attractive—if somewhat buxom for his taste. But somehow she seemed off limits, too much the Peter-Pan-collar sort; the girl you'd invite to see your etchings and have some Madeira, and who'd actually expect to see your etchings and have some Madeira.

Then Maria, considerately enough, had gotten her headache right on schedule and asked to be taken upstairs. When he'd come back down the p.r. man, Burr Whiteside, had stopped him in the elevator foyer and asked if he'd like to be on hand for the wrap-up of the TV program. And before he could answer, Ted Vassily and Grace Colello had emerged from the adjoining elevator.

"Ted," Whiteside said, "I've been looking all over for you. Spats wants you for the wrap-up."

"Come on, Grace," Ted said. "Say goodnight to your folks on TV."

She smiled. "No, I think I'll just go up and say goodnight to them in person."

"Tell Spats I'll be there as soon as I escort Miss Colello to her apartment," Ted told Whiteside.

"Well, Ted, I don't think there's time . . ."

Joseph Williams, almost without thinking, found himself offering his arm and saying, "I was about to go up myself, Miss Colello. It'll be my pleasure to escort you."

Ted and Whiteside exchanged looks. "Uh, Miss Colello," Whiteside fumbled, "this is Mister Joseph Williams, who also lives in Three-oh-five East."

"Of course," she said easily, "I'm pleased to meet you."

Ted wanted to say something, but Grace stopped him with, "It's okay, Ted. I'll be fine."

"Which wing, Miss Colello?" Williams asked, leading her away.

"West."

"A coincidence, my studio is in the west wing . . ."

As they crossed to the opposite bank of elevators, he recalled the second impression he'd had of her, something in her look that modified the initial Peter-Pan-collar impression, the sparkle of . . . mischief in her eyes, perhaps a gleam of intelligence and imagination . . . a challenge. He also wondered if it were mere coincidence that she was getting off the elevator with Vassily. Or had the ex-quarterback been with her in his apartment, and if so . . .

Whatever, Miss Grace Colello struck him as a fetching prospect, a worthy prospect, no doubt too much for Vassily and his unsubtle jock approach. It was, as it seemed so many good things in his life were, fate conspiring to reward the worthy . . .

"Do you believe in fate?" he asked her.

She laughed. "I'm afraid not."

"Extrasensory perception, then?"

"Let's just say I'm patiently skeptical."

"Which means?"

"I've heard there's some evidence for it, although I believe the scientific establishment doesn't accept it. I don't always go along with the establishment, but in this case I'm not interested enough to dig deeper on my own. Why do you ask?"

"Actually, I was just trying to account for my being in the foyer at the moment you got out of the elevator."

"How about coincidence?"

A bright young lady, indeed. There was a head above the Peter-Pan-collar. He'd chosen well. "I suspect I was looking for a more romantic explanation. My cross." They were at the west elevator bank, where he ushered her into a vacant car. She took out the key for her floor. He held the hand in which she held it and, smiling lightly, displayed his own key. "Would you have a nightcap with me?"

She hesitated.

"A quick one, if you like. I just feel the need to wind down from that business downstairs, and especially with such pleasant, if unexpected, company."

My, how he did go on . . . but she had to admit it was pleasant . . . and she was intrigued. Well, why not . . . ?

As the elevator rose she thought how comfortable she felt with Joseph Williams, despite his formidable position and reputation. There seemed no strain at all to the conversation. She didn't feel the slightest intimidation . . .

none of the unease she'd felt with Ted . . . which made her uneasy all over again thinking about it . . .

She wondered if Williams would try to seduce her, then smiled at her own naiveté. A man didn't generally invite a girl to his studio at one in the morning to compliment him on his draperies. Well, she had some winding down to do of her own. This moment—and the ones likely to come—with the famous conductor had none of the mixed feelings built-in that she'd experienced with Ted. Only a small, remote corner of her brain seemed involved. Eventually she might want to think more on it, but for now it was enough to enjoy the pleasant, superficial rapport she seemed to have with the maestro. It was, in fact, a relief.

The elevator stopped, and Joseph Williams led her down the corridor, opened his double-locked door and led her inside. He manipulated a switch, and the lights slowly brightened, as in a theater.

She found herself in a huge room that did, in fact, look like a movie set, with four symmetrically situated overhead fixtures and half a dozen lamps all working on the same switch and providing dramatic silhouette lighting.

Dominating the room was a Steinway concert grand, its huge leaf raised. At a right angle to the keyboard was a mahogany desk fully half as large as the piano, its supports being pillars half a foot in diameter, the tops of which were lions' heads, the bottoms paws. Behind the desk and opposite the keyboard was a row of mahogany filing cabinets, their tops forming a huge rectangular table. Beyond the piano's wing was a sitting area featuring unmatched Victorian furniture—a couch, a love seat and three chairs all ornately carved and lushly upholstered. The boundaries of the area were defined by a thick Oriental rug. On the opposite wall, set off by another Oriental rug, was a carved Chinese rosewood bar with six stools.

"What a fantastic room!" Grace said, and privately blushed as she recalled she'd had a similar enthusiasm to express about the view from Ted's place. Ted . . . with or without him, he was there . . .

"Feel free to look around while I get us something. Some cognac?"

"All right, fine."

While he busied himself at the bar she wandered

through the room, examining the exquisite carved pieces. She went to the U-shaped arrangement of piano, desk and filing cabinet. "You work here, of course."

"To compose, yes. I have a desk in the next room for administrative work."

She went into the adjoining room, which was no less stunning, its four corners given over to floor-to-ceiling bookcases, a windowless wall featuring two oil portraits. "I recognize Mr. Beethoven," she called. "Who's the other?"

"Gustav Mahler."

She examined the desk, which sat in the very center of the room. It was intricately carved ebony, the designs of tree branches and pieces of fruit; even the faces of the drawers were carved. On each flank of the desk was a low filing cabinet, also ebony, but not matching. The rug was Persian. Four overstuffed leather armchairs with lions' paw arms and legs completed the ensemble.

An open door led to an adjoining office, smaller and more businesslike. Wall charts described Joseph Williams' upcoming concert, rehearsal, lecture and travel schedules. There was also a bulletin board labeled "Potpourri."

"My secretary's office," he said, appearing in the doorway, brandy snifters in hand. Grace took one and followed him back to the main room. "It's a great studio," she said.

"Yes, well, I do all my writing here so I have to be comfortable . . . sometimes I don't go back to my apartment for several days . . ."

"Not even to sleep?"

"I have a bedroom here. I often work all night long, so it makes more sense to sleep here than to disturb my wife by stumbling home at five or six in the morning."

The mention of his wife took Grace by surprise. She'd known he was married, but had managed not to think about it. Now that he had mentioned it, though, she was sort of glad. It was somehow . . . well, a gentlemanly reminder of the limits on their affair . . . if, of course, they were to have one . . .

"Sit, make yourself comfortable," he said, gesturing to the couch. As she sat, she noticed the records he'd put on the stereo. Mozart. Just the right mood, not too passionate, not too cool. Mr. Williams was quite a conductor, all right.

He sat next to her, but not close enough for their bodies to touch. He stared thoughtfully at his brandy. "You're quite something, Grace Colello. Behind that sweet air of innocence is, I suspect, *real* innocence . . . which is to say, decency . . . openness. Not the phony artifice of so many of your peers . . . not to mention mine."

She smiled and couldn't think of a thing to say . . . why spoil it? Or deny to herself that she was flattered. Even if he didn't mean it, he thought her worth impressing.

"I am very taken by you, Grace," he said, putting down his brandy.

"I'm glad," she said softly, and honestly.

He kissed her. Gently. Making no effort to put his tongue into her mouth, even though her lips were parted. He held her face in one hand and backed off momentarily, admiring her. He kissed her again, this time more firmly. "You're an exciting woman, Grace." He took her face in both hands and kissed her again, this time putting his tongue into her mouth. As she welcomed it, he put both arms around her and pressed her against him.

It really was strange, she thought: the way she didn't feel uncomfortable about slipping into this so . . . well . . . casually—so different from the uneasy intensity with Ted. And then the little girl inside her took over and—faintly naughty—she giggled inwardly with the thought that this would be . . . what did they used to call it in school? . . . a double-header, for God's sake. She remembered a girl friend who'd told her she'd done it once, and how shocked Grace was . . . the next step to an *orgy*—and yet here she was with Mr. Famous Joseph Williams, without any of the you'll-be-sorry forebodings she'd felt so deeply with Ted Vassily . . . And now, damn it, the very lack of such feelings was beginning to make her uneasy . . . Stop it, Grace . . . relax . . . You *like* being with Joseph Williams . . . you're impressed, but not *too* impressed . . . So . . .

He guided her into a different position, her back toward him so that she could lean across his lap and put her legs up on the couch. The position reminded her of Goya's "Maja Desnuda," and the image made her smile. Joseph asked what she was smiling about. When she told him, it made him smile. What an *intelligent* young lady . . .

He kissed her again and gently stroked her body, taking his time, giving her time, and she appreciated his taking the pressure off her this way, respecting her feelings, realizing that she might need time . . . and she thought, what a contrast to those sweaty younger guys who'd always made her feel that she wasn't there . . . going right for their adolescent scores as if there was nothing more to her than the "box" they liked to talk about so much . . . And thinking of "younger" made her consider Joseph's age—surely he was in his late forties, perhaps even fifties! The oldest man she'd been with before was—tonight, Ted Vassily! Again she told herself—sternly as a Mother Superior—to *stop* it . . . don't be ruled by the old litany of clichés, the conditioning from girlhood . . . She'd broken its grip, and that had been the start of her intellectual and emotional liberation. Don't slip back . . . it's been a long hard road to here . . . *fuck* them . . .

Joseph Williams' fingers had found their way to her breasts, stroking ever so gently. It seemed more an act of tactile adoration than an attempt to stimulate her, though the effect, of course, was powerfully stimulating. She moaned softly as he kissed her throat, continued kissing a path downward until his face was between her breasts.

His hands now stroked her legs through her pantyhose. He touched the waistband, then gently—almost hesitantly—slid it partly down. When there was no resistance, he slid it farther. She raised her hips to make it easy for him.

"You feel so good," he said, touching the bare flesh of her legs.

"Your touch is lovely, Joseph." It seemed natural to use his first name. "So gentle . . ."

His hand went to her crotch. She tensed, suddenly remembering that she had left her panties at Ted's.

Obviously pleased, he mentioned how deliciously wet she was.

For a moment she couldn't help wondering how much of the wetness was excitement over Joseph and how much was residue from Ted—then, quickly, she dismissed the thought as gross . . . gratuitous . . . and went back to her pleasure in the subtle—yet so effective—way he was touching her. She wondered whether she should take the initiative fondling his penis or wait until he put her hand there—or was that strictly a college-kid maneuver? . . . Well, she would take the initiative, Joseph might appreciate that . . . certainly he wouldn't object . . . She stroked him through his pants, then unzipped his fly. His penis grew to full stiffness in her hand. It was neither very thick nor very long. It was kind of cute, really. Sort of a little boy's penis. On a man of his towering artistic stature. It gave him a human dimension.

He fondled her for a few more minutes, then led her into the bedroom, where he took her in his arms and kissed her as he unbuttoned her dress. She helped him help her out of it, watched as he folded it carefully, placed it on the dresser, then took off his own clothes. He embraced her again, and after a long kiss led her to the bed. They lay side by side and resumed stroking each other.

He kissed her breast, then slowly began kissing his way downward. She trembled with excitement as his tongue approached her pubes. Somehow she hadn't expected him to do this. It seemed too . . . well, basic, animal, for a man of his gentle dignity. But she loved it. And he was so good at it . . . he seemed to know exactly the right places, his tongue creating an excitement that fed on itself, driving her to higher and higher levels of desire without any irritating sense of impatience for satisfaction.

His tongue crackled noisily through her pubic hair, then found the tendons of her groin, pressed hard against them, toyed with them, strayed toward her vagina, then back to the tendons. Now into the hollows of her groin, back to the vagina, back to the hollows. Now down one thigh, now back again.

And now he was easing his tongue inside her vagina, only a short way at first, then deeply. And somehow his chin came to rest on her clitoris. And he began moving his jaw, massaging her clitoris with that area between his mouth and chin. Fantastic.

He shifted his body so that his hips were over her face, his penis at her mouth. She started to take it into her mouth, then decided to treat him as lovingly as he had her. She licked around it, toyed with his testicles, found the hollows of his groin. She heard him moan.

Now his chin action seemed to accelerate, his tongue to thrust deeper. She felt something wild begin to happen deep inside her. A warm glow. Slowly spreading. Oh, yes . . . this was going to be a tremendous one . . .

She felt herself writhing, squirming. The glow seemed to intensify. And now a preliminary flush washed over her . . . and then it happened—crashing, jarring her, shaking her. She heard herself scream. And she nearly bit his cock—quickly easing off when she realized it. And still the fantastic sensation continued, rattling her, electrifying her. She knew her body was bucking and bouncing, but it was happening without her, independently of her, beyond her control. She had no sense of space or place, she didn't know whether she was vertical or horizontal, she felt herself crash into his body but didn't know how it happened to be where she could crash into it, didn't know what position it was in, only knew his legs were somewhere around her face and his belly above her. There was a huge final spasm, and then she collapsed beneath him. And he continued to lick inside her, keeping alive the sensation.

Finally, when she was nearly unconscious, he got off her and repositioned himself the conventional way. She scarcely felt his penis enter. She scarcely felt his body on hers. She was almost numb.

She made herself move side-to-side with her hips, as far as she could go. And he liked it, he told her it felt very good. And she continued. And now he was pumping harder against her, slamming his pubic bone against hers, the feel of it penetrating her numbness. He came—the suddenness and speed of it made her think slap-slap-slap-slap-*pop*. Now he lay motionless, drawing long, groaning breaths, his belly swelling against her with each of them—but his weight not on her. A gentleman through and through, he used his elbows even now.

They lay silently for a long while, then he lifted himself off her, said he'd be right back, and returned with two snifters of cognac.

"*That* was exquisite, Grace."

She felt giddy—really great. She wanted to tell him he was a dynamite lover, in exactly those words. Instead she said, "I enjoyed it very much, Joseph. I really did."

"My man, you did it!" Nate Elefante appeared in Ted's path as Burr Whiteside hustled him from the elevator foyer.

"Did what?" Ted asked.

Nate grinned, then gestured with his head toward Grace Colello and Joseph Williams as they retreated toward the west wing. "Tha's my man, I knew you'd do it." He draped one arm over Ted's shoulders and the other over Whiteside's.

"Yessir, Burr, baby, they ain't no flies on this Instant Replay motherfucker. People think he lost his stuff, they dead wrong. He zips it in an' zips it out, just like in the ol' days." He banged Ted on the shoulder. "Now you jus' remember, Mister T, who it was set you up with that little business."

Ted managed a cheerless smile. "Why don't you just go on TV and tell the whole country about it, Nate?"

"Aw, I wasn't that loud, was I, Reep? Jeez, I'm sorry." He slapped Whiteside on the shoulder. "See that, Burr, baby? Is my man a gentleman? He may kiss, but he'll never tell."

"Ted," Whiteside said, sensing Ted's annoyance and changing the subject, "I talked Spats into doing a short bit about our security system. Just in case any prospective burglars got the idea watching the show that this might be a lucrative place to knock off."

"Good thinking."

"He'll do the bit at the door with McCollough and Kulikowski, just before the wrap-up. He wants you and the other guests he's picked standing nearby, so he can segue directly to you."

"Yeah, okay . . ."

Nate, getting impatient, added quickly, "Hey, Reep—the best is yet to come. We got us an invitation to another party. You may not dig the host, but you're sure gonna approve of the guest list."

"Well, now," Spats told the TV camera, "it looks like we're coming to the end of the road. But before we call it a night, I want to show you an aspect of Three-oh-five East that I personally find *most* interesting—the security system. Yessir, when your ol' buddy Spats tucks himself in for the night, he wants to make sure nobody disturbs his beddie-bye. And here's the man who makes sure nobody does, our security chief and former linebacker for the Chicago Bears, Sammy 'Rock' McCollough." The camera pulled back to reveal both men flanking a wall arrangement of twenty-four small TV screens.

"Spats," McCollough said, "with the security net we've established, it's as tough for an unauthorized person to get into Three-oh-five East as an inmate to get out of Sing Sing. Notice these monitors. They cover every entrance, plus the elevators, plus the courtyard, plus the garage. This set, as you can see, is here at the main entrance, where the doorman can watch it. There's a duplicate in the security office, where one of my guards or myself watches twenty-four hours a day."

"So," Spats summarized, "there's no way a person can come in or leave without being seen."

"That's right. If a tenant comes home late at night, we can watch him from the moment his car pulls into the garage until he leaves the elevator at his apartment. Tenants have specially coded plastic cards that open the garage doors. Apartment keys are required to activate the elevators. People making deliveries are escorted by security personnel, who stay with them the entire time they're in the building."

"How about guests? Suppose I wanted to have some buddies over to play poker?"

"A guest not accompanied by a tenant is escorted by a security man. All guests are given a pass envelope that contains a tiny transmitter. They turn this in when they leave. If a guest leaves the tenant's apartment and doesn't proceed directly out of the building, our equipment can identify his location by the transmitter."

Spats grinned at the camera. "Well, I guess I'll sleep well tonight. And I hope you do, too, my friends out there in TV-land, because it's getting to be about that time . . ."

Nan Loomis started for the elevator and found Nate Elefante in her way. "Hey, Miss Loomis, did you forget about the party?"

She blushed. She had hoped to get away undetected. Maybe she'd have better luck with her old, admittedly feeble, excuse . . . "Gee, Nate, I'm sorry, but I've got this awful headache—"

"I'm sure there'll be aspirins there." He took her arm, gently but authoritatively. "You can't change your mind now. I told everyone you're coming."

"Oh, I don't think they'll be disappointed. I don't know any of them—"

"That's just it. Everybody wants to meet this dynamite lady in the red dress they all saw on TV. Now come on, you can make it for at least one drink. If your headache's still bothering you, you can leave then."

She really wanted to say no. But she couldn't make herself do it . . . What else was new? she asked herself.

Joe Mandino's houseman, Angie, raised a puzzled eyebrow as Spats and company crowded into the elevator. "Does Joe expect so many guests, Spats?" he asked under his breath.

"Change in plans, Angie." Spats chucked him on the shoulder. "I'll explain to Joe." Angie turned the key, and the elevator rose. "There's five or six more coming after us," Spats said casually. "Ted Vassily's with them. Go down for them in about five minutes, okay?"

The elevator doors opened. Except for a few minor touches, Mandino's new apartment was a replica of the one on Fifth Avenue. Spats led his group through the foyer, with its pink marble floor and pillars, into the sunken living room, with its forest green marble floor and olive-colored silk wallcloth.

"What a setup," said one of the girls, who had danced on the TV show.

"This could pass for the lobby of the Excelsior in Rome," said Buffy Weiss. "I didn't know talk show hosting paid off so well."

Spats laughed. "This belongs to my friend. But mine's okay too." He refrained from winking.

They'd gotten halfway across the room when Joe Mandino appeared in an adjacent doorway. "Hello, Spats!" he called out, crossing to meet the group. "Wonderful show!"

Spats exchanged hugs with him, then introduced his guests. He'd expected Joe to show some surprise at the number of them, but the older man's face revealed no emotion. "A pleasure to meet you, Miss Weiss," said Joe, shaking her hand. "I've admired your work."

"Thank you," she replied, suddenly angry at Spats. He hadn't told her that her host would be New York's top Mafioso. She felt she should say something, do something—but exactly what? She remembered the exchange at the Algonquin between Vassily and Mandino's redneck lawyer with the tongue of honey . . . murderous phonies . . .

Joe shook hands with the others, repeating each person's name as he greeted her or him. "We were watching the program in the library," he said. "Come on in and have a drink." He led them inside.

It was a large, softly-lit room with floor-to-ceiling bookcases. A conference table was at the center, surrounded by dark brown, glove-leather swivel rocking chairs. In front of the table was an area with four leather couches arranged in front of a six-foot TV screen.

Three men sat there. They wore Brooks Brothers-cut gray flannels with rep ties, and white-on-white shirts, complete with the old-style double-roll French cuff . . . clearly men in transition. On a couch, alone, was the object of the lust of millions, Jeannie Danton.

"Meet some good friends—Lou, Mike, Petey," said Joe, gesturing to them. "Jeannie you know."

The men came forward to greet the newcomers. Buffy noted that Mandino hadn't used their full names. "Hi, *Lou,*" she said as he shook her hand. "Do you have a last name?"

"Nice meeting you, Miss Weiss," said Lou, and turned to one of the dancers.

The houseman appeared with a tray of glasses containing a cloudy yellow liquid over ice. "It's Amaretto, a Sicilian liqueur," Joe told them. "If anyone would prefer something else, just let Angie know."

The tray circulated, and the guests separated into twos and threes as they walked off with their drinks. Joe looked to Jeannie Danton, who promptly came to his side. Petey collected one of the dancers and joined Buffy and Spats. "It was a great show, Spats," he said.

"Thanks, man."

"I especially liked the bit with your father and the band. It's nice to see a guy stay close to his father, particularly these days, damn kids treat their parents like dirt . . ."

Angie disappeared with his tray and came back a few minutes later with the second contingent of guests. Spats introduced them to Joe, who introduced them to the gray flanneled gentlemen. Angie circulated with a fresh tray of Amaretto.

"I'm glad to have this opportunity to meet you," Mandino told Ted. "I've admired you for years. Welcome."

Ted nodded, feeling uneasy. "Miss Loomis and I were admiring the marble. Italian, isn't it?"

"Yes, Carrara."

"Did you pick the colors yourself?" Nan asked.

Joe glowed. "Everything. I chose every fabric, every stick of furniture, every piece of marble."

"It's beautiful," said Nan.

"Thank you," Joe said, moving along to another group of guests. He continued around the room until he crossed paths with Angie. Taking a fresh glass of Amaretto, he said in Italian, "Tell my small black friend I want to see him alone on the terrace."

"*Sì, padrone,*" Angie replied. He served several more drinks, then delivered the message, careful not to let Miss Weiss hear what was being said.

"Excuse me a minute," Spats told her. "I have to make an important phone call." He waited on the terrace until Joe arrived.

"Where the *fuck* did all these people come from?"

Spats smiled weakly. "There was a mixup with the bimbos, Uncle. The ones I had lined up for Petey and Lou and Mike—they wanted to bring their girl friends. So I had to line up the players to even things off." He fidgeted with his drink as he saw that Joe's expression was not brightening. "And you wanted to meet Vassily, right? I mean, it was a terrific opportunity, you know? Kill three birds with one stone—"

"That cunt lawyer, Buffy Weiss. Where'd she come from?"

Spats shifted weight from foot to foot. "She just sort of tagged along, Uncle. She heard me inviting one of the others and asked if she could come."

"You couldn't tell her no?"

"Well, I suppose I could've. Ordinarily. But under these circumstances, I mean . . ."

Joe wasn't listening. He'd turned his back to Spats and was looking out over the railing.

Spats waited.

"Get her out of here."

"Okay, Uncle, right away. Right now if you want." He waited a moment, then went to the door. "You want me to get rid of the others too?" He waited. No answer. He opened the door.

"Spats—" Joe turned to him—"come here a second, eh, *bello?*"

Spats went to him.

"Ah, *piccolo.*" Joe brought his palm gently to Spats' chin, cradling it as one might with a baby. With his other hand he pinched Spats' cheek. "Ah, *mio piccolo cioccolato,* you never learn from your uncle, do you?" He smiled sadly.

"I try, Uncle. I really do."

"What you have to understand, *piccolo,* some people don't like surprises. Like the cowboys in the Wild West, you know? They wouldn't sit with their back to the door. They knew, ninety-nine times out of one hundred nothing would happen. But ninety-nine percent isn't good enough."

"I wanted to clear it with you first, Uncle, but I just didn't have time . . . I was on TV and I had to set everything up before everybody got away. I used my best judgment, Uncle, I really did . . ."

Joe shook his head. "You're not listening, *piccolo.* What I'm saying is, some people don't like surprises. Maybe they're here and they don't want anybody to know it. Maybe they don't want people asking their last name. Maybe they're in the mood for a little privacy. Maybe somebody else is here that you didn't know about. So when you say you're coming here with bimbos for Mike, Petey and Lou, plus one for yourself, that's what you bring, no more, no less."

"But, Unc—"

"And the one for yourself is a bimbo like the others that won't cause any trouble, not a *lawyer*, I don't care how bad you want to get into her pants."

"But—"

"Listen to *me*," Joe hissed, twisting Spats' cheek till it stung. "I don't want explanations now, I'm explaining things to *you*. In the future, under no circumstances do you surprise me—under no circumstances. *Capisci?*"

"Yes, Uncle."

"If there's some need to change plans, you call me first to make sure it's okay. And if you can't call, you cancel whatever it was we planned. *Chiaro?*"

"Yes, Uncle."

"Now get Miss Weiss out of here. And then come back and get rid of everybody else except the three broads with Lou, Mike and Petey—if they still want them."

"Yes, Uncle."

Spats waited to see if there would be further instructions. Joe was silent. Spats went back to the library. "Hey, Buf, I took care of everything I want to do here, so what say we make it over to my place?"

She looked at him curiously. "What happened to the party?"

"Don't ask questions." He squeezed her arm. "Just come *on!*" He hustled her out.

A moment later Joe came back into the library. He walked among the clusters of guests, smiling graciously and bowing slightly to each group as he passed. He noticed Ted Vassily, Burr Whiteside and Nate Elefante standing with three girls. He enjoyed the way the one introduced as Nan Loomis was cuddling against Ted. Wasn't she the banker's daughter? He wondered if her old man even suspected she was running with pro football players.

"Mister Vassily," Joe said, approaching the group, "before it slips my mind, I want to tell you what a terrific crew I think you have. Mister Elefante here—well, they just don't make building superintendents any better. And Mister Whiteside's p.r. work—well, I guess I don't have to say anything, the results speak for themselves."

Nate and Burr said their thanks.

"Mister Mandino," Ted said, "we were just about to take off. So—" he didn't extend his hand.

"Hey," said Nate, when they were in the elevator, "what the hell you suppose happened to the party all of a sudden?"

Ted shrugged. "You guys have your own party. I'm going to show Miss Nan Loomis the best view in New York City."

"Now that we're out of that rat's nest," Buffy Weiss said as she and Spats descended in the elevator, "are you going to tell me what the *hell* is going on?"

Spats clenched his jaws, glared at the floor and did not answer.

"I asked you a question."

He kept silent.

"Coffee Joe Mandino," she said. "And those greasers in the Brooks Brothers suits. Do you realize you brought me to a mini-Appalachian convention?"

Spats' eyes rose slowly to meet hers. "Listen, lady-lawyer, I'm going to tell you three things. Number one, *I* didn't invite *you* anywhere. You invited yourself. Number two, those people are my friends. If you think you're too goddamn good for them, stay the fuck away from me, too. Number three, I've had a long night. I'm not in the mood for anybody's bullshit. You want to come up my place for a drink and a fuck, be my guest. But take that hot shit goddamn attitude of yours and shove it, 'cause this here nigger ain't kissing any chick's ass, white or black, lawyer or goddamn toilet cleaner."

She forced an obliging smile and moved closer to him. It was easier to take from him than Ted. "I wasn't trying to piss you off, Eddie." She straightened his collar, then rested her fingers on the muscles of his neck. "I'm sorry I reacted that way. Maybe it was because the whole scene scared me. Anyway, man, I promise not to bug you again . . . not for the rest of the night." (Bug . . . bug-eyed . . . she almost giggled . . . and then shivered . . .)

He looked at her uncertainly for a moment, then made himself smile. "Okay. Sorry I hollered on you."

The elevator door opened. He led her across the lobby to the west wing elevators and inserted his key in the penthouse lock.

She leaned against him as the elevator rose. She found herself thinking that he was shorter than she. In fact, the top of his head barely reached her ear. And he was so skinny. She'd never been with a smaller, thinner man. She'd always preferred them big, real beefos . . . Ted Vassily . . .

All the same, he turned her on. His vitality and energy. And, of course, his talent. And the way he asserted himself just a few moments ago. It excited her for a man to respond that way to her needle. It always had. She'd been through the whole thing with her analyst, a reaction to her nice-guy weak father . . .

"Look, I'm going to bring you up to my place," Spats said, "and then I want to go back and make sure everybody's checked out of Joe's."

"Do you have to go back?"

"Not *have* to. *Want* to. You lose your ears or something?"

"Don't get so upset." She toyed with his collar again. "It's just that I'll miss you." (Like playing with a little animal . . . an angry little animal . . .

"I'll be back right away." He held her close against him and told himself that he really had to be horny tonight to still want to ball her after all this bullshit. And she wasn't that terrific either. There wasn't one dancer from the show who didn't have a better body. And he could've had any of them. What the hell was Buffy Weiss' appeal to him? Just that she was a civilian instead of a show-biz chick? Hell, she wasn't even a Clean! She was a fucking dust-o, wearing goddamn jeans to a formal party. Matter of fact, she was even wearing that goddamn old hippie perfume—Pat Julie, or whatever they called it—the one the druggo-freakos wore. Yeah, he must really be horny.

The elevator opened, and he followed Buffy into his apartment, flicking on the lights. "It's—" she hesitated—"really striking."

He laughed. Why did chicks never like modern? They

always liked old shit that looked as though it would fall apart when you sat in it. He started toward the bar to make her a drink, then changed his mind. "The booze is over there," he said, gesturing. "I'll be back."

He rode down to the lobby. Jeez, what a bummer tonight had turned out to be. Joe was one hell of a difficult person to get along with. Of course Spats could respect the reasons for his touchiness. He should've known better than to change plans on him. He certainly should've known better than to bring Buffy Weiss to the apartment. The goddamn problem was, who the hell can think clearly under so much pressure? You've got fifteen seconds to put on your mike, get to the bandstand, take your cue—then some cunt says "fuck" a few inches from the mike, you're pretty shook, how the hell are you going to think clearly about goddamn parties? What he needed was someone to take care of this piddly-diddly horseshit. An all-around detail man. Somebody to serve him the way Nasty Nate served Ted. But somebody a lot sharper than Nasty Nate. A guy who could make reservations in restaurants, set up his travel schedule, talk to TV executives, even line up chicks if necessary. He'd once read somewhere that a shipping billionaire used to keep six guys on his staff whose only job was lining up chicks. Whenever his yacht docked someplace, they'd go ashore and hustle up the best local talent. Now *that* was the way to live.

Starting across the lobby, Spats saw Ted, Nate, Burr, and their chicks leaving the south elevators. The Loomis broad was hanging all over Ted. You'd think they were college sweethearts. Goddamn! She was the reason for this whole fuckup. He should never have tried to get to her this way. What he should've done was wait to phone her tomorrow and say he thought she was a really gorgeous lady and how would she like to audition for a part on his show. Or some horseshit like that, instead of leaving her wide open to be bird-dogged by Vassily. Of course, who could've known Ted would be interested? (Oh, shit, Spats—how could anybody not be interested in a dynamite chick like that?) You had to give the sonofabitching T-bone credit, he didn't waste time nailing her down . . .

Spats waited until the group was away from the south elevators—he wasn't in the mood for chit-chat right now—then got into a car, reached for the penthouse button and suddenly remembered that he needed a key to activate the elevator. Goddamn, nothing was happening right tonight. He'd probably get back to his own place and find that Buffy had cut out. And wind up beating his meat.

He went to the main entrance and got Joe's houseman on the intercom.

"It's okay, Spats," Angie rasped, "all the others left right after you did."

Spats hung up, then wondered if Joe might be angry that he hadn't gotten the okay from him personally. You never could tell when stuff like that would piss him off.

Spats dialed the apartment again.

"Yeah, it's okay, *bello,*" Joe said. "Give your lawyer a good fucking, eh? Reverse the usual order of things."

Spats smiled and went back to his own apartment. Goddamn, what a night. He couldn't remember wasting so much movement on piddly shit. He'd start looking tomorrow for a personal assistant, a real handsome dude, to make it super-easy with the chicks. Better yet, a white guy. That was really the only way to do the thing with white chicks.

Getting out of the elevator, Spats smelled smoke. Not regular smoke. Goddamn marijuana smoke . . .

"What the fuck are you doing?"

Buffy was sitting on the couch sucking a joint. She giggled, "I'm writing a letter to Santa Claus, lover."

He grabbed her wrist, twisting the joint away from her mouth. "You think every goddamn spade in the world is a junkie? Is that why you light up in my place without even asking if it's okay?"

"Eddie, it's only a joint!"

"Well, put the thing out if you intend to stay here. I don't want grassheads nodding out on me when I'm trying to talk to them."

"All *right,* don't get excited." She looked for an ashtray, couldn't find one, and went looking for a bathroom to dump the joint into the toilet.

Watching her retreat down the hallway, Spats felt a little guilty. He really shouldn't be so rough on her. She wasn't a bad chick, all things considered. But she *liked* him to be rough on her. She was one of those please-shit-on-me honkies.

She came back from the bathroom, displaying her empty hands. Spats smiled. "That's better, babes. Now come on over to Uncle Spats." He spread his arms, and she stepped into his embrace.

He kissed her, driving his tongue deeply into her mouth. After a moment, her hands went to his cock.

"Let's take us a shower," he said.

"Oh, you're into that old routine?"

"Well, yeah, I guess I *am* into that old routine." Also, Miss Lady Lawyer, it should help get rid of the stink of your fucking hippie perfume.

Ted led Nan Loomis into his apartment. "Champagne?"

"Thank you."

He wondered what he should do about the bottle and glasses he and Grace had used. Where were they, anyway?

He touched his glass to hers and thought how *comfortable* he felt with her . . . had felt, in fact, from the very beginning. Partly, he suspected, it was because her undemanding chatter relieved him of the old up-tight problem of making small and easy talk.

"I just noticed," she said, "you don't wear a ring."

"No."

"How come?"

"I guess it just strikes me as kind of goofy, at least for men."

"But don't you have a championship ring? I mean, they award them for the Super Bowl, right?"

"I have a couple, yeah." He hesitated. "Would you like to see them?"

"Yes."

He laughed.

"Did I say something funny?"

"No, I just thought of an old Lenny Bruce routine."

She looked at him curiously.

"I'm sorry . . . Well, the rings are in my bedroom, and that sounds like such a hokey variation on a make-out ploy that it reminded me of this old Lenny Bruce story

. . . A guy comes on to a girl in a bar and invites her back to his hotel room. She won't go because the words 'hotel room' have such a bad association—you know, cheap affair, tramp, that sort of thing. On the other hand, said Lenny, if the guy had a house trailer, it'd be okay because house trailers, after all, suggest healthy, innocent family things, great outdoors, babbling brooks . . . So the same guy coming on to the girl in the bar invites her to his 'house trailer.' And she says, 'Of course, I'd love to. Where is it?' And he says, 'In my hotel room.' "

Nan laughed, not exactly uproariously.

Ted shrugged. "Well, I guess it loses something in the telling. Anyway, with all that as prologue, would you like to come into my bedroom and see my rings?" He tried a Groucho Marx leer as accompaniment, which earned him a rather tepid smile.

"You should ask if I'd like to come into your house trailer."

"All right, would you like to come into my house trailer and see my rings?"

"I'd love to, where is it?"

"In my bedroom."

They both laughed, she more openly than she had all night, and, with relief, he picked up their champagne glasses and led her into the bedroom.

She really was fun to be with, he told himself, sort of cool and relaxed about everything. When Nate had introduced them, she'd seemed a little reluctant, but then, as they rode the elevator to Mandino's, she'd started chatting, asking questions about him that had put him completely at ease. And feeling that way, he'd found an excuse to put his arm around her, which she didn't resist. And then he took hold of her hand, which she didn't resist either. By the time they'd left the party she was cuddling up against him as if they'd already been to bed. It felt great, but he wondered if she'd be as easily responsive to something heavier later, and suspected that would be a different story . . . a banker's daughter, all-American clean-cut looking as she was . . .

"Here they are," he said, taking three small velvet-covered boxes from a drawer and popping them open.

She took the boxes one at a time and studied the rings respectfully. "They're huge," she said, lifting one from its holder. "They must weigh half a pound."

He shrugged. "Big fingers." He popped open another box. "This is the one I'm most proud of."

She took it from the box. It was even bigger than the others. It had a huge red stone, surrounded by small clear diamonds. She read the inscription: "Pro Football Hall of Fame."

"That's quite an honor," she said. "What position did you play?"

That question startled him. Didn't everybody know?—at least everybody who knew he played football! "Quarterback." He hesitated. "That's the guy in the backfield who—"

"Yes, I know, I dated a wide receiver in college."

"What was his name?"

"George Mellini."

"Where'd *he* play?"

"Harvard."

"I guess that explains it."

Her brow wrinkled, then she smiled. "Oh, you mean because Ivy League players usually aren't nationally known? Yes, George used to tell me that."

She gave him back the ring and he returned the boxes to their drawer, wondering whether he should try something now that he already had her in the bedroom—accommodating as she'd been so far, he decided he shouldn't rush things, risk putting her off . . . and he was suddenly aware of his unmade bed, which apparently bothered him more than Nan—she hadn't seemed to notice.

Hopefully she would be equally as indifferent—or non-observant—about the two glasses he and Grace had used . . . and which were where they'd left them, on the table by the window where he now led Nan to admire the view. God, sometimes he wondered if he'd ever grow up . . . Ted Vassily—superstud, masterbuilder, and with all the sophistication of a goddamn school boy, deep-down where it counted . . . He looked at Nan, who'd finished admiring the view and, as with the bed, apparently hadn't noticed the further source of his unease.

He took a deep breath, sat down on the big reclining

chair and took her hand, half-leading her into his lap. No resistance. He held her against him, kissed her on the cheek, then turned her chin toward him. Still no resistance. He kissed her on the lips. Her mouth opened to receive his tongue. He slid his hand up her side, brushing the underslope of a breast with his thumb. No resistance. Now his thumb over her full breast. Still no resistance, nor to his palm over her breast.

Was it possible?

He stroked her breast, delighting in its firm roundness, pleased that she wasn't wearing a bra. It was magnificent. Not as large as Grace's . . . stop thinking about her, stop comparing, she's different and apart, keep her that way . . . but for her slight build Nan's did seem startlingly large . . . He wanted to touch her bare breast but couldn't figure out how to get inside her dress. There were no buttons in front. Probably a zipper in back, but that would be too awkward.

"Hey," he said softly, "we're probably wrinkling the hell out of your dress. Why don't I get you a robe so you can take it off?"

"Oh . . . well, thank you, that would be very nice."

What an incredibly easy-to-get-along-with lady. He got out one of his robes, which she changed into in the bathroom. Back in the reclining chair, he wanted to reach underneath the robe immediately, but forced himself to hold back and be content for the moment with holding her, rubbing his hand up and down her back. And then he was kissing her again. And back to the breast, step-by-step . . . graze the underslope, thumb on top, palm on top, play awhile, okay . . . now inside the robe. First, just the thumb in the cleavage, no resistance, now pull the robe slightly open, heel of the hand on the breast itself, still no resistance, now all the way in to find it even more desirable in the flesh. He teased the nipple some with a finger, but mostly attended to the whole breast because he loved the texture of it, the fullness of it. And then he was taking it into his mouth . . .

She accepted all this without special enthusiasm—or reservation either. She had positioned herself so that her breasts were easy to get to, and she had a nice kind of sexy smile on her face—eyes closed, head thrown back.

There was no squirming or moaning . . . apparently not her restrained style.

He decided to go further and met no resistance as his hands eased down the flatness of her tummy and onto her long, lean thigh. He toyed momentarily with the waistband of her panties, then moved again to her thighs. They were pressed together. He put his hand between them, applied some pressure. She parted them. Almost obediently.

Up slowly. Stroke the inside of her thigh. Stop short, back down, now stroke the outside, then to the inside again. Back down, back up, linger at the crotch a moment. Still no resistance. Now press in. Yes! She was moist—not wet, really, but moist. He eased one finger into the leghole of the panties. Now into the labia. Still no problem. Okay, into her cunt and stir it up. He waited for some indication that she was getting more excited. She showed none. But still there was no resistance. None at all. All right, ease off the panties, more action in her vagina while at the same time spreading her thighs wider, for psychological effect as well as easier access; now shifting position, her thighs straddling his. Out with his cock and rubbing it first against her thigh, then against her pubes, now against the labes. Fantastic—fantastic flat belly, fantastic lean thighs . . . okay, press against the labes. Still no resistance. Rub around a while, lubricating himself with her . . . Now pressure, and she's pressing back, so a little harder now. In. In slightly deeper . . .

"Shall we go into the bedroom?" he asked after what he hoped was a respectable interval.

"If you like."

He thought of trying to carry her in while keeping her impaled on his dick—as he had with Buffy—but decided she was too restrained for that kind of showboating. Better to play it straight. He embraced her patiently alongside the bed before guiding her onto it, although by now he was wildly aroused, much more than he would have expected possible after what had already happened that evening—uneasily, he tried to force that out of his mind. Maybe it was her cool nonchalance that was turning him on so . . .

She parted her legs to await his entry. He approached

gently, guiding himself in. Her body against his now felt terrific—large cushiony breasts, the slimness of the rest of her. He took up a slow easy rhythm. Her hips fell into cadence. After a few of his head-on strokes she shifted to side-to-side movements that created unique sensations in counterpoint to his continuing head-on movements.

He knew he wouldn't be able to last too long, but he wanted to give her hers before he came. "Put your legs straight down," he said, touching her thigh.

She did.

"Now over mine."

"Like this?"

"Perfect."

He angled for the optimum clitoral pressure and waited for some sign from her that he was providing it. She wordlessly resumed her side-to-side movements.

"Am I positioned right?" he asked.

"What? Oh yes. It's fine."

He wasn't accustomed to *this* kind of cool. He put on more pressure. Still no sign that it was having an effect. He shifted slightly. Still no sign.

"What can I do to make it better for you?"

"It's fine just like this." She hesitated. "Don't try to make me come, Ted."

"Why not?"

"I usually don't."

He slid his hand between his abdomen and hers, finding her clitoris with his index finger.

"Really, Ted. I'd rather you didn't try."

Okay, if that's the way you want it, he thought, feeling faintly guilty nonetheless as he lengthened his strokes, giving himself the kind of glans pressure that would put him over very quickly. She seemed to sense what he needed; her hips went into a circular movement that accented his sensations, and at the same time she started licking his neck and jaw. He loved that.

It was a good one. Powerful and long. Afterward he stayed in place on top of her and kissed her gently on the lips. "I'm sorry I couldn't do more for you."

"Please don't be worried about it . . . I liked it very much."

"Don't you ever come?"

"Rarely."

"Do you need something special, something that I wasn't doing for you . . . ?"

"No. It's . . . unpredictable. But really, Ted, you shouldn't worry. It's not that important."

Well, talk about no pressure . . . Nan Loomis was the ultimate in that department, he thought, as he went back into the living room and came back with fresh glasses of champagne. She was so pleasant, so easy to get along with, and so great looking . . . really one of the most beautiful girls he'd ever seen—probably *the* most beautiful he'd ever been to bed with. "I admire your sexual freedom," he said, getting back into bed with her, and not liking the way that sounded, quickly added, "I mean, I think it's great to be so un-hung up about sex . . ."

She smiled. "How do you know I'm 'un-hung up'?"

"Well, I mean, you seem to be, and I think in a way I enjoy that . . . it's unusual for a woman—or a man—for that matter . . ." He wished he hadn't started on this line of conversation, which obviously was making her uncomfortable. Bail out, he told himself.

"I suppose you're right," she said. "I guess I was, well, pretty free."

"Look, I'm sorry, I still throw footballs better than I talk—"

"That's okay . . . but, you know, the fact is I'm not very experienced."

"A beautiful girl like you? All I can say is the whole male population must have gone to fairyland, if—" Vassily! *Cool* it.

She looked off at the wall. "Well, the fact is, there have only been two, before you, that is. I guess I'm just an old-fashioned—"

He couldn't deny he liked hearing it, felt damned flattered even, and rushed to cut off the subject while he was still ahead . . . way ahead. "Champagne?" he asked, grateful for the prop.

She looked at her glass, which didn't need refilling. She sipped. "Love some." Watching him pour, she wondered why she had lied to him. Wouldn't it have been as easy, or better, not to lie about the number of her lovers? Or at least to tell him that her past love life was none of his business. Better, she wasn't sure. But certainly it wouldn't have been as easy. Which was why she hadn't done it. Good old path-of-least-resistance Nan!

He sipped his champagne, then put both glasses on the night table and hugged her. "You know," he said, "I feel very good being with you, Nan Loomis. I hope it's only, as they say, the beginning . . ."

"I'm glad, Ted. I like you too . . ." Inwardly she felt a twinge of discomfort. If there was one thing she really couldn't handle just now it was another possessive man. One of Ted's attractions for her had been that he seemed unlikely to be difficult in that department. She did like him and hoped he wouldn't spoil it . . .

He kissed her, then guided her into a lying position and rested his face between her breasts. As she stretched her legs forward, she felt her bare foot come into contact with something silky. She thought it might be her panties but remembered he had taken them off in the living room. She hooked the object with her toe and fished it out from under the covers.

"Yours?" she asked, displaying Grace Colello's panties, and immediately felt sorry for saying it as she saw him blanch. She certainly hadn't intended to embarrass him, and if she'd realized what they were she would have left them under the covers.

"I suppose I should say I have no idea how they got there," he said, smiling weakly, "but the truth is—"

She laughed, then kissed him on the nose. "The truth is, Mr. Vassily, you're sort of cute, and why don't we let it go at that?" And so saying, she snuggled against him, thinking to herself that he really was cute, and that actually the panties were reassuring. With somebody else in his life he wasn't as likely to be possessive, which was just fine with her. She could relax and enjoy a relationship with a man like him if he gave her the kind of breathing room she needed. Needed? For what? Well, for her peace of mind. She had spent the better part of twenty-one years being pressured into doing what *other* people wanted. Who knew, maybe if given her free choice it would have turned out that they were the things she wanted too. But she hadn't been given that choice, and until she became accustomed to having it she was going to avoid letting anyone—even an "anyone" as attractive as Ted Vassily—put his brand on her. After twenty-one years of feeling like an instrument for other people's wishes and desires, it was time she began to become her own person.

"You must be tired," Jeannie Danton told Joe Mandino as they watched the elevator doors close behind the last of his guests.

He took her hand. "Never too tired for you, Jeannie."

She kissed him on the cheek. "I didn't mean that. I just meant, it's probably been a very long day for you."

He went to the couch opposite the fireplace, where half-finished glasses of Amaretto waited on a marble table. She sat next to him, sliding down slightly in her seat in response to his pressure on her shoulder. He reached inside her bodice. "I'll bet there are fifty million guys in this country that'd give their right arm to be able to do this. Left one too."

She smiled. "Flattery will get you everywhere."

"In this case it isn't flattery, it's truth."

"Is that why you want me, Joe? Because so many others do?"

He let go of her breast long enough to take another sip of Amaretto. The question went unanswered—a sure signal to her that she shouldn't have asked it.

"I really love being alone with you," she said, reaching inside his jacket and stroking his belly. "I also like it when we're with other people, of course, but even more when we're alone."

"You're a good girl, Jeannie. You know all the right things to say."

Her hand went slowly to his crotch. "Well, what have we here? Something nice and hard!"

"Looking at you in that dress, any guy would get one."

She took it out and ran her thumbnail teasingly around the glans. "Nice and big, too. It must be those great Sicilian genes."

He laughed.

"Remember what a time you used to have getting it up when we first started seeing each other?" His frown told her she had asked another wrong question. Three strikes and out with Joe Mandino. "Well, it's sure nice and stiff now," she added quickly.

He put pressure on the back of her neck. She held her head in place over his penis for a teasing instant, then kissed the tip, then looked up at him and winked. "Ready?"

He nodded.

She slowly took the penis into her mouth.

The houseman Angie appeared in the library doorway with the Amaretto bottle. Joe nodded to him. Angie walked softly to the marble table, filled both glasses, then retreated to the kitchen and closed the door behind him.

Jeannie Danton did not look up from her work.

SIX

TED WOKE with a start and realized the bed was empty. He found a note on the dresser. "Didn't want to wake you. Thought you might need the sleep. Thanks for a lovely evening. *Ciao*. Nan."

He felt an unusual sense of loss. Though Nan had been with him only a few hours, he had quickly developed a sense of her, an attachment to her. That beautiful face, slim body, those accented breasts—she was as close to his female physical ideal as . . . well . . . as close as he'd come since the days long ago when he used to take her kind of near-perfection for granted. Nan Loomis in one night had become an invitation for him to fall in love.

Almost as an afterthought, he checked his wristwatch. Ten-forty-five. Little wonder she'd left. He took a quick shower, brushed his teeth, inspected his face and decided he couldn't forego a shave. But he skipped the usual heat treatment for his knees. They ached like hell as he hurried to his office. Nice thing about living and working in the same building, though, he told himself—no commuting.

Emerson Wade was waiting in the outer office when Ted arrived. "You might say our show was a hit," he said, displaying a foot-thick stack of telegrams.

Ted's secretary, Bonnie, displayed a slightly smaller stack of phone messages. "Everyone from the governor on down is congratulating you."

"Anything of immediate interest?"

"Two possibles." She handed him the top two slips. "They asked for you to return their calls."

"Joe Mandino," Ted read. "From First American Investment Corporation. And Hartford Loomis. You're sure that wasn't Nan Loomis?"

"Yes. Mister Loomis' secretary placed the call from BankUS."

Ted led Emerson into the inner office. Bonnie served coffee. Ted studied the slip with Loomis' name on it. He doubted the banker would phone to congratulate him. Had Loomis found out that Nan spent the night with him? If so, would he do something as corny as phoning to raise hell?

"Joe Mandino," he said, going to the next slip. "What do you suppose he wants?"

"Something fairly benign," Emerson said. "If it was his kind of serious business I doubt he'd put the call through a switchboard."

"I've never heard of First American."

"Probably his corporate front. Maybe he wants some of the paper on the building."

"Why make the offer now? The best time would've been when we were hassling with the banks and Ron-Cor."

"You've got me, Reep."

Ted crumpled the note and dropped it into his wastebasket. "Okay, there's no law that I've got to return his call. If you're right about his intentions, that should be the end of the matter."

"And if I'm wrong?"

Ted forced a laugh. "I get myself a new financial vice president." He buzzed Bonnie and asked her to phone Hartford Loomis. "Seriously," he told Emerson, "if Coffee Joe is planning something, the worst thing I can do is roll over when he snaps his fingers. So if he's offended that I don't return his call, fuck him. Let him move out of the building. Break my heart." He sipped his coffee. "Now, let's get on with our own business."

Wade took a manila folder from his attaché case. "Reep, the press and public reaction this morning strongly supports our confidence in Three-oh-five's viability. I just checked with Jay Kasselman. As of a week ago, we had three hundred and eighty names on the waiting list for apartments—or virtually one backup for every present tenant. As of this morning, thanks to the media blitz, we've got six hundred and ten names—all with a cash deposit, needless to say. By the time the month is out, we'll likely have eight hundred."

"Okay, tell Kasselman to stop accepting applicants. No point making people wait when there's no chance of getting in."

"Consider another approach, Reep. I've put together some figures here on three older buildings in the immediate neighborhood." He leafed through his manila folder. "These are all sound structures, all very luxurious when they were built, but the managements have let them slide. We can pick up any one of them—or all three—for a song, refurbish, and offer the apartments to our waiting list. If we want, we can make it a condition of the waiting list that tenants live in one of our other buildings."

"No, I don't like that, Emer. It cheapens what we're doing at Three-oh-five."

"Okay, we don't make it mandatory. I'm sure we'd have no trouble filling the apartments anyway. All we have to do is let it be known that you're running the show . . . spin-off effect."

"In other words, we'll exploit our good name."

"Not 'exploit' in a negative sense, Ted. We'll be giving tenants sound value, but we'll be able to deliver it a lot cheaper than at Three-oh-five because these other buildings are available at distress prices . . . it'd also boost our cash flow considerably and do wonders for our balance sheet."

They were interrupted by the buzzer on Ted's phone. Bonnie reported that Hartford Loomis was on the line. Ted activated his speaker attachment.

"Hello, Mister Vassily," the banker said. "It occurred to me last night that you and I never really got an opportunity to chat. I thought it might not be a bad idea for me to get to know my landlord better. Perhaps if you're free some afternoon, you might come over to the bank for lunch."

"Sounds good," Ted said. He consulted his datebook. "How's next Thursday?"

"Friday's better."

"No, I'm tied up. The following Monday?"

"Fine. Twelve-thirty? My office?"

Emerson smiled as Ted flicked off the speaker. "An invitation to Hartford Loomis' private dining room. You know, there are guys on Wall Street who'd pay a hundred thou to eat there, just so they could say they did."

"I wonder what he wants." Ted was thinking that if Loomis was upset about Nan he'd have tried to schedule a meeting much sooner.

"What he wants," Emerson said, "is to get a little closer to *you*. You may not realize it, my man, but you've suddenly become a very hot property. From the golden arm to the golden touch. You pulled off the impossible and now everyone who said it couldn't be done wants to get close enough to have you do something for them." He gestured toward his manila folder. "Which is why I think we ought to move on these other buildings now, while we've got optimum psychological leverage. You know better than anyone, Reep, no one stays hot forever."

"Leave me the figures. I'll think about it. But my immediate reaction is negative . . . I guess it's just a gut reaction."

Emerson handed him the folder and took another from the attaché case. "I respect gut reactions, Reep, but whatever you decide on the buildings, I think it's important that we take advantage of our momentum. We're never going to find money easier to borrow. I've worked up a few other ideas . . ."

They involved a radio station, a proposed television production company to syndicate college football games, and a national newspaper devoted entirely to pro football, to be published weekly during the season. At first glance each proposal seemed very attractive, but Ted didn't want to think of any of them right now. He wanted to think of —and be with—Nan Loomis.

He took the folders and quickly wrapped up the rest of the morning's business. When Emerson had gone he got Nan's number from information and dialed it. No answer. He considered phoning her at her parents' apartment, then quickly dismissed the idea. Instead, he drew her name in elaborate letters on his scratch pad. Laughing at himself for being so schoolboy-romantic, he crumpled the sheet of paper, dropped it into his wastebasket and buzzed Bonnie. "Have a dozen white and red roses delivered to Miss Loomis. Have the card read 'Ted.' "

He hung up and started going through the telephone message slips. Midway through, he realized he'd flipped more than a dozen without noticing the callers' names . . . Because now the name Grace Colello had taken over his consciousness . . . It bothered him that he had reacted so much more positively to Nan, especially so soon after being with Grace. Ted Vassily, who shared so much more background with Grace, should at least have a sort of underdog's loyalty to her, and here he was doing what the rest of the world had no doubt done since she was a kid, rejecting her, for a beauty-queen daughter of affluence and privilege who'd never had to lift a finger . . .

Oh, come on, Vassily, you've already reminded yourself you can't argue with a limp dick . . . well, you can't argue with a stiff one either. Hell, you didn't reject Grace. You've just responded honestly to the way you feel . . . well, haven't you? . . .

The question nagged him. "Bonnie," he said, buzzing, "order a second dozen roses, for Miss Grace Colello, fourteen B. Same thing on the card."

Bonnie played it as cool as if he'd just ordered another container of coffee, for which he was instantly grateful. "And by the way, I'd like to speak to Miss Loomis. Phone her apartment every fifteen minutes until she's in."

He went back to his message slips, then after a while buzzed Bonnie again. "Put in a call to Miss Colello too, okay? If she's out, leave a call-back with her parents. If there's no answer, keep trying her every fifteen minutes too."

And back to his message slips. He had worked his way through all of them and half the telegrams, returning phone calls or dictating thank you notes, when Bonnie reported she had Miss Loomis on the line.

"Are you busy?" Ted asked.

"Oh, well, I was just out shopping."

"How about a drink?"

"Oh . . . when?"

"Now."

"But don't you have to work?"

"I think I can talk the boss into letting me off. Meet me at the east elevators, okay?"

"Well, Ted, I'd really like to, but I have so much to do this afternoon . . . I'm on a flight tomorrow and I have just scads of things—"

He laughed. "I won't tie you up too long. The invitation was just for a drink, okay?"

"I really shouldn't—"

"I'll meet you at the elevators . . ."

He waited for her to agree or object. She said nothing. "In five minutes," he prodded.

She hesitated. "Fifteen minutes. But I really can't stay for more than a drink, Ted. It's not that . . . well, I'm just so awfully busy today, I'm sure you understand . . . you do, don't you?"

"Sure. Fifteen minutes. See you then."

She was wearing a short white two-piece suit with green trim. She looked deliciously crisp . . . fresh. And beautiful. Her hair was fluffy-light and seemed almost to float toward her shoulders. Her face was sparklingly alive. And those breasts moving against the restraining fabric of her blouse . . . "You're gorgeous," he said, and meant it.

"Why, thank you," she said, feeling somewhat uneasy.

He guided her into the elevator, inserted his key and took her in his arms as the doors closed. She only momentarily resisted, then relaxed into his kiss. When the elevator stopped, she waited for him to back away. When he didn't, she eased away from him. "Somebody may be waiting for the elevator . . ."

He took out his key, took her by the arm and executed a militarily precise sidestep into the apartment—his way of saying, "Now that that's out of the way, there's no excuse."

Standing there next to him, she understood he was waiting to resume, and his impatience annoyed her. Also his presumptuousness. He'd never considered, apparently, what she might or might not want. She decided not to resist, though. To really put him off she'd need to do it in such a way that would anger or insult him, and she was more uneasy with that kind of scene than with being kissed . . . Fact was, she wasn't really adverse to being kissed, she just wasn't in the mood *now*. She was harried, tense. She had too many things to do, she'd told him she only could stay for one drink, and he should have taken her at her word . . .

Except now he was hugging her, relishing the feel of her breasts, his heart pounding so hard he was sure she must feel it too. God, she was incredibly exciting to him, he couldn't get enough of her. He *had* to have her . . .

"Ted," she was saying, "could I have a glass of cold water."

Cold water! Great . . . he filled a glass with ice, then water, and as an afterthought poured some white wine for himself. He led her to a pair of facing armchairs in the room's lower level and sat opposite her. "I guess I should apologize for pressuring you to come up," he said. "I didn't realize how busy you are. Look, I didn't have anything in particular I wanted to talk about. I just wanted to be with you—"

"Oh, Ted, that's sweet, and I'm sorry I've made you feel that way." And now . . . damn it . . . she felt guilty . . . "I wanted to be with you too, that's why I came—"

He reached across the coffee table to take her hand. "Nan, corny or not, I get so damned turned on just looking at you that I get ahead of myself . . . of you too, I guess."

"I'm flattered, Ted, and I wish I could get turned on as quickly . . . not, of course, that you're not a very handsome man. You really are . . ."

He let go of her hand, took a large swallow of wine and leaned back in his chair. "I guess it must be rough for you. With all the guys, I mean. I'm sure I'm not the only one who responds this way . . . it's just that you really are so damned beautiful, well, it's impossible to relax with you and pretend that sex isn't a part—hell, basic part —of what's going on. What little we've seen of each other so far just creates a tremendous appetite in me to see more of you, to get inside your feelings and your thoughts . . . but"—he shrugged—"I'm afraid this stiff dick of mine keeps getting up front."

She knew her blush was breaking out all over and tried to mask her discomfort with an academic line. "I think we're sort of casualties of the sexual revolution, don't you? I mean, a generation ago people kept their feelings bottled up until they knew each other well in other ways. We rebelled, but we haven't worked out the details too well."

He sipped his wine and said nothing, wondering how he could have let things take *this* turn. Hell, she had him feeling as though he were practically assaulting her.

She pressed on. "Were you ever with a girl who wanted sex when you weren't in the mood?"

"I guess so." He wanted to forget the whole thing. "I guess I've still got some details to work out."

She smiled. He really was cute, especially when he was discouraged.

"Look, Nan, I'll try not to make any more unfair demands." He stood, finished his wine and turned toward the kitchen. "Are you game for another glass of water, cold water, that is, or—"

"Ted, you're offended by what I said."

"Of course not."

She watched him retreat to the kitchen and felt a sudden panic. She was afraid that if she didn't say something, do something—do it immediately—he would end this, and if she let him do that it would be the last she saw of him. She didn't want that. Suddenly it was very important to her that they not end here. The feeling was an old one, a familiar one. . . . She would have liked to talk things out, but that could turn into an all-afternoon session and she really didn't have time for it, not today. Better just *do* it and . . . take the easy way out. "Ted—"

He materialized in the doorway.

"On second thought, I think I'd like to trade in my ice water for a glass of your wine."

His expression brightened. "White or red?"

"White will be fine."

He returned with two glasses. She stood to accept hers. "I'm sorry if I made you feel I didn't want to be with you." She let her body drift within brushing distance of his. "It's not that at all. It's just that I need a little more time than you do . . . do you understand what I mean?"

Ten minutes later they were in bed. He was amazed at the change in her mood. She seemed much more aroused than the previous night.

He enjoyed the way she moaned as he moved against

her. Abruptly her body tensed. Then her fingernails dug into his shoulders, and she groaned, "oh, Ted, oh, Ted." Her movements intensified, then her body went limp beneath his.

"Did you?" he asked uncertainly.

"Did I come?" She smiled. "Of course I did. Couldn't you tell?"

No, in her case he really wasn't sure, but he didn't want to get into a big discussion about it, not now. He wanted to go for his own.

She seemed to know precisely what to do. Her hips took up the circular motion that had done so much for him last night. At the same time her fingernails began tracing patterns up and down his ribcage. And her hot, slick tongue went to work on his neck and jaw. He came quickly.

"Was it good?" she asked.

"Very. Was yours?"

"Terrific."

He didn't believe her, he had a feeling she was faking.

"It was really overpowering," she said. She wondered if he could tell she had faked.

They lay silently for a few minutes. Then she sat up. "I really think I should be going, Ted."

He watched her body in the dim light of the closed venetian blinds. It was an incredible body. Her waist seemed thin enough to encircle with his hands. Her breasts were unbelievably solid—not the slightest bit of sag, even with her arms down along her sides.

"You know what I'd like to do tonight?" he said. "I'd like to cook dinner for us. I make a great moussaka. We'll go Greek all the way—some Demestika red, some feta cheese—"

"Gee, I'd like to, Ted"—she smiled sadly—"but I have so much to do tonight—"

"What could possibly take a whole evening?"

"I have to do my hair, I have to get my clothes ready—"

"You're making excuses."

"Ted, you don't own me." She was pleased with her assertiveness. And very angry again with him for his *pressing* her so . . . "I'm going to leave now." She started to dress.

"I'm sorry." He stood behind her and brought his hands to her arms. "It's just that . . . well, damn it, I've already told you."

"I'm sorry too." Her expression softened as her eyes found his in the mirror. "We can be together when I get back."

When she'd left he filled his wineglass to the brim and polished off half of it with two gulps. None of the afternoon had gone the way he wanted. Worst of all, he hadn't been able to resist crowding her. He was damn near foaming at the mouth for her—mad dog Vassily—and begging for the opportunity to kiss her ass. He'd have to get this thing under control. He'd have to discipline himself, show the kind of indifference that came naturally when he really didn't give a damn about a woman. Show them you don't care and *they* kiss *your* ass . . .

Which meant another girl, an . . . alternate receiver. He enjoyed the metaphor. Go to the same target all the time, your passing attack winds up on its ass. And you do on yours.

He downed the rest of his wine, dressed, went back to the office and tried for the rest of the day—mostly unsuccessfully—to concentrate on his work.

Joseph Williams woke with the taste and fragrance of Grace Colello still on him. Such a delightful woman, such an uninhibited woman, and brains!

But there was more—something vastly more important. She was of the earth . . . peasant Calabrese . . . she had an inherent naturalness and openness that summoned images of *I Pagliacci, Cavalleria Rusticana, Vespri Siciliani.* The intellect he could find—he had found—in hundreds of "Cliffies" and Vassar and Sarah Lawrence girls that he had tipped upside-down over the years. But Grace Colello was the first woman in recent memory—in fact, the first in five or six years—he felt no hostility toward the morning after. Indeed, he wanted her more than before they'd made love.

He savored the subtle, tangy aroma of her genitals, still—or so it seemed—faintly present in his nostrils. He recalled the firm, cushiony feel of her body, recalled it so vividly he could practically perceive the texture of her flesh against his. Closing his eyes and lying back, he remembered—he came close to re-experiencing—their bodies locked together, his arms wrapped around her trunk, his face buried in the smooth sweet-slick of her vulva while her fingers dug into his thighs and her teeth and tantalizing tongue gently assaulted his penis.

The image gave him an erection, and because he wanted neither to masturbate nor suffer an hour's tense frustration, he forced himself to get up and shower. Grace Colello was a prize, he told himself as he relished the hot needles of water that intensified what remained on his body of the scent of her. Twice they'd made love in less than an hour—something he hadn't done in at least ten years. And he'd have been able to do it again, at least once more, if she hadn't had to get back to her parents' apartment.

He had to see her again. Soon. Before she left they'd arranged to meet on his next free evening. But that was Friday, two nights away. He couldn't bear not seeing her until then.

He got out of the shower and briskly rubbed himself dry. He would phone her today and arrange something sooner—even if only lunch or an afternoon cocktail. In fact, he'd phone now. Perhaps she hadn't left yet for her classes.

He hurried into the bedroom, found the slip of paper on which he'd written her number and punched out the digits on his telephone. He waited six rings and was about to hang up when she answered.

"Joseph!" she said, astonished to hear his voice, "is something wrong?"

He smiled. "Nothing that couldn't be put right if you were here."

"Well, uh, I'm very happy to hear you say that, Joseph."

"Was I wrong to call? You seem strained."

"I was just on my way out. I'm running late. But I am happy you called. I'll say goodbye now, okay? See you Friday."

"I won't be able to live with myself if I have to wait that long. Meet me today. For lunch."

". . . Where?"

"I'll be at the auditorium. We can eat nearby."

"But that's an hour each way. I only have forty-five minutes between classes."

"I'll send a car for you. Could you consider cutting one class? To give us a little more time."

She hesitated. "I'm finished for the day after my first afternoon class. I'd planned to work in the library . . ."

He arranged for his car to meet her at the door of the building where she had her last morning class, then made himself a cup of cappuccino and went to the piano. He was, he decided, in a most peculiar state. He took a sheet of stave paper from a pad, printed "Grace" across the first line, then struck a G-major seventh-eleventh-sixteenth chord and picked out a sprightly figure two octaves above it. He changed chords twice, picking out additional figures, then experimented with variations on the pattern. Finally he had eight bars that pleased him. He pencilled them on the pad, played them to confirm his notation, inserted a double bar sign at the end, and wrote *"fine,"* the traditional Italian word for the close of a composition. Beneath this he wrote, *"Ti amo, carissima Grace. Tuo, Giuseppe Guglielmi."* He added the date, put the pad aside, shook his head in disbelief . . . Joseph Williams, *the* Joseph Williams, afflicted, smitten with a schoolboy's crush.

Sipping his coffee, he recalled the first time he had used "Giuseppe Guglielmi," an Italian translation of his name. He'd been at Harvard. She was at Radcliffe. An Italo-american, a rarity at a Seven Sisters school in those days. She hadn't been a first night conquest, but he'd bedded her on the second, which also was a rarity in those days, at least with a *nice* girl. The excitement of it all had inspired him to compose something for her, and he'd signed it "Giuseppe Gugliemi." Their affair lasted the better part of a year and consumed him emotionally. He'd been certain no other woman would have such an impact on him, and for almost ten years none had. Her loss probably would have driven him to a psychiatrist if it hadn't been so inspiringly Mozartian. (No, she did not die of cancer; the following summer, working as a waitress at Cape Cod while he was studying in Leipzig, she threw him over for a law student.)

He wondered if she still had that inscribed composition.

Today it was probably worth at least a few thousand dollars. And would be worth much more in the years ahead, despite his having produced several dozen similar ones over the years. In his immediate post-college period he concocted one for every new girl. Now, of course, with his stature as perhaps America's most celebrated living composer and conductor, it was a nigh irresistible . . . device. But there weren't that many women these days that he really wanted to impress. Grace was the first in years.

She arrived at the auditorium while he was rehearsing the orchestra, as he had calculated she would. He felt his early morning excitement take him over once more as he came down from the podium and saw her sitting alone in the auditorium, knees pressed together, hands folded across her lap, expression so bright and alive. The Victorian properness of her position heightened his excitement, contrasting as it did with her performance the previous night. He thought he felt his cock stiffening as he walked toward her.

She got up as he neared her seat and for a moment was uncertain whether to shake hands or offer her cheek to be kissed. She ended up doing both. "I love you," he whispered as his lips brushed her ear.

She said nothing but managed to reply by squeezing his hand. The smell of her perfume reignited his memories of their bodies together. "Let's have a lovely drink first," he said. And almost as an afterthought, "in my dressing room, all right?"

"Fine." She smiled and squeezed his hand again before releasing it.

He led her through the thicket of music stands on the stage and down a bare, brightly-lit corridor where musicians were clustered in twos and threes. They nodded or spoke greetings as he passed. It seemed to Grace that they neither took special notice of her nor especially avoided taking notice.

"Sherry?" Joseph asked, opening the door to his room and letting her precede him inside. "Or perhaps you'd prefer brandy, or white wine, or—"

"Sherry," she said, looking around. She had expected a dressing room like the ones she'd seen in movies—bare walls, a mirror surrounded with light bulbs, a bench.

This was a full-blown living room with a Persian rug, soft leather couch, carved Chinese liquor cabinet.

"But first," he said, closing the door . . . She stepped into his embrace. "Grace—my delicious, incomparable Grace."

They held a long kiss, then he stepped back and scrutinized her at arm's length. "I had to keep pinching myself all morning to persuade myself I didn't just imagine you. I can't tell you the . . . impact you've had on me, Grace."

"I'm pretty impacted myself, Joseph." She smiled at her bad pun. "It's not every day that I'm met after class by a chauffeured limousine."

"I didn't embarrass you, I hope."

"No, just sort of knocked me off my pins."

He opened a walnut cabinet that she now could see housed a refrigerator, poured two glasses of Pando and handed her one. "Frankly, Grace Colello, I *wanted* to knock you off your pins. I hope I'm not being too flamboyant—"

"Be as flamboyant as you want, Joseph. I'm enjoying every flamboyant minute of it." And she was.

He went to the couch and gestured for her to sit alongside him. As she did, he kissed her. She welcomed his tongue and fitted her body against his. Soon he was easing her onto her back. His hand closed over her breast. "I hope I'm not coming across like an overeager schoolboy"—second time today he'd thought of himself in those terms—"You've got me so aroused I'm afraid I can't restrain myself—"

"What makes you think I'm any less aroused?"

He dived into a fiercely hungry kiss, then his hand found her leg—he was pleased it was bare—and slowly moved upward. She shifted position to make it easier for him, and he responded with pleasure as he reached her hip and found no panties.

"I thought you'd like that," she whispered, and thought to herself that this time, as opposed to last night, it had been intentional.

He tantalized himself by proceeding very slowly across her hipbone and into her thick mat of pubic hair. He eased a finger inside her, marveling at her wetness—

though not quite as wet as last night. "Grace Colello, you are a wonder."

"Likewise, sir."

He moved into place between her legs, opened his fly, considered removing his pants but decided he couldn't wait that long. Her hips arched to receive him. The hotness inside her was its own language.

He pressed hard with his pubis, moving quickly, hoping somehow to ignite her orgasm before he had his. But he knew he was too intensely aroused to last more than a few strokes. Steeling himself, he withdrew and brought his face down her body, stopping at the knee, then kissing his way upward. He buried his lips in her fiery wetness, driving his tongue deep inside, then pushed hard and rhythmically at her clitoris with his upper lip, at the same time pushing up at her buttocks with his palms to force her pubis more firmly against him.

Her moans told him she would not need much more. He intensified his efforts, and her body suddenly erupted, thrashing about even more fiercely than last night, sustaining wave after wave of climax long after he would have expected her to be spent. Finally she eased off, her movements subsiding to gentle undulations, and then she was limp. He quickly stripped off his pants, positioned himself for his own orgasm.

"Ah, Grace," he whispered as he lay alongside her afterward, "there never has been another one like you . . ." He kissed her gently. "And you must be famished. I promised you lunch more than an hour ago. Come on, let me show you where the showers are."

They were off a small hallway that connected the room she had been in to a bedroom. There was one shower stall on each side. As she used hers, she thought about the two shower stalls in a single dressing room—was she just one more revolving-door visitor?

Somehow, the thought did not disturb her as she might have expected it to, probably because the whole relationship seemed so unreal. Somehow his very status and fame . . . removed as it was from her ken and expectations . . . made whatever pleasure she took from their relationship a kind of bonus. Joseph Williams, the man, didn't really overwhelm her . . . as Ted had, did . . . it was Joseph Williams the institution that tended to awe, which was far less threatening, more a wonderful bubbly kick. Relax, she told herself, and enjoy it.

An enormous Lejon bath sheet was folded over a stool outside the shower door. She caressed herself with it, luxuriating in the soft thickness of the terrycloth. She had never touched a softer, more cushiony towel. Embroidered in one corner, fully six inches high, were his initials and four notes on a musical scale.

He was in the bedroom, toweling himself. He let his bathsheet drop away. "Come here, Grace," and she stepped into his welcoming arms. He pressed her body to him, as if somehow to absorb it. "You feel wonderful . . . I think I could make love to you again, right now."

She smiled. "If you want to."

"Well, perhaps we really should eat something."

She dressed quickly, feeling strangely ill at ease with her inexpensive clothes in the plushness of his bedroom. The bedspread was embroidered silk. She guessed that it cost more than her entire wardrobe.

He adjusted his ascot in the full-length mirror-doors of his chifforobe. "Before we leave," he said, leading her back into the living room, "there's something I'd like you to have." He took what appeared to be a scroll from his desk, and she unravelled it. "I wanted to give you something as unique as the experience you've given me. Can you read the notes?"

"At a piano, I'm sure I could pick them out. But I can't sound them in my head."

He sang them to her. "So now, Grace Colello, you have your own song."

"Oh, Joseph, that's lovely, thank you." She moved into his arms.

"I love you, my dear Grace. I mean it." He slowly released her. "And now, before you collapse of hunger, shall I take you to lunch?"

His limousine deposited them on East Fifty-second Street. A doorman bowed, and she found herself in a large, dim, paneled room whose walls were covered with individually lighted western sketches. "Original Remingtons," she thought aloud.

"Yes. The largest private collection in the world."

"Then we must be at Twenty-One. Oh, Joseph, I've read about it, but I didn't notice the name as we came in."

They rode an elevator to the third floor, where a captain brought them to a corner table. She noticed someone staring at her. A man who looked familiar. Yes, of course—the man with the red sport jacket from the party at 305 East—the drunk who had said "ass" on television. Happily the captain was seating her with her back to him.

Joseph ordered a bottle of Sebastiani Gewürz Traminer. "To us," he said, touching her glass. Sipping, he added, "Delightfully fresh and fruity, isn't it? Perfect for lunch, too early in the day for anything heavier or more complicated."

She sipped. "Yes, it is delightful."

Over lunch he turned to a discussion of helping raise funds for the South Dakota Indians' legal defense fund, which he said might have been a more appropriate beneficiary of Ted Vassily's bash the previous night than 305 East, though he did have a certain admiration for Vassily's innovation. "I'm not really sure how to go about it," he told her, "an ordinary theater party or night at the opera probably wouldn't draw many contributions; people aren't familiar enough with the case and the issues. I've thought of a public meeting, perhaps with speeches by Buffy Weiss and one or two of the defendants, but the wrong people always attend those affairs—potential big contributors never go."

"What kind of affair would attract them?"

"Something social, something like last night's party. The secret, I think, is to arrange something so appealing on its own that they'll come no matter what the appeal of the cause. Then we can, so to speak, infiltrate them—perhaps a few short speeches, or perhaps just by letting the guests chat individually with some of the defendants."

"You'd have to be careful not to make it appear that you're putting the Indians on display."

"Yes. That would be demeaning. At the same time if you don't give people an opportunity to perceive them as injured flesh-and-blood human beings, you won't develop the kind of rapport that inspires major contributions."

"Then why not simply invite people to a party?"

He thought for a moment. "Yes, why not! I could draw

up a list of important potential contributors—thirty or forty couples. Add in the mayor, perhaps one or two other sympathetic politicians, and the defendants and their wives. All told, about a hundred people. Maria and I could accommodate them comfortably in our place . . ." He hesitated, suddenly aware of, and apparently uncomfortable about, the reference to his wife.

Grace was careful not to notice. "I think it would be important, though, to arrange it so that the Indians don't feel the other guests were coming to gawk at them."

"Oh, absolutely. I won't announce it as a 'cause' party. I frequently just have people in for cocktails. I'll simply give another party, but with a carefully drawn guest list. During the evening—or better still, afterward—someone can approach the guests for a donation."

"It sounds fine, Joseph. I don't see why it wouldn't work."

"But, dearest Grace, if it does it will be because of your idea, and I can't properly share it with you. Oh, you'll come, of course. But—well—I naturally will have to be with Maria."

She sipped her wine and said nothing.

He stared at his plate for a long moment, then looked up. "We're going to have to confront this sooner or later. I suppose we might as well now."

"You haven't promised me anything, Joseph. I know, as they say, what I'm getting into. I enjoy being with you and want to be with you."

"But it's more than a casual affair now, Grace—at least for me. Isn't it for you?"

"Well, I suppose, but it has, after all, been less than twenty-four hours since we met. We know what we feel now, but in two weeks, or even another twenty-four hours . . ."

He sipped his wine and seemed to study the glass. "If in two weeks I feel what I feel now, my impulse would be to take you off to some desert island, except to tell the truth I'm really not very impulsive. My career, my wife, my children—they're all very much a part of a picture that I need and want to keep." He took another sip of wine. "What I'm saying, I'm afraid, is that there *is* no future for you with me. I want to be with you, Grace, I want you in my life, but I don't believe it can ever be more than this between us, never more than clandestine, never more than . . ." He seemed to be searching for a word, then gave it up.

She covered his hand with hers, not entirely certain how much was performance, well-rehearsed, and how much heartfelt. And smiled inwardly, because, of course, it didn't *really* matter. She had already made up her mind on that. Relax and enjoy it . . . "I understand what you're saying, Joseph, and it's okay, really." She smiled at him. "We're adults. You've been one a lot longer than I"—should she have said that?—"but I'm responsible for myself too."

He squeezed her hand and sighed, with pleasure or relief—she wondered, and decided a little of both.

"Well," he said brightly, changing the subject, "would you like to come to the performance tonight?"

"Tonight?"

"Yes, it's the premier of a new production of Verdi's *Don Carlos,* the first opera I ever conducted. I'd like very much to share it with you." Quickly he added, "I'm afraid I won't be able to see you afterward. Maria and I will be attending the usual Opera Guild party, but I'd at least like very much to share the opera with you, and your thoughts about it when we see each other tomorrow evening. I'll leave two tickets for you at the box office."

"You're inviting me to bring a friend?"

"I certainly don't expect you to come alone. And I have no right to be jealous."

She hesitated. "I'd love to come, but it's short notice . . . I'll have to get something to wear—"

"Let that be a present from me. Please."

She really did want to accept. She told herself that her reluctance was mostly thinking in terms of *her* financial bracket—to Joseph, several hundred dollars was no big deal . . . would she turn down a five-dollar gift from a boyfriend her own age? "I'm not sure I can find a friend to come with me on such short notice."

He smiled. "I doubt that. I'll be looking for you when I get to the podium. I'll be very unhappy if you're not there, Grace."

By the time luncheon was over she'd decided to accept,

and went directly to Saks, her first time there. The setting intimidated and enchanted her. Models walking the floor wearing the featured clothes, salespeople hanging on her every moué . . . it was the sort of thing she'd seen in movies—*Breakfast at Tiffanys*?—but never imagined being part of. A little nagging voice inside said there was something evil about paying several hundred dollars for a dress when entire families had to eat for a month on less, but damn it, if Joseph Williams wanted to be generous with her it wasn't at anybody's expense. All right then, why shouldn't she accept? No reason . . .

She looked at a dozen gowns, finally narrowing the choice to a conservative blue and a daring black with a high gathered neckline and generous armholes that revealed enough of her breasts to be sexy without being vulgar. "You have a stunning figure," the saleslady commented as Grace looked at herself in the three-way mirror. Yes, she told herself, she did, and damn it, it was time she stopped hiding it. "I'll take this one," she said, and had to struggle not to gasp as she signed the sales slip—three hundred and seventy-five dollars.

On the way back to 305 East she wondered how she would explain the gown to her parents. And how, if it came up, would she explain her late return last night? No more "my date ran out of gas," which was an option 305 East had taken away. She should, she knew, have resolved the old issue of her independence years ago when her parents first pressured her about dating. But she'd postponed confronting them, not wanting the unpleasantness of a confrontation and anticipating that in a short time she would move into her own apartment. And then had come 305 East.

Happily they hadn't returned from work when she got home. There was a card under the door telling her that the concierge had a delivery for her. She phoned the desk and a messenger appeared with a dozen long-stemmed roses—white and red. The card read, "Ted."

She smelled the roses and, for God's sake, suddenly wanted to cry. She recalled her peculiar feeling of the previous night after she and Ted had made love. She was crazy about him, and didn't want—was afraid?—to see him again. She still was certain she would never be able to have anything permanent with him, even if Joseph were not in the picture. And yet she *did* want to see him now. She wanted more of the loving tenderness she knew was behind the roses. She also *needed* it to . . . well, insulate her from Joseph? Or was it the other way around . . . ? Jesus, life was getting complicated.

She phoned his office. "The flowers are lovely, Ted. And they couldn't have come at a better time. I was in one of those moods."

"Hey, you know what kind of mood I'm in right now? A mood to cook dinner for us . . . a Greek extravaganza, taramasalata, moussaka, Demestika red—"

She hesitated. This wasn't quite the way she wanted it to go. She hoped he'd be more low-key, more quiet and understanding . . .

"Hey, you still there?"

"Yes. Sorry. I was just thinking, Ted, how would a supermacho football hero like yourself feel about letting a lady take him to the opera after that Greek dinner?" She was almost surprised to hear herself invite him. She hadn't thought of it until she heard the words coming out.

"What's this supermacho jazz? It happens that I like opera. Where are you taking this rockhead, the Met or the City?"

"The Stuyvesant . . ."

"Are you kidding? For the premiere of *Don Carlos?* They've been sold out for months."

"I have two tickets. Would you mind, Ted . . . ?"

"Are you kidding? . . . and now about dinner—" He stopped himself short. "Say, where'd you get the tickets?" He suddenly recalled Williams intercepting her at the elevator the previous night.

"Oh, a friend had them." She remembered that she had been with Ted when she met Joseph, and suddenly wished she hadn't been so bold as to invite him . . .

He wished he'd thought more quickly, there was no need, he had no right—right?—to confront her with Williams. "So about dinner," he went on quickly, "I think we should give ourselves decent time. Shall we meet at my place, around five?" He calculated backward from an assumed seven-thirty curtain for an opera of *Don Carlos'* length and decided this didn't leave enough time . . . "Better yet, say four-thirty, just to be on the safe side?"

"I had a late lunch. Can we eat afterward?" She wished there were some way to take back the invitation.

"Sure. Make it six o'clock then. We'll relax over a glass of wine before we leave."

She put down the receiver, went to the window and looked down at the landscaped quadrangle that served as 305 East's atrium. Things were moving too fast for her. Until two days ago she was practically playing teenybop games with guys whose chief concern was what to do about their acne. All right, the games often included fucking, but somehow it was more innocent, or rather less committed. She'd wanted out of that old boring scene and into this fascinating adult world of 305 East. Well, here she was, girl into woman, delighted and excited by the big new world—and scared to death along with it . . .

Relax, she told herself. It's just that so much has changed so fast. Remember, nothing will happen that you don't let happen. And remember Henry James's line about—what was it—not regretting the things he did but the things he didn't do. She went to the refrigerator, hoping to find some white wine, saw only a six pack of beer. She opened a can and thought about the exact line Henry James had written, surely something more elegant than "the things I didn't do." She rummaged through her bookshelf, found a copy of James's *Letters,* and flipped through the well-worn pages, fully one third of whose sentences she had underlined. She located the quotation in a letter James had written in his seventieth year to Hugh Walpole: "I think I don't regret a single 'excess' of my responsive youth—I only regret, in my chilled age, certain occasions and possibilities I didn't embrace."

Beautiful. "Possibilities I didn't embrace." She lifted the beer can to her lips and got only an ounce. Could she have drunk it all so quickly? She opened another and returned to her book, reading underlined quotations at random. "It takes a great deal of history to produce a little literature." "The terrible fluidity of self-revelation." "It's a complex fate, being an American, and one of the responsibilities it entails is fighting against a superstitious valuation of Europe." "If the picturesque were banished from the face of the earth, I think the idea would survive in some typical American breast."

She sipped her beer. For years she'd wanted to know a man who could share her delight in thoughts like these, language like this. Now she thought she knew not one but possibly two—Joseph and Ted. There might be dangers. Deep water was always more dangerous than shallow. But it's no problem if you can swim. . . .

She finished her beer and started getting ready for the evening. She didn't have a really good pair of formal black pumps, damn it. Fortunately the gown was long; she could get by with her black patent leather casuals and matching purse. Fortunately too, the dress was fine enough so that she wouldn't need jewelry. She would carry one of the roses from Ted's bouquet. And maybe she'd wear a string of "pearls." Or nothing at all.

She put on her makeup, then the dress. Somehow it seemed more daring at home than in the store. The outer sides of her breasts were fully visible. And the fabric was so clingy that her nipples not only popped up but you could practically make out the goosebumps around them. Not that she was embarrassed about being seen this way in public, even though it would be the first time. In fact, it kind of turned her on. But boy, would her father and mother go crazy if they got a look at her.

She still hadn't figured out an explanation for how she happened to have the gown. No use lying about the price and saying she bought it with savings; her mother, who had taste if not money, would instantly recognize its true value. And in any case, how would she get past them with her tits poking out like a pair of cannon?

On that thought she heard a key turning in the door. Her mind raced. She could wear her black lace shawl, at least until she got to Ted's. But the shape of her bodice—and the outlines of her flesh—would be visible even through that.

"Grace, are you home?"

"In the bedroom, Mom." She remembered her white rabbit-fur shawl, a remnant from high school prom days. It was dated as hell, but at least it would get her to Ted's. It should be tucked away somewhere in her closet.

"What time did you get in last night? Your father is furious."

Why did her parents insist on carrying on conversations from three rooms away? She rummaged around on the floor, looking for the shoebox or hatbox the stole probably was stored in.

"Did you hear me?" her mother called, louder now.

"I'll be right in, Mom."

"I said"—this at the same volume—"your father is furious. You didn't get in till after three."

She stood on a chair and searched the shelf over the clothesbar.

"Do you hear me, Gracie?"

"I said," Grace yelled back, "I'll be right *in*." Her eye caught a white tuft of fur sticking out of a paper bag. She pulled out the bag, knocking three other packages to the floor. Ignoring them, she unwrapped the fur, which was dusty and smelled of mothballs. She quickly pulled it over her shoulders as her mother entered the room. "Must you broadcast our business to the entire building?" she demanded, deciding to take the offensive.

"Your father's going to kill you. He got up at three o'clock and went to your room and you still weren't—where did you get that gown?"

"I borrowed it from a friend at school. I'm going to the opera with Ted Vassily tonight."

"Vassily? He's old enough to be your father. Is that where you were till three this morning?"

Might as well let it all hang out. "No, as a matter of fact I was with Joseph Williams."

"What? My God . . . he's even older. And he's married!"

"I only said I was with him. It's possible, you know, to be with a man and not go to bed with him."

"Don't get snotty with me, Miss. Your father and I have a right to know what you're doing. You're still under our roof, you know, even if"—she hesitated, then went on in a lower voice—"you are the one that got us this place."

Grace decided to take advantage of the change in tone to make her escape, hopefully before her father got home. "Well, for whatever interest it may have for you, I was with Nan Loomis—she lives in Three-oh-five too—and we were invited to a party at Mr. Williams's studio. His wife was there, of course. So was Nan's father. Ask them if you don't believe me. And that's where I met Mr. Vassily, who's a gentleman and very intelligent, even if he is *older* than I am. And he asked me to the opera, which neither man nor boy ever did back in Flatbush, let the record so note. And I was delighted to accept his invitation." She spun away, scooping up her purse from the dresser. "Now I'm running late, so please excuse me. And don't wait up tonight. I expect to be in before midnight, but then again we may be in a group and it might be hard to break away, so if I'm home later there's nothing to be upset about."

"Grace, wait." Her mother's expression was softer now. The hint of a smile lifted a corner of her mouth. "Why don't you calm down and let me see your gown?"

Grace twirled around, affecting a model's movements, careful all the while to keep the stole in place.

"Open the stole. Let me see the top of it."

"Mom, I'm terribly late. I really must run—"

"Grace, I just want to *see* it. Why, look! You can't go out like that. That stole is all dusty." She flecked it with the backs of her fingers, producing a dust storm.

"I'll shake it off in the elevator. I'm really late—"

"Don't be ridiculous. Dust it off now."

Oh, hell . . . let it really all hang out.

Her mother's jaw, quite literally, fell as Grace removed the stole. "You can't tell me you're going out like that!"

Grace smiled. "Does it shock you, Mom? I'm sorry." She turned another circle. "But maybe it's time we both stopped kidding ourselves about these things. I'm not an innocent little girl anymore, Mom."

"Gracie! Was it . . . Joseph Williams?"

"Oh, get serious, Mom. It happened long before Joseph Williams, and I think you must know it, even if you've not wanted to accept it." She turned another circle, spreading her arms to emphasize the display of her breasts. She wondered where she was getting the nerve to do this. Surely it couldn't have been just the two beers. "I like my body, Mother," she went on, continuing to surprise herself. "I'm not a kook or exhibitionist, but I enjoy having other people like it too. I'm sorry if this shocks you, I'm not trying to shock you." She looked directly at her mother. "I guess what I'm trying to do is grow up."

"Quick, give me that wrap," her mother said softly, taking it from her. She brought it out of range of Grace's dress and hastily beat the dust from it. "Now cover yourself up and get out of here before your father gets home. He'll kill you, Grace, he really will."

"No one is going to kill me, Mom. This is twentieth century America, not feudal Naples."

"Hurry." She pushed Grace toward the door. "Go meet your Mr. Vassily. And don't get home too late tonight. Please, Grace . . . not too late?"

Grace rode the elevator to the lobby. It was, she realized, only five-forty-five. Should she wait in the lobby until six? Or would she run the risk of seeing her father there? She certainly couldn't spend fifteen minutes walking around the block in her new gown.

What she really should do, she told herself, was go back to the apartment and confront her father if he got home before six. Confront him the way she had her mother . . . who had shown herself to be surprisingly warm and understanding. Well, if her father couldn't accept her, accept the truth of her growing up, that would have to be his problem. What could he do? Throw her out? No, he wouldn't throw her out. But he might hit her. He had before, as recently as two years ago. He had hit her on the face and blackened her eye. She couldn't risk having that happen, not with tonight's date with Ted and tomorrow's with Joseph.

The elevator opened at the lobby. She went to the main entrance and asked the doorman to announce her for Ted. "He'll be right down, ma'am," said Walt Kulikowski. "Say, that's a lovely gown."

"I'll tell Mister Vassily you approve," she said, not liking his tone.

"Yes, ma'am. Thank you. Have a pleasant evening, ma'am."

She went to the east tower elevator. It seemed to take forever to arrive. The crowning touch would be for her father to arrive and make a scene just as the elevator door opened. She was sorry about being curt with the doorman.

Maybe he only seemed to be leering, maybe he was just paying her an honest compliment. God, she was acting like a real bitch. This family hassle had her so damn tense!

"Hi!" The elevator door had opened. Ted was waiting for her inside, his arms opened to welcome her. She stepped into them and felt a huge relief as the doors closed. She kissed him quickly on the lips, then pressed her face against his neck. The hugeness of his chest and shoulders again felt so good, reassuring. She'd almost forgotten what he felt like.

"You're early," he said.

"Am I? I don't have a watch . . . I thought I was late. I'm sorry."

"No problem. I haven't finished dressing yet"—he showed his shirtsleeves—"but help yourself to some champagne while I finish."

She took off the stole, suddenly feeling burdened by it.

"Hey!" He held her at arm's length. "I love it!"

She felt tears coming and couldn't hold them back.

"Hey, I'm sorry, did I say something wrong?"

She buried her face against his chest and dug her fingers into his shoulders. She was sobbing. Not just crying but actually sobbing, and there was no way to turn it off.

For a moment he stood silently, then began patting her back as though she were a baby. "Okay, honey, let it all out." His voice was soft, reassuring. "That's it, don't try to hold back."

She felt herself being guided across the floor, as if she were dancing, her face still pressed against his chest. She tried again to restrain herself but only sobbed harder.

"Let them come, baby, let them come. Don't fight. You're among friends . . ."

She carried on for what seemed to her like hours, aware of his leading her to a seat but seeing only her hands in front of her face, one of them trying somehow to contain the tears while the other alternated between reinforcing the first and searching for a handkerchief that she knew she wasn't carrying. "Here, use this," she heard him say. Magically there was a handkerchief in her hands. She felt him standing over her, his fingers kneading her neck muscles. And then he was gone, and then back, pushing two fresh handkerchiefs into her hands as he took away the first.

Finally the tears ebbed and she looked up at him. He was holding a snifter of brandy. "Drink it," he said.

"I—I'm sorry, Ted."

"Drink," he commanded.

She took a large swallow, shivering as the fiery sensation worked down her throat. "What a way to begin a night at the opera, right?" She smiled up at him. "And I don't even have my old Groucho Marx jokes to go with it . . . seriously, Ted, I am sorry. . . ."

"And just as seriously, Miss Colello, I am telling you please don't be. Now, are you ready to start on the old quarterback's bottomless champagne bottle?"

"I guess . . . and I've just decided old quarterbacks have the best shoulders in the world for crazy mixed-up girls to cry on."

"You better, as they say, believe it."

She watched him retreat to the cavernous room's upper level, grateful he hadn't subjected her to a barrage of questions. If he had, she would have had to leave, she simply would not have been able to stand it. But his unquestioning acceptance of her outburst made her feel thoroughly comfortable with him. It was exactly the kind of tenderness and understanding she had come seeking. And now she *wanted* to talk.

He came back with a bottle in an ice bucket and two of his tulip glasses. Wordlessly he peeled the foil and cage from the bottle, removed the cork with a soft *thump,* and poured a dollop into one glass. He held it up to the light, then nosed and tasted it. "Perfect," he pronounced, handing her a glass. He waited until she nodded agreement, then filled his own glass and sat opposite her. "A challenging opera, *Don Carlos,*" he said, "also long. Some people might even call it tedious. But the melodies are wonderful and that basso duet between Don Carlos and the Grand Inquisitor, it's one of my favorite things in opera." He looked to her for a response. Any response.

"Ted," she said softly, "it hardly rates as grand opera, but may I tell you the miserable story of *my* life?"

"Shoot."

"I really mean miserable. It's maudlin, sobby, sentimental, maybe even a little goofy. But I have a terrible urge to spill it out, and it looks like you're the victim. Okay?"

"Be my guest."

She began with her reaction to him the night before. She held back nothing—the way at first she was "snowed" by him, her ambivalence about going to bed with him, her strange depression when it was over. She told him about her high school "rabbit" days, her church hassles, her hang-up about privacy and propriety versus her feelings. She finished with an account of herself and Joseph Williams.

"I may sound childish, Ted, but in a way I think I love him. Oh, not some big grand passion or anything like that—which in a way is an attraction. I feel so unhassled with him . . . and I guess the *idea* of him is exciting. . . . I know there's no future in it—at least no conventional future, rose-covered cottage and all that sort of thing, but I really don't care. I don't think he understands that, but it's true. I just want it to continue on for its natural life, whatever that may be, and I honestly don't think I'll regret its end, whenever it comes." She took a long drink of champagne. "And then when I got the roses from you, I felt this tremendous need for you, for you as *you,* and the strength and tenderness that just seem to pour out of you." She hurried on, afraid he would interrupt and she'd never get it out. "I wanted very badly to be with you. Not to fuck you. Just to be with you. I wanted to happen exactly what did."

She took another gulp of champagne. "Ted, I don't know where that leaves me . . . us . . . except that I guess I'm asking if it's still possible in this not exactly best of all possible worlds to be a loving friend . . . or is that too impossibly corny, even for a schoolgirl who's not as innocent as she looks?"

"Not corny at all. I want your friendship too, Grace. Maybe in very much the same way you want mine. There's a long story to it on my side too, but"—he glanced at his watch—"you're in luck, there's no time to tell it now."

At the opera house, waiting for the first act curtain to go up, they avoided any reference to what had been said at his apartment. They talked instead about opera and symphonies, plays and books. She was surprised at his broad range, although sometimes his taste was a little hard to track. He loved *bel canto,* especially Donizetti, and most of Verdi, but didn't go at all for Puccini. On the other hand, Ginastera was one of his favorite composers and he particularly liked *Don Rodrigo,* which she thought usually appealed only to the most far-out modernists. A classic like Rostand's *Cyrano* was one of his favorite plays, but he also liked experimental theater. Which definitely did not include *Hair,* which he remembered thinking of as garbage way back when he saw it, or Joseph Papp, now retired, "the most overrated asshole of all time."

He was pleased at their talk, to find he had so many interests in common with her. Unlike most he'd gone out with, she really knew the music and plays she talked about—she hadn't cribbed her opinions secondhand from some knucklehead's music-art appreciation course or from the latest bullshit critic in velvet pants. The lady definitely had a *feeling* as well as an opinion about things, and so thinking he felt a twinge of envy toward Joseph Williams and the way she had told him she felt about the maestro—not that he'd be prepared to handle something really heavy. But still . . . you're a greedy bastard, Vassily, do you know that? What was it a high school coach said long ago?—you want to score every point, make every tackle, throw every block. Well, no, not really, coach, I'll settle for making every cheerleader . . . forgive me, folks, I was young. . . .

After the performance they decided it was too late for him to cook his Greek dinner, so they agreed to rain-check it and have supper at the Brasserie. "It's my turn to tell you my story," he found himself saying, somewhat to his astonishment. And he told all of it—at least, all of it since he'd come back to New York: the abortive affair with Buffy Weiss, the memories of Chris, the situation with Nan.

"It's really wild," she said. "I mean, our timing. You with Nan and me with Joseph. And"—she smiled mischievously at him—"you and me in between."

"Which reminds me," he said, laughing, "that tonight we're Mr. and Miss Inbetween. Right?"

"And we're true loving friends?"

"Well . . ." he said, hoping she wouldn't be too literal.

She kissed him on the cheek. "Don't worry, loving friend . . . even friends have been known to fuck each other." And they broke out in delighted laughter that had heads turning at nearby tables.

Back at his penthouse Ted poured champagne and brought the glasses to the reclining chair by the window. She nestled against him and shivered as his fingers traced sexy patterns on her legs.

"Ready?" he asked after a while.

She actually giggled, heard herself and didn't care. "You know I am." He already had two fingers inside her, all the way to the third knuckle.

It was a long, slow, incredibly sensuous fuck. He seemed determined to prolong it to the absolute limit, determined to extract every last drop of sensation from it. She accepted his teasing for as long as she could stand it, then guided his hips with her hands until they were in the best pressure position for her. "Do it for me, Ted," she whispered. "I need it *now* . . ."

He let it happen. As her moans and thrusting told him her orgasm was almost there, he let himself go for his. It wasn't precisely a simultaneous climax, but the closest thing to it—his first vibrations were starting before her last had ended. Everything was perfect . . . except, to his surprise, he found himself triggering his climax by fantasying Nan in Grace's place. Well, at least it was no longer Chris to haunt him. . . .

Afterward he lay quietly on top of her, kissing her gently all over the face. "I really do love you, loving friend," he said.

"Me too, superstud. You saved my life tonight. Just give me a ring if you need the favor returned. . . ."

They kissed some more, then he lay silently alongside her, listening to the beat of her heart and savoring the fragrance of her body. He found himself getting drowsy. "Goodnight, loving friend," he said, reaching for the light.

"Ted—I'm sorry—I can't stay."

"You're kidding."

"No, I wish I were. That's one dreary chapter I left out of my autobiography." She told him some about her parents' attitudes and the scene with her mother tonight, the worry about her father . . . "The irony is," she said, "I was looking for an apartment of my own when I first read about Three-oh-five East. Your setup specified family applications only, and after we were accepted I was so excited about living here that I postponed my escape."

He smiled. "You've just identified an injustice in Three-oh-five East that I'd never thought of. I'll get to work on it tomorrow. By the end of the week there'll be apartments here for hard-up *singles*. Seriously, would you like to be the first to apply?"

"No, Ted. I'm grateful for the opportunity but—"

"There's no reason for gratitude. If anything, I should be grateful to you for giving me an idea about how to improve this place."

"But—"

"No buts. If rich-bitch singles like Buffy Weiss and show biz types like Spats Johnson can have their own apartments and millionaires like Hartford Loomis can rent one for their daughters, it's only fair that the less well-heeled singles have a shot. I got too carried away about poor *families*."

"Well, do it if you want to, Ted, but I won't be one of the applicants." She took his hand and pressed his fingers to her lips. "I love you dearly, Ted Vassily, and I *am* grateful, even if you tell me I shouldn't be. But I'm really not ready to make the big move. I don't have a job and—"

"I'm sure I can find room in our setup for a bright young—"

"No, Ted, I mean it." She kissed his cheek. "I'll be out of school in another semester. I can hang on till then."

"But why, if it's unnecessary?"

"Because I'm an old-fashioned girl who wants to make it on her own."

"That kind of thing doesn't stop the rich folk, you know. They take every edge they can finagle. Besides, no one really makes it on his own. Or hers."

"You did, didn't you?" She kissed him again. "Time's up, superstud. Don't forget your little ol' loving friend."

"Not bloody likely. . . . I'll walk you to your apartment."

"Don't bother, Ted. With the security you've got in this building, I doubt a tank could get in. And the quieter Grace's approach, the lower her risk of parental hassle."

He watched her dress. "At least let me walk you to the elevator."

"A deal."

He pressed the call button, then took her in his arms and gave her a long kiss. "Sleep tight, loving friend," he said as the doors opened and she stepped through them.

"I love you," she told him just before they closed in front of her. And, in the privacy of the car, knew she meant it . . . in a scary, deep, forever way, not the easy exciting schoolgirlish fashion of her crush on Joseph Williams.

"Goddamn," he said out loud as he started for the bedroom and knew he wouldn't be able to sleep. He found the champagne bottle, which still contained a few ounces. He downed them, then buzzed the doorman. "Mike," he said, "is Nasty in the building?"

"He should be in his apartment, Ted. He got in about half an hour ago."

Ted dialed the number.

"My man! What you doin' on the horn at this hour? I figured you'd still be doin' the ol' push-pull."

"Feel like a few drinks with an old buddy?"

"Hey, Mister T, you know that's an offer I never refuse."

They sat at the window and drank until the sun came up.

Buffy Weiss woke with a start. She had been dreaming she was being interrogated by police. It was a thirties B-movie setting—the bright overhead light, the sadistic cop complete with dangling cigarette, much shouting and shoving and threatening . . .

"W-whassa matter, babes? You okay?"

She looked toward the voice and saw Spats Johnson peering at her through one cloudy eye, the other squeezed tightly shut against the few rays of light that managed to get through his thick draperies. She remembered where she was. "Everything's fine, just a little bad dream."

"Okay, babes. Back to sleep, huh?" The lid on his open

eye fell slowly. His head returned to the pillow, and he snuggled against her.

Buffy stared at the ceiling. She would not be able to go back to sleep, but she didn't mind lying awake with him. She felt comfortable, more than with any man in a long time.

It had started as a rocky night, but it quickly got better. The double shower seemed to turn him around. Before it he'd been abrasive to the point of near-brutality; if she'd been less than excruciatingly horny she never would have stayed. But in the shower he became totally different—tender, solicitous, attending to her every imaginable sensation; virile and assertive along with it. When she came it was the best since—since—well, since Ted Vassily.

She forced herself to push Vassily from her mind. The worm didn't even acknowledge her last night. Granted, their parting had been mildly hostile. But it hadn't been knock-down-drag-out. She had remained cordial with ex-lovers from whom she had parted on much worse terms. He should at least have come over and said hello. But enough of him. She became aware of Spats's bony knee against her leg. He had to be the thinnest man she'd ever known. But a good fuck. A very good fuck. In his case, it really wasn't so much what he did as the way he did it, the patience with which he did it. Other guys, even superstuds like Vassily, often gave you the feeling that they wished you'd hurry up and come. With Spats, you felt that he'd be delighted to stimulate you all night, to just keep going until you got tired, it was as much fun for him as for you. Come to think of it, blacks in general seemed to be that way. Maybe that was one of their attractions to her. Plus their big cocks, of course. In any case, she had never been with a black guy who made her feel rushed. And she'd been with more than a few.

Big cocks. It was true. Piss on that Masters-Johnson business about blacks being bigger only when flaccid. They were bigger in erection, too. On the average, a full inch or two bigger, in her experience. And Orientals were smaller. They had real pencil-peters, at least the four or five she'd bedded.

As for Spats, well, he wound up—she smiled . . . unwound was more accurate—somewhere on the long side of black, but on the thin side too. He really was nice and long, though—a good eight inches, but not much thicker than a finger. A real hot dog. If there were some way to combine his length with the horse-choker thickness of a guy like Vassily, well, now, that'd be a cock to build your dreams on. . . . She'd heard tell that old Frank Sinatra and Sammy Davis Jr. had endowments like that. A Las Vegas showgirl she'd once interviewed claimed experience with both of them, and reported that Frank carried a full—and incredible—thirteen inches, as big around as a girl's wrist, while Sammy came in just under twelve and equally full-bodied.

Ah, cocks. She thought of Spats Johnson's, and how nice it felt slithering in and out of her last night, moving in that easy rhythm, unhurried, never stopping, in-out, in-out . . . hey, Buffy Weiss, you're getting the hots.

She eased her hand beneath Spats's arched hip. She hoped he wasn't one of those guys that got grumpy in the morning. She made back-of-the-finger contact with soft flesh and waited to see if he stirred. So far, so good. She increased her pressure. He stayed motionless. She slowly let her fingers close around it.

"Mmm," he said, pressing close to her. "Feels good." She ran her fingernail around the head, and the shaft quickly swelled to full erection.

She used it as a handle, urging him toward her. "Hi, babes," he murmured, eyes still closed as he moved on top of her. She lubricated the head against her vulva, then eased it inside. She felt like a sword swallower, she found herself thinking. Oh, Buf, can the fucking head trip, just *ball* him, will you?

In, out; in, out. She wondered if he was still asleep. She managed to get a look at his eyes. Still closed. "That's really great, Spats," she whispered. "Do it harder." Like a machine whose gears have been shifted, he increased the force of his movements without altering the rhythm.

She whipped the sheet aside and looked down his sleek hairless body. She loved gazing at that glistening brownness. She remembered her first time with a black man. As she watched him undress, she was astounded at the vast areas of darkness being exposed to her eyes. It shouldn't have surprised her, of course. She certainly didn't expect his body to be a different shade from his face, except that in a way she must have. All her previous exposure to blacks had been in social or business circumstances, with everyone fully dressed. All she ever saw was faces and hands; maybe, occasionally, arms beneath a short-sleeved shirt. Now here was this incredible hulk of brownness coming toward her. It startled her. Terrified her. Excited her. She climaxed for the first time just a few seconds after he was inside her.

The experience had set her on a black binge. She balled about five in one month, then ran another six months averaging two or three a month. The first few were entertainers, then she went on an athlete kick. She deliberately took sports assignments with magazines to insure easy access. Football players were her favorites. She loved their mammothness. There was nothing like having those immense forms hovering over you, all chest and shoulders and pungent sweat. In a way, the penis seemed almost superfluous—in any case, a bonus, not the main kick.

In, out; in, out. Spats was a metronome. But even in his apparent stupor he seemed able to sense her needs. The clit pressure was there. The sexy little rub at the end of the thrust, that was there too. Each time.

She wanted to see more of his brownness. She wanted to get on top of him, so she could raise up to gaze at his entire body. Should she risk turning him over and disrupting things? What the hell, nothing ventured, nothing gained.

His body responded compliantly, almost in anticipation of her pressures. Contact was broken when her knee got in the way as she tried to roll over on top of him, but she quickly reinserted him and the act resumed. In, out; in, out. She contemplated his brown sleekness against the brilliant white of the sheet. Aesthetically, there was no comparison: black bodies won out over all others, going away. Why, she suddenly wondered, did they call themselves blacks? Strictly speaking, mostly they were browns. Same deal for "whites," of course. Watch it, Buf, you'll lose your liberal credentials. . . .

In, out; in, out. His eyes were squeezed shut, his lips

drawn tight in a smile, as if he were lost in a private dream.

In, out; in, out. Her sensations started building now. Slowly. Very slowly. Much more slowly than she would dare let it happen with another man. But with Spats she wasn't worried. Ol' Man River . . .

The warm fuzzy ball of orgasm started to take form inside her, gathering size now. Spats seemed to sense it. His thrusts grew stronger, deeper, more rapid. She bore down on his pubis. Oh, it was glorious, sitting there on top of Old Smokey . . . *watch* that, Buf. . . . It was almost like being on horseback, a very special kind of horseback—with one's own very special saddle. Oh, buck away, you sexy brown-co, buck away . . . (God, Buf, you've really got to improve your puns. Of course, if you don't risk the really bad ones you never get a shot at the really good ones . . .)

The feeling built inside her. Then, suddenly, it erupted. "Oh, Eddie!" she gasped, "Oh God, Eddie, it's so good, do it, do it, Eddie, it's so good . . ." His hips rose so swiftly that she almost was thrown off him. No restraint on his part now. He bucked, bucked again. His cock felt huge, thrashing around inside her. "Oh, it's good, don't stop, Eddie, it's so good, please don't stop!"

Finally the wave crested, and she brought her hands to his hips to let him know he needn't continue. Magically his movements slowed in exact cadence with the diminishing of her sensation. A machine, a veritable fucking machine, now slowing down, down, down . . .

His eyes opened.

"My word, sir, that was *fantastic,*" she said.

He grinned. "Wait till you get me on one of my good days."

"Don't put me on. You can't get any better."

He sang a full volume from the Irving Berlin song, "Yes I can, yes I can, yes I can!" Then he laughed and said, "Pardon the zanies, lady, but I very seldom get up this early and when somebody wakes me I act very weird."

She smiled. "Just stay as 'weird' as you are."

"We'll give it our best shot . . . and now don't just sit theah, lady, be so kind as to move your ahss. You've had yours, now I want mine."

Obediently she began moving.

"Bettuh yet, dear heart, flip ovuh on your back. I much prefuh it that way."

She obliged. He supported himself stiff-armed and looked down at her body. "Seriously, Buf," he said in his natural voice, "you're a wonderful fuck. Frankly I never thought we'd hit it off."

"Well, I dig you too. Hey, at what point did you wake up? When I came?"

He smiled. "I'm still not awake, baby. This is all part of a wonderful dream." He brought one hand to her thigh and slowly moved it up to her shoulder. "You've also got a terrific figure. I'll bet you look great in miniskirts."

"*Mini*skirts? No one has worn one of those in about a hundred years."

"And a damn shame, in my opinion. They were the sexiest outfits ever invented."

Minkskirts. Didn't Ted Vassily have a thing about miniskirts too? Or was that just skirts versus pants . . . ? Whatever, the whole damned world was on a body binge. Well, lie back and enjoy it.

"If you really want to turn me on some night," Spats said, "just show up in a miniskirt. Or a trench coat with *nada* underneath. Or if you want to blow my mind completely, a cheerleader outfit—sweater, short skirt, bobby sox, the whole shmear."

"You really have a thing about clothes, don't you?"

"That kind, yeah, I guess I surely do. Forgive ol' kinky Spats."

Her voice became calculating. "What do you like about that outfit you just described?"

"The way it looks."

"But what specifically?"

"I don't know."

"Think about it. I mean, a trench coat looks pretty much the same whether you're naked under it or not."

"I don't know, Buf. It just turns me on."

Cool it, Buffy. He's losing his hard-on. "You know what I want you to do?" she said quickly. "I want you to imagine I'm a cheerleader."

His expression brightened.

"You've got a date with me," she went on. "I ring your

doorbell, you open the door, and there I am. I came over right after the game. I'm even still carrying my pom-poms."

"I got it. Go." He closed his eyes. His thrusts intensified. "Tell me more."

"You're so turned on that you can't wait for me to come in. You grab me around the waist and pull me inside. I'm so flustered I just drop my little ol' pom-poms outside the door and . . . you kiss me, then you step back to take a good look. I'm wearing a bulky white sweater with a big letter 'R' on the front. And a pleated skirt that barely covers my ass. And thick cotton *bobby* sox. And white and black *saddle* shoes with rubber soles—"

"Oh, babes, you are something else . . . all right, what do I do to you? What do I do?"

"You kiss me really hard."

He did. "Then what do I do?"

"You caress me gently. And slip down my panties. And then you take me over to the couch. You're fingering me, but I'm still wearing the uniform, everything except the panties, even the shoes. I've got the panties dangling around one ankle."

"Oh, babes, this is dynamite. I'm gonna come."

"On the couch, Eddie. You stop fingering me and climb on top." She shifted position smoothly and spoke rapidly, trying to match the acceleration of his thrusts. "You put your cock inside me. I wrap my legs around you." She did it. "You can feel my calves against your back. And my bobby sox, Eddie. And my saddle shoes . . ."

His body tensed, was stone-still for a moment, as if electrified, then went limp. For a while he said nothing, then, softly kissing her cheek, said, "Baby, you are unbelievable. . . ."

Give a little, get a lot, she told herself. "You're one considerable dude yourself, Spats."

They dawdled in bed a while longer. He wanted to drink some Scotch and have some more fun. She would have liked it, but she had work to do. She already was running late. "We'll do an encore tonight," she suggested as she finished dressing. "That is, if you're free."

He grinned. "Right after I tape the program. And

don't forget your saddle shoes," he called after her as the elevator doors closed.

She went to her apartment and checked her answering service. Along with messages from her usual business contacts was one from Joseph Williams. She dialed the number and got his answering service. Eventually, she told herself, the world was going to reach a point where answering services or those horrible little recording devices communicated with each other and people became superfluous. She left her number and said she would be in all afternoon.

His call came a few hours later. "I've been thinking about those fellows you're defending in South Dakota," he said without prologue. "I suspect I can be of some help to them."

She wondered if he remembered that she'd been to bed with him. Of course, he *had* to remember; even Joseph Williams wasn't *that* cool. But judging from his phone manner, they might be total strangers. "I'm sure they'll welcome all the help they can get," she answered, taking up his tone.

He explained his plan for a fund-raising cocktail party, and she agreed it was a natural. The more he told her, emphasizing Grace's approach about a party, not a solicitation—though not mentioning Grace's name—the better she liked it. Not only would guests at the party contribute to the defense fund; if she maneuvered things properly it could be the start of a city-wide effort. She wouldn't solicit contributions herself, of course; that would be improper for a lawyer. But she knew dozens of people who'd be happy to serve as chairperson of a fund-raising committee, particularly if that job meant an invitation to a Joseph Williams party.

Later, as she started getting ready for her meeting with Spats, it occurred to her that he could help the cause too. If she asked him, he almost certainly would interview one or two of the defendants on TV. The court had issued no gag order, so there was no problem there. Spats, as a member of a minority, would certainly be a sympathetic interviewer. And when one of the Indians said he was soliciting contributions for his defense fund, money should start coming in from all over the country.

Of course, she would have to synchronize appearances carefully. She couldn't have the TV show precede the party, or it would defuse newspaper and magazine stories. Ideally, the program should come a week or so after the print exposure. That would keep the issue alive in New York—a sort of one-two punch—at the same time that it broke in the rest of the country. Meanwhile, other magazines and newspapers would pick up the first stories; there would be requests for interviews, for backgrounders, maybe even opportunities for some ghosted articles under various defendants' by-lines.

This, she told herself, was what the defense effort had needed all along. Once the money started coming in, she'd be able to farm out the nuts-and-bolts legal work to top-flight attorneys rather than relying on the well-meaning but less-than-brilliant youngsters who presently were donating their time. There would be money for expert witnesses—psychiatrists, ballistics experts, electronics specialists. She could afford private investigators, interviewers, even sociological consultants for jury selection. This was the kind of defense every defendant needed today to hold his own against the power and majesty of a government prosecution.

She excitedly began listing the people she knew who might be best on the fund-raising committee. It certainly would help to have one or more distinguished citizens as honorary chairpersons. Then as many celebrities as possible on the list. She was so absorbed in her plans that it was five minutes after she was due at Spats's apartment when she realized the time.

Well, she thought, smiling, one of the nice things about balling your neighbors was that you never had to hassle transportation. She started for the door, then stopped herself. The idea was goofy, she knew. But what the fuck . . . give a little, get a lot.

She went to her closet, rummaged about, finally located a worn cardboard box labeled—well, she'd thought it sort of clever at the time—"Dated material, Do Not Disturb," looked through it, and came up with a flame-red skirt. She shook the wrinkles out of it, held it to her waist and laughed at its length. Did she ever really wear skirts that short?

She considered pressing it but decided Spats could hardly care less. Besides, she didn't expect to have it on that long. She took off her jeans, put on the skirt, laughed again at the way she looked in it and left the apartment.

Next time, if he went along with her on the TV thing, she might even be able to manage a pair of saddle shoes.

Tom Donohue had the entire conference table covered with newspapers. "Look," he said, "the coverage this fellow is getting is absolutely incredible."

John Malloy scanned the mastheads: Washington *Post*, Los Angeles *Times*, Cleveland *Plain Dealer*, Miami *Herald*, St. Louis *Post-Dispatch*.

"And these," Donohue went on, "are only the early stories, written before the event. AP and UPI had photographers there last night. Vassily's p.r. man, Burr Whiteside, had *paparazzi* of his own, and they stayed up all night making prints so they could get them in the mail first thing this morning. Come next Sunday, this story is going to be a one- or two-page spread in damn near every paper in the country."

"All of which, Tom, confirms your good judgment in recognizing Whiteside's value to us and recruiting him for our team. You spoke to him this morning, I take it."

"Matter of fact, I did. He's surprisingly modest for a p.r. man. Says he really can't take credit for more than the routine things that any p.r. guy would do. The coverage, he says, owes entirely to Vassily's charisma."

"Maybe he was just looking for a polite way to say no."

"To the contrary. He'll be happy to work with us, billing only for expenses and a modest compensation when our stuff takes him away from his bread-and-butter accounts. He just doesn't want us to expect miracles."

"Which brings us back to Vassily and his charisma, which I suspect is your choice for item one on today's agenda."

"Yes, John, for two reasons. First, of course, is the media coverage, which speaks for itself. Second is a phone call I got this morning from our plant in the camp of our distinguished opponent. It seems our opponent's people were approached by someone from the White House."

John's eyebrows arched. The President, it was true, was

a lifelong friend and strong supporter of the incumbent senior senator from New York. But why should he approach the candidate from whom John Malloy hoped to capture the opposing party's nomination for that office?

"The President's man," Donohue went on, "was apparently very frank. He told our opponent that the President has always disliked your family and dislikes you even more than the others."

"Unusual candor for that distinguished gentleman."

"He also said that the President is ready to do almost anything in his power to see you lose the nomination. Shades of Richard you-know-who."

"Ah—so at least we're getting through to him. He's worried."

"Exactly. He knows his friend the senator will stand a much better chance against our opponent than against us. So he's volunteering to cooperate fully with our opponent in the primaries, insofar as he can do so without compromising the incumbent. And if our opponent thinks his campaign would benefit from attacks by the President, why the President will oblige and attack him. If he'd rather be ignored, the President will ignore him. And if he feels it would help for the President to endorse some of his positions, the President will endorse them—again, of course, to whatever extent possible without compromising the incumbent."

"Interesting."

"Yes, particularly with respect to the timing. Our intentions have been known for well over six months. It could, of course, be mere coincidence that you happened to be on our asshole-in-chief's mind this morning. But—"

"But it could also be that he has seen some of the Three-oh-five publicity, ties me in with the building and suddenly decides that I represent a more serious threat than he'd anticipated."

"Yeah. Maybe he even watched last night's telecast . . . before his favorite *late movie,* that is. Anyway, I can imagine his reaction if he tuned in, expecting to be regaled by some just-among-us-jocks chatter, and saw your sweet little Irish face on the screen."

John laughed. "Which brings us back to your agenda and Vassily."

"There's no doubt he can help us and no doubt he'll be happy to. The question, as I see it, is whether we should tie in further to the current publicity push on Three-oh-five East, and if so, to what extent. The most obvious possibility is to move up the formal announcement of your candidacy. Schedule a press conference next week, maybe in the Three-oh-five East quadrangle or lobby. Immediately in the public mind you're linked with the magic building. And Vassily and Whiteside wind up having spent the last six months working as your advance men."

"The disadvantage, of course, is that an early announcement exposes me to front-runner treatment by the press—tough questions on issues where I don't want, or am not ready, to take a stand."

"Conversely, if we don't exploit the current publicity, your link with the building can weaken. If we suddenly surface three months down the line, the public not having been reminded that you were a charter tenant and one of Vassily's earliest supporters, you may be seen as just another guy who lives here. In fact, you could be seen as a Johnny-come-lately trying to ride the Three-oh-five East bandwagon. The opposition could make hay calling you a limousine liberal, surrounding yourself with celebrity types and practicing tokenism to snow the peons."

"So . . ."

"A two-pronged attack. We want you to be among the Three-oh-five East celebrity crowd, but not of them. At the same time we want to reinforce your connection with the non-celebrity aspect of the building. The latter part is easy. I can manage to wangle from the rental office a confidential list of occupants of the subsidized apartments. We make it a point to establish some kind of contact with them. One family, for example, lives on your floor. You and Peg learn who they are and keep an eye out. Maybe Peg bumps into the lady some day in the elevator. They start talking, Peg invites her brood for dinner. Meanwhile you just happen to hear gossip that one of the kids on another floor broke his arm playing ball. Okay, you're a former athlete and a great supporter of physical fitness. You and Johnny visit the kid to lift his spirits and encourage him not to let this misfortune discourage him from future athletic participation. Meanwhile, you meet his parents and they get invited to dinner too. Then I let my favorite newslady know that you and yours are socializing with the poverty families, but I insist you don't want it publicized because you don't want to invade these poor folks' privacy. This, of course, makes her all the more eager to tell the world what a wonderful egalitarian you are—"

"Hey, Tom, hold it. The scenario doesn't need to be so carefully managed. I think we can and should be direct about it. No need to get the poverty list surreptitiously. If you'll recall, I moved into this building because I happen to believe in economically integrated housing and the social integration that it implies. So why not go that route? I'd actually *like* to invite each of the poverty families to dinner with my family—not a banquet, knocking them off wholesale in a way that suggests I really don't want to do it, but one family at a time, just them and us, a different one each week. And if any of them wants to return the invitation, my family will be delighted to go to their place for dinner. If we tell Vassily this is what we have in mind, I can't see why he wouldn't be willing to give us the list."

"I think you're right, John, except my source in the rental office says that Vassily is adamant about not identifying the poverty families to anyone. He feels that would set them up for treatment as second-class tenants."

"I think he's a little off base there. Realistically, you don't have to publish their names on a bulletin board for their neighbors to know who they are. On the other hand, if Vassily gives me their names and I start inviting them to dinner, they're participating in the kind of social integration that is—or at least should be—one of his chief goals. Explain the situation that way when you ask for the list, and I'm certain he'll be glad to provide it. If he refuses, well, maybe then we'll try it your way."

"Well, okay. And now on the celebrity front. I was thinking mainly that we want the celebrities in the building to be seen around you, urging you to run for office rather than any more publicity that might create the impression you're just another tenant here. If, in other words, Spats Johnson is going to throw a party for show business buddies, you don't show. We don't want people to see your picture in the paper and say, 'Ah, there's that Three-oh-five East crowd again—Spats Johnson and Ted Vassily and Joseph Williams and John Malloy . . .' What we want is the celebrities of Three-oh-five East to be meeting without you, talking among themselves about how they can persuade you to seek the nomination."

"Well, come on, Tom, don't lay it on too thick. These people aren't exactly on your payroll, you know." Tom was a good and true friend, and his heart was in the right place, but sometimes his Byzantine plotting seemed to be an end in itself.

"What we might do," Tom went on, warming to his subject, "is to get a few of them to form a committee, or a series of committees, on your behalf. Joseph Williams and Spats Johnson, for instance, the Performing Artists for John Malloy Committee; Buffy Weiss, the Lawyers' Committee for the Nomination and Election of John Malloy. You still aren't a declared candidate suffering front-runner syndrome, but naturally you aren't going to discourage these people from working on your behalf; you respect them and their judgment, you're grateful for their support and confidence in you and you are seriously considering answering their call—"

"Enough! I get the picture, oh Machiavelli."

Donohue didn't miss a beat. "Shall I invite one of them to dinner to float a little old trial balloon?"

"No! Just list a few you think would be helpful—and because they agree with our approach to public matters, we'll invite them for cocktails—*privately*, not compromising them in any way—and I'll simply tell the truth, that I'm seriously considering seeking the nomination and I'd like their reaction. If, as we hope, they're in favor, then you can propose your committees . . . actually a few like Williams have volunteered already."

"Sounds fine," Donohue said, and the discussion then turned to other matters. An hour and a half later Donohue came to the last item on his agenda. "You'll be interested," he said, "in what I've learned about Miss Colello."

John Malloy's expression didn't change as he waited.

Donohue smiled. He took great pride in his thoroughness, in *all* areas. His computerized file on those who wrote letters of support or opposition was, if he did say so himself, a thing of beauty. Grace Colello was clearly one of John Malloy's most fervent supporters.

He handed his boss a photocopy of her letter, retrieved from the microfilm unit. "Shall I check her out as a potential organizer of Students for Malloy?"

"No, just say I received her letter and would like to meet her." Not only was Tom a good and true friend, he was also trustworthy.

"But, John, she wrote six months ago."

Malloy finally allowed himself a smile. "Blame yourself for not calling the letter to my attention sooner. That should be a real test of your p.r."

SEVEN

GRACE HESITATED at the door, then obeyed the WALK IN sign and identified herself to the receptionist. "Oh, yes, Mister Malloy is expecting you," the girl said sweetly. "Please have a seat."

Grace went to a handsome overstuffed walnut and leather couch, took up the current issue of *New Republic* from an adjoining end table and tried unsuccessfully to read. Her eyes kept darting from the printed page to various places in the room, taking mental pictures of them which she then thought about while looking at without seeing the print. The office was elegantly appointed. Against one wall was an eighteenth century French armoire that she was sure was no imitation. Highlighting another was what she felt confident was an original Gainsborough. Her eyes kept returning to the receptionist, also disconcertingly beautiful, who was now saying, "Mister Malloy will see you now."

Grace entered a large office with many more French pieces and two enormous paintings of bare-breasted nymphs in stylized woodland settings, à la Boucher and Nattier. At the far end of the room was an intricately detailed oak table that served as John Malloy's desk. He now came around from behind it and offered his hand. "Grace Colello. Thanks very much for coming."

"Thank you for inviting me," she said uncertainly.

He went to an armchair and gestured for her to sit on

the adjoining couch, then looked at her with his cool blue eyes in a way that made her feel naked. "I'd be very interested," he said, seeming all business, "in your opinions on what the key issues will and should be in this year's Senate campaign."

"My opinions?" She hated herself for sounding so dopey. Why was she freezing up with him?

"Yes. I think too many politicians accept advice only from so-called professionals—staffmen, financial backers, power brokers. I can't think of a single candidate—for any office—who really has sought out articulate young people to find out what they feel."

"I—I'm not at all sure that my opinions are representative," she said uneasily. And so far my delivery is hardly articulate, she added to herself.

"Nonetheless, I think I'd benefit from hearing them. . . . Is there any particular issue, for example, that you feel especially strong about right now?"

"Representative democracy," she responded without hesitation, "and whether it can work." She was on home turf now; this was the classroom revisited. He might be sorry he asked. "The problem is, the little person—you know, the proverbial man-in-the-street—hasn't any real say in the process. Party bosses pick candidates. Usually there's little difference between them. If you don't like them, your only choice is not to vote at all—the way increasing numbers have been doing lately."

"There's the write-in vote."

"In practice, it's meaningless. The last candidate to get a significant number was Eisenhower in nineteen fifty-two, I think, and even that was in a campaign orchestrated by the Republican establishment. Anyway, whoever gets elected, once in office, he needn't—and usually doesn't—reflect the will of his constituents. His loyalty is to the power blocs that got him elected and hopefully will get him reelected—the money guys, industry, labor. If the ordinary guy is worked up about an issue, he can write a letter that a clerk will read and file. His opinion doesn't count unless it's one of a huge number of identical opinions, which means an organized campaign—which brings us back to power brokers."

John smiled. Grace Colello, once started, was something else. A bright young lady, no doubt. "What about decentralization and revenue sharing?"

"I don't believe revenue sharing really helps the little guy—it just increases the power of local politicians, in exchange for which they are undyingly loyal to the administration that gave it to them. As for decentralization, I can't see that there ever was any. Local governments were made stronger, but not at the expense of the federal government, which didn't give up any of its power. It was at the expense of the same little guy who now had *two* strong enemies instead of a strong one and a weak one."

"So you think there has to be an adversary relationship between the citizen and government?"

"Theoretically, I suppose not. But yes, in practice. The most successful politicians—the ones who most consistently are returned to office—buy off the power blocs. Bring something home from the Washington pork barrel for the unions, something else for business, and something else for every other power center that's managed to get your ear, and you'll probably stay in office for as long as you wish. Meanwhile the seniority system, even modified as it now is, increases your opportunity to bring home the bacon. So the longer someone stays in office, the longer he's likely to stay. The process seems to feed on itself, and the little guy pays the price."

"Well, Grace, that sounds pretty gloomy. Especially from somebody so young. What's your solution? Revolution?"

"No, because the same people—or people like them—who manipulate things now would find ways to manipulate the new institutions."

"Then what's left?"

"Well, I'm for staying with the basic system, but I'd like to see governmental power drastically cut back. Really limit government to the smallest role possible consistent with maintaining order. People have got to stop turning to Big Brother in Washington to shape their lives. Let them shape their own." As she said that last, she thought of how much it applied to "a little guy" named Grace Colello and "Big Brother," her father. . . .

"Other than a magic wand," John Malloy said, interrupting her thought, "what do we use to accomplish this? You just said the system perpetuates itself." His eyes fixed again on hers, and he smiled. "I don't entirely disagree with you, you know." And, he added to himself, from what he'd heard, he suspected that their mutual landlord wouldn't either. Had the old pro and the young lady perhaps been keeping company?

"How about mini-revolution," she was saying. "You find candidates like . . . well, like John Malloy, who at least agree that change is necessary. You support them and hopefully elect enough of them to overcome the others, in spite of the pressures of the power brokers. If you don't elect a majority, at least you show you're a significant opposition, and that you've got to be met half-way. It did work once with Eugene McCarthy and the Vietnam war."

John's marvelous smile came at her again. "Listening to you, Grace, I get the feeling you should be the candidate and I your supporter."

She smiled back, nervously. Was he patronizing her? "I feel pretty strongly about these things, Mr. Malloy."

"It's John. And I can see how strongly you feel. And I respect you for it." He gazed across the room. "Mini-revolution. I think I like that. What was it Shaw said about a good cry being half the battle?"

"I think," she said, "we sometimes rely too much on slogans, especially in politics." And saying it, was afraid she was sounding pompous as a politician herself.

"Granted. But it's like old age—not so bad when you consider the alternative. And now I guess I'm borrowing from Mark Twain. Anyway, lacking a magic wand that would make the electorate listen to argument as carefully reasoned as yours, I'm afraid slogans will have to be part of my war chest. To go on with them, I think it was Adam Clayton Powell who said the fundamental duty of every politician is to get and stay in office. Some of my supporters don't quite grasp that. They want me to take positions that couldn't possibly win the broad base support a candidate for national office needs to get elected."

"Politics is the art of the possible?" she said, succumbing.

"Exactly." He stood. "I'd like to go on with this, Grace,

perhaps some evening when we've more time and I'm not under the pressure of an office schedule. Before that, though, I'd very much like you to do something for me. As you of course know, I'm seriously considering running for the Senate. I'd like to have your analysis of the issues you think we might face in the upcoming primary—what they are, what you think my position should be on each of them."

"That's quite an assignment . . . I'm flattered, and I'll be happy to try."

He walked her to the elevator. "Draft a memo, something I can circulate among my staff for comments. Try to hit the issues and perspectives you think young people would be especially concerned about."

"As I said, I'll try. It may take some time, though. I want to be as thorough as I can—"

"By all means be thorough, but not compulsive, please. Which is my way of saying I'd like to have the memo as soon as possible. I'm going to have some sensitive decisions to make over the next few weeks and I'd like to take your ideas into account." He took her hand, and once again his eyes fixed on hers—his incredibly blue eyes. "I very much enjoyed meeting you, Grace. I want to see you again very soon." He was certain she got the message. He had gotten, and liked, hers.

"He wants to fuck me," she told Ted.

He didn't exactly enjoy hearing her say it, but he smiled. "I'm hardly surprised. You're not exactly repulsive looking."

"Is that so important?"

"When you want to fuck someone, it tends to be."

"I didn't mean it that way." She sipped her wine. "What I meant was, sex seems so terribly all-important to some men—you among them. You're not satisfied—you, plural—simply to do it when you happen to be with someone attractive and willing. You're constantly, well, structuring your lives so that you're surrounded by sexy attractive women. And if they don't feel like fucking you, well, out they go, there are others waiting in the wings, right?"

"I can't speak for 'you, plural.' But me, singular—damn right."

"But doesn't it strike you as somehow wrong? . . . Immoral?"

"I don't consider fucking immoral."

"I'm not talking about the fucking part, I'm talking about the discrimination."

"Let's blame it on my sense of efficiency. I like fucking. I also like going to the opera. It makes sense to do both with the same person. Hey, what the hell got you onto this anyway?"

She told him about how uneasy she'd been in John Malloy's reception room, the beautiful things, the beautiful receptionist, and from there, later on, to the way certain powerful men could order their lives with beautiful women as showpieces, as though they were available on call. . . . The women at the 305 East coming-out party, in Ted's own office at 305 East the time she'd been there to settle something about the lease, the women in the restaurant Joseph Williams had taken her to. . . . "And then I got to thinking about Joseph's party for the South Dakota defendants. I think I made a contribution to the idea, and I'm sure he appreciates this. But if he hadn't found me attractive and if I hadn't gone to bed with him, our relationship would never have gotten to the point where he'd even have discussed the matter with me—"

"I don't see the problem."

"One thing shouldn't have to follow the other." She took a large swallow of wine, went to the window and turned back to him. "I think what I'm trying to say is, I don't want to have to depend on sex as my passport. I'd like to think men like you and Joseph and John Malloy would be interested in my ideas even if you didn't find me attractive."

"You're getting yourself worked up over nothing. You happen to be a very bright girl with a great deal to contribute, and anybody with an eye and a brain cell who spends a few minutes with you can't help realizing it. But—"

"But, damn it, that's exactly what I'm talking about! No one spends a few minutes with me unless they want to fuck me." She laughed and shook her head. "See how shook up it has me? It's even got me talking ungrammatically. I meant to say, no one spends a few minutes with me unless *he* wants to fuck me."

"Come over here. Sit next to me for a minute." She obeyed. He put his arm around her. "Let me talk to you like a Dutch uncle. There are things worth getting worked up about and things that aren't. The things worth getting worked up about are the ones you can do something about. I got worked up about economically segregated housing, so I put up this building. Okay, there are certain other things that no matter how exercised you get, you can't affect in any way. One of them is the way people get together. You don't just walk down the street soliciting ideas from everyone who passes by. Even you, with your all-men-are-equal bit, wouldn't patrol the Bowery looking to the bums there to make any real contribution to your wisdom except the obvious object lesson they provide."

"I suppose you're right—"

"Of course I'm right. People get together because of the expectation of pleasure or profit. I repeat, the *expectation,* not just the possibility of it. So here I am, big Ted Vassily, out of Penn State and pro football with a head full of ideas. Do people seek me out to find out what I'm *thinking?* Hell, no. Certain broads come calling for sex, certain guys because they think they can exploit me for business purposes or because they get a bang out of running with jocks. Now, I can get pissed off about it, but there's no profit in that. So I trade what I have for what I want, and in the process I get people to listen to my ideas and support my plans and that's how come a building like Three-oh-five East is standing on this site today instead of me sitting in a bar someplace bitching that nobody gives a shit about fallen heroes, old soldiers, and similar crap."

"I'm beginning to feel a little foolish."

"Don't. Just recognize the truth of the situation and don't let it frustrate you. And the truth is, everybody needs a passport—not just you and me, even the rich. Their money is their passport. Or their social connections. Or in the case of someone like Joseph Williams, his artistic achievements. If they didn't have whatever it is they have, you and I wouldn't be interested in them. If we didn't have what we have, they wouldn't be interested in us."

She sighed. "I think what I've really been trying to say is, I do find John Malloy attractive. But I don't want his interest in my ideas to depend on my going to bed with him."

Ted sipped his wine and said nothing.

"No comment?"

"I think you should do what you feel like doing."

"Would it bother you if I balled him?" She looked at him closely.

"Of course not." He said it too quickly.

"You're not the slightest bit bothered about my going to bed with another man? Not even Joseph?"

"No." Fucking liar.

"Do you think it bothers Joseph that I'm balling you?"

"I don't give—I have no idea. Did you tell him?"

"We never discussed it, but I imagine he assumes it, what with my inviting you to the opera and all that."

"He has no right to be possessive."

"Because he's married, you mean? Yes, he said that. . . . Ted, if I were to start seeing John Malloy, at the same time continuing with Joseph *and* you—wouldn't you begin to wonder about me, wouldn't you begin to think I was some kind of a, well, my mother used to call them round-heels."

"Definitely not."

"Are you absolutely certain of that?"

"Absolutely." Bullshit.

She drank some wine, then moved closer against him. "Ted, sometimes I'm afraid things are just happening faster than I can handle. That first night with you—God, I was so *impressed* with you." (Still am.) "At first I didn't want to make it with you, I was afraid, but once we got to it I was glad we did. And then . . . well, Joseph Williams the same night. And now John Malloy . . ." She shuddered, then laughed. "The thing is, I love to fuck, Ted. I really do. But I can't stand it to be the only reason people are interseted in me. There's more to life. There's more to me."

"Of course there's more."

"Then why do you have all these terrific, gorgeous, wonderful receptionists and secretaries and who-the-hell-knows-what-else—"

"Because all other things being equal, I'd rather as many of my associates as possible be desirable women. That applies to secretaries, receptionists, business partners, friends, whatever. Not because I want to fuck them, necessarily. Just because I like being around them. It keeps life stimulating."

"And, of course, if you fuck them, so much the better."

"Oh, come off it, Grace. Is that old Roman Catholic background of yours acting up again?"

"Maybe." She sipped some more wine. "Or maybe it's just the newness of this whole scene to me. It really brings out my old anxieties. I feel as though I have to be a tightrope walker, and I'm not very surefooted. Did you ever smoke grass? You know, marijuana."

"I know. But I think I missed the transition."

She laughed. "What got me thinking about it was the tightrope thing. When I started college, I went through an anxiety period very much like what I'm going through now. It wasn't just that I worried I was in over my head. It was that everything was so new to me, and I was so excited by all of it. I desperately wanted to do everything right, so that these new people I admired so much would admire me too. I felt like a tightrope walker—oh, I could put one foot in front of the other, all right . . . but with the stakes so high, even the tiniest slip could be fatal, and that kind of pressure can make the simplest things incredibly difficult. Do you know what I mean?"

"As an ex-quarterback who occasionally has thrown on third and too long, I guess you could say I have the general idea. But I still don't see the tie-in with marijuana."

"Oh, well, back during this old anxiety period was when I discovered grass. I mean, it had been a big thing in high school, but I'd kept away from it. I associated it with the class jerks. Plus, I was propagandized—you know, *Reefer Madness* and all that. Anyway, as a freshman in college I met people I admired who used it. So that took away the old stigma of users being jerks. I also saw they weren't foaming at the mouth or suffering other visible signs of mental degeneration, so I tried it. My first time was with a new boyfriend in Greenwich Village. We got high at his apartment, then went to Washington Square Park and sat near the fountain. It must have been really good grass because although I hadn't had too much of it I was really high—which is unusual for a first experience, I'm told. Anyway, I felt so incredibly serene. Then I got thinking of my tightrope metaphor, and I noticed the curbstonelike border that circles the fountain. I decided to walk it. I got on it just as I imagined a tightrope walker would, and I started around—being terribly dramatic, of course, extending my arms, carefully planting one foot immediately ahead of the other. And I felt terrifically confident. I felt as if there was nothing in the world that could upset me. People could shake the tightrope, they could throw rocks at me, they could drop an atom bomb alongside me. The Amazing Grace would just keep walking till she got to the other side. And that's what I did, all the way around the fountain." She waited for him to say something.

He sipped at his wine.

"You didn't like my story, did you?"

"It was okay. I still don't see its relevance."

"I guess I was trying to relate my college-freshman anxiety to what I feel now. And maybe I'm looking for some sort of psychic equivalent of grass to steady me."

He said nothing.

"You don't approve of grass, do you?"

"I don't approve or disapprove. I think it should be legalized, of course. What people put into their bodies is none of the damn government's business."

She smiled, thinking of *her* recent speech to John Malloy. "But on a personal basis you don't approve?"

"What's to approve? It's like driving to Idaho. I don't particularly want to, I don't think it would do anything for me, so I don't do it."

"Do you put down people who do?"

"No, I just find them pretty lousy company, so I avoid being with them when they're high. Why the questions?"

"I don't know. I guess I'm just feeling insecure. Did you ever use it yourself?"

"A couple times."

"Didn't like it?"

"Not much."

"Did you get high at all?"

"Yeah, but I also got very tired. And hungry."

"The munchies. It's a common phenomenon."

"Well, from my point of view, it was a real pain in the ass. I was sleepy and hungry and not in full control of myself. And while everything tasted better, I couldn't help thinking I was deluding myself, it wasn't a naturally better taste, I had simply made a chemical alteration of my brain's response to certain stimuli. The phoniness of the experience soured it for me. And then, after I slept, I was fuzzy the whole next day. When I added up the pluses and minuses I had to decide the nays had it. I never tried it again."

"Maybe you're a grass puritan—I mean, a closet grass puritan, sort of like my being a closet sex puritan?"

"You mean really opposing it on moral grounds and not able to enjoy it for that reason?"

"Yes."

"I frankly never thought of it. Nor do I give a shit about it."

"The whole subject turns you off, doesn't it?"

"Yes."

"Sorry." She sipped her wine. "Do you appreciate my point, though, about being anxious in all this newness?"

"Yes." And hearing her ask it that way brought back his old, good, protective feelings toward her. And looking at her brought back other old good feelings too . . . "And I think you're handling it very well, taking things as they come, responding in each situation as your feelings suggest—"

"My feelings suggest something right now. . . ."

"That a fact?"

"Cross my heart, loving friend."

They had a real bell-ringer. Afterward she lay in the crook of his arm and pressed her cheek against the thick hairs on his chest. "I really love you, loving friend."

"I can stand you too."

"Such flattery . . . watch out, you may turn this poor girl's head. . . . But enough of the perils of Grace. . . . I'm so self-centered I haven't even asked you about Miss Loomis."

"I'm having lunch with her father tomorrow."

"The question, *friend,* was about the daughter."

"I'm playing hard to get."

"On the theory she won't feel crowded and will come running back?"

"Maybe."

"I advise against it, friend. Chicks like her don't moon over a guy. If they said yes to only half their offers, they'd be booked solid for the next three years."

"What do you suggest, friend? Beg for the opportunity to kiss her ass?"

"No, be a tightrope walker. Slow ahead, but always moving forward."

"Such wisdom from one so young. Well, she's been home from her flight two days now, I calculate. Do you recommend I pass or phone?"

"You might. Or wait till she's back from the next one. I wouldn't let it go beyond that, though. Better press your advantage while her memories of that great cock of yours are still fresh." Listening to herself, she could hardly believe this was she talking . . . and realized that it really wasn't. Fact was, the whole subject of Nan Loomis depressed her more than a little.

"She's not too interested in cocks."

Back to the big front, the smart talk . . . "Barring lesbians, which I will assume she isn't, there ain't a chick alive that's not interested in cock. It's just that some are a little shy about letting you know." She laughed brightly and said something of what she'd been thinking a moment earlier. "I can't believe I'm talking like this. Me! Sweet, innocent, super-romantic Grace Colello giving strategy points to a loving friend I'm having an affair with—"

"It's the way life should be. No barriers. No hang-ups. If it feels good, how bad can it be?" He believed it, but he didn't feel it.

"Slogan time, huh?" And again she thought of her exchange with Malloy and promptly put it out of mind. . . . "Okay, if it moves, fondle it." Her hand went to his penis. "And this one is *moving.*"

It took longer this time. Much longer. He wasn't even sure he could sustain his erection long enough for her to come. But he fantasied Nan and intensified his pubic pressure, and soon Grace's hips were doing that hungry action of theirs, arching off the bed, bucking him, higher, higher. And then she was moaning and her fists were clenched tightly at her sides, pushing down on the bed. And then she bucked way up . . .

"That, sir, was just terrific," she said after he'd come. "Hope it was for you too."

"It was."

She drew her leg over his middle, enjoying the feel of his still tumescent cock against her. Nature's tranquilizer. "Hey, I'm exhausted. . . ."

They fell asleep, and woke to the buzzer of the doorman's intercom. "Sorry to bother you, Ted, but there's some guy down here—one of the tenants—his name is Mr. Colello—he, uh, says his daughter is in your apartment and he wants her. He's kind of pissed off."

"Oh, my God," Grace said, "I should have forced myself to stay awake." She frantically pulled up the bedclothes, as if worried that her father could somehow see through the intercom. "What time is it?"

Ted showed his watch. It was four-forty-five.

"Tell him I'll be right down," Grace said. "No, wait. He'll kill me. Tell him I left at midnight and you don't know where I am."

"Tell Mr. Colello," Ted instructed the doorman, "that I'll be right down."

"What are you going to do?"

"Invite him up and try to talk to him." Ted got out of bed and started dressing. "Tell him we were together and you fell asleep. Which is the truth."

"He'll know, he'll kill me."

"No one's going to kill you."

"You don't know my father."

"Well, I'm about to."

"I'll go down with you. No, wait, I better not. He loves scenes. He'll make a whopper in the lobby—punch you out, call me a whore, the whole number. Maybe I'd better go down alone—"

"I'll go alone and bring him back. If he wants a scene,

we'll be the only audience." He checked himself in the mirror, ran a brush through his hair, then went to the elevator.

Marty Colello was pacing the lobby. He started toward the elevator doors as they opened, his arm raised as if to deliver a backhand slap. He stopped when he saw that Ted was alone. "Where is she?"

"In my apartment, Mr. Colello. Please come up and have a drink."

"I don't want a drink. I want my daughter."

"She's in my apartment."

"Send her down."

"No, you come up."

"Are you telling me you're not going to release my daughter? You want me to file kidnaping charges against you?"

"Don't be ridiculous. No one is holding her against her will. She's waiting for you to come up and talk."

Marty eyed Ted uncertainly. He couldn't say why, but he was certain that he should not step inside the elevator. Somehow that would be giving in, and if he did it once he'd wind up doing it again. That was the way the rich bastards brought you to your knees. "I'll wait here. Send her down."

Ted stayed inside the car. "I'll gladly take you to her, Mr. Colello, but I'm not going to send her down."

"I said," Marty repeated more loudly, "send her down."

"No, sir. But I'll take you to her."

Marty felt his fingernails digging into his palms. His face, he knew, was red. He could feel the heat in his ears and on the back of his neck. He shouldn't get into the elevator. Except what could he do? "I said," he shouted, "send her down!"

"You can scream as loudly as you like, Mr. Colello, it's not going to change things."

"Send her down, goddamn it, send her the hell down!" His fists were clenched in front of him, as if waiting to throw a punch. Suddenly, to his surprise, he found himself punching his own thighs. "You arrogant son of a bitch, you think you're some kind of big deal! You think I need your goddamn apartment? I don't have to live in this goddamn shithouse. I'll move out tomorrow!"

Ted said nothing.

"You want the world to think you're such a goddamn saint. You're the big goddamn saint that's going to help the poor people. Well, I don't need your charity, Mr. Touchdown. You can shove your charity up your ass."

Ted kept silent.

Marty stared at his clenched fists. He had delivered his entire blast at full volume. Now his throat hurt, his head was so hot he felt it would explode, and Vassily was still standing there looking at him as if nothing had happened. He raised both fists, stared at them as if trying to decide what to do with them, then slowly let them fall to his sides. "Well, if I have to come up for her," he said hoarsely, "I will. But there'll be no goddamn bullshit about having drinks. You're no friend of mine, fella. Don't ever get the idea you are." He stepped into the car.

Ted turned the key. The doors closed. Marty waited for him to speak. Ted said nothing.

"You think you can buy everything, don't you?" Marty glared up at him. It isn't bad enough the rich bastard screws your daughter, he also has to be fourteen feet tall so you can't talk to him without looking up at him. "You rent an apartment to a guy like me, you figure it makes my family your slaves. You want my daughter, you take her. You want my—" He struggled for another example, couldn't think of one and disgustedly turned away. "Well, you can go take a shit for yourself, Vassily. I'm moving out of your goddamn building. Find some other sucker to parade in front of the TV to show the world what a big-hearted bastard you are."

The doors opened. Marty found himself looking into a room that seemed as big as a church. It took a moment for him to realize that his daughter was sitting on a couch down on the lower level. She seemed hundreds of yards away. "Get over here," he called to her.

"Come in, Mr. Colello," Ted said. "We can talk inside."

"There won't be any talking." He didn't take his eyes from Grace, who stood but did not start toward him. "Get over here. I'm taking you home."

She did not move.

"You heard me," he said more loudly. "Get over here."

She took a step toward him.

"Not yet, Grace," Ted said. "Come in, Mr. Colello. Sit down."

Marty felt his ears and neck getting hot again. "Hey," he yelled at Grace, "who you taking orders from, him or me?"

She stood motionless.

"Get over here!" Marty started toward her, arm raised. "Get over here or I'll break your back."

It took a moment to realize that something was preventing him from going to her. His arm. Someone had hold of his arm. He tried to jerk it away but could not. It was like having your wrist in a vise.

"You're not going to touch her," Ted said softly. "You're never going to hit her again."

Marty tried once more to jerk free, then threw a punch with his opposite fist. Immediately a huge hand closed around that wrist. Goddamn it, he was helpless. Vassily was holding him like a baby. And it all was happening in front of Grace. "Let me go, you bastard. Let me go or I'll sue you for all you're worth."

"Sit down," Ted said.

Marty tugged again to free himself but realized even before he felt Ted's resistance that the effort was futile. It was futile, and the whole goddamn night was futile. He never should've got in the elevator. He never should've let Grace talk him into taking an apartment in this goddamn building. He sat.

"Will you have a drink?"

Marty stared at the floor. "No."

Ted sat opposite him. "It was my fault Grace didn't get home last night. She was ready to leave at midnight, but I asked her to stay for one more drink. We were watching a movie. We fell asleep."

Marty did not look up. "I really don't care how it happened."

"Dad," Grace said, her voice small, "I think it's time we talked about us—you and me . . . I love and respect you very much, really, but respect is a two-way street. I'm not a child anymore. You have to respect me some too. . . ."

Marty continued to stare at the floor. "If you want to

talk, you can talk in your own apartment. I don't need a referee when I talk to my daughter."

"The only reason we're here," Ted said, "is because she's afraid you'll hit her. From what I've seen tonight, that's not an unreasonable fear."

"What I do with my daughter is no business of yours."

"It's against the law to hit people, even your own daughter."

"Somebody named you policeman, huh? Where's your uniform?"

"I'm Grace's friend. I'm not going to let it happen."

"Ted," she said, "let me try. Dad, I don't want to make you unhappy, but I've got to—"

Marty turned away. He didn't want to hear any more. He kept remembering how helpless he'd felt when Vassily had had him by the wrists. What can you say when a big son of a bitch can pick you up and put you down wherever he wants? "Do whatever you like," he said. "I'm going." He started toward the elevator.

"Wait, Dad—"

Marty turned. "I don't care what you do. The only reason I came looking was your mother was afraid something happened to you."

"Do you want me to come down with you?"

"Stay with your boyfriend. I really don't give a shit." He started toward the elevator again, then turned to Ted. "As for you, big shot, be proud of yourself. You proved you're stronger than a fifty-year-old man. But you'll get yours. Believe me, you'll get yours."

"You're being unfair, Mr. Colello."

Marty went to the elevator, looked for a call button and couldn't find one. "Do I need a key to get out of this goddamn place? Is that part of your idea of how a big shot lives?"

"The button is underneath the shelf."

"I'll be down in a few minutes," Grace said as the doors opened.

Marty silently got into the car and stared at the floor until the doors closed.

"I don't quite know what to say," Grace told Ted. "I mean, thank you. For protecting me and for handling him so gently. But it's so sad. I didn't want it to happen this way."

"Do you want a drink?"

"No. Yes. Yes, I guess I need one."

He poured two glasses. "I don't think you need to worry about him hitting you anymore."

"I know. It's one of the things I feel bad about. I mean, ambivalent about. Oh, damn, what I mean is, I'm glad I don't have to worry anymore, but it saddens me that it cost him his self-respect."

"Do you really think it did?"

"How would you feel in his place? It was—it was like a turning point in his life. I mean, ever since I was a little baby he was this huge commanding presence, towering over me. Now, all of a sudden"—she snapped her fingers—"he's a midget, to be pushed around like a little boy."

"I'm sorry if you feel I acted out of line."

"No, you showed restraint and compassion, and I love you for it. But I feel very sorry for him. Scared for him. In just a few seconds he's had to change his whole image of himself. It can't be an easy thing to go through."

"I'm sure every father does, though maybe not as suddenly."

"I guess so . . . don't get me wrong, honey"—she kissed him—"I'm not blaming you. I'm blaming him, damn it. I'm blaming him for not having opened his eyes sooner, for not seeing what's been happening in the world around him, for thinking he's still in the nineteen forties or whenever it was that he got the crazy notion that being a good parent means being a tyrant. I'm blaming him for putting us in a position where you had to confront him and where I feel guilty even when my head tells me there's nothing to feel guilty about. Damn it, Ted, I'm losing my knack on the tightrope. The world's spinning so fast, so many new things are happening—I just can't keep up."

"Don't try to keep up with anything right now." They sat down on the couch. "Sometimes you can think something to death. Sometimes it's better to back off a little, try to relax and let what happens happen."

She nodded, moved up against him, and felt a little

better. "How about your father?" she asked. "Did you ever have this kind of confrontation with him?"

"In a way." He remembered an evening at Dempsey Field in Nanticoke, where his father had the hot-dog concession. "It wasn't unpleasant for him, though. Probably because I was a lot younger and I made it on his own terms."

"Football?"

"Business."

"You never talk about your family. Are your parents still alive?"

"Yes."

"Are you close to them?"

"In an emotional sense, yes. I love them. But we aren't exactly buddy-buddy. We don't share much."

"Does it bother you to talk about them?"

"No."

"But you don't."

"I go out to Pennsylvania every few weeks to visit them. Look, if you'd like to come some weekend, I'd really like taking you. But their kind of life isn't mine . . . not anymore, not for a long time."

"Does that upset you?"

"I wouldn't say 'upset.' They're happy. But it limits what I can share with them. This building, for example. They can't understand why I'd want to build it."

"You mean rich and poor together?"

"Yeah. If they were running the show, the tenants would all be rich but their own friends would still be the down-home blue-collars they grew up with. They'd bring them over every few weeks to gloat. They'd have a big Greek feast, with lots of ouzo and music. And they'd congratulate themselves on not having lost their simple tastes, on not letting money corrupt them. I don't know, maybe I'm selling them short . . . you'll decide for yourself."

"You really want me to go to Pennsylvania with you?"

"Very much."

"Why?"

"Because, lady of a thousand questions, you're my loving friend. And friends should share their lives with each other. Besides, I think you'll have a good time."

"That's very sweet." She kissed him. "I mean that in the best possible—"

"I understand. Stop already with the explanations." He smiled.

"Well—okay. And I accept your invitation."

"Which is more like it."

"Ted," she said after a silence that he welcomed, "it really bothers you to be . . . well, you know, from a blue-collar background, doesn't it?"

"I make it a point not to trouble myself about things that can't be changed." Yup, you sure do, buddy.

"But if you could change it, you would."

"Let's put it this way—all things being equal, I suppose I'd have chosen to grow up with more cultural richness, more intellectual stimulation, more . . . well, more of everything that I used to associate with the upper classes. When I say all things being equal I mean assuming I'd have the same energy and motivation. I certainly wouldn't want to have been brought up in luxury and turn into the sort of ding-a-ling I've seen in so many well-off families."

"Is that where Three-oh-five East comes in? The best of both worlds for the working class?"

"I guess in a way, although I don't think of it as a reaction to my past. I think more in terms of my own personal idea of what the best of America should be. What the individual tenants get from it, well, that remains to be seen. Maybe I should ask you."

"Me, personally? You know what I'm getting from it. It's the best thing that ever happened to me. But I wonder if I'm an exception. I'm thinking about my parents now. Forget gratitude for the comforts they didn't have before—maybe they're less happy about it because they feel, well, sort of a culture shock. Maybe they feel put down. Maybe they think they *ought* to feel happier and are angry they don't . . . I don't know . . . maybe I shouldn't be saying any of this. Who am I to say how they feel . . . ?"

"Frankly, I don't care whether they're happier or less happy."

She looked at him, startled.

"I mean it. My satisfaction comes from providing a break, a chance for happiness. If people choose not to take advantage of it, or if they try and louse it up—well, that's their problem. I did my part."

"Out of a sense of duty?" She felt herself bristling a little.

"No, out of a sense of feeling like doing it."

"It was selfish, then, not altruistic."

"Fuck altruism. That's a myth loaded onto the guilty by people who want to separate them from what's theirs."

"Are you quoting?"

"The gospel according to Saint Theodore, a Greek bearing gifts."

The edge in his voice made her uneasy. "Ted, I'm afraid I've offended you."

"Hell, no."

"I didn't mean to. I—"

He laughed. "You didn't. Sometimes I get carried away with my rhetoric. Besides, it's too late in the night for loving friends to fight."

She looked at her watch. "God, a quarter to six. Almost time to rise and shine."

"Or better yet . . ."

She got his meaning. "Really? You're up for it?"

"I want it."

They went into the bedroom, and this time it was less a recreation than a release of tension. But it felt good, even if necessary.

"I think you'll like Pennsylvania," he said as they lay together afterward. "It's a refreshing contrast to the city."

"I'm looking forward to it." She pressed against him, thinking how good it felt being here with him, and at the same time that she should be getting home. Her father, beaten down, wasn't likely to try to reestablish his old tyranny, but there was no need to add insult to injury. She should at least get home in time to have breakfast with her parents before they left for work.

She also was thinking how wildly awake and alive she felt, and suddenly remembered a novel by Jack London, *Valley of the Moon*. . . . The hero takes his girl friend to a promontory overlooking the Sonoma Valley. She asks what he wants out of life. He makes a sweeping gesture that takes in the entire horizon. "This," he says.

For the first time that she could remember, Grace Colello felt as though she were in that league, as though she had a shot at all of . . . this.

"What are you thinking?" she asked when he remained silent.

He hugged her. "That it's very damn good to be with you."

He was also thinking that in a few hours he would be having lunch with Hartford Loomis, whose daughter was Nan Loomis, who had him damn near crazy out of his head. Damn her.

The dining room was splendid—carved mahogany corner pillars extending inward at the top to form an X against the domed ceiling; frescoes in each wing of the X, extending onto the walls; a sixteenth century Florentine buffet sculptured with biblical figures; a mahogany fireplace with an antique marble clock on the mantel; and in the center of the room, elegant in its starched-white-linen-and-silver simplicity, a table for two.

Ted, recalling the advice of a mainline Philadelphia girl friend of many years ago, stifled the impulse to comment on the beauty of a host's set-up. But he made a mental note to start thinking about a private dining room for his own office. Why not? Besides, it was tax deductible, which would please Emer.

An ancient black waiter in a starched white jacket emerged from a door Ted hadn't realized was behind the buffet. "Arnold makes the best martini on the Street," said Hartford Loomis. "We also have some champagne."

Ted considered the situation's potential for intimidation and wondered if Loomis had set it up that way. Should he defer and order the martini, even if he preferred the champagne? Should he show his independence by asking for an unnamed drink? He reminded himself he had nothing to sell. Fuck psychology. Order what you want, and piss on Loomis's game playing. "I think I'll test Arnold's specialty," he said, smiling at the old man, who expressionlessly turned to Loomis.

"I'll have one too, Arnold."

Arnold nodded and moved away.

"Ted," said Loomis, "you deserve kudos for a variety

of things, but none more than for your taste in women."

Ted was startled. So Nan would be the subject of today's meeting, after all. And old Hart was leading with a roundhouse right.

Loomis continued, "I was impressed by your party. I don't think I've ever seen as many beautiful women in one place."

What's this? Hardly outraged-daddy talk. So maybe it wasn't going to be about Nan. "I'm glad you enjoyed the party."

"Surely not all of them live in the building."

"No. I understand several were models and actresses."

"Hired for the night?"

"Invited. Theater people call it 'papering the house.' "

"Interesting. I don't have many theatrical contacts. None, in fact. Like most bankers, I lead a rather insular life."

Ted felt much better. Somehow the discussion had turned around. Loomis had put himself on the defensive.

"I don't suppose that's much of a virtue, insularity, I mean. I'm probably missing a great deal."

Ted said nothing. He noted beads of perspiration on Loomis's upper lip. Whatever the hell the man was leading to, he was all wound up about it. So do you stay silent and enjoy watching him squirm—at the risk of maybe intimidating him into a retreat? Or do you say something to draw him out—at the risk of losing the unspoken advantage you hold? "I'm sure most people feel that way at one time or another. . . ."

The corners of Loomis's mouth arced in a nervous smile. "But one feels it more intensely after fifty. Take it from an expert, Ted."

Arnold returned with the martinis. Ted sipped his—it lived up to its billing—and waited for Loomis to go on. The banker seemed about to, then changed the subject to football. He wasn't exactly a superfan, but he knew the game and seemed to have some vivid memories of several of Ted's better days.

"I read a *Wall Street Journal* story once that said of all business executives who played football in college or high school, at least half were quarterbacks," he said.

"Interesting."

"You've never come on that statistic, I take it."

"No."

"It makes sense, of course. The decision-making position and all that."

"Lots of quarterbacks don't make decisions, though. Every play gets sent in by the coach. Happens even in the pros. Especially in the pros."

Hart laughed. "Then it's even better preparation for the business world. The art of appearing decisive while taking orders. I know executives who've built careers on it."

"Not top executives."

"No, you're right there."

Ted sipped his martini, wondering when Loomis would get to the point of the lunch.

Arnold reappeared with a short bespectacled man in chef's whites.

"Lars," asked Loomis, "what are you going to tempt us with today?"

The temptations included sole *meunière*, salmon with cream sauce, and trout *veronique*. Of course, Lars added quickly, he also could prepare a steak, chop, crêpe, or omelette, if monsieur desired.

Ted opted for the sole *meunière* and declined a second martini, at which point Arnold offered the wine list. Ted's eyes widened as he noted some of the vintages: Lafite in '55, '53, '48, '34 and an incredible '28, virtually unseen these days; Margaux and Latour in '55, '53, and '45; Mouton in '34 and '28; the exceptional 1937 Château d'Yquem; and Richebourg in '37 and '29. Surely Loomis didn't offer this selection to everyday guests.

"My compliments to the sommelier," Ted said.

"I'll take the bows personally, thank you. Actually, it was a stroke of luck. BankUS was holding paper for a wine wholesaler who went into bankruptcy. He'd been accumulating this stuff for three decades, and the referee awarded it to us at cost rather than fair market value." Hart smiled. "Sure you don't want to change your order to accommodate one of the Bordeaux or Burgundy heavyweights?"

What Loomis should have done, Ted thought, was show the wine list before offering cocktails. He certainly wouldn't have ordered a palate-killing martini if he'd known these wines were available. "No, I'll stay with the sole. I can make my first wine the Sterling Vineyards '75 Chenin Blanc, which will hold up against the martini, then go to the '37 Yquem for dessert." Try that on for size, buddy.

Hart nodded to Arnold, who went off with the list. "It's a pleasure to share wines with someone who appreciates them, Ted. The more I get to know you, the more tastes I find we have in common."

Great, ol' buddy. But I still don't believe that's why you invited me to lunch.

"I guess I recognized that when you served the '66 Taittinger at your party. I still can't get over those women! One in particular, a girl who, as I recall, was wearing a dress with a sort of X-shaped top. Large breasts, long blonde hair. I believe she was introduced as some sort of movie star . . ."

Ted noticed that Hart's upper lip was perspiring again. So Jeannie Danton turned him on.

"Do you know the girl I mean?"

Ted put on an innocent smile. "Not off hand. Of course, as you say, there were so many beauties there—"

"Yes. This one's name, if I recall, was, uh, Denton—Jodie Denton—?"

"Doesn't ring a bell."

"Then Julie, maybe. Or Jeannie?"

Oh, let him off the hook. "Jeannie Danton. With an 'a.' "

"Ah, is that it? I don't go to the movies too often."

Sure, baby. That's why you're sweating.

"In any case, seeing her that night, I found myself wondering, what does it take to get a girl like that in bed?"

Ted laughed. Sweat it out, Hart. I'm going to make like your question was rhetorical. In repayment for the way your man Delvecchio made me kiss ass when I was looking for *my* action for 305 East.

"I'm assuming, of course, that it's possible. You know, the casting couch and all that business. I assume people still have to pay some sort of sexual dues to make it in the movies." He wished Ted would say something instead of just staring at him like that. He brought his empty martini glass to his lips, sucked at the remaining droplets, touched a napkin to his perspiring upper lip. Where the hell was Arnold with the wine?

Ted smiled serenely, said nothing.

"Do you agree?"

"That there's a casting couch?"

"That sexual availability is still pretty much taken for granted among aspiring actresses."

"Well, I'm not really in a position to know." The ball's back in your court, baby.

Arnold appeared with the wine. Hart tasted it, nodded his approval and watched as Arnold poured for Ted. He wondered whether to make another try on the Jeannie Danton thing or wait till later. Either Vassily was very goddamn dense or was getting a perverse kick out of putting his host through the wringer. Maybe better to abandon Danton for now.

He did, speaking instead of wine, comparing French with Californian. From wine the subject shifted to European versus American culture. Lars brought the food. The conversation returned to football, then broadened to sports in general and mankind's apparent need for them.

"In the broadest sense," Ted suggested, "all human endeavor is sport, once it gets beyond providing for your own and your family's basic needs."

"Of course. After a hundred thousand a year, it's all numbers."

"Still, as Huizinga said in *Man the Player*, there seems to be some sort of compulsion to participate in or at least observe the formal recreations, like tennis, versus such disguised ones as banking and politics."

"Huizinga?"

"A social psychologist. In any case, I find his argument persuasive. The formal sports have great appeal."

"Yes. The ease of scorekeeping. The clarity of the rules. The lack of ambiguity in the outcome."

"Exactly." This was deteriorating into the kind of bull session Ted remembered having with sophomore sociology majors back at the Hub in Penn State.

Arnold cleared the empty plates and returned with the '37 Château d'Yquem. Lars brought some fruit and cheese. And Hart decided to hit the Jeannie Danton subject head-on. "A girl like her, Ted—do you suppose she ever transacts on a cash basis?"

Ted's brow furrowed. "It's hard to say." Loomis had come back to her three times now. Was *that* the only purpose of the lunch? "Are you personally interested, Hart?"

Hart sipped his wine. "I could be, I think." And by way of self-evident afterthought: "I find her very appealing."

"Apparently so does most of the rest of the world."

"The question is, is she available?"

"I don't know." Ted thought about her being with Coffee Joe. Sure as hell she was available; the question was, how widely. "Would you like me to ask around?"

Loomis was acutely aware of the beads of perspiration on his upper lip, which now seemed to swell. It was excruciatingly awkward to confront the thing this way. At the same time, he felt relieved to have it out in the open. "I'd be interested in anything you might hear."

"I'll be in touch." Ted could sense Loomis's relief. Who'd ever have thought the dried up old bastard would get so wound up about a twitch like Jeannie? Or any twitch?

Hart busied himself peeling a pear. "This is, of course, strictly confidential."

"Of course."

"I, ah, appreciate it."

They finished their fruit. Lars brought some pastry. They finished their Sauternes. Arnold brought coffee. The conversation never returned to Jeannie Danton.

"I've enjoyed this very much, Ted," Hart said, escorting him from the dining room. "I'd enjoy getting together again."

"So would I." They went through Loomis's office to the elevator. "As I said, I'll be in touch," Ted said as he watched the doors close between them. Riding down, he wondered why Loomis had so exposed himself? Was it *that* hard to score in your fifties?

Hartford Loomis, watching the elevator doors close, felt a sense of secret excitement that he hadn't known in over thirty years. He went back to his office, sat at his desk and stared at a memorandum for ten minutes without comprehending a word of it. "Bring me this morning's *Times*," he told his secretary. He leafed through the entertainment pages, hoping to find a movie ad with a picture of Jeannie Danton. No luck. Where to find a picture of her? *Time? Newsweek?* He sent for them. Nothing.

Oh, well, he didn't really need one. He could fantasy her as she looked in that first movie, nonchalantly lifting her T-shirt, letting those incredible breasts pop out.

He went off hurriedly to his private bathroom.

"Hey, we've been invited to the same cocktail party," Eddie Spats told Buffy Weiss on the telephone.

"Really?"

"Yeah. At John Malloy's."

"Oh, that. I guess I wasn't even thinking of it as a party. It'll be very political, I'm sure."

"But you're going, aren't you?"

"Yes."

"Great, we can go together."

Buffy's silence at the other end of the wire spoke volumes. It was the same silence Eddie Spats had met years ago when he happened accidentally into a then-segregated restaurant. The last person in the world he would have expected it from was Buffy Weiss, defender of the people, Indian-lover, partisan of black-is-beautiful—at least in the sack.

"Hey, you still there?"

"Yes," she said. "I was just checking my appointment book . . ."

Spats said nothing.

"Oh, damn, Eddie, I did make plans. I'm awfully sorry. I didn't think you'd want to go to a boring thing like that—"

Uh-huh. "Okay, babes, see you around."

"Eddie, you're not sore, I hope."

"Of course not. Hey, we never said we owned each other, right?"

He hung up and took an ale from the refrigerator. He really didn't give a shit about Buffy Weiss, he reminded himself. She was just an average white chick, very white when it came down to it, who threw a decent fuck and had the sense to tune in on his sex vibes. There was nothing serious between them. Still, it hurt to get brushed by her. Oh, well, the old story—a nigger in the hay is okay, just don't show him to your friends.

Man, would he enjoy showing up at that Malloy party with some really dynamite black fox. Like a collegian. A real super-Clean. Black or white, it didn't matter so long as she had that Halls of Ivy look. Of course, black would be better, show the fucken 'fays you don't need 'em.

He touched a button on his telephone that activated a buzzer in a room at the opposite end of his penthouse. Until a week ago the room had been a guest bedroom. Now it was the office of the latest addition to Spats's staff: a tall, handsome, very dark and self-assured detail-man named Reese Wilson.

"Yes, Mr. Johnson."

"I need a fox for a party next Tuesday," said Spats. "A very hip political type, liberal stripe. John Malloy's the host, so she should know what he stands for and all that shit."

"Yessir. Shall I set it up blind, or would you like to screen a few candidates?"

Spats grinned. This was the way a detail-man should operate. "I think I'd enjoy screening a few, yass," he said in a W. C. Fields voice. "Maybe we can have a little preliminary party of our own. Say tomorrow evening after the taping?"

"Yessir. At the penthouse?"

"Solid. Invite the political science clubs at Hunter and N.Y.U., if you can get to them in time. No point limiting our choices, eh?"

"Yessir."

Spats replaced the receiver and took a long swallow of his ale. This, he reflected, was the way to live. It had taken a long time to get here, but goddamn it, now that he had it he was going to enjoy it all the way down.

He buzzed Reese again.

"Yessir."

"Get Ted Vassily for me."

He savored his ale as he listened to the exchange between Reese and Ted's secretary.

"T-Bone? Eddie Spats here. How's your hammer hanging?"

"Down and dirty, ol' buddy."

"How'd you like to meet the political science club of Hunter University? I'm told the wool is absolutely incredible."

"Fine."

"Tomorrow, my place, after the taping. Bring the amigos—Nate, Emer, et cetera. Oh, yeah, I understand we're both invited to a little soirée at John Malloy's Tuesday next. You bringin' a chick?"

"Probably."

"Okay, what say the four of us have a taste at my place before we go? Say, seven-thirtyish?"

Ted agreed and Eddie hung up, finished his ale and opened another. Yes, he told himself, this was the way to live. This was what the fella was talking about when he wrote, "I'm Sittin' on Top of the World."

Spats sang eight bars of the tune, holding his ale can at arm's length as if it were a dancing partner. Then he whistled a stop-time version, doing a soft shoe to it. He laughed and switched into a heavy swing chorus, doing big back-steps. The phone buzzed.

"Mr. Vassily, sir," said Reese.

"Spats," said Ted, "that Jeannie Danton . . . I gather she's Joe's friend, but I'm wondering, does she take any free-lance action?"

"Well, you know, man, they all do *some*thin' every now and then. Why? You interested?"

"Not personally. A friend asked me about her. He's an older guy, very respectable, rich."

"Let's put it this way—if he feels like financing a movie, or pretending he's about to finance a movie, all he has to do is call her agent. I'm sure she'll be very interested in talking."

"Suppose he just feels like being with her some evening, cash-on-the-barrelhead?"

"I doubt it. If it's important to you, I can find out."

"I'd appreciate it."

"Who's the friend? Nobody that would compromise Joe, I hope."

"No danger. He's a bank president. He doesn't know anything about her and Joe."

"I'll see what I can do, T-Bone. No promises, but I'll try my level best."

He hung up, took a large swallow of ale, and went to the north bank of windows. He stared out over Central Park, barely able to distinguish in the twilight haze the boundary between the park and Harlem. Yes, he told himself, he had come a long way. And this definitely was the way to live.

He went back to the phone and buzzed Reese. "Get my father," he said. When Big Spats came on the line, Eddie said, "Hey, old-timer, how'd you like to have dinner tonight in the best restaurant in New York?"

"Hey, Little Spats, what you been doin'? Drinkin' all day?"

"Never mind that shit, I want to take my old man out to dinner. You pick the place. Or you got so much wool on the line you can't break away?"

"Shee-it, you know they ain't no wool."

"Well all right then. You ain't gonna take care o' your pud, you might as well take care o' your belly. I'll send my car for you. Seven o'clock, okay?"

He hung up, took a long swallow of ale, and danced across the room. "I'm sittin' on top-tip-top of the world . . ."

Peg Malloy extended her hand to the new arrivals and instinctively repeated their names. Ordinarily the repetition served two purposes: It made the guest feel at home (people loved the sound of their own names) and it helped Peg remember the name. Tonight, remembering was no problem; she knew just about everyone by sight. But the habit stayed with her. And, she reflected, it was without question the least troublesome of all her habits.

Unfortunately, one of her more troublesome habits—indeed, the most—was asserting itself tonight. Peg Malloy was drunk. Not falling-down drunk. Not even giggle-and-thick-speech drunk. But drunk enough, unfortunately, that she had to concentrate to avoid swaying as she stood and to make sure she didn't talk too loudly. Every once in a while her concentration would break and she'd feel herself sway ever so slightly, or she'd notice John looking at her in a way that said he was receiving more decibels than she'd realized she was sending. Control, she told herself. The answer to everything is control. (Just as the nuns said in grammar school so long ago! Wouldn't they be proud that she remembered?)

"Maestro, it's good to see you," said John Malloy. "Maria, how good of you to come."

Control. "Joseph," said Peg, "it's been so long. We adored your *Don Carlos*. Maria, my dear, you've cut your hair, it looks wonderful." Control.

"Dr. Wattley," said John, "nice to see you. Miss Bernstein, how do you do?"

Control. "Doctor, it's good of you to come. Miss Bernstein, I'm pleased to meet you."

She should have practiced more control today, Peg told herself. There really was no excuse. It wasn't as though John had sprung the party at the last moment. But she had been weak. She should not have gone to Lutèce for lunch. She could never lunch at Lutèce without ordering wine. And once she started with wine, a cognac after the chocolate mousse was irresistible. Which had been the start of the toboggan ride. Back at the apartment she had drunk Scotch for the rest of the afternoon. Fortunately she'd had the good sense around five o'clock to switch to Drambuie, the sweetness of which upset her stomach; otherwise she'd really be blitzed.

"Burr, thank you for coming. Mrs. Whiteside—Jeannie —it's a pleasure meeting you."

Control. "Mr. Whiteside—Burr—thank you. Jeannie, how do you do?" Control.

The real reason she'd let herself get drunk, of course, was Ted Vassily. It was obscene, the things that man did to her. It was his nonchalance, she calculated. Combined with that mischievous air. He was the boy in grade school who always dipped the little girls' pigtails into the inkwell. (Do they still have inkwells in grade schools nowadays? Probably not.) Steady, Peg. Steady. Control.

But Vassily, damn it, was so incredibly masculine, virile. So cocksure. (Good word, that.)

Vassily, in fact, seemed cock personified. His body was like an extension of the phallic entity. His head was the glans, his torso the stem. And that smile, always flashing so damned mischievously. Jesus, she had better pull herself together. She was really loaded. Control.

Yes, control, but she still was going to think about him. She couldn't help thinking about him. Not that he seemed all that interested in her. Matter of fact, he scarcely noticed her. But maybe she would work on that. Maybe she would do as she had with that ski instructor at Vail last year. Athletes had always found her attractive, even in high school. Especially in high school. And college too. And they still did, judging from good ol' schussbooming Sigismund at Vail. So why not Vassily too? She would be good for him. He probably was accustomed to those mindless little twitches with their tight teenybop bodies who lay there like corpses while a man knocked himself out trying to please them. She would show Ted what a mature woman could do in bed.

"Ted, Eddie, thank you for coming. Miss Colello, how do you do? Miss Gardner, a pleasure to meet you."

Control now, Peg, if you never exercise it again. "Mr. Vassily, it's good to see you again. We had a wonderful time at your party. Miss Colello, how do you do? Mr. Johnson, Miss Gardner, a pleasure to meet you." That's it, Peggy, you handled it just fine, now keep it that way.

"Mr. Wade, thank you for coming. Miss Kelly, how do you do."

"Mr. Wade. Miss Kelly."

"Miss Weiss, I'm so glad you could come. Mr. Young, how do you do?"

"Miss Weiss, thank you for coming. Mr. Young, a pleasure to meet you." (Interesting that Buffy Weiss would bring a black escort.)

"John," said Tom Donohue, "that's everyone."

"Good," said John.

"I think," Peg said, "that I'll just slip into the kitchen for a cup of coffee."

"Fine," said John, his smile as sincere as a Boston Irish ward heeler on election eve.

There was a maid in the kitchen, but Peg told her she felt like making the coffee herself. Idle hands were the devil's workshop, et cetera. Besides, she didn't like the new maid, who was French and haughty. Their maid in Connecticut, Arthurine, had been perfect. But Arthurine was black, and one didn't have black servants in New York—not if one was a political candidate seeking black votes. She laughed. The fruits of civil rights. Now you discriminated because it was better to discriminate than to demean, better to let people starve with their pride intact than to fill their bellies while treating them as, quote, inferiors, end quote.

Peg made the coffee, quickly drank a cup, then poured a second cup into a stemmed glass and added an ounce of brandy. She realized that, legend aside, coffee was not sobering, but somehow, returning to the living room, she felt more in control.

John was standing next to the piano, doing his you-may-not-believe-this-but routine. "You may not believe this, folks, but I really haven't yet decided whether to seek my party's nomination for senator from the state of New York."

Ha. Ha. Ha.

"Seriously, I would *like* very much to be a member of the Senate. But I'm not at all sure that now is the time and this the place to seek election."

Get it, folks? You're supposed to overwhelm him with encouragement.

"Before planning further, I thought I'd solicit the reaction of some New Yorkers like yourselves—do you feel I'm the person you want to represent you, and frankly, if that's true, do you think I can win?"

Peg tuned out the words and tuned in on the eyes of John's audience. If there was one talent she possessed above all others, it was the ability to read eyes. Other people could look and guess, often accurately. But with her it was a science.

Buffy Weiss. Her eyes testified to an awareness of Spats Johnson. She wasn't especially interested in him, wasn't lusting after him—at this moment anyway—as Peg herself lusted after Ted Vassily. But Buffy was concerned with Spats's reaction. Perhaps because of her black escort? Or was there more? Had they dated in the past?

Joseph Williams. Proper, as usual, and attentive to his wife. But occasionally his eyes would stray in the direction of the Ted Vassily/Spats Johnson party. More precisely, in the direction of young Grace Colello. And she was glancing at him too. It was a knowing glance, too intimate for strangers getting interested in each other. Yes, they had something going. If they weren't lovers, they at least had considered it, talked about it. No—they *were* lovers. It showed in her direct acceptance of his gaze. If she were still thinking about it, she would not be so casual. Her main worry now would be to not let his wife know she was so aware of him.

His wife. Maria. She was aware. She was aware of Grace Colello and of Buffy Weiss. Was Buffy sleeping with him too? Presently, certainly not. He was too comfortable about looking at her. But perhaps in the past. At least Maria thought so.

Eddie Spats Johnson. He was definitely interested in Buffy Weiss: They *are* lovers. He was also interested in his present date, cute young thing that she was; but not nearly as much as in Buffy. Did they have a lovers' quarrel? Did they make a secret pact not to appear together in public? If so, why?

Grace Colello. She seemed very aware of three men—Joseph Williams, Ted Vassily . . . John Malloy. She kept glancing at Vassily in a particularly intimate way—not necessarily sexual but certainly intimate. Were they lovers? Almost certainly. And Williams too? (My God, when did these girls find time to wash their hair?) And John? No, not John,—at least not yet. There was a tentativeness in her look that argued against it. But it would come, no doubt of it . . . it took only one look at John to know, seeing him studiously ignoring Miss Colello. He'd already made his decision—perhaps had even made his move—and didn't want Peg to suspect.

She wondered how, with all the other demands on his time, John could possibly link up with as many women as he did. Did they all just fall into his bed at the proverbial snap of a finger? Didn't any of them need to be taken to dinner, romanced, seduced? Well, however he did it, he did it. Yes, he most certainly did. . . .

She forced herself to look away. Ted Vassily. Yes. Ted Vassily. Rugged Adonis. He seemed unaware that his companion's interests also were elsewhere. Because he wasn't bright enough to recognize it? No. Because he didn't care? Or knew he couldn't stop it? Or was confident it would end? Whatever, he was checking out every woman in the room—with the exception of Maria Williams.

And Peg Malloy.

Damn it.

Why wasn't he interested?

All right, she wasn't the tight-bodied little lady she'd once been. Well, he wasn't the tight-bodied jock of yesteryear either. Didn't these men realize that there's more to sex than a rock-hard set of juvenile or pill-inflated tits? Why didn't Vassily at least check her out, the way he did all the other women in the room?

Because he was loyal to John? Or more likely because he assumed *she'd* be loyal to John. Yes, that was it, she hadn't given him a sufficiently clear signal. He was holding back because he was afraid she'd let John know that he'd propositioned her.

Nonetheless, he should be looking at her. He should at least be looking. . . .

But restraint is the better part of valor. Without an indication of her interest, any gentleman would hold back. Of course. It was just natural shyness on Ted's part.

Well, she'd give him an unmistakable sign. The only question was, how?

She would have to be blunt, unambiguous yet not crass. It would be simple enough to brush against him during the evening and, certain no one was in earshot, say with a very straight face, "I'd like to suck your cock." But she couldn't *do* that. The fact was, she did not want to suck his cock—that is, she did not want *merely* to suck his cock. She wanted a . . . well, an affair. She wanted to be romanced, pursued, seduced, told she was pretty—all those things that John's chippies apparently didn't need, all those things boys used to do when she was in high school and college, things John had done when they were dating, things Sigismund had done at Vail.

She noticed that her glass was empty. But the damned French maid hadn't noticed! She caught the girl's eye and sent her for a refill, then tuned in on what John was saying. And where he was looking. And where he wasn't looking.

He was saying the usual about uncompassionate government and uncaring legislators lining their pockets while serving as puppets for big business. (Oh, to give him his due, he was sincere enough in his views, she knew that . . . Whatever else he was, on that level he was absolutely sincere and even dedicated. And so different on the personal level with her. . . .) He was looking about the room now, establishing eye contact, receiving nods of agreement but meticulously keeping his eyes from the women's bodies—most particularly Grace Colello's. Yes, no question he had made his approach to her. Any day now she would turn up on one of his volunteer committees. Followed by a trip—Washington, Boston, wherever. All would happen most circumspectly. Ms. Colello would have her own room. She and Mr. Malloy would not be seen together publicly, except, of course, on campaign business. She would not sit at his table during dinner. But later, after she'd broken away from the other campaign workers, she would show up in his room. And he would fuck her little twitch ass off, goddamn it! Why did men have to *be* that way!? How could they get any real satisfaction from raw animal rutting? How could the women give themselves to it? Didn't they feel degraded? How *did* they feel?

She sipped her coffee-and-brandy, realized she had already consumed half of it and decided it tasted awful. She sent the maid for a Scotch on the rocks. To Grace Colello and her little twitch ass, she silently toasted. How could the little snip do it? Why, she was screwing half the men in the room! Well, a third of them, anyway. Peg took a long swallow of Scotch.

John had finished speaking, and now the party broke into small conversational groups. This was the part of the evening when the really heavy business would get done. Not by John himself; he would simply circulate and act charming. But all the while, Donohue would be twisting arms and collecting commitments.

So it was time for her to join her beloved husband and do her charm act. But first she wanted another drink. She noticed the maid, who seemed to look past her. What the hell was wrong with that French twitch? She signaled with her empty glass. The girl still seemed not to notice. Had Donohue ordered that she be cut off? If he had, the bastard, he was due for a lesson. He had no right to interfere in the operation of John Malloy's household. She, by God, was in charge of *something.*

She drained her glass, sucking on the ice cubes, and signaled again for a refill. The maid turned away. Well, if that didn't tear it! All right, she would go into the kitchen and fetch the goddamn drink herself. And tonight, or tomorrow, or as soon as she was sober, she'd issue the edict—Donohue goes. Imagine the nerve of that cabbage-eating bastard! Not one generation removed from the shanty and he's telling *her* when to drink. Telling Peg Malloy! Whose grandfather built the law school where Tom Donohue had to wait on tables in the cafeteria while he hustled for his degree! Well, he'd get his, the impertinent asswipe.

She realized she was walking but didn't remember where she wanted to go. She put her glass to her lips and recalled that it was empty. Yes, the kitchen, that's where she was going. She almost bumped into someone. She excused herself. She was a little dizzy. She'd have to fight it. Control. Control! No way she could get John to do anything about Donohue if she made a spectacle of herself.

The kitchen. Yes. Straight ahead. Bump someone else. Excuse, please. Ah, inside. Good. The bottle. Fill the glass. Down the hatch. That's it. Ah, feels good. Fill it again. Goddamn Donohue. What's he doing here? He saw her, did he? Well, let him try to catch her.

She ran with the glass back into the living room and felt her foot snag on something. And then she was in the air, and the booze and ice cubes were flying out of her glass, and there was a flurry around her, and somebody was holding her like a baby—yes, someone had caught her when she fell and was now cradling her in his arms, big strong arms, gorgeous big arms . . .

She looked up into the face of Ted Vassily. "I want you," she said. "Can't you see how damned much I want you?" And then she passed out.

"How'd you folks like to hear Little Spats sing a few songs?" he asked on the way to the elevator.

"Great," said Grace Colello.

"Ditto," said Dorian Gardner.

"Unanimous," said Ted Vassily.

They rode to the lobby.

"A chariot, my good man!" Spats commanded Walt Kulikowski. "Hail us a chariot."

Kulikowski flicked a switch that lit a blue lamp on 305's Second Avenue face, signaling to passing taxis. "With this rain," he said, "all I can tell you is 'lots of luck.' "

They waited for five minutes.

"Maybe," said Kulikowski, "I better try to hail one on Second and bring him around." He took his umbrella and trotted down the stairs. Five minutes later he returned in a cab.

"Stellar performance, big fellow," said Spats, pressing a ten dollar bill into the ex-fullback's palm. "Above and beyond the call, and all that jazz." To the driver, he said, "The Place, my man. Corner of Lex and Fifty-sixth."

The cab pulled away.

"If you wanted to burglarize Three-oh-five East," Ted said, "you'd be smart to do it on a rainy night, wouldn't you?"

"Why's that?" asked Spats.

"You'd stake out the place till Cooler went to fetch a cab for somebody, then walk right in."

"I don't think he'd leave the door ordinarily. He probably just did it 'cause he knew you were there."

"If he'd do it with me there, he'd do it when I wasn't there, especially if the tenant was a big tipper."

"Jeez, sorry I tempted him."

"It's not your fault, it's mine. We need a better system."

"Wouldn't intruders be seen on the TV monitors at the central security desk?" Grace asked.

"Yes, unless the security man and Kulikowski happened to be goofing off at the same time."

"Isn't that unlikely?"

"It's the kind of longshot you have to take into account when you want things to run right." Ted scribbled a reminder in his wallet memo pad to attend to the problem the next day.

"I can see," said Dorian Gardner, "why Three-oh-five East is so successful. It must be very exciting to be responsible for it."

"It is."

She nestled against Spats. "And it must be very exciting

to be able to take your friends to The Place and sing for them. I have to confess, I'm knocked out by all this. A week ago my idea of a big deal was getting asked out by a seminar leader."

"I know how you feel," Grace told her.

"Well," said Spats, "it's a big deal for us to be with two dynamite chicks like you."

"But doesn't it feel a little weird to be with girls who are so young?" Dorian asked.

"Not at all." Spats hugged her, savoring the feel of her firm breasts against his chest. This was the kind of black super-Clean he'd wanted for years, the kind that normally rejected him for the Arthur Ashe types. (So why, damn it, was he still thinking about Buffy Weiss?)

"It's not 'weird,' it's part of life," Ted added. "Women begin to tap out after twenty-five. Either they're married or hung up about not being married, or they let their bodies go to hell—"

"Don't you think that happens to some men too?"

"Sure. But I'm not interested in men."

Dorian had a feeling Spats and Ted were beginning to think her argumentative. She didn't want that. "Well, I'm glad we don't turn you off." She pressed her face into Spats's neck. "Man, am I glad I don't turn you off."

He kissed her, at the same time letting his hand come to rest on her breast. He wondered how Buffy happened to be with a militant like George Young. Was it really accidental that she'd asked Young to take her to the Malloy party before she knew Spats was invited? Did she really think he wouldn't want to go? Or was there some kind of special Jim Crow rule about these things—it's okay to be seen in public with an intellectual-political type, but not with a ditty-bop entertainer?

"What will you do about the security thing?" Grace asked, wanting to change the subject.

"I have to think about it. Maybe put an extra doorman on when it rains. Or hire a limousine to give tenants courtesy rides," Ted told her.

"Won't that be expensive?"

"Not in the long run."

"Why not just order the doorman never to leave the door?"

"Issuing orders doesn't solve problems, it just cons you into thinking you have a solution."

"I don't get it," said Spats. "If the guy never leaves the door, where's the problem?"

"The problem is, people do things that seem reasonable to them. A tenant wants a taxi in the rain, it seems reasonable to a doorman that he can hustle some extra money by running for one. You tell him not to, he'll do it anyway whenever he thinks he can get away with it. The trick is to structure the situation so that the way you want people to act always seems the most reasonable way to them."

"But," Dorian said, "if a person's afraid to lose his job, won't he be sure to obey—"

"Yes, provided the fear is genuine and always there. But that makes you a policeman, and you wind up with employees trying to hide things from you. That makes them your enemies instead of your allies. The only way to keep them in line for sure is to play Stalin, who executed innocent people every now and then just to keep the others on their toes. That's not exactly my style. No, when a tenant pays top dollar, any dollar, to live in a building like Three-oh-five East, he shouldn't have to go running after his own taxi. So the real problem isn't the doorman, it's that I didn't fully anticipate the needs of my tenants and make arrangements to satisfy them."

"You know something, T-Bone," said Spats, "you oughtta be president of these United States."

Ted laughed. "I agree. Now get me nominated."

The cab pulled to the curb at the Place. Spats led the way to the service door. The doorman stood to bar him, then recognized him and hugged him. "Spats, baby, where you been?"

"Benny, baby, how's your hammer hangin'?"

"Jes' fine, mah man, jes' fine. When you gonna come back and work for us again?"

"Hey, man, you wanna tire me out? The TV thing is enough. Besides, I gotta give other cats a chance."

"Hey, I watch you on TV all the time, man. Me an' the ol' lady. How's your father?"

"Just great, Billy." Moving so quickly that no one but Ted noticed it, Spats extracted a bill from his pocket and passed it to the doorman. "I'll tell him you said hello. Give my regards to the missus, huh?"

"Yeah, my man. Yeah."

Spats led the way down a narrow gray fluorescent-lit corridor, then up a flight of stairs to a backstage area. A band was playing onstage and a stagehand was manipulating the switches of a light board. "I'll be right back," Spats whispered. He ducked through a curtain and returned a few minutes later, motioning for the group to follow.

Ted found himself on the main floor of the Place. A captain in a tuxedo was directing two waiters, who hoisted a table over the heads of rows of diners and placed it at ringside. The waiters disappeared and returned with four chairs. "Right this way, Spats," said the captain.

"How's that?" Spats grinned at Ted. "Do I take care of my friends?"

People murmured recognition as Spats led his party through the tightly packed tables. A man at ringside got up and asked for his autograph. Spats obliged with a hasty scribble, then slipped into his seat. "Well, all right," he said as Ted and the girls joined him. "Do I get my people the best seat in the house?"

A waiter took drink orders. The band finished an uptempo number and started a ballad. Spats led Dorian onto the dance floor. Ted followed with Grace. After one chorus the drummer broke into a rock rhythm and a spotlight picked up Spats and Dorian. Other dancers stepped aside. There was a smattering of applause. Spats beamed at the audience, then turned a full circle to louder applause before returning to Dorian to resume dancing.

Ted led Grace back to the table. The band picked up the tempo. Spats's dancing become more flamboyant with spins, jumps and even a split. Dorian kept moving in rhythm, complementing him without competing. The crowd applauded. His movements became even more spectacular. He did a series of ice-skaterlike spins across the entire floor, then fell into a Russian cossack-style series of squatting kicks, then spun back to Dorian's side, executed a spin-into-a-split, rose, bowed and gestured to her. "Go to it, baby, show them your stuff."

She was stunned. "You've got to be kidding."

He pointed to her again, seeming not to hear. The audience watched expectantly.

Dorian wanted nothing more than to leave the floor but feared that would cause her even more embarrassment than staying there. She stepped in front of him and moved with the music, very conservatively at first, then more freely as the drums and bass and guitar led her on. "Yah!" she heard Spats say as her hips moved in widening arcs. She faced him and went into a series of thrusts that got the audience applauding again. "Yah!" he said.

"Goddamn, man," she hissed, coming close to him, "get me out of this."

"You're doing fine."

"I *mean* it," she fairly shouted, "bail me *out*."

He flashed a broad grin and went into a spinning split alongside her, then rose to his full height, took her hand and with his free hand signaled the band to stop. The applause was tremendous.

"How about that chick?" he said as they returned to the table. "Is she terrific, or is she terrific?"

Ted and Grace agreed that she was.

Dorian said, "I wish you'd found out if I could dance *before* you put me through that."

"Aw, come on, babes, you were terrific."

"But you had no way of knowing when you brought me out onto the floor."

"Sure I did. You're a sister." He grinned sheepishly. "You know what they say, natural rhythm and all that—"

"You made a fool of me."

"Aw, that's ridiculous."

"Hey, folks," Ted interrupted, "what'd the group think of John Malloy's cocktail party?"

The abrupt change of subject broke the tension.

"That's better," Ted said. "We're having a nice evening out, plenty of time to hassle tomorrow."

"Roger," said Spats.

"Dorian," Grace said, "I'm on my way to the ladies'. Coming with me?"

"Sheesh," Spats said after they'd left, "fucken sensitive cunt."

Ted sympathized with Dorian but didn't feel like arguing the issue. "She'll get over it."

Spats seemed not to hear. "They're always ragging you about how *good* it is to be spontaneous. Hang loose. Do your own thing. Then you do it and they get pissed off." He shrugged. "I dunno, big fella, sometimes I think you just can't win."

The girls finally returned.

"Speaking of Malloy's party," said Spats, "what's the story with his old lady?"

"I guess she likes a taste every now and then," Ted said.

"What'd she say to you when you caught her?"

"I couldn't make it out. She was mumbling too much." He had heard her clearly. He wondered if anyone else had. "What did you think of Malloy?" he asked.

"Smooth. Heads-up dude. He's going to win."

"I was impressed with him," Dorian said. "Sometimes a person is really impressive on TV but a dud in person. I thought John Malloy was even more impressive in person."

"Did he strike you as just a little too smooth?"

Spats shrugged. "He's got his act together, that's for sure. But I don't read him as phony."

"Neither do I," said Dorian. "It might be different if he and his family hadn't done so much good over the years."

"Right," said Spats. "When you consider what most people did who were born with his kind of money—you know, yachts and hundred-thousand-dollar paintings and all that shit. I mean, this dude wouldn't've had to work a day in his life if he didn't want to."

"And he's no Johnny-come-lately to good causes," said Dorian. "He was pushing national health insurance when everybody else in Congress was spouting that A.M.A. jazz about socialized medicine being the ruination of the greatest health system in the world."

Spats looked to Ted. "Don't you agree?"

"Oh, sure," he replied quickly. "I just wondered how he came across to you tonight." He pointedly had not asked Grace for her opinion. He already knew it . . . too well. Oh, come off it, he told himself, you're just her good *friend*, remember? . . .

On stage the dance band gave way to another group of musicians. There was a timpani roll, the lights dimmed. "Ladies and gentlemen," an offstage announcer intoned, "the Place proudly presents its world-famous chorus line, the Placettes." And the band broke into a snappy rendition of the old standard "That's Entertainment."

The music was too loud to talk over, so Ted sat back to watch. He positioned his chair next to Grace's and found her hand under the table.

The Placettes were followed by a bad comic, then more changes among the musicians and another timpani roll as the announcer announced, "Ladies and gentlemen, the Place very proudly presents Mr. Gene Carter!"

The celebrated crooner ambled on, his immaculately pressed tuxedo and ruffled shirt in striking contrast to his general air of dishevelment. His eyes, Ted noted, seemed perpetually about to close. His face was puffed with fat—he had to be fifty pounds heavier than when he first became a star all those many years ago.

Spats waited until he'd sung the first notes of his opening song, then jumped from his chair. "Hey, Gene," he called, "wait for me, my man!" He seemed to cross the dance floor in a single hop, threw both arms around Carter's neck, and began swinging from his shoulders, almost knocking him to his knees. "I wanna sing witcha, man! I wanna sing!"

Forty-five minutes later they were still singing. "Eddie," Gene said, "I think it's time for the boys in the band to take a break."

"Let 'em go," said Spats. "We can sing with the dance band." He stopped one of the exiting saxophonists. "Hey, man, let me use your clarinet a while. I promise I won't nigger-lip it." The audience liked that.

"Ted," said Dorian, "do you have any idea how long he plans to stay up there?"

Ted shrugged.

"I'm enjoying it, of course, but I have a nine o'clock class, I should be leaving before too long."

"I wouldn't think he'd be much longer," Grace said.

Two hours later, Spats finally left the stage. "Hey, where's my fox?" he asked, returning to the table.

Ted explained that she'd left. "I put her in a cab," he said.

Spats heaved a mighty sigh. "Sheesh, what a kick in the ass. I really liked her, too. Fucken cunt—who can figure them out?" He suddenly remembered Grace. "Jeez, I'm sorry, babes, I forgot you were there."

"Don't be silly." She turned to Ted and imitated Spats' sigh. "Fucken pricks—they just don't know how to talk in front of cunt."

Spats laughed so hard he almost fell off his chair. "Well," he said, motioning for another round of drinks, "I guess I better find me another fox."

He went backstage and returned ten minutes later with a petite brunette wearing the heavy makeup and elaborate upswept coiffure of the Placettes. "This is Gerri," Spats said. "She does her last show in about fifteen minutes, then we can all head back to Three-oh-five for a nightcap."

"Spats fucked us up," Gerri observed nonchalantly. "We shoulda finished our last show ten minutes ago, but he stayed on mike too long."

"That's show biz, babes." He drained his drink and motioned for a refill. "The problem with nightclubs these days is everybody wants to punch a time clock. Like everybody else. That's why the country's on its ass."

She finished a drink with them, then went backstage to change. "Nice chick," Spats observed. "Not a lot up here" —he touched his head—"but she's all heart." He looked from Ted to Grace, then back to Ted. "Hey, tell me something, man, am I fucked up? I mean, am I really such an asshole that chicks can't stand me?" He turned to Grace. "I mean it, babes. Don't hold back. Say what's on your mind. Am I an asshole?"

"I think you're very nice."

"Was I so wrong with Dorian? I mean, did I do such a terrible thing? I'm an entertainer, right? I show up in a spot like this, people expect me to do my act. It's part of *keeping* my act, right?"

"We knew you were going to sing," Ted reminded him. "You said so before we left Three-oh-five East."

"Right. So what's the problem? Was she pissed that I got a little flashy when I was dancing with her? Whattaya expect when you dance with Spats Johnson? Am I supposed to stand there like some mummy?"

"I think she just was tired," Grace said. "She has an early class tomorrow—"

"You think that's all it was? I hope so. The thing is, I

really like the chick, I'm flipped over her. If I'd figured she'd get pissed, I never would of brought her here. Really, the only reason I wanted to come was I thought it'd turn her on."

"I'm sure she understands that," Ted said. "Give her a call tomorrow, she'll be happy to hear from you."

"Did she say that?"

"Not in so many words but it's obvious that she likes you too."

"Really?"

"A girl can always tell," Grace told him.

He stared at her expectantly for a moment, then seemed to relax. "Well, I hope you're right. She's what I've been looking for for over twenty years, you know?" He emptied his glass and looked around impatiently for a waiter. "Hey, whose ass do you have to kiss around here to get a drink, huh?"

A waiter appeared, took away the empty and returned with a refill. "Ah, much better," said Spats, polishing off half of it with one swallow. "Much, much better."

The bands changed and the announcer again introduced the Placettes. "I'm gonna duck out now," Spats said, "so people don't see me leaving during the comic's or Gene's act. Meet me backstage after the Placettes' last number. I'll grab the check on my way out." He took a roll of bills from his pocket, peeled off the top one and tossed it on the table.

"That's a hundred," Ted said.

Spats smiled sheepishly. "You know, man, gotta maintain the image."

When the Placettes finished, Ted led Grace through the curtain. Spats was waiting with Gene Carter, who gave Ted a warm handshake. They talked football while waiting for Gerri to get into street clothes and then Spats led the way out the service door and hailed a cab on Lexington Avenue.

"My place for a nightcap?" he asked in the 305 East lobby.

Ted looked uncertainly at Grace. "How early are *your* classes tomorrow?"

"Very." She looked at her watch and laughed. "I might as well stay up for them."

"Okay," said Spats, "nightcap time it is."

In his apartment, he led them to a huge round table in the center of the living room surrounded by four reclining corduroy chairs, each as wide as a double bed. "My latest addition," he said, demonstrating one of the chairs. In its full-recline position it could serve as a bed. "Great when you've got unexpected overnight guests," observed Spats. "Also not bad for orgies. Had 'em custom made. What the hell, you only live once, right?" He snapped his fingers, as if pulling a thought from deep in his memory. "Hey, drinks! We need some drinks!"

Ted helped him prepare them, then got comfortable with Grace on one of the recliners. Spats put a Miles Davis album on the stereo, which he tuned to near-performance volume. "Yah, that's what I call music," he shouted over it. He undid his tie, then yawned mightily, stretching his arms high above his head. "Man, it feels good to relax with friends. I need it. To come down after the gig. Hey, y'all wanna watch me on TV?" He started across the room, then stopped himself. "Ah, piss on it, you saw enough of me at the Place. Let's just relax."

Gerri took something from her purse. Ted first thought it was an ordinary cigarette, then perceived its narrow hand-rolled shape.

"Aw, man," Spats said as she lit it, "you ain't gonna do one of them."

She smiled. "You come down your way, I'll come down mine."

He seemed about to renew his protest but instead shrugged at Ted, then emptied his glass with one swallow. "Ready for another, T-Bone? Gracie?"

"We'll play these," Ted said. He wished he hadn't accepted the invitation for a nightcap. The session at the Place had dragged on much longer than it should have, and now the music on the stereo seemed part of the same nerve-wracking roar. He wondered how Spats could stand it. Interestingly, Grace was taking everything in stride.

"Anybody want some?" Gerri asked, proffering the joint.

Grace took it, brought it within an inch of her lips, then turned to Ted. "You'd rather I didn't, wouldn't you?"

"I can't hear you," he said over the music.

She brought her mouth to his ear and repeated the sentence.

He brought his mouth to her ear and said, "It's not for me to say yes or no."

She brought her mouth to his ear. "I was right, you'd rather I didn't." She held the joint to her lips and pretended to draw on it, turning her head so that Ted could see she was only pretending but Gerri could not. "Thanks," she shouted to Gerri, handing it back. In Ted's ear she said, "No point hurting her feelings, right?"

He hugged her tightly.

Spats returned with his fresh drink, took a large swallow of it, placed the glass on the floor and snuggled against Gerri, pushing the recliner three quarters of the distance to its horizontal position.

Ted wanted to leave, thought they should leave. No question that Spats would start making out with Gerri, which ordinarily would be a cue for Ted to start with his girl. Which would be a cue to lower the recliners to full horizontal. Which would be a cue to fuck. After which it would be a simple matter for the men to get up—to make fresh drinks—and return to the other's recliner. Ted *could* enjoy that. He hadn't tried it since California, and Gerri was certainly attractive enough. . . . Oh, come off it, he told himself, this isn't an ordinary setup. This is *Grace,* and if he wasn't going to over-protect her, he also wasn't going to kid himself that she was just another potential player in a four-sided game. Hey, enough of this . . . leave the soul-searching to the likes of Buffy Weiss.

He sipped his Scotch, uncomfortably, and then was taken off the hook when, as Spats lowered his recliner to full horizontal, Grace said in his ear, "Ted, let's go back to your place."

Spats accompanied them to the elevator, where he handed Ted a slip of paper. "I almost forgot, T-Bone, tell your banker to give Miss Danton a call. Here's her number, and this is the name of a movie she's up for the lead in. Have your boy tell her he's considering investing and would like to meet her before he makes a decision."

"It's that simple?"

"Assuming his credentials are legit, yeah. She'll check him out first, naturally. All he has to do is ask her to dinner and she'll take it from there. Of course if he wants her after the first time he'll have to make it worth her while—fur coat, trip to the moon, whatever."

"That's his problem."

"One more thing—under *no* circumstances do you tell him about her relationship with Joe. And don't say a word to anyone, *especially* Joe, that I set it up."

"My lips are sealed."

"That's good, old buddy, 'cause if they aren't, mine will be." He laughed humorlessly and drew his thumb across his throat.

Grace and Ted boarded the elevator. "I feel sorry for Spats," she said.

"He's doing all right for himself."

"Professionally, maybe, but personally he seems a wreck."

It occurred to Ted that most girls would be insatiably curious about the parting conversation with Spats, suspecting that the two men were talking in code, with "banker" being a substitute for Ted himself getting fixed up with the girl. Grace wasn't most girls. "All Spats needs," he said, "is the tender loving care of a girl like Grace Colello."

"But he'll never get it, because he won't sit still long enough for her to get interested. Dorian was very taken with him earlier tonight—"

"He felt the same about her."

"Which makes it even sadder that he blew it with that dance routine. He just seems to have no sensitivity to other people's feelings." She leaned against him. "Unlike you, loving friend."

They arrived at his penthouse. "Drink?" he asked.

"Let's take one to bed with us." She looked at her watch, feeling wonderfully earthy and at ease with him now. "I calculate I've got time for a good fuck and a two-hour nap before the school bell tolls."

"Wine? Or do you want to stay with Scotch?"

"Scotch. I'll get the glasses." She went to the kitchen. "Come to think of it, we could make that two fucks and a one-hour nap."

He laughed, feeling himself unwinding in the spirit of her mood. "Just call me the sixty-minute man."

They went to the bedroom and wordlessly undressed.

Ted noticed that Grace automatically went to the side opposite him. They were getting to be very much like a married couple. And he was getting to like it.

Their bodies came together under the covers. He took her in his arms and pressed her against him. He loved the feeling of totally nude contact from the start. It was so much better—so much more a mutual thing—than when you had to undress a girl.

Her legs coiled around his and she pulled him on top of her. He felt the hot wetness of her vulva against the tip of his penis. He shoved and sank quickly inside, without ever having to use his hand, or she hers, for direction. He didn't remember that happening before. Except with Chris.

It seemed at first that they would have a very quick fuck, but as they got into it she began moving her hips in a teasing way that told him she wanted to make it last. And then he got a tease action of his own going—alternate zig-zag and sideways movements that made her so wet he could scarcely feel her vaginal pressure. They stretched it on and on until finally, almost magically, they both seemed to agree tacitly that it was time. He repositioned himself, lining up his pubic bone against her clit. Totally aware of what he was doing now, she needed only a few strokes to set her bucking beneath him, her buttocks coming way up off the bed, her fists pushing frantically against the sheet. He started moving for himself now and came almost instantly. "Bounce those gorgeous big fuckers against me!" he said, savoring the rolling and jumping of her enormous breasts.

"Oh, you fantastic fucker," she murmured, "oh, you incredible *fucker.*"

He stayed on top of her for a long time, doing the gentlemanly elbow-support bit. Finally she eased him to one side, keeping their hips flush so their genitals wouldn't separate. "Well, we do fuck up a storm, don't we?" she said.

It hardly needed an answer.

She had expected to be tired, considering the hour, but the fuck had rejuvenated her. She put down-pressure on his penis as if to squeeze extra drops from it. They stayed in the side-by-side position until her back tired, then they separated and he got up to freshen their drinks.

Afterward, lying against his chest, idly running her fingers through the thick hair, she said, "You weren't too impressed with John Malloy, were you?"

"I'll support him."

"Hardly an overwhelming vote of support. Do you have a better candidate in mind?"

"Sure, me." He smiled when he said it.

She raised herself on one elbow and looked at him. "Ted, I think you half mean it."

"Not really. I mean, I know it's impractical. I have no backing, no plans—"

"But you'd like to!"

"Eventually, maybe. Who knows?"

She kissed him. "Loving friend, you'd be the best goddamn candidate in the history of democracy."

"You know something? I think I agree with you . . . but I suspect that's the extent of my constituency."

"And I disagree. I'm sure plenty of people would—"

"Well, the whole thing is a ways down the pike, and in the meantime I guess I'll line up with everybody else behind good old John."

"You don't really like him, though, do you?"

"Why do you say that?"

"It comes through. Not when we were with him, of course. But I sensed it at the Place and now again here."

"I never thought about it, but I guess he does rub me a little the wrong way."

"You mean he's too smooth—was that the word you used at the Place?"

"Yes, but more than that. Somehow I think I question his sincerity . . ."

"He's been consistent, Ted. He's held his positions even when they were very unpopular—and sometimes it hurt him."

"I know. Which makes my reaction illogical. Still, it's there. I keep thinking of John F. Kennedy. Damn, how people loved and admired the man! Humanitarian—elegant, sophisticated proprietor of Camelot—cool, steel-nerved poker player, calling Khrushchev's bluff in the Cuban missile crisis. He could do no wrong. And when some people reminded you that he played dirty pool too, dumping on old Hubert Humphrey in West Virginia, playing the game with Daley in Chicago, browbeating allies and opponents—well, you persuaded yourself it was necessary, that that's the way the game is played, either run with the rats or get out of the race. So the man gets canonized—when he was assassinated in the same year that Pope John died, newspapers all over the world featured the two of them as though they were somehow interchangeable. And then you learn he was apparently involved in plots to assassinate Fidel Castro. Oh, yeah, there's no proof he actually approved them. But you figure he had to know what was planned. Lower-echelon bureaucrats don't do these things on their own. So this guy that you worshiped was, for all intents and purposes, also involved in international murder. . . . And that, goddamn it, is not the way the game is supposed to be played. There's no way you can rationalize or excuse it."

"And you think John Malloy would operate the same way?"

"I worry about it. Which may be entirely unreasonable. Maybe the only similarity between him and Kennedy is that they're Irish."

"No, I think John Malloy, consciously or unconsciously, does model himself after Kennedy. The question is, how far does it go? From the little I've seen, not very far . . . he hardly seems to have the Kennedy ruthlessness that I've read about."

"Well, I guess I don't really have any good basis for feeling otherwise. As I said, I guess I'm being illogical . . ." He sipped his Scotch.

She covered his hand with hers. "That's one of the things I like about you so much. You really are fair."

He winced a little.

They held each other silently for a while, then he said, "Speaking of Malloy, has he asked you out yet?"

"No, but I could tell tonight that he soon will. There was something in his eyes when we shook hands. A kind of edgy anticipation . . . My goodness, what a shameless one am I . . ." She took a large swallow of Scotch, waiting for him to say something, and when he didn't she said brightly, "Hey, speaking of coming attractions, what's the latest with our friend Miss Loomis?"

"Nothing. I haven't phoned."

"You really should." (She was glad he hadn't.)

"Eventually."

"No, right away. I told you, chicks like her can grow cold awfully fast." (So freeze, already.)

"I'll get around to it. I think she's due back from a flight on Friday. And speaking of which, do you want to spend this weekend in Pennsylvania?"

"Yes, great!"

"You don't have anything else on? I mean, *Malloy*-wise. Or *Williams*-wise or—"

"Nor *other*wise. Hey, I don't mean to be presumptuous, loving friend, but . . . well, *do* you resent my seeing them . . . ?"

"No. Of course not."

"You sounded kind of testy."

"Blame it on the hour." He kissed her. "I encouraged it from the start, didn't I? I think it's great for you, and I think our relationship, exactly as it stands, is great for both of us." (Sure, just great.)

"Okay, okay . . . and I agree." (I guess . . .)

"And so to Pennsylvania. We'll leave Friday evening—about seven, to avoid the traffic."

She touched his cheek. "I'm really looking forward to it, Ted. I appreciate your wanting to share your family with me."

He hugged her. "Hey, you feel good."

"Good enough to fuck?"

"I'd say."

"I mean now."

"Hey, friend," he said, putting his finger inside her and enjoying the wetness that was part him, part her, "you'll be late for school—"

"Shut up and get on."

Joseph Williams and Spats Johnson centered themselves beneath the "Malloy for U.S. Senate" sign and smiled at the cameramen.

"Does this make it official?" a reporter asked.

Williams made sure the cameramen were finished before he turned. "It's certainly official that we and many of our fellow artists are uniting to support the nomination of John Malloy for the U.S. Senate."

"But," said a second reporter, "is he officially a candidate?"

"Gentlemen," said Burr Whiteside, "let's get a few more pictures here beneath the banner. Then we'll break out the refreshments and answer all your questions."

Tom Donohue appeared with Spats's clarinet and Joseph Williams's baton.

"Lift the baton, maestro," said a photographer, "as though you were conducting while Spats plays."

Williams laughed. "A solo clarinetist wouldn't have someone conducting him."

"So just pretend," said the photographer.

"You don't mind, do you, maestro?" asked Burr Whiteside. "It's much more interesting than two faces staring at the camera."

Joseph Williams pretended to conduct. The shutters clicked.

"Now, gentlemen," said Burr, "if you'll go to the table on my left you can help yourself to the refreshments and we'll answer any questions."

"Spats," a reporter called out, "why are you supporting John Malloy?"

"Fella," Spats said, "this is a man who deserves every citizen's support. I mean it. You talk about politicians not caring for the little guy—never in the whole time I've been voting have I known a man who cared more about the ordinary cat than John Malloy. This is a guy with compassion, a guy with feeling. And I'll tell you something—the brothers in New York know it. You mark my words, come election day, the black community will support John Malloy one hundred percent."

"Maestro," another reporter called, "how do you justify supporting an out-of-state resident for senator from New York? Don't we have any qualified New Yorkers?"

Williams smiled. "John Malloy is originally from Connecticut, I'm originally from Massachusetts, and I dare say most of the so-called New Yorkers in this room are originally from some other state. One of the nice things about New York—indeed, one of the chief sources of its tremendous zest and vitality—is its ability to absorb new ideas and influences. The history of twentieth-century immigration in the United States is the history of New York.

We New Yorkers don't care where a person comes from or how long he's been here. We only want to know what he or she can contribute."

"Oh, come on, maestro," said another reporter, "we all know this residence thing is a sham. Malloy wants a shot at the senate here because he thinks he can win more easily than in Connecticut."

"Gentlemen," said Tom Donohue, "I think I can put some light on this. First of all, Mr. Malloy has not announced for the senate and may never announce. He moved to New York for a number of reasons, the main one being that he wanted his children to have the opportunities for cultural exposure uniquely available here, the opportunity to grow up with children of all racial and ethnic and religious backgrounds, to participate in a wide variety of life styles. Now, Mr. Williams and Mr. Johnson and some of their colleagues believe he would be a good man to represent them and this state in the senate, so they've formed a committee to campaign for his nomination."

There was a chorus of disbelief.

Donohue laughed. "Gentlemen, I respect your cynicism, knowing the various strains that have been placed on your credulity over the years, but I assure you, everything I tell you is the truth."

"Off the record, Tom," said the first reporter, "when is he going to declare?"

Donohue took a long time finding a glass of champagne and just slightly less sipping it. "He hasn't made a decision. Naturally he's pleased by the support of New Yorkers like Mr. Johnson and Mr. Williams, and I can assure you he will do everything in his power to advance the causes he and they support, whether as a senator, a congressman, an elected official in some other office, or merely as a private citizen."

"Off the record, Tom," another reporter reminded him.

"I'm being very candid and frank with you when I say he hasn't made a decision, one way or the other." Donohue looked directly at the questioner. "Off the record, it's safe to predict he'll be making his decision in six to eight weeks."

"I see you're becoming quite the politician," said Joe Mandino, displaying the front page of the *Daily News*.

Spats laughed, uncertain of the response expected from him. "He's a good man. He deserves support."

"They're all crooks, every last fucken one of them. They'd cut out a baby's heart if they thought it'd get them in office." Joe tossed the newspaper aside. "But I suppose there's no harm in supporting him. The worst that can happen is he loses and you don't get anything. If he wins, you got a friend at court if you ever need one."

"I really do think," said Spats, "that he's a good man."

Joe studied him for a moment, then shrugged. "Okay, for your sake, I hope he wins. For mine, I couldn't care less. One or the other, they're all out for my balls."

Spats took an envelope from his jacket. "Anyway, the reason I wanted to see you today—" He handed it to Joe, who opened it and whistled under his breath. "One hundred thousand dollars," said Spats. "The final installment."

Joe scrutinized the check. "You sure you don't want to hold back some of it? Just in case you need it?"

"No, I've got more coming in next week. I'll be okay."

"If you say so." Joe tucked the check into his pocket. "I appreciate it, *piccolo*. So many people, they never care if they pay back. Then, when a fella asks for a favor, they get upset, as though you wanted something you didn't deserve."

"I never was that way, Uncle."

"I know, *piccolo*. That's why we get along so well, you and I. You're not one of these *schifoni*, you always paid back a hundred cents on the dollar."

"I can never pay you back fully, Uncle. You know that. The things you did for me—going to the mat for me when I was down, when nobody else would give me a shot—I'll never forget it, Uncle."

"I know, *piccolo*. I know."

The message to return John Malloy's phone call was waiting when Grace got home from school. She reached him at his office.

"I was hoping you might be free this evening," he said.

"I haven't finished your memorandum."

"Well, I'm sure we can use the time profitably in any case. Will you have dinner with me?"

She arranged to meet him at his office. "Well," her mother said as Grace replaced the receiver, "you're getting to be a very busy young lady."

Grace smiled.

"It's a wonder you have time for your school work."

"It's no problem. I could coast out for the rest of the year if I had to." Thinking aloud, she added, "I'm on a personal basis with people my *teachers* only read about."

Her mother followed her to the closet, where Grace tried to decide which of her three semi-dress outfits to wear. "This life is what you always wanted, Gracie, isn't it?"

"To know exciting people who do something in the world? Yes. But you know what surprises me, Mom? It's no different from dealing with kids at school or the people back in the old neighborhood. It's easier, in fact. These people are much more open to me, to what I think and have to say."

"Then I'm happy for you, it's what you deserve. I'm only sorry your father and I can't provide better for you, nicer clothes, all that—"

"Don't worry, please, I'm doing fine." She settled on a conservative red suit for which, fortunately, she had matching shoes.

When she came out of the shower her father was home from work, sitting at the kitchen table and drinking beer from the bottle. Grace's mother set two places.

"Aren't you eating with us?" Marty Colello asked his daughter.

"She's eating out. She was invited to dinner by *John Malloy*."

His eyebrows went up. "The politician?"

"None other."

"She dates married men now?"

"Oh, Marty, it's strictly business, she's working on his campaign."

Marty silently turned back to his beer as Grace went to her room and dressed. When she was ready to leave, her mother followed her outside and tucked a twenty-dollar bill into her hand. "Just in case you need it."

"I won't." Grace tried to give it back.

"You never can tell. You may be someplace and have to take a cab or something." She stuffed it into Grace's pocket. "And Gracie"—she cocked her head and pursed her lips—"if he tries to get fresh, remember, honey, men don't respect a girl who's too easy."

Grace laughed. "You said it yourself, Mom. It's strictly business."

John Malloy's receptionist had left by the time Grace arrived at the office. "In here, Grace," Malloy called from the inner office. She found him sitting at the oak table that served as his desk. It was covered with newspapers and reports. His shirt sleeves were rolled up. It was an attractive picture, especially as framed by the window behind him, its light a hazy grayish-blue. For a moment she wondered if possibly he set the room up that way because he knew how he came across—and then decided it was an unfair notion, maybe inspired by Ted's skepticism.

He came around from the table and greeted her with a handshake. A lingering one, she thought. "I made reservations at Chez René," he said. "I'm in the mood for someplace small and intimate."

"Fine," she said. His ice-blue eyes were as intense as ever. She had a feeling that if she let her body drift the slightest bit closer to his, he would certainly try to kiss her. She eased away. Not that she didn't want him to. She just didn't want to be rushed.

He went to the closet and got his suit jacket. "Shall we?" He offered his arm.

She took it and they went to the elevator. Interesting, she thought, how men set it up. Establish physical contact and keep reinforcing it. Then when it's time for sex it isn't such an abrupt thing. She wondered if John Malloy calculated this or did it instinctively. Probably some of both.

Over dinner he asked about her family, what she was studying, what she planned to do after college. He seemed genuinely interested. She was pleased. She found that she was very comfortable with him. Except for those incredible blue eyes. They seemed to look right through her.

After dinner they walked west on Forty-ninth Street. He turned toward his office building, and she thought of asking where he was going, then decided that would be impossibly coy. She decided not to play games.

In his office he locked the elevator door and led her to the inner office. "Would you like something to drink?"

"White wine, if you have some."

He went to a bookcase and opened a door on the bottom shelf that masked a refrigerator. He poured a glass of wine for her and whiskey for himself. After setting her drink in front of her, he quickly put his arm around her. She pressed her body against his. His hand covered her breast. "I've wanted to make love to you from the first," he said.

She stifled an impulse to say, I know. His couch was also a convertible bed. It was freshly made, the sheets crisply laundered. She enjoyed their texture as she turned them down. The fabric was elegant—far more delicate than most sheets, sort of like those at Joseph Williams's studio . . . Oh, lord, Grace . . .

He came over to her and she undid his belt, and for a moment they fumbled with each other's clothes, then, laughing, gave it up and stripped themselves down. They came together in bed. His body, she saw, was flabby. He had a barrel-like torso, and his thighs were thick as logs. His penis was small. Strangely, she didn't mind. Those blue eyes held their own erotic power, coming closer to her now, fixing her, boring in on her.

Ted gave Hartford Loomis the information about Jeannie Danton.

"Why, ah, thank you very much, Ted," the banker said, tucking the slip of paper into his vest pocket. "I, ah, really appreciate it."

Ted waited for him to say something else—something to the effect of, how are your business plans developing, do you need any money, can I be of service to you in any way . . .

Loomis sipped his wine and started talking football.

Ted reminded himself that a man like Loomis probably would be fairly subtle about such things. You don't talk quid pro quo, you take it for granted that your favor will be repaid when the time comes that you need repayment. Still, he'd feel better if something were said, even a hint—

Ted, I've been thinking, now that you and I have become friends, why don't you deal directly with me instead of George DelVecchio at BankUS?

Instead, Loomis turned the conversation from football to wine.

Ted wondered whether to leave things unsaid or at least get a word on the record that he expected something. Maybe something like: Hart, Emerson Wade has several proposals before George DelVecchio. I wonder if you'd look them over and tell me what you think . . . Maybe, though, it would be better to say nothing for now. Let Loomis get his dick wet, then hit him up to repay the favor. On the other hand, once he got his dick wet, he could tell you to go to hell. Then what?

"Hart," Ted said, "getting back to football, Emerson Wade and I have worked up a couple ideas we'd like your opinion on." He described Emerson's proposals for a television production company to syndicate college games and a national weekly newspaper devoted to pro football.

Loomis listened courteously but, it seemed to Ted, with little interest. "Both projects sound reasonable," he said finally. "Of course, they'd be particularly attractive to investors if it's known that you personally are involved."

"We were thinking of financing them chiefly with bank loans rather than a stock issue. Emerson has proposals before your man DelVecchio right now."

"I've got a great deal of confidence in DelVecchio. I'm sure if the proposals are sound, he'll make you as attractive an offer as you'll find anywhere."

Was that a go-to-hell? "I'd like you to make it a point to look them over personally, Hart. As you said, it's good if people know the head man is personally involved." Ted smiled. "Not, of course, that I'd expect you to overrule DelVecchio if the proposals seem unsound. But I'd like *your* advice once you've reviewed them." There's the *quo,* baby. Quiff pro quo.

"Well, I'll be happy to give them a look, Ted."

"Thanks, Hart."

On the subway back to 305 East Ted wondered if perhaps he'd been too heavy. Not that heaviness would affect Loomis's judgment of the proposals themselves. But in a borderline situation it might be enough to turn his "maybe" into a "no," Jeannie Danton notwithstanding. It might also prejudice him against future personal dealings with the heavy-hander—say as a prospective father-in-law. Hey, where the hell did that thought come from? (Now, Mr. T, you know you've been thinking about her. Fact is, according to your calculations, she should be getting back from a flight just about right now.) . . .

Hartford Loomis considered whether to place the call to Jeannie Danton personally or have his secretary do it. While he weighed the matter, he buzzed George DelVecchio. "I understand Vassily has some football proposals before you."

"Yes, Hart. Highly speculative under ordinary circumstances, but with him and his people behind them, interesting prospects."

"Well, his people may hint to you that I'm interested in the matter. I'm not. I expect you to make the same judgments you would if I didn't live in Three-oh-five East."

"Of course."

"However, when you've made your decision, let me know. Whether it's affirmative or negative, I'd like to tell Vassily personally."

He replaced the receiver, then buzzed his secretary and asked her to try Jeannie Danton.

"Mister Loomis," said Jeannie, coming onto the phone, "I've been expecting your call. I'm looking forward to meeting you."

EIGHT

"DEAR MR. Vassily," Ted read, "I've been telephoning you twice a week since the grand opening of 305 East. I'm both sorry and puzzled you haven't found time to return my calls. I greatly admire what you've done and would welcome the chance to discuss your future plans. I hope you'll phone me at your earliest convenience. I'd like to take you to lunch and get to know you better." The letter was on the engraved stationery of First American Investment Corporation and was signed "Joseph Mandino."

"Persistent cuss, isn't he?" Ted said.

Emerson Wade examined the engraving on the parchmentlike letterhead. "None of it makes sense. If he's not planning to muscle in on the operation, what does he want with you? If he is planning to muscle in, why would he leave such a visible trail of phone messages and now a letter?"

"Maybe he's planning one of those J. P. Morgan deals—you know the old story about how Morgan helped out a friend's son by walking with him across the floor of the New York Stock Exchange."

"You mean Mandino wants someone to see him with you and think the two of you are connected? Reep, granted you're one hell of a hot property these days, I still don't see Coffee Joe kissing your ass for the pleasure of being seen in your company."

"You're right."

"If you're in the mood for Byzantine scenarios, though,

it could be not that Mandino is looking for points by being seen with you but that maybe some third party is trying to discredit *you* by having you seen with Mandino. And Coffee Joe might or might not be aware of his role."

"That's a little far out . . ."

"Maybe you're not the primary target. Maybe it's somebody you're associated with, somebody the third party hopes to discredit by smearing you . . ."

"Except who's the 'somebody'?"

"Well, there's one way to begin to find out."

"Accept his invitation?" Ted shook his head. "It goes to the idea of acceptable risk, Emer. Whatever possible good could come of it doesn't outweigh the potential for harm—keeping in mind that if Joe's acting on his own and for himself only, he'll eventually have to give it up when he sees I won't have anything to do with him."

"Should we rule out completely that he's acting in good faith?"

"We should rule out completely any contact with the Mafia. Under pressure I can go along with accepting financing from a corporation like Ron-Cor, whose link to the mob is only rumored—although frankly I'd like to buy back their paper as soon as our situation permits—but it's something else to get buddy-buddy with the Manhattan superboss, even if he is our tenant." He dropped the letter into his outbasket. "What's next on the agenda?"

Wade consulted his legal pad. "Still nothing from George DelVecchio on the two propositions. Meanwhile I've been talking to Chancellor-Cambridge Trust of Boston. They're interested in a package deal under terms I can't believe any bank would offer, much less an outfit with their conservative reputation. Get this: ninety percent financing of the TV syndicate and the weekly newspaper; eighty percent of the two radio stations; eighty-five percent of an apartment building in Boston, modeled after Three-oh-five East, including the same ratio of subsidized tenants; and for our respective ten, twenty and fifteen percent shares of equity they'll accept a second mortgage equal to whatever amount of cash we raise."

"A second mortgage on what?"

Emerson shifted uncomfortably. "Those three old

apartment buildings I suggested we pick up for a song and rent to our Three-oh-five East waiting list."

"No, Emer, I've said that's out."

"I wish you'd reconsider. If you want to talk in strictly humanitarian terms, think of the poor people in Boston who'll be able to enjoy the same advantages as the subsidized tenants of Three-oh-five East. If you want to talk business, consider the leverage we're getting. We need equity of about three million dollars. With this package, raising it will be a piece of cake. Once we have it, Chancellor-Cambridge will stake us to an operation worth close to a hundred and fifty million. We can earn back that initial three million in less than a year. From then on, the name of the tune is 'Santa Claus Is Comin' to Town.' "

"But if Chancellor-Cambridge thinks we're such hot shit, why do we need the three apartment buildings?"

"Two reasons, Reep—one, the guaranteed rentals, thanks to our waiting-list situation here; two, the tax laws allow us to depreciate the ass off those buildings, offsetting profits from the two radio stations, in effect making those profits tax free."

"I'm always delighted to screw the tax collector, but I've got bad vibes about those buildings."

"What could happen?"

"Too many things. We're putting all our time and energy into Three-oh-five East and it still isn't perfect. Imagine what a time we'd have managing these three, a Boston building, and media properties all over the country."

"Tenants don't expect a building to be perfect, Reep—particularly an old building."

"If people move into a building because they know I run it, they're entitled to expect certain minimum standards of excellence. I don't want to let them down." He came around from his desk and went to the glass case that contained the game ball from his first game as the owner, coach and starting quarterback of a pro team. "When I took over the New York franchise, guys like you and Mikey DeAngelico didn't sign because I was paying top dollar. You signed because you trusted me to give you my best. If I didn't think I could deliver, I wouldn't have asked for your trust . . . sorry to sound heavy, but—"

"I appreciate all that, Reep. But on the other hand you're not the only guy in the history of the human race that ever managed a well-run apartment building. We can deliver sound value on the satellite buildings even if you don't personally inspect the doormen's fingernails every day." He turned away. "Sorry, I guess I'm just too caught up in my own enthusiasm—"

Ted put his hand on Wade's shoulder. "Hey, old buddy, if it weren't for you *and* your enthusiasm, Three-oh-five East would still be on Axel Wessman's drawing board." He went back to his desk. "I'll review the proposals again, Emer. If I can see any way to pull it off, without compromising the standards I want to maintain, I'll give you the go-ahead. Meanwhile, believe me, nobody is hungrier for that hundred and fifty million than yours truly—not even his financial v.p."

Wade left and Ted went to the window to stare out at the 305 East courtyard. A mother with a baby in a stroller was reading the granite slab on which was engraved the name of every person who had worked on the building. An elderly man was sitting on a bench, watching two pigeons peck at something in the grass.

Ted was tired. It had been a long week. It had been a long year. He was glad it was Friday. He needed that weekend in the country. He looked at his watch. Only ten-fifteen. It felt like four p.m. He really needed more than a weekend. A few weeks on the beach at Mykonos. Lots of nude bodies bronzing in the sun. A hut on Paradise Beach, a bottle of ouzo and, fantasy time—two girls sucking his cock . . . Nan and Grace? . . . starting at his knees, licking their way upward, and when they reached his balls, each would take one in her mouth, and simultaneously four hands would be stroking his ass and pubes, and then they would work their way up his cock, together, sharing it, and when they reached the head—

The delightful possibilities of that were defeated by the sound of his secretary's buzzer. "Miss Colello on the line."

He was glad she couldn't see his double-take.

"Ted," Grace said, "I'm afraid I've got an awful dilemma. I don't know what to do . . ."

It seemed that Joseph Williams had just phoned. The conductor of the Paris Opéra was ill. Williams had been asked to take over his next three performances. He was leaving for Paris tonight and would return on Wednesday. He had invited her to go with him.

"I told him I had plans," she said. "I really want to be with you, Ted . . . but I've never been to Paris—I've never been outside the United States—it'd be such a tremendous chance—"

"Of course . . . have yourself, as they say, a great time . . ."

"Oh, thank you, Ted. Friend. God, I'm so excited, I'll think about you the whole time I'm there and I'll bring you back something perfect . . . a flower from one of the sellers in Montmartre that I've read about . . . or a bottle of your favorite wine. What is it, by the way? I should know."

He forced a good-natured laugh. "Bring me the cheapest Beaujolais you can find. If you pay more than three francs, you're getting robbed."

He went on—his heart decidedly not in it—to tell her about some of his favorite spots in Paris—a sidewalk café at the intersection of Boulevards Saint Germain and Saint Michel, a brasserie opposite Gare Saint Lazare, the bookstalls at Pont Neuf, the cathedral ceiling of Galeries Lafayette . . .

"I hadn't realized you'd been there," she said. "I guess everybody has but me."

"Well, here's your chance. Go to it."

"Thank you for being so understanding, Ted. I really appreciate it. And I can't wait to go to Pennsylvania with you. We'll do it very soon, okay?"

"Okay." He put down the receiver and tried to keep back his anger. He wasn't really angry with her, he told himself. He was very pleased for her. It was just that he'd got himself juiced up to spend the weekend with her. He couldn't hack two nights patrolling the local gin mills for dummies who'd reject him because locally it would be more of a status thing to turn him down than to screw him. Fucked up Pennsyldummy values!

Of course he could put his cock on ice and invite Nasty Nate over to kill a few cases of down-home beer. But he wasn't in the mood for a stag weekend, not keyed up as he was for two days with Grace.

He went through his address book, hoping he'd be reminded of someone at least tolerable. Spats no doubt could turn up somebody, but he didn't want a total stranger. Kill him for being old-fashioned, but what he really wanted was someone he felt something for, someone like a loving friend named Grace . . . or maybe—

Nan! She should be back from her flight. He reached for the phone, then drew back. She'd probably have more excuses than—terrible image—a pregnant paraplegic. It was chore enough getting her up to the apartment for a drink. He certainly wasn't in the mood for a resistance session. Still, nothing ventured . . . He dialed the number. Now—what do you want to bet there's either no answer or the goddamn line is busy?

She answered on the first ring. "Ted, I'm so glad you called. I was beginning to think you'd forgotten I existed."

He got to the invitation—hesitantly, damn near cringing as the words came out, certain she'd find some excuse.

"Gee, I'd love to," she said, "except I've already made plans for Saturday night—"

"Uh-huh, well, sure, I understand, short notice . . . See you around."

"If I can get out of it, I'll call you back."

"Yeah. Okay. Fine." He resisted the impulse to slam the phone. Might as well keep your temper under control, you'll only make yourself feel worse. He'd go through the address book one more time, and if he couldn't come up with someone he'd phone his parents to cancel.

He started flipping pages. Ten minutes later his secretary buzzed. "Miss Loomis for you."

"Is that invitation still open?"

"It is."

"Well, I can make it—that is, if you still want me to."

She wore a cranberry-red knit suit with a high collar. On a rack in some store it would have suggested nothing but modesty. On her it seemed to have been designed to raise hard-ons. The knit fabric stretched across her breasts, accenting their shape, and he had to fight the impulse to bury his face between them there and then. He was determined not to give her any excuse for feeling pushed or put-upon. But damn, she was delicious looking!

"You're looking good," he said, smiling as his eyes toured her body.

"You're looking pretty good yourself, sir." Like hell I am, he thought, acutely aware of his gut, which seemed to be pushing against his belt today with special force. Was he down on himself because he wanted her so damn badly and was afraid he couldn't make it? Or was his body really going to pot?

As they got into the rented car she automatically sat close against him, and the feel of her body, the smell of her perfume, the softness of her voice—aah, damn, it was driving him crazy . . . but he would control himself, he would not touch her until they were in bed. He was going to play this the way it had to be played.

They rode across New Jersey on Interstate 80. He let her carry the conversation. She was not, thank God, one of those women who sank into prolonged silences every few sentences. She talked about her life as a stewardess, the places she'd been, the things that impressed her. He shifted toward politics a few times, but she seemed uninterested so he let the conversation drift back to her. The main thing now, he kept reminding himself, was to hang loose. Don't say or do anything to make her feel the slightest discomfort. And keep your mind off her box.

He kept it off for all of New Jersey and most of the northbound Pennsylvania leg of Interstate 81. But as they approached Hazleton she started doing something with her leg against his—a kind of jiggling action, with her knee easing over the top of his thigh. He couldn't help resting his hand on her thigh. It was bare. He couldn't resist easing groinward. She didn't object; in fact, she slid down in the seat and parted her legs to give him better access. He reached her panties. They were damp. He eased a finger into the leghole. She was wet; she was very wet! He slipped a finger inside her vagina. She started squirming on top of it. Oh, man, how do you resist something like this?

He kept watching for a rest stop and after about five miles found one. He pulled into the parking stall farthest from other cars, angling his so that he could see anyone approaching. He took her into his arms and kissed her.

She sucked hungrily on his tongue as he drove it deep

into her mouth. He guided her against him, and she pressed hard with her breasts. "Let me get over on this side," he said.

She obediently rose to let him slide beneath her.

He resumed kissing her, now working his hand back into her crotch. Her hot slickness made crackling sounds as his finger played with her genital flesh. The sounds excited him even more. He tried to take off her panties.

She held his hand. "Ted, what for?"

He was stunned. "I'd say that's sort of obvious."

"Not here. We might be seen."

"Nobody's going to see us."

"We could be arrested."

"We won't be." He sighed. "But never mind . . ." He started to go back to the driver's seat.

"Wait." She put her hand on his arm. "Do you want to very much? Oh, I'm sorry, that's a stupid question. You do . . . and I do too. I guess resisting is sort of instinctive with me." She smiled. . . . "Besides, it's been a long time since I made love in a car." She slid off her panties and knelt over him, straddling his thighs with her knees. "I really do want to, Ted." She kissed him, at the same time opening his belt. "I've thought about it a lot since our last time. I've missed you."

He kept silent, wanting to believe—yet not believing. He slid off his pants and shorts. She rubbed the head of his cock against her vulva, then guided it inside. "Don't try to make me come, Ted. This one is just for you."

"But I want you to enjoy it too."

"I'll enjoy it, I just don't want us to wait until I can come. I'll save that for tonight, when we're in bed and have plenty of time . . ."

He didn't feel good about it, but he was in no mood for hassling. She was the one who'd stiffened his cock. Okay, let her play Santa Claus, if that was what she wanted.

She lowered herself onto him, then started a circular movement that he'd never experienced, at least not in this position. He pressed against her, relishing the hotness inside and the roughness of her pubic hair against his. He came faster than he had in a long, long time.

He started the car and pulled back onto the Interstate. She rested her head on his shoulder. "I'm sorry I gave you a hard time"—she missed her unintentional pun—"especially since I deliberately turned you on. I guess at the last minute I got into my old ambivalence."

"It was great," he said truthfully. "I just wish you could've enjoyed it more."

"I don't have to come to enjoy it, I told you that." She put her hand on his thigh, letting the backs of the fingers rest against his penis. "Tonight . . ."

He rounded a turn past the Hazleton exit and they found themselves overlooking the Wyoming Valley, which seemed to have been scooped away from the Interstate by a huge steamshovel. Scattered lights glowed in the deep blue twilight. Abandoned mounds of slate formed the horizon, a dragline still working near one of them, its string of lights looking like illumination for some amusement park ride.

"What a fantastic view," she said.

"It's a graveyard. The coal barons bled it dry and then left the locals to suffocate in their own stink. The sad part is, the locals like it. They think someone did them a favor. They still kiss the asses of the politicians who sold them down the river and the priests who promised they'd get paid off in heaven for the shit they ate here on earth."

She smiled hesitantly. "I can see you feel very strongly about it, but I don't quite understand . . . if the local people like it, why is it sad?"

He thought for a moment. "Maybe because they don't realize there's so much better—"

"But if they don't realize—"

"Ignorance is bliss, huh?" He remembered her father was one of the robber barons.

"Not 'bliss,' but if people like where they live—for whatever reason—isn't that good? If they lived somewhere else—Three-oh-five East, let's say—and didn't like it, wouldn't that be sad?"

"I suppose so . . . They were certainly willing collaborators in putting themselves in the hole. Why should I get pissed off at the people who showed them the way?"

"You're either appeasing me or making fun of me."

"No, I'm taking your point. I think I've been imposing my own attitude on the people here. I guess I still resent having been brought up here, taking shit from the power boys until I built up my own power by playing ball. I didn't realize that other people might be more comfortable in the shit . . . hell, might not be able to handle anything else."

"I still think you're being sarcastic."

"I'm not, really."

She found it hard to believe that he could change his views so abruptly, but she didn't want to challenge him. She certainly didn't want to quarrel. She wanted a nice, pleasant, affectionate weekend with a guy who—so far as was possible—happened to turn her on. And whom she wouldn't offend for the world. *That,* she couldn't bear.

She hadn't realized his effect on her until a few days after their last date. It was on a layover in London. She'd gone to bed with the flight engineer. At first he'd seemed terribly attractive. He had a sexy, very man-of-the-world way about him. She liked his casualness, his nonchalance, his seeming indifference to whether she responded to him. She especially appreciated that. But when they got to his bedroom and she saw how scrawny he was, and hairless, and—funny she hadn't noticed it before—how short, he couldn't be taller than five-six . . . well, she went through with it because, as usual, that was easier than hassling about why she didn't want to. But, when she thought about it, it was like having sex with a twelve-year-old boy. And then she'd thought about Ted—his size . . . *bigness* . . . she'd always been attracted to what the girls in school had called "beefos" in their bull sessions. They were her weakness. One girl whose father was a shrink had said it was because big guys reminded her of her father. But that didn't make sense when she thought of her father, who, much as she loved and respected him, did seem more fat than beef. Her girl friend had said that didn't matter, that as a little girl she'd seen him as huge, a monster, and that was the image—and the attraction—that had stuck. Well, maybe, maybe not, but whatever the reason, she knew she did like the feel of a big male hulk on top of her. She'd been that way ever since high school. Sometimes she regretted it, because the beefos tended to be emotionally insensitive—mostly me Tarzan, you Jane types—but on the other hand who, as Ted might put it, could argue with a wet cunt? Yes, that's exactly how he'd put it. . . .

"Well, this is Nanticoke," he said, pulling off the Interstate. They descended a hill, rounded a few turns, passed a garishly lit shopping center and emerged onto a narrow street whose houses, standing cheek-by-jowl, dated to the turn of the century.

"It's . . . charming."

He navigated another turn, then came to a traffic light and turned again. "Main Street. That vacant lot on the corner is where we used to hang out when I was in high school. It was a soda shop then. It burned down about fifteen years ago."

She started to ask the year of his graduation, then held back. But it did seem strange being with a man—a lover—who had graduated when you were at most six years old. "It's . . . interesting," she managed. "I mean, that a property on Main Street would stay vacant for fifteen years."

"That's northeastern Pennsylvania for you. Not exactly the progress capital of the world."

"The buildings are lovely, though. That Queen Anne house over there. And that Tudor."

"Yeah. Next year the redevelopment agency'll tear them down and put in a parking lot."

He waited for a traffic light, then turned onto another hilly street. "Now there's a place I'll never forget." He pulled to the curb.

It was a luncheonette, closed for the evening but illuminated by a night light. The facade comprised eighteen-inch squares of white-faded-to-cream tile surrounding a four-by-six-foot picture window. Behind the window was a hamburger grille. Above the grille was a neon Stegmaier Beer sign. Over the window, set in the tile, were black art-deco letters: "Lackawanna Jake's Red Hots." They got smaller as they ran uphill around the drawing of a man's head. He wore a chef's hat and had a big handlebar moustache.

"Another high school hangout?"

"My father's place. First one. He has a chain now."

Ted remembered how proud and excited he had been as a child when his mother brought him to the luncheonette in the afternoon and he saw his father through the window—Demetrios Vassilikos, the happy Greek, always smiling, always twirling his handlebar moustache, always wearing his big white chef's hat. He would wave his spatula when he saw them, and by the time they were inside he would have come around from behind the counter. His big strong hands would close around Ted's tiny chest, and he would lift him high in the air, and he would call out to everyone eating there, "Hey, everybody, look at my big boy!" And there was nothing in the world that Ted liked better than being there and feeling those strong hands around him and hearing that big deep voice.

Nan saw that Ted's eyes were moist.

He looked at her. "A cinder, I guess"—he made himself laugh—"here in coal country there's dust all over the place." He pulled away from the curb. "Let's check in with the family. If I'm not there by nine-thirty my mother starts calling the state police every five minutes for accident reports."

They arrived at nine-forty-five at the large white frame house on the hill overlooking the city. The door opened before the car had come to a halt in the driveway. Half a dozen people spilled out. Nan tried to keep track of them—a man with a moustache, a fat woman with an apron, another fat woman with a black dress, two teenage boys and a thirty-fiveish man in a cardigan sweater. They draped themselves over Ted and seemed to notice her as an afterthought. But when he made the formal introductions they embraced her warmly.

"Come in, come in, little lady," the man with the moustache sang out. "You must have a glass of ouzo."

She followed him into the kitchen, where a formica table with paper napkins had been set for eight places. He brandished a bottle of colorless liquid, then poured eight glasses.

"Stin igya sas!" he said, raising his glass toward Nan.

"Khronya pollá!" she replied, toasting, then sipping.

"She speaks Greek!" he said excitedly.

"Only enough to get through the airport," Nan said.

"Pos isthe?" the man in the cardigan sweater tested her.

"Kalá, ifkharisto; kai sis?"

"Poli kalá!"

"She speaks better than you, Teddy," said his mother.

"I guess so," he acknowledged.

"Well, I've exhausted my entire vocabulary," Nan said.

"Isthe poli ouraia," said Ted's father, raising his glass to salute Nan's beauty.

"Ifkharisto," she replied, thanking him.

Everyone laughed.

Ted's mother started putting food on the table: *bakalaos* and a tomato salad, deep-fried *gopa* and cold *kalamari,* a huge loaf of hot homemade bread. Ted's father made sure Nan had something on her plate from each platter, then heaped his own. "Tonight we eat Greek," he told her, swabbing a chunk of bread in the juice of the tomato salad. "Tomorrow I take you to Lackawanna Jake's and make you an authentic red hot."

"A real frankfurter," Ted translated.

"A *special* frankfurter of my own invention," said Demetrios Vassilikos. "With my own chili sauce that people come from as far away as Pittsburgh to taste. Some day get this big boy of mine to tell you how he sold forty-eight dozen in one night when he was only eleven years old."

"How did you ever manage that?" Nan asked.

Ted laughed. "That's a story for another day."

"Very modest, this big fella," said Demetrios, slapping Ted's shoulder. "A millionaire when he was thirty. And not just from football." Demetrios jabbed his forehead with his index finger. "All with this, he did it, Miss Loomis. *To kefali.* You know what means in Greek, *to kefali?"*

"The brain?"

"Literally, the head," Ted told her.

"We have two words in Greek, Miss Loomis—*kefali,* for head, and *kefaleo,* for capital, money. If you've got the head, that's all the capital you need in this world."

A bottle of retsina was emptied and replaced. The plates were refilled. At one in the morning, everyone was still eating. Finally at one-thirty Demetrios said, "Well, you young people must be tired after your drive. A glass of Metaxa, eh? Then we call it a night." He produced the brandy bottle and displayed the label to Nan. "Seven star. That's the best, Miss Loomis. For my big boy and his girl, we have nothing but the best."

Two glasses of brandy later, he ushered them into a bedroom and told them goodnight.

"We're sleeping together?" Nan asked when Demetrios had gone.

Ted shrugged. "What else?"

"They don't mind?"

"Honey, I'm a grown man, even in my parents' house."

"I know, but still—well, I guess I expected them to be more old-fashioned." (Did she mean "old world"?) She pressed against him. "But I'm glad they're not. And I'm very glad you brought me here. I just love them, Ted, I can't remember feeling more quickly at home. . . ."

They got into bed quickly. He put his hand on her hip. She took his penis in hand, feeling almost pacified by its hugeness, its hardness . . .

He laughed. "Hey, lady, don't fall asleep on me. There's more to come." He touched her vulva, and finding it wet eased a finger inside. She accommodated the one so effortlessly that he added another. He moved to get on top of her.

"Are you sure we won't disturb them?"

"Their bedroom is two away, Nan."

"I'm glad, I'm really in the mood tonight. All that drinking got me really high . . ." She immediately realized how that sounded and added, "I mean, it's you, not the drinking, but I guess it did lower my inhibitions . . . do you know what I mean?"

His answer was to enter her. They started moving. She noticed that the bed squeaked. "Are you sure they won't hear?"

"They won't. Don't *worry.*"

She resumed her movements, beginning to abandon herself to this wonderful huge body above her, but the damn squeaking distracted her, brought her back to her old self. . . . "I don't want you to wait for me, Ted," she said after a while. "Go ahead—for yourself, I mean."

"Really, hon, they won't hear."

"Do it anyway . . . I guess I had too much to drink after all . . . tomorrow I'll be better. You'll see . . ."

Goddamn, he thought, she sounded like Scarlett O'Hara . . . well, nothing to do now but go along. The damned springs *were* pretty loud, though. He altered his movements to produce the least possible noise. She fell into the zig-zag pattern that she knew he liked so well. He came in less than a minute.

"Was it all right?" she asked.

"More than that," he assured her, and meant it. No question, she could *fuck*, but . . .

They fell asleep in each other's arms and were in the same position when they woke to the aroma of brewing coffee. After breakfast with the family he took her for a tour of the area—his high school, the library, the river-bank, the Wyoming monument, the city of Wilkes-Barre nearby, its museum, and the Victorian houses that hadn't been washed out by the disastrous flood of 1972. "The mansions of coal barons," he said, driving along North-ampton Street, then Riverside Drive. "Built by fortunes made off immigrant miners paid fifty cents a day. Fifty cents a day and all the shit you could eat."

She didn't answer.

"I guess I shouldn't knock it. Bad as it was, it was probably worse in the old country. And at least there was the chance here to do better—if not for themselves, at least for their kids." He looked at her. "I do go on, don't I? . . . Sorry."

"Don't apologize, Ted. But I admit it is hard for me to identify with all of it."

"That's the problem—"

"What problem?"

"Forget it. It was a bad choice of words."

"Seriously, Ted, what do you mean? Do you expect me to apologize for my father's wealth?"

"No, of course not."

"Well, I don't feel guilty about it, Ted. Not a bit. I realize a lot of people think I should. I get my fill of them at N.Y.U.—especially the sociology profs."

"You're right. I'm sorry I brought it up. Forget it."

"Please don't dismiss me, Ted. Do you think I should feel guilty that my ancestors were skillful enough in managing their affairs that they could leave me a legacy, while other kids were raised in poverty?"

"No. I told you, it was a bad choice of words. I was talking about big-time rip-off artists like good old Jay Gould and Cornelius Vanderbilt and that crowd."

"But are you sure you don't really feel I ought somehow to do penance for the Loomis ancestors—for my good fortune?"

"Hell, no . . . I don't even know who your ancestors are."

"It doesn't matter. The point is, I'm not apologizing for them. I don't feel guilty. Even when I see those pathetic photos of starving people in CARE magazine ads, I don't feel guilty. I may feel sorry for them, but I don't feel guilty."

"Hey, cool it, Nan, nobody's suggesting you should—"

"But you *think* I should."

"No."

"Didn't you feel guilty enough about your good fortune to build Three-oh-five East?"

"It wasn't an act of atonement."

"Then what was it?"

"Something I felt like doing."

"That's all?"

"That's all."

"But why?"

"I never questioned that. I don't pry too deeply into motives. My policy is to trust feelings. Introspection is usually a waste of time."

"Well, I'll say amen to *that.*" She kissed him on the cheek.

He drove back to Nanticoke and pulled into the parking lot of a dilapidated stadium. "Last stop on the tour: Dempsey Field, home of the Nanticoke Bombardiers—at least that's what they used to call us. Now, with school-district consolidation and all that, it's something like the Southern Luzerne Area Golden Warriors. Which I guess is a partial steal from the California basketball team, and about as apt as a fart at a Junior League picnic."

She laughed. "You do have a way with words, sir."

And come to think of it, he was surprised at himself being even this vulgar with her. Fancy Nan Loomis. But she evidently enjoyed it. Well, rich broads usually did.

He took her hand and led her through the open gate into the empty stadium. "It's been a long time since I've been here. I almost forgot what the old place looked like."

They stood at the railing separating a section of bleachers from the playing field. During baseball season they were third-base bleachers; for football, they were at midfield. He remembered how the dirt basepaths of the baseball diamond played hell with runners of visiting football teams. Psyched everyone out. Especially the pitcher's mound, which somehow never worked out to be perfectly level, try though the ground crew did to flatten it. . . .

"George Mellini—he's the guy I told you about, the wide receiver I used to date at Harvard—he said the most impressive thing he ever felt was running into the stadium with his team and hearing the tremendous roar from the stands. I didn't really understand until he got me a sideline pass for a game. I was right at the runway when the team came on. Wow, the roar that came down from the stands! I'd heard it before from up in the seats, but it was entirely different down on the field." She smiled foolishly. "I guess I don't have to tell you."

He nodded. "You ought to hear it at Yankee Stadium."

"Do you miss it?"

"In a way. I guess every former player does. But there are other things you don't miss, things you'd never want back."

"You mean the fear of getting hurt?"

"No, you realize it's possible but you never think of it happening to you. If you did you'd never get out there in the first place. I'm talking about the pressure. You've got to perform under very exacting circumstances and for very high stakes. If you make a mistake, you let a whole lot of people down. The difference between winning and losing the Superbowl comes out to something like ten thousand per player. For an underpaid lineman with a relatively short career span, that translates into a once-in-a-lifetime shot."

"I guess I never thought of it that way."

He laughed. "The game was a lot more fun when I didn't, either."

They walked through the playing field. A groundskeeper noticed them, started to shoo them away, then recognized Ted. They chatted for a while—the inevitable we-read-about-you and what-are-you-doing-now? chatter that he got into with hometowners. Then the old man moved off, and Ted and Nan continued their walk.

"I'll bet you especially remember your games here."

"A few, maybe. But most of the pre-college stuff blurs from this distance." He looked up at the first-base bleachers, now badly in need of paint, with parts of the upper fence rotted. "What I remember better than anything is selling hot dogs."...

"Theodoros!" His father's impatient voice startled him. He'd been so wrapped up in the game he hadn't heard anyone behind him. Sighing, he turned to face the inevitable tirade.

"Are you watching the football again?"

"Aww, Pop..."

"How many times do I have to tell you? You don't sell hot dogs watching the football."

"Jeez, Pop, I was only watching for a minute. Nobody wants one anyway."

"How do you know if you don't ask?" Demetrios Vassilikos took the steamer box from its resting place on top of the rail separating the stands from the playing field. He held it up to make sure the side reading "Lackawanna Jake's Red Hots" would be facing the public. Then he looped the strap over Ted's shoulder.

"I did ask, Pop. I just came down from the stands."

Demetrios seemed not to hear. Holding index and middle fingers before his son's eyes, he pantomimed ascending and descending a stair. "Up the stands, down the stands, up the stands, down the stands." He cupped his hand alongside his mouth like Johnny in the Philip Morris ads. "Lackawanna Jake's red hots! Come an' get 'em, Lackawanna Jake's red hots!" He lowered his voice to its usual Demosthenean roar. "Maybe somebody who doesn't think of it before decides now he wants one, eh, my boy?"

As if on cue, a man in the stands gestured. Demetrios beamed triumphantly. "See!? Now go sell him, boy!"

"Dad, I just went by that guy a minute ago."

"So now you get my point." Demetrios made pedal-like movements with his fists. "Go, boy! You hear? Go sell him!"

After the game, Demetrios counted out one dollar and three cents. One penny for each red hot Ted sold. Then Ted helped him load the unsold food into the panel truck parked next to the concession stand.

"Dad?"

Demetrios's silence was permission to speak.

"Are you ever gonna let me come to a game just to watch?"

Demetrios's head turned slowly, his olive-black eyes reflecting the disbelief he might have felt if asked if he planned to grow a third arm.

"I checked with the other kids, Dad. None of them sold more than five dozen tonight. I sold close to ten."

Demetrios's raised eyebrows said that he failed to follow the argument.

"If I sell more than anybody else, I should be able to take it easy sometimes. If I keep selling more for the rest of the season, can I come to the last game without working?"

Demetrios fixed his son with a bewildered stare. After what seemed like days, he slowly scratched his head. Ted wondered whether the old man really didn't understand or was just putting on one of his acts. Finally Demetrios moved aside a box to clear a space on the floor of the truck, picked up his son by the armpits and sat him there.

"Theodoros," he said softly—very softly for him—"there are two kinds of people in this world. The kind that go to the games to watch and the kind that go to the games to work. You and me, we're the kind that go to the games to work."

"We don't have to be. Billy Sposino goes to watch. They don't have more money than us."

"That's why. They spend it all going to the games to watch." Demetrios took his son's face in his hands. "There are two kinds of people in the world, my boy. The ones that work and the ones that have fun. The ones that work are the ones on the way up. The ones that have fun are the ones on the way down."

"But don't you ever want to have fun?"

Demetrios hesitated, scowled, then, to Ted's surprise, laughed. "When I'm on the top, Theodoros, that's when

I'll worry about what to do on the way down." He picked Ted up and planted him on the ground. "Now we have work to do."

They finished loading the food. Demetrios drove into town and parked in the alley alongside the luncheonette. "Careful with the sauce!" he called as Ted bumped the pot while taking it from the truck.

"Don't worry, I'm not going to drop it." It pissed young Ted off that the old man never let him do anything on his own. It pissed him off so much that he didn't pay attention to the corner of the counter, which struck the pot, making half a cupful of chili slosh over the side. And this pissed him off so much that when he tried to hide the spill from his father he bumped the bottom of the pot against the grill and sent a pint of chili spilling over the front of his white shirt.

Demetrios was strangely calm. "Okay, don't worry." He gently took the pot, placed it on the grill and gave Ted a towel to clean the shirt. "Accidents will happen." He wiped the pot clean, held it up to the light to inspect it, then lowered it into its hole in the steam cabinet. "If you're too tired, you don't have to help."

"I'm not too tired."

When they finished, Demetrios took two fistfuls of ground beef from a bin in the cooler and slapped them into a pair of thick patties. "And now a nice chiliburger for my big boy and his old man, eh?"

Ted's spirits brightened. The old man could really be okay when he felt like it. And his chiliburgers were terrific.

Demetrios took an unlabeled green bottle from under the counter and poured each of them a glass of dark red wine. Then he cut two thick slices of raw onion and placed them on buns to await the chiliburgers. "To my big boy, eh?" he said, raising his glass.

"*Siyien,*" Ted replied, the Greek coming automatically.

Demetrios leaned his elbows on the counter and looked down into his son's eyes. "You think the old man doesn't like fun, eh, big boy? You think he likes work, work, work?" He laughed. "Teddy, my boy . . . Teddy, my boy—"

"Well, you work harder than you have to. Don't you?"

"Teddy, my boy . . . There's no standing still in this world of ours, my boy. It's one way or the other. You don't like to work hard? Okay, my friend, neither do I. But there's only two ways to go, Teddy. Up or down. Now sometimes a guy on the way up says to himself, well, it's going pretty good, I can take it easy for a while. You know what happens, my boy? He closes his eyes for a minute, and the next thing you know somebody stole his watch and somebody else took his car and his accountant walked away with his business. And then he's on the way down, Teddy. Now I don't say it happens to everybody. But it happens to somebody. If it happens to you, it don't make you feel better to know it ain't happening to anybody else. You understand, my boy? There's absolutely no satisfaction in the uniqueness of these circumstances, my boy. No satisfaction whatsoever." He drained his glass and exhaled with satisfaction before refilling it. "You're falling behind," he observed.

Ted finished his glass and watched his father refill it.

"Yes, my boy, your old man is telling you what life is all about. You think I like being Lackawanna Jake? You think I like standing here all day making red hots and going to the games at night? My boy, it isn't fun. I tell you from the bottom of my heart, it isn't fun. But I'll tell you something else, my boy. It's not as bad as the coal mines up in Lackawanna Valley. When I came to this country, eighteen hours a day, Teddy—under the ground, always dark, always cold, always dust in your face, you can't breathe. During the winter, the only time you saw daylight was Sunday. Then my brother, your uncle George, he gets a job washing dishes in a restaurant. By and by, he becomes the cook and I wash dishes. I learn to cook, I save my money. George buys his own restaurant down in Pottsville, I buy mine here. I make good red hots, Teddy. I make 'em very good. I make 'em so good and sell 'em so cheap that everybody buys them. At the games, there's an Irisher, he has the concession. But Mr. Olman from the stadium, he tastes mine, he says they're good, they're cheap, Demetrios, you can have the concession." He took a large swallow of wine and stared thoughtfully at the glass. "There are no short cuts, my boy. There is no substitute for hard work, I'm sad to have to tell you. I wish

I could tell you it's different, my boy. But that's life. Believe your old man, that's life." . . .

Ted liked all the games, but he especially liked football. He loved standing down at the rail and hearing the crunch of shoulder pads when the guys hit. Or seeing a kick or a pass. On the radio, baseball was more fun. But at the ball park you couldn't beat football. Sometimes there'd be as many as four different games a week, and he'd get to see them all—when, of course, he wasn't in the stands hawking red hots.

He loved playing football, too. During the fall, the kids played at recess and after school. The only problem was, he wanted to play tackling and the others would only play touch. They'd play tackling when he wasn't in the game, but they wouldn't play with him. They said he played dirty. What they meant was, he was too strong. It took three or four of them to tackle him when he had the ball, and none of them could ever get away from him when he came in to tackle.

He had never realized he was so strong. Maybe it came from lugging stuff around with his father. Or from eating so many red hots. Whatever it was, there wasn't a kid in his school that could beat him up—even the sixth graders, and some were a lot bigger than he. He couldn't wait till junior high. They played tackling there and even wore uniforms.

Touch was okay as long as he passed a lot. The only problem was, nobody would play if the good pass catchers were on his team. The best catchers were Tommy Ganahan and Mikey DeAngelico. Sometimes the three of them would play an imaginary team and just throw passes. Everybody was amazed at how far Ted could throw the ball. One day a man was walking through the playground and saw him throw. He asked him to throw again. He was a very tall man with a funny patch of white in the middle of his blond hair, and he spoke so softly you had to really listen to hear him. He showed Ted how to grip the ball to throw a bullet and how to set up with his weight on his right foot for more throwing power. Ted tried, and it worked. Before the man left, he wrote down Ted's name and address. He said he was a high school coach.

He told the boys his name, but after he left no one could remember it. Anyway, it felt good having a real coach like the way you passed. Ted hoped that when he was in high school he'd be good enough to make the team—*if* his father let him try out.

That night at dinner he told them about the coach. Demetrios Vassilikos regarded him with raised eyebrows. "Did he try anything funny, Theodoros?" He gestured toward the boy's genitals. "Did he try to touch you?"

Ted laughed. "Jeez, Pop, he wasn't queer. He was a *coach.*"

Demetrios patted him on the shoulder. "Don't think about coaches, Teddy. There are three kinds of people in this world. The ones that play the games, the ones that watch, and the ones that go to the games to work." He took a healthy swallow of wine, then patted his stomach and smiled. "Be like your old man. Go to the games to work, and you'll never have to worry about something to put in your belly."

"Some of the players get paid, Pop."

"The ones who don't get their heads broken first, maybe. No, my boy, listen to your old man. There are no short cuts in this life. I wish I could tell you otherwise, but sad to say, the whole thing is beyond my control." . . .

"Pop," Ted asked, "how much do they make you pay for each kid you bring into the stadium to sell red hots?"

"Nothing," Demetrios said.

"Then how come you bring only five?"

Demetrios's eyebrows rose, reflecting the puzzlement he would have felt if asked why the sun was hot or the sky blue. "Because I have only five steamer boxes. You ain't thinking about sneaking some of your friends in free, I hope. If you are, my boy, forget it. Demetrios Vassilikos doesn't operate that way."

"Who would it hurt?"

"Mr. Olman, who owns the stadium. And the teams that would've sold them tickets."

"But suppose they actually sell red hots like the rest of us? Nobody'd get hurt, and you'd make a lot more money."

Demetrios sighed patiently. "Theodoros, my boy, I have

five steamer boxes. That means five kids selling red hots. Otherwise you have cold red hots, and pretty soon you don't have customers no more."

"Buy more steamer boxes."

"I don't need them. One boy is enough for each section of bleachers, if he works hard enough." He smiled. "Now suppose you leave the business thinking to your old man, eh? You concentrate on getting up and down the stands and selling all you can."

Two games later Demetrios was astonished to find that Ted had sold eighteen dozen red hots. The following game, he sold twenty dozen; the next game, twenty-three dozen. Demetrios was kept so busy cooking and serving them that he didn't even have time to go into the stands to beam proudly at his suddenly industrious boy.

The pace continued for a month: twenty-five dozen, twenty-eight dozen, thirty dozen, thirty-three dozen. The incredulous Demetrios had to hire his assistant from the luncheonette to come up and help him at the grill. One night his brother George came from Pottsville to visit. The two men worked the concession stand during half time, then Demetrios turned things over to his assistant and took George to the stands to show off his enterprising son.

They found Ted sitting high in the bleachers, just off the fifty yard line, munching a red hot and sipping a Nehi. His steamer box was nowhere in sight. But three other boys with steamer boxes were fanning through the rows beneath him, hawking red hots to beat the band.

"Theodoros," intoned a dumbfounded Demetrios, "who are these boys? Where did they come from?"

"They rode in with us in the back of the panel," Ted said. "I figured it'd be okay as long I had steamer boxes for them."

"But where did you get the steamer boxes?"

"Mikey DeAngelico's father made them out of stuff we got in a junkyard. I got the idea that night when you sold a red hot to that guy that didn't buy one from me. People need to be reminded. The more sellers they see, the more they buy."

Demetrios couldn't decide whether he was furious or delighted until he saw his brother's reaction. George was laughing so hard there were tears in his eyes. "Oh, he's beautiful, Mitsos, just beautiful. You never have to worry about supporting yourself in your old age as long as you have that one around."

That night when they were cleaning up at the luncheonette Demetrios made Ted an extra-large chiliburger. "Well, Mr. Theodore D. Rockefeller," he said, toasting him with red wine, "I bet you think you're pretty smart."

Ted grinned. "You gotta admit we're selling lots of red hots."

Demetrios nodded, at the same time tapping his temple with an extended index finger. *"To kefali,"* he said. "You use it well, my boy. I never said you had to work with your hands. With the head, it's even better." . . .

The junior high tryouts were held a week before school started. Ted wouldn't have known about them if Mikey DeAngelico's mother hadn't read it in the paper. Ted, Mikey and Tommy Ganahan showed up together. They'd been practicing passing all summer.

The coach was a tall, mean-looking guy with a huge gut. His name was Baird Mueller, and everybody said he was a real prick. Ted had been excited about meeting him. Most of the great coaches were supposed to have been pricks. But Ted quickly got the feeling that Baird Mueller was a different kind of prick. He looked at you as though he thought you were dirt. It was one thing to be a prick because that was the best way to get your players to win. It was something else to think you were better than everybody.

Baird Mueller had one of his assistants line up all the guys who were trying out. He walked down the line looking at them, asking how much they weighed, sometimes feeling their muscles. "You're a tackle," he'd say as he went down the line. "You're an end, you're a guard, you're in the backfield."

"You're in the backfield," he said to Mikey DeAngelico. Then, patting Ted's shoulders and arms, he said, "You're a tackle."

"I'm a quarterback," Ted said. Gesturing with his head toward Mikey and Tommy Ganahan, he added, "They're ends."

Baird Mueller looked at him without saying anything, then continued down the line. After he had assigned everyone a position, an assistant coach designated areas of the field for the different units to practice. Ted went to the backfield area.

"Hey, wise guy," Baird Mueller said, "I thought I told you you're a tackle."

Ted smiled. "How about watching me throw a few passes?"

Baird Mueller's face, which was very pale to begin with, seemed to get even paler. He put his hands on his hips. "Kid, I give the orders around here. Everybody else obeys. The tackles are practicing over there, and the gate is over there. Take your pick."

Ted's impulse was to head for the gate, but he knew that would be the end of junior high football for him, so he joined the tackles. The ends were practicing nearby. One of Baird Mueller's assistants was telling them how to go out for a pass. "Go deep. Don't look back for the ball. Just keep your hands out in front of you and run as fast as you can. If you run fast enough, you and the ball will get there at the same time."

Ted ran a few blocking drills with the tackles, then got on line with the ends. He watched the assistant throw to the others. Each time, the ball was so far ahead that the receiver couldn't possibly catch it. And each time, the assistant pretended it was the receiver's fault for not running fast enough. Ted knew this wasn't true. The passes weren't going all that far. They were just being thrown too soon and not high enough. There was no way a receiver could get under them.

When his turn came, he started downfield before the center snapped the ball. He resisted the temptation to look back and continued running with both hands ahead of him. Seconds passed, and there was no ball. Then he heard a groan from the other ends and turned just in time to see the ball hit the ground a few feet behind him.

"You started too soon," the assistant yelled. "Nobody throws balls that far."

Ted calmly picked up the ball and threw it ten yards beyond the assistant, who was flabbergasted. "Let's see you do that again," he said, throwing the ball back. Again it landed short of Ted. Again Ted fired it over the assistant's head. As the assistant chased it, Ted looked around for Baird Mueller. Unfortunately, he had left for the day.

The next morning Ted, Mikey DeAngelico and Tommy Ganahan got to the field an hour before practice. They were dressed and throwing passes by the time everybody else got there. First Ted would throw to Mikey while Tommy defended, then to Tommy while Mikey defended. As the other players came out of the clubhouse, they gathered around to watch. So did Baird Mueller's assistants. Ted heard one of them say, "Jeez, this kid puts it thirty-five yards in the air."

Ted held back a smile. He could throw over forty in the air. During their summer practice sessions he, Mikey and Tommy had laid out yard markers. They'd made a rule that before they could quit practice each day, each receiver would have to go around-the-keyhole on passes, catching them at five-yard intervals from ten to forty and back. If one pass was dropped or misthrown, they'd have to start again from ten yards.

Ted continued to throw, pretending he was unaware of his audience. He fired two short bullets, having Mikey and Tommy cut in from the sidelines to catch them over what would be the center of the line. Then he sent Mikey long and fired a real bomb. It went almost forty-five in the air, hitting Mikey's fingertips high above his head while he was still running full stride. He pulled it in beautifully, took another couple steps downfield, then turned around and started back toward Ted. The players applauded, and Mikey, already a ham, bowed deeply to them.

Baird Mueller arrived just in time to see the show. "You," he said, pointing to Ted, "come here. What school are you transferring from?"

"Transfer? I was in grade school."

"Don't lie to me. You're only in the seventh grade?"

"Starting next week, yeah."

"How old are you?"

"Going on thirteen."

"Where's your birth certificate?"

"Jeez, I don't know if I even have one."

The coach walked away a few steps, then turned back.

"If you're over age, Vasley-goats, you're not gonna get away with it. I'm not playing any kid I'm not a hundred percent sure of. Before you suit up, your records are gonna be checked. Understand?"

Ted had no idea what he was talking about, but he nodded that he understood.

"Okay," said Baird Mueller, "you're practicing today at quarterback. Your buddies are practicing at ends." He turned to an assistant. "We can't have Vasley-goats playing quarterback in a lineman's jersey. Tomorrow suit him up in number thirteen—for luck." He started to walk away.

"Coach," Ted called.

Baird Mueller turned.

"The accent's on the last syllable. Vas-sil-li-*kos*."

"Vasley-goats," said Mueller, "you're gonna need all the luck you can get."

As he was leaving practice that afternoon Ted found his path blocked by a very tall man with a funny patch of white in the middle of his blond hair. "Hi," he said, extending his hand, "remember me?"

He looked familiar, but Ted couldn't remember from where.

"We met a couple years ago at the playground. I showed you some things about throwing a ball."

"Sure! The coach!"

"My name is Eddie Witkowski," he said. "I coach the Bombardiers. I see you've learned a lot more than I ever showed you."

Ted smiled. "I've been practicing a lot."

"I can see that. I hope you stay with it. I'd like having you on my team three years from now."

Ted laughed. "Save number thirteen for me. It just became my lucky number." . . .

"Is it true," asked Nan, "that you threw a touchdown pass your very first play from scrimmage?"

"In junior high? Yeah, as a matter of fact. Was my old man bragging on you while I was taking my shower?"

"No, I read it."

"Where?"

"The *New York Times*."

"Did they write something about me recently?"

"It was an old story. I read it at the library."

"How'd you happen to see it?"

"I checked you out. They have a complete file of newspapers, you know, cross-indexed by name and subject. It goes all the way back to the eighteen hundreds."

"You checked me out?"

"You're not angry, I hope."

"I'm flattered. You actually went to the trouble of looking in old newspapers?"

She smiled. "It was no trouble. It's all on microfilm. You just look in the card index for the name you want, then get a list of dates when stories appeared . . ."

"When did you do all this?"

"A couple of days after we met. It was a rainy day and I happened to be in the neighborhood anyway." She wanted to change the subject. "What else was it I read? Oh yes, you were the only player-owner-coach in the history of pro football?"

"It was one way to make sure I got my own way." He laughed. "Actually I was owner-coach for only a year, then I brought in Eddie Witkowski as coach and sold stock in the team to the players who wanted it."

"Witkowski was your high school coach, wasn't he?"

"Yeah."

"It was very nice of you to remember him."

"I wasn't being nice. He's one hell of a coach, as his record shows. I brought him in because I couldn't handle coaching and playing at the same time. A quarterback—any executive, for that matter—needs someone to evaluate his performance. If you rely on yourself for everything, your emotions can run away with you and lead you into crucial mistakes. When you're under the gun you want to be able to turn to someone and say, 'What am I doing wrong?' The trick is finding someone you can trust and knowing when to turn things over to him."

"One writer in the *Times* credited you with making football replace baseball as the national pastime."

"No, television did that. Baseball is exciting on the radio, when you're doing something else besides listening to the game, but it's too dull for TV. Football is perfect. The action is fast, and the camera can pick up things you normally wouldn't see from the stands. . . . On the other hand, maybe I'm just prejudiced."

"The *Times* story also said you originated things like having each player introduced personally over the loudspeaker as he came on the field."

"True, but I didn't do that for the fans, I did it for the players. Except for backs and receivers and an occasional stick-out defensive lineman or linebacker, players get very little personal recognition. I felt it would boost morale to have the announcer give each player's name, his home town, his college and his jersey number as the guy came on the field. That's also why I encouraged players to buy stock in the team. I wanted them to feel an intense personal involvement in how we made out, whether they sat on the bench or were all-pro."

"Does it feel strange to have all that behind you and still be a . . . relatively young man?"

"Hey, take that 'relatively' and shove it up your ass. Seriously, it doesn't feel one thing or another. Everything happened so long ago that thinking about it now is like thinking about a movie you saw."

"It must be more personal than that."

"I guess. But there's still a remoteness to it, a feeling that it all happened to someone else—someone you know very well, maybe, but not you yourself right now. It's strange, I grant you."

"That bowl game against Notre Dame when you got the nickname 'Instant Replay.' Does that seem remote?"

"Hey, you really did a research job on me, didn't you?"

"I came on that story by accident. My birthday is December thirty-first. On a lark I checked the stories of games played that day."

"You were *born* the year we played Notre Dame?"

She smiled. "Can I unshove that 'relatively'?"

"You've got a point, but please don't push it." He thought about the date. "Hey, how about old Hart Loomis screwing the tax collector even with his daughter's birth?" When she didn't laugh, he explained, "A baby is a tax deduction for the full year even if it's born on the last day."

"Oh, right, Daddy always kids me about my excellent timing. Actually I was a couple of weeks premature."

"Are you close, you and your father?"

"What? Oh, I guess so . . . though not the way you are with yours. We really get along very well, though . . ."

"Does he know we're seeing each other?"

"I've never mentioned it. Would you rather I didn't—I mean, with your being his client and all?"

"He mentioned that?"

"Well, he's mentioned that BankUS has a mortgage on Three-oh-five East. Why?"

"Nothing. I just wondered. It doesn't matter."

"I guess if we ever got serious it would have to come out—" She covered her mouth with two fingers, as if somehow that would prevent the words she'd just pronounced from escaping. "Now what in the world made me say that?" She was speaking as much to herself as to him. She was supposed to be the one terrified of getting involved. . . . "I'm sorry, Ted, I don't want you to feel I'm trying to make more out of this than there is—"

He took her in his arms. "Please don't apologize, I'm damn flattered you'd even consider it." *Flattered* . . . a bullshit hedge if he'd ever heard one. . . . He kissed her, which beat thinking peculiar thoughts. Then, abruptly, she backed away.

"What's the matter?"

"I'm not sure, I guess I'm a little afraid—"

"Of making a commitment? Don't be, I'm not asking for one."

She flashed a relieved smile. "Say, on the subject of fathers, didn't yours say something about making me a real frankfurter today?"

He looked at his watch. One o'clock. "Yeah, on to the treat of your life."

Munching the huge burger, she was inclined not to challenge that description. After lunch they took a ride to Harvey's Lake and rented a rowboat. As he rowed she asked, "Did I also read that you won more games than any quarterback in history?"

"Maybe, but I doubt it's still true. You know what's interesting, though? In the pros, which is what counts, my win record was only sixty percent."

"That seems low."

"Exactly. You remember that line about it's not whether you win or lose but how you play the game? To be accurate, it's not whether you win or lose but when. In the pros, every team beats every other team at one time or another. The secret is to win the ones that count."

"How do you manage that?"

"That's what separates the geniuses from the assholes." He smiled. "Seriously, it's mostly luck. You have to be prepared, of course. As old Pater Noster used to say at Penn State, eighty percent of luck is preparation. But that other twenty percent is all-important. Put two evenly matched teams together—and most pro teams are pretty evenly matched—it all hangs on who gets the breaks. The secret, I guess, if there is a secret, is keeping your poise when your luck is running bad. Staying cool, confident. Not letting anything break your concentration, giving the game your best and minimizing the damage the other guys inflict on you until your luck turns and you get a chance to do a number on them."

"You really like football, don't you?"

"I love it."

"Do you miss playing?"

"In the beginning I did. Now I rarely think about it."

"Why did you quit? You were at your prime—"

"That's why. If luck is eighty percent preparation, preparation is ninety percent ability. When you lose your stuff, it doesn't matter how hard you work, you're never going to cut it."

"But you didn't lose your stuff. I read about those games you played after you retired. A first-play touchdown three years in a row."

Ted laughed. "Timing again. You'll notice I didn't go back the fourth year. The secret is, quit before the other guys have a chance to figure out how much you lost."

"Do you think you've lost much?"

"Frankly, no. But I like walking out a winner. I remember back in junior high I played for this coach who was a real prick. Baird Mueller. He thought I was too cocky and wanted to teach me some humility. So he set up a little caper with two offensive linemen. We were playing a nonconference game against a real pushover team. After we took a fourteen-nothing lead, the linemen started letting their men in every time I went back to pass. I took one hell of a pasting. After six or seven sacks in a row, I figured out what was happening. My impulse was to coldcock Mueller and the linemen, then walk off the field. But with the win assured, that would be playing into their hands. Instead, I called another pass. When the defensive linemen came charging in, I handed one of them the ball and let him take off for a touchdown. Mueller almost shit. After the kickoff, I called another pass and did the exact same thing. Now it was a tied game. Mueller was ready to bust a gut. 'Okay,' I told him, 'get me some blocking and I'll put us back on the scoreboard.' He naturally pretended he hadn't set me up. But he knew I knew. And he knew I had him over a barrel because the backup quarterback wasn't worth shit. Well, Mueller called a time out and gave the line a pep-talk. Sure enough, they started blocking again, and I passed for another touchdown. Then I walked over to Mueller, decked him with an uppercut and walked off the field."

Nan winced.

"Anyway, I guess my point is that you're not really a winner unless you're in a position where you can say, 'Blow it out your ass, world,' and back it up. If you let the opposition dictate the rules, you're fighting with one arm behind your back and you'll lose every time. If you can set things up so that they fight on your terms, all you have to know is your own strengths . . . and weaknesses. But it's still a matter of timing. There are guys playing pro ball today who are older than I am. Ten years ago they were starting quarterbacks. Then they got bumped to backup, and now they're just holding the ball for field goals and extra points. By quitting when I did, I went out on top. In those three opening games, the only reason I scored first-play touchdowns was that the opposition was off balance. I dictated the terms of the action, and that gave me an advantage they couldn't overcome. But if I'd played the full game, or even one quarter, they'd have had time to figure out my weaknesses and exploit them. Now, thanks to those three freaky touchdowns, I think I could go back on the field today and play damn near a full game and still keep most of them off balance. The new guys wouldn't have me scouted, the old-timers wouldn't remember much more than the stories. With an offensive unit that was really together, I should be able to get three touchdowns on the scoreboard in the first quarter, which ought to be enough momentum to get me through the rest of the game. But if I played again the next Sunday I'd get creamed. Everyone would've had a full week to watch the game films, get a line on me, understand what I did and figure my weaknesses. Day in, day out, there's probably not a quarterback in pro ball today who can't outplay me. But as long as *I'm* dictating the terms, one time, I don't think there's a single one of them I can't take . . ." He smiled. "Just call me Ted Modest. I guess I got carried away."

"Please . . . when you talk football, you really bring to life a whole new fascinating world for me."

"Well, I think we've talked it to death for today. How about a swim?"

"I didn't bring a bathing suit."

"It's a couple miles from here to shore. I don't see anyone who'd hassle us."

She blushed. "No . . . you take a swim, I'll just lie here in the boat and enjoy the sun—"

"Then I'll lie here with you. Come on, at least let's take off some clothes." He stripped down to his shorts. She took off her jeans and, giving in to his urging, finally removed her halter. His eyes fixed to her breasts. There was a clear suntan line, but the bright pink of the untanned areas made it clear that they, too, had recently been exposed to the sun. "Hey, you've been going topless."

She blushed, despite wanting to seem very blasé about it. "Most of the girls do in Europe these days. It's not considered improper or anything. I just went along . . ."

"Hey, I'm not complaining. What beaches were you at?"

"I had a thirty-six-hour layover last flight so I went to Mykonos."

"I've been there too . . . Paradise Beach, by any chance?"

She nodded. Her blush deepened.

"Then you've been going bottomless too."

She instinctively tried to cover the front of her panties with her hands. And almost immediately . . . whether from frustration or curiosity or both . . . he reached for her, she drew away, and the sudden shifting of weight unbalanced the boat. Nan screamed and tried to compensate by leaning in the opposite direction. Ted leaned the same way, and the boat overturned.

He struggled, surfaced and looked for her. She was treading water ten yards away.

"Are you okay?"

"Yes, fine, I'm a good swimmer . . . did we lose anything?"

The oars were floating nearby, his shirt draped over one of them. A sock and one of Nan's sandals were floating near them. He quickly retrieved them.

"I got my jeans," she said.

"Which means we're missing my jeans, your halter, a sock, and three shoes."

She laughed. "Now you see the perils of being a sex maniac."

"Wrong. I see the perils of going rowing with a bashful nudist."

He dived for the missing items and managed to find his jeans and her other sandal. Then he righted the boat and started back to shore.

"What are we going to do?" she said. "I don't have a top."

He laughed. "Pretend we're in Mykonos." He tossed her his shirt. "Or, if you insist, wear this."

She wrung it out and put it on. "You think this is very funny, don't you?"

"Frankly, yes."

"You know something, so do I." Which, she decided, was progress.

Back at his parents' house, he gave his mother a bowdlerized explanation of their soaked condition, and then he and Nan showered. Afterward, in the bedroom, he opened her bathrobe and gazed at the bright pink flesh where she had removed her bikini bottom on Mykonos.

"It's gorgeous," he said. "It really drives me crazy."

"Why crazy?"

"I don't know. I guess innocent-looking girls who do sexy things just drive me crazy. Anyway, who cares why?" He knelt and kissed the pink flesh next to her pubic hair and could tell by the way she accepted him that she enjoyed it. He eased her toward the bed.

When she started to pull back for a moment he understood and quickly told her, "It's okay, I locked the door," and then guided her onto her back.

He knelt alongside the bed and kissed her thigh just above the knee, then licked his way up to her breast, covering the entire lovely pink surface, then going to her opposite side and reversing his route.

She said not a word, but something about the way she accepted his ministrations told him she was especially enjoying them. He decided to repeat himself, this time licking a path closer to the center of her body. He continued to narrow the distance until he was grazing her pubic hair. And then he started at her sternum and made his way to her vulva.

Ordinarily he wasn't much for oral sex, and sometimes it even turned him off. But today he really was up for it. Her acceptance of it, the immaculate cleanliness of her just-washed body, the beauty of it, the sexiness of her newly sunned pink flesh—all this made him want it as he never had before, even with Chris.

He lifted her legs over his shoulders and buried his tongue inside her. He licked her groin and the insides of her thighs. "Oh, Ted," she moaned, "that's so good." He did it a while longer, then got into sixty-nine position and reimmersed his tongue, at the same time using his chin to stimulate her clitoris.

"Oh, Ted," she gasped. He felt her fingers close around his cock. He felt her take it into her mouth.

He strained to get his tongue deeper inside her. The sweetness of her—the gentle fragrance, the subtle taste—was wildly exciting. And she was excited as he hadn't known her to be before. Her pubes rose to meet the pressures of his chin. Her legs tensed. She was pumping against him. He drove his tongue deeper. She pumped harder. And then her whole body tensed . . . slapping against his, once, twice, half a dozen times . . . more . . . and she groaned—so loudly he suspected this time his mother had heard. And then, finally, she went slack.

He silently repositioned himself and entered her. She

waited till he established his rhythm, then moved against it. It took less than a minute for him to come.

"Well," he said, lying next to her afterward, "you had a real one that time, didn't you."

"Mmm-hmm." She smiled.

"Have I discovered your secret?"

"It's no secret." She blushed. "I mean, it's not just oral sex that did it for me today. It was the whole day—talking with you about your life, falling into the water, going to the stadium, being with your family last night . . ." She hesitated, then frowned. "Oh, let's not talk about it."

"I'll drink to *that*. Let's just do it, and do it, and do it."

As they drove back to New York she found herself thinking that being with Ted was more than just another pleasant experience. She really did care for him. Maybe she could even love him. Now if only there were some way to divide, or divert, his sex drive . . . no, she admonished herself, don't try to change him. Accept him as he is or reject him. Well, she could accept him, his sexual demands weren't intolerable . . . just sort of annoying. Actually it wasn't so much his demands as his expectations. He was so damn hung up on her coming all the time. Male ego, she guessed. By this time she ought to be used to it . . . well, at least she should be able to handle it. And really, she should be flattered that he found her so attractive. Maybe after they'd spent more time together he'd cool off some. . . . And meanwhile, if he didn't get too dependent on her, not demand that she be with him every waking hour . . . and she not back off when things became too, well, close—yes, if they could just keep things as they were. . . .

Ted had his own thoughts. No question, she excited him in a way no one had since Chris. Now the trick would be not to smother her, not to drive her away with his horniness. Yes, he'd need to play it cool. Of course, it was a pain in the ass to have to play games, but he knew from bitter experience what happened when he didn't. He wound up with his dick in hand, that's what happened. And Nan was just too perfect to risk losing . . . someone he couldn't get enough of, and yet at the same time didn't involve him too deeply. Getting involved was something he doubted he was ready for . . . even after all these years. Unless, eventually, he and that little loving friend of his . . .

Grace could not believe that it was all really happening. It surpassed all her dreams, her fantasies of out-of-this-world luxury and elegance.

They flew first class to Paris. She'd flown only once before, an Easter break round trip to Miami. She'd had stand-by reservations and had had to wait a day and a half at Newark Airport for a seat. Now she walked past the long queues of tourist-class travelers to the first-class check-in station, surrendered her bag and ticket to an impeccably polite young man with a charming French accent, and was assigned a seat as wide as a living room chair. A steward brought her a newspaper and then a glass of champagne.

Joseph arrived about fifteen minutes later. (They went to the airport separately because his wife was seeing him off.) They kissed and toasted each other while waiting for takeoff. Once airborne, they were served a fine dinner. He'd made reservations in the upstairs dining room, whose skylight permitted them to look out at the stars. After dinner they watched a movie, then she fell asleep in his arms.

He woke her to see the sunrise. It was magnificent. As the darkness thinned, tinges of red and orange took form on the horizon. Then the whole sky was suffused with color, and finally the blinding yellow sphere eased into view. She napped again, waking as they neared the Scottish coast. She stared fascinated at the land masses that passed slowly beneath the plane, amazed that she was able to make out the same shapes she'd seen on maps.

At Orly Airport an airline agent brought them to a special customs station for V.I.P.'s. A limousine was waiting outside. They were taken to the George V, where they had a suite that reminded her of the rooms she had seen in photos of Louis XIV's palace at Versailles.

After lunch Joseph rehearsed the orchestra and singers as Grace sat in the opera house marveling at his command, frankly thrilled to be with him. Later they had dinner with the manager of the opera and his wife at Tour d'Argent. Wherever she went, people addressed her as *madame*. Not *mademoiselle*. *Madame*—she was the maestro's lady.

The next morning before he left for rehearsal he made an appointment for her with a designer. "I obviously didn't give you time to shop for this trip," he said. "There are three performances, so I suggest you select three gowns. You'll need four or five street outfits too." He put his finger to her lips. "No arguments, please. Decide what you want and take it."

"I won't need three gowns," she said. "I brought along the one you bought me for *Don Carlos*."

"Then by all means wear it. It's lovely. But get three anyway. After all, there's no law against bringing the third back to New York unworn."

She attended one more rehearsal, then, on his suggestion, spent mornings and afternoons at the Louvre, the Madeleine, the Eiffel Tower and Versailles. On their last evening they stayed up till dawn, going from the opera to a supper club to a sidewalk café to a discotheque to another discotheque to a brasserie for the traditional Paris nightcap of onion soup gratinée in the area that used to be Les Halles. Afterward they giddily walked the boulevards near the George V until it was time to get ready for their return flight.

As the plane began its descent into Kennedy Airport she took his hand. "Joseph, there's absolutely no way I can tell you how much this trip has meant to me. I know it sounds corny, but I honestly think if I had to die at this moment I'd have no complaints."

He kissed her. "Fortunately, dearest Grace, that's not a likely prospect. But looking forward to more of the same is." As the plane taxied to the terminal he told her about his plans for the party for the defendants in the Indian trial. "I'd certainly like you to be there. And considering that Maria saw you with Ted Vassily at John Malloy's cocktail party—it might be convenient if I invited him, assuming he'd bring you. Of course if you'd prefer some other arrangement—"

"Oh, no, that's okay. I think it probably would be best with Ted. Assuming, of course, he wants to go with me. I'll ask him and get back to you."

The plane had come to a halt now, and Joseph kissed her. "Dearest Grace, I can't imagine what I would do without you." And saying it, he was astonished to realize that he almost meant it.

"Are you sore at me or something?" Buffy asked.

"Why should I be?"

"You haven't called in a couple weeks."

"You know how it is, babes. Busy schedule and all that."

"Too busy to see an old friend?"

Spats hesitated. Should he tell her the truth or wait to see if the action was worth swallowing the anger he'd felt since she snubbed him for the *acceptable* nigger at John Malloy's party.

"I was shopping today and I bought this perfectly super pair of brown and beige saddle shoes. Interested?"

No time for false pride, he decided. "I might be."

"I just got in. Give me fifteen minutes."

She arrived at his penthouse wearing the shoes, bobby sox, a short brown skirt and a beige sweater. He fucked her the first time on the floor, just beyond the elevator doors. The second time it was on a reclining chair while she still had on everything but her panties. They managed a third in bed before falling asleep and number four when they woke in the middle of the night. The fifth was in the morning before she left for work.

"You may have heard about the Indians I'm defending," she said just after the fourth. "They'll be in New York early next month for press interviews. How are chances of getting them on your TV program?"

"Hey, babes," he said, "you know you don't need to ask. I'm all heart, just like you."

NINE

NATE ELEFANTE was not accustomed to getting phone calls from girls. Even in his prime, which would have been at Michigan State or his first couple of years in the pros, he had to beat the bushes for every whiff of cunt he got. Accordingly, when he answered his phone and a girl with a sexy voice told him she'd like to meet him, he not unreasonably suspected she had dialed the wrong number.

"My name's Elefante," he said. "Nate Elefante."

"I know. I'm Debbie Wilson. I've heard lots of nice things about you. Why don't you invite me out for a drink?"

Nate now more than suspected that one of his buddies had put her up to it. Either that or she was a real loser. Still, business was never so good that he could afford to turn stuff away.

She suggested that they meet at a cocktail lounge on Second Avenue. He arrived expecting the worst—and could not believe his eyes. She was a knockout. Long red hair, green eyes, a tight orange dress that showed off a great set of jugs and an ass that wouldn't quit.

She sat close to him in the booth and ordered a whiskey sour. "You look even better in person than on TV," she said.

"When did you see me on TV?"

"The night they had that party. You looked so handsome with your tuxedo on." She tickled him under the goatee. "I really go for big men. I took one look at you and said, 'That's for me.' "

"Who told you about me?"

"Let's just say a little bird did."

"A little bird, huh?"

"Yeah, like this one." She reached between his legs. "Only this bird isn't so little, is it? No siree."

"Listen," he said, draining his drink, "what say we finish these off and I'll mix a couple fresh ones at my place?"

She brought her mouth to his ear and touched him lightly with her tongue. "I thought you'd never ask."

She gave him the wildest session he'd ever had. It started with straight screwing. Then she went into the kitchen and came back with a cloth and a pot of hot water. "A man like you shouldn't have to do anything for himself," she said. "He should have a slave to take care of everything, even to wash him." She wet the cloth, wrung it out, then sponged his cock. "Do you have any brandy?"

"Sure." He started to get up.

She pushed him back down. "I'm your slave. Just tell me where it is."

He directed her to the liquor cabinet. She returned with about an ounce in a whiskey glass, spilled a few drops on his belly, then licked them off. "I love brandy this way. It's much better than in a glass." She spilled a few more drops closer to his genitals. "Mmmm, you like the way this feels, don't you?" She touched his stiffening cock. "Yes, you certainly do."

She spilled more brandy, letting it trickle into his groin before licking it. Then she dipped the head of his penis into the glass and licked it.

"This," said Nate truthfully, "is not to be believed."

"Yes, my master likes the way his slave treats him, doesn't he?"

"You know it, babes, you know it . . ."

She continued to dip, spill and lick until the brandy was gone. Then she took his penis in her mouth and one testicle in each hand.

After about a minute he told her, "I can't hold off much longer . . ."

"Come in my mouth. I want to swallow it."

Afterward she sponged him again, then lay next to him. "You're so good," she said, "you're just fantastic."

"Me? It's you that's doing all the work."

"I'm supposed to. I'm your slave, remember?"

After a while she looked at her watch and told him she had to leave for work. She was, she said, a cocktail waitress in a lounge on the West Side.

"Why don't I meet you after work?" Nate said.

"Sure, if it's not too late for you. I get off at three."

He grinned. "Debbie, for somebody like you, no time is too late."

They got together that night and the next and another after that. Nate could scarcely believe his luck. He could see himself falling in love with her. At the very least they would do a long-term sex thing.

After they had been seeing each other for a few weeks she asked if he and Ted Vassily were friends.

"Friends?" Nate laughed. "Baby, there ain't no better friends in the world."

She seemed to think he was bluffing, so he told her about their years and years of friendship. "I used to be his protector. Ain't nobody ever got by me to tackle him. He had the lowest record of sacks in the league four years in a row. If you ever went to a game when we were playing, you'd see where I stood with him."

He told her about how the announcer would introduce team members individually as they came on the field—first the bench-warmers, in the order of their jersey numbers; then the starting defense and offense, in order of playing position; then the co-captains; then Ted himself.

"There were four co-captains. Jerry Janowski on defense, and me, Mikey DeAngelico and Emerson Wade on offense. I got introduced last—right next to Ted. They didn't do it by position or jersey number or any of that. Ted picked the order himself. Now when you consider that Emerson Wade was with him all the way through Penn State and Mikey DeAngelico from junior high, but I got announced last, right next to him—well, that should tell you how close friends we are."

Debbie said, "A friend of mine thinks he's a real hunk. Any chance you can fix them up?"

"Sure. She's gotta be good-looking, of course."

"She is."

"I mean really good-looking, not just average. He's very fussy about that."

"What type does he like? The fashion model look? The *zaftig* type?"

"He likes them skinny with big tits."

"That's my girl friend exactly. He'll love her."

Nate seemed dubious.

"I'll tell you what," Debbie said. "The two of us can meet the two of you for cocktails. We'll have a drink together and he can check her out. If he doesn't dig her, he can split. No hard feelings. Fair enough?"

Nate conveyed the message. Ted was hesitant. He wasn't much for chasing after blind dates who might turn out to be turkeys—an ever-present possibility when Nate was doing the fixing. But Nan was away on another damn six-day flight, and lately Grace seemed to be very involved in politics and music. What the hell, it was worth risking a wasted couple of hours to help Nate out with his own action.

As they sat in the cocktail lounge on Second Avenue waiting for the girls, Joe Mandino walked in. He looked about as if hunting for someone he was supposed to meet, did a double-take when he saw Nate and Ted, and went over to their table. "An unexpected pleasure, gentlemen." He offered his hand. "May I buy you a drink?" Without waiting for an answer, he sat and motioned to a waiter.

"We're waiting for friends," Ted said.

"I'll leave as soon as they arrive. Meanwhile, there's no harm in a neighborly drink, eh?" Nate rose protectively. Ted signaled him to relax. The Mandino thing had been hanging fire for too long. Might as well get it out in the open.

The waiter appeared. Joe ordered a round. "You know, Mr. Vassily, I'd like to be one of your friends. But you don't seem to want my friendship."

Ted chose his words carefully. "There are responsibilities in friendship, Mr. Mandino. At the moment, I've got all the responsibilities I want to take on."

"Maybe if you had the right friends it would take some of the responsibilities off your shoulders. Your people and mine—the Greeks, the Italians—we don't have the advantages of some other Americans. We have to work twice as hard to accomplish the same thing. But if we help each other out the same way the old-line Wasps do or the Jews, we can make life a little easier."

"I've never found it a disadvantage to be Greek."

"No? Then why change your name from Vassilikos?"

"Mr. Mandino, you seem to know an awful lot about me."

"It's a matter of public record. You played as Vassilikos in high school."

"What makes my public record so interesting to you?"

"I think you're going to be hugely successful. I'm an investor. I'd like to invest in your success."

"Thanks, but I prefer to go it alone—"

"That's not true. You've got investors in Three-oh-five East—BankUS, for one. What makes Hartford Loomis's money better than mine?"

"Not better, just"—he wondered whether to say it and decided that the time for bluntness had come—"cleaner."

Joe smiled. "If you knew as much about Loomis as I do, you might change your mind."

"I've never heard of his mortgagees winding up in the East River with their feet in cement."

"Are you saying mine do? Mr. Vassily, you disappoint me. You know nothing about me, and yet you make these outrageous accusations."

"Yeah, I went through the whole thing with your lawyer." The waiter appeared with the drinks. Ted took a large swallow of Scotch. "Look, Mr. Mandino, I have nothing against you personally and certainly nothing against Italo-Americans. To coin a cliché, some of my best friends . . . and one of them happens to be sitting next to me right now. But he's never been identified by the *New York Times* as Manhattan superboss of the Mafia, and you have. The Open Housing Act of nineteen-whatever may say I have to rent you an apartment, but it doesn't say I have to be your friend."

The muscles in Joe's eyelids tightened almost imperceptibly. His voice remained low and very calm. "What's the Mafia, Mr. Vassily? I'm not aware that such an organization exists."

"Yeah, your lawyer told me. But the police say it does and you're one of the guys who runs it. They've never been able to convince a jury, but in my personal dealings I'm not bound by the test of reasonable doubt. A prima facie suspicion is enough."

"You use legal terms very well, Mr. Vassily." Joe smiled patiently. "But you're not too consistent. This alleged organization you're so troubled about—this so-called Mafia"—he pronounced it *Maff*-ee-a, and his smile broadened to accent the deliberate error—"what does this organization do? Bribe politicians? Defraud the public? Make under-the-table deals to force out legitimate competitors?"

"For starters."

"You've got your organizations mixed up, Mr. Vassily. That's not the Maff-ia. It's big oil, big steel, big airlines." He chuckled dryly. "Does this Maffia traffic in drugs? Does it order the murder of its enemies? Does it violate federal and state laws with impunity—and the laws of countries throughout the world? You're not talking about the Maffia, Mr. Vassily, you're talking about the C.I.A." Mandino leaned across the table, fixing Ted with an intense stare. "Mr. Vassily, there's not one crime of which the Maffia has been accused that hasn't been committed in recent years by leading figures in the U.S government or the business community. The difference is, the so-called respectable criminal has power so that he doesn't get caught, or if he does, like a certain late ex-president, there's always some club member waiting in the wings to sign a pardon. And then a day later he goes out and makes a speech about how important it is to stamp out organized crime."

Ted remembered saying something not so different himself recently. "I never said the country is perfect, Mr. Mandino. But it still gives every citizen certain constitutional rights, including freedom to associate—or not associate."

Joe sighed. "I'm not getting through to you. Don't you understand what I'm trying to say? There *is* no Maffia today—no organized-crime syndicate. It's all a myth, promoted by the politicians to play on the fears of the public. The late J. Edgar Hoover, your friend Malloy's brother—they all built their careers fighting something that does not exist. Sure, there was a syndicate back in the twenties, with fellows like Bugsy Siegel, Meyer Lansky, Mickey Cohen, maybe even an Italo-American or two like Al Capone. But Capone's old moonshining business has been legit for years. Lansky's old numbers racket has become the state lottery. There's no real money in crime today. You remember that line from *The Godfather*, 'A lawyer can steal more with his briefcase than any man with a gun'? It's true." He took a long swallow of his drink. "I'm no saint, Mr. Vassily. I won't say I might not be tempted to get into crime if it was as profitable as people think and if the doors of legitimate business were still closed to my people as they once were. But things have long since changed. You don't have to shoot people today. It's cheaper to buy them."

"And you want to buy me."

Joe smiled. "I want to invest in you."

"I translate that as 'buy,' Mr. Mandino, and I'm not for sale. Now I'm getting tired of this conversation. I hate to be rude, but we're past standing on ceremony, so why don't I just ask you to leave?"

"I will, Mr. Vassily. But before I do, let me make one point. You've already been bought by the Ron-Cor Corporation. They paid dearly—more than you realize. But let a few things happen that they expect to happen, and they'll get it all back and then some." He smiled at Ted's expression of renewed interest. "You made a spectacular publicity smash with Three-oh-five East, but in strictly business terms it's not such a big success. Your balance sheet is highly leveraged. Any one of several misfortunes could cut your income and force you into default. As the bankers correctly pointed out to you and your investors at your meeting in the Tuscany, the subsidized apartments force you to charge unrealistic rents for the other ones. Let something happen that makes it no longer fashionable to live at Three-oh-five East, or something that reduces your ability to deliver the current level of services, or let the national economy take a sharp downturn, you could be out of business overnight."

Ted was stunned. "Where'd you get your information about the meeting at the Tuscany?"

"Come on, Mr. Vassily. I protect my sources. That way they can trust me, and I can trust them. But I'll tell you something else. It wasn't an accident that you had to turn to Ron-Cor for money. And they didn't give it to you, or incur their many other expenses on your behalf, just to earn a few hundred thousand in interest."

"What other 'expenses'?"

"The building inspector you beat up. They had to grease a lot of palms to get that cooled down. Or the union thing. You don't think the New York building trades caved in just because you threatened to hold Eddie Fassnacht's head underwater in a toilet full of shit, do you?" Joe laughed. "You don't want to tangle with the Maffia, Mr. Vassily, but you came riding into town like Jesse James. People who live in glass houses shouldn't throw rocks. Anyway, Ron-Cor has been helping to pull your chestnuts out of the fire from the day you got here."

Ted tried to conceal his astonishment by staring into his drink. "To hear you talk, Mr. Mandino, I might get the impression you're intimately involved with Ron-Cor."

"As I said, Mr. Vassily, I never reveal my sources. But if I were with Ron-Cor, would I tell you any of this?"

"You said it wasn't an accident I had to get money from Ron-Cor. Are you saying the banks deliberately boosted their equity demands to force me into it?"

Joe smiled. Cocksure hotshot Ted Vassily didn't sound so cocky for a change. "Maybe not the banks themselves, like by a resolution brought to the board of directors. But officers of a bank have some discretion . . ."

"Why would officers of two huge institutions like BankUS and Chase set me up for Ron-Cor?"

"Mr. Vassily, for a big-deal strategist on the football field, you sound pretty naïve about the business world. Suppose officers at these institutions happened to have a personal financial interest in Ron-Cor. Or don't go that far—suppose just one officer at one bank had a stake in the company. Wouldn't it be simpler to let the competing bank know his reasons for demanding more equity?—reasons that make sound business sense."

"Are you telling me that's actually what happened?"

"Draw your own conclusions."

"If Three-oh-five East is such a lousy investment for the banks, why did Ron-Cor offer to buy as much stock as I wanted to sell?"

"They knew you'd want to sell as little as possible. If you'd made more than a few percent available, they'd have withdrawn their offer."

"But why take even a few percent? What's their interest in the building?"

"They're not interested in the building, they're interested in you. Just as I am. Don't you see, Mr. Vassily, you do have a tremendous ability to put a project together and attract lots of favorable publicity. Your building is up now. You're not going to stop there, are you? You'll build another. Or you'll try another kind of venture. The idea was that if you got along with Ron-Cor the first time, you'd be willing to play ball again, right? Only next time they'll want a little more control and they'll want to pay a little less for it. If you go along, fine, they've bought a partner. If you don't go along, they'll wait for Three-oh-five East to go under, which eventually it will—maybe not this year, maybe not next, but soon enough. When it does, they'll take it over, sell out to a dummy corporation, take a nice tax loss, throw out the poor people, turn the apartments into condominiums and sell them for a fat profit. It all happens very legal, no boom-boom, no broken noses, no bodies in the East River. And that's why the so-called Maffia is out of business."

Ted stared at his glass. "So what's your advice, Mr. Mandino? Dump Ron-Cor and tie in with you?"

"No, my advice is to dump Three-oh-five East while it's still popular. Sell it to some big real estate outfit and walk away with the cash. Or do what Ron-Cor would do—turn the building into condominiums and walk away with even more cash."

"I didn't build Three-oh-five East to turn a quick buck."

"I know. You also didn't build it to lose your ass. But you will if you don't unload fast enough. I know how these newspaper pricks are, Mr. Vassily. You should too, from when you played ball. They praise you to the skies for a while, then they get pissed off that people believe what they wrote. So now they have to tear you down. They'll watch Three-oh-five East like the vultures they are, waiting for something they can hang on you. It won't even have to involve you personally, as long as it smears the building's name. Once they find it, they'll hack away.

You'll be lucky if you get out with your jockey shorts." He shook his head sadly. "So my advice to you, Mr. Vassily, is to get out now. If you won't do that, get out the first time you read something bad about yourself in the papers. From then on, it'll be all downhill."

"Sorry, *Mister* Mandino, that's *not* why I built Three-oh-five East. It also isn't my style. It's yours."

Joe drained his glass, stared at it as if contemplating whether to order a refill, then put it aside. "I know, Mr. Vassily. Which is why I don't expect you to take my advice. But I want you to remember what I've said. Sometime in the future you may decide to explore a relationship with a man of my business judgment and connections. If so, I'll be happy to hear from you." He pushed his chair back. "One more point, then I'll leave. From the very beginning I've tried to be sensitive to your situation and the problems you face. As a tenant I had the right to attend your grand-opening party, but I stayed in my apartment and watched on TV because I didn't want to embarrass you or create problems for the building by calling public attention to the fact that notorious Joe Mandino lives there. It's an outrage that such a stigma should attach to someone who has never been convicted of even a parking violation, but that doesn't make the stigma go away, does it? I'm aware of it, and I'm careful never to compromise my friends." He stood. "I know you've had your troubles over the years with people who represented themselves as part of a crime syndicate. I know about your uncle's problems years ago in Pottsville and what happened when you were in college. I know about a few other things too. But Mr. Vassily, take it from me, eighty percent of the punks in this country who want to scare people say they're part of a syndicate. If there was a national crime syndicate, one thing you could be sure of is the people in it wouldn't admit it. As they say about political gossip, those who know don't talk and those who talk don't know." He touched his head as if tipping a hat, then went to the bar.

Nate faced Ted in complete bewilderment. It was the longest Ted could remember Nate keeping quiet.

"Well," Ted said, "whoever's doing his research is pretty damned good."

Nate nodded. "Jeez, he knew shit that nobody knew but you and me—"

"And I didn't tell anyone."

"Well—hey, now wait a minute, Reep. You don't think I did!"

"Of course not."

"Wow, you had me going there for a minute. . . . But if he didn't get it from us, where the hell did he get it?"

"I don't know." Ted didn't want to talk about it now. He wanted to think it out privately—or maybe with Emerson Wade. "Well," he said, making a production of looking at his watch, "where are those ladies of yours we're supposed to party with?"

Nate checked his own watch. "Jeez, Reep, I dunno." He finished his drink and motioned to a waiter. "Reep, getting back to that other thing—you think Mandino might be right about dumping Three-oh-five East?"

"You getting tired of being superintendent, Nate?"

"Hell, no. But if he's right that things are gonna turn around—"

"There's only one way I'd consider selling, Nate. If things ever got to the point where you guys stood to lose money—you, Emer, Mikey, the coach—then I'd dump in time to let you out with at least what you put in."

"Oh, shit, now that's not why I brought it up."

"I know. I'm just telling you." He really didn't want to talk about it now. Where the hell were—

And as if on cue, they appeared. Nate beamed as they came through the door. Ted's was gorgeous. Better looking than his own.

The girls came to the table. Nate ordered drinks. The rest of the scene played out for Ted as it had dozens, perhaps hundreds, of times. Talk a little about football. Talk a little about what you're doing now. Laugh a little, drink a little. Talk about where everybody is from and where everybody lives. Order another round. Talk a little more, laugh a little more. Raised eyebrows from Nate to Ted. A nod from Ted to Nate. "Hey, everybody"—this from Nate—"you wanna see a dynamite pad?"

That next phase proceeded routinely. Admire the decor, admire the view. A little music, a little more to drink. Hug, kiss. More booze. Now a heavy make-out on the couch.

Ted found himself thinking that his girl—what was her name—Cindy? Sandy?—was really pretty decent. Good tits, nice ass, great legs—long and well-muscled like a dancer's. Too bad his other preoccupations kept him from concentrating fully on her.

"That feels good," he told Cindy-Sandy, who had her mouth against his ear and was making sexy, crackling sounds with her lovely wet tongue. She really was okay, he told himself. Easy to get along with. Of course she had asked for this fix-up.

"Hey, that's some body you have," she said when they'd stripped down in his bedroom.

He slapped his gut, and then, as much to himself as to her, said, "I've got to get rid of this. Maybe now that the building's set, I'll join a gym or build my own in the basement . . ."

"It must be nice to be able to build your own. I mean —you know—to do whatever you want."

"Yeah." He moved to cut off the talk, which he'd had one night's fill of, courtesy of Joe Mandino. "Let's get along with what we're here for."

He was pleased that he had no trouble whatever getting it up. She had great hand movements, and then she popped down and gave great head. Terrific tongue action, great capacity—she almost managed to deep-throat him, a not inconsiderable feat, given his dimensions.

He let her suck until he was approaching the danger zone, then mounted her and used short strokes that minimized glans friction so he could cool off while working her up to her orgasm. It didn't take long. She had a good one, judging from her movements and groans. He pressed hard at her clit to maximize her sensation, then, as her movements slackened, he went for his own, and she never eased off until she knew he was drained.

It felt nice to team up with someone who knew all the moves. Sort of like running pass patterns for the first time with some really practiced receivers.

"You're an incredible lover," she said.

"Same to you. More Scotch?" he asked her.

"I still have some." She showed her glass.

He emptied his own, opened the night table, broke out

some ice cubes and dropped them into his glass. He freshened his drink, took a long draught and got back into bed. He guided her body into place alongside his, kissed her, lay back on the pillow and promptly fell asleep.

When he woke it was dark and she was shaking him. "Hey, I gotta get going. Time out for work."

"Okay, sure, I'll get up and—"

"It's all right, I can let myself out." He noticed she was dressed. "I just wanted to say goodbye. Thanks for a lovely time."

"Oh, yeah. It was great. I mean, thank you too . . . I'll give you a call."

She found a piece of paper, scribbled her number on it, kissed him and said, "Thanks again. 'Bye." She turned off the light.

He lay back and listened to her making her way out. She was really a decent chick. Just like the old days. Joe Mandino and nostalgia. What a night . . .

His thoughts drifted back to the scene at the cocktail lounge. The girls had been half an hour late . . . they'd come in right after Mandino had left the table. Not that such a coincidence was beyond belief, chicks were often late, particularly easy-fuck types. Still . . .

He dialed Nate's apartment, hoping he wouldn't be interrupting anything.

"Hell, no," Nate reassured him. "She left a couple hours ago. I'd've called you but I thought you might still be at it."

"Let's get something to eat," Ted said. They walked down Second Avenue toward the Golden Coach. "Did your girl ever tell you how she got your phone number?" Ted asked.

Nate thought a moment. "No, but I'm in the book."

"Was she late the other times you met her?"

"I dunno. A little, maybe."

"How do you suppose Mandino happened to walk into the lounge exactly when he did?"

"I dunno. Maybe he hangs out there." Nate frowned. "Hey, Reep, you don't think I set you up for him."

"You, hell no. The ladies, maybe yes."

"But—I've been seeing Debbie for, how long now? A month? Jeez, you think the whole thing's a setup? Like, they're hookers working for Coffee Joe?"

Ted shrugged.

"Would he go through all that just to make a meeting seem accidental?"

"I don't know."

"If I find out Debbie was using me that way, I'll—"

"What's her place like?"

"I never was there. She always came to mine."

"Where does she work?"

"Some cocktail lounge on the West Side."

"You don't remember the name?"

"I don't think she ever told me. You know how it is, Reep. Who thinks of this kind of shit when you're getting laid?"

"You have her phone number?"

"Jeez, I don't think I ever took it. We always made plans for our next date before we said goodbye on the last one." He sighed. "Oh, man, did I let myself get suckered into something?"

Ted took a slip of paper from his pocket. At the next street pay phone he dialed Cindy-Sandy's number. A recorded message told him that the number was out of service.

"Well," he told Nate, "the next move is up to them."

When he got back to the apartment he telephoned Emerson Wade. "Do you still go jogging every morning before work?"

"Without fail, Replay. Otherwise I might develop the kind of pot belly certain colleagues have acquired of late. Care to join me?"

"Yeah. Tomorrow morning."

They met at six-thirty in Central Park. "I wanted to talk out here instead of on the phone or at the office," Ted said. "I may be getting paranoid, but I don't want to take the chance that our conversation might be bugged." He told everything that had happened with the girls and Mandino. "Well," he concluded, "we wondered what was on Coffee Joe's mind. Now we know. Correction—we know what he wants us to believe is on his mind."

Wade thought about it. "I've put this question before—is it possible he's acting in good faith?"

"You mean he only wants to invest in us legitimately?"

"It's not impossible."

"Where's he getting his inside information about our operation? Nate?"

"Impossible."

"I don't mean he'd cross us deliberately. But you know how he likes to brag. If the right girl played him the right way, he might have been conned into spilling some beans without realizing it. Mandino certainly knew stuff that I thought only Nate and I knew—"

"Forget it. Maybe the two of you were the only ones who knew all of it first-hand, but lots of people knew parts of it. A few—I'm among them—knew all of it second-hand. Remember, I turned you onto Ron-Cor. If there's a honkie in the woodpile, heh-heh-heh, maybe he ain't a honkie after all."

"Cut the crap, Emer."

"I'm only trying to put things in perspective. Maybe everything is as sinister as you think, and then again, maybe you're being overly suspicious. Maybe Mandino pieced the story together from several sources—the union, the bankers, somebody in Ron-Cor—"

"He's competing with Ron-Cor. Or so he says."

"Maybe there's a honkie in *their* woodpile. Or maybe Joe doesn't know as much as it seems. Maybe he had some inside dope on just two or three things and guessed the rest."

"That'd be one hell of a lot of smart guessing."

"Some guys are good at it. . . . Look, my point is, don't worry so much about it. You'll only immobilize yourself. If you get real evidence of a threat, act then."

"That's a good way to get caught flat-footed."

"On the other hand, you can overdefend and waste your energies."

"You're right. Still, there seems to be too much happening to be entirely explained away by coincidence."

"Hard to say, Reep. I remember when we were at Penn State. There was this white girl I was crazy about. It took two weeks to work up the courage to ask her for a date.

When we went out, I was so shook up I didn't even try to lay her. But before I kissed her goodnight—lips tightly closed, a real chastity number—I asked to see her again the following Saturday, and she said yes. Hosannah . . . I was riding on air. Then, come Thursday, she phones to cancel. She says this old boyfriend has suddenly asked her to marry him and they're going to elope. Obviously a phony story. How transparent can you be? I tied myself in knots theorizing about what I might have done to sour her. Was she having second thoughts about dating a black? Or was she down on me for not being more sexually aggressive? I thought and thought and came up with a good twenty or thirty reasons why she'd canceled. It turned out they were all wrong. She did elope with the old boyfriend, and that was the last Penn State—or I—ever saw of her."

"I think my speculations are a bit less remote—Mandino, Jeannie Danton, Hartford Loomis, Ron-Cor . . ."

"Less remote, but still . . . let's not overdefend." He laughed. "That's one of the things I really miss about football—the clarity of it. You know who the opposition is, you know where the goal is, you know what you have to do. All you have to work out is how."

They were at the Ninety-sixth Street cutoff. His wind, he realized, wasn't what it should be. Damn it.

"Want to make the full circuit?" Emerson asked. "In case you forgot, that hill on the other side of the swimming pool is a real bitch."

"I'll take the cutoff."

Ted slowed his pace as Emerson continued along the bike road. He definitely was out of shape. Too much booze, too many late nights. It took a good run to show how much of your stuff you'd lost. Especially a run with a guy like Emer. The guy was a goddamn gazelle.

Ted really would have to get himself together. Maybe in a couple of weeks, when some of the pressure eased. No, not in weeks—now. A man who can't control his body can't control much else. A man who can't control his body belongs back in Nanticoke-goddamn-Pennsylvania sitting in a saloon pouring draft beer down his gullet and bitching about how life has passed him by.

He reached the bike road and headed south. A few

minutes later Emerson caught up to him. They didn't talk. Ted listened to their breathing and the rhythmic thump of their sneakers. There was something about running . . . running with another man. Once you got your rhythm together you seemed to communicate without saying a word. There were just the two of you and the road. And you—no, the two of you together—were going to beat it. It was as simple as that.

"Emer," he said, "we've got to do this more often."

"My man, as I said, I do it every morning."

"I'd like to do it with you. Starting tomorrow."

"Welcome aboard."

Ted looked down at the road and enjoyed the synchronized thump of their feet.

"It must be tremendously exciting to be a banker," Jeannie Danton said.

Hartford Loomis smiled at her over his glass of Dom Ruinart. "I expect most people think it's pretty dull."

"I doubt that. With all the responsibility and power" —she leaned across the table—"I'm turned on by power."

He felt his pulse throbbing, was afraid his hands might be trembling. "I turn you on?"

She took his hand. "If we were somewhere private now, I'd show you how much."

He attempted what he hoped would come out as a debonair chuckle but which, to his great embarrassment, sounded more like an aborted hiccup. "This is a private dining room."

"Your waiter wouldn't bother us?" (Watch it, she told herself. Don't be too obviously coy.)

"I assure you he wouldn't."

She leaned further across the table. Hart, bringing his mouth to hers, couldn't avoid glancing at her breasts. She was wearing a silk blouse, generously unbuttoned. As she leaned, they threatened to spill out.

His lips touched hers. Hers parted. He experimentally advanced his tongue. She touched it with hers, then sucked it into her mouth.

When she released it he suggested he ask the chef to hold lunch while "we, ah, relax with our champagne."

"I think I'd like that." She kissed him again.

He touched a button underneath the table. The butler, Arnold, materialized from behind the buffet. "Miss Danton and I will chat a while longer before lunch. I'll buzz when we're ready. Please don't disturb us until then."

Arnold executed a slight bow and started to withdraw.

"Uh, Arnold"—Hart cleared his throat—"under no circumstances is anyone to enter the room until I buzz. Do you understand?"

Arnold understood.

Hart waited until he heard the door close, then stood and motioned toward the couch along the far wall. "Perhaps we'll be more comfortable there?" He smiled uneasily, realizing that he had an erection that must be obvious to her.

If she noticed, she gave no indication. She sat next to him and raised her face up to his. He took her in his arms and thrust his tongue deeply into her mouth. His heart felt as though it were pounding through his entire body. He wanted to touch her breast but was afraid to be too aggressive. He stroked her arm, grazing a breast, and felt a current go through him.

Suddenly, inexplicably, his leg seemed to shoot out from under him, as if the knee reflex had been activated by a blow. He couldn't understand it—or the accompanying sound of breaking glass. He turned quickly from her to find that he had kicked over his champagne. "Clumsy of me," he muttered, going to the table for a napkin. "I don't know how that could have happened."

She smiled. "You can share my glass, if you like."

"Oh, yes, yes, that would be fine." He picked up the pieces of broken glass. How, he wondered, could he possibly have done that? Was his excitement making his body go out of control?

He sat next to her again. She raised her glass to his lips as if feeding an invalid, then put it aside and moved into his arms. They kissed again. Her hand went to his hip, then his thigh. And then it was in his crotch. Yes, he found himself thinking, this was the way these people operated. No need to be hesitant. They were naturally free about these things—this was a woman who exposed her entire nakedness to the movie cameras. He covered her breast with his palm, started to reach inside her blouse, then retreated. "I remember a scene in one of your movies." He described the one he had fantasied so many times. "I found it very exciting . . ." Would she re-create it for him?

"Oh, that scene." She stood and paced back and forth in front of him. "It's been so long, I think I've forgotten exactly how I did it."

"You were wearing a bulky T-shirt. Of course, I'm sure it would have been as effective with any other clothing . . . with what you're wearing now . . ." He was having a hard time breathing.

"Let me think . . ." She paced some more. "Oh, yes, I remember." She turned away from him and stood with her hands on her hips. "Did I do it like this?"

She slowly turned on him. Her eyes met his. Very slowly—very, very slowly—her hands rose to her buttons. One by one, she undid them. Then she opened the blouse wide.

As many times as he had imagined the scene, he was not prepared for this. He went to her, knelt at her feet and buried his face in her breasts. Their soft smoothness, the innocent-whorish way she'd revealed them—he was a bomb, ready to explode any second.

"Would you like to make love to me?" Her voice was soft, above his head, close yet strangely distant.

"Yes, *yes*." Would he have a heart attack? His body was throbbing with every thunderous beat.

She led him to the couch. "No, don't take off your clothes." Her hand covered his as it approached a vest button. "I want to undress you."

She did it slowly, kissing each area of flesh as she exposed it. When he was naked he moved to undress her.

"No," she said. "I'll do it. I want you to watch."

She walked away from the couch, like a model on a ramp. She stepped out of her shoes, then turned away from him. "I really don't have too much to take off." She eased her blouse down to her elbows, exposing an expanse of bare back, then turned to show him her breasts—high, the nipples sassy. "I don't like bras, I like the free feeling I get without one." She stood for a moment with the blouse dangling from her wrists before tossing it aside.

Now she eased her skirt over her hips and midway

down her thighs, revealing lacy black bikini panties. Her flat tummy, gently rounded hips and lean thighs looked even better in the flesh than on film. She let the skirt fall to her ankles, then stepped out of it and approached him. "Now I want you to take off my panties."

His trembling hands slid them to her knees, and he pressed his face against the golden softness of her pubic triangle.

She caressed his neck. "Would you like to make love to me now?"

He nodded.

She lay on the couch, guided him into place on top of her and took his penis in her hand. It was hard when she touched it, but as she brought it into place against her it went soft.

"Oh, no! Damn it, I can't do it—"

"Relax." She kissed him on the neck, then moved so that he could lie beside her. "Don't get uptight, it happens to lots of men."

"Not with someone like you."

"It's not important. Just relax and let me enjoy touching you." She stroked his belly and hips, frequently letting her fingers approach his penis but never quite reaching it. "It's really very nice to lie together this way."

"But I want to satisfy you—"

"Don't think about that now, I'm satisfied just to be with you." She kissed his neck, touched it with her tongue. "Don't think about anything now. Just relax and enjoy what I'm doing."

She licked a path down his chest, all the while continuing to stroke around his penis.

"Now," he said, feeling himself stiffen.

"No, not yet. I'll tell you when."

She continued downward until her lips were in his pubic hair. She teased the shaft of his penis with her tongue while her fingertips gently raked his testicles.

"Oh, now," he said. "I'm ready now."

She positioned herself on top of him and continued to toy with his penis as she brought it into place. He entered her, and lost his erection.

"No! How can this happen—"

"Please don't be upset. I told you, it happens to lots of men. I'm in no hurry. Now just lie back and relax."

She repeated the whole procedure, much more slowly this time. He begged her to let him enter, but she wouldn't. After what seemed like forever she told him to let her lie beneath him. She had him kneel over her so that she could reach his penis with her mouth. She licked the glans, then took it into her mouth. She sucked on it for a long time. Then she guided him again into position. She continued to stimulate his testicles with both hands after his penis was inside her.

His erection held this time—and he promptly ejaculated. He shook his head sadly as he lay on top of her. "I didn't want it to be that way. I wanted to satisfy you."

"Please don't worry about it. I liked it very much."

"You couldn't have."

"I did. And I'm sure I'll like it even more next time. Now, why don't we have something to eat?"

They dressed and went back to the table. He buzzed for Arnold, who brought a fresh bottle of Dom Ruinart while Lars prepared lunch.

"I feel very badly," Hart Loomis, ever the gentleman, said, sipping his champagne. "I know how much better it must be for you with younger men."

"I wish you wouldn't talk that way." She smiled and took his hand. "I don't like younger men very much. They're too immature. Why do men always expect women to judge them strictly on physical performance? Do you think we're incapable of relating to a person in other ways?"

"No, but the physical is important—"

"A girl likes to be touched and kissed and to know that a man enjoys her body, but she doesn't need a stud every time out. At least *I* don't."

"Well, I still can't help feeling I disappointed you—"

"But you didn't. As a matter of fact, I was very pleasantly surprised. You're much more handsome than most men your age. And more virile too." Before he could answer, she stopped him with, "I wouldn't say it if it weren't true, Hart. And remember, this was only the first time. It takes almost any man quite a while to get relaxed enough with a girl so that he can perform at his peak." She smiled her best screen-test lascivious. "I'll bet that after we've been seeing each other for a while you'll be a real stud. Even I may not be able to handle you." Her smile threatened to blossom into a laugh, then quickly vanished. "But I'm being presumptuous, aren't I? I don't even know that you'll want to see me again—"

"Of course I will."

"Well, I'm glad. Very glad. I like you very much, Hart."

When she'd left, he realized that she had not once mentioned the possibility of his investing in her film. A very smart cookie—smart enough to know she'd likely do much better playing to his masculine vanity than openly trading sex for dollars.

Well, play on, Jeannie Danton. You'll get what you earn.

He was on *his* grounds once again.

The call came on Joe Mandino's red telephone, the one with the unlisted number only three people knew. "This is Walter," a familiar voice said. "I haven't heard from you in a long time. I was wondering how you've been." "Walter" meant "Washington," and the rest of the message meant that Joe Mandino should go to a coin telephone and dial the number of a predesignated pay phone in the nation's capital.

"I was just on my way out," Joe said. "I'll call you back."

He went out to a corner phone booth and placed the call.

"I want to see you as soon as possible," said the voice.

Joe took the Eastern Airlines shuttle to Washington—he was one of only three passengers who paid for his ticket with cash—got a cab to the Washington Monument, walked to the Smithsonian's Air and Space Museum and met his contact at the Kitty Hawk exhibit. They walked across the Mall to the National Galleries and continued their conversation as they admired the paintings. When they reached Leonardo da Vinci's *Ginevra dei Benci* Joe's contact exited in one direction and Joe in the other. He took the shuttle back to New York and phoned Spats

Johnson from the airport. "We haven't had dinner in a long time, Eddie. How about we meet tonight?"

"Gee, Uncle, I have a date—"

"I'm sure she'll understand. I'll be at Gino's at eight." He hung up without waiting for an answer.

Eddie was at the restaurant when Joe arrived. "What's the big deal?" he asked.

"Eddie. Eddie, my boy." Joe took on an expression of astonishment. "The way you talk to your uncle. I could get the impression you don't respect me any more."

"Well, Uncle, I don't much like being ordered—"

" 'Ordered'? What 'ordered'?" He reached across the table, pinched Eddie's cheek and smiled. "I ask my boy to dinner and he calls it 'ordered'?"

"Well, I did have some very heavy action, Uncle . . ."

"Eddie, *piccolo,* the way you talk. You're a big man now, you write me checks, you don't need your uncle for anything, so I can go to hell, eh? *Disgraziato.*" He released the cheek and inspected his fingers as if he expected them to be stained.

"Hey, come on, you know I don't feel that way. I just don't like—"

"*Piano, piccolo.*" He made a palm-down gesture for silence. "We can talk about this some other time, eh? Sometime when nobody's around to see how a boy disrespects his uncle?"

"I—"

"*Basta.* Now we talk of more pleasant things, eh? Tell me how's the TV show."

Joe did not approach the purpose of the meeting until they were on dessert. "This Irisher that wants to be a senator," he said. "I don't think you want to stay on his side."

"What do you mean?"

"You need to reconsider, get off that committee. Make them take your name off the newspaper ads and letterheads."

"Oh, now wait a minute, Uncle. Nobody's gonna tell me who I can support for public office—"

"Lower your voice," Joe said sharply.

"I'm sorry. But—"

"You know I wouldn't ask if it wasn't important." He took a sip of tea, dabbed his lips with a napkin and smiled. "You understand how it is, eh, *piccolo?*"

"Uncle, I'll look like a goddamn fool if I turn on him now."

"Eddie, Eddie, why don't you trust me? Do you think your uncle doesn't know the importance of saving face? *Giammai perdere la faccia,* eh?" He drank more tea. "You should hear what they wanted you to do before I went to bat for you."

"Who wanted me to do?"

"They wanted you to make a public spectacle. Renounce him. Say he was two-faced and prejudiced against your people. They got some cockamamie law he voted on when he was a congressman, a civil rights amendment to another bill. He voted against the amendment. They wanted you to talk about it on TV, say how he screwed the black man when he thought he could get away with it. I said, 'Hey, fellas, we can't make Eddie do that. He'll look like a fool. What kind of guy makes speeches for a candidate one day and against him the next?' I said, 'I won't tell him to go that far. We have to compromise.' "

"What 'they' are you talking about, Uncle?"

"That doesn't concern you. Now here's what I worked out. You don't have to make any public spectacles, no TV speeches or like that. You just tell Malloy's people you're leaving the campaign. Take your name off the stationery, don't use it any more in the ads."

"They'll have to throw away lots of stationery."

"Give them a couple hundred dollars to make up for it. Cash, not a check."

"How do I explain changing my mind?"

"What explain? You don't owe these people anything."

"I can't just quit without saying why."

"It's better never to explain. You give reasons, they can talk you out of it, then where do you go? Just have that fancy valet of yours call them. Mr. Johnson is sorry, blah-blah-blah, no, I can't give reasons, it's all very unfortunate, yes, the decision is final, I'm sorry, goodbye." He made a gesture of brushing imaginary dirt from his hands. *"E finito."*

"I couldn't do it that way."

"One thing more—there's gonna be a rally for the President at the Astrodome, some cockamamie committee that wants to give him a vote of confidence or something. Gene Carter's gonna sing. You should be there too."

"Oh, now wait a minute, Uncle—"

"Don't get tense. You don't have to endorse him. Just sing a couple songs, clown around with Gene, that's all. And be on stage when the President comes up to take his bows. Give him the old buddy-buddy, you know the routine."

"The Astrodome! Geez, Uncle, you know how I hate to fly—"

"You'll sprout wings, *piccolo*. A regular little angel of mercy."

Eddie winced. "But what'll people say? Everybody knows what a prick he's been to the black man."

"Nobody's asking you to like him. Just be on stage."

"You're asking me to sell out."

"I'm asking you to do me a favor." He pinched Eddie's cheek. "You understand, eh, *cioccolatino?*"

"I don't have much choice, do I?"

"I knew you'd understand."

Joseph Williams surveyed the gathering in his living room. It was exactly right. The tone, the people mix—*perfetto*. His only dissatisfaction was that he could not be with Grace, and—damn it—she did look so happy with Vassily.

Buffy Weiss calculated the assembled money. Joseph had certainly delivered, and people were responding to her clients exactly as she'd hoped. Clusters of four and five couples surrounded each defendant, asking questions, soliciting opinions, listening raptly. White-haired men in tuxedos and their jeweled wives hung on the words of men in jeans and buckskin, while waiters circulated with trays of caviar and champagne. The apparent incongruity was, Buffy decided, appropriately symbolic of the way America—all America—should integrate.

Ted Vassily, looking about him, reflected that at least a dozen of the men here were worth a hundred million. With their loot you could house a city the size of Miami. If they really cared about poverty and oppression, why didn't they do more? If they didn't care, why show? Was their defense fund contribution merely a ticket to Joseph Williams—a social investment like an endowment to a university or a patronship at the symphony?

John Malloy decided he would be lucky to net ten votes from the whole bunch. He knew them well. They liked to put on a charitable face, but in the voting booth they'd invariably opt for the guy who favored defense spending over social programs, the guy who promised less government (unless it was a government subsidy of *their* business, in which case you called it "stimulating the economy").

Eddie Johnson did not survey the gathering. He did not because he had not been invited. He resented that. He resented it doubly because both Williams and Buffy knew he wanted to go. He hadn't come right out and asked for an invitation, but he certainly had inquired often enough about their plans. Did they think he was just making conversation?

Spats sipped his drink and gazed across the lobby. Kulikowski was opening the door for a middle-aged couple in evening clothes. Two more for the party, no doubt. Yes, they were heading for the west wing—Williams's wing. And they had money written all over them. Old money, as in Rolls-Royces and summer mansions in Southampton. The kind who kept their jewelry in safe deposit boxes and sneered at the likes of Spats Johnson for wearing his.

He finished his drink and motioned to the waiter for a refill. Normally he kept away from the lobby café. Normally he didn't like to expose himself to stares of recognition or to cornballs who wanted to shake his hand and tell him what was wrong with his show and ask him to give their tap-dancing daughter an audition. But tonight he wanted to be recognized. He wanted some of them to ask Joseph Williams, "Wasn't that Spats Johnson we saw sitting in the lobby?" Let Williams know that he knew he'd been snubbed and didn't like it.

Why had he been snubbed? Was it the Malloy thing? The waiter appeared with the drink. Spats took half of it in one gulp. "Better stack up one behind it, fella. Make that two. Just bring 'em over and put 'em here on the table."

"Yes, sir."

Spats finished the remaining half. He was really hitting it heavy tonight. But damn it, he was pissed. All week long people had been ragging him about that picture of him carried by the wire services shaking hands and beaming at the President. He was getting static from the brothers, cold stares from the liberals—a couple of guests had even mentioned it on the TV show. The network was getting letters. Damn it, what right did people have to hassle him about stuff like that? Hell, he'd done what he had to do, and if he showed up at a function for the President of the United States, for Chrissake, what was the big goddamn crime?

But who said that was why he had been excluded from Joseph Williams's swinging soirée? No, more likely he'd been shut out for the same reason twenty-four million Americans for all those years had been made to sit in the back of the bus and in the "Coloreds Only" section of theaters and courthouses. Damn right . . . that was it . . .

He raised his glass and found it empty. He looked up just as the waiter approached with the two refills, grabbed one of them from the tray and took a large swallow. "Better put two more behind these, old buddy. I'm afraid my throat is a little dry tonight, heh-heh-heh."

In the Williams apartment Buffy Weiss looked over the shoulder of the *New York Times* reporter who was her escort and found that Ted Vassily was looking at her. She smiled. He smiled back and waved, then took Grace Colello by the hand and started toward them.

Buffy was happy to see him. She welcomed the opportunity to show off the reporter from the *Times*—let Vassily know that other attractive men considered her worthy even if he didn't. She also was pleased to show off Ted to the *Times* reporter—let him know she could handle animals as well as intellectuals. And, damn it, she still felt the spark. Maybe Ted was feeling it again too.

The introductions were made, followed by the usual party small talk. A butler appeared to replenish their champagne and waitresses to offer steak teriyaki and cheese hors d'oeuvres. A few minutes later Joseph Williams's major domo reported that the people Miz Weiss had been expecting had arrived. She went to the door, greeted a writer for *New York* magazine and her husband, and brought them back to her group.

"I thought," said the *New York* writer, "that I was going to be the only magazine here."

"You are," said Buffy.

"Well, somebody better tell Toby Tanner."

"Toby Tanner?"

"Yeah," said *New York*. "I just saw him sitting in a car parked in front of the building."

"He wasn't invited."

"Who's Toby Tanner?" Ted asked.

The *Times* man liked that. "I'm sure he'd be devastated that someone in New York doesn't recognize the name."

"He's a writer," said Grace.

"That's what he calls himself," said *New York*.

"I'm surprised you haven't read him," said Buffy. "He writes for *Uptown,* also books and screenplays."

"Anyway," said *New York,* "he's parked in front of the building."

"Yes," said *Times*. "He was there when I got here, too."

"That was more than an hour ago," said Buffy.

New York laughed. "Maybe he's spying on us."

"Terrific," said *Times*. "Life not only imitates art, it imitates *Kojak*."

"There's Joseph," said Buffy, taking *New York*'s arm. "Come on, I'll introduce you."

Ted and Grace found themselves alone, but only for a moment. "Hi," said John Malloy, approaching with his wife. "It's good to see the two of you again . . ."

Peg Malloy was not drunk tonight—at least not visibly. But she still had it for Ted. Her eyes kept being drawn back to his, try though she might to avert them.

She didn't look bad at all tonight, Ted thought. Maybe it was her suntan. And short cocktail dress. Her legs were very decent. She should show them more often. She also was fair game now. Malloy and Grace . . .

The Malloys moved on, and a middle-aged couple approached and introduced themselves. Ted recognized the name from *Fortune*. The dude was a real honcho. He did the usual number about admiring what Ted had achieved with 305 East and if-I-can-ever-be-of-service-don't-hesitate. Ted would not hesitate. If there was one thing he could not have too much of, it was *Fortune* Five Hundred honchos wanting to be of service.

Another couple approached and were greeted by the first, then introduced. *Barron's*. Investment banking. The couples moved on, and Ted turned to greet their successors. There was no one. He munched a stuffed olive and sipped some champagne. Hanns Kornell Sehr Trocken, he believed. Excellent. He really was in the mood to shake hands with a few more honchos, but no one else seemed to notice him. The Indians were getting all the play now.

Ted led Grace to the far end of the room, where a string quartet was playing Vivaldi. He enjoyed it, but he also had a weird sense of foreboding, as though things had been going too well for him and were going to turn around. Relax, he told himself, it's only the Greek in you —you're a born tragedian. Plus Coffee Joe probably has you spooked. But he couldn't shake the feeling. He reminded himself that he'd felt the same way at the start of his second year in the pros. The team had gone on to the championship. Right? So fuck Euripides.

He and Grace strolled to the opposite end of the room and again found themselves with the Malloys. "Ted," Malloy said, "you're good friends with Spats Johnson, aren't you?"

"I know him, yes."

"Has he ever mentioned what made him change his mind about me?"

"We never discussed it."

"Curious."

"Well," said Peg, "you can ask him yourself. There he is."

Spats had pushed his way past the door tender and was standing at the edge of the foyer, glaring into the room. Obviously drunk, tie askew, jacket sliding off one shoulder, shirttail coming out of his pants, he said, "Well what the hell you looking at? You got some rule against *niggers* at this party? Or is it just red that's beautiful these days?"

The crowd drew back, which at once made him angrier and gave him a stage. "What's the matter, do I smell bad? Or do I have the wrong week? Yeah, that must be it. This is be-kind-to-Indians week. *Last* week was niggers' week."

Ted went to him.

"Get out of my way, T-Bone," Spats said, straight-arming him on the chest. He pulled a batch of crumpled bills from his pocket, not noticing that half a dozen of them fell to the floor. He glared at the crowd. "Is it money you're worried about? You think I don't have money?" He took another batch of bills from another pocket and held both in front of him, as if offering them at an altar. More bills spilled. "I've got more than any of you. I make twenty thousand dollars a fucken week. Anybody here match that?" He threw his money in the air. "Here, you fuckers, there's lots more where this came from." He spotted a buckskin-jacketed Indian and strode over to him. "Hey, brother, what's the story? You want paleface money but you don't want mine? Ah, but you wanna be on my TV show, right? Well, you can kiss my black ass before I put you on TV."

Williams started toward him.

Spats wheeled. "Here he is, my ol' buddy. Him with his baton, me with my clarinet. Just us two talented—in our fashion—musicians, uniting behind good old John Malloy. But he doesn't want anything to do with me any more. Now that I found out what a hypocrite old John is—now that I know how he voted against the black man—I'm not welcome, am I, *maestro?*"

"You're welcome here any time, Eddie."

"Then how come you didn't invite me to your goddamn party, *Joey?*"

"I didn't *not* invite you, I—in any case, please come in, have some champagne . . ."

"Not now, Joey. It's too late for that. I've already, as any of these fools can plainly see, got quite a load on. But let me ask you a question—in front of your distinguished goddamn assemblage—how come there's no goddamn black people in the New York Symphony Orchestra?"

"We've got blacks in the orchestra, Eddie."

"Yeah, two goddamn token back-up men that you just hired. Hey, you think we can only play *jazz,* man?"

"Eddie, come in and relax. There's no need to shout."

"There is a goddamn need to shout," he said at full volume. "Nobody listens to a goddamn nigger unless he shouts!"

Buffy Weiss came up to him.

"Cunt! You're the worst of them all! Miss no-bra women's lib. Go ahead and bounce those little tits around, I've seen better on twelve-year-olds."

"Eddie, you're out of line."

"Your ass is out of line. I'm okay to fuck but not for your parties, huh? Do all your friends know you fucked me?" He turned to the crowd. "That's right, folks. And she sucked my *big black cock.* She did it in a goddamn cheerleader's uniform, just to turn me on. That's *Miz* Women's Lib for you. She'll kiss ass, she'll eat shit, she'll fuck, she'll suck—she'll do anything to get these goddamn Comanches on TV. Only you ain't getting 'em on the Spats Johnson show, lady. This heah nigger has *had* it with you."

He looked around contemptuously at the stunned guests, picked up a crumpled hundred dollar bill, started to put it in his pocket, changed his mind, threw it at Joseph Williams, then kicked into a bunch of balled-up bills, sending them scattering, and strode out.

The guests, who seemed to be holding their collective breath, remained silent until the door slammed. Then, as if on command, the room filled with incredulous murmurs. Everyone was looking to Joseph Williams.

He considered apologizing but decided it would only make things worse. Somehow he had to get people relaxed again. He raised his hands for silence. The murmurs slowly ebbed.

He smiled. "Ladies and gentlemen, for an encore the quartet will play Haydn's Opus Number Four in B-Flat."

The crowd broke up, with relief. The quartet quickly took the cue, and the party resumed. But things were not the same. Several couples asked for their coats. Others made preliminary moves to leave.

Williams went to Ted. "How did he get up here? My

man in the lobby would never admit him without an invitation."

"He lives in the building, maestro."

"Not on this floor. Where did he get the key for the elevator?"

"I don't know, but I intend to find out." He went down to the lobby, where Williams's elevator tender reported that the doorman had activated the elevator for Spats with his master key. Ted confronted Kulikowski.

"Cripes, T-Bone, he said he lost his invitation and didn't want to bother Williams for another one. I figured he was your friend, so he must be okay."

"Couldn't you see he was drunk?"

"He had a few, yeah, but that's not my business. I'm just a mucker, T-Bone. My job is to open and close doors."

"You got a nice tip for opening this one, didn't you?"

"He gave me something, yeah."

"Well, get this, Cooler, and get it straight—your job is not to let anyone past you without authorization, no matter how much he tips. If you can't handle that, let me know and I'll find someone who can."

Ted went back to the party. Most of the crowd was still there, but the ambience had deteriorated even further. Buffy Weiss was with Williams and his wife. She was, in spite of herself, crying.

"I'm sorry," Ted said. "I know apologies are no comfort, but I want you to know I feel very badly about this."

Williams—gracious host—said, "It wasn't your fault, Ted . . ."

"It was, and it won't happen again."

Ted brought Grace back to his penthouse. In the elevator he wrote himself a note to have Nate fire Kulikowski. Then, thinking about it—and all those years together—he told himself that Cooler had, after all, been acting in good faith, he knew that Ted and Spats were friends . . . Well, okay, don't fire him now, but damn it, keep a close eye on him. And if Cooler ever again did anything even slightly out of line that'd be it. Maybe a letter ought to go out to all tenants requesting that they refrain from tipping building employees. That would make the employees mad as hell, but in the long run it probably would work out for the best. The distance between a tip and a bribe was too small. A building like 305 East couldn't afford to employ bribable people.

"You're way down, loving friend," Grace was saying.

Ted kissed her. "Down, but not out . . . and—if you can stand it—I love you."

She felt a shiver go through her but thought it best not to react as though he really meant it. . . . "Don't be angry with yourself, no one expects the building to be perfect all the time—"

"As I said once too often before, at the prices tenants are paying, they have a right."

"Well, their rights can wait until morning. For now, come on to bed and fuck me."

He did.

Hartford Loomis reviewed the study he had ordered of motion picture financing. It contained some surprises. Movies were, of course, a speculative situation, but they weren't exactly a horse race if you controlled certain variables. The secret was not to be too greedy. If you went for the brass ring, you were talking big-budget pictures—which meant high risk. If you were content to select low-overhead projects, you reduced your chances of scoring big but you also almost insured that you wouldn't lose money. Someone who knew what he was doing and who had the self-discipline to avoid the excess that the industry's high rollers so often fell into should be able to earn a consistent twenty-five to thirty-five percent on capital.

"I've decided not to invest in that movie you're up for," he told Jeannie Danton at lunch.

She frowned.

"I've decided to do something that will bring considerably more benefit to both of us." He had Arnold bring him a telephone. "I want to meet with our trust people," he told George DelVecchio. "Before the meeting, have them estimate the dollars they can free for investment in motion pictures—not, mind you, in corporate securities but in individual film productions. My beginning target is twenty million, but I'm sure if we work at it we can come up with triple that."

Jeannie Danton looked at him with glowing eyes.

"My dear," he said, "I want you to start looking for properties that are right for you. Don't limit yourself, think of TV pilots and legitimate theater too. The main consideration is that they should be you and they should be sexy—which is another way of saying they should be you."

She covered his hand with hers. "Hart, seeing you in action is a turn-on just in itself." Not to mention the sound of all those dollars . . .

He looked pleased. "Risky decisions are my business," he told her. "I know what they say about bankers being conservative, but it's not true with the good ones. Our business is making investments for profit. Every decision is a risk, the bigger the riskier. To me it's second nature. I love it."

After they'd made love—much, much more satisfactorily this time—he lay on the couch stroking her breasts and thinking out the details of the upcoming project. He would need, first of all, a knowledgeable film executive to put together a production company. Then, to make sure the executive didn't go bananas on him, he'd need a hard-nosed overseer, preferably one with the sort of recognizable name that would make contributors to the trust funds confident that their moneys were being invested prudently.

Getting a film executive would be a breeze; they were coming out of the woodwork. As for an overseer—who better than Ted Vassily? He was a big enough ego to consider himself up to any job and enough of a Boy Scout to handle this one without even thinking of trying to take over the operation for himself. He also, thanks to 305 East, had the kind of name that would make the trust fund crowd feel as comfortable about their investment as if they were in—well, a bank.

Yes, it could be quite a picnic. Indeed, a smorgasbord of delights. After Jeannie Danton there would be others—all young, all lovely, all so hungry for success that they would not only place their bodies at his disposal but also convincingly pretend that they enjoyed it.

They went over it at lunch in Ted's recently installed private dining room. "It sounds good," he said. "Give Emer and me a couple of days to think about it and we'll get back to you."

When Loomis and DelVecchio were safely out of hearing, Emerson Wade said, "Do you realize what this means, Reep? We've tapped a pipeline to the mint."

"I see it being potentially profitable," Ted said. "I don't see the mint."

"We tie everything into one package: Three-oh-five East, the radio stations, the TV syndicate, the weekly paper. Loomis is so hungry he'll take just about anything."

"Why tie in Three-oh-five East?"

"It's the linchpin. It gives us a solid equity figure to make the rest of the balance sheet look good."

"And if the rest of the operation goes under, we lose the building, too."

"No. We incorporate each operation separately and swap stock with an umbrella corporation. With Three-oh-five East, we swap only forty-nine percent. That dresses up the umbrella's balance sheet but keeps control in our hands. Meanwhile, it's an opportunity to get Ron-Cor off our back."

"You think Loomis will pick up their paper?"

"If I read him right."

"What about Coffee Joe's theory that the bankers—or one of them anyway—set us up for Ron-Cor?"

"He may be full of shit. Or he may have been spinning tales to sell you his own package. We should find out soon."

"Well, it's worth a try."

"I'll put some figures together tonight. We can go over them tomorrow morning." Wade started to leave, then turned back. "Reep, we'll have a much more attractive package for Loomis if we go with my original idea of buying additional buildings."

"Come on, Emer, you know I closed the door on that."

"Maybe you ought to reopen it. If your own financial profit gain doesn't grab you, think about the rest of us. It's a chance to secure our front money and maybe even double it in a year."

"Okay, I'll think about it. But my leanings are still negative."

Ted spent that evening with Nan, whose immaculate beauty made the not so immaculate reality of everything else seem far removed. She didn't come, despite his going down on her, but she urged him not to be disappointed, to realize please that she just wasn't as highly sexed as he was. . . . They made it again in the morning before he left to jog with Emer. He hadn't intended to wake her, but she was a light sleeper and he figured, what the hell, as long as she's awake . . . She accommodated him, but he sensed that she resented it. Well, who could blame her? She had, after all, leveled with him. And instead of respecting her feelings he'd pushed himself on her again. But, damn it, in a peculiar way her sort of detached air about sex was a turn-on, or at least seemed to make him want to get at her, again and again. To change her . . . ? Goddamn, still playing games. And at his age . . .

"When will I see you again?" he asked.

"This weekend?"

"Great. How'd you like to go to the country?"

"That would be nice."

"We can spend Friday night with my folks, then take a ride Saturday to Penn State."

"I'd really like that," she said, and kissed him.

He felt much better about the morning as he jogged to the park . . . until he remembered he still hadn't made good on his invitation to Grace for a Pennsylvania weekend. Of course, that was hardly his fault. She'd canceled out for the pleasures of Paris with the Maestro. Not that he resented it, as he'd made clear to her. What the hell, as she said, it was too good an opportunity to pass up. . . . No hurry, he'd take her in the fall, they'd go to all the Penn State games. . . .

Emer was waiting for him at Fifty-ninth Street. They headed north on the bike road. The morning was cool and misty and beautifully quiet. The only sounds were their breathing, the occasional call of a bird, the distant whoosh and rumble of a passing car on Fifth Avenue and the thump of their sneakers on the pavement.

They didn't speak until they had passed the Ninety-sixth Street cutoff. "I've decided to go with your plan," Ted said.

Emer couldn't resist jumping in the air. He turned a full circle, jumped again, then ran with a high-strutting pace until he was some thirty yards ahead of Ted. Finally he turned around and jogged backward until Ted caught up with him. "Don't mind me, Reep, I always act this way when somebody tells me I'm going to be a millionaire."

"I won't force our waiting-list people at Three-oh-five East to rent one of the other apartments."

"I can live with that. Will you settle for letting them know we're managing the other buildings, in case they'd like to make that decision all on their own?"

"Yeah, I'll go for that."

Emer did another circular jump. "Replay, you can't believe how good this is going to look on the balance sheet."

They said goodbye at the corner of Fifty-ninth and Fifth. Ted jogged back to 305 East, hoping but not really expecting that Nan would still be in his bed. She had left. He proceeded to do thirty push-ups—he was really feeling physical this morning—then took a long leisurely shower and phoned Nate to join him for breakfast.

While they were eating, the sense of foreboding that had come over Ted at Joseph Williams's party—and that had proved out with Spats's weird performance—returned with disturbing urgency. Forget it, he told himself, you're acting goofy. He pushed it out of his mind and talked football and good old times with Nate for another hour before going to the office.

Emerson was waiting when he arrived. The happy-millionaire look had given way to a worried frown. "Those folks on the waiting list, Reep—I have a hunch we're going to be losing some of them."

"Why so, Emer?"

"Do you ever read *Uptown?*"

"Not often."

Emerson handed him several pages that had been clipped from the magazine. Stapled to them was a note on the engraved memo paper of Joseph Mandino. "Dear Mr. Vassily: I would interpret this as a dump signal. *Carissimi saluti*. Joe."

"Evidently he thought we might have missed it," Emerson said. "He took the trouble to send these tear sheets by messenger first thing this morning."

Ted skimmed the article. It was by Toby Tanner and entitled "Minority Chic." It was about Joseph Williams's party.

Ted's first impression was that it was generally complimentary. It described the elegant setting, the clothes of the guests, the food and champagne, the string quartet. Apparently Tanner had done an extensive job interviewing the guests from his post outside the building as they left. Curiously, there was nothing whatever about Spats's outburst. Could that have been Buffy's influence? Maybe . . . except Toby Tanner hardly seemed her type— But why was Emer so upset?

"The magazine went on sale yesterday," Emer said, interrupting his thoughts. "Subscribers will begin receiving it in the mail today. Yesterday four people on the waiting list asked Jay Kasselman to refund their deposit. So far this morning we've had requests from another three."

"Seven apartments, from a waiting list with eight hundred names. Not exactly a disaster," Ted said with more equanimity than he felt.

"Replay, we haven't had that many cancellations in a single month, let alone two days. Maybe you should give the article a more careful reading."

Ted did. It was a put-down, all right—but in an ingenious way that wove a series of items that appeared complimentary if taken separately but were snidely derogatory in their total impact. Toby Tanner had created a portrait of jaded, social-climbing types trying to bring meaning to their lives by socializing with Buffy Weiss's Indians, who it turned out were part of the evening's entertainment along with the string quartet and the champagne and the hors d'oeuvre. Tomorrow, after the novelty had worn off, the guests would doubtless pursue new entertainments.

What made the article particularly devastating was the way Tanner managed—without ever actually saying it—to characterize 305 East as an extension of the party. The subsidized apartments were just one more amusement —hey, everybody, look at us, aren't we cute and wonderful and warm-hearted to let these peasants live in our building? Minority chic, the rich goofing on the poor.

"This is damned unfair," Ted said to Emerson.

"Nobody ever won an argument with a writer in his own magazine, Reep. The only thing we can do is sit back and hope it blows over. Meanwhile, I suggest we get our asses in gear on the BankUS deal. I'd like to get something in writing today—at the very least, a letter of intent. Maybe Loomis and his people haven't seen the article . . ." Some chance.

When Emerson had left, Ted reread the article. He couldn't understand the writer's motives. Why do a number on 305 East?

Why, for that matter, do a number on anybody. He remembered what Mandino had said about journalists . . . Now that Tanner had fired the first round, would others follow?

By the end of the week he decided that others didn't have to follow: Tanner had done damage enough on his own—twenty-six people on the waiting list had asked for refunds. Fortunately—although it was hard to believe—Loomis didn't seem to realize what was happening. He signed the letter of intent. Well, don't look a gift horse, etcetera. . . .

"We've got it, we've got it!" Emerson sang out, dancing into Ted's office clutching the document high above his head, much as he'd danced in the end zone after catching a T.D. pass. . . .

Thank God it's Friday, Ted told himself as he helped Nan into the car he'd rented for the drive to Pennsylvania. Maybe he'd come back from the weekend and find that the week's bad news had been nothing but a bad dream. Maybe.

Joe Mandino was on the toilet when the call came. "It's Walter," Angie called through the door.

There were two times when Joe could not stand to be interrupted: when he was eating and when he was on the throne. But Washington was Washington.

He went to a phone booth. "I want to see you as soon as possible," he was told.

Two and a half hours later he met "Walter" at the

Museum of Science and Technology. They walked along the Mall to the Washington Monument, then north on Fourteenth Street. "I hadn't expected to hear from you so soon," Joe said.

"Yes. Well, I wouldn't have called if it wasn't urgent. I'm going to need more help regarding our friend Malloy."

"I don't know how much more I can do for you. My little friend has taken a lot of heat for what I've had him do so far. He is not happy."

"Well, we did protect him with Toby Tanner—not a word in that piece about his freak-out, if you noticed. I think we did pretty well on that one—Malloy's supporters coming off looking like real phonies, and his macho bleeding-heart all-American showpiece getting it where he—and they—really live."

Joe had to acknowledge as much, though he didn't add that if the net effect were to drive Vassily into his investment company it would be a most welcome—to him—fallout. He really could, he figured, make money with the guy. . . .

"Besides," said his contact, "what's on the fire won't involve the little man at all."

Joe listened with growing disbelief as "Walter" spelled out the new assignment. Malloy, the man said, in spite of defections such as Spats's and embarrassments to other supporters, was still gaining strength too rapidly. Something had to be done immediately or the fall election could cause New York to be lost for the President. The contact took a deep breath and went on. Now, it seemed there was a certain chemical that had been developed—a drug something like L.S.D. in its effects except that it didn't make a person hallucinate. Instead, when added to an alcoholic beverage, it significantly magnified the effect of the alcohol. If a quantity of this drug were added to Malloy's liquor supply—

"Are you serious?" Joe said incredulously. "You expect me to break into Malloy's apartment and—"

"Not you personally, of course. Our people will make the actual entry. Your job is to get them into Three-oh-five East. They're all clean, so there won't be a problem with police surveillance or anything of that sort."

Joe shook his head. "It doesn't make sense. How do

you help the President by mickeying Malloy's booze?"

The other man smiled. "Frankly, it strikes me as an off-the-wall scheme too. But it came straight from the top. I guess the thinking is, let Malloy start overreacting to his liquor and he'll start having problems—maybe start worrying about his health, maybe start making a spectacle of himself in public, maybe even going to see a psychiatrist. You know what a kiss of death that can be. Whatever happens, it won't help his campaign and could do considerable harm—"

"Suppose he's smart enough to smell something and throw out the bottle. Or give it to the newspapers and have them get it analyzed."

"We'll cross that bridge, as my superiors like to say, when we come to it. Anyway, the decision has been made that this is how we're going to proceed. As for getting someone into Three-oh-five East, we've decided that the best approach would be for you to have some guests for dinner. Two couples. We'll have things checked out well in advance. It'll be a night when the entire Malloy household is away, hopefully for a weekend. Our people will come to your place for dinner, register with the doorman, all very kosher. Your houseman should go through all the motions of planning the dinner, buying the food, cooking it—on the outside chance that someone later is questioned about what happened that night. When they're at your place, our people will set up the Malloy entry. One couple will go to the apartment. The guy is an expert lockman. He'll pick the elevator lock to get to Malloy's floor. The girl will stand watch in the corridor while the guy breaks into the apartment. Meanwhile, the other guy is riding up and down in the elevator with a miniaturized walkie-talkie so he can warn the girl if someone is approaching. The second girl is in your place with her own walkie-talkie, keeping track of the whole show."

"You know what I think?" Joe frowned. "I think you guys've been drinking too much of that spiked booze yourselves."

His contact smiled. "As I said, Joe, it's not my idea. I'm not particularly crazy about it, but mine is not to wonder why. Look at it this way . . . assuming there are no hitches, the whole thing will be over in two or three minutes, and The Man owes Joe Mandino another big favor."

"Yeah. And a couple days later, when Malloy figures his booze is mickeyed, it's time for Joe Mandino to do one more favor. Only what this time? Put L.S.D. in his breakfast cereal?"

The other man's face hardened. "I'm sure there are people who'd like nothing more than to have me tell them you refused to cooperate."

"I'm not refusing, I'm just trying to explain something to you. Look, I don't know how you guys do things in Ethiopia or Zaire or behind the iron curtain or wherever the goddamn hell, but I want to tell you I think this idea is a cockamamie crock of shit. You put something in Malloy's bottle . . . suppose he doesn't drink it. Or suppose his wife drinks it—"

"We understand she's a lush. Who would notice?"

"Okay, but suppose they serve it to guests one night and everybody gets sick."

"It's not supposed to be a one-shot deal—"

"Not *supposed* to be . . . Look, if you really think Malloy is such a big problem, do it right. Hire some pro to fuck him and blow the whistle to the newspapers, they love that shit. Or if you can't do it any other way, get rid of the problem permanently—"

"And make him a martyr . . . like the Kennedys?"

"Well, whatever you do, this shit is gonna get somebody in trouble. For Chrissake! You got four people on the job, and all of them will know what happened. You know and I know, so that makes six, plus the assholes that thought it up and probably had a couple hundred committee meetings to discuss it. What happens if somebody somewhere starts talking and a senate investigating committee starts handing out subpoenas?"

The other man smiled humorlessly. "Let me worry about that, Joe. All we want from you right now is an invitation to a dinner party."

Mandino knew it was pointless to argue. He and his companion had reached M Street. They walked over to Fifteenth, then ducked into the cocktail lounge of the Madison Hotel.

As they sipped snifters of brandy, Joe's contact motioned to a young couple sitting side by side at a wall table near the piano. "Two of your dinner guests," the contact said. "You'll know them as Mr. and Mrs. Draper —John and Nora. Within a few days you'll get a letter from him inquiring about a job at First American Investment. Interview him at your office, then invite him and his wife to your place for dinner. The same with the other couple."

Joe studied the faces of the so-called Mr. and Mrs. Draper. The guy was about twenty-eight and mostly looked like an old-time F.B.I. man. His hair was closely cropped on the sides in a way that accented the squareness of his jaw, but he also had a black handlebar moustache that looked real enough, if incongruous with the rest of the image. Just below one eye was a thin, fairly recent scar that reached almost to his ear. Joe wondered if the scar were a fake, designed to draw a witness's attention away from other features—a ploy frequently used by stick-up men and others who did not want to be identified. John Draper did not look in Joe's direction, but somehow Joe got the feeling of being studied by the guy. A really top man would not put out that kind of vibrations.

Nora Draper looked about twenty-five and very collegiate. An attractive broad. Her long straw-blonde hair hung below her shoulders and fell around her face as she leaned forward to speak. She wore a clinging blue sweater that outlined her high-standing breasts. Her eyes were green and catlike, and at least twice they drifted toward the table where Joe was sitting. Strictly amateur night. Apparently the recruiting was tough these days in the spook business. He wondered, though, what attracted a kid like her to this kind of work. Jesus! It wasn't as if she'd grown up on the wrong side of the tracks like Joe Mandino. You could tell just by looking at her . . . him too . . . that they'd never worried about a meal in their whole lives. Ah . . . to hell with them.

"Shall we?" said Joe's companion, draining his brandy snifter and gesturing toward the door.

Joe finished his drink and followed the man outside. They waved off the doorman who asked if they wanted a cab.

"I still think this deal is ridiculous," Joe said as they walked down Fifteenth.

His companion smiled. "I know how you feel, Joe. But one thing I've learned in this business, you never argue with the top."

Joe stared out the window as his plane rose over the Potomac and banked north, revealing the entire Washington metropolitan area beneath its wing. Watergate and some of the post-Watergate cheap shots apparently hadn't taught anyone anything. They were still carrying on like assholes—every last one of them. The "top" says this, "they" say that—Jesus, small fucken wonder the country was going down the tubes. And what was *he* doing playing in this sandbox? Well, he'd gotten into it too long ago, and too deeply, to get out now. Maffia . . . shit . . . what a laugh. If Vassily only knew who the real strongarms were. . . .

They stayed at the Nittany Lion Inn. The campus was virtually empty for the summer, but Ted could well remember being here in September when the stone wall on College Avenue was packed solid with people sitting and talking and necking a little, and the dinner line at The Tavern was two hours long.

He took Nan walking up the mall and into the rotunda of Old Main, where the walls were covered with Depression-style frescoes of the history of the state. They listened to the recordings of the history of the university—the nation's first land-grant college, chartered by Abraham Lincoln, originally an agricultural school. They went walking on Ag Hill—on what *used* to be Ag Hill, the location of stables and granaries for the agriculture students, now the site of seemingly endless blocks of dormitories. They walked past the tennis courts and the public TV station (WPSX) to Beaver Stadium and climbed the stands to the press box and looked down at the field. "This is a lot bigger than the stadium at Harvard," she said.

"Yeah," he said.

They went back to The Creamery for ice cream—was there any better in the world?—then ambled through the museum, where the current exhibition was of three Swiss artists.

They walked to the rec building and he suggested checking Pater Noster's office on the outside chance the coach would be using a summer Saturday to catch up on paperwork. As they entered the building Nan glanced at the framed photos over the doors leading to the basketball court, then did a double-take. "Hey, Ted, that's you!"

Yep, there he was, flat-top haircut, white sidewalls around the ears, straight-arming an imaginary tackler for the camera. Right up there with the likes of Milt Plum, Dave Robinson, Tony Rados, Richie Lucas, John Cappelletti . . . He'd forgotten the picture. If he'd remembered it, he wouldn't have taken her into the rec building.

Pater Noster's office was dark. Ted and Nan strolled fraternity row and admired the Victorian houses.

"I was a Kappa Sig," she said.

"On this campus," he said, "it was a big deal to make out with a Kappa Sig. They wouldn't let a girl into that sorority unless she was blonde and had a thirty-six-inch bust. We used to keep a chart in the locker room to keep score on the guys who had balled Kappa Sigs and how many."

"And who was the winner . . . ?"

"Well, I guess a quarterback enjoyed certain unfair advantages . . ."

"It's still a matter of pride with you, isn't it? Women are targets, conquests, the more the merrier."

"Who knows?"

"But isn't it?"

"It was then, I guess."

"And now?"

"Now, sweet Nan, I'm all grown up and would like nothing more than to spend the rest of my life with my face buried in your cunt."

"Ted, do you have to be so crude?"

"You asked an honest question, I tried an honest answer."

"I like your romantic side."

He sighed. "Okay, I'll show you the most romantic place on campus."

They walked back to the mall, and he brought her to a monument that looked to her like a stack of rocks but which, he explained, was really a sort of geological phenomenon, a collection from all the various strata that existed in the state.

"There's a legend," he said, "that if a virgin ever walks by this, the rocks will disintegrate and the bells in Old Main will begin pealing the alma mater."

"Hasn't happened yet, right?" She laughed, then let herself fall into his arms. "You know, you're sort of an asshole in your own right."

"Now who's being vulgar?"

"When in Rome . . . or Penn State . . ."

They both laughed, and he was pleasantly surprised at her suddenly loosening up. They went on then to the Hub, where he showed her the Lambert Trophy—awarded to the outstanding team in the East and which Penn State and Pittsburgh had managed to monopolize for years. From there they walked back across the mall to College Avenue and he showed her a frame house, the main floor of which was a haberdashery. "My most nostalgic spot on campus."

"Did you work there?"

"It's the first building I owned."

She remembered his father saying he had been a millionaire at thirty—and this when some football players were lucky to make twenty thousand dollars a year. "Is that how you made your money? Real estate?"

"At one time I used to own half of College Avenue. It quadrupled in value in less than ten years."

"Making money excites you, doesn't it?"

"Yes."

"Daddy, too. I don't think I've ever really understood it."

"It's one way of keeping score."

"Score of what?"

"How about life? On the football field, you measure your success in points. In business, it's dollars."

"And that's all life is? Dollars?"

"No, but it's the measurable part."

They went to The Tavern for dinner, then to Schwab Hall for a chamber music concert. Afterward, at the Nittany Lion Inn, he fucked her. Tenderly. She came. Or at least seemed to. (This time, he believed, she wasn't faking. And she got there without his going down on her.)

"I love you," she told him.

"Do you really?" He was beginning to feel uneasy.

"Yes, I think I really do. You don't know how hard it was for me to say that."

"Why?"

She told him about her problem about allowing herself to be taken over, usually resenting it, being afraid of it but often too afraid to tell the truth and risk offending . . .

"I hope I don't make you feel that way."

"You don't, at least not now. I think that's why I was able to say it."

He held her close. He wanted to reassure her that her mood, and resistance to an involvement, wasn't so different from his. He even thought of telling her about Grace —and quickly dismissed it. This kind of truth-telling could be more self-indulgent than productive. Better, he decided, to keep his mouth shut, let each of them handle his own feelings on his own as best he could, and meanwhile not louse up the moment . . . Well, well, Vassily, maybe you *are* beginning to grow up a little. . . .

Driving east on Interstate 80 he felt remarkably at peace, still removed from the hassles of the city. This had been his very best time with Nan. At the same time he was looking forward to seeing Grace. It had been too damn long. . . .

He pulled into the toll booth at the Lincoln Tunnel and collected a snarl from the woman on duty when he failed to have the proper change in hand. Ah yes, back to New York. To reality.

He drove across town and got a feeling that something was wrong even before he pulled up in front of 305 East. The flashing red light, he would later reflect; he'd seen the flashing red light as he rounded the corner at Third Avenue.

The flashing red light was on a police car. It was parked in front of the building. A crowd had gathered. His first thought was an automobile accident. Yes, some hophead had been roaring through the street and had struck a pedestrian. He devoutly hoped it wasn't a tenant.

He identified himself at the police barricade and was

let through. Lou, the weekend four-to-midnight doorman, was standing at the curb. He looked shaken. Nate was with him. His face was tight, his eyes red.

"Oh, Jesus," he said, putting his arms around Ted. "I wish I didn't have to be the one to tell you . . ."

Absently—almost as if willed there—Ted's eyes went to the floodlights a dozen yards away, the floodlights where policemen were keeping people back from a roped-off area, an area where there was a splattered redness on the sidewalk, a redness around which the silhouette of a body had been drawn in chalk. The wing of the building immediately behind was completely lighted, as if every tenant were somehow participating in what was going on below.

"A suicide?" Ted asked.

Nate was crying now. His arms closed tightly around Ted. Ted felt Nate's rough beard against his face and the wetness of Nate's tears on his cheek.

"What's going on?" he demanded.

"Oh, God, Ted," Nate finally got out, "it's Grace."

Joseph Williams had been spending a quiet evening at home. Ever since the *Uptown* article he had been turning down social invitations. Tonight he and Maria dined alone, then watched television. After the eleven-o'clock news he went out for a copy of the *Times*. There was a commotion at the entrance door, but he didn't pay much attention until he saw a middle-aged couple sobbing hysterically and heard the building superintendent, who was trying to console them, address the woman as Mrs. Colello.

Joseph struggled to contain his alarm. He certainly hoped that whatever they were upset about did not involve Grace. Or was something minor. Italians tended to overreact.

Joseph went to the door. There were police barricades. Looking past one of the policemen, he saw a canvas sheet covering something on the sidewalk. Yes, it had to be a body. But not . . . her! Oh, no, God, not her! A friend. It could be a friend visiting her. Her parents would be upset about that. He asked someone in the crowd. The details came in fragments. A suicide, apparently. Nobody knew the floor, but it had to be a high one. People actually *heard* when the body landed. Blood was splattered thirty yards away. The name? Uh, Crillo. Or Crello. "Colello, Mr. Williams," the doorman told him.

"Her first name . . ."

"Grace. Young girl, a student, I understand . . . very tragic thing."

Joseph told himself that he had to maintain his composure. It still could be a mistake. The parents didn't really see her. Maybe she was visiting somewhere and this had happened to someone else, they only *thought* it was she. It was dark. If it *were* true—

Composure. If it were true, there was nothing he could do about it and there was much needless harm that could come to himself, and to others, if he did not maintain his composure . . . He forced himself to walk to the opposite side of the lobby and out the Second Avenue doors. He would buy his newspaper and go back to his apartment, just as if nothing had happened. Maria must not see any change in him.

He walked uptown on Second. The cool air was good. It was as if by contact with the familiar sensation of coolness he could wipe out the alien, the unreal thing he had just brushed with.

Cool. He would act coolly. He would think coolly.

He thought about the place where the . . . body was, the sidewalk on the south side of the building. But Grace didn't live in the south wing! It *was* a mistake after all!

No. The doorman would know. And the parents would certainly know.

Then why the south wing? Did she have a friend there? Perhaps—but does one commit suicide from the terrace of a *friend?*

Malloy! *His* apartment was in the south wing!

Joseph had suspected that her interest in Malloy went beyond working on his campaign. And that Malloy's in her went beyond her doubtlessly legitimate contribution. She had never volunteered any information, and he had never questioned her, but he had eyes to see the way Malloy looked at her. And he knew that when Malloy found a woman appealing he did something about it.

But what could have happened? Had he tried to force himself on her, had they struggled—and she retreated from him, backing onto the terrace—? Not likely. It was hardly his style, or hers.

But neither was suicide.

Stop it . . . He had to stop thinking about it. Go back to Maria as if nothing had happened. Think of something else!

He tried to lose himself by running a musical score through his mind. The Ode to Joy from Beethoven's Ninth. It kept getting crowded out by the melody he had written for Grace after their first night.

Stop! Now go to the newsstand. Yes. Buy the paper. Back to the building. Into the elevator. Yes. Calm. Cool . . .

"You look as though you've seen a ghost," Maria was saying to him.

"There was an accident. A suicide, they think."

"One of the tenants?"

"I believe so." Did she have to interrogate him about it?

"Not anyone we know, I hope."

"You've met her, though you probably don't remember. She was with Ted Vassily at our party."

"Grace Colello?"

"You do remember, then."

"Oh, Joseph!" Her tone, her expression told him that she knew everything. "You—you must be—" She went to him, took his hands. "I'm so very sorry for you."

"Oh, Maria!" He dropped to his knees, wrapped his arms around her legs and pressed his face against her. "Darling —I need you so much now. Need your help. Need your understanding."

"Yes, darling." She massaged the back of his neck. "I understand." And to herself: I should break your neck, not massage it.

John Malloy had no idea where she was. He remembered being with her in the living room, and then suddenly she was not there any longer. He could not remember whether he had left and come back to find that she had gone, or whether she had left and would soon return. Time was distorted. Had she already left for the evening? No, that couldn't be. They hadn't even been to bed yet.

He was really in terrible shape. So was she. It was uncanny. A couple drinks and *pow!* They had sat on the floor listening to music. And he had nodded out. She woke him. She was very worried about Peg coming back to the apartment and finding them. He explained to her that his wife and young Johnnie were in Connecticut for the weekend; that that was why he'd brought her here to the apartment rather than the office; that there was nothing whatsoever to worry about. At least, that's what he'd *meant* to explain . . . right now he was damned if he could remember whether he'd gotten it all out before he'd nodded off again.

He'd awakened at least once more while she was still there. They had talked about something else . . . music, he thought, though he couldn't remember for sure. And then? Maybe he'd nodded off again, maybe he hadn't. In any case, she was gone. . . .

His watch. Yes, why not look at his watch? Maybe it was late. Maybe she'd gone home. Of course, the thing to do now was look at his watch. He would, as soon as he could get up the energy. . . .

There was another time-warp. Maybe he'd nodded again, maybe not. Anyway, he now felt a breeze. The terrace door was open. He worked up the energy to get up from the floor and take a look. He rose, swayed, stumbled and righted himself. My God . . . what was wrong . . . now steady, John. One foot in front of the other. Across the floor. That's it.

He stood at the door for what seemed a long time before he realized there was some kind of commotion down below. A flashing red light reflected through the hazy night air. Maybe an accident. He would go to the railing and take a look.

He reconnoitered the path between himself and the railing. Three steps, more or less. He should be able to handle that.

He noticed something about the railing. There was a break at the top, right next to one of the supports. Funny he'd never noticed it before. He'd have to have the super get it fixed. Somebody could come out here, lean against it . . .

Something happened inside his gut. It was as though a

hand had taken a grip on his stomach. The railing, the open door, the flashing light.

He inched cautiously toward the railing. He touched the support post. It seemed solid. He tested it by pulling toward himself. It did not budge.

Okay, now the railing. He pulled it toward himself. The support post stopped it. Holding firmly to the support post, he tried pushing away the railing. It yielded. An inch. A few inches more. He pushed harder. Nearly a foot . . . at least. Maybe a little more. Enough for someone to fall through . . . someone . . . who? . . . how . . . ?

Maybe the commotion downstairs had nothing to do with any of this. Except where was she? . . . Grace . . . He looked at his watch. Eleven o'clock. Would she have gone home so early?

He went back inside, stumbling over the threshold. God, he had to pull himself together! And get out of here. Just in case . . . Should he try to tidy up the place before he left? No. No time. He had to get out. Find Donohue. Yes, find Donohue. Fast—before anyone saw him like this.

He put on his jacket, straightened his tie and checked himself in the mirror. Fortunately he was thinking a little more clearly now. Yes, the thing to do was get out. People couldn't tell how he felt by looking at him. Unless he swayed when he walked. Damn, he was doing it now.

He ran a brush through his hair. Ouch! There was a knob the size of an egg at the back of his head! How come? Did he fall? Did something fall on him? Well, there'd be time enough to figure it out later. Right now, he had to get out. Find Donohue.

He left the bathroom—how had he gotten into the bathroom?—and tried to walk a straight line across the living room. On the fourth step he swayed, tried to right himself, overcompensated and fell flat on his ass. Holy living Jesus! He had to pull himself together!

He went back to the bathroom, splashed water on his face, toweled it. Okay, he felt a little better. Now out. Go.

He found his keys, left the apartment, went to the elevator. So far, so good. No one in the corridor. Hopefully, no one in the elevator either.

The bell rang. The doors opened. He told himself he

had better hurry and get into the car, but by the time he could put thought into action the doors had closed. *Damn it, John, pull yourself together!*

He pressed the call button. Another car. Empty. Good. Inside. Fine. Now the lobby. No, he didn't dare walk across the lobby in this condition. The garage.

After what seemed like forever he found his car and managed to drive out. Nobody in the garage, nobody to see him. Good. Now to Donohue. Turn left at L Street, then right at Twenty-eight—No, damn it, that was two years ago . . . this was New York, not Washington . . .

He made his way to Third Avenue and headed downtown. Horns were blowing all around him. Obviously he was doing something wrong. Okay, keep cool. Ease over to the side. That's it. Ah, the curb. Relief. Now a phone booth.

He found one and dialed Donohue, who, when he arrived, found Malloy sitting on the curb, head forward, asleep. The car was angled in, with its tail in the traffic lane. Fortunately no police were around. And New York being New York, nobody did more than give Malloy a sidelong glance as they hurried by. Donohue put Malloy inside, then drove to his own apartment. There he forced Malloy to drink a cup of black coffee. How the hell much booze had he consumed? And what the hell had happened?!

The story came out slowly. "Maybe it's nothing, nothing at all . . . maybe she just went back to her own apartment . . ."

"Let's not guess about it," Donohue said. "I'll go to the building and see what I can find out. You stay here."

He drove downtown on Second. There was a crowd at the corner of 305 East. He found a parking place two blocks away, then stood at the fringe of the crowd listening to the talk. A suicide. A girl. Someone had seen her jump. Donohue wondered if he dared ask one of the policemen her name. If it was Grace, and if they tied her to John it might be a bad idea to have witnesses place him on the scene.

Or maybe it wouldn't be so bad. Maybe his genuine ignorance of what was going on would support whatever story they ultimately decided John should tell. In any case he had to act fast. If it was Grace, there were things to be done.

Donohue used his outdated Congressional aide's identification to get past the police lines. The doorman recognized him, and confirmed that Grace was the victim. He added, "The weird thing is, nobody can figure where she jumped from. Her apartment's in a different wing."

Donohue went to the elevator and activated it with his key to John's apartment. It would, of course, be only a matter of time before people figured out where Grace had been. She could not have gotten on the roof except through the penthouse. Quite possibly someone had seen her with John or on the way to his apartment. She may have told someone she was going to see him tonight. Even if not, she certainly must have told people she was working on his campaign. Vassily had taken her to John's party, and others would doubtless remember her being there. John would be questioned. If he denied being with her and evidence later contradicted him . . . Damn it, why did John have to bring her here! And why so much booze! Wasn't life complicated enough without going into the bottle so close to the election?

Donohue let himself into the apartment. The living room was a wreck—chairs overturned, pretzels and potato chips all over the place, wet spots on the rug where drinks apparently had been spilled.

He inspected the terrace. John had been right about the railing. The opening was big enough to fall through. But she would have had to be leaning pretty hard against it to make it snap. Why would she be leaning against it? Just to look over the side? Why would anyone do that? Of course, if she were as drunk as John she might have done anything. As *he* might have . . . including pushing her against the railing if he was trying to lay her and she was resisting . . . Except that wasn't his style. And from what he'd gathered she was not exactly the least available girl in town.

But even if there had been a struggle—for whatever reason—and no matter how hard John might have pushed her or she might accidentally have pushed herself against the railing, it shouldn't have broken. The lawyer in Tom Donohue decided there definitely was a negligence suit here. But all that still didn't explain how she came to be in a position to topple over when the railing snapped. The people downstairs were talking suicide. If so, had the railing snapped when she climbed on top to jump? . . . But it seemed damned unlikely she would come to John Malloy's apartment and suddenly be inspired by depression, or shock at his advances, to do a header. Ladies favored by John's attentions were rarely depressed *or* shocked.

But if she hadn't jumped and hadn't been pushed and hadn't leaned, what the hell *had* happened?

Well, there was no more time to think about that now. Somehow he had to get John out of the picture, before the police put him in the middle of it and destroyed him. He went back inside the apartment and tidied it up. Grace's purse was there, as was the memo she'd written for John on what she believed young people perceived the campaign issues to be. Now how to explain all this when the police and the press followed the trail here, as they inevitably would . . .

The only answer was to place John out of the apartment when Grace Colello died. But how to explain him leaving her alone in his apartment? Well, she was known to be working on his campaign. If they'd been working together, perhaps on that memo she'd written, and if something had happened that made him leave . . .

But that hardly explained why she had jumped—or fallen—or whatever. A convincing story would take all this into account. Damn it, he needed more time to think . . . except there was no time, too much had already gone by.

He left the apartment, and as he rode down in the elevator a story finally did start to take form in his mind. To give it maximum credibility he should go immediately to the police and tell them he believed Grace had been in John's apartment. But he didn't dare . . . first he had to make sure John would be able to hold up his end.

He went to the doorman and asked, "Have you seen Mister Malloy?"

"No, sir."

"If you do, tell him I'm looking for him. It's urgent." He started out the door.

"Yes, sir. Where shall I say you'll be, sir?"

Donohue hesitated. "I—I don't know. Out looking for him. Better just say I'll be back in about an hour."

At his own apartment, Donohue found John Malloy asleep. He slapped him awake and gave him a dishtowel filled with ice cubes to hold against his face.

"We have to act fast," he said. "Are you with it enough to talk about this thing?"

"I'm pretty rocky."

"Well, listen and try to understand. Your story goes like this . . . You met with her at your apartment as a matter of mutual convenience, since you both live in the building. I was scheduled to be there too but I phoned to say I'd be late. With me so far?"

"I think so . . ."

"Okay, what time did you start to get plastered?"

Malloy looked up. " 'Plastered'? Yes, I guess I must have, except I'm damned if I remember drinking that much . . ."

"Never mind all that . . . just try to give me a time when you remember having a drink."

"Okay, okay . . . about eight-thirty, I guess."

"All right, at eight-thirty you were talking to Grace about restructuring the presidential cabinet to be more representative of young people and minorities. She was helping you sketch out a position paper and speech . . . You wanted to refer to something I wrote on the subject —by the way, I really did, remember?—but it was back at your office. You left her at the apartment and said you'd be back in no more than half an hour—"

"Why didn't I take her with me?"

"I don't know, let's see . . . you suggested it but she said she'd rather stay and work. You parked your car near your office, got out, and that's when the lights went out."

"I passed out?"

"You were mugged. The last thing you remember is getting out of your car and hearing somebody behind you. That lump on your head will support your story."

"I don't know, Tom. It sounds a little—"

"If you can think of something better be my guest. But you'd better do it right now because any moment people are going to put together the obvious and figure out she was in your apartment."

"What *happened* there, anyway?"

"I wasn't there, John . . . Now, come on, we don't have much time."

In his car Donohue gave him the rest of his plan. Malloy didn't like it but had to concede he couldn't think of anything better. Admitting the truth—at least so far as he knew it—would be disastrous and solve nothing.

Donohue drove to Madison Avenue, uptown to Ninety-sixth, then west to Central Park. Half a mile inside the park he got out of the car and looked about. Good. No one in sight.

Malloy got out too. "Are you sure this trip was necessary? I mean, couldn't I just stay mugged in my own car by my own office?"

"We've been over that, John," Donohue said, trying to mask his impatience. "We have to account for the time you've been away. Nobody would buy your not being found by now if it happened outside your office."

"Yes, but does it make sense from a mugger's viewpoint to drag me all the way out here to the park?"

"I hope so . . . I hope they'll figure that your attackers didn't want you found for a while either. Maybe they'll even pin it on the opposition . . . which would really be coming out of a mess smelling like roses. After all, there have been some peculiar goings-on from the other side . . ."

Malloy knew that in his own mind Tom was reaching, that he was more trying to convince himself than convince John, but maybe it wasn't all that farfetched that the opposition might have been trying to set him up. . . . Except to go to the extreme of murder . . . ? That hardly seemed likely . . .

"Look, John, I'm sorry, but we've got to get at it."

Malloy nodded and, making a face, lay down in the grass alongside the road.

"Give me at least five minutes before you get up and start looking for 'help.' "

"Five minutes! Why—"

"John, *five minutes.*" Donohue started back to the car,

then remembered his boss's wallet. He should have thought of that first. . . . "Give it to me," he told Malloy, and impatiently reached into Malloy's inside pocket. It was a miracle no cars had come by . . . oh-oh, here came one now . . . He held his hands at his fly, as if urinating. The car passed. His anxiety didn't.

Playing the role of mugger, he searched John's other pockets, taking some folded bills and a fountain pen. He started to get back into the car, then remembered the wristwatch. Okay. Enough! Get the hell out of here!

He engaged the starter, half-expecting that the engine would refuse to turn over. Happily it whirred to life as efficiently as in a television commercial. He drove around the northern perimeter of the park, then exited on West Eighty-sixth and made his way downtown on Broadway. His hands, he realized, were trembling. Small wonder!

At Columbus Circle he maneuvered to Fifty-seventh, then headed east. There still was so much to do . . . He found a parking place near his apartment, then went to John's car, which was half a block away. He found a parking place for it a block and a half from John's office, then hailed a taxi for 305 East. Much of the crowd had dispersed, but a dozen people were still around. A new doorman was on duty.

"Have you seen Mister Malloy?" Donohue asked.

"No, sir."

"I can't understand it." Donohue scratched his head. "I was supposed to meet him here several hours ago. He's not at his office, either."

The man with the scar did not like domestic assignments. Overseas things went much easier. You got to the right people, you gave them what they wanted and they did the job. There rarely were slip-ups, and when there were it wasn't your problem, the locals always took the heat. Domestically you got assignments that were nearly impossible, you got assistants that couldn't coordinate, you had to worry about city and state police as well as whatever federal agents your people couldn't get to, and if there were slip-ups it was your ass on the line.

When the man with the scar got assigned to the Malloy case he had a feeling there would be an outbreak of foul-ups. Somehow these political craperoos always turned left on you. The problem was, you didn't have professionals calling the shots. The guy who dreamed up your battle plan was usually some dip-shit from Stanford who got the idea from something the assholes in his fraternity used to do to harass candidates for the student senate. They thought like Batman comics—ray guns and crap like that. They gave you something farfetched, then if it didn't work they put the blame on you.

This Malloy caper, for instance. From the moment he was assigned to it he knew it was one of those funny farm deals. Spike the guy's booze with some secret chemical! Jesus Christ! A thousand things could go wrong! Even if nothing went wrong, there was still no way to be sure the thing would accomplish what you wanted.

He made that point to his superior when the operation—if you could call it that—was assigned. And his superior, as he'd expected, pointed out that the orders had come from *above*. The *top*. Nothing he could do about it, followed by sheepish smile. Time to play Batman again.

The first maneuver, surprisingly, went without a hitch. Mandino was a smart old guy who carried out his end perfectly. The electronics gear picked up Malloy's burglar alarm, which was easy enough to deactivate. The break-in was a piece of cake. In two minutes the job was finished. Three minutes after that, the four members of the team were sipping drinks once again with Mandino.

But the man with the scar had had a hunch that darker moments were ahead. He was right. For whatever reason, the chemical in John Malloy's rum didn't work. That is to say, for the better part of a month, Malloy didn't do a damn thing that suggested his mind had been fucked up by the spiked booze. So it was back to the drawing boards. And that led to the order for a re-entry to spike the rum with a heavier dose on a weekend when it was determined Malloy and his family were to be in Connecticut.

The man with the scar argued vociferously against it. If the Batman mickey finn didn't work the first time, why expect it to work now? Suppose Malloy had figured out that his booze was spiked and asked the F.B.I. for a stakeout. Or the New York cops, who were harder to get to. Or suppose he had hired a private detective. Or suppose he had simply stopped drinking rum.

The reply, of course, was that the decision already had been made. So it was back to Mandino—who fought like crazy before once again agreeing to play host to the new raiding party. And it was back to 305 East.

This time the man with the scar decided to stay in the Mandino apartment with a walkie-talkie while the other members of the team did the frontline Mickey-Mouse. As events unfolded, he found himself wishing he hadn't made that decision.

The first storm signal came from the look-out girl who'd been riding the elevator. "He's here," she said over the walkie-talkie. "Malloy . . . with a girl. I got off the elevator in the lobby when they got on."

"Clear out!" snapped the man with the scar. "Fast!"

A few seconds later he heard the voice of the girl who was standing by outside the Malloy apartment. "No, David. Stay inside! The elevator is here!"

There was a pause of about a minute, then her voice came on again: "I'm in the elevator now. Malloy and the girl should be entering the apartment any second."

"I'm in a fucking closet," David said. "I hear his key in the lock. Stand by."

The man with the scar waited. A few minutes later the two girls returned to Mandino's apartment. No word from David. Fifteen minutes passed. Half an hour. Finally after almost an hour David reported via walkie-talkie that he was on his way back to the apartment.

He arrived looking very pale and started to blurt out his story. Mandino held up a silencing hand. "Not here. I have the place checked out for bugs every few weeks, but there's always a chance one of your feds planted a mike my people didn't find."

The man with the scar nodded agreement. At least Mandino was a pro. That's what was wrong with this caper—it needed more pros like Mandino and fewer amateurs like the assholes who had thought it up.

David, the two girls and the man with the scar left the apartment. They made a big deal of saying goodbye to Mandino at the elevator, and of asking the doorman what had happened as they made their way through a crowd that had gathered at the entrance. They then hailed a cab for Times Square.

At Broadway and Forty-sixth they left the cab and started walking uptown, looking very much like tourists having a night on the town. "Now," said the man with the scar, "what the fuck happened?"

David's story was just the sort to go with such a wild-hair caper. He'd been in the apartment for only a minute or two when Malloy arrived. He'd just added his chemical to the rum bottle in the liquor cabinet and was looking for additional rum bottles when the lookout girl alerted him.

He'd listened from the closet as Malloy and his girl friend came in, had a drink and started talking. Malloy was apparently putting the make on her, and from the sound of things it was going to be a long night.

Then the girl complained that she felt weird. Malloy tried to calm her. But then he said he was starting to feel peculiar too. Evidently they both had drunk from the spiked bottle. And this time the dose was really heavy.

The girl said she was having a hard time breathing. Malloy suggested that they go out on the terrace for fresh air. She had the wit to want to go to the hospital—she said she was afraid they might be poisoned. Malloy told her to wait a few minutes, maybe they'd feel better . . . besides, if they showed up together at a hospital it would require too much explaining.

David next heard the terrace door opening. Then silence for a few minutes, then more movement in the apartment. The girl was now insisting that they go to a hospital. Malloy told her he'd call a doctor he knew could be trusted. He said she should go back out on the terrace, she seemed to feel better out there . . . Maybe the problem was some kind of psychoactive chemical in the room. He'd had a milder version of the same experience a few times during the past month . . . Maybe it was some damn cleaning chemical or the coolant in the air conditioner or something like that. He'd meant to say something to Vassily next time he saw him. Now he damn well would. . . .

David had waited. There was movement but no telephone call to a physician. Malloy seemed to be pacing, perhaps looking for the phone number. Then came a thud. The girl screamed. More movement. Then a slamming door.

David listened. No sound. He guessed that Malloy had fallen and the girl had run for help. He decided that if he didn't get out now he'd be trapped in the apartment. He could hardly pass himself off as an ordinary burglar. His presence would be linked with the strange feelings that Malloy and the girl had experienced. There would be questions, maybe a correct assumption of political espionage, followed by a congressional investigation. . . .

He stepped out of the closet. Malloy, indeed, had fallen. He was sprawled on the floor next to the liquor cabinet. But the girl had not left the apartment. The slamming door notwithstanding, there she was in the living room, telephone in hand. She must have opened the door, seen somebody coming, gotten panicky at what they'd think . . . she alone with Malloy, he passed out on the floor . . . and slammed the door shut.

David's first impulse was to run. But suppose she followed him, yelling now for help? Or suppose she told the doorman on the intercom and he sealed off the building?

David jerked the telephone from her hand. "Don't move. If you make a sound I'll kill you."

He hadn't meant that, of course. He had intended only to quiet her so that he could tie her up and get the hell out of there. But she fought him off and went for the telephone. He got it away from her again, but when he tried to subdue her she managed to break free, grab up a book end and hit him over the head with it.

She ran for the door. He managed to tackle her before she could reach it. Holding her in a headlock, he struggled to take off his belt so that he could tie her arms. Again she broke free and ran in the opposite direction.

He was amazed at her stamina and strength. Apparently she hadn't drunk as much of the spiked rum as Malloy. In any case, she was a real demon.

He chased her toward the kitchen. When it appeared that he was about to corner her, she managed to elude him and rush toward the door again. When he blocked her in that direction, she ran onto the terrace and started screaming for help.

He never intended to push her off. All along he'd only wanted to subdue her, tie her up so that he could leave the apartment without being caught.

He still couldn't quite understand how it had happened. There must have been something wrong with the railing. One minute he was struggling with her, trying to get his hand over her mouth to stop her from screaming. The next minute, he felt her body falling away from him. It happened so unexpectedly that he almost went with her.

Her scream was lost in the chasm below him as she plummeted to the ground. He was frightened, overwhelmed. He had never killed someone at close range before. With a rifle, yes. But that was less personal, a wholly different feeling from having a warm body in your arms and then, an instant later, knowing the person was dead.

He almost blacked out but remembered his training—remembered what they had said about this kind of shock reaction following an up-close kill, that if you realized it was coming you could deal with it.

He pulled himself together, and was sufficiently controlled before leaving the apartment that he could wipe his fingerprints from the telephone, empty the bottle of spiked rum down the toilet, flush the toilet five times to remove any possible trace of the chemical, and wipe his fingerprints from the bottle before dropping it into the kitchen garbage can. . . .

"Well," said the man with the scar, "you used good judgment. It was an unfortunate result, but you did the best you could under the circumstances." The problem, he told himself, was the assholes from Stanford.

The four federal agents reached Fifty-seventh Street, retraced their path to Times Square, then separated. David and his girl headed for the Port Authority Bus Terminal. The other girl and the man with the scar hailed a cab for LaGuardia Airport. . . .

Back in Washington, the man with the scar met with his superior. "It could have been a disaster," he said. "It worked out much better than we had any right to expect."

His superior nodded. "There is still, of course, one piece of unfinished business."

"Should we risk finishing it so soon?"

"Not immediately. But soon."

The man with the scar shook his head. "He's a good man. It's unfortunate that this is necessary."

"Yes. Unfortunate. But necessary." He raised his eyebrows to underscore the instructions that would follow. "I'll tell you when. And this time, don't trust subordinates."

Joe Mandino learned what had happened from Angie, whom he had sent out for his nightly paper. Joe's first thought was that it was a shame an innocent bystander like Grace Colello had been the victim of this horseshit. His second thought was that Washington had stumbled across the goal line—for sure Malloy's political career would be finished when the story hit the newspapers. His third thought was, if an innocent bystander had to be victimized, it couldn't happen to a better person than Ted Vassily's girl friend. So the arrogant bastard thought he was too good for Joe Mandino, did he? Maybe this would take him down a notch, not to mention even a score.

Joe's fourth thought brought him back to his first—whatever her relationship to Ted Vassily, Grace Colello was a nice Italian girl who didn't mean anyone any harm. The sudden recollection that she was Italian rattled him. Here it was, the whole thing happening again—Italians being victimized by the *'Mericane*, by the rotten drunken dry-cock pasty-faced freckle-assholed beer-bellied cocksucking no-good Irishmen.

God damn it. Goddamn those rotten exploitative fuckers. They took and took and took, and even when you thought you had them against the wall they seemed to figure out some way to turn things around and take some more. No-good pricks . . .

And now? Now there was nothing to do but try to put the whole thing out of mind. If you let shit like this bother you, you couldn't function. You had to draw a curtain over it and go about your business as if nothing had happened. If you couldn't do that, you didn't survive. As Harry Truman had said long ago, if you can't take the heat, you don't belong in the kitchen.

Joe told Angie to draw him a bath. While in the tub he placed a call to Jeannie Danton. She said she was busy but would break the date as soon as she could and be at Joe's apartment within two hours.

He sent Angie to fetch him an Amaretto. Yes, he told himself as he lay in the hot water sipping the sweet liqueur, you had to draw a curtain over it. That was the only way to survive.

Ted could not believe his reaction. He didn't feel anything. He was numb.

Nate put a drink in his hand. Ted stared at it. Nan—hastily briefed by Nate about Ted and Grace—guided it to his lips. "Leave me alone," Ted said.

Tears were on Nate's expressionless face. He wiped them away. "I was the one who introduced you to her."

"I suppose I should go see her parents," Ted said.

"Maybe it would be better tomorrow," Nan said quietly. "They're probably too much in shock now to want to see anyone."

"Yes, tomorrow. You're right, that would be better." Ted sipped his drink and thought about John Malloy, and that Grace had to have been in his apartment . . .

The intercom buzzed. Nate answered. The doorman told him that Emerson Wade wanted to see Ted. Nate went down to the lobby to bring him to Ted's apartment.

"I'm sorry for you, man," Emerson said, embracing Ted.

"How'd you find out?"

"Burr Whiteside called."

"I told him," Nate said. "I figured the reporters would be asking questions. I figured we should have somebody around that knew how to handle them."

Ted stared ahead, barely hearing the talk that swirled around him . . . talk about Grace, what a great person she was. For him, the whole thing felt . . . well, surreal. He had accepted that she was dead—but he really didn't. He couldn't bring himself to speak about her in the past tense.

The intercom buzzed again. The doorman announced Spats Johnson, and Nate went to get him.

In Ted's penthouse, Spats glanced uncertainly at Nan. "She knows," Ted said. "Everybody here knows everything. Except me. I don't know anything."

"I'm really sorry," Spats said. "If there's anything I can do . . ."

Nate served drinks. They talked a while longer, everybody except Ted, who finally said, "I'm knocked out. Let's get together again in the morning. Okay?"

The men left. "Will you stay?" Ted asked Nan.

"Of course."

Their bodies came together in bed, more therapy than sex. Nan seemed especially willing and understanding. He dozed in her arms. When he awoke he thought it was morning, then saw it was still dark. He looked at the night table clock and realized he had slept for only a few minutes.

"Nan," he said, "will you stay—I mean for a few days, until I can get myself together?"

"I have a flight tomorrow at four . . ."

He waited.

"It's just that they don't like crew members to cancel, it creates all sorts of headaches for—" She stopped short. "Oh, forgive me, Ted, I'm thinking so selfishly. I'll cancel. Of course I'll stay as long as you want."

He fell asleep in her arms and awoke calling out Grace's name. "I'm sorry," he said.

"I understand, Ted. Just try to rest."

It was a long time before he could get back to sleep, and when he next awakened it was nine o'clock and for a few moments he was completely blanked out on what had happened . . . until memory rushed in and over him. He held tightly to Nan, as if somehow he could absorb strength from her.

"They'll need me at the office," he said after a while. "I'll be back as soon as I can."

"I have some things to do too. Shall we meet at five-thirty?"

"Not that late, eleven-thirty."

"Noon?"

"Sure, noon."

Emerson Wade and Burr Whiteside were waiting for him. "This is a terrible time to talk business," Emer said, "but I'm afraid some things can't wait."

"Let's talk," Ted said. He welcomed it.

Emer displayed the morning newspapers. The *Daily News* had made the story its banner headline:

"Mystery at Celeb House:

"COLLEGE GIRL DEAD,

"JOHN MALLOY MISSING."

Below the thick black type were a grainy high school graduation photo of Grace, a more recent photo of Malloy and a long shot of the apartment building, with a broken line tipped with an arrow showing the path of Grace's fall.

The *Times* played things more quietly but still gave it two columns, page one.

"Aides Report John Malloy Missing;

"Campaign Worker Plunges to Death"

Burr Whiteside winced as he looked up from the papers. "Ordinarily a suicide in New York doesn't even make the inside pages, but the Malloy tie-in is big news. I can't ask reporters to play down the Three-oh-five East angle. I think our best at this point is to cooperate and wait for it to run itself out."

Emerson nodded. "They probably wouldn't hit the celebrity house angle so hard if it weren't for that damned Williams party. One of the TV anchormen this morning began his report something like this . . . 'The celebrity apartment house where composer-conductor Joseph Williams served champagne and caviar to South Dakota Indians on trial for murder is in the news again today—this time the scene of a mysterious death and the no less mysterious disappearance of undeclared senatorial candidate John Malloy—' "

"What's this about Malloy?" Ted broke in.

"He was missing until a few hours ago," Burr said. "He was found, believe it or not, in Central Park, apparently a mugging victim. That'll be this afternoon's headline."

"Central Park? Mugged? Jesus . . . how did the paper link him up to Grace?"

Burr and Emer condensed the morning articles: Grace had told her parents she was going to see Malloy. Police found her purse in his apartment. They also found a lengthy memo and outline for a speech she had written about issues in the forthcoming senatorial primary. Tom

Donohue told police he believed she had been there, though he couldn't confirm it from first-hand knowledge.

Donohue, according to the account he gave police, had been scheduled to meet with Malloy at eight-thirty at Malloy's apartment. Though Malloy hadn't told him that anyone else would be there, Malloy frequently invited others to political meetings of this sort.

Donohue took a nap after dinner and overslept. When he awoke—around ten-thirty—he hurried to 305 East. When he arrived, a covered body was on the sidewalk and a crowd had gathered. He learned from the doorman that it was Grace and rushed up to Malloy's apartment to tell him that his young campaign worker was dead. He found the apartment empty. He went looking for Malloy, couldn't find him and returned to 305 East. By this time police had connected Grace to the Malloy apartment—but Malloy was still nowhere to be found.

"And now they've found him in Central Park," Emerson said.

"It doesn't make sense," Ted said.

"I'm with you," Burr Whiteside said. "A well-known married man, likely senatorial candidate, leaves a single girl campaign worker alone in his apartment and goes for a walk in Central Park? While he's gone she decides to commit suicide?"

Emerson saw Ted's face take on a pained expression. "Maybe," he said, putting his hand on Ted's shoulder, "we'd better postpone this meeting."

"No, let's talk. Sooner or later I've got to face it."

Emerson got a glass of water for Ted, then, not wanting to seem overly solicitous, poured glasses for himself and Burr Whiteside. "I never got to know the young lady, Reep, but I find it hard to imagine anyone committing suicide under circumstances like those."

Ted stared at his glass. "I can't imagine her committing suicide under any circumstances."

"If she didn't jump," said Burr Whiteside, "the railing snapped while she was leaning against it. But why would she be out on Malloy's terrace on a chilly windy night when he wasn't in the apartment? No wonder the press is skeptical. Would you like to take a look at the railing?"

Ted's jaw tightened. Really, he had to force himself to

confront it. If he came apart at the seams, that was the chance he'd have to take. He couldn't turn away. "Yes," he said. "Let's look."

A policeman on duty outside the door of the apartment recognized Emerson and let the group in. A rope that another policeman stood behind had been stretched diagonally across the living room. "Apparently they're not taking any chances that someone will tamper with the evidence," Burr told Ted.

The policeman behind the rope lifted it, then followed the group to the terrace. Emerson manipulated the railing to show its range of movement. Ted examined the break.

"The theory," Emerson said, "is that it snapped when . . . she jumped."

Ted winced, then forcing himself to confront it, said, "She didn't weigh more than a hundred and thirty at most . . ."

"The compression as she pushed off, like on a diving board." Emerson embarrassed himself being so graphic. "The railing should have been able to withstand hundreds of pounds, thousands . . . It was defective, obviously."

"And we're responsible," Ted said.

"For what?"

"For putting a faulty railing on the terrace, that's for what."

"Well," said Whiteside carefully, "I believe the railing manufacturer is ultimately responsible. . . ."

"I don't see any jury finding liability in an accident where the victim was attempting suicide," Emerson said briskly.

"If she was, which I don't believe," Ted snapped.

"Then what was she doing on the railing?"

"I don't know. Maybe just sitting there—"

"On the thirty-eighth floor? Alone at night on a windy terrace?"

"It's no less plausible than suicide, if you knew Grace." Plausible . . . maybe she was a little loaded, he thought to himself, and had been doing that old tightrope walking number for real that she'd talked about—except she'd have had to be really loaded, and Grace was hardly a heavy drinker, a little wine was about the limit . . . And then he remembered her story about walking the curb like a tightrope in Washington Square when she'd been high on pot—except so far as he knew she didn't smoke any more, and even if she occasionally did, she'd hardly do it with the likes of John Malloy . . . He led the way back through the apartment to the elevator. "All right, file a claim with the insurance company, and get me some money from our general fund for Mr. and Mrs. Colello —two or three thousand, to cover . . . expenses."

"Do you really think we should, Reep? Courts could interpret that as an admission of culpability—"

"Fuck the courts."

They went back to the office. "The press is going to want to talk to you, Ted," Burr said. "Today would be the best time to let them in. They'll be so preoccupied with finding Malloy in Central Park that anything involving you or the building will probably wind up on page ninety-three."

"Okay, set it up."

"I'll keep out everyone but the majors—the networks, the *Times, News* and *Post,* and *Time* and *Newsweek.*"

"All right." Ted yawned. Suddenly he felt totally exhausted, his legs very weak. "Let me know when. I guess I need a little more sleep . . ."

"Reep"—Emerson displayed a sheaf of papers—"just one more thing. You know that letter of intent Hartford Loomis signed? Well, if we wind up getting all kinds of bad press on this . . . accident, he'd be legally entitled to back out of the deal. I hate to push it on you, but I really think we should get contracts signed as soon as possible—"

"Get them drawn up."

"I did." He handed Ted the sheaf. "I got Teddy Epstein out of bed last night right after I left your apartment. We stayed up all night working on them. I'd like to present them to Loomis today but you'll need to review them first."

"I'll take them with me."

"I'll send someone for them around—say, two o'clock?"

"Yeah." Ted took the papers. He felt that he couldn't stay on his feet a minute longer. He left the office, crossed the lobby, took the elevator to his penthouse and fell into bed. He lay awake for what seemed like hours before drifting into a fitful sleep. He was sure he'd been asleep only minutes when Emer was on the intercom asking if he'd reviewed the contracts. "Tomorrow morning . . . I'll have them for you then . . ."

He tried again to sleep but could not. When he finally dozed, it seemed only seconds had passed before his private telephone was ringing.

Burr Whiteside. He'd set up the press conference for four o'clock, late enough to miss the six o'clock news. Hopefully early evening developments with Malloy would preempt the eleven o'clock broadcasts and the stories in the morning papers. "He's still at the hospital being checked out," Burr reported, "but Donohue tells me he'll probably be released tonight."

Ted said thanks and hung up. He was still bone tired. What the hell time was it anyway? Hadn't Emer said he'd buzz at two? That had been a nap and a half ago.

He remembered he was wearing a wrist watch. It was an effort to make a separate decision to look at it. Everything was running together—thoughts, movements, time. Time . . . his eyes fixed on the big hand and little hand, and he computed three-forty-five. He had to pull himself together.

He took a shower, which made him feel a little better. And then while he was getting dressed he remembered asking Nan to meet him at noon. He found her note on his dresser. "Ted, I didn't want to wake you. Anyway I have a lot to do and this afternoon is a good time. See you at five-thirty. *Ciao.*"

He was jolted by the intercom buzzer. It was Emer. "Four-fifteen, Reep. I thought we might go over what you're going to say to the press."

Four-fifteen! Jesus, where did it all go? Wasn't it just three-forty-five a minute ago?

"Reep, you still there?"

"Yeah, I'm here." He tried to picture himself getting slapped across the face. He had to make himself more alert. "I'll be right down. I'll just stop on the way and see her parents for a minute—"

"Ah, Reep, maybe it would be better to let that wait until after the press conference."

"Hey, I'm not a total moron, Emer. I don't need you and Whiteside to give me my lines."

"Sorry. No offense meant."

"Okay, none taken." On top of everything else he was too goddamn edgy. He'd damn well better pull himself together or he'd really blow it with the reporters.

He hurriedly finished getting dressed, then phoned the Colello apartment. Her mother answered. She seemed surprised he would want to speak to her. She hesitated when he asked if he could stop by, then quickly said yes, of course, that would be fine. . . . As he replaced the receiver similarities between the mother's voice and Grace's eerily reverberated in his head.

It was Grace's mother who answered the door when he rang the bell. He recognized her immediately, even though he'd never seen her. Her face was different from Grace's, but certain features were identical—the deep-set, almost brooding eyes, the faintly downturned corners of the mouth. It was as if they had been transposed from one photograph onto another older version.

"I'd just gotten back . . . I mean, from a weekend in Pennsylvania, when I learned . . . what happened." How else could he refer to it except as "what happened"? "I just wanted to tell you and Mister Colello—"

"Come in, Mr. Vassily," she said.

He followed her into the living room. Half a dozen heavy-set women and four men sat talking over cake and coffee. The scene translated immediately for Ted—Greek-Americans and Italian-Americans reacted to death the same way.

The mother introduced him as "Grace's . . . friend." Almost as an afterthought she added, "Mr. Vassily owns the building."

Ted shook hands with everyone.

"I saw you play," said one of the men, introduced as Uncle Charlie. "I sure never thought I'd get to meet you in person." He turned to one of the other men. "You remember that Penn State–Notre Dame Orange Bowl? You ever think we'd get to meet the guy in person?"

"I wish," Ted said quietly, "it were under other circumstances."

"What's that?" Charlie asked.

"I wish—" He wished he had never said it. "I wish I could have met you at some other time, instead of under circumstances like these."

"Oh, yeah. Sure. But better now than never, huh?"

"Come, Mister Vassily," said Grace's mother, "sit down."

"I can't stay very long, I just wanted to come by . . . you know, and offer to help in any way I can—"

"We don't need your help, Vassily."

Ted turned to face Marty Colello, pale, red-eyed. "Sure, I understand, Mister Colello." Ted offered his hand.

Marty did not take it. "Get out of my apartment, Vassily."

"Marty!" his wife said, shaking her head.

"He's overwrought, champ," Uncle Charlie said, coming to Ted's side. "You understand."

"I'm over-goddamn-nothin'," Marty said, pointing to the door. "I want this bum out of here now."

"I—I just wanted to offer—"

"Offer my ass," said Marty, his index finger still extended toward the door, his entire arm trembling. "Get out."

Ted started toward the door. "I'm sorry," he said.

"You goddamn oughtta be sorry. You put up a building like this . . . the goddamn railings don't even hold—" Suddenly he threw a punch that landed on Ted's ribs. It had little power, but the unexpectedness of it made Ted double over. Charlie jumped between them.

"I'm sorry, Mister Vassily." Grace's mother hurried him to the door. "Please understand, he's overwrought."

"Get out of my apartment!" Marty screamed. "This is your building, but it's my apartment! I can throw you out any goddamn time I please!"

Ted went to his office, thoroughly shaken. Emer and Burr were waiting. "The press is in the lobby," Emer said. "We're feeding them drinks. You look pale."

"I'm all right, goddamn it, just get me a brandy. Bonnie knows where it is."

The snifter seemed to materialize even before Ted finished the sentence. He took a large swallow, winced, then drained the snifter.

"Another?" Bonnie asked.

He nodded and she quickly poured it.

"Okay," he said, "let's get at it."

"Shouldn't we first talk a little about what you're going to say?" Burr asked.

"I know what I'm going to say."

Emerson shrugged and led the newsmen into his own office, then brought in Ted. "Gentlemen," Ted said, "I don't know how many of you know it, but Miss Colello and I were close friends. I'd appreciate it if you'd leave that alone. Her family's suffering enough, they don't need to be embarrassed. They're very conservative old-fashioned people. Good people . . . At this point I honestly don't know what happened or how, but whatever it was, we in Three-oh-five East will do whatever we can to see that—"

"Hey, Ted," said *Daily News*, "when're you going to give us something we can print?"

"I'd appreciate it if you'd give me a break on this, fellas. I think you know I've cooperated with you over the years. This is special, and I'd really—"

"Do you think she committed suicide?" asked *Post*.

"No."

"You don't accept the police report?" asked *Newsweek*.

"I don't know what the police report says. If they decide it was suicide I'll look at their findings and decide whether I agree. For now, I don't think it was."

"Do you suspect foul play?" asked CBS.

"I don't know what to think, except that, knowing Grace, I don't believe she would commit suicide."

"If it wasn't foul play, what could it have been? An accident?"

"I don't know, maybe . . . I really haven't been able to think very logically about it."

"Ted," said *Time*, "how do you feel about your close friend being alone with John Malloy in his apartment?"

Ted glared at him.

"That was your description, not mine, Mr. Vassily."

"And," said ABC, "they were there alone, weren't they?"

"I don't know. I was in Pennsylvania."

"Well, *if* they were there alone, would you have objected?"

"I don't—I didn't have any special claim. We were just very good friends." Very good loving friends . . .

"She never told you about any relationship with John Malloy?"

"I knew she was working on his campaign. I believed—I *believe*—that was the extent of it."

"You sound like you're trying to convince somebody, Ted."

"Oh, stop it. What's to convince? It's none of my business, or yours—"

"Fellas," said Burr Whiteside, "what say we call it a day? Obviously Ted is upset. We all are. Now, if you TV people have camera setups in the courtyard we'll go out and do a couple of short answers for each of you, but that will really have to be it for today."

Ted turned to Emer, who put his arm on Ted's shoulder. "I didn't do very well, did I?" Ted asked when they were in his own office.

"Have another brandy," Emer said.

"How badly did I blow it?"

"You want the truth?"

"I just got it."

"The biggest damage was saying unequivocally that you don't think she committed suicide. You gave them a sure-fire headline: 'VASSILY SAYS IT WASN'T SUICIDE.' "

"I never bullshitted them, Emer. Never in my life. I don't want to start doing it with Grace's death . . ."

"But giving them headlines on a platter . . ." He took Ted's arm. "Sorry, Reep. I shouldn't be climbing all over you on this. I know how tough it is. And I know why you said it."

Ted's eyes were moist when they met Emer's. "And I should be holding up better, old buddy. I shouldn't be coming unstuck on you this way."

"You do what you can do, Reep. Like most of us humans. Now drink that brandy and let's do the TV setups."

In the setups all the reporters asked the suicide question, and Ted, after thinking about hedging, decided to answer exactly as he had earlier. The cameramen and soundmen packed their equipment and everyone left.

"Well," said Burr Whiteside, "we'll get more space than I wanted, but you were direct and honest, the kind of thing people expect from you. Hopefully, there'll be enough on Malloy that you'll wind up a 'meanwhile' segment."

"A 'meanwhile segment'?"

"You know, after they do the main part of the story the anchorman says, 'Meanwhile, Ted Vassily, the builder of Three-oh-five East, says he doesn't believe it was suicide.' . . . Still, I wish you'd used slightly different words. You're *not certain* it was a suicide. You aren't *fully convinced.* But to flat out say—" He noticed Emerson Wade's stern glance. "Oh, well, water over the bridge. Let's just hope that whatever Malloy says, it's enough to keep the spotlight off you."

Emerson walked him to the elevator, took a deep breath and said, "Reep, how much of the BankUS contract did you get a chance to read?"

Ted sighed. He wasn't in any condition to take this kind of pressure.

"I wouldn't bug you about it," Emerson said, "but we really should act as quickly as possible."

Ted restrained the impulse to tell him to get lost. "More waiting list cancellations today?"

"Matter of fact, the reverse. We got a dozen new applicants. But they're, well, lower calibre. I think we're starting to get the thrill-seekers, the kind of dip-shits that would have bought Lee Harvey Oswald's rifle. We need to get the deal closed before Loomis has a chance to figure out we've had a change in demographics." He smiled apologetically.

"I'll have a decision first thing in the morning, Emer. I promise." He went back to his penthouse, took out the contracts, tried to read and found he had passed his eyes over the first sentence a dozen times without comprehending a single word.

He loosened his tie and went to the refrigerator. He found a bottle of Hanns Kornell *Sehr Trocken.* For once he couldn't have cared less about the label. He went to one of the chairs at the window, poured a glass and stared out over Brooklyn and Queens. He had a vague feeling of inappropriateness, a sense that somehow he should not be here. Then he remembered Grace—their first night together, in this chair . . . He lay back and stared at the ceiling. He wanted to yell out, curse out at somebody. Everybody. Nothing would come.

He lifted his glass, studied the bubbles in it, then put it aside. He stared out the window. His eyelids grew heavy. Nan was due, wasn't she? The glass was sitting there on the end table, its bubbles slowly dissipating. Slowly, slowly, not like Grace, who had gone very quickly. . . .

Nan looked at her watch. "I really must go."

Stonington Wattley smiled. "I don't think I'm going to let you."

"I must, Stoney."

Without looking, he reached for her crotch and found himself precisely on target. "I really think I'm going to hold you prisoner forever." He let his fingers roam through the delicious hollow formed by the juncture of her sartorius and long adductor muscles—he'd already mockingly defined them for her . . . what the hell, he hadn't always been a plastic surgeon. . . . he had started as a *real* doctor. "Maybe I'll chain you in the closet, feed you nothing but bread and water. Yes, I'll make you my prisoner . . ."

She moved out of his reach and groped about the floor for her panties.

"I really don't want you to go," he said.

"He's very upset. He needs me."

"He doesn't need you. He has dozens of girls. *I* need you. I—Stonington Wattley."

"I don't want to talk about it, Stoney."

"And I don't want you to leave. Damn it, at least tonight was supposed to be mine, not his."

She found her panties and hurriedly slipped into them. She was fifteen minutes late. "It won't be long. Only a few more nights. Wouldn't you want me to do the same for you if you were in his place?"

"Want!" Wattley made a sweeping gesture, as if somehow to push the word away from their conversation. "Who's he to want? What about me? What about you? You're always talking about what other people want. What do *you* want?"

He was on target again, but his timing was off. Way off. I want, she reflected, to be very far away from here. I want—and I would if it were possible—to turn back the clock and erase my first meeting with Ted Vassily *and* Stonington Wattley. "I want to go now," she said, pulling her dress over her head.

"And I want you to stay."

She forced herself not to respond the way she felt. He was always hard to take when he'd been drinking. "It won't be long." She kissed him lightly on the lips. "Another week at most. Then everything should be back to normal." Why, she asked herself, couldn't she simply tell him to mind his own goddamn business? He didn't own her. She didn't even like him. Not very much, anyway. Not any more. But, damn it, as usual she let herself get into these situations. Too damned weak to say no.

"I'll phone you," she said, hurrying from the room before he could get out of bed.

"When?"

"Soon," she called over her shoulder. "G'night, luv." Once out the door she practically ran to the elevator. She worried that Stoney would get his robe on and come after her. Now if only the car would come. Damn, where was it?

It arrived and with relief she stepped inside and punched the lobby button. Yes, she told herself, she had done it again, she'd let herself get hemmed in, by both of them, and now she had to run. She didn't like to, but at least it was better than fighting.

The elevator door opened at the lobby. She crossed to the east bank and used her key to Ted's apartment to activate that elevator. What she would do, she decided, was put in for a transfer. New York was too hectic anyway. It always had been. She never should have talked herself into moving back after Kansas City. What she really needed was someplace more *peaceful*—without the crazy New York pace and people—some place like Boston, or San Francisco. She probably wasn't senior enough for San Francisco, which every stew and pilot in the company wanted as a base. Boston, though, was fairly junior. And so was Dallas. Or L.A. For that matter, Kansas City wouldn't be all that bad to go back to. Of course, she'd have to avoid Bob. Well, maybe he'd be transferred by then.

The elevator doors opened. Ted, in his chair at the window, awoke with a start.

"I'm sorry I'm late," Nan said. "I was doing so many errands I lost track of time. And the traffic was awful."

He met her halfway across the room. She stepped into his arms. "I was dreaming," he said. "I dreamt you'd run off somewhere."

"Never, baby." She stroked his hair as he pressed his face against her neck. She wondered if her father would get stuck with the price of the full two-year lease when she vacated the apartment. Probably not. All sorts of people were just dying to move into 305 East.

"I really need you, Miss Nan Loomis. I don't think I've ever said that to anyone before. Maybe there was no reason to. Well, there is now. I hope you don't mind."

She smiled and hugged him. Mind? She couldn't stand it.

TEN

THE DAYS and nights seemed to run together. He would wake up and not know whether it was morning or evening. His only focal points were communications from other people—Emer on the intercom asking if he had finished with the contracts, Nate asking if he wanted to go out for a bite to eat, Nan reminding him he hadn't shaved for two days, Eddie Witt inviting him to dinner, Emer telling him it was time for the funeral, Burr reporting the latest developments in the press, Nate asking if he wanted to go out for a bite to eat . . .

He responded to each one as he received it, but afterward they were lost in his memory. He could not remember which had come when, or how he had responded, or what more was expected from him, if anything. He could not be sure which were real and which were dreams. . . .

There was Eddie Witt's invitation to dinner. He was supposed to go to Witt's house with Nan. Witt had made a big deal about him being able to find the place, did he know Long Island, where would he get a car, all that shit. He wasn't interested in the questions but he somehow managed to answer them, to put an end to them, but later he couldn't remember what he had said, or whether it was dream or reality. And then his phone rang and it was Witt wondering if he was okay, and he answered, "Sure, I'm fine, coach, just give me a couple plays to catch my breath," and Witt said, "Don't go anywhere, I want you to stay right where you are, I'll be right over."

And then Nate was there and Nan and Emer and finally Witt and his wife. And somehow it came through to Ted that he'd fucked up on dinner and it wasn't a dream, and Witt's old lady had probably knocked herself out with *pierogen* and *halupki* and *kolutz* and all sorts of down-home crap and goddamn it how could he have let it all get past him?

"Teddy," Witt said, "I want to take you to a doctor." . . . "What for, coach. Whatever you say." . . . N.Y.U. Hospital, the emergency room, a look at you anyway." . . . "I told you, coach, I'm okay. Just a little tired, that's all. After the funeral I'll spend a few days in the country and everything'll be fine." . . . "Teddy," Witt said, "the funeral was three weeks ago." . . . "My God, I missed it!" . . . Witt touched his wrist. "You were there, Teddy. I was with you." . . . And suddenly he remembered the church service and all the photographers waiting outside and Marty Colello coming over to him and pummeling him with his fists and calling him a ripoff artist and a hypocrite. "Sorry, coach," he said, "I must be losing my marbles." . . . "Let's go see a doctor, Teddy." . . . "Okay, coach. Whatever you say." . . . N.Y.U. Hospital, the emergency room, and a nurse asking him lots of questions while she filled out a pink form, then another nurse telling him to put on a white gown and lie on a cot in a narrow area surrounded by sheets, and a young doctor coming in and pressing on his stomach, putting a stethoscope to his chest. . . .

And then the scene faded and Nan was telling him he had better get up in a hurry, because they were expected at Eddie Witt's for dinner. So the whole craziness scene was part of a dream too? . . .

He read the newspapers, then piled them on the floor next to his chair, and when Nan wanted to throw them out he wouldn't let her. They were his link to reality. Somehow, if he kept them long enough, he might manage to absorb their contents, and they would fill in the blank spaces between then . . . that awful *then* . . . and now. He read the stories over and over, sometimes passing his eyes over entire paragraphs without registering a word, at other times remembering everything. . . .

Malloy was released from the hospital. He said he had

no idea what had happened. He had been working with Miss Colello at the apartment, reviewing her memo and speech outline about what the main issues of the senatorial campaign should be, discussing how young people might react to various positions on various issues. Donohue was supposed to be there from the start of the meeting but had phoned to say he'd be late. He'd wanted to refer to a position paper Donohue had written—something on restructuring the presidential cabinet—but had left it at his office. He went to get it. He parked his car a few blocks from the office, got out, took a couple steps, and the next thing he remembered was being on the ground in Central Park and having a terrible headache.

At first the press was, to put it mildly, suspicious, so he and Donohue decided to hold a press conference in an effort to clear things up. Why had Malloy gone to the office for Donohue's position paper? Why hadn't he simply phoned Donohue to pick it up on his way in? He had phoned Donohue, but there was no answer at either Donohue's apartment or his office. Why hadn't he taken Grace with him when he went to the office? He had suggested it, but she'd wanted to stay at the apartment to work on the draft of the speech. Where was the draft now? He had no idea, he only knew that when he left she said she would work on it.

How did it happen that he got mugged outside his office, which was on Second Avenue, and his body was found a mile away in Central Park? He had no idea. He didn't see anybody, didn't remember a thing. Except waking up with a king-size bump on his head, his pockets emptied and his watch gone. But why should somebody take him to Central Park? It didn't make much sense, unless maybe somebody wanted to give the impression that he'd somehow gone out of his mind and taken to going on nighttime strolls through the park. Had he any idea who such a "somebody" might be? None at all . . .

(It was going better than he'd expected, Donohue thought, at least for the moment. If the press even entertained the notion that the opposition was involved, farfetched as it might seem—John had thought it farfetched when he'd mentioned it to him, but he still wasn't so sure—well, they'd be on their way to salvaging something positive out of this mess. Still, to give a more prosaic explanation, Donohue added that maybe someone had struck Malloy and then driven him to the park to rob him—nobody paid much attention to such actions in the park, sad to say—rather than take his property in a lighted, high-traffic area like Second Avenue. Of course, Donohue said, he was only speculating, and if it didn't entirely make sense, well, so be it, except that he supposed people didn't always act rationally when committing a crime . . .)

The questions kept coming. Why was Donohue late for the meeting? He'd overslept. Didn't he hear the phone when Malloy called? No. How come the phone could ring in his own apartment and he didn't hear it? Well, the phone was attached to a jack. If it was unplugged, there would be no ring. Was it unplugged that night? He didn't remember. Could it have been unplugged without his knowing? Yes, the maid might accidentally have unplugged it while cleaning and replugged it the next day. Or his wife might have. Or one of his kids might have. It had happened before, now that he thought about it.

Would Grace Colello have had any reason to commit suicide? None that Malloy or Donohue knew, but then again, neither of them really knew her that well. Was she acting strangely when Mr. Malloy left his apartment? No, not at all. Had she had anything to drink? Only one, as Malloy remembered. Was it possible she'd been using any drugs? He certainly doubted it, she seemed perfectly lucid.

Was his relationship with her strictly business? Yes, strictly. Did his wife know he was entertaining a young lady in their apartment? He didn't recall specifically discussing it with her, he frequently had political meetings at the apartment both when she was and wasn't there. Did he frequently have political meetings alone with young ladies? No, there always was at least one other person. Then why not this time? As he'd said before, Mr. Donohue was supposed to have been there but arrived late.

Again, did Mr. Malloy *believe* Grace Colello had committed suicide? Again, he couldn't, of course, be certain but he doubted it. Then did he think she fell through the railing accidentally? He didn't know. Maybe—he stressed he was only speculating—she had been leaning against the railing, leaning too far over it, looking down to the ground. She had admired the view. If the railing had snapped under such circumstances, she might have fallen over it. Did he think the police were remiss in not considering that theory? He wasn't sure that they hadn't considered it. He assumed that the police would investigate the matter thoroughly. He was prepared to accept their conclusions, whatever they might be.

The press conference did not satisfy the reporters about what had happened to Grace Colello, but it did help offset their suspicions that Malloy and Donohue might be dissembling. Actually the flaws and inconsistencies in the story became its greatest strength. As several reporters noted, if some sort of cover-up were going on, wouldn't the likes of John Malloy and Tom Donohue have been able to manage it more skillfully?

Ted rejected that. Never underestimate the stupidity of anyone, he told himself, suspecting that he was quoting H. L. Mencken. Which reminded him of that long ago first time with Grace and her cleverness about language, and that business about cliché quotations with . . . was it Buffy? All right, enough of that, back to now, and to wondering what was the truth if Malloy and Donohue were lying. . . .

"Ted . . ." Nan was standing next to him. She looked strikingly somber, dressed entirely in black. "You should be getting dressed. We're due to leave in fifteen minutes."

The funeral was in Brooklyn. The church was packed. Police lines had been set up and curiosity-seekers stood twelve deep behind them. At the main entrance, Ted presented himself to the priest, who scanned a typewritten sheet of names and told Ted that he was not on it.

"I'm a good friend," Ted said. "I own the building where she . . . please . . ."

The priest shook his head. "At the family's request, we have reserved seats for the people on this list. All other seats were filled first-come first-served."

A policeman recognized Ted and made room for him and Nan in a roped-off area where TV cameramen and photographers were waiting to take pictures when the funeral procession left the church. A reporter with time on his hands decided to try an interview.

"Ted Vassily, it seems you haven't been invited to attend the service. Can you tell us why? We understand you were a friend of the deceased." He thrust a styrofoam-covered microphone into Ted's face.

"An oversight. Unimportant. Her family obviously is very upset."

"There's been some talk that you've exchanged harsh words with her father, that the family even holds you responsible for her death."

"That's crazy."

"But you were very close friends, weren't you?"

Ted felt his fists clenching. He bit on the inside of his cheek to control the violence he felt coming on, but while he managed not to swing at the reporter he couldn't hold back the words. "Don't you have any decency, man? This girl is dead. Is this your idea of hard-hitting journalism?"

"Do you refuse to answer the question?"

"I won't say another goddamn word to you, you little ass-wipe." He turned away, feeling his ears burn as the camera continued to whirr.

"I'll ask it again," said the reporter, following him. "You were her lover, weren't you?"

Ted wheeled around and grabbed the man by both lapels. He lifted him away from where he'd been standing and pushed him against a crowd of reporters and photographers on the opposite side. He heard shutters clicking and cameras whirring. He knew he shouldn't be doing this—it was disaster in the making—but he couldn't help himself. "You little shit," he heard himself screaming, "I'll shove that fucking microphone down your throat." And so saying he tore it from the reporter's hand and tried to literally carry out the threat. He felt hands pulling on his arms, but they weren't strong enough to keep him from lifting the microphone and going for the reporter's face. Now he heard Nan scream. Suddenly there were pains in his arms, then they both went numb and to his surprise fell helplessly to his sides.

Only then did he see the policemen who had hit him with their billy clubs. One of them was poised to hit him again, but a second one stopped him. Someone behind Ted grabbed him in a chinlock. A sergeant held a raised billy near his face. "Don't fight us, fella, or we'll really have to hurt you."

Ted nodded, not saying a word. The sergeant looked at him uncertainly for a moment, then lowered the club. The policeman holding Ted from behind let go. "Come with me," the sergeant said. He led Ted up the steps of the church and into an entrance arch. "I'm sorry we had to do that," he said softly. "I'd've liked to see you stick one mike down his throat and another up his ass. But we were on camera, Mr. Vassily. We had to stop you."

"I think you broke my arms," Ted said. He couldn't lift them.

"Nah, they'll just be numb for a while. Listen, I really didn't want to do it, you know? But what could I do?"

"Yeah. I know."

"If I let you go now, you promise you won't go after him again?"

"Yeah."

"I'll put you on the opposite side of the church with no reporters near you. Only promise me, no more rough stuff or I'll have to arrest you."

Ted nodded again and started away.

"Wait a second," the sergeant said.

Ted turned back.

The sergeant smiled. "I just wanted to tell you. I saw you play. Yankee Stadium. The national championships against Philly. That bomb to Emerson Wade . . . I never saw a prettier thing in my life."

"Thanks."

"How about an autograph for my kids?"

"Okay, what shall I use?"

The sergeant patted his pockets. "You don't have any paper, huh?"

Ted started to reach for his pocket but could scarcely lift his arm. Some of the numbness was gone, replaced by a dull ache. "Your guys hit hard."

"Sorry. Want me to look for you?"

"In my inside pocket," Ted said. "There are business cards in my wallet."

The sergeant took out two, then a third. "Sign three,

okay? I've got three kids. All boys." He offered one forearm as a desk, lifted Ted's arm into writing position, then held the card in place to be signed.

Ted managed three shaky scrawls. "If they can't read that, bring them by my office about a week from now and I'll do it again—if I've regained ths use of my arms."

"Don't worry about them, they'll be okay in a couple minutes. We hit guys like that all the time."

The sergeant brought him to the police barrier on the opposite side of the church and ushered him into position in front of some grumbling curiosity-seekers. "He owns the building where the deceased lived," the sergeant explained. "He's a friend of the family." Another policeman escorted Nan to Ted's side. "Take care," said the sergeant, tipping his cap. "I may just take you up on that thing about bringing the kids to your office."

"Please do, I'd be happy to meet them."

Nan assessed his mood before saying anything. "Are you okay?" she finally managed.

"Nothing serious."

"That reporter was disgusting."

"Yeah, well, I suppose he was only doing his job. The prick." He half smiled, then thought of Grace and his expression froze.

"Are you really okay?"

"Yeah. Yeah. I'm *fine*."

He stood staring at the stairs to the church, occasionally hearing a snippet of the ceremony within as doors opened and closed. Finally the service was over. The crowd poured out, policemen urging everyone to keep moving so that the funeral party could get through. The curiosity-seekers had been in the back of the church and exited first. They were followed by the family's friends. Ted saw that John Malloy was there with his wife, and Tom Donohue with a woman Ted assumed to be his. A moment later Spats Johnson appeared in one of the archways. As he descended the stairway he noticed Ted and hurried to the police barrier.

"Hey, man, how come I didn't see you inside?"

"It doesn't matter . . ."

A hush came over the crowd as the funeral cortege came through the central arch. The pallbearers were students. An altar boy swinging a censer preceded them, and two others with thick orange candles followed. They in turn were followed by a somber priest carrying a prayer book, then Grace's family—father and mother, an elderly man and woman presumably grandparents, the people Ted had seen at Grace's the day after she died, several other couples and a dozen children.

Shutters clicked and television cameras whirred as the cortege made its way down the stairs and through the police lines to the hearse. Ted watched Grace's parents. Marty Colello seemed to be staring blankly at the ground, but after every few steps he'd raise his eyes to scan the crowd. Eventually they met Ted's. The gaze was held for an instant, then Marty looked away.

Considering her feelings, Ted found it a bit ironic that Grace would have a Roman Catholic funeral—doubly so as a suspected suicide. He turned to Nan, who was watching him intently. He squeezed her hand, a silent way of telling her how grateful he was for her support since Grace's death . . . *Grace* . . . Oh, God . . .

He saw a look of fear on Nan's face and for an instant thought she was reacting to something she saw in his face. And then he realized that she was looking beyond him, and he whirled around just in time to catch a solid punch in the mouth from Marty Colello.

"You son of a bitch," Marty screamed. "It's not bad enough you kill my daughter, you have to come to the funeral?"

Suddenly Marty was surrounded by cameramen, reporters and policemen, but nonetheless managed to get off a second punch before the police could restrain him.

"Mister Touchdown," he continued to taunt with his arms pinned behind his back. "Mister Big Superstar that bleeds for the poor people. Hah! We're just furniture to you! You want us around so you can show off the poor folks next door. Well, I don't need your handout, Mister Touchdown. I'm moving out!" The police tried gently to steer him away. He seemed to go along with them, then abruptly spun back to Ted. "But I ain't leaving before I say goodbye. You ready?" He looked around as if to make sure the cameras were on him. They were. "Here it is, Superstar—goodbye!" And he spat in Ted's face.

Ted wiped himself with a handkerchief as the photographers zeroed in.

"Mr. Vassily," said a familiar voice, "what's your reaction to Mr. Colello's accusations?" It was the reporter Ted had confronted earlier, and once again he shoved his styrofoam-covered microphone toward Ted's face.

Ted looked at him a moment—fists clenched at his side—and walked away without saying a word.

"Well," said Burr Whiteside, "it could have been worse."

"How?" asked Emerson Wade.

"I don't know offhand, but I'm sure it could have been."

"I guess it's my fault," Ted said.

No one responded.

"You all think I should have kept my mouth shut with that reporter the whole time. Well, I tried but—"

Emer chuckled sardonically. "In a way, it's good you didn't. They had to cut your four-letter words, which meant cutting half the film they shot."

"Don't patronize me, Emer."

"I'm not." He raised both arms as if about to make a point, then let them fall to his sides. "I'm—I'm just frustrated, man. I see this fantastic thing that we put together—that *you* put together, with the rest of us just sort of hanging on and helping where we could—and now I see the whole goddamn thing ready to bust apart."

"What should I do?"

"Okay the goddamn contracts with BankUS." Emer seemed about to strike out at Ted, but suddenly his expression softened. "I'm sorry, man, I really am. I know how this whole thing must be tearing you up. But understand my position—here we are about to convert Three-oh-five East into a multi-million-dollar conglomerate, and we're having one disaster after another. Any second now the whole thing can go down the goddamn drain."

"Were there more waiting list cancellations today?"

"It stayed about even. But it won't forever, Reep. People are watching their TV's. They're going to start thinking, who needs to live in that zoo? Any day now our list could get chopped in half. If that happens, or if your buddy Loomis suddenly wakes up to what could happen

—which I'm surprised he hasn't done already—it's the end of the old ballgame." He put his hand on Ted's shoulder. "Please understand that I appreciate what you're going through, but I've got to have those contracts. If you don't okay them, we could wind up kissing the whole thing goodbye."

Ted turned to Burr. "You agree?"

"I'm just a hired hand, Ted. It's not for me to agree or disagree."

"You've got shares in Athletes, Inc., so you're more than a hired hand. Do you agree with Emer or not?"

"Let's say if I were the one to make the decision, yeah, I guess I'd go with Emer."

Ted made a tent with his fingers and stared at it for so long that Emerson asked, "Reep, you nodding out on us?"

"I want you to call a meeting," Ted said, still not looking up. "Get all our people who have a major interest in this. Mikey, Nate, the coach. No Ron-Cor or other outsiders, just our old gang. Get them over here tonight if you can."

"I'll get on the horn right now."

"Set it for after dinner. Ten o'clock."

"Do you think nine might be a little better?"

"Ten," he said, and started out.

Emer stopped him. "Reep, one thing. I know how fond you and Nan Loomis are of each other, but remember that her father's our target of opportunity. If you were planning on bringing her to the meeting—"

"I may be an emotional wreck, Emer, but I'm not a total jerk."

They assembled in Ted's office. Nate served Scotch. Everyone eyed Ted warily.

"I haven't gone bananas," he said. "Don't worry."

They laughed nervously.

"But I know when I'm giving it my best shot and when I'm not. Right now, I'm not."

They all found things to look at other than his face.

"Coach, when I played ball for you, I was very big on back-up quarterbacks. Other guys wanted to play the whole game. I wanted a two-touchdown lead, then out and let the back-up man run the show."

"That's true, Teddy. And there were times you were happy to pack it in with a one-touchdown lead."

Everyone laughed.

"Right. Well, I don't know what kind of lead we've got now, or whether we're even ahead, but I know I'm no longer giving this team what it needs. So if it meets with you guys' approval, I want out."

There was a murmur. The abdication announcement was not totally unexpected, but no one seemed quite ready to hear it pronounced.

"Effective immediately, I'm resigning as chairman and C.E.O. of our corporations. I'm keeping my stock, but I'm going to proxy the voting rights to you guys as a committee of the whole, with a unanimous vote required to exercise them. I'll make my recommendations, then I'll leave the room and you can play it any way you like."

There was nervous laughter.

"For our parent corporation and all the subsidiaries except Three-oh-five East itself, I recommend as my successor Emerson Wade."

"Thank you, Reep." Emerson obviously was pleased but also puzzled—he didn't expect 305 East to be split from the corporate parent.

"As chairman and chief executive officer of Three-oh-five East, I recommend Nate Elefante."

"Jeez, Reep, I don't think I can handle it."

"You can handle it." Ted shrugged. "But if you don't want to work that hard, take it up with your fellow stockholders. I've just cashed in my chips." He started toward the door.

Eddie Witt blocked his path. "Teddy, I think I speak for everyone when I say this is entirely unnecessary. None of us doubts your ability to continue."

"You don't have to. I do. That's enough."

"I for one am willing to keep my shares behind you all the way."

"Thanks, coach, but I'm out." He stepped around Witt. "Have a nice night, fellas. See you around."

"Reep." It was Emer.

Ted turned.

"I want you to know . . . if the group follows your

recommendation and gives me full authority, I may do some things you wouldn't approve of."

"The game's all yours, friend. No plays from the bench."

"I may decide Three-oh-five East could be more profitable for the corporate parent if we sell it off as condominia."

"Take that up with Mr. Elefante if your fellow stockholders elect him as I've recommended." He went to the door.

Back in his penthouse, he threw up. Mr. T. had given up the ball, and it wasn't something as easily passed off as he'd pretended at the meeting. He looked in on Nan, sleeping . . . or perhaps pretending to be? Never mind . . . this was one night when he knew without testing that he'd never be able to get it up.

When she got up in the morning Nan found him fast asleep in the chair he had first shared with Grace Colello.

He waited for the oppressive curtain of grief to lift. It didn't.

It was no longer only the loss of Grace, he decided. It was a combination of losses. It was the failure of 305 East to become what he had dreamed. It was the feeling that he somehow had wasted two years. It was the feeling that ultimately everything was a waste, because ultimately everything was a game and it didn't really matter who won. It was the feeling of being tired and getting old and past the point when he could give his best to the one game he really played best.

He kept running in the morning with Emer. And now that he didn't have business to attend to, he spent a good deal of time during the day chucking balls at kids on playgrounds. It felt good. It felt particularly good to be out from under all the pressure of the past two years. But it did not feel the same as running Three-oh-five East —or taking a championship team on the field and making it play its absolute best.

He talked a reluctant Nan—though she smilingly tried to hide her feelings—into making a complicated swap arrangement with some other stews so she could have ten days in a row with him. They went to Penn State, stayed at the Nittany Lion Inn, had dinner every night at The Tavern, watched the football workouts. One day after the regular practice Pater Noster invited him to throw a few, and he gave the receivers all they could take in a workout. The quarterbacks stood around with their mouths open. "I'd give anything to be able to throw like that," said a young man who was being touted as the first Penn Stater to win a Heismann since John Cappelletti. It felt good to Ted. But it was still far removed from the feeling of taking a championship team on the field and making it play better than its best.

He and Nan walked under the elms in front of Old Main. They sat in The Hub watching kids walk by who seemed to Ted like babies. Was it possible he was once that young and capable of feeling the emotions he now could only remember? Come to think of it . . . Nan was scarcely a year or two older than that now!

He took her to Beaver Stadium and she asked, "Is this where they used to do that individual-introduction thing that Nate's so fond of talking about?"

"No, that was Yankee Stadium, in the pros."

"I'll bet it was exciting to play here too."

He thought about the Blue Band rushing onto the field in double time. And playing "Fight On, State" after a touchdown and having the mascot in the lion's suit do one push-up for every point scored in the game. There was one day when Ted was responsible for making the poor bastard do sixty-eight push-ups.

They walked from Beaver back toward College Avenue, going past the TV stations and the tennis courts. A pair of really boxy chicks walked by and didn't notice him looking at them. Was that what being an old man was all about? The box stops noticing you, and eventually everyone else does, and you just fade the hell away?

They attended a road company performance of a Broadway musical at Rec Hall. They sat in on English Department lectures on Chaucer, who Nan said was her favorite storyteller. He thought about that a little, but not much. They ate ice cream at The Creamery and sat with the after-classes crowd at The Skeller. (Christ, these kids really looked young!) On the seventh of their planned ten days, she told him she had to make a routine phone call to crew-scheduling, just in case the airline needed her. She came back from the phone to report that she was needed in New York immediately. He knew her explanation was bullshit. He wasn't sure why she was cutting the trip short, but it didn't matter. If you're being bullshitted, what does it matter why?

They went back to New York. She left on a flight. He had a hunch he wouldn't see her again. He was wrong. He saw her half a dozen times more. On the first of these occasions she reported that to her great surprise she'd been transferred to Kansas City, effective the end of the month. On other occasions she told him how she would miss him and would think of him all the time and would be sure to call whenever she was in New York. He offered to help move her stuff from the apartment, but she said her father was taking care of everything. He offered to accompany her to the airport, but she said she hated long sad goodbyes and would rather do it nice and clean right here in his apartment. He kissed her and watched the elevator doors close after her, and he told himself this really was the last time.

He saw her once more. Actually it was the next night. He happened to be sitting in the lobby nursing one of many Scotches and hoping some spectacular new quiff would walk by. Sometime around one in the morning Nan came through the door with Stonington Wattley, holding onto his arm, smiling and leaning against him, tossing her long brunette curls as she responded to his hilarious banter. She saw Ted and sort of pushed herself against Wattley, as though it might somehow be possible to hide in the folds of his flaming green sports jacket. Then she clutched his hand and forced him to turn a quick about-face. The last Ted saw of her was her cute little ass as she and Wattley walked hand-in-hand out the door.

He told himself that he really shouldn't let it throw him. All along, he told himself, he had expected something like this. Especially during the last week or so.

All right, so Nan Loomis hadn't broken his heart—nor he hers—so they'd quit all even. As she'd said, break nice and clean. He should've known better than to rely so completely on Nan, but after Grace—

No, damn it, enough self-pity. Onward, upward. Back, God help him, to the hunt! Make that, Bacchus help him. The other guy was down on sex.

He spent time with Spats Johnson. They chased chorus girls. A couple of times, Ted scored. But they were real air-heads, they couldn't get their act together without dope—how he hated that!—and they were lousy lays.

One of them started moaning and bucking before he'd even gotten all the way in. Her movements made it impossible for him to penetrate, like trying to thread a moving needle. He asked her to lie still, and she said she would, but somehow she never did. Giggling apologetically, she explained that she couldn't help herself. After losing his hard-on three times he finally managed to get it in and to squeeze out a quick come. But, damn, it was hard work.

Another broad was into water games. A few minutes after he'd brought her to his place she excused herself to go to the bathroom, then called for him. He figured maybe the maid forgot to put out toilet paper. When he got to the bathroom the door was wide open and this dippy broad was sitting on the john.

"What's wrong?" he asked.

"Nothing," she said. "I just feel like talking." Whereupon she commenced to take a piss. She smiled naughtily at the sound of her stream hitting the water. When Ted didn't respond, she pouted, "Don't I turn you on?"

"We can talk when you finish," he said, retreating.

He considered developing a headache, a hernia, a flare-up of an old football injury—you understand, I'm sure—except he was still too horny. He focused on her legs, which were lovely, and forced himself not to think of the toilet scene. By concentrating powerfully, he managed to get an erection and have a tolerable fuck.

Afterward, he got up from the bed to go to the bathroom. "May I come?" she asked.

"What for?"

"I want to hold your wee-wee while you tinkle."

Wasn't *anybody* into good old Kentucky straight anymore?

And the answer came back that, yes, Buffy Weiss was into good old Kentucky straight. He was surprised to find himself thinking of her. But cuntiness notwithstanding, she had been a really decent lay. Well, not such a good lay, really, but a turn-on. He remembered that first day in his room at the Tuscany. . . .

"You're probably wondering why I'm here."

"The question crossed my mind."

"I've heard you're one hell of a fuck."

Yeah, she was something. Maybe he should call her. . . . "I've heard you've got some new tricks and I wanted to see if it was true."

No, that wasn't his style. Besides, he'd get himself all psyched up worrying about being shot down, and her phone would be busy the first few times he called, and when she finally answered he'd stutter and she'd realize she had the advantage, and she'd rub his nose in shit to make up for what she considered to be the number he had done on her. Fuck, forget it.

But he couldn't forget it. He toyed with the idea of phoning her and went so far sometimes as to pick up the receiver and dial the first few digits of her number before hanging up. And he hung around the lobby between five-thirty and six-thirty in the evening, when everyone was getting home from work, sort of hoping he'd see her. And after a couple of weeks he did. He watched her, waiting for her eyes to meet his so that he could smile and she would in return. She looked through him and walked right past.

He decided not to let it go at that. He called her name, and when she didn't answer he jogged after her. "Hey," he said, catching up just as she reached the elevator, "long time no see. What've you been doing?"

She looked at him with mock-uncertainty, then managed a frosty smile. "Ah, I remember. Ted Vassily . . . you used to own this building, didn't you?"

She stepped into the elevator and the door closed before he could think of anything to say.

But he thought: *Cunt. Cunt!!!*

One night he got drunk and decided to phone Chris. He dialed her number, listened to three rings, four, five, was about to hang up, and heard a voice. It wasn't Chris's. The number had been changed some time ago.

He looked her up in the directory. Had she got married

again? No—his heart pounded—she was still listed under her maiden name!

He dialed the new number. Six rings, no answer. He waited half an hour. Same scene. He drank some more and dialed again an hour later. Busy signal. He dialed again in fifteen minutes. A man answered.

"Miss"—he started. "Mistake," he amended quickly. "Wrong number. Sorry. Goodnight."

He ripped the phone out of the wall, threw it across the room, emptied his bottle of wine and went to bed.

Eddie Witt invited Ted and Nate to dinner. They talked politics and old times and the stock market and just about everything except what really was on their minds.

"Teddy," Witt said finally after his wife had left the three men alone, "I think I could use your help with something."

Ted smiled. "Translation—you think I'm going down the drain and you want to bail me out."

"That happens to be true, young fella, but it's not the subject I was about to introduce."

"Sorry, coach."

"What I was about to introduce was the subject of those three season openers where you ran the first play from scrimmage. I was going over the attendance figures of those games versus our subsequent openers. You know, we had three capacity crowds, versus nothing better than sixty percent in the years since."

"So you're going to ask me to do you the favor of running another first play and making lots of money for the team. And in the meantime if I happen to get motivated and rehabilitated, well, that's just a fringe benefit, huh?"

"Will you stop acting like a self-pitying young punk and listen to the rest of what I have to say?"

"Sorry . . ."

"I've been talking to Willie Coleman in Detroit. We're on against each other for the first pre-season exhibition game. I don't know how closely you've been following attendance figures for exhibition games, but lately we haven't been able to draw flies."

"Small wonder. Nobody wants to get hurt before the season opener, so nobody plays a decent game of ball."

"That's part of it, yes. Anyway, Willie and I got to talking about various gimmicks to fill a ball park and it occurred to us that pro football never tried its version of that baseball classic, the Old Timers' Game."

Ted laughed. "For a damn good reason. Most goddamn football old timers are on crutches."

"An exaggeration, Teddy, but in the general direction of the target, yes. Anyway, Willie and I remembered your first-play-from-scrimmage capacity crowds and decided it might not be a bad idea to do our own variation on it for our opening exhibition number. Instead of one play we'd make it one series of downs, the New York Old Timers versus the Detroit Old Timers. We'd get sportswriters or some other outside group to pick each team's twenty-two starters from the all-time roster—using, of course, only those who wanted to play."

Ted swirled his wine, watched it slosh around in the glass. "A few problems with that, coach. Number one, most of the guys would be in such lousy shape they wouldn't be able to run a play. Number two, most of them would've played in different years and not be on to each other's moves. Number three, you'd have style differences—the old single-wing leather helmet guys versus the wide-open style of the late fifties and early sixties versus today's highly controlled game. You'd wind up with twenty-two old farts playing junior high bump-and-fall football. With a big letdown for the fans."

"Maybe you're right, but the basic idea—"

"The basic idea is sound, but you'd have to set up a first-class game of football. Use old timers sparingly. Mix them in with the first-string lineup. Forget about old timer running backs or defensive backs. They'd be too slow and couldn't take the punishment. Quarterbacks could handle it, there's less contact. Kickers, of course, and maybe a few linemen. Some receivers, if they really stayed in shape, like Mikey and Emer."

Witt smiled. "You think you could put together an old timers' team for me, to go up against Carm 'the Arm' Camaratta and the Detroit Old Timers?"

"You kiddin'? Give me Nate and Mikey and Emer—I'd blow those guys off the field." Ted halted in mid-smile.

"You slipped one past me, coach. I let myself get faked out."

"It's no fake, Ted. It's a good idea. Lots of fans get a chance to see their old favorites play again, the team makes a pile of money and we all have some fun."

"I could go for it, coach. I could really go for it." He sipped his wine. "But we have to make a few more changes. Let's not run just one series of downs. Make it a full quarter. Or a whole game. Yeah, a full game. Get the commissioner to allow you an extra twenty-two slots per team, and mix the old timers in with the regular lineup. Bring out old Horst Springer to do the opening kickoff. If he can handle it, let him kick field goals and extra points too. If he starts screwing up, bring in the regular first-stringer. Maybe let Kulikowski run a few from the fullback slot, but not with the rest of us old farts in the backfield. Give him a shot with a young line and backfield so he can have decent blocking and show his stuff."

"How does it sound to you, Nate?"

Nate laughed. "Co', you jes' tell your equipment manager to find a number seventy-seven jersey and pants with a fifty-two waist."

"I'll want lots of practice with the team," Ted said. "Nothing that would screw up your regular sessions, of course. But I should work for at least a couple of weeks with the center. Either that or bring in one of my own. No, use yours—an old timer couldn't take the punishment. And I want lots of work on handoffs with the backs. I've seen some of these pro bowl games on TV. Christ, the guys look as though they're handing each other cups and saucers."

"I don't see where we'll have any problems setting up practices."

"One thing more, coach. If you really want to make it a media event plus get maximum performance out of each player, try this—you know how they pay in the Super Bowl, twice as much for the winners as the losers? You want to really have one hell of a game, set aside a certain percentage of the gate for the old timers, with the winning players getting two thirds and the losers one third."

Witt laughed. "Teddy, you should never have left the

game. You should've fired me as coach and run the show yourself."

"No, coach, I said it all when I shook loose from Three-oh-five East. I'm okay when it comes to setting things up, but I'm better off leaving the operations to other people."

"So what do you think you might set up next? After the Old Timers Game, I mean."

"I don't know. Something . . . sooner or later."

"You really plan to look, Teddy, don't you?"

"You're worried about me, coach?"

"I hate waste, my boy. I know the kind of ability you have. I hate to think of it being squandered."

"I'll be okay, coach." He laughed. "Just give me a couple plays to catch my breath."

"I believe that now, Teddy."

"You didn't before?"

"I wasn't sure, I am now."

An hour later Ted and Nate said their goodbyes to Witt and his wife. "Coach," Ted said, gripping Witt's forearm, "thanks for everything. I really mean *everything.*"

"Teddy"—Witt's eyes fixed to his—"don't mistake my having confidence in you with doing you a favor. When you brought me up from high school to coach pro ball, it was a tremendous break for me. But you didn't do me a favor, Teddy. You gave me an opportunity. There's a difference. If you didn't think I could handle it, you wouldn't have let me try. Or you shouldn't have." He clapped Ted on the shoulder. "I'm not doing you any favors, young fella. I know how good you are. Your talents have helped me come a long ways from the coal fields. I'd be a darned fool if I didn't give you the opportunity to take me even further."

As Nate drove them back into the city, Ted leaned back in the white Eldorado convertible and remembered the night Nate had picked him up at the airport. Only two years ago . . .

"You really want me on that old timers' team?" Nate said.

Ted made himself laugh. "Come on, Nasty, you know better than to ask."

"Seriously. It was a good point you made about guys being old and out of shape. I'm no spring chicken, you know."

"Nathan, the day that you can't take out any two defensive linemen in pro football is the day I start voting Socialist."

"Well, I just want you to know I won't be offended if that's what you figure would be best for the team . . . Like Witt said, nobody wants favors."

"How about opportunities?"

Nate punched him on the thigh. "I'll take all I can get, you prick."

They rode silently for a while.

"Reep?"

"Yeah?"

"I'm interested in your answer to Witt's question about what you might set up next."

"I told him the truth. I haven't decided."

"You haven't even thought about it?"

"I've thought I'd better get my ass in gear and do something, but it hasn't gone beyond that."

"You know, when I was a kid back in Shreveport I had a buddy that was a lot like you. When he finished high school he didn't know what he wanted to do or even where he wanted to go, but he knew he had to get out of Louisiana or he'd go under with the rest of the locals. So one day he packed everything he owned in his car and drove to the junction where Route Eighty intersects with Seventy-one, Seven, One, and One Seventy-one. He wrote down all the possible directions on pieces of paper: 'Seventy-one north,' 'Eighty west,' 'Eighty east,' and so on. Then he crumpled them up, put them in his hat and picked one out. It was Eighty west and he stayed on it till he got to California. He's a big-ass aerospace honcho today."

"You think that's what I ought to do?"

"I think you ought to do something."

"I will."

Nate hesitated. "When you do, Reep, I'd like to come along."

"You're already tired of honchoing Three-oh-five East?"

"Not tired." Nate smiled sheepishly. "I know I'm in

over my head. Eighty percent of the time Emer is carrying me. Besides, it's like you said tonight—some guys are good at one thing, others at another. I'm no honcho. I'm a Sancho Panza."

"A what?"

"You know, the guy in *Don Quixote*."

Ted laughed.

"Don't be so surprised. You're not the only football player that ever read a book, you know. All right, actually I didn't read the book, I saw *Man of La Mancha*. Anyway, some guys are Sanchos. I know it ain't the great American dream. We're all supposed to want to grow up to be president. But piss on it, Reep, that's not my style. I'm a Sancho."

"If you are, you're the best of the lot."

"You think so?"

"Yeah."

"All right, I know so. So what more do you want? When you decide to make your move, let me know."

They rode through the Queens-Midtown tunnel, then headed north on First. "How soon do you think it'll be?" Nate asked.

"My move?" Ted shrugged.

"You waiting for some particular thing to happen?"

"Not really."

"Doesn't it drive you nuts living the way you are now?"

Ted let a few seconds pass. "Yeah."

"You have any idea what you want to do?"

"Nope."

"Not even a hint?"

"Nope."

"Well, Jesus, you ain't gonna just sit around being the fucken emeritus forever, are you?"

"Maybe."

"Emer was saying the other day you'd be really valuable as the company's new-projects honcho. In other words, every time we got—"

"—a new thing going I'd do the organizing."

"Right. Did he talk to you about it?"

"No, but I know the way he thinks."

"It could be great—for the two of us, I mean. Go out

to L.A., get the new radio station off its ass, ball some Triple-C Clean Califo'nia Cunt. Finish there, back to New York and honcho something here. Then, who knows, maybe Miami."

"Yeah, sounds good, Nate."

"So when do we get started?"

"I don't know."

Nate sighed. "Jesus, Reep, whatta we gotta do to get you off your ass?"

Ted didn't answer.

The days passed. Ted made himself think about his body. If he was really going to play a full game of ball, he had to toughen up.

He pinched the roll of flab above his belt. He'd lost about three inches since he started running with Emer. Three more and he'd be fine.

Yeah, fine to look at. But it takes more than a skinny waist to stand up to four quarters of football. Some of these new linemen were monsters.

Of course, there was no law that he had to play the full game. He could take himself out after one play. Except he knew he wouldn't.

So that meant getting in shape. And the harder he worked at it, the more distant the goal seemed. The first plateau hadn't been bad. The second had been tough. The third was working out to be a real killer. And the two after that would be tougher still.

"Remember what you used to tell me at Penn State?" Emer said. " 'Play the game one down at a time.' "

They ran silently for a while. Ted wondered if Emer was picking up speed. If not, Ted was really dragging ass today.

"Hey, Emer, how go things these days with the old corp?"

"You ought to start attending directors' meetings. Maybe you'd find out. What do you do all day? Sit around and drink?"

"I've cut out drinking, except wine with meals. No, these days I sit around and think. I've become a very big thinker."

"Not very healthy, old buddy."

"I know . . . Anyway, what's happening with the corp?"

"We're right on target with *Football Weekly*. I hired away a top editor from Magazine Management, the old Martin Goodman company. This guy trained under Goodman personally. We'll have every statistical service available, plus picks and point spreads from the top Vegas oddsmakers. Great photo coverage—all the wire services, plus two staff photographers—one of whom is female and a real box. All we need now are some provocative columnists. Interested?"

"You serious?"

"Am I ever anything but?"

"Aw, I'm no writer."

"You weren't a quarterback either until you got out on a field and started throwing some balls."

"Nah, I'll skip that one. What else is happening?"

"We bought a property for Hart's girl friend. Hey, there's something you could get your teeth into. The property, I mean. The girl friend too, of course, but mainly the property."

Ted said nothing.

"Seriously, Reep, the corp could use somebody to honcho the movie. Those Hollywood bastards could steal us blind."

"Will you stop trying to find work for me?"

"You'd love it. Think of all the ass you'd get."

"I'm retired, Emer. Period." They ran silently for a few moments. "What else is happening with the corp?"

"Not much, really."

More silence.

"What's happening," Ted asked finally, "with Three-oh-five East?"

"Not much."

"Same old shit, huh? The elevators still go up and down, the door still opens—"

"Well, you know I converted to condos."

"Yeah."

"None too soon either. About sixty percent of the tenants bought their apartments. A month after the . . . funeral some of the buyers were trying to renege and the rental waiting list was down to practically zilch. Mandino had it about right. New York is trendy. The trend turned against us—"

"Did Malloy buy his apartment?"

"No, he bought a brownstone in Harlem."

"Funny."

"Seriously. It was in all the papers. You given them up? He's having the place renovated and plans to move in as soon as the work is done."

"Why?"

"Publicity. Conviction. Some of both, I guess. Anyway, he probably figures if he can dissociate himself from Three-oh-five East he can also blur voters' connection of him with Grace's death."

"Any developments . . . about Grace, I mean."

"You really don't read the newspapers, do you?"

"Not much."

"Well, her parents say they're convinced it was an accident. They wouldn't authorize an autopsy, and the police seem willing to let it go at that. Certain writers—Toby Tanner up front—keep harping that there has to be more than meets the eye, that Malloy was somehow involved, but everyone else seems willing to accept it as an accident."

"What do you think? Could she have fallen, the way Malloy said?"

"She'd have to have been leaning over awfully far."

"You don't believe the suicide business?"

"I don't not believe anything."

"Is our insurance going to pay off?"

"No, they're claiming it's suicide."

"Cocksuckers."

"Yeah, insurance people are worse than lawyers. Speaking of whom, I spoke to Mike Epstein, and he checked with a top liability man. The best strategy, they decided, is for Grace's parents to sue Three-oh-five East and us to bring in the insurance company as an additional defendant."

"Okay, do it. Meanwhile don't pay any more premiums and let the fuckers cancel us."

"Uh, Reep, aren't you forgetting something?"

"What?"

"You abdicated."

Ted was embarrassed. "Sorry, Emer."

"So am I."

They ran in silence for a while.

"What else goes at Three-oh-five East?"

"Not a hell of a lot."

"Grace's folks move out?"

"Yeah, as soon as their last month's rent was used up."

"What're you going to do about the subsidized apartments in the condo setup?"

"We can't do anything."

"How's that?"

"Once fifty-one percent of the apartments were sold, we lost the controlling vote. Now we're just the management company, with the condo owners calling the shots."

"What're they calling on the subsidized apartments?"

"I talked them into letting the current leases run."

"And then throw the people out?"

"And then not renew the leases, yeah."

"Oh, great. I put two years of my life into that place to turn it over to a bunch of fat-assed selfish pigs."

"You knew before you resigned what I'd planned—"

"I'm not blaming *you*."

They ran silently for a while.

"Maybe," Emer said, "you shouldn't blame yourself either, Reep. The bankers, Mandino—I guess they called the shot right from the start. It was a beautiful idea, rich and poor together, all under free-enterprise capitalism. But it just wasn't practical—not now, not here."

"Maybe you're right."

"Look at the bright side. For a while, anyway, we pulled it off. The people got to live in their subsidized apartments for a year. We made money, and we're going to make more. If the building eventually goes under it's not our loss, it's BankUS's."

"Yeah. Beautiful."

"All right, it isn't the way we'd work it out if we had a magic wand. But be realistic, Reep. When you add up the pluses and minuses, we got dipped in shit and came out smelling like a rose."

"Yeah," Ted said. He thought of a line he had read

somewhere but couldn't remember the source. "Tread softly, sir, for you tread on my dreams." Grace, he thought . . . Grace would know the source.

When Joe Mandino got Emerson Wade's letter that 305 East was being converted into a condominium, the first thing he did was invite Emerson to lunch and offer him the presidency of First American Investment Corporation at one hundred and fifty thousand dollars a year. The second thing he did—after Emerson turned down escalations to three hundred thousand dollars a year—was instruct his lawyer to find him a new apartment. Not only rats desert a sinking ship . . . anybody with half a fucken brain deserts a sinking ship.

Joe did not reveal to anyone except his lawyer that he planned to move. He had learned over the years that the less people know about you, the less you have to worry about. These days, of course, were a picnic compared to the old days. He was far removed from the front lines. He was an elder statesman, highly influential, well-liked. He was the man people called on to arbitrate disputes, never one of the disputants.

Still, the habits of a lifetime of caution were deeply ingrained. A less cautious man than Joe Mandino, now entering the lobby of 305 East, probably would not have given a second thought to the fellow with the red beard sitting at one of the lobby tables sipping a drink. People lounged at the tables all the time, watching the passing parade. But somehow this fellow did not look as though he belonged. He was too alert, too ready, for someone who supposedly was lounging.

"*Attenzione,*" Joe told his man Angie. "*La barba rossa.*"

"*Si, padrone. Lo vedo.*" Angie's hand slowly went inside his jacket.

The man with the red beard seemed not to notice. He continued to sip his drink and look toward the door.

Joe Mandino did not take his eyes off the man. And now, as Joe neared his table, Joe noticed the scar—a thin, fairly recent scar, almost but not quite covered by the beard. It started just below one eye and reached almost to the man's ear. Of course . . . the government man, sent to make sure he didn't talk . . . he, Joe Mandino! Crazy fucked-up amateurs . . . judge everybody by themselves. . . .

"Fucilalo!" Joe yelled, at the same time wheeling toward a pillar which, if he could get behind it in time, would offer temporary cover.

Angie was getting on. At twenty-five, he could have got a shot off before the man with the red beard had a chance to blink. Even at fifty he could have blown away the kid before he could go for his own piece. Not at seventy-two.

The kid was firing while Angie's pistol was still in its shoulder holster. "Don't!"—Joe heard himself screaming and hated it—"I'll pay you more than they—" Something in his lungs cut off the last word. By that time the kid had pumped one bullet into Angie and was firing another into Joe.

The gun was a .357 Magnum, which at six feet can knock over a horse. The second bullet caught Joe in the neck and opened a hole as big as a fist. A fine shower of blood came from the circumference of the wound like the spray from a lawn sprinkler. A moment later a thick red jet shot from the center. Then a mass of bluish-pink flesh dropped out, looking like the innards of a butchered animal.

The next shot hit Angie in the center of the chest. Its force knocked him over a table. The next went into Joe's face, along his nose and just above his teeth. It came out the back of his head, creating another showerlike red spray. The final shot tore open his shirt, which quickly turned dark red. His hands closed in front of the fast-spreading stain, as if to conceal it, and he toppled face-first onto the marble floor.

Nate was with Ted in the penthouse when Kulikowski reached him on the intercom with the news. "Jesus, call the police," Nate said.

"I did," said Kulikowski.

"Have security close off the area. Nobody leaves the building, not even tenants. And nobody gets in but tenants."

"I did that too."

"Okay, call Burr Whiteside. Have him get here as fast as he can. I'll be right down."

The security cordons were up when they got to the lobby. The first wave of policemen had arrived. Sirens outside heralded reinforcements.

"How did it happen?" Ted asked.

Kulikowski was pale. "I dunno, Reep. It was nice out, so I was opening the door from outside instead of inside. I let Mandino and his guy in. Next thing I know, there's shots and there they are on the floor."

"Who did it?"

"I dunno, man. I didn't see anyone."

Security chief Sammy McCollough and the cocktail waiter began jabbering at once. The waiter had seen the guy with the red beard. He'd been sitting there for almost two hours, drinking ginger ale.

"Where did he go?"

"I don't know," said the waiter. "When I heard the shots I got behind the bar."

"He went out the front door," said McCollough.

"No way," said Kulikowski. "I ran in as soon as I heard the shots. Nobody got past me."

"He walked right past you," said McCollough. "I saw him on the monitor. Maybe you didn't see him."

"No way," said Kulikowski. "Maybe you were looking at the garage monitor. Nobody got past me."

"How come," Ted said, "that a guy who wasn't a tenant was sitting in the lobby for two hours without anybody checking him out?"

"I figured he was a tenant," said the waiter. "Cripes, the way this place has been turning over lately, I hardly recognize anybody."

"Nobody got past me that wasn't a tenant, going in or coming out," said Kulikowski. "He must've come in before I went on duty. Maybe he's some tenant's guest. Maybe he's a new tenant."

Ted sent Kulikowski for the guest log. "Check out everybody," he told McCollough. "Don't settle for a tenant's word that the guest is in his apartment. Demand to see him. And don't go alone. Take a cop, just in case anybody starts wondering that you might be in on a setup."

"Jeez, Reep, you don't think this is an inside job—"

"No way it's anything else."

The police sealed the building. Tenants who had been out were checked carefully before being permitted past the barricades. A table was set up in one corner of the cocktail lounge to interview witnesses. Orders went out that the press would not be given its usual privilege of crossing the police lines. Burr Whiteside got on the phone and had someone hunt up a Winnebago camper, which he parked a block away to serve as press headquarters. Coffee and donuts were served while reporters took turns at the barricades waiting for a statement. Photographers used telephoto lenses to get pictures of what little action they could see.

Not long after the barricades were up Spats Johnson came home with a date. The policeman who checked his identification told him who had been killed just as stretchers bearing the bodies of Joe and Angie were being carried to a waiting hearse. "Uncle!" Spats said, running to them. Flashguns popped. Spats grabbed Joe's blood-soaked hand, then dropped it quickly. More flashguns popped as police tore him away.

Ted and Nate had gone back to Ted's penthouse. "Kulikowski set it up," Ted said.

"How do you know?"

"If the gunman had Cooler in his pocket, he could pull it off without anyone else. The deal must have been that Cooler would let the guy in, no questions asked, and look the other way when he was ready to leave."

"Why would Cooler want to do it?"

"Money. Plus he figured he would never get caught. He was gambling it would all happen too fast for McCollough to see anything on the monitor. Anyway, it's McCollough's word against his. He'll say right down to the wire that nobody got past him."

"A bummer. He should've known how something like this could hurt us—"

"He did know." Ted went to the intercom. A policeman answered the buzz. "This is Mr. Vassily," Ted said. "I'm the owner of this building. Please tell the doorman to check with me before he goes off duty."

He leaned back in his chair and stared at the ceiling.

"You know," he said, more to himself than to Nate, "I'm kind of sorry to see the old bastard get it this way."

"Coffee Joe?"

Ted nodded.

"Well, so far as we know he was always straight by us."

"Except he did use the broads that time to get to us. Yours never did call again, did she?"

"No. Scheming cunt. Of course, I got a decent ride. She was one of the best I ever had."

Ted sipped his Scotch, jiggled the ice cubes, then studied them. "All along I had these weird premonitions about Coffee Joe. I saw a direct line from him to the hoods that hassled me in college to the ones that muscled my uncle. I was sure he'd be the guy to ruin Three-oh-five East on me." Ted laughed. "So it winds up that he gives me good advice and Three-oh-five East goes under pretty much the way he predicted. Meanwhile, it seems I helped get him killed by hiring a doorman who sells out. I guess the whole thing appeals to my Greek sense of irony." . . . Except, he reminded himself, he might be stretching things a little to fit that sense of irony. Put in another perspective, Mandino could still be the centerpiece of his troubles. Mandino's interest in him, beginning with his insistence on moving into Three-oh-five East, could have been for more than just legitimate business reasons. Spats and Mandino were known friends, which meant Spats owed the man. Spats's abrupt turnabout from supporting to attacking Malloy . . . And Grace's death . . . Ted had pushed the thought out of his mind he-didn't-know-how-many times, but how to dismiss it entirely? If someone were using Mandino—hell, it had happened before, with those guys back in the days of Kennedy and the Cuban thing—what better way to bury Malloy politically, at the very least, than to stage the death of a lovely young female campaign worker in his penthouse when his wife was away? . . . He brought himself up abruptly, reminding himself he had no real evidence, none at all. There were no neat answers in this deal and not likely to be any. If he didn't want to drive himself crazy, he'd better settle for that and get on with some living. . . .

The buzzer sounded. Kulikowski reported that he was ready to come up. Nate went down for him.

Kulikowski entered the penthouse uncertainly. Ted remained seated. Kulikowski walked to a point three yards from the foot of Ted's chair and waited. Ted did not offer him a drink or invite him to sit. Ted's eyes fixed to Kulikowski's, then he looked away. There was a long minute of silence before Kulikowski finally said, "Reep, I had nothing to do with it."

"You sold us out, Cooler. You sold out me and Nate and Mikey and Emer and the coach."

"I had nothing to do with it, Reep. Maybe McCollough was right, maybe I got shook up when I heard the shots and somebody got past without me seeing him, but—"

"I don't believe you, Cooler. But that doesn't matter. All I can do is fire you. What matters is, Mandino's family is going to know this was an inside job. They're going to put it together and figure out who had the only opportunity to set it up. If I were you I'd get my ass out of here right now and go to the guys that hired you and ask their protection. Or I'd go to the cops and make an immunity and protection deal for fingering the killers. Or if you got enough money out of it, get on the next plane to some city where you don't have any relatives and—I'll bet you've planned that already, Cooler. I bet you have a spot all picked out and a broad waiting there for you. Where is it, Cooler? Miami? Las Vegas?"

"You got me wrong, Reep."

"We'll see. Meanwhile, you're fired."

Cooler started away, then spun back. His brave front was gone. "You can't fire me, Reep. That'll be telling the mob I'm the guy."

"You sold me out, Cooler. Why should I do you any favors?"

"I didn't sell anybody out." He looked to both sides, as if expecting someone to pounce on him, then went over to Ted, knelt alongside the chair and grabbed Ted's arm. "Please, Reep—you don't have any proof I set anything up—you just think it happened. Don't do this to me, buddy . . ."

"Cooler, if you don't get your ass out of here the mob isn't going to have to kill you. I'll do it myself."

"Please, Reep—" Kulikowski clutched at his arm. Ted jerked it away. Kulikowski reached toward it again, then drew back, stood, looked around and backed to the elevator. "Please, Reep," he said once again from the doorway. Ted did not answer. Kulikowski waited a long time, then stepped into the car. The doors closed.

Nate's hands shook as he filled a glass with Scotch. The ice cubes chattered as he lifted it. He almost spilled it before finally managing to get his lips around the rim and take a large swallow. "Isn't it going a little overboard to get the guy killed?"

"I'm saving his life, you dumb bastard. If he uses his head, he'll go straight from here to the airport. If he thought nobody was on to him, he'd probably hang around long enough for Joe's guys to figure out what we know."

Nate finished his Scotch and refilled the glass. "It's like I always said, Mister T. Deep down, you're all heart."

Buffy Weiss moved out. She knew that New York law didn't permit a landlord to post an eviction notice until a tenant was twenty days late with his rent and that another ten days had to elapse before the landlord could seize assets in payment of the debt. Accordingly she ignored the first-of-the-month rent statement and the tenth-of-the-month overdue reminder. When the eviction notice was posted she went to the courthouse and filed a request for a hearing. It was set for the thirtieth. On the twenty-ninth, movers came for her furniture. Her new apartment was on Central Park West, with a lovely view of the park.

Stonington Wattley moved out. Instead of waiting for the eviction notice, he vacated the apartment on the nineteenth and flew to Kansas City for a two-week vacation.

Hartford Loomis moved out. He considered having BankUS take over the leases on his and Nan's apartments, using them as hospitality suites for out-of-town clients. Then he ran a few figures through his desk calculator, bought both apartments in his own name and promptly resold them at a profit: one to an aerospace manufacturer who had a ten-million-dollar line of credit at the bank, the other to the government of Saudi Arabia. The profit was useful in his additional financing of Jeannie Danton's motion picture projects, which even without Vassily's overseeing seemed likely to turn into gold mines. With Mandino removed, the lady was now totally available. Truly a dream come true.

Eddie Spats Johnson bought his penthouse, the late Joe Mandino's and three other apartments. He moved into Mandino's, turned his own over to his father and donated the other three to the Lenox Avenue Baptist Church to make available to deserving families.

Joseph Williams moved out. He told Emerson Wade he would continue paying rent on the vacant apartment until it could be rented or sold. He told Ted, "If the original arrangement had remained in force I probably would have stayed indefinitely. Now, there's really no point." Softly he added, "And the memories are very painful."

"I know," Ted said. They shook hands.

Ted went to Nate's office, ascertained that Malloy hadn't yet vacated his apartment and got the unlisted telephone number from the tenant file. Even as he dialed the number, he wasn't sure what he was going to do. Or rather, he wasn't aware of having this day made the decision to do it. Actually he'd known ever since Grace's death that eventually he was going to do it.

"Malloy residence," answered a French-accented voice.

"Mrs. Malloy," said Ted, and then identified himself.

Nate's eyebrows arched. "I thought you didn't like juicers."

"I owe her something." Not to mention her husband, he thought . . . the would-be next senator for New York and the last known man to see Grace Colello alive.

She seemed nervous about her hair. Why did women always get so tense about their hair? Didn't they realize guys don't give a shit about hair? Her perfume was strong. And expensive, he was certain. Probably one of those fifty-dollar-a-drop deals from Saks or Tiffany's.

"Champagne?" he asked. "Or would you prefer Scotch?"

"Either. Actually, Scotch, I think."

He poured, handed her a glass and touched his to it. "To Peg"—he smiled—"who paid me the highest compliment a woman can pay a man."

"Which was?"

"To tell him you desire him. That night at your party, remember?"

"How could I forget? But you didn't seem very interested at the time."

"Discretion is the better part of valor, and so forth."

She came without hesitation but stiffly into his arms. They kissed. Her breath reeked of stale booze. The strong perfume could cover only so much. The odor sickened him.

"I've often wondered," he said, quickly tucking her head against his chest, "how a woman as attractive as you manages to avoid being constantly propositioned?"

She laughed. "That's what the Irish call blarney."

"It's what the Greeks call disarming with candor."

"Disarming, maybe, but certainly not with candor."

"Don't sell yourself short."

"Please . . . I can see what other women look like and what I look like."

"I think you look great."

"When I was younger, maybe. Not any more."

"Stop putting yourself down." Someone, he thought, should tell her that a smart woman never deprecates her own appearance, that it's like a pastor telling the congregation not to put buttons in the collection plate . . . some people get the idea who might never have thought of it on their own.

He shoved his tongue deeply into her mouth and held his breath.

"A girl could get very excited being kissed like that," she said when he finally backed away.

He gave his best knowing-scoundrel chuckle and buried his face in her neck, at the same time grazing his palm against her breast. He methodically went through his repertoire of approach techniques—graze the breasts, stroke them, clutch them, now under the dress . . . pantyhose! "Why don't you slip these off while I freshen our drinks?"

She seemed hesitant.

"Unless," he quickly added, "you don't want to—"

"No. I mean, I do." She blushed. "I mean, I'm not very good at this sort of thing, am I?"

"Stop putting yourself down."

She followed him into the kitchen. "Inexperience, I guess. Would you believe I've never had an affair in thirteen years of marriage?"

"No, I don't think I would, not a woman as attractive and—"

"Well, one. Two, actually. But I don't think of them as affairs. They were more, well, in the old days we called them 'pecadillos.' "

He handed her a full glass. "Well, one person's pecadillo is another's affair, I guess. Anyway, cheers!" He touched her glass with his.

"Yes." She took a large swallow. "I think I needed this, to relax me, you know?" She drained the glass. "Would you think me terrible if I asked for another?"

He suppressed a grimace and poured. "Let's take the bottle with us." He led her to a couch and brought his hand to her leg. "Ah, Peg . . . the pantyhose?"

"Oh, yes. Sorry." She took a drink. "I feel so, well, inept, and a little foolish . . . where's your bathroom?"

He showed her.

Like pulling teeth, he thought, and then told himself not to be unfair.

When she came back he got her talking about herself. She seemed hesitant to discuss the present, but she warmed up considerably when he asked about her college days. She told him about the boys she'd dated before John Malloy, and about football weekends, and about going with John to a pro game in New York when none other than Ted Vassily had been playing. "As an athlete, you were his idol," she said. "He always had mixed feelings about being an Ivy League quarterback. He loved Yale and wouldn't have traded its academic prestige for anything, but he knew it wasn't big-time college football." She laughed bitterly. "The bastard! Here I am cuckolding him" . . . she smiled and shook her head. "There's really an old-fashioned word for you. Anyway, here I am doing whatever it's now called and I can't even get him out of my mind. I'm sorry . . ."

He touched her crotch. "I think we'd be more comfortable in the bedroom."

She undressed hesitantly, shyly. She wore unsexy waist-high white panties. (Let's face it, some broads just don't know how to play the game.)

She looked at her breasts in the mirror. "I feel so old . . ."

Oh, for Pete's sake, get off it. Actually they weren't bad at all. A little saggy, at worst. "They're very attractive," he said. He took them gently in his hands and pressed his face between them.

"They're too flabby. It happened after I had Johnny—"

"I repeat, I think they're very attractive. And your legs —they're lovely. Come on over here and take off your panties."

She did and got into bed with him. He guided her into place alongside him and traced patterns over her body with the balls of his fingers.

"That feels good," she said.

He put her hand on his penis. "So does that."

Her hand lay limply on top of him. His response was equally limp. Maybe when he put his fingers inside her, if he found her wet—and if he thought very hard, thought *himself* hard about someone else . . . But who? Certainly not Grace. Not Nan. Or Buffy Weiss. Or Chris. Goddamn, he'd come to a point in his life where there wasn't even anybody acceptable to have fantasies about!

She was wet, and he felt himself stiffening. Good. Now, beach at Mykonos. That's it. Nude bodies all around. Gorgeous chick with nice bouncy tits—not too big, just nice. Thick, free-falling hair. Sexy eyes. Yes, could be any one of a hundred.

Is it stiff? Yes, right. Certainly not super-stiff, that's not going to happen today. But usable-stiff? Maybe.

He mounted her and rubbed the head against her wetness. He pushed forward. Something was wrong. Her hips weren't angling to receive him.

He tried to adjust his angle. He felt the stiffness leaving him. Damn it, she didn't know how to position her own cunt . . . Well, okay, one down, let's work at getting it back up.

He lay alongside her and resumed fingering her. "Touch me," he said when she didn't do it spontaneously.

Now back to Mykonos. Semi-stiff again. Should he risk it?

Might as well, it wasn't going to get better no matter what.

Mount. Shift. Push. Again. Shift. Push. *Nothing.*

"It's my fault, isn't it?"

"Don't be silly."

"It is. I'm a lousy lay, aren't I?"

"I don't know, I haven't laid you yet." He made himself laugh.

"This happens to me all the time. . . . Vaseline can help. Really."

He got the jar from the bathroom, opened it and presented it to her.

"Do you want me to put it on you?"

"Right. And I'll put some on you too. It makes everything much easier, much nicer."

Semi-stiff. Good. A little stiffer. "That feels terrific, keep doing it." Three-quarters . . . "Yes, terrific, wonderful."

Now. Mount. Shift. Push. In. Move. Wait—*not that way*. Out. Goddamn.

"Just relax. Don't be nervous. It'll work this time."

"I'm a real dud, aren't I?"

"Relax. You're doing fine."

In. Oh, hell, not stiff enough. Well, in anyway. Okay. Now . . .

"Put your legs straight down. Let me put mine over them."

"Like this?"

Out.

She turned away.

"Don't be disappointed. Sometimes it takes a long time."

She was crying.

"Aw, come on, Peggy. Take it easy—sometimes it takes dozens of times before two people get the feel of each other's bodies . . ."

She sat up. "Don't work at being nice to me, Ted. At least spare me that." She looked to the night table, seemed relieved to find a box of Kleenex, tugged out three of them and blew her nose. "It's so—so—humiliating . . ." She burst into tears and buried her face in her hands.

He put his arm around her. Without looking up, she extracted half a dozen more Kleenex and wiped her eyes and nose. "It's so easy for men. You can stay attractive till you're sixty. For a woman, it's all over at thirty. If she's lucky—really lucky—she can hang on till thirty-five. I'm not lucky. There's too much young . . . what do you gentlemen call it? . . . *stuff* around, too many firm bodies, too many pouty-sexy little faces. And they don't want boys their own age, the way we did when I was young. They want older men, married men—"

"You need a drink." He handed her her Scotch.

"Yes, I need a drink." She gulped, wiped her eyes again, then looked up at him. "Look at me, if you can stand it. I'm washed-out. A has-been. Over the goddamn hill. At thirty-five."

"That's ridiculous."

"Go ahead and make fun . . . you're a man. You can't understand what it feels like."

He took a long drink of Scotch. "Yes I can," he said quietly.

He walked slowly through the lobby, admiring the beige draperies, the dark brown and burnt orange rugs. They still looked almost new. The secret was to buy super-high-quality merchandise. It held up.

He went to the mahogany Victorian loveseat with peach velvet fabric where he had fucked Buffy Weiss and shared a bottle of Taittinger Comtes '66 that day when the building was under construction. It seemed so long ago.

"Something to drink, Mr. Vassily?"

"Scotch on the rocks," he told the waiter. "Make it a double."

He gazed out over the lobby, imagining all the furniture and fixtures vanishing, picturing the immense room as it had been that day with Buffy, just marble and plaster, the chalky dust from the plaster coating everything. He remembered taking her up on the skeleton of the building, feeling her body tremble as she looked over the side, walking together against the wind, hearing the snapping sound their sleeves and cuffs made in the breeze. He remembered Nate patrolling the site in his hardhat, with his clipboard always at the ready.

"Here you are, Mr. Vassily."

He signed the check, then took his drink out to the quadrangle. He touched the granite slab with the names of all the people who had worked on the building. He remembered the meeting at the Tuscany with the bankers, and the game of touch afterward in Central Park, and coming here to the site at nine in the morning and watching the demolition crew raze the last of the three-story brick buildings that had stood on the block for probably a hundred years.

He walked to the center of the quadrangle and looked up at the four towers. What was it one of the bankers had called it? A Florentine fortress? Who had said that, anyway? DelVecchio? Kraft? Whoever, it was apt. What could be more dignified than a Florentine fortress? It certainly beat the shit out of all those central-core matchboxes whose economics the bankers were in love with.

He walked around the outside of the building, then through the lower lobby, then back to the loveseat. "Another," he said to the waiter. "And have the doorman buzz Mr. Elefante. Tell him I'd like him to have a drink with me if he's free."

Nate appeared within minutes. "My man! I detect a look in your eye—one I haven't seen in a long time. Did you give her one she'll never forget?"

"I'm sure she'll remember it for quite some time."

He retraced with Nate the earlier tour he had taken of the lobby and courtyard. They reminisced about the night Nate met him at the airport, the building inspector whose face Ted had rammed into a window, the grand party in the lobby. They got refills for their Scotches and contemplated the granite slab in the quadrangle. Then they rode the elevator to Ted's penthouse and let themselves out onto the roof.

They leaned against the waist-high wall surrounding the roof and stared out into the humid New York night. "Let's do it again," Ted said.

"Do what?"

"The whole fucken thing."

"What whole fucken thing?"

Ted laughed. "What was my specialty in football? The instant replay, right?"

"Right."

"So, why only football?"

Nate looked at him for a long time. "You mean put up another building?"

"That's what I mean."

"Where?"

"Does it matter? As long as it's better . . ."

Nate was flabbergasted.

"We'll do like your buddy in Shreveport. Get a road map, pick a direction. You like California? Okay, they have poor people in California—Los Angeles, San Francisco, San Diego—"

"You wanna do subsidized apartments again?"

"Yes, the whole thing, top to bottom. But as I said, more and better. We'll get Axel to design it—radically different design from Three-oh-five but even more luxurious. If Emer and the other guys want in, fine. If not, I've got enough equity in the corporation to handle it on my own."

"I want a piece of it, deal me in."

"You're in."

"So when do we start?"

"Right after the Detroit game."

Nate drained his Scotch, looked at the glass for a long moment, then threw a sudden punch that caught Ted square in the gut. "Eat shit, you fucker," Nate said with delight.

Ted struggled to conceal his pain—actually, he was having a hard time keeping on his feet—but he managed to lift his glass, take a sip, lower it and get off his own punch.

Nate groaned. His belly seemed to suck in Ted's arm up to the wrist, then spit it out. Slowly, like falling timber, he came forward—and in the process unleashed another punch.

Ted was ready for this one, was able to smile and throw a counter.

Nate clinched as he took it, then turned to drape one arm over Ted's shoulders, sucked the remaining liquid from his empty glass, looked at the glass pensively for a moment and threw it high in the air. "Whooppee!" he sang in a loud falsetto. "We're rollin' again, Reep. We're rollin'!"

Ted laughed. "If that doesn't land on this roof, Emer could be up to his ass in insurance claims."

"Fuck the insurance claims. And fuck the Superspook! We're *rollin'!*"

ELEVEN

THEY WAITED in the runway under the stands as the announcer gave the names of the regular players.

"I should have my head examined," said Emerson Wade. "I have no more business out there against those young mastodons than I have performing brain surgery."

"You know what I always liked about you, Superspook?" said Mikey DeAngelico. "Your positive attitude. Always givin' everybody a lift, makin' us feel there's nothing we can't do."

"Those young fuckers ain't gonna shit," said Nate. "They nevuh seen His Nastiness in action. He gonna sit on them like a big mothuh hen. I only wish this was one-platoon football so's I could block the shit out of 'em on offense, then put some manners on Carm the Arm on defense."

Mikey held his hands in front of him for balance and dropped into a quick series of deep knee bends. "I feel good, T. I really feel good."

"You should," said Nate. "This fucker been workin' our ass off for a month an' a half." He made a fist and punched his opposite palm. "You heah me out there, Carm the Arm? When ol' Nasty Nate gets you, your ass ain't gonna be jes' grass, it gonna be Astro-turf!"

Ted heard clicking sounds behind him. He turned and did a double-take.

She was tall and slim with enormous breasts. She wore tight blue denim shorts that barely covered the underslope of her buttocks, and a bright yellow tank top. She had a thirty-five millimeter Nikon in front of her face.

She pressed the shutter release, then lowered the camera. She had a pert turned-up nose, a bow-shaped mouth, blue-green eyes that sparkled behind granny glasses. Pigtails decorated her straw-blonde hair. A press pass was pinned to her shirt just above a nipple that stood out like a bullet.

"Hey, Nate," said Mikey, "they could put them in the whale museum."

"Try 'sexy newspaperperson,' " she said.

"Gentlepeople," said Emerson Wade, "meet Miz Sally Hall of *Football Weekly*."

"Hey, that's our magazine," said Mikey.

"Sally Hall," said Nate, "you can take my picture any time. How'd you like some nudes?"

"Hey, Nate," said Mikey, "they could put them in the whale museum."

"Ladies and gentlemen," said the stadium announcer, "the co-captains of the New York Old-Timers—"

"Mike, you're up," called one of the equipment boys.

"—from Nanticoke, Pennsylvania, and the University of Alabama, wearing number twenty-one, Mikey DeAngelico."

"Feels great, T-Bone," he said. "I almost forgot what it sounded like." He jogged onto the field as a roar rose from the stands.

"From Chattanooga, Tennessee, and Penn State University," said the announcer, "wearing number eighty-four, Emerson Wade."

Sally Hall moved in close to Ted and Nate, clicking her shutter as they listened for the announcer's next call.

"From Shreveport, Louisiana, and Michigan State University, wearing number seventy-seven, Nate Elefante."

"Sally Hall," Ted said, "I'm getting ready to put up a building in California. What would you say if I asked you to come out and take some pictures of it for me?"

Without seeming to pay attention to the camera, which she held at her waist, she pointed it at Ted and tripped the shutter. "I'd say you ought to look at samples of my work before you offer me an assignment."

Ted felt terrific. Giddy. "What would you say if I told you I fell in love with you the instant I laid eyes on you?"

"I'd say you're an asshole."

"Ladies and gentlemen," said the announcer, "from Nanticoke, Pennsylvania, and Penn State University, wearing number thirteen, Ted Vassily."

The cheers reverberated through the stadium as he jogged onto the field. They seemed to build and build and build. Just when he was sure they had reached their crest, they built even more. And *still* they kept building. Then, slowly —very slowly—the sound subsided. Mikey was right—it felt great.

He led Mikey, Emer and Nate to the center of the field for the reenactment of the toss. Carm the Arm Camaratta and his co-captains got there first. Carm looked as magazine-advertisement-suave as ever, helmet in hand, thick black hair slicked down. "Hello, Mister Touchdown," he said, grinning as they shook hands. "How's the apartment business?"

Ted laughed. "Not bad, Carm. You still modeling pantyhose?"

"Over-the-calf socks, Theodore. Namath was pantyhose, remember? You're getting your generations mixed."

"Generate this, Arm," said Mikey DeAngelico, grabbing his cock with both hands. "You're gonna lose your ass today."

Carm exaggerated a snarl. "Be quiet, Michael, or I'll press the down button on your elevator shoes."

"Har-de-har-har."

"Hey, Carm," said Nate, "how'd you like me to break off that famous arm and shove it up your ass."

"Is this your offensive tackle, gentlemen?" asked Carm.

"You goddamn know it," said Mikey.

"He's the most offensive tackle I've ever met," said Carm.

"Gentlemen," said the referee, "we've got heads. New York, the choice is yours."

Ted chose to defend the south goal.

"Playing your cards close to the vest, are you, Mister T?"

"Just trying to psyche you out, Carm. Elect to kick and I'll show you how close we're playing them."

"We'll receive," said Carm.

The referee gave the appropriate signals to the press box as the co-captains trotted to the sidelines. Horst

Springer jogged from the New York bench and set up the ball on the thirty-five. Ted stood at the fifty-yard marker to watch.

"Hey, why you letting 'em receive?" Nate asked.

"Strategy, Nathan. Strategy."

"I'm hip. But what's the strategy?"

"How's your mother, Nate?"

"Oh, shit, you ain't gonna start that number again—"

"Watch the game, old buddy."

Springer's kick was deep into Detroit territory and was returned to the twenty-five. Camaratta called a pass on first down and overthrew the intended receiver as the New York defense broke into the cup. On second, Carm completed a play action pass to his fullback in the flat for a five-yard gain. On third, he sent receivers out for a bomb and got sacked.

"That's the strategy," Ted told Nate as Detroit punted on fourth and fifteen.

The runback was to the New York forty-five. "Give me Marshall and Riggs," Ted told Eddie Witt.

"You got 'em."

Fullback Otis Marshall and tailback Preston Riggs, who were current starters, joined Ted and Mikey DeAngelico in the Old Timers' backfield. Ted sent Marshall off tackle. Detroit was expecting a pass and had called a blitz. Marshall got past the linebackers for twelve yards before a cornerback brought him down.

"Your turn, Preston," said Ted in the huddle.

Still expecting a pass, Detroit gave up another nine. The ball sat on the Detroit thirty-four.

Detroit correctly diagnosed a fullback misdirect, stopping Marshall for a loss of one. Then Riggs went inside tackle for six and another first down.

"T-Bone," said Mikey DeAngelico, coming back to the huddle, "they're giving me lots of room. Wanna throw one?"

"Not yet," Ted said. He called a power sweep. It was stopped at the line of scrimmage.

"I'm wide open, T," said Mikey. "Meanwhile, these bump-and-run fuckers are poundin' the piss out of me."

"We'll try a screen," Ted said to him. "I want our line to get their confidence up before I throw from the pocket."

The screen worked, but an alert linebacker held Mikey to a four-yard gain. On the twenty-one-yard line with fourth and two Ted called for Horst Springer to attempt a field goal. Mitch Poe, the back-up quarterback, came in to hold. There were scattered boos as Ted walked off the field.

The attempt was good. There were more boos as Springer kicked off.

Emerson Wade joined Ted on the sideline. "New York fans," he said, gesturing to the stands. "Who else boos a score?"

Ted laughed. "They want an aerial circus. I want to play football."

The runback was to the Detroit twenty-nine. Carm the Arm opened with a quick play action pass to the tight end that was good for ten yards. He followed with one from the pocket, hitting the wide receiver on a post pattern for twenty yards. There were cheers in the stands.

Carm called a draw that was good for six, then went back into the pocket and got caught in a blitz for a loss of twelve. On third and sixteen, he sent three receivers deep. The New York defense broke through, the pass was rushed, it fell short and old-timer safety Bill Bates intercepted at the ten.

"That," Ted told Emer, "is what happens when you let the fans call your plays."

He put together another running attack, mixing in a few screens and short passes into the flats but nothing deep. He got four first downs before Detroit dug in at its own forty-five. On fourth and four he called for Nick Adamo, the punter. There was another chorus of boos as Ted trotted to the sidelines. He raised both hands in a victory salute, which inspired more boos. Adamo's punt rolled out of bounds on the four.

Carm was gun-shy after the interception. He called two running plays that moved the ball five yards, then threw a hurried short pass that his tailback dropped. Old Timer Hank Messner punted under pressure to his own forty. The runback was good for five yards.

Ted stayed with the running game and short passes. His attack ran out of steam on the twenty, and Horst

Springer kicked another field goal. The boos were ferocious.

Pappy Sanderson, the backfield coach, and Eddie Witt joined Ted at the sidelines.

"You're calling a brilliant game," Pappy said.

Witt patted Ted's shoulder pad. "I always said, Pappy, there's lots of fellas around that can throw passes. But this man is the best field general ever to play the game." He walked around in front of Ted and looked up into his eyes. "How you feeling, son? You holding up okay?"

"Just fine, coach."

"You find yourself getting tired, don't be a martyr."

"Don't worry, coach, it's not my style."

Pappy said, "Our guy in the press box says they're speculating something happened to your arm. They want him to find out what's the story."

"Have him say I said no comment. Then let's hope the rumor gets to the Detroit bench."

"I'm sure it has already."

Springer's kickoff was run back to the thirty-five. Carm managed two first downs on short passes, then got sacked twice and overthrew a third. Old Timer Hank Messner's punt sailed to the New York twenty and was run back five.

Ted mixed runs and screens for two first downs, then met resistance and had to call a punt from his own forty-five. More boos.

"T-Bone," said Mikey DeAngelico, "these bastards are giving me enough room to plant a garden. When the fuck're you gonna throw me a bomb?"

"Soon," Ted said.

Camaratta connected on a first-down pass for twenty, then was sacked twice. His next pass was good for forty and would have been a touchdown except for a diving tackle by the cornerback. Then he got sacked two more times, fumbling on the second.

On first down Ted passed to Otis Marshall over the center for ten yards. "T-Bone," said Mikey, "I'm telling you, I got enough room back there to lead McNamara's band."

"Okay," Ted said, "let's do it."

The defensive line was still thinking run. Back in the pocket, Ted had all the time in the world. He put the ball up and started walking off the field. Mikey snagged it on the ten, a full five yards past the nearest defender, and crossed the goal line in a near-walk.

The fans were cheering now. Ted didn't look up. Eddie Witt came over and put an arm around his shoulder. Ted noticed a pair of legs and a camera pop out from behind one of the defensive tackles. The shutter clicked. He smiled. The shutter clicked again.

Sally Hall started toward him. Eddie Witt discreetly stepped away. "You're good," she said. "You're really good."

"I'll bet you're really good too," he said.

"Seriously. I've seen lots of pro football, but I've never seen anybody call a game like you've been calling."

"Thanks." He noticed that one of her feet was touching the white in-bounds line. He tucked a finger into her belt loop and guided her away.

"Oops, sorry," she said.

"No problem." He left his finger in place on the loop and maneuvered the rest of his hand so that it was resting on her hip. "I'll bet you're more than good," he said. "I'll bet you're great."

She smirked. "At what?"

He exaggerated feigned innocence. "Photography, of course."

"I was sure that's what you meant."

"What else?"

She laughed. "I like you. You're horribly obvious and a terrible sexist, but I like you."

"I like you too, Sally Hall. How about a drink after the game?"

"Love one."

Thank God, a lady of few words . . .

Detroit ran back Horst Springer's kickoff to the New York forty. Carm the Arm got sacked on the first play.

"Poor guy," Sally said, "he's taking an awful beating."

"He's asking for it. You go for a bomb every play, the defense knows right where to find you."

Carm went back for another one, got chased out of the

pocket and ran for the sidelines. Ted got a close look at his face. He looked like a kid being chased by a street gang.

On third and twenty-three, Carm dropped back again. This time a New York defender fell, the pass sailed beautifully high and far, and Old Timer Denny Dembrosky took it on his fingertips in the end zone.

The kickoff was run back to the New York thirty. Ted went back to the ground game and screens for two first downs, then called a first-play bomb. Detroit diagnosed it. Ted saw the blitzing corner linebacker and wheeled to the opposite side, hoping to salvage a short one to Preston Riggs in the flat. He turned just in time to see a blur of blue and white. And then he was on the ground. The ball, he found himself thinking. Did he fumble?

The blue and white hunk got off him, then offered a hand. The face behind the mask looked like a child's. "Hope I didn't hurt you," the guy said, seeming to mean it.

"Good hit, big fella," Ted said. "Good clean hit."

"It's an honor to play against you," the kid said. Then he was gone and Nate was pulling at Ted's elbow. "You okay, Reep?"

"Yeah." Actually, his back felt as if it had been cracked by a baseball bat and his knees as if someone had driven a nail into each of them.

"I'm sorry, Reep. He was my guy. I let him outsmart me."

"It happens."

"It won't again. Call the same play. I promise you, that fucker don't get by me if I have to tie a rope around him."

The referee hadn't signaled a change of possession, so Ted knew the last call was an incomplete pass rather than a fumble. He called a medium-range pass play that had both Mikey and Emer buttonhooking.

He dropped into the pocket and waited for their moves. Mikey made his, but was covered. Emer made his, and also was covered. The second alternate receiver, Preston Riggs, was in the flats but had a safety on his back.

It occurred to Ted that he was getting an awful lot of time. He watched Mikey and Emer make moves against their defenders. And now Mikey was free, and

Ted threw. Mikey made a diving catch that was good for thirty yards, but a flag was down. "Not me, Ref," Nate was saying. "I never touched the guy."

"Nasty," said the ref, "you had him in a full-nelson. The call is offensive holding—ten yards."

A runner came in from the bench. "Witt says he thinks they're vulnerable to the flood, if you think now's a good time to try it."

Ted nodded. "The flood" was a gang-up on the cornerback whom Witt and Ted had decided was Detroit's weakest pass defender. Emer and Mikey would start out on flag patterns, then Emer would suddenly cross toward Mikey's flag, giving the cornerback two receivers to worry about instead of one. The tight end, Stan Dubinski, would also enter the zone, but not as deeply as Emer and Mike. At the same time Preston Riggs, running at tailback, would make a token attempt to block a linebacker, then follow Dubinski. If Detroit didn't diagnose the moves, the zone would—for a few seconds anyway—be flooded, two defenders against four receivers. The problem was, with the tight end and tailback out for passes, the blocking would be extremely thin. The deep receivers would have to get deep really fast, and Ted would have only an instant to get the pass off.

"Okay, let's flood 'em," he said.

He took the snap from center and stepped back—one, two, three. The cornerback was back-pedaling fast to stay with Mikey. Emer feinted to his right, faked his man out and quickly cut back. Ted fired the ball and turned away just in time to dodge a hit by the center linebacker. Emer eluded the safety and cornerback, cut crossfield, then downfield and picked up another fifteen yards before he was brought down. First and ten on the Detroit thirty-five.

"Let's do it again," Ted said.

The play developed identically. This time, though, Mikey outdistanced the cornerback and was racing for the flag. Ted lofted one high and deep. Mikey jumped three feet into the air to let it hit him on the numbers, then came down with both feet neatly in the end zone.

The fans were going bananas. Ted spotted Sally Hall's long bare legs on the sidelines and trotted toward them.

Players clustered around and pounded his shoulder pads as he accepted Pappy Sanderson's congratulatory handshake. "Pap," he said, "I've got two bottles of San Martin Brut in the clubhouse refrigerator. Don't let these clowns pour them over each other at the victory party. They're for me and my friend Miss Hall here."

"You are good," she said, her mouth close to his ear. "You are so goddamn good."

Detroit returned Horst Springer's kick to the thirty. Carm threw three incompletes and called in his punter. New York ran it back to the fifty.

"Okay," Ted said in the huddle, "let's do a replay."

This time he threw to Emerson Wade, who took it at full stride and got to the two-yard line before the cornerback knocked him out of bounds. Ted ran Preston Riggs inside guard on a second-man-through for the score.

"Now," he said, coming toward the sideline with one arm draped over Nate's shoulder and the other over Mikey's, "let's give the kiddies a chance."

The cheers echoing through the stands sounded like thunder. Ted stopped short of the out-of-bounds marker, raised both hands high over his head in a victory signal, then made a fist and slapped his elbow-pit in the classic Italian gesture. Blow it out your ass, world, he said to himself, and jogged the rest of the way off the field. As he'd once told Nan, if you say it—even to yourself—be able to back it up. He had. One time more.

It was enough.

ABOUT THE AUTHOR

PAUL GILLETTE is a native of Pennsylvania. His previous novel, *Carmela,* was called by *Publishers Weekly* "absorbing and dramatic . . . believable and entertaining." He now makes his home in San Francisco.

Bantam Book Catalog

Here's your up-to-the-minute listing of every book currently available from Bantam.

This easy-to-use catalog is divided into categories and contains over 1400 titles by your favorite authors.

So don't delay—take advantage of this special opportunity to increase your reading pleasure.

Just send us your name and address and 25¢ (to help defray postage and handling costs).

BANTAM BOOKS, INC.
Dept. FC, 414 East Golf Road, Des Plaines, Ill. 60016

Mr./Mrs./Miss ______________________________
(please print)

Address ______________________________

City ______________ State ______________ Zip ______________

Do you know someone who enjoys books? Just give us their names and addresses and we'll send them a catalog too!

____

Mr./Mrs./Miss ______________________________

Address ______________________________

City ______________ State ______________ Zip ______________

____

Mr./Mrs./Miss ______________________________

Address ______________________________

City ______________ State ______________ Zip ______________

FC—6/77